SPECTERS

IN THE
SHADOW OF GOD

ISBN: 978-0-578-16958-3

This literary work is dedicated
In memory of

Mae Jean Wade
(August 1940 – July 2009)

About The Author

Until recently, authoring this book, or any book, was nothing more than a distant memory while conventional printing was seemingly out of reach, as well as a headache. Only those with tremendous capitol or celebrity status could truly capitalize on such a venue; neither of which I have. But like so many out there, I too have a story to tell.

I enjoy art; graphic design, animation, and have become an avid truck enthusiast. Among other things, volleyball, the great outdoors, sci-fi thrillers, and building things seem to help me keep my sanity. When writing, I enjoy combining science, religion, and real-life stories; especially from the perspective of an older person's point of view.

I wrote *Specters InThe Shadow of God* because I see so much of myself in the main character, though not as smart. He is intellelgent and capable of handling so many things in his company, but like many, he is unappreciated in the eyes of management; and in essence seeks out a way to prove that he is so much more than the perverbial 'label' that is placed on him.

Sharing this book with others is reward enough, while in advance, I would personally like to thank each and every one of you who has taken the time to read this story.

I sincerly hope you enjoy it – thank you so much.

Gerald A. Wade

Specters – (English variant of Spectres)
An incorporeal spirit, a ghost or phantom, possessing a terrifying nature. But in the constitution of man, such apparitions take the form of many disguises that foster the severe plight of human degradation.

War rages in the Mesopotamia as several terrorist cells carry out their vicious religion. Fueled with a deadly objective, they slaughter thousands in the process. In addition, an idealistic extremist uses the war as a smoke screen to cover his own agenda and spearheads a group of fascist radicals who propose a threat greater than the war itself.

To combat such a threat, Colonel Ducet, head of bio weaponry research in conjunction with Rowland, director of GenoSyss and lead geneticist, assembles a team that produces several hybrid prodigies. However, Rowland's bond with Ducet forms a deadly union.

Inevitably, they seek the talents of Arthur Robinson. Arthur's creation of a creature known as Gjhe'nan (project 429) ironically puts all the power players closer to their clandestine purposes; yet, project 429 is as much a mystery as it is an answer, plunging all involving participants into the depths of human despair.

~~~~~Contents~~~~~

"…In the shadow of His hand He has concealed me;"

Isaiah 49:2

Arthur Robinson

~~~**Remember Me**~~~

Death baptized her, having granted nothing less than freedom as a silent outcry whisked past her distressed lips. Tender eyes that gazed upward while trustedhands held tight, loosened upon the gentle turn of her head. Peaceful and still, warm crimson rivers course no more.

And yet, she comesto me again – even to this day...

Nostalgia, how fitting is her name. Her ever-essence glow brings the sweetest of memories to the inner depths of my soul. Such an overwhelming presence yields tremendous undeniable power that humbles me in a way like nothing else can. To gaze upon her, to interpret every line, every contour, every texture, to imbed her visage into my senses are by far the noblest of gestures. However, unbending guilt wields its merciless shadow and drives me deep into the inner sanctions of my heart. We meet occasionally in our minds but it is she who determines the time, and the place is – wherever. This time, she deliberately goes through eight phases of her journey and I have memorized them all as she kindly caresses my bare skin with her light. This is our connection...this is our affair and I must never forget.

Most of the time, Texas weather is kind to all its residents on this brisk night in March. Like most citizens here, we herald the coolness with a gracious welcoming for all know that in a few months, sweltering temperatures will crush those it cannot forgive. With that in mind, there is little motivation to exercise or listen to music. Such activities in times past has successfully induced sleep but tonight, such a passive interlude will go unsuccessful. With nothing else of interest, making the decision to indulge myself in the mindless entertainment on one of technology's idiot boxes becomes the next focal point.

In reaching for the remote, there is hardly an appreciation for the turquoise marble end-table upon which it lays. Repetition of the daily grind causes such attitudes but for now, if I placed it there, then there it should be, just as we were supposed to be where we were a long time ago. "Why would we be anywhere else," speaking aloud for a brief moment. Realizing my outspokenness, I quickly shake my head, which brings me back to the present. It is a funny thing how the mind can go into so many directions – all at once.

I make my way to the couch in the living room and finally manage the company of the monitor. Choosing not to voice-activate, I take the remote and view several stations, but unfortunately only a few stations airing programs at such a time are actually worth while the effort. To make matters worse, even the movie vault is less appealing. There are no quick remedies for my condition — though I take comfort in the words of a man that walked this earth so long ago. But until His words become the peace that surpasses all understanding, I will immerse myself into the vanities of this world. Spurts of anger and agitation often cross my mind, but who is to suffer my wrath. Drugs, alcohol, a sexual playground; all could easily become my friend – but I can't.

Channel after channel, I find a man who appears to be a type of mediator between two very outspoken individuals. One person is an unhappy woman and the other a very disgruntle man. The two engage in an extreme argument. The crowd, viewing the confrontation erupts in loud applauds and shouts the mediator's name. "Interesting…" But soon, the memories return. I reach for the remote and quickly silence the mayhem.

Now, the silence of the night quickly looms throughout the house. It comes with unimaginable power as though to subdue all activity in its presence. "Who am I kidding," I whisper, but then, I know she is here and she is calling me…because she wants me to remember. I want to forget so badly.

Time stops for no one as the silence engulfs everything. Lying still, a subtle exhale passes through my lips and into the emptiness. It is here in this labyrinth of quietness that the active world goes aside and one can cherish one's own inner thoughts. There's true value in this state of existence, because it is a moment when chaos cease and an inner calm blankets me from within. Yet, as time goes on, peace yields its clarity. As I ponder such thoughts, I slowly turn towards the east wall. As fate would have it, upon the wall, ruling the night in soft light is – Nostalgia.

Elsewhere, on the mantle, there is a plaque that I received years ago. It denotes a commemorate effort when I worked for GenoSyss. The inscription on the plaque states: 'Admirable Service Award to Arthur Wade Robinson.' It is as though that humble piece of wood is my only tie to a meaningful existence. It reminds me of a time when efforts meant something and the labor of one's own hand could benefit everyone in society. It reminds me of a time when larger-than-life dreams were worth the efforts and that selfish subtleties were nothing more than poor excuses. At times, I swear it cries out "risk everything for something greater" or sadly, it delivers an omen of why some things should never take place. In the end, it ties me to an inescapable reality.

In other parts of the room, silhouette shadows blend together forming other bizarre images, and yet, my mind separates each image independently as I pan the room even more. Exquisite décor adorns the walls of our home in such a way as only the passionate eye of my loving wife can give. Dark images of fish looms within their clear water prison, gracefully making their way back and forth along the wall of glass, simply living out their lives as only the Creator intends. They have no worries, no fears, but only to live peacefully – if only I were them. Renditions of my handy work proudly occupy a portion of space near the mantle. One painting depicts wild mustangs running down a hill and onto an open plateau. The other painting captivates a caring humpback whale with calf navigating their undersea realm. Again, another depiction that tells the story of freedom...most importantly, the freedom to enjoy life without regrets.

The animals within the paintings remind me of my genetics team. I can see each of them, one by one. It is the pureness of intent; that my former colleagues and I shared, which embeds deeply within these two paintings; and yet, knowing that, I humbly turn away.

The quietness of the world grows more prevalent by the tic-toc sound generating from the clock. The sound softly echoes as a slight chill forms in the air. I drape myself with a blanket. As I walk the dark room, a soothing refreshment of silence cascades my mind even more. If only I could stay within this sea of tranquil stillness. Silence passes into my mind like a sweet voice preluding a lover's attention; how needful it is...but time waits for no one. Such a mental state soon accompanies a deep breath of relaxation, a well of complete passiveness, a moment to finally die while alive. "Dear God, please let this remain," I whisper, trusting that such words do not go unheard.

However, the rest is short-lived. She calls for me, knocking on the door where matters-of-the-heart seats deeply within. She is no stranger. I jump to my feet, making haste to enter the meeting place. Lunging forward, I grab the curling doorknobs on both French doors and pull with such force as though to announce my own presence. There I stand expectantly with intent. There is no resistance, no bargaining, or holding back. The power to face the truth in transparency has finally come. No more lies, no more running. She wants me to remember her so that I will never forget.

Progressing slowly, she bathes me with a subtle glow while baring herself as usual. Just as I am, so is she – there are no boundaries between us. The time has come for us to meet, and as always, gazing upon her prompts the memories to begin.

While standing in the middle of this room, a gentle breeze softly caresses the hairs on my arm. Such actions in effect pacify my state of thought even more. There, in the quietness of a once raging mental storm, I gaze upwardly through the sky windows and yes – without fail…she is there, beautiful as ever. Her lunar body captivates the night sky as the time of her waning crescent appears. Sleep will elude me this night, because both of them are here and they are one. Strangely, I lay a path to escape towards the doors, purposefully walking as if a mission besets me. Upon approach, a brief pause, and my course reverses without hesitation. Just as a child lifts his head to his mother for acts of retribution or a man facing his own mortality in the wake of an illness, I slowly look up once again, and behold whom else, "Nostalgia" I whisper.

In complete awareness, my memories yield persuasions of good and evil, searching for information that has been buried for so long. As Nostalgia's presence enters the room, she reminds me of what I had done. How could any one know that such success would breed a deadly ambition the likes of which few have ever known? Whether a prisoner of inner thoughts or a refugee from outer turmoil, escape is futile.

Light-headed, I sprawl myself upon the floor and close my eyes.

In doing so, the main hallway that leads to the Delegation Room begins to appear. Voices become significant as mysterious powers start to play out the uncanny events that took place some *time ago*.

~~~ **Temptation's Prowess**~~~

10:30 AM marks the start of a labor intensive March morning. GenoSyss receives a hefty contract from the Department of Defense. A mandatory meeting convenes in the Delegation Room. The room is given a more colorful name by many workers as the *Divine Hangout*. Dignitaries, senators, diplomats, politicians, celebrities, and even foreign officials walk these floors. Armed guards intentionally make their presence known, reassuring that information is the only thing that comes and goes. Most information that pours from this room is privy only to the executive levels of GenoSyss, but today, everyone will hear.

Casually approaching the room is a familiar presence. His mannerisms and discrete personality projects a rather melancholy character. Short-cropped hair and dorky-styled glasses make for an oddly decent looking fellow. His 6-1 thinly built frame virtually blocks the entry as he gazes upon the word Delegation while others press their way pass him in order to gain entry. With binder in hand, he stands at the threshold and takes into account the security monitors that line the white ceiling. His name is Arthur Wade Robinson.

Arthur leans upon a post while a security guard suspiciously stares at him. But the guard turns away. Perhaps he knows as well as Arthur that the inevitable gathering must go on or maybe that some of the employees are uninterested. Frustration paints the lab technician's face as his eyes look downward. "You should not have come today," he says, but the rules of GenoSyss lacks mercy and are quite known for granting its version of due benevolence for an employee's disobedience.

Locked in frustration, a kinder sound echoes in his ears. "Good morning Arthur." The sound gleefully pours from the mouth of a fellow employee as he passes. "Hello to you too," Arthur responds. "Good morning," from another and yes, a response in kind. Then, another person approaches, but this time eye contact prolongs. The man does not smile nor does he gesture towards Arthur. Walter Grant Pierson displays upon his name badge as he passes. With no expression, both men turn opposite of each other.

Arthur wages his reluctance to enter the meeting room once more. With casual interplay, a happy facade paints his face, a kind gesture for others daring enough to be the recipient of an emotional lashing. "Just another gathering, another pep talk, and another song and dance routine," he says. Slowly turning from the passing crowds, Arthur walks away from the room. It is simple for him, because there are those who are chosen and then there are peons. Either the corporate mold fits or not, and any success that spawns as the result of a peon's hands is absorbed in corporate's greater schemes. Management sees to it.

Grappled in silent turmoil, Arthur continues his progress until another voice catches his attention. "Just were do you think you're going?" With a broken train of thought, wide eye, and quite awaken, Arthur's peering glance unfolds non-other than Gracella Jobet-Andreas. Fast pace and full of emotion, this 5-7and sternly built modern day female is quite capable of holding her own with any one she meets. Dawned in a white lab coat and black-laced stockings, Gracella blocks the surprised technician's path. Gracella's relationship to Arthur has produced a quirky togetherness that teeters between unquestionable loyalty and that of head-butting siblings.

"Just where do you think you're going Arthur?"

"As if you of all people would be asking..."

"Still having group gathering issues?"

"You mean look-the-other-way while we lords piss on you sessions."

"I take that as a yes."

"You should."

"Well…you should know by now that's exactly how management wants us – half human, half peon."

"Not bad, especially coming from the only real half-breed hybrid I know. I told you before; you're a white Mexican with Black in you – minus the neck movements."

"Really…"

"Yes."

"Suck it up Arthur. Everybody else does. Just because management denied you a cross-lateral assignment, that doesn't give you leeway to recant on your contract."

"I'm well aware of that Grace."

"Then *git'ya* butt in there because I think Aniah will have something to say about you coming home with a pink slip."

"What propaganda can they shove at us this time?"

"Well…my point, you won't know *til'* you get in there. Since the change in Directorship, everything comes under scrutiny. Now let's go."

Upon entering, Arthur immediately observes the entire infrastructure.

"Now you know why we don't get raises. This room spans at least a hundred feet in length, while the extending walls stretch maybe ten to twelve feet high. Those other walls are solid glass, laced with fancy etched embroidery from top to bottom. That's a lot of *fancyism* just for a place to show and tell."

"Think of it this way Arthur…by this afternoon, no one will care."

Spectacular mahogany trusses span the arch ceiling, concluding its rise to the 18-foot fourth wall. Four sculpted Cathedral pillars stand majestically between the fourth wall and the platform. Red marble emanates from the floor throughout the room. Velvet-padded chairs appear to mark conceivable arrangements according to numbers, suggesting that the room serves more than one purpose. A high platform rests centrally in front of the pillars, silently inviting speakers to make their statements known. Such declarations come from behind a nicely crafted crystal podium that shares the company of two elegant Japanese Andromedas, each posing on both sides. Recess lighting cast spans of luminance in eight-foot intervals, thus creating a comfortable mood. Track lighting illuminates the speakers and the climate control makes the room acceptable for all seasons. Such comfort, such beauty – no expenses spared.

Making their way towards the rear of the room, Arthur and Gracella hear conversations amidst the crowd. *"This could be the union that sets us free." "Don't have to worry about federal re-location for employees, huh?" "Something good should come of this?" "Rumor has it that outsiders are interested."* Person by person reveals conversations that spur a barrage of curiosity. As time passes, a cloud of excitement intensifies as people help themselves to refreshments in the rear of the room.

Gracella seats herself centrally in a row of chairs. Placing her purse aside, she pulls from within a small mirror and checks for facial flaws and imperfections. Finding contentment, she streaks her fingers through her black hair and shakes it to her satisfaction. Afterwards, she removes a tablet from her purse and begins to write. She fills the page with words, words that carry a meaning perhaps only valuable to her. As she crosses her legs, anyone can see that her penmanship is elegant and comprehendible as ever.

Approaching quietly from the rear of the aisle, Arthur maneuvers between the seats and gets near Gracella. "I was beginning to wonder if you had gotten lost," she says.

"Who…this old boy scout? Don't count it. I see you're writing the chronicles of BS Gathering 101. "

"I'm comparing my notes from the last section meeting to this one."

"Why?"

"My journals show that each time a new director or major discussion takes place; our company's goals become more reckless than ever. Remember when they tried to grow a human's nose on a chimpanzee?"

"Oh yeah, but that was in the name of primate advancement – The chimp's nose wasn't good enough by nature – Right?"

"That was a waste of time and money Arthur."

"Haven't you heard Grace? Only fools scoff at the fool hearted deeds of the foolish."

"And you pulled that out of whose ass?"

"Amen *sista* Andreas, now pass the plate and the money too?"

"You wouldn't be one of those *brothas* who'd keep the money now would you?"

"I'd keep it and give it back to the poor."

"Lord helps us all."

"He is, by making people like me take the financial burden from organizations like this and put it back into the hands of the people, who actually pay for this mess."

"What ever…but I don't see you complaining about the pay."

"Oh…I'll admit, there are benefits."

"Then shut-up and sit down."

"So…bossy."

"Arthur, rumor has it that the military is interested."

"Rumor may be true, since that woman over on the far side is wearing dress greens. Not only that, a military humvee is in the prestigious parking spot."

"Well if that's the case, we shall know soon enough."

"Why?"

"I think we're about to find out."

Suddenly, the room erupts with a loud applause as several stand to their feet. Entering from a side door is a man, average height and robust in size. His motions are slightly awkward as he clacks his cane to a rhythmless stride. His body sways as he bears down on the nicely crafted instrument of aid. Waving at those who cheer him, his progress is quite good, yet the clacking sound is always present. Flanking him is a military officer and two men in nicely gray-tailored suites. Soft lighting illuminates the man of the hour as he sways with wayward motion, concluding his journey directly behind the podium.

"Arthur, recognize that walk?"

"No."

"Don't you know this guy?"

"Should I?"

"Oh my God... It's Rowland."

"Rowland who?"

"Rowland Krenshencov. He's Henderson's replacement. I heard him speak on cellular mitosis a few months ago; this guy virtually wrote the modern day book on genetics."

"Then why haven't I heard of him?"

"Because some people actually read their electronic mail; now *shhh…pay attention.*"

Roland'sdistinct skin features bear record of his history. Mild gray eyebrows with deep defining cheek-folds accent a rather nice composition of facial features. His complexion bears the brand of the Texas sun. With a balding head and piercing blue eyes, his countenance seemingly leaves the impression that a congressional delegate is ready to solicit voters. As the applauding admirers settle, Rowland steps forward and takes charge.

"Umm hummmm…umm, "*Zdravstvuite…Zdravstvuite Menia zovut Vladik Ivonovich Kreshenkov…* ZrDRAST-vet-yah… ZrDRAST-vet-yah, Men-YAH zoh-VOOT,"* he says, smilingly. Laughter fills the room.

"I tell you hello, two times. My name is Vladik Ivonovich Kreshenkov. For new faces, you call me Rowland. For old faces, you may call me many *theengz'.*" Again, the room immediately burst with laughter. "To fear any company, organization, or persons, *eez* to *rre-main* static and die without knowing *dereez* some-*ting* better ahead; a sad travesty for any person *eez* to perish without having tried something new. Better to try and fail than to have failed and not have tried – at all.Opportunity comes to us all – Yes? You either ready for embrace, or you…allow good condition to pass bye – hear me all! Today *veel* mark revolutionary moment and make everlasting solution to any problem where human life…would otherwise be in jeopardy! This fate of *weech* I speak *eez* determined not by what coincidentally comes our way, but what we *crr-eate* with the materials given to us, thus resulting in profound actions!"

"He must have been a preacher or politician."

"He's doing good Arthur – just listen."

"I want to know what he means by solution to problems that puts human life in jeopardy." Gracella gives no verbal response to Arthur's reply as she casually watches Rowland unbuttoning his jacket.

Rowland continues. "As for each one of you, I am proud to be part of some-*teen* bigger than life. Each of you put hard emphasis on success, and compassion for mankind. Your deeds often go unappreciated. But the work you perform is far more important than you realize since*eet* can *brr-ing* cures to those that suffer from diseases, deformities, and the social pressures of foreign dictatorships!"

Rowland's charisma rises as he unbuttons the last button on his coat, exposing his yellow tie and white shirt. He sportingly animates the emphasis of each topic of his speech as he forcefully shakes his fist, driving home words to imprint minds daring enough to accept his challenges.

"Though society sees clones far lower than sublevel entities, they are shortsighted to possibilities. We can *geev* people organs that work without causing others to pay large sacrifice. We can select genetic strengths and root out weaknesses, even such illnesses that prey on many. We can even *crr-eate* desirable companions for those who choose not to go through the complexities of social selecting. *Thees* ability was once unthinkable or deemed unethical *eez* now at fingertips of your hands. *Weeth prr-opper* backing; even cloned soldiers of fortune can take the place of enlisted loved ones, thus to someday raise clones to higher acceptance! *Unteel* then, we steady hold true to our course."

With a pause in his delivery, Rowland lowers his head as though to gather the next set of thoughts, stretching his moment of silence. But soon, he raises his hand in trembling fashion and positions his palm just beneath his nose while covering his mouth. His apparent actions suggest a moment of reflection; however, the microphone faintly picks up the word, "Dunyasha." Tears begin to stream down Rowland's check and across his trembling lips as the audience watch with sorrowful curiosity.

"What's going on Grace?"

"*Shhh*…I don't know."

The man who gleamed with exuberant joy only moments earlier now stands as a broken container of sympathetic emotions; yet somehow, beneath the layers of cloth and fleshly exterior, Rowland summons the courage to press forward.

"You must understand that we are chosen not only to solve great deal of world's problems through genetic research, but to save *thees* world, we must also protect. I have spent weeks debating if GenoSyss should take on more projects that are ambitious, or remain were we are and perfect what currently exists. Comrades, we have weathered difficulties from human-rights activists, moralists, and even *rr-ight*-wing politicians, but their lack of vision makes us *strrr*-ong. And because of that, we now have major interest group. Behold, Department of Defense! Detailed study of projects and workloads pushes me to believe we are able to accommodate their interest. So…*wee*-out *rrr-*eservation, I have decided to accept challenge of Defense Department. Together, their foresight and our ingenuity *veel* make *thees* union new era in genetic research. *Dasvidaniya – Dazav-tra*."

With poised shoulders and a gleam in his eye, Rowland continues to sway the crowd to his rallying agenda as the masses respond with cheers, erupting in a broad band of praise.

"That explains the dress-greens," whispers Arthur.

"Das vidanya to you too Rowland. Well that's it…we now have an official contract. Our new director has taken a tempting offer from Uncle Sam. So, what do you think about that Arthur? Arthur, are you listening?"

"Huh?"

"Oh no…there's that look in your eye again."

"I didn't know this meeting would be so interesting."

"Though rare, that does happen on occasion – when you do attend; but that look on your face is sending out red flags – so let me be the first to warn you. Take it easy this time."

"Grace, that contract is a security blanket and I want to know more about Rowland's proposal."

"All I'm saying Arthur, is don't put your heart into whatever they have to offer…too soon. Remember the last time?"

"We all live and learn."

"Yes – but you heal very slowly; and I prefer not to see you go through that again."

"Aww, how sweet, you care."

"Shut up – I'm serious."

"Sometimes a tempting offer can be the best antidote, or best, A-miracle cure. I declare I'm *heeeealed*."

"Arthur, you're going to…so…fall on your ass."

"That's why the good lord put cusion back there."

"Never mind…that I told you so."

Soon, bodies stir throughout the room as some congratulate Rowland while others immediately exit. The crowd dwindles, yet words begin to pour over the p.a. system. "COULD I HAVE YOUR ATTENTION PLEASE…could I have your attention?" As Gracella, Arthur, and a few other colleagues turn in the direction of the sound, the room grows silent. "YOU ARE EXCUSED FOR THE DAY!" Excitement fills the room once more.

"There is a God in Heaven," states Arthur.

Gracella simply looks at Arthur and walks away.

~~~~Justifying Cause~~~

My eyes open only to find that Nostalgia is still here. I reach for her, only to watch my hands wave through empty space. In the still of the moonlight, she appears and then vanishes as quickly as I can find her – But was she really there?

Rowland's speech vividly fills my thoughts – even to this day. It was a grand occasion for GenoSyss and the meeting went well. There were people dancing, cheering, smiling, and speaking to those whom they have not spoken too for quite some time.

While thinking in silence, the short couch against the far wall comes into view. Even in dim light the maroon, almond, and blue pastel colors of the flower patterns are quite distinguishable. Dark streaks of green on the stems of the plants are recognizable amidst the collage of patterns as well. As I watch, the cool breeze that caressed my skin earlier passes once more. This time, it over whelms my senses. But these feelings tenderly succumb to the state of a mental awareness; an awareness that sets the stage once more within GenoSyss.

Rowland's acceptance of the military's proposal was a miraculous time for us all. It marked the beginning of a new era in clone-bio engineering. Staring at the ceiling, my eyes slowly close again as I uncover those events from long ago.

The buzzing sound of an alarm clock pierces the darkness. Arthur's eyes open as he beholds his long time companion, but instead, one continuous motion of his arm silences the alarm. "Baby…baby…wake up, you're late," she says.

"Oh shi…." "Don't even finish that statement; that is if you intend to live out the rest of your days…fully intact. From now on, you need to get to bed on time."

Rising upon silk linen, Arthur pushes himself to balance upright. He places one hand over his forehead as Aniah watches. "See…you guys were the party animals last night. That's what happens when you act crazy."

"What time did we get home?"

"We were among the last to leave because you couldn't keep your mouth shut."

"And you couldn't stay away from the Long Island Ice Tea."

"I did my share but you were well into that green fizzy stuff."

"I didn't have that much."

"Much of what; the tea or the company?"

"What do you mean?"

"Arthur, each time you behave as you did last night, it usually has something to do with GenoSyss. Either they have made a decision that you strongly disagree with or they coaxed you into a comfort zone – again. Usually, they get what they want while leaving you with nothing much to show for."

"Yes, the company has successfully invoked apartheid – and took my balls in the process."

"Watch your mouth…dear," responds Aniah as she zips her dress and makes her way towards the bedroom mirror.

Arthur steps inside the shower as the crystal door slides shut. "Temp eighty-nine, Fahrenheit, jet stream…intermittent." In an instant, pristine water spews from the showerhead, but Arthur simply stands there.

"Did you hear me?" Aniah attempts to gain Arthur's attention, but he ignores her. He stares at the sprinkling water as though it possesses a hypnotic allure. Afterwards, warm air blows from several ports, rapidly drying his body as he exits the shower bay. Entering the bedroom, Arthur encounters a finger pressing firmly against his chest. There to confront him is Aniah, adjusting her head to assure eye contact.

"Did you hear me talking to you?"

"No…not exactly."

"Honey, I think you are very talented, but you still hold on to old things; and it's those *things* of the past that are making you bitter. GenoSyss is only a stepping-stone, yet I believe you may try to move ahead at the wrong time. You really have a heart for what you do, but you have to be patient."

"Thank-you for letting me have fun with the guys last night – even if we did drink a little too..."

"Momma use to say that you can't tame a fool, if he's already a fool...so don't let the fool's foolishness tame you."

"Ouch."

"Seven years has given me more insight into you Mr. Robinson than anyone you may think you know. Now just remember, I'm still with you, and that alone should tell you something."

Aniah's expressions strike deep within Arthur as he looks away, realizing that she can touch the most sensitive implications of his male-*ish* factions. Whether such power becomes her by fate or the relinquishing of his will, she controls the highs and lows between them with each beckoning word. She walks her fingers upward, along his chest until her hand comes to rest just behind his neck. Gently pulling his head, she embraces him. "I know why I married you," she says, concluding with a kiss while standing on the tip of her toes. Their benevolent actions breathes a joyful moment, yet both realize that time becomes a factor and conclude their embrace. Shortly afterwards, standing near a window, Arthur waves goodbye as a black sedan takes her away.

Arthur's attire is everything but the desire of management as scruffy denim touches the heel of hiking boots. A long black sweatshirt drapes partially over his thighs. He places a bracelet upon his wrist and punches code keys to lock it in place. Approaching the front door, he grabs the doorknob with haste and exits. Upon entering his vehicle, Arthur slides his wrist past the ignition slot and the mighty machine roars to life. Soon, he propels the white transport into the business of the day.

Arthur's travel eventually brings him to a large barbed-wire gate. Security personnel check the identification badges for each driver entering. Glancing above, Arthur sees a sign that he has seen far too often which displays: GenoSyss, Genetics Systems Research Site, The Future is in the Genes. "The future is more like...he who controls congress," he mutters. Arthur flashes his wristband and the guard waves him through.

Shortly afterwards, a dull noise thumps loudly as Arthur flings his briefcase upon a desktop. Stretching his neck, he plants himself before a monitor. In routine fashion, he turns on a lamp, prepares a bowl of oatmeal, fills his water canteen, adjusts his chair, and allows music to gently fill his space. Arthur's area is clean and simple. Pastel frosted walls and a glass desk form a modular cubical that grants him freedom to move about, yet invokes a cell block sense of containment. A philodendron scarcely survives under artificial lighting while a miniature military humvee proudly displays near a picture of he and Aniah. Surprisingly, few plaques dress the walls as drawings of four horses, three Siberian tigers, and a photograph of YellowstoneNational Park hangs noticeably. Adhering to a moment of silence, Arthur begins to pray. He concludes his prayer by asking God, "Lead and guide me this day – Amen." After executing a process on the computer, Arthur quietly stares at the pictures of the tigers and horses. For him, there is always time to observe. Perhaps it is an act to secure a subliminal connection. The horses are running somewhere and yet nowhere. Before them lies an open field that stretches far into the horizon; no fences, no boundaries – only freedom. The tigers are together and looking in the same direction; a partnership of unity perhaps – only Arthur knows. The wall calendar displays the only job related accomplishment, a ten-year service award certificate. He smiles.

"System on, AR35706, operation manual," he says. Soon, the dark screen displays several elements for viewing. Arthur accesses his electronic message account. Scrolling down, he goes through the fun portions first, reading jokes and watching videos sent to him by co-workers. Once complete, only then does he render attention to the urgent reply message. "More junk," he utters. Moving the cursor into position, he readies the delete option…until, "Whoa…this was sent late yesterday evening." Arthur leans back in his chair and opens the desk drawer. He discovers a sealed envelope specifically with his name printed on it. Carefully opening the document, he reads the information contained within. His curiosity swells, but he holds back like a cat playing with a mouse just before the kill. Soon, his anxiousness gets the best of him and without further hesitation; he finds a map inside the envelope. In one breath, he reads the entire message, looks at his watch, and turns toward the monitor. "System end," he whispers while leaning backwards in the chair once more.

Flickering lights illuminate the office as the sound of voices begins pouring in. Far across blue partitions, coffee pots brew the dark fluid as bodies begin to move about. "The morning crew is in," he says. Arthur looks away in disarray as he reaches for his leather binder, tucking it snugly underneath the pit of his arm along with the envelope. "Morning Arthur," bellows from a passing co-worker.

"Morning to you too – Oh…Trent."

"Yeah…"

"I'll be in the warehouse today."

"So?"

"Well…if any one is looking for me… Got it?"

"Sure – I don't care. Just stay out of trouble…"

"No problem."

Arthur quickly departs. Other employees pass Arthur, but the technician acts as if he does not hear or see them. Pressing his way downstairs, Arthur navigates through a maze of lowly lit corridors until he finally comes to a room. Stopping in mid motion, he views a small metallic gold marker just above a door. "Room 47-C Conference." As he reassures himself, he gently slides his bracelet across a scanner. The sound of unlocking mechanisms echo as he grabs the door handle, but he does not go in just yet. Pausing, Arthur takes a deep breath and moves the door handle downward. As the door slowly opens, an atmosphere of gayety eases his concerns as he pokes his head past the entry. Immediately, Arthur scans the room and eventually steps inside only to realize that he is not alone. Sitting at the head of a table is Rowland. "Ah…there you are *MeesterRrr-obinson.*" "Yes," Arthur responds, nodding his head while maintaining focus. Arthur makes his way to the only seat available. Much to his surprise, other faces are staring at him.

"Sorry I'm running late Rowland."

"*Eet eez* good you join us…we were expecting you. I realize electronic messages are sometimes unpredictable, but you did read it this time – good for you. Now you may shred envelope; leave no paper trail. Curious eyes are undesirable. Also, we took liberty to have your bracelet encoded so you could enter *thees* room."

"It was a surprise to me Rowland."

"I'm quite sure. We meet down here because *thees* place *eez* very confidential – Yes? Do sit."

Arthur positions his binder directly on the table. He gives the appearance of preparedness though his tardiness renders a very awkward presentation. Rowland speaks quietly with two outsiders, thus allowing time for Arthur to observe the room. For Arthur, there is always time to observe. Three men conduct business beneath a ten-foot cork-panel ceiling. The ceiling trails with one long central rail of track lights. Some lights efficiently strike subjects within the room while other beams paint the room with a soft glow. High-back leather chairs take nothing from the beige walls that contain subtle streaks of gray, green, and yellow hash marks. The marks lay random patterns throughout a pastel color scheme. Each element compliments a large wooden table that sits in the middle of the room. Most strikingly, the table radiates a glass-like polish, which astoundingly reflects the images of everyone sitting close enough to view the craftsman's handy work. Underneath the base of the table is a dark emerald-green carpet.

With much to view, Arthur focuses his attention on those sitting around the table. Each participant pairs off in groups of two. Relaxed bodies rock back and forth as conversations rise. Then, an enchanting sound draws Arthur's attention. The sound comes from three twinkling bracelets on a small pale wrist. The stylish ensemble belongs to Alexis Hawthorne. Such jewelry coincides with an undeniable perfume, a partial smile, tinted cheeks, and fluttering eyelids. Alexis' smile grows wider as she invokes her girlish mannerisms into the ears of the older and seemingly wiser Jade Vjekoslava.

Jade casts a wonderful tan, dark hair and green eyes. Her accent fosters a warm greeting. Gesturing with Alexis, she briskly responds, "Yeah – I'm sure he has a cute butt…but in time, that butt will become a bag so you better get interested in something else. Now until you become a full-timer, men should either become a relic or all together dormant." Alexis' eyebrows curiously rise as her mouth partially opens.

Arthur smiles, but then focuses his attention to another duo, Tuan Nguyen and Gracella, who both engage in conversation as well. "You can eat fish with chicken…eat with pork; any thing just about – I ate much back home. Rice is good," Tuan explains. "*Mmm,* you know I can go for red beans, ground beef, and rice, with *chile'* and *chiportele'*, and some jalapenos," replies Gracella with her eyes closed, rubbing her belly while sinking down into the chair.

"Grace always loves her food," notes Arthur, whispering aloud.

Then, a pounding noise draws every one's attention and the room quickly becomes silent. Frank Guilford forcefully slams his hand face down on the table, making a profound statement, word for word.

"They…can…do…what…they…want," he expounds. As he does, his partner, Walter Grant Pierson responds by pounding his fist on the table in like manner. "Okay, okay…so what if Congress does. Is it a sin…huh, is it a sin? Tell me!" Others take interest in their conversation, but Frank does not smile as he stares at Walter. Instead, he breathes heavier as his right eye begins to twitch. Walter returns the gesture.

As both men stare at each other, a boisterous deep voice intervenes, commandingly taking president over their uncanny conversation. "You *wanna* know what I think?" The question spews from none other than Nathaniel Keech. Leaning closer to Frank and Walter, Nathaniel's voice bellows. "Hell…I'll tell *ya* what I think." Without warning, Nathaniel's thick chubby hand flattens upon the surface of the table. Then his arm moves slowly up and down as he points his finger aloft. Deep folds within his skin conform to a rigid tightening of his eyebrows; tensely, and his leathery face exudes a deep redness. "*Yous* two…and Congress can kiss my Midlothian Ass!" Nathaniel leans back in his chair as though a monumental task has been achieved. Chuckling fills the room.

"Oh Lord, they're at it again," notes Arthur.

"Gentlemen…that *weel* be enough. Let us begin – shall we?" Rowland acknowledges Tuan with a head gesture.

Tuan approaches a console panel on the wall. "Secure all," he says. Immediately, the door locks and electronic shields cover the walls. "Sound masking complete Professor; we're good to go."

Rowland quiets the teams. "We must not be disturbed. Only you in *these rr-oom* receive e-message and envelope. This was done in part as to leave no suspicions or electronic information that can be linked to you, with regards to this meeting. You were selected because of your *skeeelz* and your position on the pecking order of *theengs;* fair representation – so to speak. So, *heer* you are... *Weeth* out further waiting…ladies, gentlemen, I want to introduce Michael Gladestone from McCormick Affiliates Law firm and Colonel Mortimer Ducet of United States Marine Bio Development *Dee*-vision.

"Hello," acknowledges Michael in formal fashion while placing a portable computer on the table, but Ducet's acknowledgement is with less enthusiasm.

"At *thees* time, I *weel* let Colonel Ducet address you."

"Thank you Rowland," replies the colonel. The solemn commander places his elbows on the table. Clutching his hands in a prayerful manner, the officer's broad shoulders proudly bears epaulets, which boldly displays his ranking insignia. He is a stoic piece of militant discipline. With feet planted firmly and back straightly upright, Ducet's posture is correct as can be. Prominent facial ridgelines cast distinguishing hard shadows over rock solid jaws. His neatly crew cut, sandy-brown hair frames a rather stern looking and well shaven face, which accents the standard dress green uniform. Spectacular awards and decorations cover his chest while a large gold ring glistens upon his finger. Taking a deep breath, the colonel stares upward towards the ceiling, then downward again to confront the assembly. It is clear that Ducet is gathering his thoughts, but what he has to say is far more expecting.

"Ladies…gentlemen, thank you for coming. What you are about to hear in this room stays in this room. If there is any breech of confidentiality, plausible deniability will go into effect. Should any information leak out – you will not win. Your account of this meeting and the involvement of others will have no supportive evidence whatsoever, and we will see to that."

The colonel bears no emotion. His piercing hazel eyes leave no room for an unforgettable encounter. Only the sound of Gladstone inputting information into the computer fills the room.

Ducet continues. "A long, long, time ago on August 9th, our Commander in Chief, at the time, gave his approval for stem cell research and supported it with more than two-million green-backs. The money was to fund at least 64 stem cell lines. Now, it is a free-for-all to whoever wants it. As you know, cloning, manipulating DNA, and replacing organs have long been a hot topic and I'm sure you can understand the reasons why. In the case of war, the military has always shown an interest in healing wounded soldiers, or replacing worn out parts on humans – so to speak. But old directives have always favored antiquated approaches. In other words, people should sacrifice their lives and die, all in the name of honor. That is not a bad way to exit this world; however, it's just too costly in more ways than just financial. But thanks to advances in science, we now have the freedom to explore, which brings us to you. Few facilities can match the success of this company. Months ago, my department made contact with your director and the rest is history. In short, congratulations people, your facility was chosen to host a governmental project that will help us to explore a more contemporary approach to sparing a soldier's life as well as securing the future of this country."

Colonel Ducet receives a glass of water from Rowland. As he drinks, Walter jumps to his feet with astounding exuberance. "Yes" he says while bearing a smile and shaking his fist in triumphant agreement.

"Thank you Mr. Walter Pierson." The colonel wipes his face with one swiping motion from forehead to chin as though the hardest part of his delivery is over. He leans back into his chair placing one hand on the handle and his elbow on the other handle, thus causing his body to turn sideways.

"In addition, our department's mandate is to see whether or not a new species can be cloned, altered, or manipulated from raw genetic material. That material is either fabricated or taken from a living subject – which is highly preferable. If we incorporate our concepts with your impressive genius, we can only step into the annals of greatness. Technology and radiation are key factors for success, based on what we have seen so far. And you can trust me when I say that I would not be here if what I am asking you is not possible. We have seen the impending effects of radiation on plants and animals in ways unimaginable, and that brings us to the ultimate reason why we, as a group, are here. Any questions so far?"

Colonel Ducet continues his deliberation with such proficiency that one cannot help but wonder about the reasons for the urgency. In the mist of his speech, Arthur roughly sketches bizarre characters on white paper. As he does, no one leaves the room or takes a break. Everyone sits in captivation.

The room again locks down in silence as the colonel reaches into a black briefcase. He pulls from within the case four-color photographs and proceeds to pass the photos one by one to Frank who is nearest. Frank receives the photos and attempts to make sense of the images. He stares at the imbedded elements, gritting his teeth while frowning with discuss. Saying nothing, he passes one of the photos to Jade. Her eyes lock directly onto the photo. A hard sternness covers her face while her mouth slowly opens. Several seconds pass and she slowly gives the photo to Alexis.

Noticing their reactions, the colonel leans forward. "These were taken some time ago. Our visual lab specialists concur that the images are real."

Gracella receives the next photo and her reaction is no less abhorrent than the others. Then, Tuan receives the first photo and he too becomes deeply concerned with the images. "What the hell," whispers

Nathaniel as he turns and faces Frank just before giving him the next photo. Tuan and Alexis both cover their mouths. The clockwise delivery proceeds as minor metaphors and verbal gander fills the atmosphere. Finally, the first photo reaches Arthur. Using both hands, the technician assures that the image does not move. Staring closely, Arthur summons Ducet.

"Colonel, am I seeing what I think I see?"

"What exactly is...*it*...that you think you see?"

Arthur stares at the colonel as if pondering a foolish question. "For the record - sir, the photo displays three Bedouins, apparently carrying some type of assault riffles. It does not appear that they have an association with the military, but in that part of the world – who knows. Just beneath the feet of one the men is the body of something laying face down. Partial human-like torso is visible and the rear appendages of an animal's hind legs – a fawn or goat of some sort. Fine hairs cover much of the nude body and of course, large amounts of blood."

"An accurate assessment Mr. Arthur Robinson."

Arthur passes the photo to Rowland as Colonel Ducet rises to his feet and slowly walks around the room. "What you see before you is authentic – I can assure you." Silence looms throughout the room once more.

The second photo arrives into the hands of Gracella. "Colonel, is this a closer look at the body? It appears that the men have turned the body face up, exposing the chest cavity and legs. There are large chunks of flesh torn out of the side of its body. What happened?"

"As the story goes, a farmer heard noises one night coming from his livestock bin. He investigates. What you see in the photo is what he found gnawing on one of his sheep. In haste, he fires several rounds directly into this – creature. According to him, *it* made a sound that pierced his very soul. Even to this day, he reports of ongoing nightmares."

"Wow."

"*'Wow'* is an understatement. Amazingly, the beast did not die from the initial shot. The gunmen, or Bedouins as Mr. Robinson says, found a pack of wolves tearing into the creature. The men scared the wolves away; a noble gesture, considering it happened after five deaths with sixteen severely wounded. That creature was found eleven miles from the farmer's property – still bleeding."

"According to the gunshot wounds, it should have died on the spot."

"True, but what intrigues me about this whole situation, is the kind of stamina this beast exhibited. This type of exertion is not found in the natural or conventional world as we know it."

The third photo comes into Arthur's possession. "This can't be," says Arthur as goose pimples cover his forearms. He raises his head and notices Walter placing his hand over his mouth as though to prevent regurgitation. The colonel paces the floor before proceeding on with his debriefing.

"Observe the area where the torso and leg portions join. Note how the torso joins the waist and thigh areas."

"What am I looking for?"

"Do you see a seam, remnants of stitches, or scars…or any other mark to suggest a separate addition of bonding, or Frankenstein connection – if you will?"

"No. This is impressive work."

"Pan," says Jade. "Pan…who," replies Frank. "Pan, the mythical Greek half-man half-goat forest dweller, or something like that."

"You mean…chimera; a political correctness for modern time – Yes?" Rowland's statement beckons profound stares as he unfolds his hands and approaches the table.

Alexis asks, "What's the difference Professor?"

"*Pan has* same original DNA, born that way of course. The chimera has multiple DNA, which exist as one in the same animal. As you know, many of us believe that *mee-xing* human and animal DNA will make better specimens to study."

As Rowland speaks, curious interjections from all surrounding persons begin to fill the air.

"We do know that a long time ago, scientist in China fused human cells with rabbit eggs. The embryos were allowed to develop for several days but were destroyed after the scientist harvested the stem cells," explains Gracella.

"Did you also know that history records that a clinic in Minnesota successfully created pigs with human blood flowing through their veins and that StanfordUniversity attempted to grow mice with human brains? Those institutions were quite successful, so what you are seeing is not entirely incomprehensible," adds Tuan.

Frank draws Ducet's attention. "That's all fine, but Colonel, where did these photos come from?"

"That information is classified. I can; however, tell you that not long after local officials got word of the incident, attempts were made to retrieve...this Pan – as you call it."

"Owners? You mean that *thing* belongs to someone? "

"I mean...that, this creature is not a freak of nature. Someone is responsible – but how we know is classified." The colonel glances around the room, capturing the eyes of all who are listening.

Alexis raises her hand. "Scuse' me umm sir, but where were these pictures taken?"

"That information is classified ma'am."

"Well...can you tell us who took them?"

"That too...again...is classified."

Alexis grows impatient. "Then what can you tell us Colonel?"

"I've already told you more than you need to know. However, off the record, I have reason to believe that a factious group may have something to do with the creature. But more importantly, such creations are possible, and that makes this creature all too real."

Frank draws the colonel's attention in a sarcastic manner. "So the photographs bare the Authentication of the U.S. Government...eh?" Ducet is void of expression and simply looks at him. Frank picks up one of the other photos and carefully examines it. "Sounds like movie material."

"This is the got-damnedest thing I ever heard," expresses Nathaniel as he looks towards the colonel.

"Oh it's real…I can assure you Mr. Nathaniel Keech."

After responding to Nathaniel, the colonel sits within his chair as the fourth photograph enters Arthur's hands. "Colonel Ducet, this image in the photo displays a close up of the creature from chest to head. The head bears a partial human-like appearance as half of its face remains, bearing what appear to be bite marks. It also appears that something fed on it – the wolves undoubtedly."

"You are correct."

"Something fed well, because only the top row of teeth remains. Did the wolves take the lower jaw?"

"Possibly…"

"Small slits appear to represent a nose while the skull is partially exposed. Even more interesting is the olive-blue skin? Is it possible we can see this creature in person?" Ducet simply looks at Arthur."I know, I know…classified or on-a-need to-see basis," replies the technician.

"There are several strange anomalies surrounding this beast, but for he most part I want you all to pay close attention to the animal's makeup. Note the eyes. What do you see?"

"The pupil is hard to see. It blends in with the sclera. In humans, that would be the white part of the eye; which is oddly dark in color for our friend here," replies Gracella.

"That's the physical assessment. We all can see that Mrs. Gracella Andreas. What I really want to know is what Mr. Robinson sees."

Arthur cants a childish grin. "The look upon its face…even in death, this pariah is seemingly trying to tell us something."

"And…what do you think it is trying to tell us?"

"Honestly?"

"Sure – we are in secret."

Arthur winces for a moment. He looks sternly at the photograph once more. Afterwards, he places the picture on the table and observes the surrounding partisans. Taking a long deep breath, he tells them, "Some things are an abomination and should never exist."

Silence lingers. Without anticipation, Colonel Ducet addresses the room again. "Rowland assures me that you all can produce some promising results. The others within this facility will be given routine assignments so they can carry out their daily business while you, within this room, will conduct an experiment of extraordinary proportions. As the result of your success record, this additional task befalls you." Ducet leans back into his chair crowning the moment with a drink of water.

Rowland steps forth, "Thank you Colonel. *Thees* now brings us to major point. There are always matters of ethics. *We* have seen such things before. You know what we are up against. Now; for major question... Though you were selected, we need final approval as to *weech* of you will participate?"

One by one, affirmations slowly accept Rowland's invitation in one shattering moment while leaving Arthur to give the final acceptance. "Well Arthur?" he asks. All eyes fasten on the silent technician as he ponders his thoughts. A lurid quietness looms within the room. Then, in a small monotone voice, without reservation, "Can we control an abomination?" Curious faces stare without expression. Suddenly, piercing the cloud of silence, Michael Gladestone, the lawyer brazes the moment. "Control is a relative term Mr. Arthur Robinson."

"With all due respect, is it the relevance that justifies our dealings in this matter?"

"Your point?"

"The existence of this creature suggests that someone successfully manufactured a hybrid. Well...controlling it...failed. Now, *we* are trying to prove that we can manufacture the same thing, but with control – Am I correct?"

"As I said earlier Mr. Robinson, control is relative...indeed," reiterates Gladestone, crossing his legs while clutching his hands upon his kneecaps, nodding his head as though to assure everyone that *yes* is the appropriate answer.

Arthur slants his head in a questionable manner, and then gestures a nonverbal concurrence.

"Then *eet eez* settled," Rowland smilingly replies.

~~~The Enlightened Ones~~~

As I open my eyes, I find that a blanket covers me. Rising upright, the realization soon strikes me that Aniah assured my comfort while I slept. While smiling, I stand to my feet and make my way directly to the fireplace. Smoldering coals dimly cast the glowing remnants of a once dancing flame. The remaining heat brazes my bare hands. The warmth is comforting. Yet, having no sense of urgency, I make my way to the library.

Upon entering, I slowly open the closet and remove a plain gray scrapbook. Staring at the book seems to be the right thing to do while holding it. The leather binder feels new and smells like rawhide. But such things are of no importance since the book is only good for one thing – memories. Taking a deep breath, I make my way down the dark hall to the master bedroom. Gently pressing the bedroom door, a mild squeak sounds as the hinges turn upon each other. The door opens just enough to reveal Aniah sleeping. Reserving the right to wake her, the destination to the den becomes my objective once more. Upon arrival, still awaiting me is the essence of Nostalgia but this time, her presence is faint as the moon positions farther across the sky.

Reoccupying the sofa, I lay open the pages of the scrapbook. Picturesque paraphernalia fills several adhesive 11x14 pages, which commemorates a five-year legacy of some of the finest moments at GenoSyss. One photo reveals Gracella attempting to sing while another catches Walter and Tuan in the act of mimicking the former Director of the company. Alexis poses with cashmere beside Jade and there is Nathaniel bearing the resemblance of the bull terrier that sits beside him. The laughter, the smiles, jesting, pranks, newspaper articles; all give a pleasurable glimpse into the past, everything from slimmer bodies to Rowland with hair on his head. A fine account from photo to photo.

Turning the pages reveals a very special project; a donkey named Bartimaeus. We thought the name was colorful, since Jackass would be too sarcastic, but no one joked too long about it. We toast to celebrate our successful cloning of Bartimaeus, but he was not just any ordinary clone. We called him Bart for short.

With Tuan's input in genetic accelerants, the growth rate of Bart propeled the sandy brown Abyssinian from conception to adulthood in less than two weeks. What a remarkable time it was. Bart was healthy, vibrant, and full of excitement. We were all so proud. But how were we to know that three months later would mark the end of him. His metabolism burned him to death. To our ignorance, such knowledge came too late. Bart was often warm and having brought him to life fell far short of desiring expectations. I gently rub the picture, telling myself that minor alterations were okay. Maybe I deeply tell myself that God's creation came with missing pieces, so…we mere mortals had to assist the Almighty in completing His design. My feelings succumb to a deep emotional attachment that results in a teardrop. Only later did the direct modification of certain endocrine glands prove too practical, effective, and humane – as if God forgot something. I close the book.

Silhouette images prance in their darkened world, parading as though to elude my attempts to distill their luring haughtiness, while elsewhere before me, Nostalgia stands amidst. Gazing at her congers memories as the theater of my mind gives precedence to bloodstain performances and acts of heresy; they're all here – contained well within my mind. My eyes gently close again.

Walter unloads materials to the others in room 47-C. As he does, Rowland approaches. "Very *guud* information yesterday – Yes?"

"About as good as it gets for Texas, "replies Walter.

"In reference to cloning?"

"Of course…"

"Isn't it interesting how other countries seem to embrace questionable acts before US? China for *eenstence*, now have laws for therapeutic cloning. England argues for stem cell research, and even Australia is pushing for more progressive measures."

"Cloning humans is still a blasphemous act for some people Rowland."

"Most Americans…too *beezy weeth* other matters."

"I often think about the successes of men like Hans Spemann, how his work virtually paved the way for our successes."

"Yes, I am aware of *heem*; not to mention the cloned lamb, Dolly, from the United Kingdom – both were monumental feats."

30

Nathaniel hears the conversation and quickly intervenes. "Foreigners may seem like the first, only because the US had its hands in a lot of *shit* long before they came along."

"Nathaniel, our guest," interrupts Rowland in a suggestive manner while nodding towards Colonel Ducet. "That's quite all right Rowland, I've heard my share," responds the officer in a chuckling manner, but Nathaniel continues his points.

"My apologies colonel, but you know what I mean. That old boy who help discover DNA way back in 1953, Ned First cloning of calves in 94, and human embryos in Massachusetts of 01 – that seems to speak for itself."

"You tell em' Nat. We'll be the first to clone em' bigger and better in Texas," says Alexis, laughing while patting Nathaniel on the back.

"I see that you all are aquatinted with history. Much like the scenarios you mentioned. Note that all who were involved saw a tremendous need for what they had to offer. They all saw opportunity and seized it," explains the colonel. Bowing his head briefly, the soldier places both hands on the table and slowly pushes his 6' frame back into the chair. Every one watches with anticipation, anxiously awaiting the colonel's next move. Ducet methodically walks behind each person in the room as he apparently builds a deliberation for the next outpouring of information.

"As I stated before, the photos you saw earlier are indeed real. There's more information surrounding the photographs; but for now, lets just say that…if…someone is able to create such a creature, and that creature is a hybrid. Then who's to say that such capability will stop there?"

"Scuse' me colonel – sir, but *'it'* being what exactly," asks Walter.

"The *it* being intent, purpose, outcome, circumstances. Think along these lines – if you will. Why was that creature created and what was the purpose for its existence?"

"Point taken…"

"Good. Now keep in mind, if you can create a body, then why stop there when you can condition the mind to control that body?"

31

Gracella asks, "Colonel, are you suggesting that the creature in the photo somehow represents a threat to national security, or is it a threat at all?"

"Let's just say that if this creature is a threat, I hope that my presence here will convince each of you that containing such a threat is possible. And if containing such a threat is possible, then wouldn't you all agree that the playing field should be even?"

"It sounds practical."

"I want you all to know that current resources of the latest technology are at your disposal."

"Colonel, think us not too ignorant. What you're saying is that if they can do it, then…why can't we. And if *they* did create this creature and intend to use it as a weapon, then why shouldn't we?"

"We're on the same page ma'am…Gracella, but think of our product as a precautionary defense rather than a threatening offensive weapon."

Jade watches Ducet as if suspicion crosses her mind. Both sternly make eye contact, and yet, he asks, "Do you have something to add Ms. Jade?"

"Of course colonel... Earlier, you mention a radical group. Is the group named Rham-kiev and are they somehow involved in the fabrication of this hybrid Pan?"

Colonel Ducet does not answer. Instead, he leaves his chair and slowly circles the group with his head down, obviously pondering an answer. As he turns his back to the group, the officer gingerly grabs the leaf of a plant, which is nestled in the corner of the room. Tilting his head as though the flora holds a mystic interest, Ducet then strikingly unfolds his answer.

"It is interesting that you should ask, since many are not aware of Rham-kiev's existence. Therefore, let us speculate. We know that Rham-kiev is a group of radicals in Europe, who may have some cloning capability, but as to their involvement with the creation in the photo, we are not certain. I'm sure you are beginning to see where I'm going with this whole thing. If such capability falls into the wrong hands, many bad things can happen."

"Especially when humans are involved..."

"Absolutely...."

"Which part?"

"You have no idea how difficult it is to notify parents, husbands, wives, sons, and daughters that their loved ones are coming home in body bags, especially for causes that become degrading or questionable."

"Causes...on whose part, yours or theirs?"

Ducet eyes Jade, sternly saying, "Causes that sometimes revolve around a No-win scenario."

Jade watches the colonel while smirking. "I'm sure, no one here can relate."

Ducet turns away from Jade, but then continues. "Since you are all sitting here, I conclude that we are all on the same page and have no reservations about how each of you will be spending the next four to six months developing this project. Surely, you all must know that even the best of tasks, with good reason, will have some degree of ethical or moral repercussions. My point here is not to re-evaluate your position on this matter, but to give you some degree of clairvoyant perspective on the issues that surround the human aspect of this project. Far too often, events take place in this world that requires the unbiased approach of the military. The military's involvement then becomes proactive, in that it either curtails a situation or completely put it down altogether. Such drastic measures often kill innocent people in the process. Make no mistake, commanders have the guts to send men and women to their deaths and believe me, we are not afraid to do so. But over time, places like Hiroshima and Nagasaki, Grenada, Panama, IRAQ, Gibraltar, FortSterling 3; we've learned that mass destruction is not always the best answer, and that humans as collateral damage are not always a prudent choice. Only afterwards do we learn that surgical strikes with seal or marine units continue to put soldiers needlessly in harms way. With new technologies at our disposal, we can reinvent the wheel."

"Send in the hybrids," says Walter.

"Something to that effect...Mr. Pierce. You see...instead of conditioning people, why not condition a hybrid. You know as well as I that conflicts with humans arise continuously, so... Why not create a soldier capable of doing the job and whose life is more or less expendable? Now for the million-dollar question. If you could create such a soldier, would you?"

"Are you serious?" asks Arthur, causing the colonel to respon in a courious manner.

"Did you leave us Mr. Arthur Robinson? Did you not hear me already? Do you not perceive this event? Is it common that the military makes casual visits to basement rooms so that it can fill people's heads with silly notions of science fiction nonsense?"

"Sounds to me like you're looking for a clean war colonel. Should I have heard about this before I signed on?"

"No war is clean. Even you know that."

"You could have fooled me," says Frank.

Ducet gives Frank a cold hard stare. "Keep up with me people and listen carefully. What if you could create a hybrid soldier, a soldier that is not human; or an animal, but possess humanistic qualities? And yet, this particular hybrid does not exist naturally in nature. Science fiction you say – no. The photographs you saw earlier testify that someone has been at this concept for quite some time."

Gracella asks, "How would you know that Colonel?"

"That part is classified."

Gracella lowers her head, shaking it slowly to protest her dissatisfaction, however the colonel continues. "Our hybrid never existed in the natural so therefore it has no rights. Because of that, it belongs to us. We create it, special order, solely for our purpose. Gene splicing, DNA manipulation, stem cell research and cloning as you know gives us the power to make decisions that are far outside natural occurrences. So then, why not use this power to create something practical, or better yet, something far more convenient in the arena of combat deterrence?"

"The logic is sound," grumbles Nathaniel.

"*Eet* is undeniable that such *theengs* come as result of evolution in society," Rowland adds while crossing his arms.

"I'm sure you all are thinking of the money, the security, or even the federal funding, but the one thing you should all know is that you are making the right decision in order to help others. The magnitude of this project will undoubtedly draw attention in the final stages of its development, and believe me, when that time comes; I want you all to be ready – with no reservations."

"Break time – yes?" Rowland adds.

All persons rise from their seats and begin walking about the room, but Jade continues to sit, staring directly at Colonel Ducet. After watching for a moment, she uncrosses her legs and rises to her feet with poignant mannerisms. Streamline glasses lay half way down her nose as her head tilts, thus drawing the colonel's attention. Staring him eye-to-eye, no one could miss such body language. With a gentle breath, she tells him, "So then, man makes circumstances, which changes God's rules. And Rham-kiev is somewhere in the middle; you know this to be true."

Ducet simply listens.

Impish-grins lace the faces of Frank and Nathaniel as Jade casually walks out the door while leaving behind a room of speechless observers.

~~~Project 429~~~

Thirteen hundred hours gleam across the face of a clock. The clock sets high above a projector screen. For most, the passage of time is an integral part of daily existence, and maybe a crowning moment for GenoSyss. But for Arthur, there is always time for something other than the moment: a time for questions, a time to reminisce, and even a time concerning the unknown.

Arthur stares at images on the projector screen as Rowland approaches. "You are silent, more than normal Arthur Robinson – Yes?" Rowland's entreatment of Arthur comes with a sheisty grin. Yet, turning to face the geneticist, Arthur leans toward him only to notice that Colonel Ducet is watching both of them.

"Not as obvious as your friend over there. It never fails Rowland, there is always a hidden agenda."

"Perhaps, but I think the good colonel is *thinkeen*, his speech has effect by now?"

"Or maybe he intends that the group make light of any hidden propaganda."

"Suspicious, are you now Arthur?"

"Rowland, since when does the military care about human lives in this respect? Every soldier knows that they are dispensable if the overall mission calls for it. They also know that dying for their country is one hell of an honor – not that they are anxious to go out that way. With all things considered, only the final outcome will tell the story."

"Well thought *Meeser Rrr-obinson*, but I cannot answer for the colonel, especially concerning some areas of your thoughts."

All have returned and are now sitting in their respective places. As the noise lessens, Colonel Ducet rises to his feet and again, slowly paces the floor. "Well, I hope you all are refreshed and ready for the best part of this meeting. Make no mistake, conflict is eminent, continuously present, and will be with us for as long as we live. However, this meeting is not a proposal to solve the problems of the world, but to convey an attempt to make would-be aggressors think twice before they decide to carry out some sadistic plot. Since 9/11, so many years ago, we have planned, created, destroyed, and tested a concept that at one time was unimaginable. Well, after 428 times of trail and error, it is now official."

The colonel places seven beige folders in front of each person in the room in poker style fashion. "You are now the proud observers and future workers of project 429. Ladies and Gentlemen, may I formally introduce concept ENAN 429-001." Immediately, faces glisten with speechless expressions.

Alexis asks, "Umm…colonel, what exactly is an enan?"

"ENAN is an acronym for: Evolutionized Nocturnal Nomad."

"Sounds like something out of a…"

"Comic book…yes, I know."

"Well…"

"This is real people, so get use to it. The second page contains the specifications and blueprints for what we need in order to produce the hybrid."

Comments lowly utter throughout the room behind Ducet's statement.

Nathaniel casually turns the pages, and then tells the colonel, "I see your codes colonel, I see your specs, and I even see your application theory. But where's your model?"

"You're ahead of me Mr. Nathaniel Keech; however, you are quite correct. We have the applications; how it behaves, why it behaves, where it is going, even the neurological, psychological, and physiological reads, but we lack the means to put it all together in a body."

"You have all the ingredients, but you need us to bake your cake," says Gracella.

"Touché," responds the colonel, nodding his head in agreement. "The sole purpose of the ENAN is to infiltrate hostile territory, carry out instructions, and then return home. It needs the uncanny ability to wonder between scenes until recovered – hence the word nomad. Simple enough, but our hope is that once the hybrid strikes, its encounter will leave the enemy stunned by what they think they see – and notice I said *think*."

"Seal Units Colonel," says Walter.

Ducet immediately sighs with a tense countenance. "As I mentioned earlier, for those who were paying attention, conventional foot soldiers or special units comprise of men and women; two key elements we are trying *hard* to factor out of the equation. I thought I was clear on that – do keep up Mr. Walter Pierson."

"Point taken," responds Walter.

"I think best we *muv* on –shall we," says Rowland.

"Alright people, the ENAN will have no gender. Reproduction is not our intent. If you cannot bypass the gender protocols, then I recommend female. Testosterone levels in males can become a problem as the ENAN matures. Speed is a necessity and mobility is extremely needful – without saying. The hybrid will be agile and capable of sustaining severe wounds. It must possess a cognitive ability to figure out complex scenarios – learning as it covers territory. It will contain finger-type digits to handle intricate items, just as the human hand functions. Whatever other appendages you deem necessary for its missions, you add accordingly. Most importantly, the ENAN will posses the ability to operate under the cover of darkness and sustain long periods in water. Now I want you to pay very close attention to its eyes. A natural ability to see at night will give the ENAN a tremendous advantage. You and I both know how much darkness can be an ally. The ENAN will have extremely sensitive ears for high frequency hearing, powerful legs for fast mobility and defensive capability, enlarged lungs and a heart to push large volumes of oxygen. More importantly, the rate of oxygen transfer to cells during rapid expulsion must take place in a systematic rhythm or else cardiac arrest may occur. And finally, a tail – if needed."

"What about the hybrid's head Colonel? We all know what happens if the command center gets damaged," says Tuan.

"A double boned cranial encasement should do the job."

Arthur catches Gracella's attention. He scribbles on a piece of paper and passes it to her beneath the table. She reads the inscription: '2nd Timothy 3:7.'

"Colonel, it sounds as though an animal will be our model," says Tuan.

"As I said, humans are complicated. In this way, there are no visual or emotional attachments. Keep in mind that we will own the ENAN. We will grow them, use them, and terminate them as we see fit."

Upon hearing the word terminate, a ghastly silence grips everyone. Each person glances at the other as if trying to interpret the unimaginable.

Tuan asks, "Colonel, is the ENAN a prototype upon which your people will expound, after we complete our objective?"

"We reserve the right to enhance the hybrid – if that's what you mean; however, only if we don't like what we see."

"You speak in terms of one ENAN. Will there be others?"

"We will clone from the original."

"Then, can you be more specific on the guidelines of appearance?"

"The how and why it appears the way it does is your department. My job is to get the project done. Once complete your work as well as any other concerns you may have should no longer burden you."

"Sounds good…"

"Believe me, it is."

"And, how much time do we have for the prototype to become efficient?"

"The maturation of the ENAN must accelerate in order to meet timing constraints. Seventy-two hours is the mark from gestation and two to three weeks for combat readiness. I've talked to Rowland. Given the tests and other information he provided, I feel that the proposal is achievable. Also, based on your current experience with animal-hybrids, we expect to see this project in completion seven months from now. Any questions?"

Wayward glances connect as though to sanction unannounced concurrences. Smiles of all sizes grace many of the faces in attendance, except Arthur. Without hesitation, Colonel Ducet looks directly at Arthur. Arthur's transparency leaves no conclusion about his personal feelings. But the stalwart technician raises his head as his ebony skin lightens under the ceiling lamp. He looks at Ducet and leans forward in somewhat of an audacious manner.

"Since you're staring at me Colonel, I can only assume that you want me to say something."

"By all means..."

"Alright... Will this hybrid become a weapon under military control?"

"What do you think?"

"I think we're always learning how to do things, but I feel the whole truth in this matter has just passed us by."

"Sometimes, the truth of a matter is as simple as what's in front of you."

"No hidden agenda's Colonel?"

"Don't make this more than what it is Mr. Arthur Robinson."

"And so it begins."

Arthur's utterance comes under the quietness of his breath as Ducet watches with silent disregard.

~~~The Hybrid Adam~~~

Arthur accesses the elevator and presses the button for basement level. As the door opens, he proceeds down a long narrow corridor. Fluorescent lamps eerily reveal a dusty concrete floor as well as aging walls. Old furniture partially lay along side the hallway. Bypassing a dusty shelf, Arthur arrives at the end of the corridor. Noticing an entry lock, he swipes his wrist past a scanner and two large glass doors slide apart, which allows him access to another section beyond the main hall. Sterilization sensors commence operation and Arthur soon passes into the next section. Faint voices emanate from ahead. The technician finally turns the corner only to find Nathaniel and Rowland playfully engaging in verbal bantering. He draws their attention.

"Welcome to grindstone haven Robinson," rumbles Nathaniel, patting Arthur on the back as he approaches.

"I love you too," responds Arthur in a casual manner.

"This is your first time here?"

"I had no idea GenoSyss had dungeons."

"Don't let the outside fool you. Back in the day, this portion of the building saw a lot of action…that is before management closed it off. But I think the equipment here is a lot better than the others elsewhere in the building. I think you'll like it."

Rowland nears Arthur with an immediate business attitude. "Do you have your information Arthur?"

"Tucked away in these data capsules."

"After three days, we have DNA prototype from the colonel; however, there *eez* one thing that evades us."

"What is that?"

"That, which will become the embodiment of our information?"

"That shouldn't be too much of a problem Rowland. We simply need to find the proper body glove – so to speak."

"And you have idea – Yes?"

"Somewhere in my head; there are only a few hundred animals to choose from."

"After today, you should be able to narrow your list."

Papers shuffle as Arthur notices a small plaque in the corner of the room. "Fort Clone: Unit 429. Is that your handy work Rowland?"

"No, that *eez* Walter's doing. He *theenks* it to be joking patriotism."

"Oh…because of the military."

"Yes."

As Rowland speaks to Arthur, the technician periodically glances amidst the room. The spacious chamber nests in seclusion on the far side of the building. High walls encompass the area in a rectangular stoned mesa enclosure. White granite tabletops line the entire length of the nearest and farthest walls. The tables rise three feet above a black tile floor. Each long section of tables supports seven computers, which display large transparent monitors. Microscopes, flasks, and other machines conducive to genetic research lay among the electronic ensemble. The atmosphere is sterile and cool. Flowing air conveys a chilling presence, dangling strands of paper in front of all ventilation covers. Several instruments lie along stern walls, which also support three large light tables. Upon each table, X-rays lay clamped upon the viewing surfaces while an additional door for emergency exits lie just behind a high Plexiglas square enclosure, which is located in the center of the room. Faint sounds cause Arthur to fix his attention to a green light above the main entry of the door. The light begins to flare. Suddenly, thick glass doors slide open, allowing the sound of muffled voices to become prevalent as the remaining members of the team enter the room.

"Are you listening Arthur?"

"Sure…*ahhh*…yes, I heard you Professor; the whole time."

"You were looking elsewhere. Just have your *rrr*-report *rr*-eady."

As Rowland departs, Arthur watches each team member assemble. He seats himself on one of several high chairs. Closing his eyes, he gently rubs the temples of his forehead with his thumbs. Then, his concise attentiveness perks as he responds from a tap on his shoulder.

"Are we here today?"

"Grace, you know about this dungeon?"

"I guess so…seeing that I'm here. Are you focused or what?"

"Visual anomalies are the trust of fools Grace."

"Maybe, but if you leave the Mrs. alone at night, you may have a little more energy."

"I don't hear you complaining about Robert; besides, she hit the pillows before I had a chance."

"Well…I knew you weren't praying, but I also realize that your eyes are red – again."

"Really?"

"And how many cookies have you had this morning."

"My sugar is fine."

"I'll bet…"

"As if you know me so well…"

"…Like my shadow. Anyway, it looks as though Rowland put us on the same team. That being the case, I need to know if you're all together here or some where else."

"Where else would I be?"

"You tell me."

"Okay, I didn't get much rest last night, but…"

"What is it?"

"Nothing... I just realized that today marks seventeen years of blissful solidarity between us."

"That usually happens when you've known someone forever. That also gives me the ability to tell when something's bugging you. You have been very suspicious about this whole project from the very beginning."

"Wasn't it you who told me not to jump into any projects?"

"I told you don't be quick to throw your heart into this project – too soon."

Gracella dawns a quirky expression while gracing Arthur with a smile, but he remains silent. Yet, instead, Arthur looks at her, perhaps unsure whether to say anything or nothing at all.

"Arthur, I think what's really bothering you is…that the earlier projects were merely exploratory and that, the final outcome posed no harm to people?"

"Something like that, but you heard the colonel."

"Yes, I did…and I'll be the first to tell you that I share the same feelings about this fiasco, to a certain point. Though I research science, I have no desire to build some biological death machine. But, I am quite sure that signing the contracts absolves us from what ever happens. After we finish our work, the military can do whatever they want with the hybrid."

"Grace, do you think God is speaking?"

"To you… about this project?"

"Well…I'm not sure how to say it."

"In a sense, I believe that God is always speaking, in some manner. Whether or not you're listening is a whole-*nother* matter in itself. If I understand you Arthur, I think God will take you through whatever is awaiting you before He'll *subside* apparent circumstances. In the end, it's your character He is most concerned with. Why do you ask?"

"Just thinking aloud…"

"I see…"

Gracella opens a black binder as Arthur fixates upon the transparent square at the center of the room. Gracella silently stares at him. With an obvious train of thought, she examines his behavior.

"Arthur, that clear square isn't going anywhere. Why are you watching it as if something will magically appear?"

"Complacency Grace. Perhaps it's better to face these types of assignments this way. People would often turn to habituates, erratic behavior, unwanted relationships, and even religion as the recourse of failed courage."

"Complacent or not Arthur, you were picked for a reason. You could quit, run away…act as if you will never face a situation like this again, but that will prove nothing; so my recommendation is that you follow through with your agreement, because, this project is officially underway."

Air thrusts into the lab, chilling specimens at a moderate 55 degrees Celsius. Yet, in the midst of the chill, Rowland debriefs separate teams with a sense of urgency. He turns his attention to Frank, Walter, and Alexis. Viewing his clipboard, he approaches them.

"Team 2, your preliminary suggestions *eez* good, but we must find suitable host once embryo reaches maturation point – Yes? Frank, at *thees* point you may *weesh* to inject accelerate for expedition process – understand?"

"*A-ya una-ta u-ne-ga a-s-ga-ya ga-nu-ga* - boss man," utters Frank, after which an impish grin forms upon his face. Rowland simply looks at him.

Walter reaches for his binder and draws Rowland's attention. "By mentioning embryo, are you saying that the somatic cells, containing their nuclei of course, will be allowed to grow and divide inside a surrogate host?"

"Yes."

"Now, these same cells will be deprived of nutrients in order to induce suspension prior to this stage."

"Yes, go on."

"Well…I mean, once the cells reach a mature stage, then an egg cell that's had its nucleus removed is placed closely to the somatic cell. After that, both cells receive an electric shock, which causes them both to fuse together – right?"

"Then the developing embryo is placed into the surrogate host, but mother *eez* a more preferred term," replies Rowland.

"What you're saying is prep the egg, put it in the *bitch* and watch it grow." Alexis' interjected point stirs laughter, which immediately fills the room, but much to Rowland's surprise.

"That language *eez* not fitting for one such as you Ms. Hawthorne…I caution you of Nathaniel's influence."

"*Bitch*, being the operative word Professor, not to humiliate females but to accurately describe the host."

"Somatic cell nuclear transfer is the basis of our initial approach. We can remove the nucleus from the somatic cell and inject it into an egg that has *eets* nucleus already removed."

"Then we implant the developing embryo into a 'B' or surrogate, so that it will continue to develop."

"Well said Ms Hawthorne," states Rowland as he departs, flipping the pages of his binder.

Walter approaches Frank. "Hey, you were speaking Cherokee. What did you say to the Professor?" Frank, poised and in character fashion; "I *sez*…I know white man's tongue." Walter looks a Frank and simply walks away.

Rowland finally turns his attention to Arthur, Gracella, and Jade. "Greetings again team 3. The colonel's requirements for mobility will prove challenging, even for you; however, your proposal *eez* interesting – indeed."

"Interesting is hardly the word," spurns Jade with her back towards Rowland. She maneuvers her chair into position; seating her self in a casual manner as she nonchalantly crosses both arms and legs. She swings one leg with agitation wile turning, and then staring Rowland eye-to-eye.

"Professor… We are not talking about animal hybrids or mutating genes within a species or genus group. Even I am amazed at the power we have to create such beasts, but what the colonel wants is impossible."

"Not *eem*-possible, but *een*-conceivable, problem-*mat-eek* – yes?"

"Is that what the colonel told you?"

Rowland approaches Jade more closely and places his hand on her shoulder. "I know you have been hours *weeth* no sleep, as many of us, but you must know that the answer *eez* here and we will find it." Jade's eyes slowly close and her complexion grows redder than previous.

Observing Jade, Gracella approaches Rowland. "Professor, despite the difficulties, we came up with a basic approach for the crossover of team 2's product into ours. First, we isolate the abilities we want. For example, if we want to regrow arms, legs, and a tail, we must find a specimen that can virtually re-grow all its limbs, something like a newt or a salamander. Secondly, we isolate the genes responsible for such abilities, so that we can make regrowth of such items possible for our host. The process has to take place in such a way that the new body can carry out the regrowth process with few changes. If that procedure doesn't work, then the whole block of genes may need transferring to the host instead of isolating a single strand."

"A sound methodology Gracella and *eet* lessens Arthur's list of animals tremendously…good job. Now…what do you *theenk* Arthur?"

"Team 2 provides everything from the logical or human side, that the ENAN will have. We will provide everything from the host, or animal side. It all simply boils down to grafting both sides, their human zygote to our animal embryo. But the trick Professor lies in what percentage of the hybrid's thought process will either be human, or animal."

"Well noted *Meester Rrr*-obonson," says Rowland as he walks away.

In an abrupt manner, Jade sternly views Arthur and Gracella. "I do not want to rain on this parade. Rowland and Colonel Ducet seem so sure that this project will work. Did any of you stop to think that the military is using us to help them create some kind of weapon without the consent of the Pentagon or the Joint Chiefs?"

"What…where did that come from girl? You are implying something way over our heads," says Gracella.

"I know that sounds odd, but the military have their own geneticists. Why do they need us?"

"It's not unusual for the military to procure civilian services. You know that. What is wrong with you, why do you say such things? Jade, you know something, don't you?" Gracella's question leaves Jade in a moment of disarray as she stares at her with sentimental observance. Jade's mouth begins to move, quivering, but soon halts in a silent transaction of nonverbal conjecture. Then, slowly, like a child hesitant of judgmental exposure, "Did you ever consider that innocent people will die?"

"We already crossed that bridge. What's really bothering you? I've never seen you like this."

"Shhhhh..."

Jade motions Gracella to keep her tone low. Discerning the moment, Gracella gently places her hand on Jade's shoulder. "These are unexplored territories for us all; but remember; guns don't kill; only people kill."

Jade looks upward, gleaming her colleague with a trusting countenance, telling her, "You and Arthur both still do not see. There is more to this that you do not understand. I do not want either of you to get hurt." Jade closes her eyes, folds her arms, and lays her head upon the table, gently breathing, silently falling to sleep.

Gracella and Arthur glance at each other with puzzling bewilderment. "This is so strange for her. I have never seen her like this," says Gracella, watching Jade with a degree of sympathy.

Suddenly, "Hey…the party animal sleeps!" Tuan's hails catches both off guard as he struts towards them. "You guys need to let me know of your nocturnal activities, I want to have fun too."

"Pleeez," sarcastically responds Gracella, making as though she has better things to do.

Tuan points to each item on the table, while making comical gestures with his hands, and yet, casting his dysfunctional mannerisms towards Arthur. "I see you got your instruments all laid out and ready to play."

"You seem thrilled for the challenge."

"Hey, aren't you? A hefty price tag comes with this gig, and with major league funding to supply it. Team 1, with yours truly, will supervise you guys, guiding you into all truths to make sure we obtain the goal…hoorah."

"And Nathaniel will supervise team 2?"

"Yes. Rowland, Nathaniel, and I are team 1, but speaking of Rowland, where's the old Professor?"

"He went out earlier."

As Tuan scans the room, an immediate sound catches his attention. The green entry light illuminates. As it does, Rowland enters while pushing a cart. The wheeled container has six compartment doors. Biohazard decals display on all sides as a banner denoting 'PROPERTY OF U.S MILITARY' displays vividly on top. Air filled tires cushion the motion of the carrier while Rowland wheels it near one of the larger tables. Several gages display slight fluctuations in temperature and pressure readings as Rowland carefully positions the cart where all six doors are easily accessible. All team members gather closely.

"*It eez* show time, as you sayArthur – yes?"

Rowland's exuberance heightens as he removes the major locks. Afterwards, he places several contents on the cart as the curious teams stare. Then, with commanding emphasis, he acquires Nathaniel's attention. "Take *thees* specimen for the team you are to supervise."

Nathaniel removes the remaining seals across the doors. As he opens one of the doors, a gaseous cloud expels, thus allowing white misty smoke to pour onto the floor. Nathaniel carefully pulls a specimen from within. "Here it is folks. The better-than-sex revolution thanks to your tax dollars." Nathaniel smiles as he gives the sealed container to Walter.

Nathaniel opens the next door. Again, a gaseous mist expels as he reaches in and gives the next canister to Frank. "The future is here," replies Frank as he takes the container to Team 2's working area.

Tuan kneels beside the door on the other side. He removes four jars, giving two jars to Arthur and two jars to Gracella.

Nathaniel fastens his attention upon the taller silver canister. He removes the plastic seal. As he removes the cover, a ghostly mist clears, only to reveal the contents inside. He reaches in. "Ladies and gentlemen, behold…here's your precious somatic cell. The good colonel gives us chromosomes for anger, chromosomes for the immune system and… What the hell…what are these letters C9 for?"

Walter responds in coy fashion, "Don't you know? Those are the chromosomes of some poor soul who made the dead-on-arrival list."

"That can't be."

"Oh, I'm just yanking your leg Nat. The poor guy we got these from could have been minutes dead before his DNA was harvested, maybe even a volunteer – who knows."

"Well…anyway. Ducet wants us to modify these to his specs and put our results into the somatic cell. So, you handle the aggression and let Frank handle the Immune system. Alexis, you got the bloody department and you can also help me with putting our results in the somatic cell when you finish."

Meanwhile, Rowland, smiling as usual approaches the first canister. Tuan along with Arthur and Gracella, join him. With both hands, Rowland reaches for the canister. He gently rotates the silver drum, revealing an intricate wire layout, a thermometer, small lights, and a small apparatus from which two tiny hoses extend. "*Eeem*-prres-*seev* technology," he says.

"It sure is," replies Tuan. As Rowland completes the rotation of the canister, a small window comes into view. "Do you see *eet*? *Dere* they float quietly, in tinted solution lays our embryos." All gaze into the tiny window, anxious to see the potential selection; however, Jade awakens and observes from a distance.

Gracella approaches Rowland. "So…this is our cheetah," she says.

"Yes – and our thoroughbred, gray fox, ostrich, greyhound, and gazelle."

"Professor, based on Colonel Ducet's specifications, we quickly concluded that winged animals would not be acceptable. Nor snakes, since digits or appendages are easier to modify from an existing or developing appendage than from a nonexistent one. Exoskeletons are too heavy and cumbersome for silent mobility once the specimen reaches a larger size. Amphibians depend too heavily on water, while reptiles are cold-blooded which means seasonal or periodic activity. That leaves us with only mammals. Within the mammal groups, we decided to concentrate our efforts on six of the fastest and more agile animals for their body structure."

"Well noted Gracella," comments Rowland.

Surprisingly, a soft voice manages to present a familiar presence. Gently clutching both hands in prayer-like fashion, Jade rejoins the group. "I'm sorry," she whispers. Gracella embraces her. "I was beginning to worry about you. You look exhausted."

"I am – in more ways than you know."

"You need to go home."

"I will be fine."

"You don't have a boy friend or a late night routine, like pole dancing – do you?"

"You are joking – yes?"

"Of course I am; you know me."

"No, I need to sit down. Everything came too sudden and I felt overwhelmed – more tired than normal."

Jade gazes into the window of the canister. She gently places three fingers on the surface as though to connect with a lost meaning. Sighing, she mystically stares at the embryo, saying nothing as the others watch. Then, in a subtle quiet voice, she expresses, "You know not what you will become."

Later, Team 2 is well underway with their task as Frank stares into a microscope. "This was an easy assignment for me. I thought I would have to use restriction enzymes to cut out parts of the DNA and then reinsert new strands. Lucky for me, I was able to turn off all the bad genes in order to eliminate the influence of *the-one* bad gene. I'll have to use antigens as a supplement during the later stages of the embryos development – hoorah." Frank excitedly raises both hands above his head while looking at Walter.

Walter asks, "Did you do it? You were able to silence some genes?"

"Yep! Our enan will not be seeing a medicine man any time soon."

Walter peeks into the microscope and observes Frank's handiwork. A gleeful smile forms upon his face as he proudly acknowledges Frank who graciously returns the gesture. "Wish mine were that easy. I had to do some splicing and repairing."

Frank asks, "Why?"

"Anger is not something you just turn on and off with a remote control. Outwardly speaking, circumstances for causing anger are numerous and everyone responds differently – in terms of humans."

"So, what's the problem science boy?"

"What exactly makes an enan angry, how long an enan should be angry, how the enan channels that anger, and more importantly, when an enan should discontinue its anger; these are the scenarios I have to deal with."

"Those behaviors should be dealt with during the training stage. Like a child, this thing isn't going know anything when it is born. Did you not hear Rowland and the colonel say that?"

"No, you don't understand. Colonel Ducet not only wants anger management, he wants anger control. Long before our ENAN learns what behavior patterns to adapt, there has to be a switch to control that type of aggression."

"Ahhh, control…the relative term," says Frank.

Hearing their conversation, Alexis barges in. "You boys think you got it tough. Let me show you something." Alexis reaches over the counter and grabs a test tube holder. She pulls the holder closer towards her, noticing that a tube lies therein. "See this? Whether angry or not, the enan has to live; at least long enough to carry out its mission."

"Your point?" asks Frank.

"Without this, control is irrelevant."

"Looks like blood to me."

"Disease defiant and purple as ever."

"Why don't you just let team 3's developing embryo facilitate the blood naturally?"

"No, no, no, not just any old *bluuud*. This is special *bluuud*, especially during a big freeze."

Frank intensely examines the thick, dark fluid. He asks, "Is there something we're missing Blondie?"

"My little claim to fame is the synthesizing of blood that contains glycoproteins, better known as antifreeze glycoproteins; AFGPs as we call them. So, twenty-two tries and seventy-two hours later, here it is. *Ta-daaaaahhhh!"*

Alexis parades her product of wonder as Nathaniel approaches. "I heard that. What in sand hill blazes is that kind of blood? Is it in the specs?"

"Page 34b."

"That's the damnedest thing I ever heard of," rumbles Nathaniel as he reaches for the test tube, examining the dark fluid.

Both, Frank and Walter stare at Alexis, displaying a visual numbness. "I'm not stupid," she says.

"Well *scuse'* me Miss Antifreeze," blurts Walter.

Frank asks, "Were in Geronimo's name did you get that idea?"

"Look…the Antarctic cod lives in the Arctic – Right? Its family, the *Noto-the-nii-daes* is extremely adapted to frigid conditions in the sea. These specialized proteins or AFGPs prevent ice crystals from forming in the fish's blood. The same type of process also prevents tissue damage and allows the blood to flow freely."

"I knew you were working with blood, but not like this. That'll get you a promotion, and maybe a permanent spot."

"Are you kidding? I'm just a drone."

"Well…let's put it all together and give it to team 3."

Walter rubs his chin as he watches Nathaniel give the tube to Alexis. "Antifreeze for blood... Why would the first hybrid Adam of its kind need antifreeze?"

"Maybe for something we don't know about – just yet," replies Frank.

~~~Deadly Discernment~~~

A brisk coolness engulfs my senses as my eyes open. Draped in a blanket, I rise to my feet and progress forward in the darkness. "Ouch!" Reaching desperately to ease the pain, I frantically rub my toe, trying to calm the pulsating nerves. The culprit for my situation is nowhere to be found; therefore, stupidity lies in yours truly. Consoling my embarrassment, the darkness becomes more apparent since determining points of reference are no longer identifiable. "Something's wrong...different." The moon lit brilliance that graced this room earlier is no longer present. Only the sheath of darkness now fills the enclosure. Flickering dim lights on the alarm system and the aquarium heater are the only recognizable items within my entire field of view.

Using those lights as reference points, I cautiously begin feeling my way in the direction of the windows. Fumbling clumsily with eyes wide open, my hands make contact with the threshold of the window. "What happened?" Reaching blindly for the Venetian slats, a small separation reveals a more destitute darkness than my mind previously could fathom. Gazing outward, I suddenly realize that the glow of the moon is no longer there, and that the expectation of daylight is farther away. Nostalgia is nowhere, neither seen in spirit nor celestial body. My heart pounds loudly against my chest as I sit upon the mantle of the daybed. Our meeting is seemingly cut short and the story is unfinished. As the wall becomes a headrest, the window reveals the sea of darkness. It is quite immense, but the movement of a faint mist is heading eastward. I watch in disillusionment. Leaning back into my former position, the tenseness felt earlier immediately subsides. "Clouds," I whisper. Still feeling the chill of the air, I pull the blanket tightly around me, curling into somewhat of a fetal position.

Part of the blanket touches my nose. White Diamond aromatically pours into my senses, producing a feeling of gratitude that cascades the emotions of my every being. Aniah is present, even when she is absent. Though content for the moment, the black sky continues to dominate the scene. Yet, tiny openings in the unusually thick cloud cover faintly allow the light of the celestial god to touch the concrete jungle. But it is just a small speckle in comparison to the full power that filled the sky earlier. Then, it all becomes a hardening reality as droplets of water start to fall in the trees, upon the deck, atop the sky windows, and softly, gently, and so subtlety upon my skin. And then...a downpour. I close the window, but continue to stare into the black heavens; gazing until my vision shifts to blurriness and my head becomes an object of weightless thoughts. "It's not over. We were getting close."

There is something about the clouds. Just as these clouds blanket the night sky, the sun hid behind such a covering long ago. Time passes a little more as I stare quietly into the dark heavens. The darkness grows more prevalent and soon, my eyes close. There were so many dark clouds on that day.

Ominous clouds fortify a dreadful presence as thunder pounds the heavens and lightning cracks the sky. Within GenoSyss, Arthur and Gracella step into the deep basement laboratory. The two engage in whimsical conversation as they make their way into the shadows of the entryway. Gracella gives Arthur several sheets of paper.

"Looks as if I can let the good Lord water my lawn today."

"Really…well He can water my lawn anytime; especially after a five-month drought. How's the hubby?"

"Richard's okay; lazy as ever…but good. He's getting a belly."

"Good for him."

"You guys bulge around the stomach while we women pack it on everywhere."

"You're just thick and happy – what can I say," scoffs Arthur as Gracella's mouth drops open.

"Do you tell Aniah that?"

"I want to live."

"Thought so…"

"Anyway, are you up for the task at hand?"

"Ready and willing…"

"You don't look too convincing."

"I have a lot to think about these days."

"I see… I know it's hard to believe we haven't had rain for that long of a period; but then again, this is Texas."

"Texas? Arthur, are we on the same page?"

"Absolutely; this rainy day marks the passing of five months – it's show time."

Both approach the working area assigned for their team. Arthur, scratching his head, looks towards five large sectional bins. Within each bin is an animal. The bins also lay side-by-side, squared and high as the ceiling with straw upon the floor. Clear glass panels separate each bin, yet the rear wall of the laboratory room acts as the back closure.

Arthur observes with profound interest. "Nice. At this point, we can add on two and half more days for deliberations and prep work…not to mention Tuan's reading sessions."

"Sounds good... Hey, there have been people asking me about the reassignment. What about you?"

"I just tell them…whatever. People are so gullible, and can be very naïve. No body cares Grace." The two look at each other and begin to chuckle.

Rowland's timely interruption breaks their little moment as he gallantly approaches. Patting each on their shoulder, he escorts them to the holding bins. Upon approach, Rowland candidly greets two occupants. "Good morning Sasha and Mishka," he says.

As though rehearsed, the uttering sound of a horse projects outwardly. Also responding on cue is a colt, standing, eyeing Rowland with child-like interest. The colt approaches the front of the bin. Light glistens softly over the animal's black coat. The youngster raises its head to greet the extending hand of Rowland, who gently caresses the foal's nose. "Mishka, you are *beu-tee-ful* and so is your mother, Sasha."

"Magnificent indeed," concurs Arthur. Sasha stands motionless while staring at Arthur. The fixation leaves the technician wondering, as though the animal's eyes pierce his very soul. "Rowland, why does she stare that way?"

"What way? Maybe she's curious. Would you be *eef* strangers appear as you – yes? Come, let us move on."

Rowland approaches the next bin where Tuan is standing. "Good morning Professor."

"How *eez* Gertrude and Gearhardt?"

"Tests show both are doing well and on schedule. Aren't you ladies?" As Tuan addresses both ostriches, the older towering bird cautiously struts towards the group and halts just shy of the transparent barrier. Then, powerful legs bend as the animal crouches to the floor. Dull, black plumage blankets the animal, leaving only a scantly covered neck and a featherless head as visual ornaments. Flanking the large bird is a much smaller version. The fledgling invokes a keen observance as well, proudly parading its objectionable appearance. Tuan gleams, "Fascinating, aren't they?" Rowland asks, "So what does *Struthiocamelus* have for us today?" "Wait and see Professor."

Tuan extends the same invite to the others. While kneeling directly in front of the boarder, he makes eye contact with the docile beast. "Gertrude, understand, move this way," pointing his finger to the right side of the holding area. The bird simply stares at him. "Gertrude, move this way," he states again. Once more, the bird simply stares. "Come on girl, move this way," he says for a third time. The ostrich turns away, cocking its head to one side, acting as though Tuan does not exist.

Tuan approaches his colleagues. "See how she responds? Like a dog, listening without interpretation when she hears you.""Or a woman, who simply ignores you altogether," says Frank. "Hah…right. She moved her head in a manner as if she understood me, but we know better. Now watch this."

Tuan crouches in front of the fledgling. The smaller ostrich approaches. "Gearhardt," he says. Immediately, the young bird snaps to attention. "Move left." The bird stands momentarily and slowly steps in tiny incremental movements to the left. "Move right," instructs Tuan, and again, the bird obeys.

Jade observes the animal's behavior. She kneels quietly beside Tuan and places her mouth closely near his ear. "Cute, but I can train a hamster to do the same thing," she says.

Tuan quickly stands to his feet. "Perhaps, but can a hamster do the same thing by simply reading?"

Silence encompasses everyone. Rowland gleefully approaches Tuan. "Tuan, you say *eet* learned from your words, what you told it to do - yes?"

"I'm saying we taught Gerhardt basic words. Each word has a specific definition. I gave her this to read." Tuan presents Rowland with a sheet of paper. Rowland reads the inscription. Soon, his hands slightly tremble as the others stare at him with peculiar wonder.

"Professor, are you alight?" Rowland looks up in astonishment, giving the piece of paper to Gracella. She stands momentarily silent. With eyebrows raised and her mouth partially opened, her eyes fixated upon the inscription. Then, she slowly raises her head. "Tuan, you're telling me that this animal read this paper a few minutes ago and, at that point knew exactly what you were saying?"

"As I said before, Gerhardt interprets words based on a strict definition – not words with several meanings. That's the beauty of it – to have them perform a task without training."

"I thought this was going to take much longer. You're telling us that your bird can now read with an understanding," interjects Arthur.

"Why should it be so surprising? This is what we've been working on. It's also what the colonel wants."

"But to see months of culminating theory actually work," says Walter.

"Well science boy, these guys are the first to show this sort of behavior." Smiles encompass everyone as Tuan's gleaming eyes fasten upon Gearhardt.

Suddenly, a blistering scream screeches across the room, drawing every one's attention. The clamoring sound of anxious footsteps immediately fills the air as a sorrowful cry intensifies. Bodies congregate into one spot. Arthur is the last to arrive on scene. White coats quickly separate and immediately, Gracella pushes through, holding Alexis and partially covering her face as they both whisk past the technician. They depart in haste, but not before Alexis emerges with tear stains upon her face and a blood drenched coat. Some rush to their aid as Arthur pushes through the remaining group.

"What happened? Why is there blood on the walls?" Quickly searching, Arthur scans in several directions, trying to pinpoint the incident. Finally, something in the rear of the bin catches his eye. He carefully steps over the cracked patrician barrier and makes his way to a red stained quagmire of straw. Pressing his foot firmly to the ground, the technician realizes that something lies beneath the mound. Looking downward, he notices the tiny paw of an animal. "There's body parts everywhere – what happened?" Silence is the only response.

Looking further, Arthur discovers more internal organs strewn in several places. He steps once more, only to find the culmination of his suspicions. "Good Lord, Jordane," he whispers. Using one foot to sweep away the straw, he uncovers the body of a young cheetah cub. By doing so, he reveals a decapitated torso that lays wretchedly torn open. His foot motions disturb sagging skin overlaying bone, under which there are no internal organs. Crouching slowly, his bewildering actions suggest something that neither he nor his companions were prepared to see. Lying outside the dismembered cub's body is a tiny heart. Though dislodged, the organ continues pumping as the river of life pours outward and into a burgundy pool. Arthur gazes toward the ceiling as though to beckon God's mercy until he slowly lowers his head.

Then, a noise immediately draws his attention. Crouching forward, he moves closer towards a cheetah. Arthur flusters his eyes several times as thought to clear his vision. "What happened girl? Tell me." Arthur reaches for the cat, yet while hesitant to touch the animal's backbone, he realizes the condition of an emaciated feline that sits in poor posture, shivering while panting in anguish. More curious than fearful, Arthur leans closer, panning his view to see the animal's face, which lays tucked into the corner of the wall. The cheetah's blood stained skin drapes its ribs like a sagging over-size suit, a condition which also smothers a complimenting spotted pattern; all which lies hidden underneath the animal's current plight.

"What happened to you," again he whispers. Blood trickles from the feline's mouth as Arthur takes a deep breath and glances back at his colleagues. They are all silent as the distant cries of Alexis fill the room from the background. Arthur tilts his head in an adjacent manner just shy of the animal's face, which yields nothing less than a ghostly persona. Then surprisingly, the cat becomes deathly still, displaying an internal torture through deep watery eyes.

Nathaniel steps forward. "Son, the cat's lost its mind. We have to put her down."

"That may be, but we still don't know why she did it."

"Rabies is usually the culprit."

"Yeah, but I don't see any of that here."

Arthur puts his hand on the cheetah's head. His long fingers courses through the animal's fur, separating the binding strands tangled by a red dampness. He rubs the animal's head, carefully feeling the bony protrusions from underneath the skin. "Tell us your story girl." His subtle plea of alien dialect passes to the animal as though she understands, but the creature yields only silence. Arthur places one hand under the cat's chest, and listens.

"The interval between each breath is increasing."

"Not a good sign," replies Nathaniel.

Without a moment's notice, the cheetah surprisingly stares at her comforter. Arthur gazes deeply into the tattered soul of the exotic beast as if a mystical bond connects them. Silence shrouds the area while seconds tick away. Finally, the majestic cat slowly closes her eyes and slumps to the ground.

"Good-bye Jhena," whispers Arthur, slowly bowing his head and closing his own eyes as well.

"One body, one hope…now gone; an accepted loss," insights Nathaniel.

Rowland approaches. "Gentlemen, mark Jhena and Jordane terminated at 1500 hours – reasons unknown."

Arthur asks, "Professor, does the Colonel need to know?"

"No – but more importantly*eez* why *these* happen and how did Jhena loose so much weight *een* short time?"

"Tons of questions Professor…"

"Answers *weel* come Nathaniel, they *wveel* come."

"You told us that Ducet is only concerned with the idea of success."

"Yes. The *mee*-litary does not care about failures, only success."

"Well that answers that. Now what about the cat?"

Intently listening, Tuan edges forward. "I think we all knew what possibilities could happen. This event in itself is not an isolated travesty. Animals in the wild have been known to kill their offspring in times of stressful situations. It helps to perpetuate a healthy survival for the species. Whatever was wrong with Jordane somehow got past our readings and Jhena sensed it. She became stressed and acted out in the best interest of Jordane – maybe in the best interest of both for all we know. I realize that's not the answer you want to hear, but it's a start."

"You're taking this all so well," says Alexis, blurting at Tuan.

"Well…why wouldn't I? Death is a natural part of life's cycle. What Jhena did is normal and as far as I'm concerned…"

"What? You call that normal? That was not normal or **NATURAL**!!! What happened back there was insane mutilation!"

"Probably to us, but not to Jhena."

"You make it sound so convenient, like it was casual."

"In the eyes of an animal, death is…"

"See these marks on my arm? There was fear in Jhena's eyes and she saw something she didn't like and was afraid."

"Well why wouldn't she be? Jhena was the mother; death to her is something different than it is to us – How many times must I tell you?"

"You're unbelievable."

"If it were Jordane, I'd worry because Jordane had the adoptive human genes to make rational decisions."

Redness swells in the face of Alexis as tears stream down her swollen cheeks. Poised for retaliation, she confronts Tuan face to face. "Who the hell made you God or any of us?"

"*Pleeez…pleeeez. There eez no one to blame,*" interjects Rowland as Gracella gently compels Alexis to sit down.

Tuan explains, "Professor, we don't know exactly what happened. The tests show that both, Jhena and Jordane were doing well. What ever transpired happened radically within a few days."

"You're saying there was no digression of weight loss or any signs of peculiar behavior?"

"None that showed-up on any of the tests. Once team 2 gave us the developing somatic cell, we procedurally fitted it into Jhena as a developing zygote. The transfer went well. Once the developing embryo reached the point of maturation, well...the rest is history. I have no explanation for such a rapid loss in weight, nor can I explain the animal's veraciousness. For the record, I think there's a bit of over reacting here."

"Of course..."

"Something foreign has been introduced into the equation. Perhaps Jhena saw Jordane as something unnatural and chose to destroy her. Birds are known to abandon their young if they detect the scent of humans on them."

"And what of the other animals?"

"None of the other animals exhibit the same behavior – so far." Upon completing his explanation, Tuan shrugs his shoulders and closes his notebook.

Jade crosses her legs; swaying the upper leg in short distances as if impatiently waiting for something. Her actions continue for some time until she tires of the silence. Slightly lowering her head, she stares into the table. "The animals are expendable," she says as all eyes converge upon her.

"Yes...all in the name of scientific *rre*-surch," assures Rowland.

"Professor, surely you can not expect us to wait for perfection. We all have seen death in experimentation before, so what makes this incident any different? Is there something we are not talking about?"

"You of all people would know – of that, I am sure," replies Rowland.

Tuan asks, "Was this not a stressful ordeal for you at one time?"

"Tuan, maybe we should abandon the project altogether."

"What? Toss out months of work – you're crazy."

"And you are pathetic, just like this whole project."

"Maybe you should reevaluate what side of the fence you are on."

"Hell with you..." Jade immediately storms out of the room followed by Gracella, whose ill attempts to calm her falls on deaf ears.

"*Peeple*. That *weel* be enough! We sit here as *eef* worldwide tragedy occurred. We should *prr*-oceed," expounds Rowland.

"I agree Professor. We've come this far so there's no turning back now. You called us here for an evaluation of the incident, not a decommissioning. We didn't kill that cub and I don't know why the whole thing happened. Jhena freaked and I don't know what else to say." Having made his statement, Tuan reclines in his chair while making minor adjustments to his eyeglasses.

"Maybe it's how the cub died that spooks us," says Frank.

Walter asks, "Are you discerning a threatening situation here?"

"I'm merely saying that this whole situation is not about blaming us, or that Jhena killed Jordane. It seems to me that the real issue here pertains to bringing something unnatural into a natural setting. We were so *caught-up* with how we could do this project that none of us considered the types of drawbacks. We are taking human DNA, repressing what traits we do not want, cloning it into a somatic cell, fusing that cell into a developing embryo, which is nothing more than a smaller version of its surrogate host. Upon birth, we nurture the offspring, develop it and teach it things in hopes to find some human connection, which hopefully resides inside the animal's body – surely, you cannot expect normal-human results."

"We already know that these are radical procedures Frank. That is why we select more than one specimen – so... What's your point?"

"The human factor is what makes this whole thing difficult. Without human DNA, these animals are nothing more than ordinary tests subjects. The only reassurance we have that marks any worthy progress, is the human-like responses displayed by Gearhardt. Such performances are abnormal for these animals; performances that are strictly base on unrehearsed verbal commands. What happened to the cheetahs is unfortunate – but I agree with Tuan, we must proceed." Frank concludes his explanation while looking at Tuan, nodding his head in concurrence. Tuan returns Frank's gesture in kind.

Rowland taps his fingers upon the table. His heavy brows stiffen as he scans the entire room. Anticipation strews as everyone waits to hear his answer. Then, with one swipe of his hand, Rowland wipes his forehead in cascading motion until finally nesting his chin within the palm of his hand. "Wee *muuv* on, but before we do, an analysis of Jhena's brain is required. I don't want to *geev* military flawed product."

"That settles it then," responds Nathaniel. The teams gather their belongings, but before their possessions are well within reach, Walter walks side-by-side with Frank as both men approach the exit. Walter draws Frank's attention. "You know, for a minute there, I thought you were a dignified scholar – I'm proud of you."

"What is it science boy?"

"I thought you were going to get all mystified-Indian legend on us. Give us the tribal shaman wisdom-of-warnings."

"Well…since you put it that way, there is an old Cherokee legend. As I remember, in the beginning of all things, wisdom and knowledge were with the animals. Tirawa, the one above – as they called him, did not speak to man, so he got certain animals to do so."

"I don't get it. What were the animals talking about?"

Frank coldly stares at Walter. "Animals don't do stupid things, until they are involved with humans. By all accounts, Jordane saw something in Jhena that was not normal. Even animals, without human insight are wise in their own right."

"You're saying Jordane sensed something unnatural in Jhena?"

"I'm saying Jordane sensed that Jhena was an abomination."

"You're beginning to sound like Arthur, Frank."

~~~The Looking Glass~~~

A brisk October morning marks the testing of the remaining offspring. Harnessed and strapped with monitoring devices, the colt is first in line for a series of tests. Walter secures the hybrid to a large conveyor track as Nathaniel watches. "I'm ready," he says, waiving at Nathaniel who activates the large treadmill. Nathaniel sets a slow speed, thus causing the magnificent animal to step in stride. Walter takes note of his stopwatch. "Readings are normal...make her trot!" Nathaniel increases the speed and the animal responds without hesitation.

As the test proceeds, an aromatic fragrance precedes the sound of high heels, but the moment causes Walter to loose focus. Quickly turning, his field of view catches nothing less than a snugly fitting one-piece outfit, along with a glistening smile. "Whoa," he says. With a lab coat over her shoulder, Alexis throws her head back and tightly grabs her hair. With veteran skill, she pulls, rolls, and cleverly clasps her golden strands into a full-length ponytail. Afterwards, she drapes herself with the standard issue lab coat and concludes her transformation by adorning black-rimmed glasses.

As she approaches, Walter eyes her up and down but Alexis fastens her attention directly on the horse, as if Walter were never present. Walter takes full advantage of continuously watching her from head to toe. Then, without a clue, "Made *ya* look – huh," she tells him, while portraying elusive facial expressions.

"Wha...wha...oh...look...yeah. Didn't know you wore glasses."

"I've been wearing them from day 1 – stupid."

"I never noticed."

"I'll bet..."

"Glad you're feeling better."

"About what exactly?"

"You know...after the incident with Tuan and the cheetahs."

"Oh...how considerate of you, but don't mention it."

"Make *er'* run," belts Nathaniel as a startled Walter obeys, frivolously fumbling to get his timer as he blurts aloud, "Running!" The mighty conveyor track wines, forcing the powerful hooves of the beast to move in succession.

"We got oxygen and carbon dioxide readings," informs Nathaniel, but Walter returns his attention to Alexis on a much slower pace.

"You know, this baby girl is performing like a fine tune engine."

"Baby girl – she weighs 462 pounds."

"Yeah but she's showing signs of human cognitive levels."

"Really..."

"Oh yeah... Gerhardt was the first to show signs, but Mishka here, soon followed."

"What's her evidence?"

"We figured out that it starts with the eyes. It's how they look at you…how they respond to your words."

"Ah…a sensitive response. I didn't know you were capable of comprehending such behavior. How can you possibly relate to such a thing?"

"You'd be surprised."

"I'll be sure not to hold my breath."

"As you know, we teach them the alphabet as well as the basics of reading – on a kindergarten level."

"I wonder just how much they can learn on their own."

"Not sure; just hope I'm around when one gets free of this controlling atmosphere."

"Maybe if you stop flirting, you might just live long enough to see."

"Full gallop," roars Nathaniel. "Full," responds Walter while turning the dial. In a thunderous fury, the thoroughbred pounds the conveyor track while several computers calculate heart rate as well as other information. "Walter, dynamic readings surpass the mark," screams Nathaniel.

Soon, all team members marvel at the awesome force in motion; however, Walter again indulges in his fixation with Alexis. While gingerly resting his arm on a nearby shelf, he asks, "Say…you have plans this evening?"

"Well…as a matter of fact I do." Alexis, displaying girlish mannerisms looks Walter in the eyes, slowly tilting her head left to right. She nudges closer to Walter as he moves closer to her, face to face. Then, she whispers in his ear, "I love twosomes."

"Wh…wh…what...you and…me?"

A great smile forms upon Walter's face. Alexis smiles and leans even closer. "Me and Mishka. I love to read and so does she. We both have something in common; so, I'll invite her over instead." "*Okaaay…*" "Oh, be sure to tell that person you call a girlfriend hello for me." Walter slowly nods his head and somberly leans away from Alexis as she daunts a mischievous grin.

As she departs, Frank approaches. "Walter!"

"What is it?"

"You *cozying* up to Blondie?"

"What do you want Frank?"

"Well, since you asked; here are the readings for your horse, and…"

"And what?"

"You need to fix that."

"Fix that… Fix what?"

"That…" Frank yells with adamancy, conveying that Walter should look downward. Walter perceives Frank's notions and does so. His discovery produces nothing less than a startling embarrassment. Wide eyed and stiffed lipped, he quickly looks at Frank, yet in that same moment, "Shut her down," expounds from Nathaniel. Walter speedily drapes himself with his lab coat and briskly walks towards the men's room. Frank slows the conveyor, allowing the horse to experience a moment of cool down time. Nathaniel approaches the computer monitor only to find Frank standing near the controls.

Nathaniel asks, "Where's Walter?"

Frank candidly smiles, saying, "He was a bit stiff, so he's gone to *shut'er* down."

Nathaniel, void of expression simply looks at Frank.

Team 3 concludes a series of tests on the remaining animals. An exuberant Tuan delivers the results of the gray fox and ostrich to Rowland, who is conversing through a private transmission. Soon afterwards, Rowland discontinues his conversation. "Tuan, what do you have for me?"

"Here's the reports you wanted. Look at the numbers."

Rowland activates a small screen and anxiously looks through the papers.

"This is wonderful news Tuan."

"I knew you would like it Professor. Both animals performed an astounding sixty-five percent better than the best records for their cousins in strength, speed, stamina, and durability."

"I'm glad, because the colonel is coming to examine *heez* subjects."

"What? He's coming here?"

"Yes! I just spoke *weeth heem* on the phone."

"Is he coming today?"

"He did not say, but I admonish you to be prepared."

The teams indulge in conversation while the animals observe with curious wonder. Walter approaches the horse and immediately stretches his hand to rub the animal's coat. "This is your big day girl." Suddenly, his attention is taken from the animal as he responds to a tap on his shoulder. "Be careful," the voice tells him. Walter quickly confronts his prankster. "What is it this time Frank?"

"Well…you may have to *shut er'* down." Frank blurts a hysterical laugh, as well as Nathaniel and Gracella.

"I pray constipation visits all of ya'll, especially you." Walter presents his middle finger to Frank and departs.

Jade calls for Gracella's attention. "Gracella, when you finish pouring your guts out, I need to know your plans for this evening."

"Jade, *yu…yu…*you don't understand…he…"

"Oh, I think I do. Anything thing Walter does makes no sense. He is the result of…a troubled mind."

"But, if you could have seen him; then again, you would know since he looks at you all the time."

"Walter looks at everybody all the time - even you."

"He's…cute, in a rugged sort of way."

"He is scruffy – like highland sheep back home."

"Just your type…"

"Tell me, what are your plans for evening?"

"I don't know – Why?"

"There is movie I want to see, and would like you to come with me."

"I don't have any plans that I know of."

"Find time – yes?"

"My husband says I'm married to you more than him."

"I enjoy our times together."

"So do I."

"You're like, sister to me Gracella."

"I never felt anything less. And speaking of sister, how is your family?"

"Well…much time has past."

"I'm sorry."

No, it is fine."

"There is seldom a word from you with regards to your family, or your past; there is still some hurt there Jade – I can feel it."

"What *do this* have to do with movie?"

"Sometimes, you seem one way and then in another way, you seem…somehow completely different. Is there any thing bothering you?"

"Why do you ask such things?"

"Because you are my friend and I am concerned about you."

"Please, not now. Better we discuss later – *pouzdanjemeni*."

"I do trust you."

"Ah…you remember well..."

"Every word you taught me, though your English is better than my Croatian."

"But your English took me many years."

"Jade, I…just…don't…want your past to cloud your future, in any thing – even relationships."

"Relationships – such things run bad for girl like me."

"You will make someone a wonderful prize someday."

"Many fail to see that."

"Compatibility and a Godly interest helps."

"Ah…the Jesus you speak of again – In time perhaps, but as far as compatibility in relationship, I have no need for such things now."

"Time will tell."

"I can see the happiness of you and yours, Arthur and his, Nathaniel's family…but good ones somehow get away from me."

"Maybe not all the good ones. Just turn around."

"For what?"

"Turn…around…"

"What game is this?"

"Good things come in interesting packages."

Jade catches a glimpse of Walter placing items on a shelf. She immediately faces Gracella. "You are out of your mind!"

"Don't be surprised."

"What is it you see in him?"

"Not him Jade, but you."

"I don't understand."

"When you look in the mirror, what do you see?"

"I see me staring right back at me – What else?"

"And nothing more?"

"I know what you say Gracella."

"Jade, if I were the looking glass in which you stare, I would see a person far deserving of something wonderful. I'd show you a beautiful flower, a soaring bird, a palette of many colors, infinite possibilities; you are so far short of your expectations that you can't even appreciate your own worth. If you only let the past go, whatever it is, and embrace the present…and trust God for the future."

"You are good friend Gracella; you and Arthur both, but the mirror I look in shows someone far disturbing to me; far different than you know."

"Whatever it is, I'm sure it will all be fine…and yes, we can catch a movie."

A few days pass and the teams reassemble. A tall mysterious figure quietly enters the room. Under the shadows of the entryway, the figure holds a cap tucked securely under one arm. Stepping forward, the figure pauses at the edge of the lightened area and observes all the team members from a distance.

Surprisingly, Alexis notices the silhouette standing in the distance and immediately summons Rowland. "Who are you and how *did* you get in here? This *eez* secure area! I *veel* call security!"

A brief moment of silence; then a slow somber voice, "I sure hope so… After all, our investment should be protected."

With one step, the dark body enters the light and transforms into a familiar countenance. Rowland sighs with relief. "Colonel Ducet, you have mustache now. Been vacationing – yes?"

"Something like that..."

"We've been expecting you, but unsure of your arrival."

"I hope I am not intruding, but your message was too tempting to pass up."

Rowland escorts the colonel to the holding bins. "Here they are Colonel; Meshka, Gearhardt, Foxtrot, and Demora. All show good signs of progress."

"Excellent..."

"They are weeks ahead of schedule, and s*trrr-ong* and *rrr-heady* for the *wourld!*"

"Rowland, you said in your message that their mental capabilities parallel to that of humans."

"Their ability to comprehend dialect *eez* comparative to small children, but they also come *weeth* ability to learn at much…much…higher level."

"I should hope so, because we would like to test them on our terms."

"Tests…what do you say Colonel?"

"Just as it sounds Rowland..."

"On your TERMS? But I thought time *eez* for much later; a factor desiring of need – no doubt. Colonel, surely *thees* cannot be?"

"Based on your reports I feel that the time is just right. I will take it from here."

"Colonel, we cannot know the subjects full potential at *thees* point."

"Rowland, we are not interested in how smart these enans are. If they can move, breathe; rationalize simple instructions – that automatically qualify them for the job. Remember clause twenty-seven of our contractual agreement?"

Rowland steps away from the colonel. His blaring fixation upon the officer matches the rampaging beat of his heart. Ducet sternly observes Rowland. Silence looms within the laboratory once more.

Tuan confronts Ducet. "We were saving the more confidential aspects about these animal hybrids for you on the due date Colonel."

"Noted, but also know that we have our sources and the report is good."

"Sources, like what? Where? In this building?"

"Sources…Mr. Vein; not to mention clause 27-e."

"I know what the clause says and how your ownership fits in, but…"

"That will be enough. You have done your part now let us do ours. My men are at the loading dock. Either you load them or I will get my men to do it."

"You're going to take them away – now?"

"Yes."

"Professor, will you explain to him that these hybrids need more testing?"

"The colonel is *een heez* right."

"So, he just shows up and takes them away?"

Ducet firmly plants his hat and exits the room. Rowland feels the presence of all eyes bearing down upon him as he systematically paces the room. After a brief moment, he looks at his teams.Then, in a somber voice, "Like carnival mirrors; stretched glass showing many false angles of the one standing in front of *eet*. Our perilous looking glass of modern technology has revealed an ill-contortioned identity."

No one responds. Rowland sits quietly in front of Meshka's bin and slowly buries his face within his hands. The teams prepare the hybrid subjects for embarkation aboard Ducet's transports.

~~~Test~~~

0900 hours mark another day of experiments. Each team accompanies Rowland to the colonel's testing facility. Tinted windows shield the occupants as the sun's brilliance beats down upon the long stretch of black top. Sweltering heat waves spiral upward in an emulsifying dance as the transport shuttles its occupants through the barren landscape. The long journey concludes in front of four men.

Two of the men; bearing firearms, stand at an entry gate while the other two, dressed in dessert camouflage, display high-power weapons, each with one finger near the trigger. The tall gate spans to the north and south, stretching into the distance of the mountainous horizon. Razor sharp barbs lace a cyclone spiral of wire that rests on top of the high barrier; a threatening appearance that warns anyone with hostile intentions.

One of the guards approaches Rowland. Badges and IDs display after which the guard transmits a visual message. Then, he waves for both vehicles to enter. Upon passing through the gates, a sign, YOU ARE NOW ENTERING PROPERTY OF THE UNITED STATES GOVERNMENT boldly displays.

Walter leans against the window. "We're on their turf now – guess we better behave."

"That's got to be a hard thing for you," replies Alexis.

"Maybe... But take a look at the surrounding hillside. Is this the Red Sea on dry land or what? I've never seen so much red sand."

"Must have high concentrations of iron," replies Nathaniel.

Both vehicles proceed forward as distant mountains silently cast bluish hues against the dry terrain. Their journey is swift, yet Frank notices something in the sand. "A gun turret; looks like a 50 cal."

After a long trip along the main road, huge concrete ventilation shafts emerge above ground as a large rectangular opening in the earth comes into view. The road, on which the teams travel, passes into a pitch-black abyss. "Impressive," says Gracella, looking out the window with child-like wonder. Artificial lights appear and quickly line the ceiling of a tunnel as the travelers make their way around a winding road and eventually into a parking area.

Ending their trek within a vacant lot, three guards greet the teams as they exit the vehicles. "Please follow me," instructs one of the guards.

The guard leads Rowland and his teams to an oversize metallic door. The door displays as part of the natural rock surrounding. As the door slides apart, everyone passes through heavy security scanners and soon realize that they are on an elevator. With one press of a button, the subterranean capsule immediately plummets deep within the bowels of the earth until it comes to a slow halt. "Ladies, gentlemen step this way please," beckons the guard, but Walter quickly raises his hand. "Um, excuse me, but how deep are we?"

The guard simply stares at Walter and directs his attention to another officer. "Officer Keagan will lead you and answer any questions you may have." The guard departs, leaving Walter perplexed as ever.

Clear-panel doors slide apart, revealing a large room where several military and civilian personnel carry out various functions. Proceeding further, the officer leads the teams to a much larger room. Inside, the room displays a complex array of computer and electronic sophistication on a presidential scale. "Wow," faintly passes into the cavernous enclosure as each team member stand in awe. "So this is where our tax dollars go," says Nathaniel. Five enormous size windows line the front of the room with a single massive viewing window in the center and two smaller compartmental windows adjacent on both sides. Eyes widen as astonishing remarks continue.

Officer Keagan brings the teams to a prominent figure. "Sir, they're here." "Thank you – that will be all," responds the figure. Turning with both hands clasped behind his back, the tall ranking officer stands stoic before the teams.

Rowland approaches. "No doubt the man in charge – Yes Colonel? And…*weeth* mustache gone, now *thees* is how I remember you."

"I trust your trip was comfortable."

"*Eet* was, but may I say that you appear predisposed – yes?"

"Perhaps… But not enough to ignore the gods of our progenies. Welcome and please follow me." Colonel Ducet gives Rowland a firm handshake and both men move to the observation chamber.

Colonel Ducet displays nothing less than a prideful stride and the mannerisms that accompany such behavior. "Magnificent, isn't it? Just beyond those windows lies the unofficial eighth wonder of the world, a two-mile long rectangular subterranean enclosure. The *proving grounds* – we like to call it. We are more than one mile below the surface, housed in complete and total seclusion. Damn we're good."

"I see..."

"What we do here is shrouded in secrecy, safely tucked away from the curious eyes of the public. Consider yourselves quite fortunate to be here."

"Absolutely Colonel..."

"By the way Rowland, no hard feelings on our last meeting – you know, about taking the enans."

"No – I totally understand. One does what one must."

"Good... Now then, to the rest of the team – ladies, gentlemen; glad you all could come. Allow me to officially welcome you to Red Sands Research and Development or RSRD for short. I trust your journey was comfortable."

"Thank you. We see how the name relates," replies Frank.

"Oh yes – the sand. This site was selected because of the stability within the earth's infrastructure. Enormous amounts of iron ore were discovered and during the excavation, the remnants were strewed topside; thus forming the red or oxidation that you saw earlier. Without the stability, those one hundred and fifty foot high walls out there would be impossible to stand."

"That's what I call a high wall," comments Walter.

"Now forgive me, time is crucial so I'll be brief. Every thing you are about to see is classified. Six stories below this observation deck, the first of a series of tests is about to begin. Our first test subject is ready. I'm sure you all will find this quite interesting, especially you Mr. Tuan Vein."

"Then bring it on," replies Tuan.

As everyone approaches the viewing window, Jade beckons the attention of a sentinel. He asks, "May I help you?"

"Yes. Where is the ladies room?"

"Right this way ma'am, but I must scan you as a precautionary measure."

"Of course..."

The sentinel raises his forearm, bending it at chest level. A wave of light pulsates from a device strapped to his forearm, projecting a flat horizontal beam of orange light. The light weaves from the top of Jade's head to the bottom of her feet. "Registering probes indicate nothing unusual. Right this way ma'am."

Upon entry into the latrine, Jade peels off a small layer of skin from her forearm. Afterwards, she retrieves a tiny, thin, disk-like device and momentarily holds the object in her hand. "Forgive me, but time has come." She activates the disk.

Elsewhere, Rowland and his teams follow Colonel Ducet as they move closer to the main observation window. Ducet narrates the activity below. "You all made it in time to witness history in the making. Beneath us, laying in readiness is our first official test subject. The synopsis is simple. We wrote specific instructions, the test subject will read it, and if it comprehends well enough, then it will know exactly what to do."

"Um, it's a she Colonel," interjects Tuan.

"Yes...of course Mr. Vein. Goals; run the gauntlet, destroy the target, and return - alive of corse..." Laughter fills the air.

"Surely we will not use live rounds, but do know that 50 meter casings can still hurt you if you get struck by one."

Suddenly, a voice emanates from the forward speaker. "Colonel, the subject is green for go." Ducet takes a receiver in hand. He pauses and looks at Tuan. "If the ENAN, well...Gerhardt to you Mr. Vein, but project 429-001 to us, does well then you have done well." "ENAN?" "Oh...yes ENAN, Evolutionized Nocturnal Assault Nomad. Remember the term from our previous meeting?" "Yes." Colonel Ducet asserts his focus back to the speaker, "proceed," he commands.

Sirens intensely blare throughout the cavernous enclosure. Suddenly, the bird takes flight, running with great speed into the field as it rips a trail into the earthen floor. Tuan watches with high expectation as Ducet leans near by.

"An ostrich – odd choice of soldier. It is fortunate that appearance is low on our list. Your subject suggests that our enemy will die while laughing."

"On the contrary colonel; we were trying to get as close to natural as possible."

"Fair enough. But be advised, should this work, more formidable appearances must occur – Understand?"

"Point taken Colonel, but you did leave the carrier selection to us. You also took the hybrids before we were ready to deliver them."

"Yes…I did."

Near the bird's path, a thunderous explosion erupts. The force of impact brazes the animal's plumage. Startled, the awkward beast proceeds forward as rising clouds of dust cyclone in her wake. Another explosion tears into the ground, hurling more earth and ash into the air. Gerhardt continues to run, jumping, ducking, and systematically maneuvering until she enters a small white structure.

"Test subject has entered the first success stage Colonel," expels the supervisor.

"Acknowledge. Activate the high guns," commands Ducet.

Square doors slide open along the towering walls, after which, nozzles of high-powered guns point toward the field. One of the guns begins to fire.

While inside the structure, Gerhardt assures herself the safety of further entering. The bird quickly pulls a small device from within a carrying pouch and places it near the bottom of the rear wall. She skillfully pecks numbers upon a specialized keypad as chunks of concrete crumbles to the floor. Cracks tear furiously into the ceiling as the west wall of the structure receives the merciless brunt of the assault gun. Undaunted, Gerhardt pulls from the pouch and places a second device near the bottom of the adjacent wall. In like manner, the hybrid beast pecks numbers upon a keypad. Soon, a countdown process begins. Gerhardt exits the structure and runs into a nearby low-lying area. She crouches in a gangly manner and tucks her head behind an earthen barrier. Meanwhile, time expends on the devices and a blistering cloud of smoke and fire blazes into the air,dangerously reaching the ceiling of the artificial grotto. Once peaked, the flames rapidly diminish and debris falls to the ground. Nothing remains of the structure.

"First stage complete sir," yells the supervisor. Immediately, exciting cheers fills the observation room. All but Colonel Ducet partake of the festivities.

"Go ahead with second stage," he commands. The soldier hastily implements the senior officer's orders; however, he soon calls for the colonel's attention.

"Sir, we lost visual."

"What do you mean?"

"I can't find our enan."

"Then check your vitals and homing signal."

The soldier does so. Then, a small blinking dot moves across the monitor. A sigh of relief combs the soldier's face. "429-001 moves sir."

"Good. Now this time, keep up with her."

"Yes sir."

Deadly bullets blaze closely to the animal, tattering the bird's path with stifling results. With each stride, Gerhardt continues to dart forward, preceding inches beyond the piercing rounds. Another explosion erupts nearby, but the stalwart beast keeps moving. Soon, Gerhardt locates another concrete enclosure and quickly enters inside. Simultaneously, an additional gun turret activates and begins punishing the structure with disatrous results.

Inside, Gerhardt immediately rushes to a small table and locates a black box with a red and black wire exposed. A can of fuel and a barrel of gunpowder are located beneath the table. Both items lay near the rear of the farthest portion of the room. Flexing her neck, Gerhardt acquires the pouch upon her back. She pulls a small portion of clay from within the bag and presses it on the table in front of the black box. Afterwards, she presses both wires into the clay. Then, Gerhardt pulls a long stream of wire from the pouch, presses one end of it into the clay and strings the other end of the wire along the ground.

Holes form within the walls of the structure as chunks of concrete spew inwardly. In spite of it all, the hybrid continues to work vigorously. The bird takes the fuel and methodically pours a stream from the exposed wire to the floor, forming a complete stream that leads to the barrel of gunpowder. Pressing a small button with her beak, Gerhardt ignites the stream of gas, which quickly turns into a dancing wall of flames. Inch by inch, the fiery barrier cast a convincing moment of contact, and it becomes quite clear that Gerhardt has seen enough. Powerful legs propel her flightless body beyond the entryway and into the onslaught of gunfire. Soon, the fire makes contact with the barrel and a roaring sound tears through the underground field while shaking the floor of the observation room. Shadows vanish as a pillar of white fire soars upward.

Static appears on the monitors as silence falls everywhere. Moments later, the colonel approaches the supervisor. "Where's 429-001?"

"No visual sir."

Debris finally settles as huge turbines vent the field and cameras resume observation. Then, a wild gating figure emerges from within the plumes of smoke. Gerhardt comes into view, but carries around her neck a torn collar and a small dangling box. With ruffled feathers and patches of soot covering exposed skin, Gerhardt hurriedly makes her way back to the control room.

"Sir, there she is!"

"Bring her in, NOW!"

Cheers of adulation fill the room, as the success of the first test becomes history.

Tuan approaches Rowland. "Why use such powerful explosives? There's enough to level an entire city."

"That *eez* point... Yes?"

"They may as well use live ammo."

"Absolutely Mr. Vein. Remember the synopsis – if the subject reads and comprehends, then it would know that its survival is sealed, despite the staging. In warfare, you carry out your mission regardless of what's going on around you. Gerhardt succeeded, congratulations – end of story."

Celebration reigns high as Gerhardt slowly walks towards the safety zone.

Then, without warning, firearms surprisingly rattle fury upon the field once more. Personnel, both military and civilian alike, desperately take cover. "What the hell is that?" yells Ducet. The panel operator surprisingly responds. "Sir, the simulation is – still active."

"Well kill it!"

"Sir, safety protocols are off!"

"What? Are you reading that panel right?"

"No error Colonel."

"Then manually shut it down!"

"I can't...over-ride won't respond!"

"Then find a way to protect our enan!"

Immediately, an army of personnel frantically flips switches and push buttons to bring the raining hell fire to silence. In the event, a young soldier quickly approaches the colonel. "Sir, the ostrich has a failsafe diverter that tells the computers not to fire on its location when exposed to the outside."

"Yes...I'm aware of that, just like every other person out there; but in case the computer has something else in mind, I'd like to take my option under consideration."

"Sir, look!" The soldier points to the monitor. A camera barely catches Gerhardt running past the lens.

"What's that dangling around her neck?"

"Oh no, it's the diverter. It's broken. This is not good sir."

"How did that happen?" Colonel Ducet slams his hand down on the panel, "Get those guns down...NOW!"

"We may have to pull the mainframe."

"Then DO IT!"

Explosions burst outwardly in random sequence as led continue to rain upon the field. Sensing imminent danger, Gerhardt desperately runs toward the safe zone, but she soon sways in disorientation. Her left wing begins to sag, dropping lower with each stride until ruffled feathers scrape the ground. Everyone watch with hopeful anticipation as Gerhardt approaches the bay. Personnel loudly encourage the hybrid into the safety zone, but remain weary of the rain of terror.

Sadly, chunks of flesh grossly tear away from beneath the bird's soot-stained plumage as bullets cascade downward. The event senselessly pierces Gearhardt's entire body. Remarkable strides now dwindle to a staggering limp. In one ghastly breath; the torn hybrid belts a horrifying screech into the air, a sound that burrows deep into the ears of everyone listening. Lunging forward, the awkward creature stretches its entire body, falling until flesh contacts the ground. In despairing stillness, the final halt signifies a journey's end. Gearhardt's head lay within inches of the safety margin while blood oozes from her mouth; and yet, her eyes hauntingly remain open.

"Clear!" Assuring words ring forth as soldiers and civilian personnel comb the field, crossing the path of the fallen beast. Staring into Gearhardt's eyes, one soldier closely examines her. "God help us…she's still breathing," he says while gently rubbing the hybrid's head, offering as much compassion humanly possible. But soon, Gerhardt passes into silence.

Many within the control room lower their heads while others, mostly Rowland's team, hide their faces behind shielding hands.

The colonel grabs the microphone. His bare hands lock tightly around the instrument as his solemn face sinks upon his chest. Slowly leaning forward, all eyes fasten upon the officer. "Talk to me…talk to me someone."

Then, a voice projects from the panel speaker. "Sir…" "Go ahead," replies the colonel. "ENAN test subject 429-001, deceased at 1422 hours. An autopsy usually follows. What are your orders?"

The colonel stands in one spot, looking at Rowland. He removes his hat and wipes his forehead, acting as if his greatest fear has materialized. "DAMMIT," he yells, driving his fist into the surface of the panel. All eyes fasten upon him. Afterwards, he takes a long deep breath and leans near the microphone.

"I know what killed the animal…son, what I don't know is why the computer reactivated the scenario with live ammo. That is now the goal. Until we figure that out…carry on people!" The entire room looms in silence as two men carry a large black bag where Gerhardt lays. Rowland bestows a sympathetic pat on Tuan's shoulder as Jade intently watches from a distance.

~~~Recourse~~~

"**Sweet**s...sweets, wake up." Subtle words echo in the darkness, effectively drawing me into the present. My eyes slowly open. Standing before me is Aniah. A solemn embrace consumes the moment. She asks, "When are you coming to bed?" I stare at her for a moment, trying to find the right words to say. "I couldn't sleep," I tell her.

"Just resting with your eyes closed?"

"Something like that."

She looks at me with emptiness for a moment, and then gazes upward. "The moon is beautiful. I suppose the cloud cover has moved on."

"It appears that way."

"I see you've been going through your photo albums. Are you reminiscing about the glory days?"

"Sort of..."

"Those were some crazy times."

"Yes they were."

"Crazy enough to keep you awake – again?"

"Crazy enough to make me remember."

"More dreams?"

"Like clock work."

"We have been over this a hundred times. Honey, those events are in the past."

"Yes, but those events did happen and you know what it cost me – and you."

"All I know is that we're together, but I'll be damned if I share you with that infernal abomination; both of them."

"They are gone."

"And thank God, but you keep them alive in your head. At this rate, they will eventually destroy you. Not to mention…they are keeping you from me."

"I never intended that."

"I know."

"I keep replaying the scenarios over…and over…"

"Do you still desire them both so badly that you choose to hold on?"

"They are a part of me."

Aniah peers at me, as though to ask more questions without divulging a single word; probably sensing whether I'm telling the truth or not, as only God designed her to do, but her points end with a smile. She tenderly touches my shoulder with two fingers as if to bestow consent of Devine approval. Then, in a subtle voice, "let there be enough room in those dreams for me," she says. Rising to her feet, the moonlight gently shines against her smooth brown skin while she looks at me. Standing on the tips of her toes, she manages to stretch her 5' 2" frame, pulling me closer, hugging me ever so tightly. I bend slightly, realizing the warmth of her embrace and how it constantly heals my wounded soul. She places a gentle kiss upon my face and slowly walks away, leaving a pleasing rear view as she vanishes into the darkness.

Facing the window, I capture a glimpse of Nostalgia as she immerges. "There you are," I whisper. She will soon come to me, but not yet. I lay upon the sofa, strategically balancing the photo album upon my chest, realizing that there is enough light to make out the images.

Turning the pages, I find Rowland shaking hands with Colonel Ducet. Spitefully, both men had very little to say to each other after Gearhardt's death, at least openly. More photos reveal candid shots of the teams making progressive measures for more testing. "The show must go on." Yes, the show did go on.

In a matter of minutes, the album falls forward, touching the lower portion of my chin. Staring upward, the ceiling begins to fluctuate in a surge of wild movements as darkness wields its cloak of emptiness. But even in such bowels of obscurity, degrees of heighten clarity comes forth as my eyes close once more.

Room 47-C again holds its occupants as a familiar silence looms within the atmosphere. Each member sits quietly around the oak table. Rowland stares amidst as he slowly taps his fingers upon the hard glossy surface. Papers turn within binders as answers to questions elude even the most knowledgeable attendants. However, Walter spurns his frivolous point-of-view.

"They knew. They all knew from day one that if this works, they would have to hide all the evidence and make it look like an accident. I believe that this is some kind of a cover up!"

"Pretty messy cover up for a bird," interjects Nathaniel.

"I don't think so, and remember; Gerhardt was not just a bird. She was an engineered hybrid that could rival human intellect – real easy!"

As the discussion continues, a tiny light flickers upon one of the monitors. Frank answers the transmission and draws Rowland's attention. Several seconds pass as Rowland pauses. Turning his back towards the group, Rowland conveniently shields his conversation from the others.

Noticing his actions, Gracella folds her arms and immediately directs a question aloud. "How long does a formal investigation take? It's been three weeks and we haven't heard anything from the Military."

"That's because they're getting ready for the next big lie. Politics is a smoke screen. Can't you tell? And when it all clears, only then do you find that we were too late to see the truth."

"Walter, I was expecting a more educated response. I think we simply don't know all the details of what is going on, if there is anything going on. Why do you insinuate that there is some kind of conspiracy or cover-up with the military? You're beginning to sound like Arthur, or even our precious government."

"There usually is a cover up. Before you know it, they'll be tapping our butt holes just to keep account of who's producing the most piles of crap, just so they can raise our taxes per household."

"Walter, you're so stupid," interjects Alexis.

As Walter refutes the others, Rowland returns. He reaches into his pocket while staring directly at Tuan, yet neither man verbally acknowledges each other. Rowland proceeds with his lethargic mannerisms as he pulls from his coat a small silver flask. All eyes fixate upon the shiny item, but none dare ask with regards to it. Rowland takes a deep drink, throwing his head back while briskly swallowing. Replacing the lid, he concludes with a soothing exhale. The others watch in sheer astonishment, but Tuan decides to break the silence.

"Professor, you…you're not supposed to do that."

Rowland wipes his mouth with the sleeve of his lab coat. He replaces the small flask back into his pocket and rolls his chair closer to the table. Placing his hands on top of his head, the geneticist leans back in his chair with cavalier poise. "There's many *theengs* we are not to do. Today, I *weel* push that boundary. *If* any of you *weeesh* to join me, I *veel* see that a good performance report is received by all, *weeth prrro*-motion potential – of course."

"Sounds good to me," grumbles Nathaniel, sarcastically relishing the moment.

Rowland places both hands on the table as the atmosphere erupts with laughter. But the momentquickly fades as Rowland leans forward. "That was Colonel. *Heees* preliminary investigation reveals that… distracter, as they call *it*, around Gearhardt's neck was damaged during routine exercise, *wheeech*…prevent computers from diverting bullets away from…*thee* Gerhardt. When they realized…*that*…box was damaged, Gerhardt was well *in* harms way."

Arthur asks, "So…what destroyed the distracter?"

"He did not say. But he did say that Mishka did well, but was limited in dexterous functions while the fox and the others were not as impressive as they had hoped. But all were unharmed."

"That's good to hear Professor and it also answers the question of manageable digits. But for speed, we need an animal that either runs or hops."

"No matter *eef* animal can run or hop, only that *eet eez* fast. Dexterous fingers are now the focus. The colonel says that the computers should be okay. Most importantly, our contract *weel* not be affected due to…incident – Yes?"

Tuan addresses Walter as he tosses notes before him. "There goes your Big-Brother conspiracy theory – stupid." "*Hmmmph*...that's what you think." Rowland exits the room, followed by the others.

Arthur lingers behind, catching Gracella's attention as he pulls her aside. "Grace."

"What is it?"

"Did you hear that?"

"Hear what?"

"Listen. I didn't want to say any thing in front of the others."

"What is this about?"

"If the distracter was supposed to protect Gerhardt, by telling the computers to aim away from her, then how did the distracter get damaged in the first place?"

"I was going to ask that same question; but maybe a bullet hit it."

"Are you kidding? Wake up girl... A computer glitch and a stray bullet? What puzzles me is that, the distracter was on Gearhardt's underside. How can bullets from above strike something shielded so well beneath? The monitor showed that the box was busted long before Gerhardt approached the safety zone."

"You're saying that Gerhardt was okay long before those computers went hay-wire?"

"Yes."

"Arthur, do you know what you are suggesting?"

"Of course I do."

"Why would the military sabotage their own investment?"

"That's my point Grace, they wouldn't, but someone else might." Gracella remains silent, but slowly looks away, yet heavily in thought. Meanwhile, Colonel Ducet grants Rowland's teams with new mandates. Each mandate requires more results. Their previous efforts proved quite noble; however, their dire expectations are far short of what the military had hoped for.

Feeling the weight of such expectations, Arthur finds that a routine visit to a favorite place is more than a needful relief. It is twenty-one hundred hours on a brisk Thursday night as he stares at a spherical white ball of leather. Violent words pass back and forth across a high black net as two groups of six combatants privately engage in a confrontation of mortal dominance. Poised and hardened, Arthur quietly steps away from the blue boundary marker. He hears the words *"Get'em, get'em,"* ringing forth from five members of his team, but his opponents, grappling with anticipation, perch themselves with daring resistance as they watch his movements. Slowly, their bodies sway left and right, an obvious preparation for what could be their advantage or demise.

Then, with great form, Arthur tosses the ball into the air and whacks it with such force that it barely clears the net. The ball strikes a defensive player and bounces far beyond the boundary. Arthur's team immediately roars in a frenzy of high praise. While celebrating, one of the participants crosses the net, spewing profanity while purposefully agitating Arthur's team. While shouting his pathetic insults, the man is met with equal male-*ish* verbiage as an older member of Arthur's team contests their victory. Only the most discipline of minds can deal with such words ringing back and forth. Arthur laughs while his team bestows waves of congratulations.

"Alright people, your moment of glory is over! Time to go…now get out!" The commands of the attendant are carried out as instructed. Arthur is among the last to exit the building.

Fumbling for his bracelet, Arthur takes notice of a man sitting in a large truck. The vehicle sets only a few yards ahead, yet Arthur continues to approach his own transport in a casual manner. A few minutes pass and the sound of a diesel engine rumbles into the parking lot, effectively drawing the attention of everyone.

Raw black smoke billows high above twin upright exhausts as a low winding transmission unmistakably marks a workhorse of a machine. All six wheels tread to a screeching halt. With the motor operating, the door swings open and out steps a robust figure of a man. His worn blue uniform depicts the markings of a seasoned rail-roader, but his vehicle typifies the countenance of an experienced mechanic as well as a truck enthusiast.

He opens the door of Arthur's truck and casually enters. Seating himself, he belts a hardy laugh and punches Arthur in the arm.

"What's up gooseneck?" Arthur casts a frown, but soon extends a heart felt welcome as both men tangle in a contest of strength. Arthur looses. "Hah, one day, you'll gain enough weight; you string bean" screams the man.

"Well look who's here...haven't seen you in a while. I thought you were taking the gravy train in route to Austin this weekend."

"I was, but I got bumped."

"Seniority?"

"You got it."

"I see. So – what are you tipping the scales at this time?"

"265."

"Still corn fed...."

"...And loving it."

"How are things with you and Merry, Mia, or what ever her name is?"

"It's Myran and we're dandy as two pigs in the mud hole."

"Dandy...I see... You still got the country in you boy – don't you?"

"Some things never change."

"You're becoming more and more like a crusty old farmer."

"Why not? Farming's in my blood and I *ain't* changing. Not to mention that Myran doesn't seem to mind it one bit. She can field dress a deer and run a trout line – and that really gets me going."

"Freak"

"Whatever... Plus...she's got a nice rear end suspension and I like it!"

"You always had a thing for thick mountain chicks."

"So what?"

"To each his ownve... Even God graces the unusual little brother."

"Whatever. Hey Gooseneck, check this out. They finally got my name right."

"Engineer Hollis Eric Brenan."

"Good deal. You can now officially drive the big boys of the rail."

"It also gives me a side benefit."

"Oh?"

"I can train you to drive the heavy riggers and freighters."

"I've always been proud of you. I'm not surprised, but you will always be my little brother, though you outweigh me by seventy pounds."

"There is help for you bony. Anyway… When are you going to sell Ramsey to me?"

"What? My truck… Maybe when I'm pushing up daisies."

"Someday, you will part with this beast – so give me first dibs."

"That I can do…" Both men laugh while embracing the moment.

Hollis reaches into his pocket and pulls out a device. "Here's the code reader you wanted. All you have to do is plug this into the computer of Aniah's car and press this button. It's the diagnosis for just what the doctor ordered."

"Aniah and I thank you."

"Anytime. Hate to run but I got to *skid-dattle*."

"What?"

"Never mind…"

"Nobody talks that way anymore."

"Listen. I just got back in town from the farm and I need to rest. Before I go, I want to know if you found the answer to your Frankenstein dilemma."

"No. As for Frankenstein, it is the systematic manipulation of cell development, and that's (SMD) to you."

"Well SMD, STD, DSD, PMS3…whatever…did you find the answer?"

"Not yet."

"The problem has to be with your approach."

"We didn't miss anything."

"I mean the angle of your attempts."

"Nevertheless, the answer is so close that I can taste it. Right now, the teams are letting the conventional approach dictate their methodologies. They want animals close to the finish product. I see their logic, but the final products just keep falling short."

"Arthur, it seems to me that if you can change animals at will, draw up the final product first, and then change the little varmints into what you want. Why not do that; instead of letting specs dictate your approach."

Arthur ponders the information as Hollis takes a glance at his watch. At that moment, his eyes widen; and then he asks, "What did you say?"

"I said don't let the animal's specs tailor…"

"No…not that!"

"Then what?"

"You said varmints, little rascals."

"Varmints…"

"Yeah!"

"You once told me that you needed something fast and mobile."

"Speed is basic."

"Critters range from possums, raccoons, prairie dogs, armadillos - you name it."

"Yeah…yeah…I get that part."

"We see little rascals jumping out of the way of the train when rolling the tracks at night!"

"So what's your point?"

"What if you had something small that naturally grows up big and can do...some of the things you want? Whatever they lack – give it to them as they develop. You got to think way outside the box on this one."

"There are no big jumping rats that can suite our purpose."

"Sure there is. Varmints come in all shapes and sizes and four-legs *ain't* the only fast moving things on land. Look guy, I got to run...call you later."

Hollis opens the door and exits the vehicle. Arthur's mouth immediately drops open as he stares beyond the windshield. His tense captivation consumes his attention so deep that he never sees Hollis exiting the parking lot. "Small to large, two legs instead of four; alter natural course of development," he whispers.

Entering his home, Arthur rushes into the office. Careful not to awake Aniah, he accesses his computer. "Alright... Show me what I'm looking for." His actions continue until morning.

Later that day, Gracella joins Arthur and both immediately depart. While in route, Gracella becomes most inquisitive. "Based on your adrenaline level, I know this is not a casual picnic. So...when do you intend to fill me in on this little mysterious outing?"

"Just hang on, you'll see. Hopefully, I'll find information that will help the project and I need someone who's familiar with the cloning process."

"Really..."

"Yes, someone...like...you."

"Why exactly?"

"You can bare witness to the information regarding a particular species, not to mention; you're on my team."

"Walter wasn't good enough?"

"Walter is with Jade."

"Never in a million years would I have thought that possible."

"I do recall you saying that stranger things have happened."

"Yes, I did say that, but those things usually don't happen."

"Entertaining hypocrisy?"

"No – I am a realist."

"Hah."

"If it works out between them, then good."

"We shall see, anyway, I will only need your approval as a witness for today."

"All right, but I'll only give you two hours of my time. Robert and I do have plans."

"Hey, the fate of man is one big orgasm waiting to happen."

"Shut-up Arthur and drive."

As Arthur guides his transport through a winding row of tress, Gracella begins to notice the area in which they are traveling. She says nothing as Arthur turns the large vehicle into a well-populated area. Parking along the outer edges of the lot, Gracella's attentiveness to a large sign confirms her suspicions.

"The Zoo? You got me up this morning to bring me to the zoo?! Arthur, we already work at a zoo. Is this your secret?"

"Have faith. Here's the tickets, lets get going."

Upon entering, both hasten towards an assembly of people near one of the zoological attractions. "Talk to me Arthur!"

"There, you see that gathering of people?"

"I see a lot of gathering of people."

"Over there…that's where we need to go." Arthur points in the direction of the crowed and they quickly become part of the large group. Several people carefully listen to a man with great interest. Though speaking, the man advertises an animal in such a way that interest peaks among the spectators. "All right folks, gather round and look closely. The answer to the question posed earlier, why the Land-Down-Under host a variety of marsupials unlike any other species in the world. Well, you can be *shur* that whatever happened way back when, is *shur'- nuff* the reason as to what we got now!" A crowed of faces immediately glee with laughter as young and old cast aloud sounds of festive rebuttal.

"This guy is a naturalist? I could have told you that," growls Gracella as a non-distracted Arthur endorses his approval on the man's comment. "*Shhhhhh...* I found this guy on the Internet."

"You…surfing for guys on the net? And you think I got issues?"

"This guy is hosting today's Down Under exhibit."

"I can see that Arthur, but what does this have to do with project 429?"

"Remember that picture I drew during the earlier stages of 429?"

"Yes."

"That picture is a view of what I believe to be the key to our next presentation."

"You've got to be kidding me."

"No. With conventional approaches to Colonel Ducet's request, I think we're off track. We need to take a more radical approach. If what I found this morning is any indication of what we can use in the lab, then this little trip is well worth our attention. That speaker is giving an educational lecture right here - now, and I feel we can benefit from his knowledge about these animals, especially that one."

"Arthur, it's a kangaroo; a baby at that, barely out of the stage of a joey."

"Then let's hear what he has to say."

The speaker takes center stage. "This here's my friend Joey. Joey is an Eastern Grey Kangaroo and is common in his part of the world. But he's not as popular as his cousin, the Red. Joey here can *git* bout' as large as a Red and weigh *jest* as much. Now our friend Joey is *jest* that…a joey. He's been *outta* his momma's pouch for a little more than 370 days. Male younglings are called joeys, and females are called jills. They prematurely enter the world *bout* an inch long. After a 35-day gestation period, they are hairless and have only their forelimbs developed. When they pop out, they make their way to momma's pouch. Once in, the baby attaches himself to the teat and begins a *suckin*.

The speaker hoists the small animal, holding it with one arm. Then, he gently stretches one of the kangaroo's hind legs. "This is one of the most fascinating *thangs bout* these animals. Kangaroos, like their kin, the wallabies have the unique ability to store an elastic strain of energy in the tendons of their large hind legs. With that in mind, the spring action of the tendons provides much of the energy needed for each jump. Even more fascinating is the relationship between *jumpin* and *breathin*. You see…when the feet leave the ground; air is expelled from the lungs; and by bringing the feet forward in preparation for landing, that action fills the kangaroo's lungs again with air, thus providing more energy efficiency. That's what I call a two-for-the-price-of-one effect. Other studies suggest that kangaroos use far less than minimal energy to hop at all. They can increase speed with very little effort and achieve the same rate of speed as that of a horse or dog. Also, very little energy is required to carry extra weight. Now, a major benefit for these animals is their ability to travel great distances in search of food, a helpful commodity in a very-hostile continent."

"Alright Grace, now tell me if that also sounds like a major part of Ducet's request."

"You made your point Arthur. I think I'm beginning to see why you came."

"Success is…*all*…in the legs?"

"Could we have gotten this information from a library or the electronic net?"

"Don't you think live information is better?"

"Why else did you really come here Arthur?"

"I want a first person's perspective. I want to hear him tell me what I already suspect and for you to confirm it."

"Well you have my confirmation – Now can we go?"

Arthur presses a sheet of paper into Gracella's hand and walks away.

"Hey, where are you going?"

"Grace, did you know that art personifies the soul, thereby preceding a factual result?"

"What is that suppose to mean?"

"Imagination Grace… The imagination always comes before the manifestation."

"Did you take your meds?" Gracella's question brazes Arthur's ears, but the technician strategically creates a path through the hoards of inquisitive spectators. He finally reaches the speaker.

Gracella sprawls the paper in front of her, sternly squinting her eyes while her mouth hangs open. "You've got to be kidding me," she says as the paper hangs open, displaying a drawing of a strange beast.

~~~The Man God~~~

Several species of birds congregate the outlining of maple trees along the roadside, singing merrily from within the thick canopies. Their piercing, yet soothing sounds signal the beginning of another labor intense week for Rowland and his teams. Again, room 47-C becomes the meeting place. Several easels hold various pictures of animal specimens that could likely serve as the next generation of 429 prospects. Input into the matter comes from every member around the table. Walter and Tuan both stand beside one of the easels, pointing out matters regarding lemurs.

Walter captures the groups' attention as he explains his points. "They can see well at night, which means minimal adjustments to the eyes. They can also jump and soar gracefully between trees making their agile abilities more beneficial than that of Gerhardt or the gazelle, or even our fox. Also note that their hands are extremely primate and dexterous for meticulous handling; something the military is very interested in."

"*Prrr-omising* Walter, but they are not fast," comments Rowland. Other team members uncover more pictures and discuss various points of views as well.

As discussions rein high, the entry door swings open. Arthur boldly enters; carrying instruments while nestling rolls of paper tucked under one arm. Placing his items upon the table, he hurriedly goes out the door and retrieves a large carrying case with a blanket covering it. He slams the door and approaches the table with a glowing countenance. Rowland extends a greeting. "*Vwell* Arthur…glad you can join us."

"Sorry I'm late Professor, but I think this is something you will want to see."

Arthur carefully places the carrying case on the table. While unrolling the paper, the case quickly becomes the center of attention. Alexis apprehends the moment, asking, "What's in the bag?" Arthur does not respond, but Frank too becomes inquisitive. "Already drinking on the job, and I thought life on the reservation was bad." "Some other time perhaps, but not today," responds Arthur as he quickly grabs an easel and secures a poster to it. He positions the wooden tri-pod in front of the group and immediately begins his presentation.

"Okay guys. As some of you may know, I am not in favor of conventionalism. I've said it before and I'll say it again; we've been trying to find an animal closely in shape and size to the final result.

Our intent is to also grant our enan with all the natural abilities for Ducet's soldier of fortune. The problem with this approach is that every gadget will have to be tailor-made for the hybrid's unique physical make up. This is okay if our hybrid encounters known elements or situations that are familiar to us. With that being said…it is my understanding that our hybrid will tread upon unknown territory, not to mention that it will be working with gadgets and gizmos that were never intended for natural animal handling."

Alexis chuckles aloud, candidly tapping her nails upon the hard surface of the table. "So…my goldfish can't shoot a rifle. Why is that so hard to believe Arthur?"

"That's my point. That also means that the military will have to make more specialized equipment for the hybrid, which adds up to more costs and more headaches when transporting the animals."

"Point made, do *prro*-ceed *Meester* Rrr-obinson," says Rowland.

"Like the military, we too must be practical. We don't put hands on a horse because the horse wasn't designed to have hands or fingers. Nor do we want to put wings on a dog because the dog's back muscles would have to be three times the animal's size in order to lift it off the ground. Tremendous amounts of energy are required for mobility, even if such a design could sustain the dog in flight. By comparison to Gearhardt, we need a hybrid that is adaptable in all the ways that matter to the assignment. Also, keep in mind that the military does not care about the hybrid's overall appearance – at least not yet."

Tuan asks, "Then what do you propose?"

"I propose something all together radical and completely out of the box. Since we have the ability to manipulate at the genetic level and alter cellular mitosis as the developing embryo progresses, why not expand the horizon far beyond conventionalism?"

"And how…exactly…do we do that?" asks Walter.

"I have before you three topics: size, ability, and potential. All which will manifest as our new subject grows older."

Nathaniel boldly leans forward. "How do these attributes or topics get introduced?"

"Look at the posters. The sub-topics, underneath each major topic, explain the sequence of events. In short, we simply alter the embryo at any time during the stages of development."

"Interesting..."

"Absolutely. The All Mighty never intended His creations to do the things that the military wants, so therefore, let us create...*hybrid*...in-our-image – so to speak."

Rowland leans forward, observing the graphic presentations. "A very *een-teresting* synopsis *Meester Rrr*-obinson. Now tell us...what *weel* be your model?"

Standing poised, Arthur slowly eyes each person in the room. Slightly smiling, he approaches the box and leans over the table while reaching for the cover. Without looking, he pulls the cloth away. "Ladies and gentlemen, I give you Macropus Giganteus." Eyes widen as astounding sighs randomly exert. Some members begin to make subtle comments while others stare in acute silence. Arthur gently pulls from within the carrying case a small kangaroo and carefully holds the animal high.

Frank smiles. "A magic trick there - Arthur?"

"In some sense – yes."

"Ah, an Eastern Grey Kangaroo," comments Rowland.

"Awwwww...it's so cute," woos Alexis while rubbing the animal's side.

"It's a damn varmint," grumbles Nathaniel.

"Yes and no. It's not a rat at all and in many ways our little friend has been considered a pest in its homeland. But in this country, he's red carpet material."

Rowland carefully removes the animal from Arthur's hands and cradles the marsupial like a newborn baby. "Macropus, Macropus, Macropus," he says. Rowland turns towards Arthur and then looks at the poster. The geneticist illuminates with a familiar glee. "I see your point *Meester Rrr*-obinson. Therefore, you *veel* have to lead team to make *thees* happen."

Arthur smiles and slowly gazes at the second poster. "This poster depicts a drawing of a kangaroo from point of origin to the conclusive stage of development."

Fascination draws the attention of everyone to the indescribable apparition that sets at the final phase of the flow chart. So striking is the final stage of the hybrid's appearance that no one questions Arthur's intent, except one.

Tuan sees differently. "Professor, I thought we already discussed the hybrid package. We can't just throw away these ideas that have already proven effective. Arthur's project has to undergo far too much testing – we do not have that kind of time."

"He put *thees* idea in my head two days ago. I think potential *eez*...very good."

"But Professor..."

"*Vwell,* what do you suggest?"

"Let Arthur proceed as he will and let us continue with what we already have. Create two teams instead of three."

"We are more effective *weeth* more heads on one project – yes? Division *weel* diminish our strength."

"Professor, I say we continue on course or I'm off this project."

Tuan folds his arms, staring at the table as though to find a responsive answer. Rowland remains silent, as do the others until Gracella draws their attention. "Rowland, may I suggest that Arthur pursue his idea with one person to assist and let the others continue with the conventional route. At first, I was appalled at Arthur's idea and...as you can see, the end result will be extremely radical – if he can pull it off. Concerning the kangaroo; there are facets regarding this animal's body that we simply cannot ignore, not to mention that we will have two chances for success instead of one."

"Then...who *weel* help Arthur?"

Gracella raises her hand; winking at Arthur who reciprocates with a smile. Then surprisingly, another hand rises. "I'll help," says Walter.

"Good. That *weel* be enough. There you have *it*. Two teams, Arthur's and yours Tuan." Rowland pulls from within his coat a wafer and gives it to the Eastern Gray juvenile. As he does, he peers into the animal's eyes as though it can understand his thoughts. The small mammal trustingly eats away, unaware of the destiny that waits.

On the following day, a cloudless sky brightens the scene bellow, allowing its brilliance to bathe every object it touches. Cased within its glare, pedestrians scour in their routines. Bare legs and sleeveless attire compliment the mood of the season as well as announcing the arrival of the Annual Trinity Fest. The occasion draws thousands.

Arthur, Gracella, and Walter are among the many participants as they gather inside a fast food deli. While sitting, Arthur's inspirational spark becomes the focus of their collective minds. Shortly, Walter approaches the table.

"Here guys; Arthur, here's chicken for you…turkey and ham for you Gracella - all on my tab."

"Thank you Walter, this is a wonderful surprise. You're not planning on departing from us - are you?"

"No…thank you very much – that I know of. I'm just very happy to try something new and revolutionized."

"I'm impressed that you would volunteer," states Arthur.

"Every now and then it's good to spread the wealth – Right? Besides, I think I actually like both of you and there's something new everyday. But if nothing else, I can always gain friendship through the stomach."

"Amen to that."

Gracella gingerly observes Walter and smiles. "How's your family?"

"You mean… how's Darlene?"

"You're quick."

"And still sharp, but the relationship…how we say…it is circling the drain."

"Oh, I'm sorry."

"Hell… I'm not. She just doesn't see me as I see her. Most of the time, she acts as if I owe her something, but the big split is imminent –

partiality will come – the sooner, the better. At this rate, I may have to be a solitary man."

"There are others you know."

"Like who?"

"Lllllliiiike…Jade?"

"What about Jade?"

"You know what I mean silly."

"I normally don't do co-workers Gracella. Besides, Jade is hard, like a rock, a closed door to the gift horse's mouth. Pandora's Box for all I know. It's like she's hiding something. Funniest thing though, we sat together a few days ago and had the best conversation. What blew me away is the fact that she accepted my invitation to take her out. That's when I thought I was going to die."

"Trust me. You'll want to take your time with her…if you're interested."

"Maybe… She is cute…and we did have a descent time. You guys on the other hand have what I want. You're married, good spouses; you both seem to have it all together. Was it love at first sight?"

"Hardly," responds Gracella while Arthur remains silent.

"I do realize that it's a daily commitment of decision making. And when a decision is finally made, you simply stick to it – if you can."

"For the gray areas Walter, you may need to lean on the only One who can truly help you, if you know what I mean."

"Are you really into that?"

"Walter, there are some things in this life that only God can help you with."

"Maybe… But someday I will know of what you speak of, but for now…I'm not ready to deal with that."

"I see…"

"As far as our teams, Tuan and the others are alright, but I can't quite connect with them. You know what I mean?"

"Of course we do Walter."

Arthur pulls from his pocket a note pad and begins to draw. Gracella and Walter give close attention to the pencil etching as the technician lays out his contour scheme. Flustering with enthusiasm, Arthur glistens before his fellow co-workers.

While drawing, he expounds. "He will have legs far, far more powerful than that of Gearhardt. They will propel him much faster than Mishka. He will be much more cunning than the fox and remarkably agile than the cheetahs. Scales will provide an excellent outer armor, small enough to allow tremendous flexibility, yet tough enough to withstand most issued weaponry. No hair will cover his body. Dexterous fingers will give him the ability to handle any test the military comes up with. And when the night comes, he shall be mobile as any of us by day. His eyes will pierce the very depths of a man's soul, leaving his victims motionless upon first contact; just enough time for him to leave his mark. Our little Joey will grant us something never before seen by human eyes." Arthur never looks up, but his words sink deep into the ears of Walter and Gracella. They stare at him as his forearm partially covers the drawing.

Arthur's gaping smile parades his rendition, but before Walter can get close enough to see the image, Arthur shoves the paper directly in front of him.

"Whoa," replies Walter.

"That's my finalized concept of the genetic kangaroo-hybrid."

"This guy is slightly altered from your rendition on the poster. Look at those legs. Why did you not show this at the meeting?"

"I didn't want the others to see it until I knew Rowland would give me the go-ahead to pursue the idea. I also wanted to know who would help me."

"This is remarkable Arthur…my god."

"I've taken care of all the transitional time periods. I've even laid out exactly when the accelerants are to take place and even took the liberty of laying out the engrafting commencements. It's all pretty straight forward; I just need someone to make sure my steps are as I wrote them. Make sure that every 't' is crossed and that every 'i' is dotted."

"You can make this a reality?"

"How can I fail?"

"Arthur, just think. If you were in ancient times, they would view you as a god."

"Flattering, but there is only one God-man that I know and I can't hold a candle to Him, but at least I can make something from His scraps."

"Carefully said," responds Walter as he and Gracella stare at the conceptual embodiment of a creature that is more surreal than imaginative.

0900 hours signify a new morning. Three attentive souls orchestrate to the snapping sound of sterile gloves and clinking containers. Arthur, Gracella, and Walter embark upon their sympathetic task as a gray kangaroo lies before them. Gracella gently rubs the animal's hair, sensing every contour of muscle beneath its scruffy hide. But her maternal actions cease as Arthur approaches.

"She's ready. Look at her, quiet as a mouse."

"Here's the somatic cell you requested earlier. It contains the engrafted-human DNA."

"Everything looks good Arthur."

"I love it when a plan comes together. Now let's get our girl pregnant."

Arthur inserts the mammal with the somatic cell and places the slumbering creature into an incubation chamber. He adjusts the heat settings and makes sure that the kangaroo is resting. "You normally take twenty days to drop your little miracle, but I'll only need four," he says as he glows with paternal care.

As time passes, Tuan relentlessly pursues his conventional method and produces another genetic hybrid. Another cheetah becomes the test subject as he successfully impregnates the surrogate host. The entire insemination process concludes well into the evening.

Meanwhile, the day-to-day routine for Arthur's team of caring for the kangaroo progresses with the highest of expectations. Then, on one sunny afternoon, "Arthur...quick – It's time!" shouts Walter as both, he and Arthur rush into the lab.

They find Gracella performing duties of a midwife as the kangaroo gives birth to a tiny hairless blueprint of herself. All three stare with wide-eyed wonder. Without intervening, the joey crawls from its mother's birth canal to the inside of her pouch. Gracella leans against the transparent cage, breathing softly and watching with undivided attention. "Congratulations girl, you are now a *momma*."

"Cigars any one, drinks all a round…I love a celebration," says Walter, mimicking antics that resemble a Vaudeville entertainer.

Arthur leans forward. "So be it. It's best to let the joey remain with its mother until its eyes begin to open. She will undoubtedly do a better job than any of us in these first few days."

"It's called a mother's instinct," proudly replies Gracella.

"Real cute…and on that note, you guys better get home and get some rest. When the others get here, I don't need them disturbing her."

Walter approaches Arthur with an open notebook in hand. "Arthur, if your timing with the developing little joey is correct, alteration of the legs and forearms should conclude by these dates."

"It checks out."

"Then all is well for the little rat."

"That's the plan and it *ain't* no rat."

"Well, do you have a name for it?"

"I have no current name for it, but you do have a point."

"Such as?"

"Timing... The protein enhancements to the tail, legs, and forearms will come later; however, blood type, and immunity enhancements should take effect immediately."

"Rock on. This critter's *gonna* kick some ass!"

"Walter, I'm not in competition with Tuan."

"Sure you are. As I recall, he didn't like your proposal. Not to mention that only one hybrid can prevail."

"I'm not worried about that. This is all for the love of the project."

"Sounds to me like your heart is into it."

"I can't help that, Walter."

"Well…try not to take an emotional spiral to crash and burn."

"I know; Gracella preached that sermon already."

"But at least Tuan's efforts will assist in the tiny one's growth."

"Hah…tiny."

"What's so funny?"

"Stay in your manual science boy."

"I do and I'm not slow. If your growth computations are correct *Meester Rrrr-obinson*, you are going to have one big hybrid on your hands."

"He may actually be too big."

"Oh well…things happen. Arthur, despite Tuan's differences with you, if you can actually get that joey to look like that drawing, then man…you are on to something."

"That's the goal Walter."

Arthur slowly leans against a nearby lab table. He locates the same drawing he sketched at the sandwich shop. Silently staring, he manifests a haunting connection. In the eve of the day, all three exit the lab. Only a small lamp dimly shines upon the sleeping kangaroo, an unusual subject for what could become the answer for the next hybrid soldier of the U.S. military.

As time passes, the entire lab displays enthusiasm for the young kangaroo, yet still, both teams are under stress and with conflicting interests. Arthur officially makes his announcement of the offspring as he proudly displays his inner feelings to his laboratory peers. Even Tuan briefly shares in the jubilation, but soon turns his attention towards the nurturing of his cheetahs.

The kangaroo eventually opens its eyes, and Arthur is there to assure that the animal imprints upon him. *"ENAN log; 1547 evening. Our little joey takes the shape and form of its surrogate mother's appearance. Its eyes are sensitive to the slightest of movements as its ears respond to the most...minute of sounds. Whiskers grow as wide as the hybrid and he possesses an appetite second to none. No longer awkward, little joey moves with bursts of energy as it hops inside the cage. Intriguingly, the hybrid shows signs of personal recognition towards Gracella, Walter, and especially me. All is going well."*

Without fail, Arthur continuously imbeds his presence upon the animal. In a tranquil moment, he reaches into the cage and gently lifts the small kangaroo. His paternal action takes place with the mother's full compliance. Little goes unnoticed as the joey stares into the eyes of its human progenitor. "It's time little fella."Arthur carries the joey from its mother. As he exits the room, the surrogate mother moves towards the side of the clear panel and observes their departure. In a mysterious manner, she presses one paw against the panel as if telling her offspring - farewell.

Days later, Arthur enters laboratory room 2 and immediately begins logging his entry into the computer. Suddenly, a dull sound captures his attention. Curiously responding, Arthur approaches the holding area and sees the hybrid quietly standing. The technician takes a mental note of what he sees. *"The accelerants are taking effect. My god...you're bigger than your mother."*

The hybrid tilts its head and stares deeply into Arthur's eyes. Excited, Arthur approaches. Removing a pin-light from his pocket, Arthur scans the hybrid's eye. "Show me what I'm looking for *fella*." The light pierces the lens of the eye, dispelling the deep blackness within. Arthur searches and searches...until finally, "It's there," he whispers.

With excitement, he immediately annotates his findings.

"ENAN Log time 1837: Within the subject's eye, I find the fluorescent red dye permeating and mixing with the vitreous humor of the eye. The cognitive enzymes are there."

While caressing the sides of the kangaroo's head, Arthur looks at the youthful fledgling face-to-face. With child-like enthusiasm, he asks, "Can you understand me?" The joey tilts its head as though making a special effort to comprehend Arthur's words, yet a speechless blink is the only rebuttal. "Oh well, you are still special." The animal tilts its head again, and again. Then without a moments notice, the hybrid finds interest elsewhere. Arthur closes his eyes, smiles, and then sprawls face-up on the floor.

At that moment, the entry door opens. Gracella and Walter enter the room. "Feeling comfy?" Gracella's question brazes Arthur's ears, yet he does not answer. She places her hand on his shoulder, gently shaking him. The mellow technician slowly responds. "He's ready Grace."

"Ready for what?"

"I found traces of the dye."

"There's detection of human coherency in the rat's eye?" Walter's abrupt question makes him the recipient of a swat from Gracella. "Ouch!"

"She's not a rat Science Boy."

"Oh, so when did Joey become Jill Arthur?"

"I know…the military wants females. I'm just not sure how to sell them…him – at least not yet."

"Let me help you off the floor. You're beginning to give me a poor workman's complex."

"At this point Walter, I think that the military wants results. In any case, the dyed opticin came through."

"Op…opticin. Can you explain that to me?"

"It is a small leu-cine-rich proteo-gly-can that is abundant in several ocular tissues, including the vitreous of an animal's eye – as well as a human's. Nathaniel and Rowland devised this method for identifying and marking human chromosomes that are responsible for the development of the eye. Their procedure grants us the ability to dye, or tag the eye during the stages of early development. The dye saturates the genetic code of the human subject and remains present through the entire development of the subject's eye, even when transferring into a somatic cell. Presence of human *cognitive-ness* is undetectable in early hybrid development, but as time passes, the red dyed opticin makes its presence known in the eyes of the hybrid. That is how we can tell when the human genes reach a level of maturation, or in layman's terms; when our creations are at a point to think like humans. Without that, it becomes a guessing game."

"Oh, that's what Tuan meant when he said 'watch their eyes.' Tricky procedure though I never understood how he did that."

"It's not too hard to understand, once you know what genes to identify."

"Easy for you to say..."

"Trust me."

"I do, and if joey is at the stage that you say he is, then his reading lessons will begin in a matter of days."

"I know..."

Several more notes are taken after which each member claim their possessions and prepare and exit the room.

During their departure, Walter is expressive as ever and leans upon Arthur's shoulder. "Umm, by the way. How did you come to the conclusion that this is a male? I don't see any *fixtures* hanging."

"There were more than two shakes before he tucked it away."

"Oh..." Bewildered, Walter simply stares at Arthur.

Misty rain covers the grassy landscape on a cool Sunday morning. Arthur and Aniah find themselves performing their usual pattern of attending the weekly morning service. For many, such activities come as a trifle act of conviction, yet for this couple, it is part of an embarkation for personal growth.

Lying on the outskirts of the county, a once rugged center for equestrian sports now acts as a hub for those seeking Divine influence. Within the walls of the newer addition to the building, a twenty-two hundred-seated auditorium echoes the sound of adulation as the main speaker presides. Styled in denim jeans and a long sleeve pullover, he pours his unrehearsed dissertation into the ears of the congregation.

"Second Timothy 3 tells us that certain types of men are always learning, and yet, never able to come to the knowledge of the truth! In addition, you have to know that these are intrinsic truths given by our Heavenly Father for our generation as well. Man is smarter, but he doesn't have the wisdom to know right from wrong on his own outside of Godly precepts. Even now, many will attempt feats while disregarding whether they should or shouldn't, and in doing so, they will try to justify their actions purely on pre-conceived notions or inconclusive information."

Several agreeable responses ring forth from those in the audience, but Arthur remains silent, not allowing the activity around him to distract his disciplined focus. The speaker relentlessly delivers his message, and soon, everything around Arthur looses its familiarity. However, at the mentioning of certain words, Arthur becomes more intent on what is spoken. He reacts as if a tingling sensation rivets within his chest; or as if chills scurry throughout his body.

The speaker continues, "More often than not, the lure of success will sometimes over shadow our judgment and we will pursue things that could ultimately destroy us. That is why Psalms 23 tells us to trust in the Lord with *all* our heart. Further reading reveals that we should acknowledge Him because our understanding of what we can't see in the future is insufficient. Every believer should acknowledge God. But most don't, because of one thing… pride. Pride is the one true thing that keeps us from submitting to the Lord's guidance."

Arthur looks onward, absorbing all that he hears. Soon, the entire auditorium rises as the dismissal of service takes place.

Driving along a winding road, Arthur and Aniah converse their recent experience. Interchanging words go well, but communication between the two deteriorates into a solitary conversation. "The service was still inspiring," she says.

Arthur, slow to respond, looks amidst the golden fields of grass beneath the gray horizon. "Hey…did you hear me?" Puzzled, Arthur turns his head, "yes."

"I was calling your name and you seem…distant."

"Oh…I was looking at the farmland."

Aniah grows more unconvincing of Arthur's response and stares at him. Determined to pursue a response, she vigorously questions Arthur. "You've been quiet for most of the latter part of the service – Why?"

"I got my reasons – So what…"

"Oh…I get it. It's a guy thing."

"What...? Where did that come from?"

"Okay...fine."

"Okay...*fine*...what?"

"Sure..."

"Sure what? Why do you do that?"

"Do...*that*...what?"

"Nothing..."

Arthur throws his hands up for a brief moment, and quickly clutches the steering wheel again. "What do you *mean* nothing?"

"Nothing..."

"Look Aniah...I really don't need this from you."

"Whatever...but would you look at the road."

"What do you think I'm doing?"

"Look at the road – will you?"

"Oh...now I can't DRIVE all of sudden!"

"Will you look at the ROAD?"

"Sure, I can look at the road."

"WATCH the *frickin* road!"

Arthur turns his head and glances beyond the windshield. In a spurring moment, Aniah takes a deep breath, clutches the inner handrails and closes her eyes. Immediately, Arthur forcefully turns the steering wheel in one direction. A horrific thump resonates within the cab as screeching wheels succumb to the massive weight of the vehicle.

In a settling moment, standing defiantly on coarse pavement is a fully-grown Black Angus. The beast makes its presence known.

Aniah covers her face while Arthur sits quietly. Slowly turning towards her, he attempts to say what only a heart-felt apology could mend, but the words fail to come forth. Then, a solemn, shaken Aniah lowers her hands, revealing tear stained eyes while looking away. "You know…what ever is going on in that head of yours; I wish you would GET RID OF IT!"

"Aniah, you know that the project is something we've never done before and those actions may boarder on what was said in the message this morning."

"And speaking of…Arthur, do you really think God cares about that…*thing*…you brought to life?"

"Look, we've talked about this already."

"*It*…is not natural."

"Gjhe'nan is no different than any other project."

"It's an abomination Arthur, and just because you put human sense in it and give *it* a name, that doesn't make it human."

"I never said it was human!"

"It is an insult to God's natural order. Do you people ever consider the moral and ethical issues about the things you're doing? Do you even think God cares about what you're doing?"

"Why in the h… no, I don't think about how God feels, because I personally think that if it puts a roof over our heads, food on the table, clothes on our backs, and it doesn't break the law, then maybe it's not so bad. It's not like we're dealing drugs or sending people to gas chambers just because…"

"You really don't get it. Do you?"

"Then explain it!"

"It's not only…the fact that you created this thing. It's also the fact that I know you too well, and I also know that those procedures will not stop with that thing!"

"What the *hell* are you saying?"

"Every time your heart gets into something, it leads into something else – a lot worse. It never fails."

"Stop ridding me. It's not like my pride is getting in the way."

"It's ALWAYS PRIDE!"

"I am on the threshold of something remarkable Aniah. But you're too shallow to see it."

"Arthur…you are not God. You're just trying to play God. All of you for that matter!"

Arthur remains silent as the sound of voices manifest in the background. Few men approach the vehicle while several others attempt to coax the animal into a trailer. The beast heeds their beckoning call as its un-rhythmic stride testifies to the earlier contact of flesh with metal.

~~~ Enduring~~~

Day by day, the hybrid kangaroo grows stronger and more trusting of Arthur. Like children, both frolic upon the laboratory floor, often engaging in a game of chase or hide and seek. Occasionally, Arthur smuggles the adolescent creature home, to Aniah's protest, and treats it as though it were part of the family. Late one evening, the hybrid drifts to sleep while nestling upon Arthur's lap.

Sensing the hybrid's slumber, Arthur writes the military's definition of ENAN upon a sheet of paper. "Enhanced Nocturnal Assault Nomad; they call you. In fact, you are a genetic joey-hybrid, enhanced as a nocturnal assault nymph. Put one word before the other, and you get...Gjhe'nan."

Arthur stares at the inscription, pondering tensely with out a single blink. He rubs the hybrid's head as the lengthy beast lay half way sprawled on his lap as well as the floor. Large paws and a long tail more than encompass the mediocre hybrid. Arthur glistens. "Gjhe'nan...that is your name." The hybrid's eyes open and then quickly close again. Arthur smiles and all seems well, but the frivolous days of secretive transports come to an end as the hybrid increases in size and strength.

Ominous clouds blanket the city. Heaven's gates open wide as crystalline drops relentlessly shower the earth, transforming a once arid metropolis into a cool watery Eden. Rushing rivers, small and great, end their journeys within lakes, ponds, and inlets; swelling everything until overflow becomes imminent. Flash flood warnings cast endlessly upon all bands of communication. Such warnings draw the attention of three very enthusiastic workers of GenoSyss.

Within laboratory 2, Arthur, Gracella, and Walter prepare to capture on video a miraculous phenomenon. Walter stands near a radio. "I hope *this* storm doesn't affect our efforts."

"We should be okay. The generators have proven dependable so far," responds Arthur.

"You remember what happened the last time it rained 40 days and nights."

"Yeah, but that's not this kind of party."

"When did you notice the changes on Joey?"

"About four days ago."

"Are we still recording?"

"Yep – "

Walter kneels beside the beast and pours through the mound of magazines and other elementary literature. "Looks like he's been busy, covering every topic from pre - K to the dictionary, not to mention his understanding of the alphabet. In two weeks, he should be able to read the first pages of the training assignments. He is a fast learner; sixty percent of the letters in less than a day; the best record yet for our hybrids."

"Less than a day? That's incredible! Did you hear that Grace?"

"Yes, I heard…but look at the size of him; almost a seventy-five percent growth factor. I had to sedate him a couple of times during last week until his normal body functions could catch up with his evolving, otherwise that metabolism of his would have burned him up."

"That explains his appetite. It also explains why he sleeps so much. Take a look at his torso. His appearance suggests that there's more human in him than I originally thought," Arthur notates.

Arthur opens his sketchbook and captures the pictorial scene in front of him. His trained eye follows every contour of the hybrid from head to tail. Walter acquires a lamp. "Will this help?"

"Thanks. Hey, look at his hands. They look like yours."

"There is a resemblance, but in a more mutated way. Do you think he's cold?"

"No. That warm-blooded metabolism compensates for that."

Gracella rubs the slumbering beast. "Arthur, I think he's changing again. Each time I move my hand across his side, more fur comes off. There's enough on the floor to stuff eight large trash bags."

"Just toss it in the pile over there."

"See…look at his forearm, more of the new skin. This is any thing but the outer epidermis of kangaroo's flesh."

"Tough stuff, isn't it?"

"Arthur, Is this normal? It feels like serrated cowhide."

"The shedding is, but the skin is an engrafting of reptile DNA. By tagging modified gator DNA into his skin's gene chemistry, it produces a tougher outer layer. Right now, you're feeling the beginning of what will later become millions of tiny scales. Each scale will become denser and tougher as he matures. Larger scales will develop and line his back while the smaller ones will line his under side. You should also see the spikes on his back."

"What is that sharp thing at the tip of his tail?"

"I engineered that to become a weapon. You'll see once his transformation is complete."

"Weapons and spikes…cool," says Walter, smiling while shaking his head.

Gracella responds with a hefty laugh. "Well… that may be a guy thing, but from a woman's view, don't you think he has some rather large hips and thighs?"

"Most women do," responds Walter.

"Real cute, but I was talking to Arthur."

"Yes he does…and for good reason. Remember the leg proportions of the regular size kangaroo and how fast they move?"

"I don't see the relevance. His legs look nothing like his smaller counterparts. I though the relationship was in the design of the leg and how the tendons fit."

"True, but if we are going to enlarge the animal and maintain a high rate of speed, then, his leg power will have to be stronger, in order to overcome gravity. We're way outside the box – don't forget."

"Yeah…but this is like, monster truck legs on a Volkswagen torso," responds Walter.

Walter gently lifts the hybrid's arm, revealing three fingers while extending the animal's left forearm. "Whoa…don't wake him," cautions Arthur. Suddenly, the hybrid opens its eyes, raises its head and glances at Walter. Walter returns the stare, intently, focusing on the event, quietly watching as if something of extraordinary proportions will manifest. A calm silence fills the air. Then suddenly, the hybrid utters a solemn shriek and quietly lays its head down, closing both eyes and resuming its prior state of rest.

Walter asks, "What was that about Arthur?"

"That could mean…that you're not important."

"Oh…"

"Do the others know how far he's transforming?"

"No. They're maintaining the conventional ways with Tuan's cheetahs, but Rowland knows what I am up too."

After answering Walter's question, Arthur resumes his sketching; intently roughing his charcoal rendition while cameras silently capture the hybrid's bizarre metamorphosis in time-lapse sequence.

In laboratory room 1, excitement fills the air. Tuan commemorates the success of his newest addition. His expressions boast high as he curtails his experiment upon a leash. He stands before the others. "Guys, I would like to formally introduce Si'ehda. She scored 75 percent on the comprehension tests and…; get this, an astounding 91 percent on course completions." Applause rings forth and Tuan graciously takes a bow.

But the cheetah has other interests and attempts to pull away. "She appears nervous," says Alexis.

"She's hungry, so I devised a little something for her in the event that this should happen. Alexis, would you give me that sheet of paper?"

"Sure."

"What time is it?"

"Ten minutes to four."

Tuan scribbles words on the sheet of paper. He holds the sheet directly in front of the cat. The animal looks upon the writings, staring while halting all forms of movement. Piercing feline eyes gaze into the depths of what reflects back to her from the paper. Tuan, recognizing such behavior motions Alexis to unlatch the leash. He places the paper on the floor and directly in front of the animal. As he does, Si'ehda's fixation never leaves the white paper. Tuan rises to his feet and steps away from the animal.

Anticipation fills the air. Then suddenly, Si'ehda explodes with a powerful burst of speed, quickly darting across the room. In an attempt to turn a sharp corner, her body incredibly twists and curves while in motion. Using her tail as a counter balance, Si'ehda remarkably makes the turn without loosing stride.

Three small boxes lie side by side in the center of the floor. The cat quickly comes upon the boxes and voraciously tears into the center box. Her actions aggressively uncover two mice. Once exposed, the rodents escape in different directions. Without hesitation, the hunter feline darts to the left, hurling her sleek body into the air as if cued for an aerial assault. Winding with style and grace, Si'ehda inevitably pounces upon one of the tiny defenseless mammals. With one swift bite, the rodent succumbs to the crushing power of Si'ehda's fury.

Witnessing the act, Alexis and Jade cover their faces, but Frank graces the moment with a candid smile.

The cat quickly scoops the limp rodent in her mouth and intently locks on to the trail of the other mouse. However, with much difficulty, Si'ehda attempts to locate the mouse. She lays the mouse in her mouth aside and begins searching for a scent trail. Scurrying through boxes and other objects, Si'ehda comes upon a canister. Displaying a readiness to ambush, she silently approaches while fixating upon an established target.

Both, Tuan and Frank follow. "Her senses are speaking to her; she can feel the heart of the prey beating. She will make a good kill."

"Well...at least for now, let the record show that this is purely scientific Frank," responds Tuan.

Si'ehda slowly approaches the canister, but before she can get within inches of the shiny container, the tiny mouse rushes into the open, desperately trying to find sanctuary. Soon, the cat locks onto the small target and with one powerful leap, pounces on the small mammal. Strangely, Si'ehda does not kill the mouse. Instead, she takes the mouse in her mouth and acquires the other rodent as well. Afterwards, she presents both mice to Tuan. The lead geneticist radiates with pride, yet unaware of the blood trail marking the floor. "See! I told you it would work. Si'ehda did exactly as I wrote on paper."

As Tuan boast of the accomplishment, the sound of footsteps echoes behind him. "Good for you *Mee-ster* Vein!"

"Professor…"

"I just got off phone *veeth* the colonel. He's adamant about…two week…extended period – given us. I take *eet* that your *demon-strr-ation* is a sign that Si'ehda is *rr-eady* for departure – Yes?"

"Yes…she is."

"*Guuuuud*. Then you *weel* have her ready by morning." After conveying his instructions, Rowland exits the room.

Frank observes the ordeal and approaches Tuan. He asks, "Could he have been any more direct?"

"It's the military Frank. It appears that they want us to create in order to destroy. This time, they're cutting back the length of time we have, which seriously hinders our tests. A two week extension is hardly enough time to know the animal's true readiness."

"You knew this would come."

"Apparently…"

Tuan reattaches the leash to Si'ehda and leads the animal to a holding bin. Before he could open the door, Alexis calls out to him. "Hey, did you feed her yet? You know that Rowland wants no distractions."

"No…not yet."

Surprisingly, both focus their attention upon the cat once more and observe the animal deeply swallowing. "What is she doing?" Alexis asks.

Tuan takes a closer look at Si'ehda's mouth. "Oh…I almost forgot. She should not be too hungry any more." "Why?" "Because at the end of the instructions, I told her, that after four, the mice are yours." Alexis, startled, curiously observes the clock. "It's three minutes passed four. Oh my God, you…you both are disgusting." Laughter fills the air as Alexis hysterically departs.

Red Sands becomes the testing field once more as orders echoe throughout the colossus underground complex. Lights illuminate the earthen floor as structures poise high into proper places. Gun turrets open, displaying powerful long-range cannons before retracting from view. Activity upon the field is nothing less of a small army preparing for the task ahead.

Inside the observation deck, Colonel Ducet, along with Rowland and his team, stands over the monitoring board. The officer gives orders to his subordinates while making sure that everything possible is in place. "Rowland, allow me to show you something. It's been the better part of eight months since you were last here. See this beauty? This is one of our newest additions. It is the eye to the entire cavernous system. From here, we see…everything."

"*Eemm-prres-seev.*"

"You bet. And a personal favorite of mine is the ability to speak and hear without technology hanging off my uniform. Now brace yourself. We're about to commence testing."

"By all means Colonel…"

Ducet faces the colossus window. He stands firm, overlooking the field before him. Suddenly, he gives one swift execution of verbal authority, "Fire!" Far from the observation deck, two large metal doors sway outward as the emergence of a large-caliper cannon comes into view.

"Fire in the hole!" The alarming siren rings forth as many take cover below. The cannon thunders aloud, spewing surges of smoke and fire from the nozzle, hurling two projectiles directly into the viewing shield of the observation deck. Many within the room flinch as each projectile explodes upon impact, bathing the room in a shimmering flash of light while disintegrating into dust.

"The shield holds sir…once more…again…and again," informs one of the operators. But Colonel Ducet continues gazing through the window. "Fascinating professor – don't you think?"

"I see that you amused yourself *weeth* this before – Yes?"

"Not asingle sound; although outside, it's a hellish deafening reality."

"Truly remarkable Colonel," replies Rowland.

"Good, because we're better prepared now."

"*Prre*-pared for what?"

"For the unexpected."

"Of course, but are you so sure you have control of 429?"

"Control is what we do Professor. And with the test subjects you provide, you will help us maintain that control."

"But 429 is not like gun or *prr*-ojectiles."

"Whether under ground or on the battlefield, when there's a crisis, we neutralize harmful threats through the use of brute force if necessary. As you realize by now, some test subjects die so that others may live."

"The fate of Gerhardt - yes?"

"Unfortunately..."

"And what of the fox and other test subjects?"

"They died, but because they were too conventional."

"*Deed*...any survive?"

"Only the horse."

"Meeshka?"

"The horse became confused with the instructions given, and couldn't determine the best recourse. Its limitations to move effectively across various terrains got it seriously injured."

"But she lives – yes?"

"She lives. Rowland you have to know that we are doing everything possible to keep these animals from unnecessary harm, but you must also understand that these are deadly scenarios to weed out the subjects that just can't cut it."

"Sounds like Third Reich's approach to humans."

"Don't insult me – we're not the got-damn Germans of the First World War."

"Now you listen, Full Bird! I have been doing genetic research...many years. My own counsel *veel* I listen too *eef* none else. My own judgment I *weel* consult. *Eeef* you want to destroy these animals *with* out proper accommodations, then you should let us handle training tactics."

"Not possible..."

"Hell *weeth* you…for all our labor when death comes foolishly."

"For god's sake man, the battle field is no wedding chapel and we're not the local Boy Scouts."

"Hear my *wuuuurds* Colonel."

Words echo throughout the room as curious eyes fasten upon both men. The colonel stands quietly, momentarily, and then in a low methodical voice, "We're not cold-blooded murderers. We can now manipulate existing elements within a species and diminish the risk factor for human involvement. That is our goal. Now tell me Rowland, how many animals died so you could take medication for your ailments?"

"Irrelevant Colonel..."

"You surprise me. You sound as if you are becoming…soft – attached."

"Don't confuse issue Colonel."

"And don't you dare get sanctimonious with me."

Ducet takes one step closer to Rowland, positioning his face closely to that of the professor's. "Where the hell were you when I watched a child's guts spill on the ground just because he was too close to friendly fire?"

"I'm no soldier – not my problem."

"Fine, but remember Kreshenkov – we have a deal."

Rowland silently stares into the eyes of the battle hardened commander and for a brief moment, contemplates his rebuttal. However, with nothing to add, Rowland departs, but before the professor could get too far, Colonel Ducet tells him in a slow, lethargic voice, "God did give man dominion over the Earth."

Rowland eyes the colonel, replying, "Perhaps. But I wonder *eef* man's dominion *eez* in best interest of God's sovereignty?" After his statement, Rowland returns to his team.

Meanwhile, Si'ehda is in position and ready to begin her scheduled test. Military technicians allow the animal to scan the given instructions. Unlike Gearhardt, Si'ehda has two monitors attached to her head with secured wires trailing into a small black box. The box lays shielded underneath her abdomen.

On the observation deck, several monitors within the control room register the cat's vital signs. Everyone watch with anticipation, hoping that the hybrid feline can bring their program one step closer to the military's quest for the ideal soldier. One of the panel operators signals Colonel Ducet. "Sir, schematic displays that the emitter registers with the bio scanner. Encephalogram activity registers…all information is uploading to the mainframe. We're green."

"Good. No bullets should come within fifteen feet of the cat," responds Ducet.

"G for 15 seconds and counting…" The cheetah perches her sleek spotted body as the monitor displays an increase in heart rate. "G for 5, 4, 3, 2, commence test 429-002-beta…go!" Suddenly, a siren rings forth and the cheetah ignites with a burst of speed. "Wow… Look at her go!"

On the sidewall of the room, a long-range camera captures the elegance and grace of the majestic feline as she blazes a path upon the earthen floor. So magnificent is her speed to range ratio that one of the tending personnel signals the colonel. "Sir, match 30 and rising!"

Tuan stands proudly and pats Nathaniel on the back. Colonel Ducet watches with high intensity, then he sends the command, "Commence artillery shower!"

"Commencing artillery shower in 4, 3, 2, 1…" The panel operator pushes a blue button and immediately, several steel panels open outwardly, allowing the emergence of long-range riffles to appear.

Without a moments notice, glowing hot lead begins to rain upon the path of the cheetah. The startled animal darts off course, momentarily, but quickly resumes her target with even more determination. "Sir, match 45," sounds the technician.

Dust rises with each touch of the animal's feet upon the ground. Si'ehda locks on to a small white structure. "Sir, match 59," sounds the technician. The colonel looks at his watch and leans near one of the personnel. "One hundred and fifty yards in eight seconds...how's that for a running back?"

Loud explosions thunder behind the darting animal as she pursues her directive.

"Sir...match 72, she's gone three-hundred yards!"

Si'ehda barrels her way into a small structure. She rests momentarily. Then, the feline pulls a device from a pouch fastened upon her back. Afterwards, she methodically makes her way to three large barrels that are different in color. The barrel to the left is red, the barrel to the right is green, and the barrel in the middle is white. Each barrel has a faucet. The cat lays the device down in front of the red barrel. Clamping down upon the faucet, Si'ehda turns the handle. Fuel pours onto the floor. Afterwards, she forcefully presses a sequencer, which displays ten seconds in red illuminated numbers.

While observing, mortar spews into the room as ammo rounds pierce the structure. With threatening circumstances, Si'ehda exits the structure and enters the midst of the raining inferno.

"Sir, she's match 30." "Looks good," resounds the colonel.

Si'ehda hastens towards the safety zone, but suddenly, her gallant pace drastically slows to a meandering gait.

"Sir, ten seconds pass, but our subject shows no sign of clearing the blast zone."

"Dammit! Now what's happening?" "Sir, match speed 15...10...3." The cat slowly walks to the side of a mound and completely stops.

"Talk to me." Bewilderment overtakes the technician as he shakes his head, signifying that he has no words to offer. The colonel grabs him and shakes him.

"Answer me!" The technician does not reply.

Immediately, Tuan approaches the colonel. "Colonel, here's Si'ehda's bio signs; she's burning up. Her heart rate is way too fast!"

"Then cool her off."

"She's not a machine that you just turn on and off. This test is over."

Ducet wildly stares at Tuan. All goes quiet.

Suddenly, an explosion pummels the ground, sending tremors throughout the subterranean chamber. Ghastly clouds of dust paint the dimly lit room as pyrotechnic splendor spews its magnificent brilliance throughout the earthen cavern. The event captivates its spectators as it wields an impetuous masquerade to become the very thing it was meant to be.

Gun turrets retract as all explosive activity concludes with the settling dust. "Clear," screeches into the smoky abyss as military and civilian personnel search the floor.

Inside the observation room, all remain silent, except for Ducet. "Would someone find my cat?"

Time passes, but then, in the midst of the chaos, "We got heart beat sir."

"Search teams move into position," commands the colonel. Teams quickly track the signal, smartly concluding that the origin of the signal is under a mound of dirt. They desperately unearth a small concrete cove, which houses an even smaller area of space. Surprisingly, there inside, they find Si'ehda, unharmed.

"Sir, she's fine!"

As the information reaches the observation room, cheers of adulation wildly expound. Tuan and the team join in the celebration. However, Rowland views the situation, and makes a hasty departure.

Colonel Ducet approaches Tuan. "You mind telling me just what the hell all that was about?"

"She can only maintain high rates of speed for a few seconds colonel, even with the enhancements. After the initial burst, she has to shorten her range; otherwise, she'll burn up or even suffer brain damage. I surmise that she exhausted her strength and sought out shelter to avoid the explosion – a very human thing to do."

"So…what you're telling me is that this cat is only good for a one-way trip?"

"If your target is five hundred yards away and you want her to get there going eighty miles per hour, or…"

"Or what?"

"Or…you initially intend for her to go on a one-way suicide run."

Hearing Tuan's remarks, Colonel Ducet conspicuously eyes him, getting closer to Tuan. "You have something to say Mr.?" Tuan pauses, staring back at the colonel. Squaring his shoulders, he steps towards Ducet. "Since you couldn't wait for proper testing in our facility, we had to rush the developmental process. We had no time to factor how large the heart should be for long distances or compensate for the rate of O2 exchange. Now with that in mind, you're going to have to learn about her limitations during your tests."

"That cat's limitations come as the direct result of your engineering Mr. Vein."

"Her direct results are the product of your lack of patience Colonel."

Ducet stands void of expression, but strongly appalled. He raises his chin and stands straight, clutching both hands behind his back. Then, in a soft manner, he tells Tuan. "We gave that animal a sheet of instructions, telling her to detonate the red barrel. To your credit, it read the instructions and carried out its mission. I'll give you that much. But I need more."

"What…out of all this? What are you really asking us to do?"

"I'm telling you to give me something that's a hell of a lot more than animal, but not much less than human."

Having made his statement, Ducet abruptly departs Tuan's presence. Tuan simply watches while shaking his head in disbelief.

The full-bird commander walks briskly atop white raised-panels with his head hung low. His muffled footsteps allow him to silently pass other personnel who barely notice his presence as well as his tightly clinched fists. Undistracted, Colonel Ducet makes his way into the cargo elevator. He presses a button marked 'field level' and descends. Upon arrival, the doors slide open and the colonel steps forward. Walking into a secluded area, he activates a small device. Within seconds, another voice resonates upon the instrument panel.

"Yes?"

"It's me…"

"I take it that your prro-duct was satees-factory – Yes?"

"Not by a long shot, and you know it. I thought we clearly had an understanding of what I'm looking for."

"Conventional methods dictate at thees point."

"Look, either deliver, or we go elsewhere and you personally can kiss your precious efforts good-bye…if you know what I mean."

"Perhaps, but be not hasty – less you forget your own dilemma as vell colonel. If I fail, then so do you."

"Just have something soon; I've endured enough."

"Then I ask you too endure a little longer – for both our sakes. I vweeel keep in touch and so weel you."

Colonel Ducet closes the device and immediately draws the attention of soldier.

"You there!"

"Yes Sir."

"I want the field prepped and ready for conventional maneuvers."

"Sir, do we have further tests of ENANS today?"

"As far as I'm concerned, it may be time to reconsider. Just get it done."

~~~ Gjhe'nan~~~

Cargo lights rotate as large bay doors retract deep inside underground walls. Afterwards, the roaring sound of an engine engulfs nearby attendants as blow-by carbons funnel through chrome-platted exhaust stacks. Eighteen wheels slowly roll in reverse, allowing a long enclosed trailer to barely clear the entry. A worker supervises the operation while standing near Colonel Ducet.

"Sir, your name is on the manifest, so is your signature for top-secret delivery. This delivery…is…marked for your eyes-only, but you seem surprise."

"I do not recall making a scheduled delivery; specially one that requires a fifty-two foot trailer."

"Maybe some gal caught your eye at the officer's club last night – huh?"

"If she did, I'm not familiar with her whatsoever – On with your job man."

"Okay…okay…*sheeeeesh* – just kidding."

Soon, an impressively designed purple rig brings the high trailer to a halt. Out climbs the driver and he approaches both men.

"I have a delivery for Colonel Mortimer Ducet. Where is he?"

"That would be me," replies the colonel.

"Please remain still."

The driver removes a hand held device from his belt and moves it from bottom to top of the officer as pulsating lights change from red to green. "Scanning optics complete. Your image matches the master files for this signature."

"*Hmph*, high security – fair enough. Where is this order coming from?"

"Texas. That's *bout* all I can tell you. But your boys sure gave me a tough time when trying to get through the front gate."

Suddenly, the trailer sways side-to-side. Curious spectators begin to assemble. The driver approaches the trailer, but Ducet, sensing something strange lays his hand on the driver's shoulder. "I know what you are thinking, but the answer is classified. I'll handle it from here."

"I'm sure you will," spurns a voice from amidst the group. Ducet turns, only to find a familiar countenance standing directly behind him.

"Rowland... You are early."

"Taking care of business – of course."

"Well good for you."

The colonel grabs the electronic clipboard from the driver and signs it, then sends the driver on his way. Rowland and Ducet walk towards the rear of the trailer. Upon approach, the geneticist pounds the door with two hard hits. Soon, the inner sound of latches loosening and chains falling quickly take place. Finally, a full-scale ramp lowers, gently touching the ground as curious eyes attempt to peek inside. Ducet peers inside, but immediately drops the clipboard. With eyebrows raised, his mouth partially opens. In sheer astonishment, he looks at Rowland. "What in heavens name is that?"

"I'm afraid that *eez* bit short of heaven colonel, but *eet iz* something you have never seen."

"Is it safe to go in there?"

"Of course, go in."

Ducet inches his way inside the sturdy container. His quivering hands cautiously touch a prevailing curtain. Exhaling with ease, he slowly pulls the draping cloth to one side.

Standing before him in the dark shadows is Arthur. "Welcome aboard Colonel."

"On your word Mr. Robinson..."

"I know this is awkward for you, but trust me – it is safe."

"Is *that*...the culmination of your work?"

"For the most part..."

Ducet steps forward, but ensures that Arthur stands between him and his uncanny prodigy. "What...is...that?"

"Arthur, would you *pleez* indulge the good colonel," interjects Rowland.

"Sure professor. What we have here Colonel is a genetically enhanced joey that is evolutionized as a nocturnal assault nymph." Ducet continues staring at the hybrid as though Arthur's definition never registers.
Then, with out hesitation, the creature looms forward, curiously eying the officer, gently moving with every motion the colonel makes while

leaving no subtleties without notice. The colonel peers deeply into the windows of the hybrid's eyes. "My god, they are so black…so deep and dark."

"Keep looking colonel."

"Whoa…there's a dark bluish glow in its eyes. Why is that?"

"We are not a hundred percent sure. It may be a reaction from the opticin tagging during his development."

"Sure…whatever; if you say so…"

Ducet scans the hybrid, realizing that before him lays a creature so bizarre that it can only exist in the depths of imagination; however, those who stand near the beast know that such notions are now a blatant reality.

The hybrid's eyes are large and lay almost strategically on the side of its head. Its ears are long and flange outward, monitoring every sound as thick blood vessels course throughout the elephant-like folds, pulsing with every heartbeat. A long, strong neck secures the hybrid's head to a human-like torso. Sleek muscular forearms bevel into hands, which posses five finger digits, such that are proportionate to the hybrid's over-all physique.

Colonel Ducet moves closer to the amalgamate beast. "Careful sir," cautions Gracella while the colonel gently rubs the mesh of shiny scales. He methodically makes his way from front to rear, missing nothing. Speechless, the colonel remains captive by the hybrid's spectacular appearance, yet putting himself in safe proximity of the animal's massive legs.

Arthur observes the colonel's behavior. "Colonel, the legs are the specialty item; a combination of human and kangaroo."

"I see... But it walks on its toes."

"Unlike the human foot, he has the advantage of an extended tibia, femur, and foot bones."

"Layman's terms – please."

"That description accounts for the 'z' shape of the leg."

"Umm…huh…."

"Like a rubber band, he'll be able to bounce or hop with virtually no effort at all – regardless of his size. As you can see, he poises in a squatting manner, awkward to us, but normal for him."

"Interesting, but the legs are almost twice the entire length of its body. Why so unusually large?"

"There are several reasons colonel, most importantly – speed and strength."

"Is it normal for it to sway like that?"

"He does that to compensate for balance."

"Yes – of course. Ha…ha…how…how big, tall… big is it?"

"We did not have much time to get exacts, but the floor scale suggests somewhere in the neighborhood of one thousand, two hundred and twenty-five point eight kilograms."

"And that calculates what…in English, please…"

"Roughly…twenty-seven hundred pounds sir, one point three five short U.S. tons."

"He's heavy."

"Yes. And as for his height, if he stays in this crouching position, our best estimation is somewhere close to eight feet; but fully extended on his toes, he could easily pass fourteen, sixteen feet at best."

While Arthur discloses the dimensions of the hybrid, a dull noise draws the Colonel's immediate attention. "What was that?" "That scrapping sound? Oh…that's a defense mechanism. I like to think of it as a tool used to motivate the enemy into retreat."

"A weapon…"

"Look at the tail."

"Tail…?"

Colonel Ducet intently scans the long muscular appendage as Arthur explains. "Closely near the animal's body, the tail is stiff, but becomes more flexible towards the end. I modified the end of the tail with extra dense bone and shark cartilage. As you can see, it's serrated on one side. The hybrid can use it in a thrashing motion while the tip is for thrusting."

"If this weapon is one of its defenses – What are the others?"

"Well…the legs, forearms, and anything else he can use to defend himself. Often times, kangaroos will run from their enemies rather than fight. However, Gjhe'nan can become formidable in a confrontation."

"What…wh…what did you say?"

"Kangaroos often run…"

"No. Not that. You called it a name."

"Gjhe'nan."

"G-*nan*…"

"It's a play on the character of words Colonel."

"G-*nan*…and…"

"The proper pronunciation is Je'-non. You called them ENAN, for evolutionized-nocturnal-assault-nomad. Well…our friend here receives the name Gjhe'nan because he is a genetic-joey-hybrid-evolutionized as a nocturnal-assault-nymph."

"Nymph?"

"Rather than nomad, which gives credence to a wonderer, the nymph is a water spirit. In ancient times, nymphs were spirits or fairies that guarded the waterways of the land – or something like that. They would strike fear into those who encountered them. In relation to nymphs, Gjhe'nan can remain for hours in water and judging from your response, he can easily frighten or confuse any one he encounters."

"I'll say…"

"Also Colonel, he is a male."

"Well… Given the current stance of our situation, I don't care, just as long as he can give me what I want…and as long as he can be controlled."

"Oh yes; control, the operative word."

"Tell me Arthur, can he read and comprehend written instructions like the others?"

"Yes."

As Colonel Ducet gazes upon the hybrid, a brilliant barrage of luminescent colors radiate into different patterns from the larger outer scales that covers the creatures' back, thighs, and forearms, to the smaller scales that covers the underside.

Ducet smiles; then calls Rowland to his side. "You and I have some work ahead of us. I've got to know what this thing can do."

"Yes…absolutely…"

The colonel bangs his fist upon the door of the trailer. A guard responds. "Yes sir!" "I want you to set up the playing field for an alpha-1 scenario. If all goes well, I want you to by-pass beta and delta operations, proceeding only to a gamma 3 scenario - got it?"

The guard listens to the instructions, but periodically looks at the hybrid. So compelling is his need to stare that the colonel raises his voice. "Did you HEAR ME?" "Y…Yes sir!"

"Now get that information to the observation deck immediately!"

The guard quickly exits the trailer.

~~~Forged Fury~~~

Dull senses respond to the caressing movement of an unexpected, yet familiar small hand. My eyes open. In addition, another heart beat softly tremors against my chest. Aniah now joins me, but in her mild slumber, she is unaware of my awakening. Darkness continues to engulf the city as the subtle red numbers of three-thirty illuminates. Time bares no transient significance, whether I've been here one minute or one thousand years, this is the time of remembrance. As Aniah lies upon my chest, I gaze through the sky window and note how beautifully it frames my celestial companion, which constantly moves farther across the black sky. She is the lesser light to rule the night, yet we in our confining wisdom decide to worship her and ultimately tread upon her, attempting to extract secrets unknown. But she is no mystery to me. With one arm, I reach for the scrapbook. Turning the pages, notes from an earlier project comes to view.

Quietly, in the moonlight, the note reads as follows:

We must somehow possess her, bring her into our world and change her virgin beauty to our glory just as we have change the mountains, rivers, forests, and grasslands. Restless and ever gathering are we; merciless in our quest to possess what no other has and to achieve what others cannot – so goes the plight of human progress. In all our glory and splendor, we have managed to accomplish tremendous feats, rise to momentous status and tread where even angels dare not, all for the sake of taking every thing from its natural existence in order to create something never before seen.

My own penmanship, laid to paper many years ago. Whether good or bad, right or wrong, agreeable or indifferent, all our actions emancipate the inert passions of a beguiling heart, and yet for this reason, Gjhe'nan was born.

I gaze at the vaulted ceiling. Though seeing nothing, I am able to draw from the catacombs of a bewildering mind where dark, hidden, irrefutable forces sublimely push against me, compelling me to kiss those things where lips of despair linger; passions become futile and wantonness goes beyond daily accommodations. It is in moments like these that men are driven mad, desperately trying to accomplish that *thing* before their debut into eternity.

But in those days long ago, GenoSyss was one of the forerunners of cloning technology. They called me the man-god, and sadly, my work suggested that God's creations were not good enough for our well-being – even for the military. Only when triumphant glory is within arms reach, decisions easily transfer without forethought and the accountability of actions merit no reprieve. I shall never forget.

Though still, Aniah's hand gently caresses my arm. The softness and warmth of her skin pacifies the moment as her head nestles motionless beneath my chin. With each breath, I feel her heart beating, forcing life throughout her resting body. Soothing is her presence that I begin to fall into a restful state once more.

The moon was high that night, though we were beneath the ground. Gjhe'nan was alive, and we were to control everything…but control was and still is a relative assumption.

"**WHAT** the hell is THAT?"

"I don't know…but it's the funkiest thing I ever did see!"

Two field workers stand awe struck at the sight of Gjhe'nan. Their candid motions signify an ongoing response felt by everyone on the field.

On the observation deck, a voice resonates through a loud speaker. *"Exercise of ENAN-429-003 will commence in 10 seconds, 9, 8, 7, 6, 5, 4, 3, 2, 1!"*

Immediately, the blaring sound of the hazard siren rings forth, sending all spectators behind protective cover. Entering the launch platform is the hybrid Gjhe'nan. Anticipation rises. Some view the phenomenal beast in such a way that their very position puts them in harms reach. A sense of awe covers the launch zone as well as the observation room. Seconds linger as time seemingly stands still. Again, sirens forcefully blare throughout the launch pad.

Then suddenly, the hybrid creature lunges forward as the saber-end tail sways. With a glance in a few directions, the hybrid quickly embarks upon the mission. Like a prehistoric biped from another world, the hybrid's gangly stride becomes a sight to see. As Gjhe'nan quickens pace, systematic explosions take place all around, thrusting rubble high into the air while bearing witness to the sea of chaos.

Fascination grows as all eyes converge upon the monitors.

"Sir, he's holding at 25."

"Zero to twenty-five for start...not bad. But for some reason, he doesn't sense a need for urgency."

"Then perhaps you should narrow the protective field sir."

"My thoughts exactly... Make his safe zone five feet, non explosives – explain it to him."

"Aye sir..."

Gracella turns towards Arthur, asking, "Will that close range injure him?"

"Only two cannons are allowed that close, but only non-lethal projectiles are fired. Upon impact, the fireworks are off."

"I hope you're right. Ducet's accident free profile is not as assuring."

Immediately, turret doors open as two cannons emerge. Each cannon hurls several projectiles towards the moving hybrid. Upon impacting the ground, mild burst of flames ignite, sending the creature darting off course and immediately taking cover.

"Arthur, is he hurt?"

"No Grace. He's just standing there, watching, appearing as though he's pondering something."

The hybrid crouches and stares at the field ahead, but the moment is brief as projectiles continuously pound within close proximity. Soon, Gjhe'nan moves forward, taking enormous strides and periodic brisk hops, combining such movements as the field stretches ahead.

Then, without warning, a projectile contacts the ground but fails to break apart. Instead, it strikes the side of the creature, brazing the scaly flesh with considerable force. The startled hybrid shrieks loudly, piercing the atmosphere with an ear wrenching yell. All stare in amazement. Afterwards, Gjhe'nan crouches, then forcefully leaps as both legs propel the majestic beast high into the air and several yards forward.

Personnel on the observation deck stare with profound amazement. "Whoa, did you see that?" Such questions echo throughout the area. Even Colonel Ducet casts a subtle smile as he delivers his concurrence to Rowland. "Now that's what I'm talking about – a little motivation to get things going!"

While in mid air, Gjhe'nan draws his legs forward, outstretching both as he prepares to land. Like huge shock absorbers, both legs absorb the impact. As quickly as the jump cycle ends, another cycle begins. A series of leaping and jumping motions propel the hybrid well into the mission as if no time was lost.

All actions are carefully scrutinized from the observation room. "Sir, he runs…*scus'e* me; his air speed moves at 65 …and climbs with each jump…leap; whatever," exerts the technician.

"From zero to…look at him go," states Walter.

Gjhe'nan easily jumps over debris, obstacles, and even fabricated trees until finally reaching a small structure. The hybrid discovers locks on a wooden door, but instead of inserting a key, one powerful kick into the barrier shatters the door into several pieces. Forcefully tearing away the outer edges of the entrance, the hybrid widens an opening in order to press inside. Once inside, Gjhe'nan stands within a few feet of the doorway. Bullets start to rain down upon the structure, mercilessly punishing the surface with a brutal outpour.

As Gjhe'nan stares into a black abyss, the observation personnel manage cameras within the structure. "Infrareds are operational Colonel."

"Good, now let's see what he does."

Though dark, the hybrid's undaunting actions yield the long awaited hope of nocturnal capability, which gives the observation deck more reasons to applaud, as well as rendering a commemorative pat on Arthur's back.

Locating a table, Gjhe'nan routes wires, sets timers, and remarkably positions four explosive devises within the room.

"Amazing," says Ducet.

"Sir, shell bombardment in three seconds," relays an operator.

A chilling silence engulfs the room.

Gjhe'nan delivers a flawless performance; then suddenly, large chunks of cement tears away from the ceiling. Heavier shells shake the ground as cracks form within the walls, but Gjhe'nan remains poised and focused. Upon completion, the hybrid quickly exits the structure.

Shortly afterwards, a thunderous sound resonates within the vast underground room, precluding yet another staggering explosion. Hot raining lead tatters the earthen floor, riveting deeply into the battle scared ground as the beast gallantly sails beyond the fiery threshold and into the confines of the safety zone. Chunks of debris follow, but are violently repelled against a magnetic barrier.

Jubilation fills the observation room while the colonel receives multiple reports. "Sir, he covered nearly two thousand yards in…"

"In what…"

"I'm sorry colonel, I was too caught up. It was under a minute whatever it was."

"Good, now finalize all your data and send it to my office."

Ducet embraces Rowland and whispers in the geneticist's ear. "I want more of these enans. And we will be well on our way." Rowland silently acknowledges the colonel with a heart felt stare.

The GenoSyss group hurriedly makes their way to the bay area where Gjhe'nan has come to rest. Moving into position, the group frantically shuns all curious spectators and outside personnel. They coax the hybrid into an area of seclusion where Arthur approaches. The technician rubs Gjhe'nan's scaly hide while daunting a smile as proudly as any father to his child.

"Let him rest and give him some water."

"I knew you were up to something, but I never knew it would be like this," states Jade while caressing the forehead of the beast.

Tuan, observing all the activity around the hybrid, approaches Arthur. "Congratulations. I think the colonel likes your design. Well done."

Arthur reciprocates the compliment. Then, Tuan slowly turns, but before he could walk away, Arthur quickly taps him on the shoulder.

"Tuan..."

"Yes."

"I want to apologize for our...well my part in our confrontations. You know...the problems we've had. I'm sorry."

"Hey, don't mention it. Those things happen. I like to think of it as professional competition. Good luck to you Arthur." Tuan exits the area, but Gracella notices the event and approaches Arthur. "He never failed," she says.

"I know...I just hope he knows that."

As both watch Tuan from a distance; Frank approaches while carrying printed material. "Arthur, guys. The bio reads for *g-nan* are all in the black; they look good, especially for an animal that size." Frank passes a print to Arthur who quickly pulls the item from his hand and immediately scans the information.

"That's good, considering we haven't had much time for testing prior to this experiment."

"But how are we to know that such readings are normal for *g-nan*?"

"Good question. And how do we know what a normal heartbeat is for him? With regards to weight, I haven't exactly gone up to a mature bull to take its blood pressure after rodeo antics."

"Yeah, well bulls don't jump forty feet in the air or leap fifty yards in a single bounce. There has to be a resting period after exertion and your animal is no exception. Bio reads dictate heart rate up during exercise. Now, the animal's heart rate is down since the exercise is over. That sounds normal to me."

"Point taken…. Thanks Frank."

"Sure…"

As time progress, Gjhe'nan's performances continue to surpass Colonel Ducet's expectations as well as the GenoSyss team. With each test, the level of difficulty rises and so does the hybrid's performance; even the hybrid's aptitude for literary comprehension.

Intently overseeing Gjhe'nan's progress is Arthur, who spends even more time with his prodigy. A strong bond develops between the two as Arthur becomes the trusting symbiotic figure to Gjhe'nan. So attaching is their bond that the hybrid develops performances based solely upon Arthur's presence. But in time, their mutual ties become an undesirable distraction to Ducet's militaristic plans. Clearly, the colonel does not share either of their sentiments.

Later, testing convenes once again and Colonel Ducet oversees the progress as usual. Standing near the forward window, the officer observes something in the distance. "What is the problem now? Someone, get me Arthur!" Angrily spouting frustration, the colonel leaves the platform, but the recipients of his verbal abuse seem inadequate to respond. No one answers.

On the field, personnel locate Arthur. He goes with them, only to find that two soldiers are forcing the hybrid onto the testing range. Several men corner the apprehensive creature, attempting to sway the confrontation to their favor.

"Mr. Robinson, the colonel wants this thing on the field, now!"

Shouting his commands, a sergeant raises his firearm and moves into position as two other men manage to place a lasso around Gjhe'nan's neck. More soldiers move in, prodding the beast, wielding long rods that dispel electrical sparks. Gjhe'nan loudly shrieks, desperately moving away from the men. Arthur's stern demeanor overshadows his logic as he grabs one of the soldiers by the jacket, but the soldier pulls away.

"What are you doing? Is this the control that the colonel wants?"

"Get out of my way man."

"What the hell's wrong with you people?"

"Listen Mr. Robinson. You interfere; you kiss your ass goodbye!" The soldier's warning lies heavily upon Arthur's mind.

Four men frantically try to subdue the beast. They each wrap the rope around their wrist to obtain a better grip, pulling and tugging with greater effort, but Gjhe'nan resists even more. One of the men violently retaliates by shocking the hybrid several times.

Then, like a slow burning flame, Gjhe'nan's eyes illuminate with a dim reddish glow; a glow that now accompanies the sound of a menacing growl.

The man and his counterpart see the transformation. "No way..."
"What did you do?" Both men step backwards.

In an instant, Gjhe'nan lunges forward, dragging all four men behind. Their bodies violently scrape the ground as the hybrid plunges forward. Two more soldiers perch upon a side railing. With weapons drawn and attitude to coincide, one of the soldiers raises his hand. "Prepare to fire on my mark!" Arthur sees the men and runs towards them, but other soldiers quickly lay in pursuit while informing Colonel Ducet. "Sir, we have a hostile situation, please advise?"

Ducet instructs his men aloud. "Contain the situation, but do not, I repeat, do not damage the hybrid!" As both soldiers hear the men scream, they become too embroiled in the moment. They do not hear the end of the colonel's orders. "CONTAIN THE SITUATION - FIRE!"

Shots ring out, but Arthur spurs into the gunman's side, shoving him into the other unsuspecting shooter as well. Smoke fills the air as one of the men lie on the ground. Yet, despite the technician's gallant effort, Gjhe'nan suffers the full brunt of the militia's standard issue.

"Where did those shots come from? I did not authorize that type of containment! CEASE FIRE! CEASE YOUR FIRE! That's an ORDER!" screams Ducet.

Workers on the field hurriedly take shelter as the hybrid sustains direct impact. Remarkably, Gjhe'nan's scales hold strong, but more bullets spray into the beast until one bullet wedges deeply between the hybrid's scales.

"NO!" Arthur grits his teeth as arteries course his swelling neck. Raging with fury, the technician clenches both fists and violently strikes the soldier, dispersing a crimson stream upon the man's face. "NO!" As the soldier falls to the ground, Arthur pursues Gjhe'nan, but the hybrid quickly takes flight, showing no mercy for the men who desperately cling to the ropes.

Once airborne, Gjhe'nan pinpoints an exit and lands. The hybrid attempts to run through double bay doors, but watchful guardsmen perceive the hybrid's intent and proceed to lower the door. Suddenly, scales collide with steel as Gjhe'nan impacts the door. With great force, the impact breaks several support hinges and dislodges most of the steel rollers from the tracks. Though dangling to one side, the door amazingly holds, thereby obstructing Gjhe'nan's escape. Other military personnel move into position, setting harnesses and preparing to bombard the creature. Nothing seems to impede the hybrid's progress.

Soon, military vehicles move in closer and a sergeant makes their position known. "Sir, we've got him cornered!" *"Proceed with caution. Now remember, I need that creature alive!"*

The hybrid steps backward as more vehicles move closer, but Gjhe'nan's agitation grows worse. Announcing a low growl, the hybrid swings its long tail and hammers the side of the nearest humvee. The violent impact shatters the windshield and jolts two soldiers to the ground. *"Shhhiiiiiit…* and the colonel says don't kill it." "Just what the hell is we suppose to do then – say please?"

The men cast a net over the hybrid, completely covering its body. In response, Gjhe'nan crouches and without hesitation propels vertically, startling his would-be apprehenders.

While disembarking, another humvee lays directly in the landing path of the hybrid's descent. Soldiers perceive their demise and frantically abandon the vehicle, except one. Their desperate efforts spare only a few seconds before Gjhe'nan's bulk crushes the canopy, in effect making the armored carrier derelict in its tracks. With talons erect and ears folding back, Gjhe'nan defiantly stands on top of the vehicle, bolstering his plea for dominance as he desperately tries to get free of the net.

With chaos abounding, one of the fleeing soldiers looks behind, yelling, "Duncan...Duncan!" His solemn cry yields no response.

In sheer view, Duncan's lifeless body lies partially across the window track of the humvee. The soldier's blood stained torso testifies to his misfortune as Gjhe'nan's frivolous motions completely sever the soldier's body in two.

"Sir, one man down," radios the sergeant.

In the control room, Colonel Ducet projects a speechless demeanor as the sergeant maintains contact. *"Sir, can you hear me? One man is down – Duncan is dead – sir!"*

Ducet slowly blinks, "Mercy," he whispers. His solemn figure turns towards Rowland, but the geneticist has no consoling words. Wiping his face in agitation, the colonel responds. "Son, think of that creature as an over-size kangaroo. Put a net over it, and then tranquilize the damn thing.*"*

"But sir, this thing just walked through our firearms. I doubt a needle will penetrate those scales."

"Then secure it by any means necessary, but don't kill it!" Ducet discontinues his transmission, after which, he drives his fist into the console.

The field sergeant looks at his men. "All right, you heard the colonel! Move in and capture!" In an instant, multiple nets engulf Gjhe'nan, restricting the hybrid's movements. Responsive enough, the unit skillfully place ropes around Gjhe'nan's head and tail. The incident creates more agitation within the hybrid.

Viewing his would-be captors, Gjhe'nan pinpoints two soldiers on approach. Then, without warning, the hybrid slams his tail into both men, propelling one of the men several yards aloft and the other violently into a cement pillar. Upon impact, the soldier's body slowly slides to the ground until ultimately resting on both knees. His eyes remain open as his head slumps awkwardly to one side. Pitiful stares converge upon the lifeless body, but ignoring the hybrid for only a moment proves foolish as the creature takes flight once more, in effect showing little concern for those attempting containment.

In the control room, Ducet approaches Rowland.
"The price is rising Krenshenkov."

"So it appears."

"Decision – now!"

"You tell me *thees* underground *rr-oomiz* two square miles."

"And your point…"

"The hybrid can not leave even *eef it* wants to."

"We may have to destroy it."

"Most unfortunate…"

"If so; can you create another one; and this time without Arthur's influence?"

"The *prr*-ocedure is possible – yes."

"Do it quickly?" Ducet leans near the console, activating his transceiver. *"Listen up…all unit commanders. Instruct your men to kill!"*

Upon Ducet's command, bullets ferociously impact Gjhe'nan's side, violently hammering against the tightly dense scales. But in the flash of a moment, retaliation sets in as the hybrid swings its tail at anything within reach. High pitch sounds blare aloud as rapid impact forces the beast to flinch. But mercy shuns the face of compassion as muffling gunfire silence the hybrid's child-like wines.

The engulfing chaos proves more than even Gjhe'nan can bear. Crouching low, Gjhe'nan catapults high into the air, and upon impact to the ground, the hybrid darts away with amazing speed. Soldiers pursue, only to find that Gjhe'nan is nowhere in sight.

"You can't hide from us. Follow the tracker!" Soon, military vehicles locate Gjhe'nan's beacon, only to find that the device lay upon barren ground near a large stone. A soldier picks up the device and disappointedly tosses it aside.

"Sir, he ditched us."

"Ditched us? Now how the hell do you loose something that big in a place like this?"

"There are lots of big rocks and shrubs on this jagged field."

As the sergeant shakes his head in disbelief, another soldier approaches. "Sir, hostile sighted just over that ridge. It ran into a bunker. "Okay – move out people!"

Several military vehicles arrive at the bunker, girding with lights and heavy artillery. The vehicles quickly surround the structure, bathing it with piercing high beams wile armaments are locked and ready to fire.

Amidst the surplus of men, Arthur makes his move. He jumps from his vehicle and runs inside of the structure.

Rowland and Ducet intently watch. "What is he doing?"

"Perhaps the only *thing* that can be done colonel... *Eef* he does what I believe, it may work to our best interest - After all, Arthur knows *hees* creature."

Arthur arrives at the edge of the structure. He takes caution upon entering and methodically makes his way through the surrounding darkness.

"Gjhe'nan...Gjhe'nan," he calls while stretching his hands forward. Finding the nearest wall, he slides his hand upon the plastered surface while cautiously sliding his feet forward. "Gjhe'nan!" Again he calls, but silence is the only response. Pressing forward, he looses his footing and braces for the inevitable fall. Contacting the ground, Arthur rolls to his side. Silence chills the air. Then, a low pitch-snarl pierces the blackness, becoming louder with each second. Immediately, Arthur realizes that his search is over.

Brazen red eyes appear and draw near as the technician senses the approach of an overwhelming presence. Arthur cowers and closes his own eyes, then turns away as if to protect himself from the unknown. Acting upon nothing more than instinct, he attempts to run but looses balance. With hands raised, the technician discovers that a slippery substance is the result of his undoing. Yet, his distraught state allows him to stare in the direction of the eyes. Apparently sensing what could be his end, Arthur remains calm.

The snarling intensifies as the eyes move closer. Taking a long deep breath, Arthur slowly rises to his feet. Perhaps realizing his lesser fate, he courageously leans forward, anticipating the nearness of his approaching prodigy. Then, surprisingly, something touches his hand and the growling subsides.

Like a sorrowful adolescent, Gjhe'nan nudges Arthur's face. Arthur responds in kind. "I would never hurt you," he says as the hybrid senses water trickling from his maker's eyes.

Arthur takes Gjhe'nan by the hand and proceeds towards the opening of the structure. At first, Gjhe'nan resists, but trustingly follows. However, Arthur continues to fumble amidst the darkness in an attempt to find his way. Sensing Arthur's handicap, the nostalgic giant takes hold of Arthur's hand and leads him towards the entry.

"I never knew that your eyes could glare red; and now they turn dark blue again. You are truly amazing."

Exiting the structure, both encounter blinding lights. "Hold your fire," yells an officer. Quickly realizing the situation, Arthur stands in front of Gjhe'nan. Though severely dwarfed by the hybrid's size, Arthur animates his futile gestures as he waves his hands in an attempt to ward off a potential attack. Yet, in his efforts, he sees something on his hands. "This is your blood." He takes notice of the hybrid's condition.

Though battered and bruised, the beautiful array of transient colors continue to emanate from the hybrid's scaly exterior. Arthur coaxes the hybrid giant into a docile state and then leads the beast away. Everyone watches in sheer amazement.

In the observation room, Colonel Ducet and Rowland observe the unfolding situation. "That creature survived an onslaught of a dreadful magnitude. My God!"

"*Emprr-esseeve* - Yes?"

"Rowland, I need more of those g-nons."

"We now have genetic codes and no longer require *Meester* Arthur *Rrr-obinson's* involvement."

"But will he be a problem?"

"Nothing that can not be handled, I assure you."

"Then we move forward."

A few days later, all teams assemble within room 47-C. After the door closes, a cloud of tension hovers. Several members cast flagrant comments aloud, even spurring shrewd responses as counter arguments. Arthur aggressively asserts as the forerunner, projecting his points while slamming his hand on the table.

"Why Rowland…why did you allow the military to force the issue?! They could have killed Gjhe'nan!"

"What care you…*eetz* their *prro-perty*. Your creature is now selected. The colonel wants more of them, you *deed* well!"

"Don't patronize me."

"There *eez* no patronization!"

"Who the hell determines the life and death my enan?"

"YOUR ENAN? Again I remind you…military owns enan project."

"Not the military…but only one person, the colonel. And his answer to everything is to kill what he can't control."

"Be not so hypocritical *MeesterRrr*-obinson. How many animals die in circus and zoos in order for you to create your hybrid?"

"Animals die because people want to control them."

"I have no time for *these*! Enough, or you are on report *weeth* suspension." Rowland turns away as Arthur hurls books against the wall. Gracella quickly directs her attention to Rowland. "Was it necessary to shoot? Did Gjhe'nan threaten the soldiers first?"

"Inconclusive, but he belongs to them to do as they *pleez*."

"Professor, even though the scales saved Gjhe'nan's life, there was still some blood lost."

"Damn right it was! He could have died out there," interjects Arthur.

"Your point *eez* noted Arthur – now that will be enough!"

"Bullshit!" Arthur belts his disapproval, violently pointing his finger to the chair where Colonel Ducet once sat. "They represent the DOD who gets paid by our tax dollars and it's my ingenuity in Gjhe'nan, not theirs. That means we own a large piece of stock in this as well."

"Your Gjhe'nan jeopardized testing and *keeled* two military men as the result of *hees leetle* skirmish. Now tell me, do you know the names of the soldiers who died?"

"What are you talking about?"

"The soldiers who died – Do you know their names?"

"What does that have to do with anything?"

"You get point; after all…they were human. And when humans die as result of experiment, and we forget their name, then we are lower than those *weeth* no conscience, do you get point – Yes?"

"I can't believe what you're implying." Arthur immediately grabs an easel and throws it to the floor, shattering the tri-pod into several pieces.

"You are on report *Rrr*-obinson! One more outburst, then you are fired! And I can assure you that you will have nothing to link this project to us, or to you!"

Frank leans forward while candidly placing his elbows on the table, eying Arthur while pondering thoughts. Then, in a calm voice, he asks, "Arthur, do you feel the heart beat of the animal?"

Arthur surprisingly looks at Frank. "What?"

"Do you feel Gjhe'nan's heart beat?"

"If this is a joke, I'm *gonna* tell you were you can put it."

"No joke. My ancestors believed that when a hunter and prey engage in their prowess, the hunter feels the animal, thinks like the animal and moves like the animal. In a sense, both become one. I don't suggest ignorant or foolish ancestral thinking, but my point is that the anger inside you burns more than ours because the creature is part of you. Both, you and your g-non are one – and that is where the problem is."

Arthur stares at Frank, but gives no response, nor does he provide the slightest hint that Frank's words are of consent.

Rowland clasps both hands behind his back, pacing the floor with a tense expression. "Arthur. I prefer your involvement. We can benefit from your talents. Therefore, make *dee*-cision. Will you continue with us or not – either way, the samples *weel* be given to the colonel."

Arthur lowers his head. He stares at his image, which emanates from the polished surface of the table. Every one remains quiet, yet in a matter of seconds, the once placid moment receives an interruption.

"Fine..."

Few nod their heads in concurrence, but Gracella and Walter sternly cast an appearance to suggest unfavorable implications. "You won't regret it Arthur," says Tuan. Rowland gingerly smiles and begins to speak, but before he can utter a single word, Arthur leans forward. "All I ask is one condition," he says.

"And what *eez* that to mean *Meester* Rrr-obinson?"

"I want to give the military a clone of Gjhe'nan, but keep the original here to study. I have information that suggests a few problems that Gjhe'nan may encounter. After all, we still don't know the long-term effects from his mutations."

Rowland carefully eyes Arthur, who displays a placid contentment; but soon, Rowland's gleeful expression turns to despondency. "And just how is *thees* Gjhe'nan too be cared for? Providing any shelter other than GenoSyss facility may incur sizable expenses and trouble."

"That's a matter of opinion."

"Might I *rr*-emind you that Gjhe'nan *eez* company property – as you noted?"

"The examinations will only be for a short while."

"So says you! But I find *eet* interesting that you changed your mind so easily. I grow tired of your games Arthur. Tell me...where did *these prr*o-ject grow personal for you?"

"What do you care?" Upon hearing Arthur's response, Rowland storms across the floor, shoving chairs beyond his path while leaving a trail of fallen paper.

Tuan immediately stops Rowland at the door. "So, is that it?"

"Are you addressing me Mr. Vein?"

"Why do you act as though Colonel Ducet wants Gjhe'nan instead of Si'ehda? Was a decision already made? Why weren't we told?"

"*Eetz* but…small matter now…"

"Did Colonel Ducet already make his decision?"

Silence lingers in the room as faces fluster with sheer puzzlement; then in one breath, Rowland points his finger towards Tuan. "Don't ever let *it* cross your mind that I would not terminate either project, as well as you and Arthur. I *vil-geev* all materials to…colonel, and no one keeps anything."

"It is as though you planned it all along."

Having heard Tuan's statement, Rowland grabs the doorknob and exits the room.

"So much for the diplomatic approach," says Frank as he and the others clear the room, leaving behind an empty and silent chamber.

~~~Blind Ambition~~~

Deep shadows dance before me as I reestablish familiar surroundings. Placing both feet upon the floor, slowly and yet cautiously, I fumble an invisible path to the fireplace. Subtle light grants just enough luminance while a brisk chill thralls my waking senses. Above the mantle lie earlier paintings; one of two leopards and two horses running free. Both are a pictorial testament to that part of me that yearns to be free.

Ironically, I choose to come here, like an animal lingering at the open door of its cage. Under the pictures lie more photo albums, apparently placed there earlier by my hand when daylight ruled. Taking the largest of four albums, I return to the den and unfold more images frozen in time. Such capsules of Gracella, Walter, and me depict our trio during a time when things were much simpler and the act of cloning was more for science than politics, more for aiding human frailties than for personal gain - such innocence.

But Gjhe'nan grew stronger and more knowledgeable of his surroundings. We drank a toast to his awareness, his success, and even his evolving. My God...Gjhe'nan shined. No one knows of this image, not even Aniah. Days, seemingly without end passed as Gjhe'nan matured and flourished, growing wonderfully into what he was to become. I was too close to him; but I didn't care. In light of that fact, since the military decided to take Gjhe'nan, they could not have known that something else was at work.

Subtle streams of gold highlight the edge of the picture as my handling of it reflects Nostalgia's presence. She wore gold around her neck that day and I can still count the lockets within the choker. Her brilliance now embodies the celestial eve of all clear lunar nights. Yet strangely, another was there that night as well. To my foolishness, I would bring Him with me.

His magnificence far outweighs us mortals, even where mere comparisons to Him simply cannot measure up. I do not profess a flawless nature in His dominion, nor do I weigh a pressing countenance of nobility; only the realization that I live day to day in the blanket of His shadow. Though a lifestyle void of impetuous deeds is possible in Him, the ambiance of that moment long ago flusters in colorful fragrances and tasteful pleasures. To this day, only the resounding silence of the moonlit night can tell the story, and that is something I must never forget. Or should I?

My hand slides across a prominent bugle in the center of the photograph. I carefully remove the picture only to expose an aging piece of paper. Curiously, I begin to unravel the prominent folds. Only now do I recollect the item before me. It is a hand written message of an old recorded point in time:

The troublesome trio, who would dare, the troublesome trio everywhere. We clone for now, we clone for then, we give you something that has never been. Signed: Gracella, Walter, and Arthur.

Laughter fills me as I replace the two objects within the scrapbook. To this day, I had no way of knowing that Walter and Gracella would mean so much to me. God's angels come in all forms.

My eyes close once more, thrusting me deeper into the fathoms of darkness. Without fail, I find a place where mortals are gods and fictitious memories rule with magnificent grandeur.

Footsteps echo towards a room far away. The room lies well beyond prying eyes and ears of all personnel within the Red Sands facility. The room consists of a large desk, a large screen monitor, and two leather swayback chairs. Patriotism laces the walls as prominent military paraphernalia strikingly display for all to observe. As the footsteps cease, two men quickly seat themselves in front of a large monitor. "Access on," says one of the men. Soon, the monitor illuminates with information privy only to those in attendance. A match strikes. Clouds of black cherry plumbs disperse into the air. In that brief moment of illumination, Colonel Ducet and Rowland Krenshenkov bask in total isolation.

Gently rocking to a silent rhythm, the colonel gazes into the monitor. "Just look at them. Less than a year ago, they were nothing more than an idea. Our first primary test subjects were a bird and a cat. Who would have possibly imagined that a modified kangaroo would win the bid? Now we have thirty-six hybrid kangaroo enans, each awaiting instructions. Sixteen of these hybrids are trained and ready for deportation to the Middle East. You did good Rowland."

"*Eet* was trying time – of course."

"Now you listen to me. The team's reluctance means nothing. All that matters now is that we can do our thing."

"*Weeth* that aside... I delivered as *prro*-mised; now for your part of bargain colonel. Do you have them?"

"Of course..."

The colonel pours Rowland a glass of wine and gives it to him. The placid geneticist sips the amber beverage while Ducet candidly stares. "Six of these enans are yours Professor."

"Good."

"However, I must say that you carry a strange and dangerous outlook. I must ask again Rowland, do you really intend to take down Rham-kiev for the alleged death of your family; your...sister?"

"Need you ask?"

"I figured the bid for project 429 was tremendously in our favor, but since it was your call, it all eventually made sense."

"I know where you are going *weeth* this colonel, but you should not be concerned *about* me. I have sources that know location of Rham-kiev."

"They are larger than you know."

"Perhaps, but...enans are deadlier than they realize."

"So be it..."

"And what of you Colonel; are your superiors aware of your intentions – *hmmm*...?"

"They only know what I tell them and that's good enough – for now."

"You *Ame-rrr*-icans...always too assure for your own good."

"Perhaps, but remember, you came to this country for the best possible chance of furthering your endeavor."

"Yes I *deed*. But I also discover that you have personal agenda as well – Yes?"

Rowland gulps down the beverage and stares at Ducet with a piercing glare. "I see that you have not forgotten," he says.

"Of course not... Why should I? Revenge is a very common enactment; but nevertheless Rowland, for a man of your distinct talents, one would think that such a primitive mindset would be far outside your motives."

"Are we not all equal in death?"

"You do realize that your ambitious endeavor can kill you."

"Vindication is justifiable when needed. Besides, American justice lies in the eyes of legislative interpretation. And let us not forget, your justice is also in the power of he who holds much currency."

"You did your homework."

"I can b*rr*-ing Rham-kiev to justice."

"How…by reducing their numbers?"

"Elimination..."

"You fool."

"*Eef* shoe *fits*…as you say…"

"Just remember, you get caught – we have no ties. Surely a man in your position can understand that."

"And you…are so above your own laws Colonel?"

"I never said I was, but make no mistake; it is hard to transport enans from place to place on U.S soil. And you want me to smuggle six of them out of the country for your revenging endeavor."

"Fair expectation – Yes?"

"You die, no problem, but if any one of those creatures is discovered, that situation could lead a trail back to me."

"You worry too much Colonel. I take care of you –"

"Are you listening? Hunting down Rham-kiev for the alleged death of your sister..."

"Alleged...alleged, damn it! How dare you? They *deed* kill her. They *keeled* her and many *othuurs*! Years later, my family die because of Rham-kiev's toxic exposures; twas` some-*teen* they *deed* – *Rrr*ham-kiev *keeld* many more...all of them die. *Thees* I know!"

"Even if you get the enans into the Soviet Union; are you sure that you can control them?"

"How are you to judge my abilities? Am I not as able as you? With that in mind, what of your excursion Colonel; can you control the enans any better than I?"

Ducet slowly fills his cup with more wine, leisurely sipping while slowly pacing the floor. "I have seen combat and I am telling you that plans always change. Situations mostly provoke the outcome. Enans in a hostile environment are no different; the tests prove it! What you are suggesting is absolute control, but even still, there are no guarantees."

"Nothing has *guaran-teez* Colonel. Did you not know that true control lies only in the hand of he who destroys?"

"It sounds poetic enough."

"Rightly so – Now do we still have an agreement or not?"

Silence grips both men as disquieted stares linger amidst the secret setting. With arms folded, Ducet scans the wall of paintings where images portray ancient veterans of antiquated battles. Soon, their professional approach comes forth as both men quickly realize the moment of truth.

"Absolutely," says Ducet.

"Good. I will then leave you. But tell me again Colonel, what *eez* difference between enans placing bomb on object than on a human?"

"The difference is having the ability to wake up the next morning and living with yourself?"

"Can you?"

Ducet glances afar off as though an audience beckons his immediate attention, peering to the walls once more; then, in a small still voice, "I have no choice," he says.

Days later, a gray canopy greets the awakening city. Dense clouds deny the slightest of sunrays to grace the concrete jungle as inhabitants pursue their daily tasks. Not immune to such behavior, Rowland's team reassembles in room 47-C. Separated into small groups, each unit provides information regarding Gjhe'nan's cloned hybrids.

With common familiarity, Rowland sits in full view of his teams. "As you know, the enans has been *dee*-livered. Colonel sends high praises for your work. I *weel* attempt to bring conclusion to *thees* precocious matter of the enans and would like your input before reassignment back to your former office duties."

"Oh, you mean we have a choice in this matter," says Arthur; sarcastically mocking Rowland.

"I *weel* not get dragged into debate *weeth* you *Meester Rrr*-obinson. A very good day today – I *theenk*."

"Then you don't mind answering the questions as to how many enans are there? Did the military create boys, girls, or both? And what's to become of the cloning samples afterwards? Those are just simple questions – by the way."

"Of all people, I know you are not happy *weeth* military sanctioning our division for care of…enans, but who better for task? Only you display sour feelings when you should be happy!"

"Rowland, our newly found bed fellows will do something out of the normality of human dignity just to get a job done."

"You are referring to the *mee*-litary's treatment of the enans - Yes?"

"No…but only one man, Colonel Ducet."

The room grows quiet as all in attendance observe both men. Gracella immediately grabs Arthur's hand and forces him to exit the room. Tuan notices the two and yells at both. "That's it, take your girlfriend and go relieve some stress!" "Kiss my…" The door closes before Arthur can add to his reply.

"What's with you Arthur? I've never seen you this upset. You are increasingly hostile since the military took the enans. It was Rowland's decision and that's, that!" Arthur hears her yet continues to stare afar, displaying an angry countenance. "Don't get quiet on me now, what's wrong? Arthur, we've come this far but if you don't want to talk about

166

it, then…you know what will happen. Look, it's almost lunch time, let's get something to eat."

Gracella gently touches Arthur's shoulder. In doing so, the door opens and Walter emerges. "Hey you two. I came to check on you. What's going on guy?" Arthur takes a deep breath but remains speechless while simply closing his eyes.

Walter looks at Gracella. "I think it's time for a ride. Clear us for leave."

Overcast blankets the metropolitan area and yields no signs of disbursing. The trio embarks on a southward journey to rural property. "The more I come out here, the less time the drive actually takes," says Walter, attempting to generate conversation. But his conversation is two fold. Gracella responds, yet Arthur remains distant as the journey concludes near a metallic gate at the end of a dirt road. Arthur's transport, Ramsey, passes through an entry gate as it deathly flattens milkweeds and other native wild grasses, creating a trail for several yards until reaching a large white barn. The barn sets in isolation upon a hill.

The property is peaceful. Several mesquite trees adorn the multi-acreage plot while partially concealing a large inland pond. Ramsey's presence draws the attention of a small herd of cattle as they cease from grazing around the water's edge. Graceful birds fly in tranquil solitude, drawing Gracella's attention as Walter steers Ramsey closer to the barn. Stopping Ramsey, Walter shrugs Arthur's shoulder and in a kind manner, he asks, "Feeling better guy?"

"Yeah," responds Arthur.

"This is a nice place your little brother has here. Fortunate for you, it has come in quite handy for us."

"Hollis and I would often come here when we were kids. His father left him this property. I never knew how much it would be a part of my life."

"Hey, therapy seems to be kicking in," states Gracella as Arthur begins to smile.

"I'm sorry about my attitude."

"No matter what happened at the office today, just realize that on the other side of that door is the reason that makes everything we do, all worth while."

After entering the barn, Arthur turns the lights on.

"Wow, nice tractor," says Walter, kissing the machine as though it were feminine.

"I'm praying for you," responds Gracella.

"Oh please do, and may she be everything I want."

"In your dreams pal and don't let your drool ruin the paint job."

Skylights cast subtle light throughout while softly bathing the straw laden floor. Hay bails lay neatly in several square rows, stacked along side the aft wall of the two-story structure. They walk quietly towards the rear of the barn. As they approach, large dark eyes stare at them with uncanny attentiveness. Arthur claps his hands. "Gjhe'nan, come on out, it's us."

As the hybrid comes into view, Walter embraces the beast by the neck. "Hey, look at this. His wounds have virtually healed and all the damaged scales have fallen off. New ones are growing in. We missed you big boy."

Once Gjhe'nan sees Arthur, the hybrid approaches with enthusiasm; awkwardly moving both legs in bipedal fashion while carrying Walter as though he weighs nothing. "Gjhe'nan," Arthur whispers. The hybrid nudges Arthur, whose benign countenance finally dawns a smile.

Gracella gently places her hand on Arthur's shoulder. "I'm glad you gave him a name, too my surprise, but I'm also delighted to see you feeling better."

"I do feel better. And...thank you for bypassing security so I could get him out here. I realize that I have asked both of you to do something very compromising."

"Hold on, not so fast. Keep in mind that if you get caught..."

"I will never put you and Walter in harms way – not for anything, especially me."

"I've known you too long Arthur. Because of that, I hope you find what ever you are looking for. I feel suspicious about Rowland and Ducet but the contracts grant them sovereign rights, despite your feelings."

"It's because of those gut feelings that I have to do this."

"And…repeat to me again why you are doing…*this*."

"I followed Rowland late one night from the office."

"You did WHAT?"

"Listen…I saw him meeting with one of Ducet's men in the park."

"And that means…?"

"It prompted me to hide out in the building late one night, in the lab. That was when I heard Rowland telling someone about *heez* portion of the *dee-livery*. Military jargon was referenced through the whole conversation."

"Really…."

"Who do we know that is related to the military; possessing knowledge of 429?"

"If there is something to hide, I don't think Rowland, of all people, will be so irresponsible; but I see your point."

"The more I listened; the more I became convinced that those two are up to something."

"Arthur, you stole Gjhe'nan, which is military and company property, in order to prove that a conspiracy is taking place? And we helped you do it."

"I took Gjhe'nan so they can't hurt him. You saw what the military tried to do when they couldn't control him."

"Was that your right to do so?"

"Grace, I'm not trying to create a weapon; that's their job. I want to create life."

"You can create life Arthur. It's called pregnancy and I think God intended females to do it."

169

"We must really like you buddy, risking our butts like that," exerts Walter, lying sprawled along the hybrid's back, attempting to avoid the large dorsal spines.

Arthur gently rubs Gjhe'nan's chin while engaging in head nudging. "It's just the way the military has taken over and how Rowland has been behaving since we fulfilled our contract."

"Are you sure it's not because you are too close to this big guy – despite his cute little *facey-waycy*."

"Maybe... In other instances, I heard Rowland implying 429's deployment elsewhere and that our teams will remain silent. There is something going on, but I'm yet to put my finger on it. I also feel that this project will be lost, just like the others. Surely you two suspect something otherwise you would not have helped me."

"The only thing we suspect Arthur is that you will go down, alone - if they find out…and I mean alone – buddy."

"Point taken…

~~~The Mission~~~

On foreign shores, soldiers quickly assemble; hurriedly preparing for debarkation under the watchful eye of Colonel Ducet. The full-bird commander parades before his assembly, interjecting assurances for a mission that he obviously believes in.

"No matter what happens today, you should know that this is the first confrontation of its kind in the history of warfare! Understand that all of you are making a profound statement for your brothers-in-arms; whose blood still cries out for justice. To this day, their corpses testify of atrocities that destroyed them; which is why we must avenge them. But keep in mind; enemies of the flag continue to taunt us without conscience as well as our own who protest against us. For that matter, no one cares for the POWs or the MIAs until political campaigns enter the scene. But hold fast ladies and gentlemen. We now have an answer for those who think suicide bombing, terrorism, or mercy killing is a means to an end. Today, our enemies will know of a judgment as never before. They will know of terror and pain, the likes of which mere mortals has never endured. They shall taste vindication that will be heard around the world. And they will think twice before they impart their hellish actions upon innocent people. So, with that in mind… Continue to serve proudly and without shame of what is asked of you today. Now go…and send our enemies back where they belong. Godspeed to you all!"

Watchful eyes gaze forward, locked sternly from within camouflaged painted faces. Poised at attention, their rigid bodies stand with intensity as arms column downward to his or her side. These modern day musketeers project a silent attentiveness that is picturesque of a deeper focus. Each of them stands loyal until their commander dismisses them.

Having made his decree, Ducet returns aboard the freighter. As he does, large cargo doors open, revealing a deep blackness within the hull. His infantry quickly run ashore and into a nearby grove of trees, leaving tracks in the cool sand under the glow of the pale moonlight.

As the men take shelter, the crew monitors radar and gauges. Colonel Ducet signals each soldier to grasp a whistle and raise the instrument to his mouth. *"Signals register, check."* Such words roll across a short wave transmission.

In that moment, the watercraft sways side-to-side as one enan emerges from inside the craft and pounces onto the deck. Afterwards, the hybrid beast lunges forward onto dry land. Five more enans emerge from the hull and perform in like manner. Receiving instructions, the enans suddenly vanish into the distant night while leaving the soldiers far behind.

"Stalker to Eagle, the payload has been deployed," informs one of the soldiers.

"Good, now monitor their progress and report frequently back to me," responds Ducet as the cargo doors tightly seal. Soon, the large craft submerges beneath the cold dark waters.

Subtle clouds of dust rise as the enans leap in rhythmic cycles, sequencing one jump after another. Each hybrid covers vast distances, gracefully, effortlessly displaying the agility of their smaller progenitors. The enan's ingrained abilities cover a stretch of land that humbles the most capable of long distance runners. But Ducet's men show no concern for marathons as they set up operations far behind the traveling beasts.

Soon, the enans arrive at an establishment outside the province of Yamur, where they halt progress. With unwavering anticipation, they wait.

Field unit commander, Essington Moore Jamison, whose code name is Stalker, begins to relay information to Colonel Ducet. "This is Stalker to Eagle, Stalker calling the Eagle..."

"The Eagle is listening, go ahead..."

"The marsupial doppelgangers are in place and awaiting instructions."

Ducet smiling, *"Marsupial doppelgangers?"*

"Yes sir – "

"Where did you get that term?"

"That is...what they are sir..."

"Welcome to the freak show," whispers the colonel. *"Fair enough... Proceed with phase two."*

"Phase two will now commence."

The faces of each soldier illuminate with a soft glow as light from miniature monitors display what each of their assigned enan sees. In like manner, each enan has a miniature camera mounted on top of its head conveying to the soldiers exactly what it sees. The hybrids fasten their keen eyes upon a nearby compound. As they wait, their heads bob and bodies sway, each rocking their massive legs while silently conjuring a ghostly stance.

One of Stalker's men coveys a report. "Sir, LandSat confirms seventeen hostiles patrolling. Four heavy guns; two east, one west, and one topside. Also, four rogue bogies on the outskirts. There is concern for the animal's body armor against mortar fire but other than that, we're good to go."

"Don't worry about the armor soldier. Trust me; the enan's scales are tuff. Just send in… What were their names?"

"Zeus, Apollo, and Mercury…sir…"

"Oh…yeah…right… Send in the gods."

"Aye sir..." The men relay the instructions to their respective enan and immediately, three enans separate from the pack and lock onto their targets.

Armed patrols ride along the outskirts of the compound. The tranquil mood of the peaceful surrounding is enough to relax the mindset of anyone within the area. But training dictates that everyone should remain alert and the guards are certainly no exception. However, a routine patrol tingle their suspicions, and they could not have known what irony waits.

Stalker cues first wave, "Engage." Suddenly, the creature's deep black eyes begin to glare with a haunting subtle red as they peer down upon their targets. One of the men on patrol sees an enan. Without warning, the creature slashes the man's body in two and decapitates the driver's head. The man's face, ghastly brazen with fear; testifies that a demonic apparition was the last thing he saw. His head rolls along the ground. The enan pulls a device from an attached harness and quickly releases it, then jumps several feet into the air. An explosion takes place as the creature descends from mid air and crushes the next unsuspecting guard.

The other two enans simultaneously crush four unsuspecting guards as well, pouncing on each and then releasing grenades as they jettison across the plateau. Explosions occur as desperate gunshots spray in the direction of the beasts; but their uncanny movements prove far too difficult for a direct hit. Sirens hasten other guards and like a disturbed hornets nest, reinforcements pour on to the scene. The entire compound quickly becomes an intense frenzy of gunfire and frantic bodies moving in all directions. Then, as if planned, the enans vanish within the surrounding hillsides.

"Attack east side and drop the payload," commands Stalker.

The men relay the information to the enans and the beasts respond accordingly. High pitch shrieks pierces the guard's ears as the outer patrol of the complex comes under attack. The hybrids cleverly widen their patterns, propelling themselves high in the air and directly into action. The enans move with surprising agility, matching that of their smaller Australian counterparts.

Elsewhere, two men patrol the outer edge of the compound. As they do, they witness an enan. "What the…hell?" "Don't know. I don't even know what I see," responds the driver.

Suddenly, an enan lands directly in front of the moving vehicle. The creature's feet absorb the thunderous impact, thus allowing the beast to hop away, vanishing as quickly as it appeared. The driver grabs his communicator. "Tower one, tower, this is patrol 3…we're under attack! We sighted something…uuuuggh!" Desperate words are cut short as the heads of both men roll outside the vehicle. And with little regard, the enan pounces high into the air, pilfering a screeching sound while bearing a fresh red stain upon the end of its tail.

So agile are the enans, that some of the men become victims of their own lofty attempts in trying to slay the beasts. With each appearance, blood spews into the night. Deadly black talons slash and tear chunks of flesh from the bowels of more unsuspecting victims.

Miles away, Stalker observes the events and relays a message to Colonel Ducet. "Sir, the situation appears to be going as planned. Preparing to send in second wave on your command."

"Stalker, if all is on course, set fire just beyond the perimeter and lay a fuel line to the side of the complex. Then, I want you to proceed with caution."

"Acknowledged... Gentlemen, send in the clowns."

Stalker's rebuttal is any thing but a circus as second wave culminates an advance near the west wall of the complex. Under the cover of smoke and darkness, the enans brutishly pound the wall, but their brutal onslaught is discovered by men patrolling the rooftop.

"Incoming!" The men fire upon the creatures, sending forth a terrible storm of hell fire; but the hybrid juggernauts savagely crash through their feeble defenses.

One enan enters through the door, another through a nearby window, and another through a second window, viciously ripping a wider entrance in order to gain access. Upon entering, the enans crush bodies while remarkably withstanding close range discharges.

Stalker's men relish the moment. "Sir, the building is breached. No hybrid casualties."

"Good, then you know what to do. After that...just make sure that no one knows what took place in that building."

"Aye sir!"

The hybrids immediately race downstairs, leaping, dodging, jumping over chairs, tables, casings, and railings; recklessly plowing a path through a gauntlet of enemy resistance.

As the enans advance, evasive happenings convene deeper within the complex. Four men desperately sort out what could be their eminent fate. One of the men turns to his associates and speaks with candid authority. "You must leave while you can Adir. You need not die just yet. Do you hear me?"

Adir despondently faces the man. His blood-shot eyes and leathery skin bears several abrasions. His only reprieve, a ripped uniform bearing the markings of bloody badges that shines as courage markers in the faces of his men.

He asks, "How did they find us?"

"Doesn't matter Adir... Become a martyr when others can witness your deeds. To die here without consequence, so dies the cause."

Adir rises to his feet and stares at the others in the room. All are silent, awaiting instructions with high anticipation.

"Barricade the door! What ever comes through will not live! Ala is with us!"

"Adir, we block the door, there's no other way out."

"Then here – is where we make our stand!"

Silence again grips the men as explosions rock the corridor outside the door.

The enans locate their target. One enan remains at the entry of the corridor while the other two proceed to Adir's hideaway.

"Stalker, they're there," states one of the operatives. "Implore the grapplers," commands Stalker. "Done!" The hybrids hang small devices to the hinges of the door and move several feet away.

One of the men inside the room asks, "What are they doing?" "We will soon know," responds Adir.

Smoke rises as the metal hinges slowly melt, dropping to the floor in a liquid form. Then, the huge vault door falls to the ground. Few seconds later, a screeching sound pierces the corridor. "FIRE!" Adir's command sends forth a current of bullets through the entryway, violently destroying everything in striking distance. However, the enans are nowhere in sight.

"Stalker to Eagle, we have them."
"Not just yet. I want visual confirmation first," replies Ducet.

As Stalker's command goes forth; the fiery lash of bullets halts.

"Reload...now! I'll try to hold them off!" Adir's cry is all but unheard as canisters roll upon the floor, releasing a deathly mist. "They're gassing us," cries one of the men. "Run for the door, fire your way through," commands Adir. Two men follow suite with preceding gunshots. One of the men enters the entryway. His desperate efforts immediately cease as he encounters an enan face to face.

The man's eyes widen as he stares into the deep red glow of the creature's eyes. Trembling and speechless, the man halts all forms of movement as the creature's visage immerges.

Suddenly, shots ring out, striking the hybrid several times at point blank range. The enan's scaly sheathing repels the onslaught and the beast lunges forward, colliding with the man and slamming him with such force that his broken body imbeds within the wall. The hybrid pounds through the entryway and claws a larger opening into the room. Adir's men furiously attack the advancing creature. Feeble attempts subside as the men find themselves lying on the floor with deep lacerations and mortal wounds.

Wasting no time, the creature dismembers their bodies and mutilates all the remaining gunmen. Only Adir remains.

Standing in disbelief, Adir manages to raise his weapon and fire off several rounds. His gun is more powerful than the others; yet, it barely pierces the creature's scaly armor. The enan shrieks and wildly slashes every thing in the room with its powerful tail. Soon, the stifling biped grabs Adir by the neck, lifts him off the ground, and chokes him to the point of suffocation.

Stalker attentively watches. "Stalker to Eagle... Is target confirmed?"

Colonel Ducet raises his head, placing both hands behind his back while staring at the monitor in a gratified manner. *"Adir Sa'ood. For ten years, you've been milking our government for your little skirmishes while prostituting our dollars. You take our weapons and conspire with your neighbors in order to attack us. Then you hide behind international laws while playing the innocent bystander. But as you can see; today, those laws will not save you."*

Adir Sa'ood, puzzled and confused, hears Ducet's voice emitting from the camera speaker. He watches with profound grief, painfully raising his voice to reply. "Wh...who...are...you?"

Ducet, reveling the moment gladly replies. *"Who am I? Someone you pissed-off a long time ago – and now – you die. Target confirmed!"* Suddenly, the enan plunges its claws into Adir's body and then violently rips him apart. Afterwards, the beast savagely crushes Adir's skull until nothing of his face remains.

"Stalker to Eagle, we have a confirmed kill."

"Good, now detonate."

Stalker's face immediately spurns with surprise. "But sir, Adir's dead and the enan is fine."

"Consider it a test – now do it!"

All other enans regroup, leaving the one enan with Adir's body. As both hybrids make an escape, the situation draws more unwanted attention.

Stalker's operative flips two switches on a remote keypad. Within moments, a gaseous cloud rapidly engulfs the enan as it stands near Adir's body. Sparks ignite within the cloud, culminating into a massive explosion. The complex crumbles as intense flames disintegrate everything. Helicopters and additional gunmen arrive upon the scene only to find a tremendous pile of rubble and bodies strewn everywhere.

Near the shore, the sea freighter quickly moves within range. Its rustic hull breaches the surface of the water, but not before Stalker, his operatives, and the remaining five enans climb onto the deck. Cascading waves slightly pound the craft as a single large cargo door opens. All enter the vessel.

Inside, Ducet eagerly greets his men. "Well done soldiers. A known terrorist is eliminated thanks to you and there are no identifying parties mentioned. Doing things this way absolves us from the UN's rules of engagement. We can now kill the enemy without them even knowing it…anytime, anywhere. Herein lies the testament of true power gentleman. Oh, don't worry about the enan because we can replace it anytime."

As Ducet speaks, Stalker approaches him. "Colonel, surely you are aware that Adir Sa'ood was only a puppet."

"Yes, but we have to fight through the pawns to get to the king. And when he shows his ugly face, I'll make damn sure I'm there to rip it off."

"Rightly spoken sir..."

"Yes, now listen; no one knows of our little escapade – not even base command or the joint chiefs."

"Understood sir…"

"Oh, by the way Essington…good job commanding the troops."

"Thank you sir."

As the door closes, the large craft departs, leaving behind mortal souls who bear the scars of chaos, confusion, and bewilderment. For such men, the holocaust of technological advancement leaves no comforting answers, no room for pity, or even a rational explanation. As the craft submerges beneath the dark waters, pooling ripples scathe the surface. Such subtleties are the only remaining signs of its presence as the craft leaves the Mediterranean Sea in its wake.

Elsewhere, deep in the Ukraine, seasoned blue eyes carefully gaze through a monitor as two enans step past four bodies that are lying face down. Both creatures exit an old dilapidated building. Outside, the enans cautiously take flight upon their powerful legs, making well their progress into the night and ultimately, taking cover inside a vehicle awaiting them. A man closes the doors as crates and cargo nets conceal the creatures.

The man, dressed in black rugged clothes, enters the cab of a ten-wheel freighter. He tells the driver to travel down a soiled road. The man, now a passenger, lowers his weapons. He retrieves a wireless microphone and a small computer.

Positioning the hardware upon his lap, he contacts the blue-eyed viewer, who is now on screen. "It is done," he says.

"Good. Do you know eef their leader was among them?"

"No, he was not."

"That eez okay. We weel find heem. Thees works, wee can get others like heem and avoid political red tape. Rham-kiev will fall and you receive good compensation – I will contact you later."

"I'll be waiting."

Both, man and driver smile as the transmission ends.

The man removes the driver's hood, exposing dark shoulder length hair, bedroom eyes, and peach colored lips; lips that compliment a devious but vivid smile. "I love it when a plan works," she says. "So do I..." The man friskily rubs her thigh, and works his way upward underneath her jacket, sensually touching. He kisses her as the large rig scurries away with a dangerous payload.

Later, forensic detachments and police arrive at the scene of the building where four bodies lay. An unmarked vehicle arrives as well. Then, a tall slender brown-haired man exits. A tanned trench coat drapes his body while touching the ankles of his heavy boots. The man observes several other bodies taken from the building and placed side by side; after which he earnestly entreats a nearby officer. "You there," he says.

"Yes," replies the officer, placing his hand on his gun, cautiously viewing his approaching questioner from head to toe.

"What happened here?"

"STOP and do not come any closer."

"I bare you no harm comrade, I assure you."

"Such matters here are privy in nature, but to whom would I be speaking, if such matters require a need to know?"

"Oh, forgive me. I am Detective Yuri Arimov of the Russian police and I have been tracking this group for quite some time."

Arimov displays his badge as the officer examines it. "And what group would that be detective?"

"Surely this is not the work of one man – do you think?"

"That is my point detective, no information has been released. Again, what brings you far down here comrade?"

Without a single word, Arimov spreads his arms and proceeds to make a semi-twist from his waist, looking around, chuckling as he alludes to the mass number of covered bodies laying on the ground and the personnel moving them.

"I see your point," says the officer.

Both men enter the building. "I did not know that the Russian police would have matters of concern down here. Perhaps you find we are incapable of handling our own incidents?"

"On the contrary," replies Arimov.

Both men carefully step over broken furniture and other structural debris. Passing personnel amidst the clamor, Arimov kneels beside the first body he encounters while the officer stands behind him. The detective raises a white sheet that covers a corpse and proceeds to examine the body. "Did you call animal control?"

The officer, appearing somewhat bewildered by Arimov's question, asks, "Are you suggesting that animals did this?"

"I am suggesting that a man may not have done that. See those slash marks in this poor fellow's chest? They are at least six inches deep. Unless you know of a man big enough to make a wound like that officer – with out a weapon of course, then we both can see that a human did not do this."

"My god," replies the officer.

Arimov grabs the dead man's hand, turning the palm side-up. He pulls the sleeve, exposing the wrist of the deceased. "See that?"

"What do you have there detective?"

"K *pacho,* a scorpion and the *monotok*, sign of the red scorpion and hammer."

"I do not understand."

"I am not surprised."

Arimov stands to his feet. As he does, the officer receives a document from one of his fellow policemen. As the officer begins reading the document, Arimov tells him, "For quite sometime we have been tracking *this* group. They disappeared for a while, but now they reappear…recently here in this town. These markings, the red scorpion and hammer are the markings of radicals called Rham-kiev. They strike with the terror of the scorpion and crush with force of the hammer. Control with fear is their intent, and as you may gather, these are not petty criminals or drug dealers – and this is not a common killing."

"Yes-It would seem uncommon; however, here is something you may find interesting detective."

"Oh?"

"According to this report, there are no survivors and the only eyewitness tells of something that looks like dinosaur with long legs, leaving the building. Or she thought she saw something like that."

Arimov looks at the officer while candidly smiling. "Then we have our first clue as to what may have happened."

"Conclusive so soon detective?"

"Would you believe that a dinosaur killed a group of radicals?"

"At this point, I do not know what to believe, but further investigation will reveal the truth, I am sure."

Both men display no emotion as Arimov leans against the wall of a nearby window.

The detective dawns a smile that quickly fades as he glances into the night sky.

"Dinosaur or not...something came and went. These people once lived, and now are dead. So where did you go my mysterious dinosaur?

~~~Farewell Team 429~~~

As Arimov's suspicions weigh heavily upon his mind, time and distance gives place to a windy morning in Texas. Sitting on a bench, near the main entry to GenoSyss is one of the more outward and colorful personalities of the company. His name is Frank Nunna'hi-tsune'ga Guilford and he is the direct descendent of a Chief by his native-born bloodline. Like his forefathers, Frank bares a name with regards to something that marks his very existence. Nunna'hi-tsune'ga means White-Path, a benevolent label given him by his Cherokee tribe as a youth since Frank chose to embrace teachings from white missionaries. Today, for reasons know only to him, Frank sits quietly, rubbing his eyes while massaging his head. Such faint mannerisms suggest tiredness.

But in an unrehearsed moment, Frank pulls a picture from within a black leather case. The picture depicts a woman whose skin is as pale and yet fair as any of her race. She displays a charming smile while wearing a blue denim dress. *'To My Husband with Love'* lavishly embroiders the front of the photo.

Frank solemnly stares. "Carolyn, if only I can see simplicity as you. I fear that I have helped to disturb God's creations. Ambition rules 429. Maybe I find other line of work. Maybe we place roots elsewhere now that Arthur's demon lives. When I see you today, we will conclude this matter." His quiet remarks fall upon deaf ears since the photo can only offer a silent image. With his head hung low, Frank places the photograph in his brief case.

He rises from the bench, but in his haste, the case opens, spilling all contents upon the ground. Frank tries frantically to retrieve the stirring documents, but the wind hinders his attempts. His feeble actions lead him around an empty parking lot and finally into bordering shrubs. "Where did you go you little…" Crawling upon his hands and knees, he finally reaches for one sheet of paper, but then he hears a whistle.

The sound captures his attention' yet to his surprise, a voice follows."Looking for this? I know it's very important to someone the likes of you."

Startled, Frank surprisingly looks upward. To his amazement, standing before him is a stern figure, dressed in black and wearing a hood – only the eyes are exposed. The figure holds the document in hand, just out of Frank's reach.

"Yes," Frank replies while standing to his feet. He cautiously approaches the figure. Frank reaches for the document while taking one-step, another step, and then another. But then, Frank slows his approach as if to determine whether or not the document is worth such an encounter.

Sensing an obvious disorder, Frank never breaks eye contact with the figure nor does he take a single breath. No words exchange between the two. Then, the figure slowly extends his arm with the paper clasped between two gloved fingers. Frank's fingertips touch the paper, and then he pauses. Cautiously, he takes a subtle breath and attempts to pull the document into his possession. Both stand motionless. Then, Frank confidently retrieves the document and turns away.

Suddenly, a cloth is placed over Frank's face from behind. He never sees it coming. Grunts and muffle screams shatter the placid atmosphere as Frank desperately tries to breathe. A scuffle breaks out. Incredibly, the hooded-figure sustains a violent kick to the chest, thus falling to the ground. Then, another stranger grabs Frank from behind. Fists collide with flesh as foul words fill the air. In a moment of direness, Frank cleverly manages to hold one of his attackers down by straddling the dark contender's chest. But even Frank's weight offers little assurance. "HELP, SOMEBODY HELP ME!" Frank's cry fills the area. His efforts are valiant; yet sadly, he never sees the blunt object in the hand of the other stranger. Frank violently succumbs to a staggering blow.

There are no deterrents as the second assailant finds the target of his intent. Frank slumps forward, but amazingly staggers to his feet. As if drunk, he tries to hold on to anything within reach. He stumbles to the ground, resting upon one knee, but quickly rises to his feet again. He places one hand on the rear of his head, desperately trying to ease the pain.

The attacker stands near with arms poised to deliver yet another blow. With no surprise, Frank falls forward, twisting and turning his body upon impacting the ground. In a convulsive state, Frank places both hands on the area where he was struck. Barely able to raise either arm, he offers no resistance as both aggressors quickly drag his body into a nearby vehicle and drive away.

The black leather case remains open while forceful winds carry off all remaining papers. Contained within the nomadic chaos is the photograph of Carolyn, adorning a blue denim dress, sailing high as the sun makes an awaking presence.

Later that day, the wind separates yellow and auburn color leaves from high twisting branches. Several of the leaves fall to the ground, congregating with similar kind, mixing and dancing to a mystifying choreography. Other leaves find a resting point on the roof of GenoSyss. Yet, the topside activity is only an act in time, corresponding with yet another activity below. Arthur and Gracella gather in an outside pavilion, taking full advantage of the scenery while seating themselves well away from co-workers.

Arthur opens a sketchpad and scans over information as well as several illustrational sketches. "It feels strange returning to our sections. Project 429 has become all but a distant memory. Grace. I can't forget what we've done."

"You haven't discussed the project with anyone, have you?"

"No."

"Not even Aniah?"

"She knows a few things."

"Arthur – you have to be careful."

"I didn't tell her everything. Besides, she's not that enthusiastic about Gjhe'nan. The last thing I need is to have more information leaking into her ears."

"Arthur, do you hear from the others?"

"I don't hear from anyone anymore, but you, and occasionally Walter. In conjunction to that, the company is also downsizing."

"All companies downsize Arthur."

"Yeah, but this is coming at a time when GenoSyss should be basking in the success of 429."

"I know. So…where did the funds from the defense contract go?"

"Is now a good time to say…I told you so?"

"Arthur, you have nothing to support your conspiracy suspicions."

"Look around Grace. Layoffs are already happening and our team is disbanded. I should have read the contract closer. I had no idea that we were not supposed to contact members of the team after we completed the project. Alexis is gone and I haven't seen Frank at all. Nathaniel is no longer in the research department. What kind of garbage is that?"

"I know…"

"What about Jade?"

"I saw Jade last month, but we had no time to talk. We don't really talk anymore. Besides…she's been acting different."

"Really…"

"Have you seen Rowland?"

"That jack-ass…"

"Arthur, stop it."

"He makes periodic appearances from time to time. Rumor has it that he may be leaving."

"I thought he was going on a business trip."

"That's what he says. At this point, you are the only person I see."

"Well, you may not be seeing me for much longer."

"Why?"

"I got my transferal papers one week ago. Problem is…I don't know where I'm going. It just says; *stand bye*."

Arthur's mouth hangs open. He rubs the bridge of his nose as a stern silence grips him.

"Are you ok?"

"Yeah…it's just…it's nothing."

"Arthur, have you noticed any thing out of the ordinary?"

"Grace, it's like, I know something isn't right but I can't figure it out yet. I haven't had much time to see anything. I've been traveling back and fourth to the farm – caring for *you-know-who*."

"How is Gjhe'nan doing?"

"He's behaving differently. He is more curious now than ever. If I didn't know any better, I'd say he's a human with long legs – which can't be too far from the truth. He has this insatiable appetite for knowledge, as if he needs to know every thing. He's even asking more questions. He's worse than my niece."

"What does he want from you?"

"He demands an explanation for every word defined. Why is the sky blue, why do people lack contentment, why are buildings made different, why lie, why trust, how many people are on earth, he even asked me if I had sex and when he could have sex."

"What? Oh God you're kidding..."

"Oh yeah...he knows about that. I just don't know if it's the animal or the human side that's talking.

"That is hilarious Arthur."

"I'll say, but of all the questions regarding any topic, any subject, God occur the most. Who is He, why can't we see Him, what is eternity, what is a spirit, what is a soul?"

"Are you saying that Gjhe'nan's got religion?"

"No – I am saying that he is curious, and I am quite sure that the human side of him is asking those types of questions. I feel that his little world is threatened."

"How does the knowledge of God pose a threat?"

"Grace – he's touching subjects he was never meant to know...and that could complicate things. The only way to pacify him is to buy time with useless subjects."

"Stalling him is not going to last forever."

"You should come and see him?"

"Well...Robert and I have plans, I think."

"He is much farther along than before. I'll show you."

"Heeeey… That's your business; I don't want to know what you two are doing in that barn."

"Get real…will you?"

Arthur playfully shoves Gracella as both return inside the building. To those who witness their meeting, it gives only a convincing impression of friendship, something normal as the sun drifting further on a westward course.

In another location, Alexis converses aloud as her earpiece relays information. Her conversation carries inside the confines of a shower, though her movements are completely without restraint.

"What? You mean he wants to see me? I think he looks great Lynn, but he's going to have a J-O-B if he wants me. You know that work is scarce since GenoSyss let me go. But it looks like Maryland will be calling me soon. GenoSyss made some hefty promises, but started letting more people go…I couldn't believe my ears. Wait a minute…"

Alexis turns towards a console. "System dry…" Muffle sounds emit as air jets bathe her with warm air, effectively drying every part of her body. With earpiece intact, she steps past frosted-glass. Shapely legs move with feminine grace side by side as high-arched feet carelessly leave a faint trail of damp footprints.

"So…what time will you be here, or do you want me to come and pick you up? -No…no…it's no problem, I can come get you. This is not like my other job where I had to get up early and become a virtual slave for some project. Look, it's no problem; I will come and pick you up. I'll get dressed and be over in a few."

Preoccupied, Alexis is unaware that a pair of electronic eyes are watching her every move. Several feet away, outside her residence, human eyes glance into a monitor as sound equipment captures her conversation. The monitor displays her form, outlining it in hues of orange, red, and yellow, with the background and other inanimate objects displayed in deep blue. Alexis grabs her wrist-key and hastily makes her way down stairs.

While approaching her vehicle, she drops the wrist-key. The impact drives the metal object under the vehicle. "Oh great…" Crouching to the ground, she extends her arm while scraping several bracelets against the concrete surface. Wide swinging motions push the key further away. After several attempts, she eventually secures the items.

"Gotcha!" With exuberance, her persona lightens, but in an instance, her actions cease as though years of perpetual instinct has taken over.

Frozen in motion, Alexis stares into oblivion, yet her overwhelming impulses prompt a curious action. She slowly turns her head. With impending concern, her eyes widen as her body begins to shake. Whatever her thoughts, the conformation could not have come any clearer.

Footsteps halt directly behind her. She makes a full turn and whisks a faint inhale. Staring at black heavy boots, she scans upward and identifies the handle of a gun that barely protrudes from the denim pocket of a silent figure. The figure is dressed completely in black and wears a hood.

Alexis never makes eye contact. "P...pl...please don't hurt me... Wh...wha...whatever you want, I...I...can..."

Her pleading offer never completes as a black bag is thrown over her head. With much contest, the figure subdues her. Muffling screams pierce the air, but no one comes to her aid. In the process, an unmarked vehicle screeches to a halt. The side door flings open and another shadowy figure emerges from within. Together, both assailants apprehend Alexis and with little effort, throw her into the back of the vehicle.

Inside, one of the assailants removes the hood from Alexis. "Is she the package?" The assailant's question secures the driver's attention, which returns a clandestine stare. "She is the package and a fine one at that."

"And how did he say to deliver this package?"

"He didn't. I assume we will handle this one like the other one."

"Is that a fact?"

"Yes. But you should know that the...*lady*...thinks otherwise and has offered considerably more capital than our employer."

"Is that so?"

"Yes."

"That's always good."

"Sure."

"Does the *ladeee*... care how this package is delivered?"

"No – if delivered at all."

Both men eye each other and begin to display lustful grins while removing their hoods. Soon, the blonde haired man approaches Alexis and violently tears her sweater apart, then turns to the driver. "Hey, take the long way around – eh?"

Alexis eyes the blond haired perpetrator, and in a furious moment strikes him in the face. Drawing blood, she immediately proceeds to attack him, but he wrestles her down and sprawls on top of her. He quickly takes a gun and presses the barrel to her throat, mercilessly forcing her into idleness. Then, he slides the barrel onto her face, cocking the trigger while concluding his demeaning intent upon her forehead.

She slowly turns away while he unzips his pants. "You cannot know the big picture Blondie; what's really going on here. But do know this...one person wants you right where you are, and another wants you exactly where you're going. But me...personally, I just want a little fun – for now – love."

Exploiting eyes scan clad laced skin while a hideous laugh divulges sublime debauchery.

He courses his cold wet hands upon her and proceeds to have his way. He kisses her in the mouth, and then raises her skirt. As his dastardly motions causes her to move in an unscrupulous manner, her hands bend downward, allowing five bracelets to unnoticeably fall upon the floor. Her pitiful cries fade into silence as the vehicle scurries away.

As time passes, an encounter of another kind takes place as Arthur and Gracella make their way to the ranch of Hollis Brenan. Ramsey, Arthur's transport, barrels down a dirt road. The transport finally halts at the entry of the large white barn. Arthur unravels a video camera. "I thought it would be a good idea to record this, but I felt you needed to see it live."

"Oh well, seeing is believing..."

"Trust me Grace; you're gonna love this."

Both enter the barn. As they do, their distinct images imprints upon deep dark eyes. Emerging from the shadows is Gjhe'nan. His sheer, yet heavy form enters the light. Turquoise and burgundy tints swirl in a spectacular borage of color as the hybrid approaches both technicians. As usual, Arthur receives a gentle head nudge. "Hey boy, how are you? I brought what you asked for. You know who this is? Remember Grace? Sure you do." Gjhe'nan responds with a head gesture and a subtle shriek. "Gjhe'nan; what do you want to tell Grace?"

Like a child, the hybrid acquires a large board and places it on the ground, directly in front of Gracella. With the aid of a marker, Gjhe'nan grasps the utensil and manifests a written prologue. Sharp claws are no hindrance.

Gracella stares with amazement. "Wow... Is this for real? "

"Sure it is... He wanted to see you after I told him more about you. But he thinks that I may have created you."

"Some of the words run together but I can still make sense of his writings."

"Go ahead, tell him."

Gracella touches Gjhe'nan's nose. "Arthur did not create me. I am my own human." Gjhe'nan tilts his head. "Does he understand that word?"

"Sure... He understands a great deal of words in the English language."

"Why is he staring at me – like that?"

"He thinks you're cute...for a human."

"Oh..." responds Gracella, while blushing. "Arthur, this is remarkable. He knows who he is but does he know what he is?"

"Not clear at this point. As you can see by the inscriptions on the walls, he's definitely working things out."

"I thought their training only aloud them to understand basic sentence structure with very specific meanings."

"So did I."

"But those writings are complex Arthur."

"I told you that you wouldn't believe me."

"You are telling me that the dictionary provides definitions while the encyclopedia and grammatical English books give him a much broader understanding of word usage?"

"And we...somehow bridge the connection of understanding between the two – for now."

"Simple enough..."

"Somehow, he reads simple, but forms a complex understanding of words. He's quite an intellectual in an undeveloped way."

"If that is so, then he is no longer the ideal candidate for the military."

"What do you mean?"

"You do recall that Ducet wants the unconditional obedience of a soldier, especially when given a direct order. How much more do you think he will allow an animal to question his authority?"

Immediately, Gjhe'nan nudges Arthur. "Oh sorry..."

"What was that all about?"

"He doesn't like to be referred to as an *animal*."

"Opps...my bad..."

"There are times when he'll try to relate to something; similar in appearance to himself, then he'll bug me for the answer. As of yet, I don't fully know how he ascertains an understanding through his thought process, but he somehow manages to read and comprehend beyond just doing what he's told to do."

"Maybe that task best suits a psychologist Arthur."

"I guess..."

"Are the other enans capable of this type of communication?"

"Capable, but they are not unique like him."

"In what way?"

"The military doesn't control what Gjhe'nan is taught."

Gjhe'nan moves one of the boards forward and gently taps on the wooden surface. "Grace, I think he wants you to finish reading."

"Oh…of course. 'U I trust …help 2 find others.' Arthur, what does it mean?"

"I believe he wants to see the other enans. It's the social part of him."

"At least he is aware of what happened to him during the procedure."

"He knows that we cloned from him."

"You told him – didn't you?"

"Even he has a right to know."

"But Rowland forbid you giving that part of knowledge to him."

"Go figure Grace. If he can read a dictionary, don't you think he can figure out what we did?"

"Well then…when reality finally hits – do you honestly believe you can keep him here indefinitely?"

"You know why I had to bring him here."

"Bringing him…is one thing, keeping him…is something else; despite that he was never yours to take."

"C'mon. If the military was ready to kill him, don't you think they will kill the other enans as well?"

"Maybe, but again, that is not your concern."

"I thought you were on my side."

"I am, but I'm also curious."

"About what?"

"Arthur, did you ask God for His opinion?"

"I didn't know God had a concern in this matter."

"That's my point. Why bother with God at all if you already have your own plans laid out?"

"This isn't about religion."

"You of all people know what I mean."

"I fail to see the relevance."

"The basis for a person's belief usually dictates his or her actions. In this case, I think you are heading for a tailspin and you will not see the relevance until something unfortunate happens."

"Why is everybody riding me?"

"Arthur, if you cannot let something go, that was never yours to begin with; then you are setting yourself up for a big disappointment – or maybe something worse. It makes me believe that you planned to take Gjhe'nan all along – Or did you?"

"I'm not hearing this."

"Then hear this. Your actions will turn into something undesirable if you keep pressing on this road of yours. I will pray for you, as well as myself, because I helped you, thinking that maybe…there was something going on."

"Having a change of heart?"

"Just…re-thinking my actions, Arthur."

"You know I wouldn't jeopardize your safety."

"I know, but sometimes good intentions can still hurt – unintentionally."

Gracella looks at Arthur and closes her eyes. Both sit upon a hay bale as though condemned to serve time. Gjhe'nan gazes at them both, as the day quietly passes into the evening.

The sun sets as a man approaches a small sports car and proceeds to open the driver-side door. A semi-empty parking lot is all but quiet as birds migrate southward on an unknown course. Prior to entering the vehicle, the man tosses a sleek brief case upon the passenger seat.

The case lands key side up, displaying the embroidery letters of T.N.V. The man is Tuan Nguyen Vein and he has concluded a long day of work. Tuan's gift to GenoSyss lay in his ability to bring strength to the molecular and cytogenesis portion of 429's development. Since his departure from Hanoi, he has delivered remarkable results; however, he shows little ethical attachments for any of the projects.

Shortly afterwards, the hum of a finely tuned engine roars to life. Afterwards, a black canopy top contracts and folds backwards into a small compartment behind two seats. Large speakers begin to pound heavy bass overtones, vibrating everything within close proximity. Screeching tires signify an exit as the vehicle swiftly moves down the expressway.

Minutes into the drive, Tuan realizes that he is the only driver traveling the road. But suddenly, his solo state ends as a large mysterious passenger van pulls along side of him. The driver of the van makes eye contact, and yet both drivers never really acknowledge each other. As the van thrusts forward, it leaves the smaller sports car behind.

Then, without warning, the van veers directly in front of Tuan and comes to a screeching halt. Tuan is unable to avoid contact as air bags deploy and the car burrows beneath the rear bumper of the van. The car sustains severe damage while coming to a gruesome halt.

Immediately, the rear doors of the van open and a shadowy figure emerges. The figure forcefully leaps into the windshield of Tuan's car. Breaking the windshield, the figure lands in the passenger seat of the vehicle. Tuan, though dazed, sees the figure and manages to open the door. He desperately runs toward a nearby neighborhood.

The driver of the van sees Tuan and quickly assists his co-operative. "Get'em before he gets away!" Both men direly attempt to catch Tuan, but the frightened geneticist closes the distance to nearby houses.

Suddenly, a car enters the road and draws their attention. "Dammit, look," cries one of the assailants.

Tuan alters his course and makes a daring run for the approaching vehicle. "Help me...HELP ME!!" His distressing alarm is barely heard, but the driver of the approaching car sees the unusual situation and stops. A man rises out of the vehicle and makes his declaration known. "Hey...what are you two doing to him? I'm calling the cops!" The man gets in his vehicle and proceeds to call.

The assailants cease their pursuit, but one of the men makes an alarming observation. "You idiot...they can see you!"

"What are you talking about?"

"Your hood man, you forgot your hood!"

The hoodless assailant quickly touches his face and courses his scraggly blond hair, only to find that his partner has made a correct observation. "Idiot, you know what we have to do...NOW!" The hooded figure's command calls for a quick response as his partner pulls out a large silver gun. In seconds, thunderous sounds resonate as six chambers rotate; blaringly hurling three projectiles with deadly accuracy until each bullet ferociously penetrates both human targets.

Tuan falls to the ground as the driver slumps within the seat of his car.

One of the assailants grabs two items from the van and sprays the license plates of Tuan's car. The solution dissolves the plates into a molten lump of silver. At the same time, the man throws a device inside the car and gets back into the van. He hurriedly pulls along side of his co-operative who drags Tuan's body inside while leaving the driver of the other vehicle lying in his place.

Once inside, the man slides the side door shut. "You...lay low now - before someone sees you mate. We've got to report; things have changed."

"How did he want this package?"

"Our employer wanted to question this one, but again, her price was higher; just drive..."

"If that's the case, then nothing's changed."

The hooded driver affirms his concerns to his blond haired partner who brandishes a demonic smile. "Cheerio then," he replies.

As the assailants hastily exit the scene, a loud fiery explosion disintegrates the sports car into countless pieces of twisted metal and burned fabric. The paramount event immediately draws a crowd of curious on-lookers. Yet, the resounding chaos leaves nothing for the imagination. Within a nearby field, a tiny faceplate baering the initials T.N.V. lays brandished among the debris.

On tranquil shoals, near a serene shoreline, two bodies leisurely walk upon rustic cobblestones on the outskirts of lake front property. Tranquil waters glisten under the moonlight as quiet inlets flow only a few yards away. Pond laden fish bobble for misfortunate insects as birds serenade the night with a subtle melody. Kerosene flames flicker inside antique lanterns, bathing each stone while painting a vivid pathway with a soft yellow luminance. Tantalizing stars speckle the dark heavens as an unseasonable warmness engulfs the surrounding elements.

Soothing winds expose his chest, separating the unbutton fabric with each wave of forceful flow. Her dress waves to a rhythm of the breeze, revealing bare legs to the cover of night. Childish laughter flows between the two as moments of conversation dwindle little by little. Masculine hands gently hold and caress soft slender fingers, fingers possessing nails of high polish and manicuring compliment. She gently lays her head upon His higher shoulder while his arm wraps her closer to his side. Though their strides are uneven in length, their understanding compensates for such dainty differences.

Both make their way down a wet portion of the walkway, yet to each other's surprise, their light garments soon bear the markings of an active sprinkler system. She quickly discards her sandals as spontaneous laughter shrouds the event. They rush forward and finally make their way to a front door, to which a porch light gracefully illuminates the letters 4A.

He wipes her hair as she wipes his shirt, manually drying each other amidst the cozy area. Soon, their actions cease as they quietly stare at each other for a moment. Charming smiles form as their eyes find a common language. He gently caresses her shoulders as she leans forward, placing her head softly upon his chest. They stand quietly for a moment; but then, she scans the key sensor and proceeds to open the door.

Upon entering, she turns on the interior lights while he remains standing outside, just beyond the threshold. Slowly, she turns, and then stares directly into his eyes. He intently watches, but then she slowly turns and walks away while leaving the door open. Communicating without words, he receives her invitation and enters. The door closes and the two find themselves within an atmosphere all their own.

She does not leave his presence; instead, she dims the lights and passively renders him a gentle kiss. He removes his shirt just as her dress falls upon bare feet, only exposing violet painted toenails. In like manner, the removal of garments continues until all that remains are silhouette bodies against the backdrop of a window. Neither barriers nor concerns become evident as both eagerly embrace, tightly holding, caressing, and stimulating one another while yet standing; continuing such actions until they lay atop white linen.

Passions ignite as ecstasy rises, giving, receiving, delivering, and reciprocating, filling each other's senses right down to the very nature of erotic indulgence. Groaning pleasantries erupt as rhythmic motions embellish human form, driving their binding expressions well into the passionate seclusion of the night.

In the waning hours, all that lingers is the heartbeat of either counterpart, as they lay interlocked in each other's embrace.

The morning sun fills the room as both awake. Her head lies upon his chest while his hand gently plows through her waves of dark tangled strands. Tilting her head, she greets him with a smile. Green eyes peer deeply into the meekness of his and at that moment, a communication of words begins to form.

"I often wondered about this moment between us," she says.

"So have I. Ever since those days in the lab, I kept thinking about you and wanted to see you but was too afraid to ask."

"Ask? What did you think silly, that I was going to bite you?"

"Praying mantises and black widows teach us males to render our intentions...very...carefully."

"You are still alive – are you?"

"A pleasant surprise..."

"So now what do you think?"

"I think you are...how you say – Easy?"

She pinches him and laughter soon follows, but silence quickly grows in the moment of their interlude.

Then, Jade leans closer to Walter and renders him a sincere expression. "It is simple. There was only one suitor in my life – so now, you have potential. At least you are here for me – Yes?"

"Jade, I always wanted to be there for you."

"After I heard you were reassigned, I looked for you. I thought I lost you."

"I thought I'd never see you again, so I moved on – didn't know what else to do."

"The agency did not release information. I had to track you down."

"That must have been hard."

"Yes."

"I'm glad you did."

"I do not see any of the team, except Arthur, and I have not spoken to Gracella in months."

"Do they know about us?"

"Gracella does. She introduced us – Remember?"

"Oh – I forgot… But I last saw those two in Ennis."

"Ennis… What for?"

"Uh…some farm work."

"You and Arthur are farmers?"

"Well, I can multi-task when the occasion calls for it."

"A jack of trades – I see..."

"Close enough." Walter tightly embraces Jade, attempting to divert his statement. "Jade, I know we've covered a lot of territory fast, but I would never hurt you. It's just that, well…this compromise…"

"What compromise? Are you referring to my past?"

"If you are not ready to tell me, I'll understand but please don't shut me out."

"Walter, you have no idea. I am trying to protect you."

"From what?"

"Not now – please."

"Jade, would I love you any less for knowing?"

"Would you love me any more if you never knew?"

"Then what's the point of those conversations with Gracella?"

"Walter, my past is just that – the past. And as far as Gracella's discussions, there are many things about Jesus that I do not understand, but I know that people who have such belief in Him do what we have just done."

"To express love…before getting a certificate?"

"It is called fornication."

"Oh… Well…I didn't see any convictions last night."

"Walter, tell me it was not a meaningless act?"

"For some…maybe, but after all this time, isn't it obvious what you mean to me?"

"I want to hear it, from you."

"What more can I say?"

"Sometimes…I need to hear."

"Jade, I have no problem with you taking this Jesus route, especially if it gives you a new beginning."

"That is not what I want to hear."

"Then what is it you want to hear?"

"Walter, you still do not get it."

"You haven't been exactly clear."

"Marriage is no guarantee for what you want - especially from me."

"Marriage...love. Is this what you want to hear from me? Jade, is that all you think I want?"

"I don't know."

"Jade, am I just flesh for your own desires or a man who simply desires fulfillment from someone he..."

"Say it."

"...he cares for?"

"Those words are not fair. You never said you loved me."

"Then what does that make you?"

"I need time."

"I don't know how long I can wait for you."

"Then love is not patient."

"I did not mean that."

"I am foolish for wanting family and normal life. Maybe I should have stayed away – and say nothing."

"What would that accomplish?"

"Walter, there is much that I want to tell you but involvement *weeth* me may not be good thing for you."

"There's another partial statement."

"Not now Walter, please...not now."

Jade clutches Walter's wrist ever so tightly and buries her head once more on his chest. Walter lays motionless as though his thoughts have taken complete control of his movements, and yet, she holds his hand until he closes his eyes, never seeing the trickle of tears streaming down her face.

While Jade and Walter ponder their thoughts, the threshold of familiarity finds its way into the walls of GenoSyss once more. Tasks and assignments are all but typical for the employees of the now weltering company. But for the remaining employees, one of GenoSyss most prominent minds stands before them, perhaps for the last time. The center's former director, Rowland Kreshenkov addresses an audience.

"We have seen the best and worst of times, yet triumphed until end. I am glad to have worked weeth such finest group of you all. Yet, again comrades, though our past projects were successful – our downsizing has not taken away our ability to supply pharmaceutical companies *weeth* ground breaking information and results. Some of you stayed while others of you go...*wheech* leaves more rrr-rubbies for me than you, I think – Yes?" Sparks of laughter break forth as Rowland continues his charming deliverance. "*Dees* agency continues doing very well. As stated before, Mr. Hues *iz* your new director and I am quite sure he *weel* do good job...well!"

Applause engulfs the room as personnel looks on. The old and new directors exchange handshakes as they both step from behind the elaborate podium and into the midst of the group.

Rowland strategically makes his way pass the mixture of bodies and into the presence of non-other than two other familiar faces. Unlike most in the audience, these two do not express sentimental exuberance, especially one.

"*Vwell, vwell*...Arthur and heez faithful companion...Gracella."

"I'm not his dog – thank you very much."

"No insult intended Gracella. *Eeetz* just that... I am surprise to see you both still here. You are truly each other's shadow, truer for you Meester Rrro-binson – I theenk. Not to denote color of your skin but your lack of adventure beyond project 429."

"I've heard worse. But then again, that's no longer your concern – *eezn't eet?*"

"Ha ha ha...very coy and nicely done...but no. My time here is finished!"

"I can remember when this room had as many as 400 or so people, now we only have about 25 percent in attendance. I suspect that over budgeting and lack of funding killed 429's blessings."

"That *iz*...ah...management issues. Much things beyond my control Arthur."

Rowland scans the scene, and then moves closer to both technicians. "*Dhere eez* something I *weesh* to speak to you. Would you *pleeez* excuse us Gracella." "Sure," she says.

"Arthur, I need not remind you of your sworn oath concerning 429's disclosures. We have your signature – Remember?"

"Get to the point, but remember, I no longer work for you…you bastard!"

Curious glances peer towards both men as Rowland skillfully plays off Arthur's heated response. "Let professional courtesy prevail Meester Rrr-obinson. *Shuush*…how dare you? Quiet your voice."

"Then enlighten me."

"Management set rules; you knew then as you know now. Others on 429 team got higher compensation because of degrees. You do not have degree from University of management's liking, so your efforts were counted as contribution – end of story."

"But you could have changed all that."

"Regardless; but, now to matter at hand... Remember when 429 was here in basement rooms?"

"Like flies on cow shit."

"I see… Well…our inventory for Colonel Ducet counts thirty-*seex* enan clones dee-livered, but our records confirm thirty-seven enans generated, including your g-nan. One record has your signature during final stages of delivery – we are missing an enan. Do you know any *theeng* of this?"

"Not off the top of my head."

"Are you sure?"

Arthur thinks for a moment. He says nothing as though a strange form of conviction paralyzes his ability to speak. Then without conscience or forethought, Arthur stares Rowland directly in the eyes and advances closer to his face. "Yes, I'm sure." A shady smile forms upon Rowland's face as he stares back at Arthur. "Of course Meester Rrr-obinson."

"Rowland…there's something about Ducet."

"Oh?"

"I don't think he's going to use the enans for inhumane reasons."

"*Vwhere* deed you get that en-formation? *Mee*litary paid for 429, *eetz* theirs for taking."

"I'm saying that in situations of mass slaughter, hell-bent executions without accountability usually merit a retaliatory backlash. Such is the case of degrading human slaughter."

"Get to point."

"Where is the love of God when such extremes are taken in order to silence the souls of men, even if they are our enemies?"

"You make good politician Arthur - I think."

"This is not a joke."

"Indeed… Now you hear me, I listen to you and your truth is a lie and your advice *eez* persuasive. I grow tired of you."

"Rowland…wait…"

"Das vidaniya Arthur Rrr-obinson."

Upon Rowland's departure, Gracella approaches Arthur. "What was that all about?" Arthur does not respond immediately. He stares at Rowland who continues making his way deeper into the crowd.

"I just lied and he knows it."

"Arthur, you know what happens if you keep digging yourself in deeper."

"And the truth shall set me free… Right?"

"I'm serious."

"Haven't you heard Grace? We the People of the United States, in order to form a more perfect Union, establish justice, insure domestic tranquility, provide for the common defense, hell…even promote general welfare for the people…blah, blah, blah."

"Oh Arthur, don't give me that line of crap! You know as well as I that every one is out for them selves; and you; of all people, are continuing to justify what you did."

"Still riding my ass… Gee, would you hand me my bow and arrow, along with my green tights so I can give something back to the people."

"This is not a joke Arthur."

"Neither is standing around and waiting for something to happen. Need I remind you Grace that taking no action when it's time to take action, is just as bad as promoting unwanted action."

"Action against whom: Rowland, management, Ducet…and for what? There are papers you sighed by your own admission that are sitting in Michael Gladestone's office – it kills me how you fail to remember that."

"You drive a hard bargain woman; just be ready when it all hits the fan!"

"Arthur, are you so close to that thing you created that you can't even see how clouded your vision is?"

"Gjhe'nan is a product, not a reason."

"Oh, excuse me – I'm not talking about Gjhe'nan. I'm talking about your ego, your pride, that thing in you that all men must complete before they turn 40 or 50, even 60, such that has no eternal significance what so ever."

"Midlife – get real."

"I'm talking about leaving your mark in life – ALL men do it – or try."

"Who doesn't? Men leave their mark; women go on bio clocks to reproduce."

"What does Aniah think about your conspiracy theory?"

"Aniah thinks what ever she wants."

"Is that so?"

"Look Grace…*dammit*…GenoSyss used me like a tramp, like a two-dollar whore. When they got what they wanted, they tossed me aside like a douche rag."

"It's called a job."

"Whatever…just know that I'll kill Gjhe'nan before I let them take him."

"So – if you can't have him then no one else can. Is that your point?"

"A great love affair – wouldn't you say?"

"It's called misguided possessive syndrome, and people with mental disorders do that."

"You're not funny."

"Arthur, you're not making any sense to me."

"What have I been trying to get you to see all along? In the right hands, Gjhe'nan can benefit others."

"Whatever... Granted, that may be true, but look at you. You're tired, glossy eyed, loosing weight."

"For God's sake, you're sounding like Aniah."

"Good."

"No…bad."

"As I told you before Arthur, this isn't about religion. This is, and has always been about you and Him."

"Make no mistake; I have more respect for demons than people. At least demons show their true colors all the time."

Gracella raises her hands in the air. "Finally…the truth."

"Enlighten me…please."

"You're trying to get back at GenoSyss by taking Gjhe'nan? And you're justifying the act because people you once trusted have scorned you, including the church? This is your act of defiance, your rebel with a cause response – Right? All that has happened to you has turned into this Robin Hood insanity of yours."

"Point taken, but even muddy waters settle."

"When that happens, it is called clarity. Everything you said has absolutely nothing to do with Gjhe'nan or GenoSyss."

"Then explain Dr. Freud."

"As I said before Arthur, you quickly jump into challenges or projects that originate from humble or justifiable beginnings. Once involved, you frequently open your heart to the cause. Your talents and skills allow you to created powerful results and for a moment, you're at the top of your game. But then, due to a decision or an opinion that is out of your control, all your efforts and results slip right pass your fingertips and into the hands of someone else. Then you are ultimately left with something far less than what you started with. That has happened to you way too often. Now, you are making a decision that you know is wrong. You have to forgive those people who hurt you and let God help you to let it all go."

"Forgive them? I curse them all to hell."

"I hope you really don't mean that. I hope you listen to Him."

"God is not my problem."

"But isn't it interesting that He always has something to say, but we choose not to listen."

Arthur's face tightens as veins swell above his brow. Gracella watches while kindly putting her hand on his shoulder. Arthur lowers his head as she departs.

Rowland makes his way through an isolated hallway of the building. Finding seclusion, he secures a position near a parlor and retrieves a wireless device from his coat pocket. A series of clicks and dial tones denotes an attempt to gain access; however, a connection soon beckons the response of an ominous voice. Familiarity sets the stage once more.

"Your suspicions were *rright*. Arthur is lying, but a misfortunate oversight for *heem*. I do not have to tell you what threat an extra enan rrunning loose can do to us. Besides, you should be well on your way by now. Oh, less I forget…good job in Mediterranean. I contact you later."

Rowland proceeds to press more numbers, and as before, he makes contact with yet another voice over the transmission. "Listen; there are five more workers remaining. Among them is Arthur Rrr-obinson. I *veel* give you *heez* schedule and you *weel* take care of *heem* like others. Now you must be careful when dealing *weeth* Arthur. Gracella *eez* close to *hem*, so time your actions *weeth* our final departure; else much attention will come to us – Understand? Now show less incompetence and cover your tracks well. Prevent your stupidity from creating more mishaps, like the apprehension of Tuan. I contact you later." Having concluded his conversation, Rowland places the small device in his pocket and departs.

Returning home, Arthur acquaints himself with Aniah, who seemingly desires information regarding the events of his day. But Arthur is not forthcoming as they sit snuggly upon a sofa. While watching a movie, Arthur grows with intrigue.

"I always love this part. This is where the whale tears up the harbor and there's nothing anyone can do to stop him."

"Why?"

"He's trying to get some guy who killed his pod, his family, so he's making a point by terrorizing the harbor. The whale is just too plain smart for the guy, as well as the whole town."

"If the whale is that smart, then why doesn't he just write his terms down on paper and give it to PETA or Greenpeace?"

"Real funny, but in case you haven't noticed, whales don't write."

"Maybe he's just not that smart after all."

"All right Einstein, just how else can that animal get his point across?"

"That whale's brain is supposed to be larger than ours – Right? Then it seems to me that it should be able to do something without smashing docks or sinking boats just to prove a point. I don't know…maybe throw a fin or tail in the air…or etch something in the sand."

"The size of a brain and the intelligence to go with it means nothing if you lack the ability to communicate. Only then does a violent act become the logical recourse."

"Says who?"

"Humanity woman…"

"Well that proves my point. That whale is bi-polar and has serious mood swings while acting out in violence. Or he's simply stupid!"

"Just like a woman," says Arthur as he tickles Aniah.

Both conjure silly jesters before one another, accompanied with facial expressions, pinching, and mock fighting. Their playful bantering creates enough noise to rival a room full of rambunctious toddlers. In the end, they hardly notice a torn pillow, broken vase, and spilled water as the result of their childish antics. Having completed their folly, both sit upon the sectional, observing the screen while recuperating from their prior enactments. Then, Aniah stares at Arthur. "What is it…what are you looking at?"

"I'm looking at you, silly. You seem to be more relaxed; at least here at home now that your secret project is over."

"I hope so."

"Don't worry Sweets. I'm not going to bring the job up, but you are a little more restful."

"If that's true, then I apparently lead a double life. Grace thinks I'm rigid and full of hate."

"You are to some degree, but you're still less tense than usual."

"I was trying to accomplish something before they took it all away."

"How long will you continue? Surely you know that, that thing…"

"Gjhe'nan."

"Whatever…Gjhe'nan can't stay hidden inside Hollis' barn forever."

"You only saw the video of him, but I tell you that he's far beyond what Rowland or the Military intend. He knows who he is and it's only a matter of time before he discovers what he really wants. Even now he wishes to find others like himself."

"Then if what you say is true, can he effectively communicate this to you?"

"Gjhe'nan is not quite like a household pet, or even the whale in the movie. He can read and write."

"That is all good, but can he interpret feelings, situations, or decipher a purpose or intent on the same level as a human? How does he interpret that kind of information? After all, does he think in color or black and white? What is his philosophy and does he have a religion to govern his actions? How much of Gjhe'nan is human and how much is animal? Are you his mentor and if so, then, how much of you, is in him? Yes, unlike the whale, he can read and write, but like the whale, if his desire outweighs his ability to achieve an objective, communicate a need, or facilitate a means to an end, then violence will more than likely become his only recourse."

Arthur looks silently at his consult. He slowly blinks, and then looks downward. "I'm sorry, I didn't mean to bring this up," Aniah tells him.

"That's okay. As usual, you bring another perspective to the matter."

"Let's get some sleep." Through voice activation, Arthur silences the screen as both prepare for the evening.

As they pass the message board, Aniah suddenly stops and reaches for a yellow sheet of paper. She draws Arthur's attention. "Oh, by the way, I almost forgot honey. There was a lady who called earlier. She wants to contact you and says that it is very important. She also says that she has something of tremendous interest to you and it's in regard to your line of work."

Arthur takes the small sheet of paper in hand. At a glance, he stares at the fluid lines, which curve into a single focal point. He lowers the paper and places it near the counter top. "Angelica Banks; never heard of her but I'll give her a call." Aniah takes Arthur by the hand and leads him to the bedroom as the hall lights soon darken and the night casts its silent cloak over the city.

Though darkness symbolizes a time of rest, the city continues to thrive with bustling movement. Part of the movement transpires in the far southern part of the county as a large van carries two men down an interstate. The vehicle winds its way upon a long narrow dirt road. The road sets in ghostly isolation from all directions. Approaching a gated entry, one of the men exits the van and attaches an electronic device to the keypad of the entryway. He presses a few buttons and the gate immediately slides open, allowing both men to make their way towards a modest ranch house. Cautiously, the men travel several yards along the outskirts of hog plums and milk berries. With lights off, the vehicle slowly approaches a gravel-laden driveway and halts. Both men cover their heads as three black mustangs lightly trot across the open field.

One of the hooded figures taps several keys on a keypad while raising the view screen of a computer. He summons his aid. "Look there. Heat signatures confirm that there are only three bodies inside the house."

"Fortunate for us, the old geezer doesn't get out much after sunset. In any case, our mistress lady has out bided the Russian again and she's put a nice price on this guy's head."

"Did she say why she wants this one?"

"You know we don't ask questions. Besides, it's beyond me. Any ways…, she wants'em done away with, and as long as the cash keeps flowing, I'll keep working."

"Nathaniel Keech is the package this time and his family may be in there with him, except for one of his daughters."

"That changes nothing, so let's nab the old bloke and come out grinning like a fox – Eh?"

"Half pass the quarter hour and there's no movement inside."

"Then it's time mate. This station is only sixty two-hundred square-feet…two-story, and we've each got twenty seconds tops. You take the low road," says one of the men; chuckling his diabolical laughter as the engine continually operates.

Bypassing door sensors, both men prepare to enter the house.

Prickly shards tatter the wooden floor as both intruders toss canisters inside. The canisters explode, releasing an ominous gas as it whisks throughout the lower rooms. Suddenly, the front door forcefully swings open, impacting the doorknob into the panel molding. As the gaseous mist waves from the motion of the door, both men enter the house, pointing launchers with one hand and holding firearms in the other. With masks tightly strapped, the men immediately begin inspecting the rooms, combing the area for the unsuspecting.

The intruders separate, as one runs upstairs into the darkness.

Suddenly, a bedroom door swings open and a young woman dashes out. She engulfs the fumes. Her dismal actions turn horrid as she immediately coughs and salivates, then falls to the floor in a desperate attempt to comfort her watery eyes. Yet, to the invader's surprise, the woman discerns trouble. She quickly rises to her feet and hurls her self directly into his chest. Fist feverishly pound hard canvass, but to no avail as the intruder raises his weapon and fires. After neutralizing his victim, the assailant proceeds to the final door.

Hearing the noise, his accomplice joins him. Upon approach, he takes a glimpse of the fallen woman. "Was that necessary?" "Only a flesh wound." His partner shrugs his shoulders and both men eventually approach the remaining door and prepare to kick it open.

Silence stirs, but suddenly, the door swings open and there to greet them both is a double-barrel shotgun held by none other than Nathaniel Keech. "GET OUTTA' MY HOUSE!" Blistering fire projects beyond two black barrels, sending one of the intruders mercilessly plummeting to the floor. The other intruder returns fire of lesser magnitude, but no less effective as Nathaniel falls forward to the ground. "Awww...my knee...you callous sons-of-bitches!" The assailant hits Nathaniel with the shoulder piece of the rifle, silencing his agonizing cries.

His fallen partner rises to his feet, feebly standing while covering the brandish area where the shot made contact. "Will you live?" His partner's question goes unanswered as he painfully assists in dragging Nathaniel's body.

But the other accomplice sees Nathaniel's wife, Mary. He slowly raises his gun, points it at her and squeezes the trigger. "No, not part of the deal," yells his injured partner as muffled sounds project loudly through his mask.

Mary pulls a blanket just beneath her chin as though it becomes a magical shield. She squirms into the headboard of the bed, drawing her legs inward while shaking like a frightened child. The perpetrator eyes Mary and lowers his gun. He pulls from his harness another canister, releases the latch, and tosses the canister upon the floor. Thick plumbs of smoke quickly saturate the room as he closes the door and severs the doorknob. Afterwards, he drives a long steel item through the panel of the door and into the side molding, seizing the door shut. Dire coughs persist from the other side of the door. "She can at least open the window and jump – even if it is a two story drop."

Both men secure Nathaniel.

They carry Nathaniel's body downstairs and drag him through the front door, though paying no attention to the shards of glass cutting deep into Nathaniel's flesh. Without hesitation, they put Nathaniel inside the van and plunge the vehicle forward, violently smashing through the nearest section of fence and vanishing beyond the foothills of the land.

Eventually, fresh air enters the lingering house as the alarm desperately summons the city's finest.

~~~Contemporary Sultana~~~

Dark times immersed GenoSyss and following those terrible events were broken families, destroyed dreams, and crushed hopes – We who remained were so afraid. Black forces were driven by lust, power, and dominance, even revenge; and yet, some of us paid dearly for someone else's decisions. In point of fact, a stark reality of man's character seizes all hopes of a trusting outlook; noting that people, in general, try to control, manipulate, or even debauch trusting believers. Such ill mortal beings perpetuate nothing less than preposterous sins – and sadly, their acts characterize events of modern day synagogues. To my surprise, I've witnessed both accounts.

However, the moon continues to radiate in the sky and even now accompanies me in the early morning hours. Gazing at her lucid body continues to stir the deepest feelings of humanity within me: sympathy, remorse, concern, compassion, and even the most celebrated but often misunderstood element of all – love.

Of all my troublesome moments, it is conceivable that my earthly possessions are cast into shark infested waters and that I am made to walk upon a lofty plank in order to retrieve them. Perhaps a lesson to be learned, or a wakening reality, nonetheless, I sit here quietly, dancing in the shadows of perilous thought. But this one flickering moment in time dares me to remain idle.

Even now, my most prized companion was once a victim when I laid into the clutches of deceit – having suffered all for the sake of a moment. Heaviness burdens me, pressing me with tiresome guilt and antiquating thoughts. But just when it seems too difficult to bear, one single truth soothes my imprisonment. God has somehow hidden me behind a mountain and protected me from my own beguiling heart. He put me in the shadow of his presence. And though comforting, several plaguing thoughts of *what-ifs* present a tantalizing appeal.

In retrospect, I did not want to hide from my iniquity. Luring imaginations foster the sincerest of feelings that drew me closer to a labyrinth of cruel acceptance. It was all too real, yet through it all, I somehow escaped.

And then, there's Nostalgia - so graceful, elegant, stunning, captivating right down to the very cells that only the Creator could have made. She was never meant to be, and yet here she is; either dancing in the pale moon light or tucked away in the chasms of my mind. I have a right to her existence. Though buried, even a man's deepest secrets lay under a mound of *male-ish* bravado, which culminates into one main question; can a man's actions truly be forgotten or must his story continue to be told, so that others will learn and never forget?

Focusing on the black binder, I ruffle through the images and paper clippings that I saw earlier. This time, a night-light provides adequate luminance, more than likely placed there by Aniah. I lay upon the floor. The soft twisting fiber of the carpet does not compare to the quilted feel of the comforters that Aniah brought earlier, but the floor serves the immediate purpose. Impatiently, I turn the pages to the exact photo that comes to mind…and yes, there she is – Nostalgia.

Her silhouetted image of unmistakable form lies captured in an ageless profile and I have memorized every contour. She was only thirty years of age at the time. Even now, virtue escapes me; knowing that part of me is part of her. I stare, and think, and stare even more. Was it fascination, or love, but if so, was she even capable of such a thing, or was it merely a flattering moment in time?

My weariness quickly overtakes me again as the playground of the Devil ceases to no end. For now, another person comes knocking upon the threshold of my mind, and yet, I carry no photo or any records of her.

Leaning against the couch, I gaze upward and then simply close my eyes. There is no reason to fight such memories any more. I awake when I awake and sleep when I sleep, but this complicated person was the reason Nostalgia came. She was the reason we were there and the theater of my mind retells the occurrence again. As it were, Rowland became a question mark, while I was given the fortitude of having met the one lady who became my blessed angel of darkness, and oddly enough, Gjhe'nan was in the middle of it all.

Maple leaves blanket the ground as a brisk northerly wind carries much of the yellow foliage to unknown destinations. The forceful surge pushes against everything in its path as it announces its presence through swaying branches. Flapping garments make bundled pedestrians fully aware of the unseen force as they walk the streets of the bustling city. The northerly presence is also noticeable to those behind walls as well; and for two employees of GenoSyss, there are no exceptions.

Arthur and Gracella observe the gray sky and activities outside as another flowing surge howls past the window. "Tell me something. Isn't it more interesting to see what's going on out there than it is in here?"

"As usual…Grace. Look at that guy chasing his cap. And someone forgot to tell that lady that mini-skirts don't behave on windy days."

"Some people do things without thinking."

"That's what makes the world a wonderful place, Grace."

"If you say so…."

"Aniah gave me the information last night, and the rest will soon be history."

"Then, you better get going – your *mystery* woman waits. Let me know how it goes."

Immediately, a loud clack of thunder shakes the building as the sky brightens. Within minutes, Arthur departs GenoSyss and sets a course to the location where his prior instructions call for. The powerful surge of wind is a constant as Ramsey plows its way through the perpetual expanse of the concrete jungle. Other would-be travelers brave the elements as well, but few more capable than Ramsey. The vehicle rocks and sways in rhythm as the underside suspension compensates for pressing moments. Speckles of ice tatter the windshield, taunting all who are caught in its gripping force. Yet, the lone technician holds faithful to his course and brings his white goliath to halt after more than an hour's journey.

"Woe," he says, waiting just outside the parking lot. "The Chateau Dijon. Is this the right place? There's not a car on this lot less than fifty grand. Oh well, so much for Guide Quest." Arthur parks his vehicle on the outskirts of the lot, exits, and makes his way pass the valet attendant.

Upon entering the building, he takes note of the lavish gold trim lacing the walls and ceilings, displaying meticulous craftsmanship that is nothing less than a compliment to its designers. High polish floor tile spans the full range of the large room as elegant debutants and socialites cast their reflections upon the clean white surface. Crystal chandeliers softly glow while enchanting columns stand powerfully between rows of burgundy draped tables. Each table supports a compliment of fine brass and porcelain dining utensils as well as sporting an array of candles with renaissance appeal. In conjunction, tantalizing flames dance atop each candle, most effective in casting a flickering delight of tranquil ambiance.

Arthur stands poised; yet, to his surprise an alluring voice accents the moment. "May I take your coat sir?"

Arthur turns with the most instinctive curiosity and notices a well-mannered Asian woman, professional to the end. "Oh…yes you may." He gives the woman his draping denim coat. She carefully folds the long piece of wardrobe, though it is almost twice her height.

"Which dining coat would you prefer for the evening sir?"

"Umm…?"

"Compliments of Ms. Banks."

"Oh…sure."

"Right this way Mr. Robinson."

Stunned, Arthur puts on the coat and follows her. He noticeably observes men wearing tuxedo laced suites and women in after-five attire. Arthur sits as the waitress instructs. "Ms. Banks has informed me that she will be running a little late due to the weather, but she will be here. Can I get you something?"

"Umm, just plain water with lemon for now." The waitress acknowledges Arthur's request and departs.

After a brief moment, the woman returns with water, on ice, and places the clear glass upon the table. Arthur glances at his watch, but soon begins relishing the live jazz harmonics. So soothing are the musical sounds that he closes his eyes, sips the water, and moves his head in rhythm to the coaxing tunes.

As Arthur indulges in the moment, he grows oblivious to the world around him, until another voice captures his attention. "I'm glad to see that you are enjoying the music." In an instant, Arthur's world collapses. Not only is the voice alluring, but commanding, heavy yet without rasp or baritone; concise, also provocative and spoken with a sultry sense of mature sensation.

Arthur turns to confirm what his mind possibly concludes, but in his observant manner, he scans the object of his attention from toe to head, taking all that he sees into a mental inventory as his mouth hangs open.

Standing proudly before him is a Negroid female whose dark-skin resonates beyond her eccentric wardrobe. Her entire ensemble cleverly displays the tanned skin of an animal. A crowning headpiece parades two drabs of gray feathers from which a single long plume extends; a fantastic trait of a large bird that waves with every motion of her head. A short jacket adorns a high neck covering, sleek shoulder padding, and an uneven length hemline. The skirt bares the same style of cut and nicely accentuates her moderate hips. Black ostrich sheer hoses enticingly contour well-toned legs right down to a pair of black open-toe high heels.

Though speechless, Arthur closes his eyes for a moment as if to gather the right words, yet for him, she is already prepared.

"Well…are you going to invite a lady to dinner or sit with your mouth open?"

"Umm…right…" Arthur proceeds to pull the chair from the table, allowing the woman to sit down. Once seated, he continues to invoke his mannerisms.

"Now you are one sophisticated lady," he tells her while maintaining his powers of observation.

"Well thank you…and you my friend are equally exceptional."

Both sit patiently as the waitress approaches. "Hello Ms. Banks, it is good to see you again. May I take your hat and coat?"

"Of course…thank you."

"I see you brought a friend Ms. Banks, very *goood*. Now what can I get for you?"

"I'll have the usual, and my friend here can have whatever he wants; it's all on me." Both place their orders and the waitress carries out her instructions.

"Well…well…well, the great man himself; finally in person…"

"Now you're flattering me Ms. Banks."

"Oh no you don't," she says, jokingly interrupting Arthur while crossing her legs and waving her finger. "You just call me Angelica. There are a few gray strands in this head, so you needn't remind me of how much older I am."

"As you wish."

"This is informal Arthur and please; stage nothing on my account."

"Well I have to admit…had I known I'd be in a place like this, I would have brought my black tie. This isn't exactly a jean scene."

"Forgive me - please. My board meeting lasted too long and the weather, as you can see is acting very Tex-*assy*. However, our waitress and I go way back; she takes very good care of me when I come here, especially when I'm in a rush. But trust me, when we walk out that door, your jeans will be the least bit of any one's concern – even yours."

"So…where are your body guards?"

"P…*leeeez* – now you're flattering me. If any one conks me over the head, they'll get nothing and I certainly don't hang out with the rich and famous. I prefer the low-key status quo. It keeps me closer to the real geniuses of society. As for protection, my laser-guided Colt does just fine. She goes with me everywhere."

"Spoken as if experienced?"

"Why sure, but for now…all I need is you."

"Well, let's hope so. I'm anxious to know why I am here, and since my wife gave me your message, I'm all ears."

"Ah, a man for the moment. I like that."

Angelica smilingly stares into Arthur's eyes. Uncrossing her legs, she places both elbows on the table and smiles. Then, she clasps her long slender fingers together while leaning her chin upon two fingertips. "First of all, I want to thank you for coming on such short notice and I really wanted to meet you; because frankly, I don't like others handling my personal interests."

"Fair enough…"

"Arthur, I hope that my coming here will entice a man of your talents as well as show a jester of good faith, even secure a degree of trust."

"Sounds good so far..."

"My sources prove quite handy, especially when I do my homework. You see...it's my business to know potential bedfellows. And should you accept, then do understand that any information between us will never leave this table, now, after, or otherwise."

Arthur moves his head in acknowledgment of Angelica's statement. After hearing her point, he too leans forward as to make sure he misses nothing she says.

"You know, there were other potentials Arthur, but none with stunning results as yours; not one. Not to mention the successful prodigy you now enjoy...bringing that creature of yours to life on a workingman's budget."

"Whoa...wait a minute. You know about..."

"Your enan, yes, you call him g-nan, or something like that...of course I know about it."

"How could you know that?"

"Information always travel; you just have to know where and when to pick it up."

"Were you spying on GenoSyss?"

"I like to think of it as simply getting to know other businesses. But more so, to the point, I'm not that concern with what the company does as a whole. My particular interest lies in one person."

"Rowland?"

"Not likely."

"Oh..."

"Is Rowland sitting at this table?"

"Um...no."

"My, oh my…are we a little slow this evening…of course it's you silly. Why do you think you're here?"

"Point taken..."

"I know you were the key to the success for a hush-hush project. I know that the military had a profound interest in that program…to some extent. I know that you and your former supervisor were at odds with each other, and I also know that you are not happy with GenoSyss."

"Can you read into my soul?"

"Almost… The grapevine also tells me that the current policies regarding non-degreed techs like *yourself*, makes you currently disenchanted with the agency. Even your faith in God is questioned. I can only imagine why."

"Should I undress now, so you won't miss anything else?"

"And show me what; something I haven't seen before? *Pleeeez*. Make no mistake Arthur, my friend, I know more about you than you may realize, and you being here is no coincidence." Arthur moves his head in a peculiar motion, watching attentively as Angelica reveals her ambitious itinerary.

"Listen carefully. It is often said that each person sees the evening-tide of his or her years as twilight descends. Only then do we hope that what we do in this life is not in vain, and hopefully someone will benefit from our works long after we're gone. The most beautiful and endearing thing in life is to *mean something* in this cycling chain of existence."

"You sound…spiritual."

"That's not so bizarre, especially when considering that every society on the face of this planet conducts some form or spiritualistic rituals to some sort of deity."

"Are you a believer of Jesus the Christ?"

"Whole-heartedly, but am I a devout churchgoer – no. That is for those who find purpose within those four walls. I never did."

"Humph…"

"But aside from that, we are all given an opportunity to give back something Arthur. You see…my father; God rest his soul, saw tremendous potential in skin regenerative therapy. He synthesized a formula for the actual treatment of cell aging. So effective was this formula that many companies – world wide were ready to pay handsomely just for the manuscripts - alone."

"Why didn't you sell?"

"Not ready. We…wanted to test the final results on a…"

"Person…"

"Not by definition."

"You mean…?"

"Hold that thought… Three years ago, we discovered that we could slow the breakdown of skin tissue. Several skin samples were taken from different parts of the human body – I won't say which parts though."

"Then I won't ask. But it sounds like the age old quest for the fountain of youth."

"More or less…"

"This wouldn't be anything you're using now - right?"

Angelica looks downward, smiling; girlishly turning her head as reddish pigmentations coats her accentuating cheeks. "How charming of you, but no…Banks Enterprise is a company that my father founded fifteen years ago. Needless to say, his works not only helped so many, but also has proven to be beneficial for our families. He actually believed he could stop cell degeneration."

"Angelica, if I'm hearing you right; you're telling me that you can eliminate the results of sin?"

"I didn't say…remove the curse on mankind, I said…that my father could slow down the effects of aging – or sin."

"I'm sorry."

"That's okay…"

"I mean…about your father."

"Oh…thank you."

"So, he never fully achieved what he sought after."

"No, but he did pass all he had to me and I don't mean just materialistic things."

"You're saying that, he trained you."

"Yes. I became my father's apprentice. I was only able to further his work with limited results – at least enough to keep financiers interested. However, my point is…he past to me something more precious than what I had."

"Mentorship…"

"As a coach mentors a player, a big brother to a little brother, a person of respect to someone subjugate, and as a mother to her daughter."

"I see…"

"Good."

"Now you want to pass your knowledge to your children or someone coming after you. It's making sense now."

"Yes and no."

"Yes and no?"

"Yes, this is where you come in, because there's a deep need for your talents from the genetic aspect. I want you to create something for me."

"That explains the yes, now what about the…no?"

"The no, simply means that I don't require you as an apprentice."

"Oh, I see. You already have someone, or perhaps since Banks Enterprise is family owed and operated, you merely want to keep things in the family – I understand."

"Sure you do, but there's one problem."

"And what might that be?"

"I have no children Arthur, and I would preferably desire a daughter to pass everything too."

"Sounds like you need a lawyer and an adoption agency."

"In a normal sense – yes."

"*Soooow*…why do I get the feeling that the meaning of *normal* is absent?"

Angelica peers deeply into Arthur's eyes, seductively smiling while leaning closer. She lightly inhales while presenting a flirtatious wink, telling him, "Arthur, I would like very much…for you to give me that daughter."

Arthur's eyes widen as his mouth hangs open. He leans back into his chair with both hands on the table. "You mean…you… you – me," he says, pointing to Angelica, then to himself. "Yes – you and me; a daughter."

Arthur remains silent – wide-eyed.

Angelica moves closer, speaking softly while casting bedroom eyes. She removes her gloves and proceeds to lay each item upon the table. Then, she gently touches the topside of Arthur's wrist and slowly moves her finger in a circling pattern while staring him in the eye.

"Arthur, I need you to give me a beneficiary."

Silence lingers; then, Arthur withdraws his hand and increases the space between them. "Angelica. I…I…ca…can…can't do this. I just can't do what you're asking me to do. I'm not supposed too. I mean you're not bad at all…in fact you got it; I mean you got it going on like dual smoke stacks…but…*but*."

Arthur takes a deep breath. Then, without a moments notice Angelica leans within a few inches of Arthur's face. While staring into his eyes, she whispers the faint words, "Got'cha," winks at him, and leans back into her chair, laughing hysterically. Bewilderment covers Arthur as his mouth gates open. Angelica relishes the moment.

"You are merciless and cruel."

"I had you…Arthur."

"Yes, you did."

"Yes I did. I can hear your heart beating way over here, and talk about a picture-perfect moment."

"That was terrible – so cruel."

"That was great!"

"Angelica, you don't quite fit the description of a CEO."

"Well, I'll leave that interpretation to you, but I've had my share of indecent proposals, and believe me, your response simply assures me that I made a wise choice."

"So…to the point?"

"The point is…I'll provide you with all the necessary equipment in order for you to clone a female beneficiary for me. I've always wanted a daughter but without the hassles of marriage and pregnancy – my choice…no questions asked."

"But, why a clone Angelica, why not adopt?"

"Oh no. Parenting is for the married-young. You also know that philanthropy regulations will not allow the outright manipulation of natural human development, especially for personal endeavors."

"True…"

"As mentioned earlier, the cell degenerative repressor we've manufactured needs testing, but not on humans."

"Oh…okay."

"Now you see the picture."

"You want to test the repressor on a cloned human female hybrid."

"*Ahhh*…see? You *caaan* think – it's not so hard – good for you. There's hope for the male species."

"Angelica, The National Committee of Cloning Ethics is going to be all in your business."

"NCCE can go to hell, and as far as my business, what happens in Banks Industries stays in Banks Industries."

"Cloning animals with human traits is one thing. What you're asking me to do is ethically *borderline* of the law."

"The law on cloning humans is still in debate, but there are ways to get around the moral issues, and in time, legislation will legitimize human hybrid cloning Arthur – it's just a matter of time."

"Speaking of cloning, who's the donor?"

"Yours truly..."

"What are the terms?"

"Arrange for leave of absence from GenoSyss – so you can keep your day job; after which, you will report to my facility."

"Absence means no pay."

"And you think you're here for the March of Dimes?"

"Oh...of course not..."

"For your inconveniences, I'm quite sure we will reach a worthy compensation for you."

"Strange...I feel honored."

"You should be."

"Incredible."

"Now I know you're dying to ask, why not other more qualified people, or companies, blah...blah...blah."

"The thought had occurred."

"It's quite simple; confidentiality."

"Sure..."

"I prefer to avoid tabloid rubbish and the involvement of large companies, which possess large egos. No one but us, need to know."

Angelica lifts a glass and admonishes Arthur to do the same. "Here's to us, a new friendship, partnership, and beginning." Both lightly toast as the waitress brings their meal. With nothing more to say, Angelica consumes her deep red wine while Arthur casts an impish grin. Consent of merit mingles with rising steam from the simmering hull of bright red crustaceans. Arthur slowly motions his head from left and right as though to ponder the fascinating offer from this woman of ambiguous, yet intriguing character.

As night engulfs the city, a voice confers within a dimly lit room. Inside, Rowland sits leisurely in a classic wooden chair, rocking, pivoting the antique piece of furniture upon a large rug. The rug depicts the embroidered face of a bear, perhaps a patriotic reminder of his homeland. Accompanying the snug floor covering are all the amenities that one could hope for within the spacious dwelling. There are white marble tabletops, classic plaster vases, lamps of Celtic craftsmanship, a grandfather clock, and a white stone fireplace that houses the rise and fall of dancing flames. Rowland's discussion carries over a device whereby he and the recipient engage in topics with complete disregard to matters at hand.

"Tell me again. Langley was shot while trying to take Nathaniel – Yes? Will he live? Fortunate...for *heem*. As stated before, your stupidity *weel* hurt us. The vests saved you both *thees* time. Now tell me, can he obtain the next package *weeth* you? Good. Police begin questions, but they know nothing! You *deed* well to des-*trroy theengs* that would link you to me; like Tuan's red car and melt the license plate. No more attempts by daylight – far too *rrisky*. Now...there are four that *rrremain*: Walter, Jade, Gracella, and Arthur. As said before, *Meester* Robinson will be difficult. Now go and do not broadcast your incompetence."

Rowland discontinues the conversation. He places another log on the dwindling fire and returns to his chair. Slightly rocking, he stares at the ceiling, rubbing his face as though to take thought of his next move. Minutes pass as the shrieking wind chills the outside air, but soon, a transmission alert rings and he answers it.

"Ah, I have been expecting you. Say again... Oh good. Yes – I am very curious to hear what the *rr*-rest of your findings mean, because *eef* what you say is true, then our little skirmishes overseas hurt your Adir Sa'ood. Also, my intelligence reports of Russian Detective Arimov finding several dead members of Rham-kiev, but their leader was not among them. The enans undoubtedly proved efficient, but we must act *sweef-tly* else your friends in Washington *veel* soon discover you...

and me."

The unfolding conversation reveals nothing less than clandestine motives of unmerciful terms. Placid walls house Rowland's cryptic communication as the grandfather clock chimes its hourly chant, echoing serene sounds aloud to the flickering shadows – shadows which mimic the dance of the yellow flames.

~~~The Hammer of War~~~

Across the North Atlantic, information reaches a man who is given a mobile computer. The man sits upon a wooden crate inside a rusting tin shed. The shed sits remotely on barren sand. The shed also nestles under the sound of surging waves and sea birds squawking in their quest for daily sustenance. Ironically, the man's demeanor and mannerisms depict something far more than his surrounding furniture as he sits behind an old shanty wooden desk. Periodic sips of water satisfy his undeniable thirst. Raising the viewer, he begins to enter information from a keypad. The screen illuminates with unreadable symbols as it electronically tiles the viewer. "My password works, but the message is encrypted. I'll have to decipher it. It shall only take a moment."

The room has no décor to adorn the stain-laden walls, nor pictures to accent the mood therein. Tattered rags hang just enough to cover a broken window that slightly presents a picturesque view of the sandy coast. The floor comprises of broken linoleum with pieces of missing sections. Battered sheet-rock and barren, weathered rafters lace the ceiling. Sun light partially filters into the small room, allowing barely enough light to shine on the contents within.

In contrast, the man sports a black suit, in which the jacket spans a single-breasted drape that casually hangs open. The rich fabric exposes subtle transitions of dual coloration. Engraved letters 'A.M.' line elegantly just out of view on a silver bracelet, and the same initials display on the face of a dazzling watch. He also dons a shiny bracelet that contains the sterling engraftment of a hammer and a scorpion. A collarless shirt vividly captures the deep fabric, as do the high polish black shoes that adorn his feet. Permeating light highlights just enough bronze skin and manicured fingernails to refute the possibility of manual labor – of any sort. His hair is as black as his wardrobe, trimmed in exquisite perfection right down to the narrow side-burns hugging the sides his face. There is no beard to line the masculine chiseling of his jaw, but the sparkling rings on his fingers more than accommodate whatever his entire presentation lacks.

Another man respectfully stands near him, acting as though waiting for a response. Soon, the man behind the desk immediately raises his head. "There, the decryption is finished," he says. Auburn eyes scan the information on the viewer as seconds unfold. He gently raises his head and slightly leans backwards. After taking a modest sip, he summons the man standing near him.

"We must return home, but before we do, I will have to pay a visit to one of our outposts. It appears that there has been an incident in the house of Adir Sa'ood. Make preparations for travel near Algiers, into the Mediterranean. "Yes," replies the man standing, and then bowing before exiting the room.

The man behind the desk rises and later exits the room as well. Approaching an entry door, two more men greet him. "Sultan, your traveling preparations are ready." "Well done…" Each provide escort to a black limousine in which everyone enters.

Inside the limousine, the men take into account a situation at hand. "Sultan, was Adir Sa'ood's establishment completely destroyed?"

"No. According to the encrypted report…most of it remains standing. As a precaution, I have sent word to the other two establishments."

"But that will draw the attention of the CIA and European Intelligence."

"There is no concern for them. If they track us here, then they will only find a worn down shack along the Angola coastline. However, something strange occurred in the house of Adir Sa'ood."

"What is it?"

"I am not sure, but when I get there, I will see for myself. And when I find out who is responsible, they shall surely know the sting of the scorpion, the crushing power of the hammer, and the terror that Rham-kiev lives, because I, Aun'war Martinet has declared it."

"So be it, Sultan." The men bow their heads to their ruling lord.

Their journey concludes at a solitary airfield. As the convoy of vehicles arrives, a party of men, guarding an aircraft welcomes Aun'war. He and his band of men board the craft. Soon, the craft is airborne and vanishes over the distant horizon.

Later, the aircraft lands in the Mediterranean near a compound. Not too far from the compound, surging waters instinctively react to the ancient powers of the moon, coming and going in tidal fashion; cycling patterns that has continued for centuries. Sea life sways in the surging embrace while its fluidic expanse sweeps primordial shores of anything tangible. Such waving actions take place under the midst of conversations, where men parade around a partially destroyed compound. Though lacking confining walls, they gather on a balcony that overlooks the resending waves.

Aun'war arrives and immediately dispense with salutations. Several men assemble before the slender speaker whose display of prominent leadership becomes clear. Their itching ears eagerly receive his information, though none dare break away from the attentive atmosphere.

Seated within the group of gatherers is another man who makes his interest known. "Sir, Aun'war, what is the current status of your development?" Upon hearing the question, Aun'war motions his hand towards a guard who is standing near a burned curtain.

The guard quietly disappears behind the ragged veil and reemerges with two other guards, and a man desperately wrestling in a state of captivity. The captive's clothes are torn and brandish soil stains. One of the guards precedes the others, carrying by his side a riffle-shape instrument while the two remaining guards mercilessly shove their unwilling captive through the room. The guardsmen carouse the poor soul until he stands in front of the assembly. Lesions of bruises cover the captive's tense body, but his eyes make it quite clear that an indomitable spirit is locked away behind his grungy flesh.

One of the observers asks, "Sultan, who is this man?"

"I don't know, we took him from somewhere – and…we do not know why he was, where he was… But he was… Who cares? Take him outside."

Crawling on the floor, the captive immediately lifts his head, yelling, "You'll rot in hell Aun'war…I swear it!" He kicks desperately and struggles to resist his bondsmen, but such futile efforts yield no release as he soon finds himself out side the railing of the balcony. Both guards continue to restrain the captive while the third guardsman readies the strange instrument.

The assembly of gatherers intently watches the unfolding situation like a pack of wolves observing a herd. "Curse you Aun'war for the motherless, curse you for the fatherless and the blood you spilled! Curse you…curse you to hell Aun'war – I curse you for all eternity – I swear it!"

The captive shouts profusely as he succumbs to several blows from his apprehenders. Their efforts are so effective that it sends him plummeting to the ground. Afterwards, both guards immediately disperse, leaving only the captive and his would-be executioner.

Perceiving an appalling situation, the crowd slowly backs away.

Though fallen, the captive manages to raise his head high enough to see his tormentor. "God sees you and you will never get away with this Aun'war!" Aun'war stares him down, "I already have," he says.

Immediately, Aun'war signals the guard. Upon acknowledgement, the guard pulls the trigger and the mysterious device fires. The captive's hands quickly cover the point of impact. Aun'war approaches the man. "The sensation you feel is the penetration of a high yielding plasma cartridge. It is so tiny that it is virtually undetectable. You only know about it because you were expecting it. Now you may go."

The captive struggles to his feet and runs only a few yards away from the balcony, offering nothing less than an adequate performance. Stride for stride, his gait appears normal but soon comes to a dreadful halt. He falls to his knees with both arms extending forward. Large drops of sweat pour down his face as his skin blisters mildly. Frantically shaking, he stares directly upon the changing texture of his skin, which testifies of more agonizing circumstances.

The assembly of watchers gathers closely around the man, though maintaining what they consider to be a safe distance, staring as to miss nothing.

Then strangely, the captive convulses, but even in his degenerative state, he observes his own disturbing transformation. Red inflammation appears on his hands and face as his skin turns to a translucent gel-like covering, revealing veins, muscle tissue, blood, and even bone. Large clumps of flesh oozes downward until it hangs virtually from his bones. Then, in a matter of seconds, all that categorizes the definition of bodily organs collapses within itself, drenching the ground beneath in a cesspool of putrescent goop.

Some within the crowed cover their mouths while others turn completely away. Many more breathe through clothing or handkerchiefs, trying to efficiently filter out the raw stench of flesh.

The man's remnants slowly dissolve and soon culminate into a fine mist. All that remains are the garments that once covered his badgered body. Stunned faces view the area where the man stood. A guard approaches and stirs the shirt and pants with a stick.

"Not a trace of him… Even his clothes are dry."

The assembly returns to the room where Aun'war addresses them. "There you have it gentlemen. The progress of what I like to call…the dismantler - the newest chapter in bio-weaponry. One shot causes the outer membrane of the cells to breakdown thus releasing the cell's inner contents. Once done, the unlucky victim's bodily fluids react with inert radiation by eliminating any remnants of what was once alive – eventually leaving no trace of the person, whatsoever. Everything biological – even his DNA, goes. The process only works on living tissue. As far as…how…well; I leave that to the real geniuses."

The room applauds, but one of the participants makes his intention known. "Impressive Sultan Martinet, please indulge us again with your reason for creating such a weapon."

"Which reason? In the greater scheme of things, governments con their people, but in return, I will con the governments."

"Many will think you a terrorist."

"All forms of totalitarian sovereignties are terrorists; whether killing Indians for land, beguiling people for taxes, or sending young men to their deaths for some foolish political agenda. Whether penalizing citizens for poor judgment, or using the mighty congressional pen for advantageous reasons, the goal of all such groups is absolute control. And the penalty for non-compliance is high. But people will ultimately obey, because of consequential fear. In the end, we are all terrorists. Do this…or that…or suffer the consequences – How often have we seen such remarks in action?"

Aun'war activates a large monitor. "Before you are the great continents of the world, a plateau for the ambitious, and a play ground for those willing to participate. In order to secure my demands, our approach will be small and mobile. We will take down public targets and leave witnesses to figure out just what happened. The X marks our next targets. We will strike randomly, using stealth with deadly accuracy. By the time anyone figures out what has happened, we will be well on our way to obtaining our demands."

"Are you a mercenary, Sultan – sir?"

"I like to think of myself as a *helper* of the people, a facilitator of good fortune. Needless to say, as the result of this weapon; the eastern regions will soon be at our disposal. Once that happens, we can be as generous with whomever we choose – be they peasant or monarch."

"And if they choose not to deal with you, what then?"

"Then…I will bring them the hammer of war. I, Aun'war Martinet' will cause them to taste me for a thousand years!" The assembly of partisans applauds while delightfully consuming drinks. An atmosphere of festive gaiety fills the entire gathering as men and women alike celebrate Aun`war's proposal.

But as the night falls, Aun'war summons a guard and retreats to a more secluded portion of the room. Leaning close to the guardsman's ear, Aun'war whispers, "Make sure that no one on the production team remains – everything from paper to people must disappear – Understand?" The guardsman acknowledges with a headshake and leaves the area while Aun'war returns to the festivities at hand.

In the morning hours, Aun'war and several of his men convene within the bunker of the compound. The sub portion of the compound surprisingly remains intact, though baring scars from the previous attack. Portions of the ceiling intermittently fall to the ground. Pillars that stood as mighty supports now lay helplessly along the sand stone floor. Several cracked walls and broken wooden pieces tatter the surroundings amidst a pile of corpses.

Aun'war's men stand in astonishment as a poor soul pitifully cries out for their attention. Aun'war stands directly in front of the man and watches as the man attempts to give an account of a gruesome situation. "Please…please I beg you…yes I survived, but I do not know what attacked us. They…were…some kind of animals!"

"You are telling me that animals did all of this?"

"It is true…I beg you Sultan," cries the man while shaking and looking suspiciously towards his inquirer.

Aun'war whispers in the man's face, "Animals," he says.

The respondent hysterically nods his head in compliance as silence looms within the room. Aun'war's countenance lightens, followed by a gentle laugh. All others laugh as well, festively complying with their disident leader.

Then suddenly, Aun'war reaches into his coat, removes a gun and shoots the man in the thigh. An anguishing cry projects outwardly as the man falls to the ground, pitifully sobbing while covering his fresh wound with both hands. "Please Sultan; please…I speak the truth!" Sweat engulfs the man's face as his shooter approaches.

Extending one arm, Aun'war presses the gun against the man's forehead. Sweat sizzles upon the barrel as the piece of iron singes into raw flesh. "*Uhhhh*…I beg you…you can't."

"Oh yes…I can. Now listen to me. We find what appears to be Adir Sa'ood's face, with no skull, lying right over there along with several pieces of a chard body – that presumably…is…his. One of his men, as you can clearly see, is imbedded in that wall. The door, which seals this room, weighs a ton, but it is on the floor, and that tells me something apparently got in! Do you really understand to whom you are speaking?"

"Yes…yes Sultan, but please, please, I beg you, I speak truth!" Aun'war cocks the gun and presses it into the man's forehead even more. The man simply closes his eyes.

Immediately, another observer comes forward. "Sir Martinet. Please…do not kill him. He speaks the truth." Aun'war coldly stares at the man. "Sultan, he speaks truth…please listen – I beg you. These were not normal animals, not like anything you have seen. These were strange beasts, and powerful, and not easy to kill. We shoot at them but they did not fall. They hit us hard and fast, and then…they disappear into the hills. All I remember were the eyes…those mysterious eyes – glowing red but not bright, yet starring into our souls."

With each passing second, Aun'war forcefully presses the wounded man's face, looking as though to find a reason to shoot, edging closer to the point of no return. Then, as quickly as it began, Aun'war withdraws his weapon. The man lies upon the ground, sobbing while covering his gaping wound.

As Aun'war approaches the man from the crowd as he begins to emphasize points with unmistakable body language. "So…you are telling me that animals did this!"

"Yes my lord."

"That being the situation, then these animals…are sophisticated."

"Perhaps…"

"And if that is true, then someone taught these animals. Do you agree?"

"Of course..."

"And if that holds true, then would it make sense that a higher mind is orchestrating such creatures?"

"Possibly..."

"Then, guess what? That means people are involved – Understand?"

"Yes sir."

"I hope you do, because there is another problem. Now that Adir Sa'ood is dead, I have to replace him. His lost means that someone in my very own...regime may be trying to kill me. Such insolence also means that I have to spend more time looking inside rather than outside. That endeavor alone will tax my men far too much and it will seriously hurt my efforts, not to mention the head aches brought on by the U.S. as well as Central Europe."

 All eyes bear upon Aun'war as he propagates his dissertations well into the night.

Time presses forward and dawn wonderfully graces central Texas. A large white transport makes its way into the town of Ennis. Inside the cab, Arthur speaks with Aniah, whose image transmits upon a small screen.

"After I take Gjhe'nan back to GenoSyss, I will destroy all the manuscripts and notes. I thought about what you said."

"Good... You'll feel much better and who knows how far Angelica's project will take you."

"Well, anything is better than making test tubes in prison."

"Glad it's sinking in. Now listen, I have to go see mom, so I'll catch up with you later. Love you Sweets – bye."

"Love you too – take care." As the transmission ends, Arthur finally brings his iron horse to the entry of the white barn where the hybrid beast resides.

Upon entering, Arthur finds his prodigy anxiously waiting. With ears laid back and squinting eyes, the creature nudges Arthur's head, wagging its over size tail; thus compelling the technician to reciprocate an embracing gesture. In their moment of adulation, Gjhe'nan unintentionally thrashes a seam in the wall of the barn. Arthur shakes his head in surprising disbelief as he watches the gleeful beast acting unaware of its destructive mannerisms.

"Hey, you need to calm down - Okay? I have to tell you something, but before I do; did you enjoy your exercise last night?" In the usual manner, Gjhe'nan acknowledges Arthur with mild shrieks and grunts.

After making their ritualistic acquaintance, the richly colored hybrid proceeds to a nearby haystack and cleverly places wooden boards upon the floor. As before, the hybrid carves markings of written text as sincere perceptions roughly unfold upon the laden pieces of wood.

Seconds pass, and the hybrid present its clawed penmanship. "C cows, bird, stars…" Arthur scratches his head and chuckles. "Well…you certainly developed an acquaintance with the locals."

Gjhe'nan shrills a mild squawk as though to give Arthur a rain check on the subject.

"Your mind is like a sponge and your appetite for knowledge is growing like weeds. It is unfair to keep you here like this, especially since your cousins are sociable. I'm sure that trait is driving the need for you to see them. But you will not have the freedom you deserve. If I let you go, Rowland and Colonel Ducet will find you. To them, you are nothing more than something to throw away. But to me…you are…so…much more. But the problem with you is that you are not the average pet, so therefore, gallivanting around in public is out of the question. Try to understand." The hybrid shrieks and silently watches Arthur.

"Gjhe'nan. Sometimes, when we get too close to something, we do bad things. Well…I did a bad thing. I took you from your true owners and they want you back. But if you go back, worse things may happen to you. Do you understand?"

Gjhe'nan tilts his head in a curious manner. Arthur looks towards the ceiling as though to find missing words to fill his staggering speech. Then, in an inexplicit manner, the technician caringly gazes into the dark windows of the hybrid's eyes and silently places the keys in his pocket. Gjhe'nan moves his head as though to question the remark of his maker, but Arthur cleverly turns away.

"I have to do some work for a lady. I will be gone for a little while."

Again, Gjhe'nan shrills softly, beckoning Arthur to convey a sense of acknowledgment to its demanding inquiries, but Arthur does not yield. Tears course the technician's narrow face, flowing across his flustered skin, and then finally dripping from beneath his chin until the floor consumes every drop. Such matters of the heart should come as no surprise, for the words 'TRUST U FRIEND' vividly displays in claw mark etchings upon the board.

The night drifts slowly into the morning, and needless to say, the transport of Gjhe'nan back to GenoSyss never takes place.

~~~Lucent Diary~~~

It is late evening and a transport carries three individuals to an undisclosed destination: a passenger, the driver, and a discontent Walter Pierson. Walter is bound with rope and lies in the cargo section. In a quiet manner, he observes the plain interior as though to make reference of his current location. With much effort, he maneuvers his body into a sitting position.

He observes the passenger and attempts to gain the man's attention. "You there. Who are you?" The passenger, hearing Walter casually taps the driver on the shoulder. "Our piker is awake. Looks like he'll be joining the party after all."

The driver ignores them both as Walter continues to entreat the man. "I see. Well…you don't have to face me, but your accent suggests that you're from Australia and your driving buddy is either Caucasian or some kind of foreigner."

"Very observant Walter," responds the passenger.

"You know my name?"

"Course I do. You were our next package Walter Pierson."

"Package eh? It's a little dark in here, so your identity should be safe."

"As if it matters…"

"My lips hurt, they feel bruised; one of you hit me – oh…now I remember."

"It was for your own good - science boy."

"There's blood on my jacket. Did you stab me too?"

"Take a guess," says the passenger while grinning.

Feeling no threat from their token hostage, they proceed to focus on their destination, but Walter continues. "I guess its useless asking how long I've been here so I won't bother. But…look guys; I'll cut you a deal. Let me go and I tell no one, or you let me go and I still tell no one."

"A comedian – are yah?"

"Diplomacy is not my strength but this throbbing headache you gave me suggests that you thought I was the right guy. But that can't be since I'm not rich and I have no wealthy relatives, and I didn't' win the lottery. I haven't done anything."

"My…my, are we talkative. You're bout to piss me off, so here's the situation. You did do something mate, now contain *yer* yap! *B-sides*…where you're going, it won't matter. You're just a package – and we aim to deliver. Get it?"

"You mind telling me…where will the drop off be?"

"Some *wheres* – nice and cozy. You will even find some *friendlies* there."

Upon hearing such words, the driver eyes the more robust passenger in a malcontent manner. "Fool, you never could shut up."

"Hey, at least I can keep my mask on when doing a job. Because of you, we had to shoot that chap with the red sports car, and watch the bloody road, you…you *whacka*!"

"Look who's talking. You're the one who shot the old man's daughter for no reason – and almost got me killed!"

"The vest did its job and saved your lily-ass Langley, so shut the bloody hell up will you!"

Hearing the two squabbling, Walter's countenance falls. He cradles himself in fetal-style position as his mouth opens and his breathing becomes erratic.

The blond-haired passenger reaches into a compartment, pulls out a large shiny pistol, and begins to insert bullets into the chamber. Upon finishing, he slams the chamber shut, forcefully making a loud noise. Then, he eyes Walter with no emotion whatsoever.

"All right you, no more messing around. Did ya hear what I said earlier? Wind up like your friends – I *says*; especially like the one with the red sports car. That's right… Now keep mouthing ya pie-hole and I may decide to do ya right hear, right now – Get it?" Silence looms heavily within the vehicle as Walter's suspecting eyes peer upon the back of the passenger's head.

Though Walter's hands are restrained, he covertly locates a sharp edge along the interior support railing, and resourcefully moves his tied wrists in a saw-like motion. Walter ponders his own plight as his confined body shifts with the motion of the vehicle. After careful thought, he again decides to chance his direct inquisitions to the passenger. "Tell me, how do you know about the man in the red sports car? How are we connected? I don't understand what…"

"Shut-up obviously means something different in this country."

The passenger cocks the gun. Astonishment covers Walter's face for he knew that he had struck a cord with the man. "Ya sit back there all tied up, running yer bloody mouth like you don't know who the driver of that red car was!"

"Tuan."

"Hard to figure out, was it? Anymore bright minded questions – science boy?"

"You talk too much," warns Langley while driving the road more carefully.

"Relax mate. The Russian pays us well to deliver these guys to the underground market, but the woman pays us more to silence them forever. This job will be just like the other four."

Walter closes his eyes and slumps momentarily as if loosing all virtue of hope. He restricts his covert actions even more. Anxiety grows as the desperate saw-like motions produce minimal results. Though in despair, he repositions himself and forcefully rubs the binding twine until the nylon threads begin to separate. So intense is his actions that small droplets of blood percolate down his wrists.

Attempting to draw no attention, Walter daringly engages the passenger again. "Umm, I…I…didn't mean to upset you sir, really. It's just that I…well if you would please be kind enough to humor a man on death row – I just want to know one more thing. Please?"

"Sorry chap, my smokes are for me. You'll have to get your own."

"That's not what I want."

"Then what is it?"

"You mentioned a Russian. Who is he?"

The passenger laughs, leaning his head into the headrest. "You want me to give up our employer - eh? I'll tell ya this much. I won't do you like I did your hot friend – Blondie; had her squealing to the very end." Laughter fills the air as the driver confirms the passenger's statement. "I see your point," says Walter.

In an instant, the passenger motions to Langley. "Hey, slow down – here's our turn off; a few more yards, bang, bang…then, we're done."

Walter extends to get a better view through the windshield. He is able to determine that street lights are distant, and that the ride now becomes hurtfully bumpy. Both, Langley and the passenger drastically sway to the violent motion of the vehicle; each bracing themselves during the current moment. Sweat pours from Walter's head, but his dreadful situation seems conclusive as he frantically attempts to brace *him*-self. Even in despair, Walter furiously tugs, desperately trying to break his bonds.

"Just a few more yards Langley, and watch the tree," blurts the passenger.

Hearing such dire remarks, Walter's eyes widen. His countenance dwindles as he lies helplessly on the floor. Sadly, he no longer attempts to free himself. His body relaxes as both arms drop, remaining still as if everything within him has gone. "Oh God…not like this," he whispers. So subtle is his plea that even the sensitive ears of his captors are unresponsive, but the passenger remains focused as ever.

"There…over there, there's the hole; just a few more feet – now cut the lights." Silence looms within the vehicle as Walter stares at the cargo ceiling. He stares intently, and stares even more; then, he stares none at all as all motion stops.

"Langley, take'em out while I attach the silencer to…the silencer." Snickering laughter chills the air as the blonde haired passenger carries out his brutish ploy.

Both men quickly exit the vehicle; however, Langley is the first to make his way to the rear doors. He opens the doors, grabs Walter by the shirt and throws him to the ground. The abrupt action brings both men face-to-face.

"Well, surprise. I am the driver who just drove you to your…hole - tell. But guess what? I'm white - just like you. Satisfied?" Langley sarcastically smiles while pressing his thumb into Walter's neck.

Walter says nothing; yet realizing his situation, he slowly rises to his feet and staggers backwards.

"Are you drunk?" Langley's question falls on tentative ears as he shoves Walter into the rear door. Upon impact, Walter snags the binding ropes on the handle of the door while Langley gets closer. "Scream all you want, no one will hear you. Besides, the hole is ready…now let's get going."

Walter stands motionless with his head hanging low. He blinks slowly as if experiencing a dream. He does not resist, nor does he speak. Langley reaches for Walter and grabs a large piece of fabric near his shoulder. Then suddenly, Walter lunges forward, furiously grunting with intensity. At that moment, the ropes break, which frees Walter's hands, but Langley never realizes it and surprisingly succumbs to the crashing blow of Walter's fist. Langley's limp body collapses to the ground. Though dazed, he attempts to reach inside his jacket, but Walter notices his actions and quickly apprehends the targeted item. A scuffle breaks out as both men combatively try to secure the item. Then, an act of desperation allows one finger of destiny to find the trigger. Soon to follow is a blaring noise that plasters the night air.

"Hey…*dammit* Langley…Langley!" The blond haired passenger calls, but there is no response. He cautiously makes his way to the rear of the transport. To his amazement, both Walter and Langley lay motionless, one on top of the other with Langley's body facing upward. The man slowly approaches. "Don't know which of you is alive…guess I'll have to do you both; you first science boy." The blond haired man raises his weapon and proceeds to press the trigger, but suddenly, Walter quickly pulls Langley's body to one side and uses it as a shield. The lifeless corpse absorbs four deadly rounds. Yet, in a blaring moment, the assailant never sees Walter pointing a gun at him. Two furious shots ring out as the blond haired assailant falls silently to the ground.

Walter approaches his fallen victim, who now lies in a pool of blood. His demising state gives Walter a clear face-to-to-face advantage. "So, thought you kill me, *eh' bloke…mate…cheerio chap* or what ever the hell you say?"

Remarkably, the man laughs while choking on his own blood. "That would be dag for you chap…you're quite funny – really…"

"So who's laughing now?"

"Always time for a good laugh…*chum*…"

"Not today."

"Well then…end it now," replies the man, gurgling with every agonizing breath.

"Not my style. Your face is red and your eyes are glazing over. I'll get help."

"NNNnnnnnoooo…nooo…no! You win science boy."

"Then tell me something if you can. What is the name of the Russian? Please, I beg you…just give me anything, or part of his name."

The man stares at Walter, then his breathing becomes dreadfully erratic as blood immensely pools beneath him, drenching every fiber of soil, cloth, and bare piece of flesh. Sensing no progress towards an answer, Walter rises to his feet. Then, surprisingly, the fallen man, void of strength, whispers, "Ro…w…lnd," and then passes into the night.

Walter stares into the dark sky. "Thank you," he whispers. Then he glances to a hole in the ground, apparently dug with the intent of a burial. Four other areas lay around the unearthed burrow that suggests recent activity. Again, Walter looks towards the sky, "You heard me," he humbly utters, whispering softly while wiping his tear stained eyes. Without a moments notice, he removes Langley's gun, enters the transport and departs the scene, leaving behind two men that will forever remain in the diary of his memory.

Finding his way into the city, Walter realizes his location. He parks the vehicle in a secluded lot and sets it on fire. Later, he locates a public booth and proceeds to place a call. The small screen illuminates with Jade on the other end of a visual transmission.

"Jade…Jade…"

"Walter, is that you? What happened to you?"

"No time to explain."

"Is that blood on you, why are you covered in blood?"

"It's complicated, but I didn't mean to leave you sitting alone in that restaurant. I had every intention of meeting you, but something happened."

"What happened...?! Tell me now!"

"Jade, I need your help."

"I'll be right there!"

"No, no don't hang up - I think I know what may have happened to Tuan, Nathaniel, and Alexis."

Jade intently stares at Walter. Her wide-eyed glance displays an acute moment of bewilderment. Walter, barely noticing her expression continues to look around, seeing if anyone is watching. Sensing her prolong silence, he questions her again. "Jade...Jade, did you hear me?"

Walter repeats his question a few times, but Jade simply stares at him in astonishment, until she responds, *"Ummm – yes."*

"Why are you staring at me like that? I'm the one hurting over here."

"I'm fine...just surprised."

"Look, something's going on and I think we all may be in danger. We have to get Arthur and Gracella. It's not safe to talk here. I'll give you another location to come and get me."

"Okay..."

The transmission ends as Walter quickly departs the scene.

~~~Nostalgic Prelude~~~

God did smile on Walter that day. He survived to tell the story.

It is four-thirty in the morning and coke with a dab of vodka becomes the refreshment of choice, though not my first selection. However, I do find that the medicinal purposes far outweigh the criticisms. As the morning hours linger, the den continues to be my resting chamber; yet, I find the same solace within my home office. There is even more serenity here than previously thought. Taking comfort in a high swayback chair, the leathery surface secures me for the moment. Past artwork, a substantial library, computers, and a light table all denote nothing less than an extension of me. After all, this is where my true work takes place. Perhaps that is the drawing element of this humble room – a place to go where my mind can roam free; whether good, bad, indifferent, thoughts of right, thoughts of wrong, my strengths, my weaknesses, it's just me and my Maker.

Yet, in these quiet hours, someone else is here, granting an answer to my extending invitation. Curse or cure, our link stirs a profound feeling within me. The moon's pastel grays undeniably mark its ancient character as it sits high amidst the dark sky, a sky that now softly fades into a deep violet blue horizon. Her presence is fainting but she continues to shine brightly enough. It was a full moon when we met and the world I once knew changed forever.

How taunting that man should fantasize of a love deeper than the ocean or beauty that parallels the face of angels, a fleshly facade that speaks to one's own imaginative pretence. Ancient scrolls herald frigid warnings of mental devices that waywardly influence the ponderous heart and it is easy to see why one should never discount such omens. So…why does the nature of man flirt with infidelity? Only God's wisdom can grant us such insight.

Amidst these products of solid technology lies one picture that I allow to remain – willingly. Within a mesh binder, compartmental pages turn frivolously until I find her. The charcoal rendition vividly captures her as I remember. As though staring directly at me, this illustration casts her void of expression, yet speaking with her eyes; eyes which hold the underlying essence of a being formed from the depths of human desire. Even now, it is as if this contemporary duchess is reading my very thoughts. I dare not cast her presence openly, as if hanging a pictue on the wall; because such a display will only bring vexation. But like all men, I choose to hold her in a secret place deep inside and away from the curiosity of prying eyes.

The vodka tastes good; however, distant memories of good and evil wildly prance before me, boldly enunciating the joys of success, the foolishness of men's pride, kind and evil faces, and the haunting apparitions that follow. How can a person truly face the mirror in honesty, knowing that the only true demon that can torment him is the image staring right back? Perhaps Jeremiah understood best when he said, "How the heart is deceitful and wicked above all things; who can know it? " My deepest sin was that I became too close to that which was already in me.

Nostalgia was created for someone else to remember, but…others of us remember all too well. She was meant to continue the good deeds of her predecessor. Somehow, seeing this image formed of charcoal exhibit the disdains of humanities capabilities, such capabilities to do things that border on the realms of sanity, morality, and even divine indictment. To touch God's heart is always a yearning act for peace, but during that time when chaos flourished, it provoked little remorseful effort from me, especially while Gjhe'nan was anything but a distant memory. My prayers to God become poor, pitiful efforts, as the theater of my mind rehearses; yet, another act.

Heavy clouds cover the majestic terrain as heaven unleashes torrential loads upon the earth. The reoccurring event sustains life as the cycle has done for centuries. Yet, these basic principles of giving for the greater good are the sole expression of Angelica Banks. Angelica is CEO of Banks Industries and within her personal laboratory, Arthur conjures his talents for her special entreatment.

Well into the advancing stages of his newly found assignment; Arthur carries out his benevolent efforts in secret. Test after test, sample after sample, the technician systematically takes the appropriate steps to secure a bloodline for Angelica. While taking a break, Arthur converses through a small transmission.

"It's going fine. I'm in the developing stages of the embryo. I should be home in a few days. Keep in mind; you are the only one who knows where I am. Hollis and Grace don't even know where I am. Besides, they will keep an eye on Gjhe'nan for me. So don't worry, this side job will compensate us well during my leave of absence from GenoSyss."

Suddenly, the sliding doors open as high-heels clack upon the tile surface.

"Oh, the boss is here, I got to go, love you too…bye."

Arthur places the device in his pocket as Angelica approaches. "Now Arthur, if you're going to be sneaky, you'll have to do better that. Besides, I encourage couples to communicate – even you. How's the wife?"

"She's fine."

"How much doe's she know?"

"No more than she needs too; but your secret is safe."

"I have no doubts. Partial confidentiality can be helpful. But you're fortunate to have someone in your corner."

"She does bring a healthy perspective to my life's journey - sometimes."

"Good for you. I'm glad to see that she is trusting of you, especially when working so far away from home. Believe me, there are spouses that will find such arrangements questionable – I know."

"You speak as though from experience."

"Should that surprise you?"

"Not really…"

"Much shouldn't these days."

"I am still curious as to why the elaborate route for someone to succeed you."

"Let's just say, there was a time I would have settled down; played the good wife, became the working girl or the typical mother, expected church girl, would-be soccer mom, the whole nine yards. Having viewed my options, I simply wanted something else in life. That's when I became engrossed in my father's work."

"So…you were the one who made the change."

"I had to be strong – even then, to say that I wanted more in life was viewed by many to imply that God's given role for women is not good enough. All I'm saying is that I did not want the conscientious norm; and of course, I also have my conservative background to thank for that."

"But, there was…someone."

"At the time, my would-be suitor protested my professional field of choice. *'Too much time from home'–* he said, not to mention the other insinuations. In short, I decided not to play the subservient role anymore – nor for any one. I have no desire to deal with children or insecure men of any sort. Now, thanks to the spoils of the modern age, I don't have too. And by the way…the number I told you earlier was free of charge."

Arthur stares in sheer puzzlement. "The number? Oh…your age…I got it."

"That's all right; I know you're a little slow Robinson. Just stay with me long enough, you will catch up – I promise."

While listening, Arthur scans information upon a monitor. "Angelica, our catalogue is sending up red flags. You're pushing this project dangerously close to violating replicate laws."

"Listen to me. Is there an altered human being developing in that room?"

"*Noooo*…but the basis of what's developing in there is human; yet again, once the accelerants enter her system, we are boarder lining the CCE's regulations. And if they find out about your prodigy…"

"Yes, yes, I am aware of that. Now explain the *damn* process again."

"Alright…"

Angelica takes a deep breath, massaging her neck while rotating her head, shrugging both shoulders in the midst of agitation. Arthur surprisingly watches, sensing that something else is stirring. "Okay. The process is simple. I take the unfertilized egg of a human, female in this case – being yours, and other genetic material as needed. Put it all in a dish and add the inhibitors as well as the accelerants before cellular division occurs – enough said."

"That is precisely why I brought you here. So that you could bypass CCE's bull...crap."

"Hold on...if you let me finish."

"Well go ahead."

"Keep in mind Angelica that the replicate laws dictate that there has to be a substitution of two major organs during the early stages of human development – long before the fetus reaches three days. This is done so that the unborn cannot be classified as human."

"Now that's what I want to hear – a solution."

"But at the moment of conception or even cloning; you and I know better..."

"Yes...yes...I realize that if left alone the fetus becomes a human being – we know this already, now get on with the solution man."

"Early altering will change your successor. In this case, she will have the heart and blood of a deer."

"Sounds fitting; a deer, for a dear," replies Angelica as she slowly moves her fingers along the side of the large crystal container.

Both observe the developing fetus as it lays dormant, suspended well within an embryonic sack as lines carry life-giving sustenance to the man-made womb.

"Just think. What was once the privilege of degreed practicing PhDs is now the common tactics of anyone competent enough to do so. If you understand the automotive world, these procedures are no more difficult than putting pieces of an engine together."

"It's the new era Arthur."

"Of course, I'll have to give her mergants in order to mask the foreign organs when they become part of her body's genetic chemistry, but she should do quite well."

"Well is an understatement and you, my friend...are doing remarkable from what I can see. Don't take your gifts for granted Arthur. Though others can do as you do, they cannot create quite like you."

"Thank you. But I leave the true compliments to the real geniuses that thought of all this. I simply assemble the pieces."

"You're too modest Arthur. Anyway, how long will her development take?"

"At this rate, a few weeks, afterwards the engrafting; and after that, the accelerants again, then the encoding; she should reach full maturity in a matter of one to two months."

"One to two months?!"

"Yes. The process normally takes much longer but now we can refine it down to a couple of months."

"Mercy sakes alive!"

"What's wrong?"

"Arthur, at what point did we separate on the road? I don't have a couple of months."

"*Wh…wh…*wait a minute. I thought you said to make sure everything is in order."

"I did…but…I can't wait that long."

"Good Lord… Why the rush?"

"You don't understand."

"Angelica, we can't go trail blazing through the process. The nature of cell replication alone takes time."

"But you said you could excllerate cell replication."

"Angelica, some developments have to take place before other changes can occur."

Angelica places her hands over her face, sighs deeply and slowly turns away. Sensing her dissatisfaction, Arthur discontinues his explanation. Silence stirs, but soon, Angelica faces him again. "Arthur, take the chance."

"What?"

"You heard me, take...the chance."

"You mean..."

"Yes! I'm paying you and this is my property so do it."

"Angelica, her metabolism could fry her insides. I'm not sure I can control the process that well."

"You did it for your *g-nan*."

"His system is completely different."

"Do it! I need her fully functional in one week."

"One week?!"

"I'll take full responsibility. If she crash and burn, we'll simply start the process all over again until it works."

"Though a hybrid, she is still human."

"Do it."

Arthur ponders Angelica's request, but concurs in silent protest.

"By the way. What will you call her?"

Angelica smiles and takes a seat near a workbench. She casually crosses her legs in lady-like fashion, watching intently at the sterling side of a large chrysalis. "This is a tremendous time in the history of Bank's Industries. In this line of work, you cannot know the things that such success brings, especially if you're a woman."

"A woman like you – "

"Though I've managed well, such blessings come with a price."

"What kind of price?"

"Time..."

"Everyone pays –"

"That is because time is the true grim reaper. It takes away a portion of our life every day – giving nothing in return as it robs us of our prime. And for reasons of my own, this child will remind me of many things; a living embodiment of hope, joy, fullness of life, sincerity, and even regrets."

"Sounds very…"

"Nostalgic? Then Nostalgia will be her name."

With child-like tendencies, Angelica immerses her curiosities into a microscope. Looking through the viewfinder, she observes the contents of a Petri dish. "Is this what I think it is?"

"Deer's blood…"

"So tell me, will she be more animal on the inside or human?"

"The procedure dictates the results. Gjhe'nan was fabricated from an animal's egg; first – a kangaroo to be exact, and secondly he was grafted with human and reptilian attributes. He is more animal in appearance, but has intrinsic human innateness. With similar regards, your unconventional daughter will be every bit as human, at least in ways that matter, but will have non-human engrafts that are more on the physical side – blood and heart does not influence perception, will, or emotion."

"Oh yes…the human soul."

Angelica sits quietly as Arthur continues his work. She gazes through the ceiling window. Then, in a consensual overtone, "Arthur, Do you think of me as a woman who spends her money foolishly?"

"I think a lot of things Angelica, but I'm not your judge, and I certainly don't tell you…, of all people, how to spend what's yours. Although, I can clearly see that this endeavor of yours is definitely a means to an end. Perhaps it is something deeper, or maybe Nostalgia, as you call her, is your trophy."

Angelica smiles at Arthur. She raises one finger and touches her mauve colored lips as thought to speak, but soon focuses her attention to an object outside the window. Arthur, noticing her actions, also looks in the same direction.

"What do you see?"

"The celestial ruler of the night…"

"The lunar moon – it is beautiful."

Suspended high in the dark heavens, the gray giant supremely glistens as the soft under girth of clouds passes by. With each opening, cascading light gently fills the laboratory. Arthur observes Angelica's tear stained eyes.Then, in a somber voice, she tells him, "I also see the past, present, and future. Thank you Arthur…" Angelica rises from her chair and pitifully exits the room.

Arthur curiously watches the door close behind her. Standing quietly, he gazes beyond the window and again observes the nimbus formations. Arthur's powers of observation are keen as he easily perceives that much has been said, though very little was spoken.

Afterwards, the technician returns his attention to the developing fetus, Nostalgia.

~~~The Hammer Strikes~~~

Within the province of the United Kingdom, sunrise renders its subtle glow to the bustling city of Westminster, a thriving metropolis in London's West End district. Though early morning, citizens comb the streets, either ending or beginning their ritualistic assignments for the day. Several food concessions prepare to open as businesses unlock doors for operation. Damp streets act as major arteries for the influx of growing crowds. Antiquated buildings combine modern adaptations to attract and entertain thousands of tourists and Londoners alike. Attractions such as Piccadilly Circus, Chinatown, Covent Garden, and London's entertainment industry bring major economic strength to this geographic region.

On a remote street near the West End, two unmarked vehicles park on the outskirts of town. Though widely visible, the vehicles conform to the rules of the city and attract little attention. Each transport carries a compliment of passengers and equipment of sorts; however, there is one distinguished passenger who rides in the front vehicle. That person is Aun'war, and he begins to address his men.

"Listen everyone. We are now on the Queen's turf, and judging from the demise of our two sister outposts, I want to make sure this demonstration goes well. Once our mission is complete, I will make a statement to the governments of the world, but until then, I will bring down any thing or any one that gets in my way."

"What is your plan Aun'war?"

"Plan? Hah…simple man. Do not make things more complex than need be. Those behind us will drive into Westminster, or near Covert Gardens; I don't care which place; then…they will shoot as many poor souls with the extractors. And afterwards, blend in with the traffic while escaping. They will rendezvous at the pick up site. Simple?" Snarling grins widely display as eyes concur deeds of deplorable merit.

"Sultan, I hear that you decided not to rebuild the Ukraine and Mediterranean outposts. I also hear that you silenced all who worked on the extractors as well. Is it true?"

Aun'war does not reply. Instead, he grasps a transceiver and communicates to others through the device. Explicit orders go forth and the second transport scurries away. Audio monitors broadcast as other sounds resonate with full functionality.

"Drive," commands their sultan. The driver hastily takes an alternate route than the other vehicle. Aun'war glances at his chauffeur and takes a deep breath while reaching towards the inside of his jacket. The driver observes Aun'war, but then, quickly looks ahead. "I...I...did not mean to question your plans sir." Aun'war looks at him, and immediately laughs, as his actions prove misleading when his hand bypasses a concealed weapon. Aun'war removes only a small silver cigarette holder; lights a cigarette and leans back. Comforting exhales fill the inside cabin as several assault weapons dangle overhead.

Aun'war continues his snickering, until he tells them, "Gentlemen, the problem with the Ukraine and the Mediterranean outposts is that someone found out about them, and hit us – and destroyed our major points of attack. Those facilities were also operational bunkers and only those in my immediate army knew about the location of the bunkers. My urgent concern is that who ever knew about those outposts can now touch us...and that is a threat."

"Those outposts were keys to our operations."

"I am aware of that - simpleton. It also occurred to me that we are spread too large, which makes us thin; and it is difficult to control several independent operations at the same time. But in light of things, we now have the sole blue prints for the extractors; making it better for us to operate small, while managing a reasonable size army."

"And what of Europe?"

"Europe shall suit our new base of operations just fine. That is another reason why I had to see this demonstration for my self." Aun'war lights more cigars and offers the men a chance to puff their plans into fruition.

The transport, in which Aun'war rides, finally reaches its destination. The driver informs all occupants, "Sir, we're here." As the broadcast echoes loudly, Aun'war douses his cigarette and the others radically follow suite.

"Okay gents; let's give merry old England a merry new makeover. Be fruitful and multiply – or die." Aun'war gingerly smiles and clicks the transmitter off. Those within his company eye one another with great concern.

The forecast for the day is clear; however, pedestrians' choice of clothing refutes the possibility of high temperatures. Piccadilly Circus, a main intersection of roads in London's West End, funnels a mass number of people on a daily basis. Neon signs, bright colors, gothic architecture, and large video signs combine to dazzle the imagination; all transpiring under the watchful eye of The Angel of Christian Charity, Eros.

But even Eros barely notices the second van as it enters the midst of the unsuspecting denizens. With skill and tactfulness, the driver maneuvers his transport into the flow of rushing vehicles. The van has no windows along the aft compartment, only the driver and passenger side, as well as the forward windshield. Also contained are three custom-fitted nozzle shutters, one on either side of the transport, and one on the rear door. One of the men addresses his cohorts, asking, "Did Aun'war give specifics?"

"No."

"Hah…bet the boys riding with him are crapping in their *unddies*; because they know he could kill'em just for breathing wrong."

"Shut up and just do your job."

"Fine... Look, over there, that's a good spot."

"Then you'd better start loading Mr. Cane. I'll drive closer."

Jumping to the occasion, Cane peers just beyond the glass covering surrounding the port of the shutter, but covertly assures that no one notices the small doors opening on the outside.

"Drive us smooth and steady – You hear?"

"Just do your job, and Saul, make good on your attempts this time," replies the driver.

Silence sterns as eyes peer beyond the ports and lock on to a cluster of people. Fingers wrap anxiously around triggers poised with deadly aim. Cane glances at his partner. "Saul, three o'clock and I got my nine." Without hesitation, Saul squeezes the trigger. The fierce recoil presses firmly against his shoulder and pushes him backwards. "Whoa," he says.

"Idiot, you hit nothing."

"Just feeling it out – relax man."

"Yeah…right, never send a mouse to do a rat's job. Sit back and pay close attention." Cane finds his mark and fires twice. A quick, turbulent sound whisks beyond the barrel as two tiny capsules strike unsuspecting victims. "Now that's power," he says.

The victims, a man and woman, experience a ghostly touch. The man swats his shoulder as if striking an insect. "Bloody bug!"

"Were you bitten?"

"I felt as if something pinched me on the shoulder. But whatever it was, it's gone, but now my chest is sore." "I too felt something earlier."

The woman rubs her chest as though a disconcerting inflammation is taking place. Her facial expressions and casual stride offers no identifiable connection to the victimizing act. Perhaps countless times before, she continues to engage in moderate conversation with her counterpart. Both walk side-by-side, as do crowds of others.

Then strangely, the woman flusters red and pulls her sweater down from the neckline. Onlookers begin to take notice, curiously watching as her counterpart asks, "What's wrong?" She does not answer, but rubs her arms in an attempt to expel something unseen. "Oh God... I'm on fire...help me; please?"

"Do you have a fever?"

Her stern eyes and red face clearly denote torment, such that words offer little comfort. She breathes deeper and much more erratic. She tears her garments in an attempt to cast the items off. Partially nude, she falls to her knees and cowers.

Two young men emerge from the gathering crowd. "Hey, is this one of those candid gigs – yeh?" The young man eyes the woman; smirking a shifty grin, unaware that the situation before him girths the beginning of human suffering.

The woman's counterpart throws his jacket over her; but then, he too collapses to the ground, drawing even more attention from the gathering crowd. In the most pitiful sense of mortal states, the woman screams as loud as her blistering lungs can assist.

In sheer astonishment, one of the young men rushes towards her and offers what little assistance he can. "What's wrong Miss…what's wrong?"

The young man's questions come in earnest, but not before the woman's counterpart rents his shirt. His actions expose his bare chest and shoulders. He frantically squirms along the ground. Suddenly, his body convulses wildly, and as strange as it began, he becomes deathly still. Sweat covers him. Blisters erupt, quickly appearing small then rapidly growing, horridly turning into boils while systematically covering his entire body.

"Good Lord Jesus," whispers their would-be helper as his driving compassion commands him to mercifully hold the woman's hand; yet in anguish, he bears witness to the red swelling progression from her chest to the outer parts of her body. Her heart beats heavily while her eyes speak for a useless tongue. Tear ducts that once flowed streams of water now course with blood.

"Get help, I'll get help now," the young man tells her, but to no avail. A groaning noise rises just behind him as the laden man's body putrefies.

An older man approaches from the crowd. "Son, get away from them…and you don't touch her. Can't you see something's wrong? And look at him; His skin is leaving his body – get away from them – Are you crazy?" Within moments, the man's body dissolves into an organic mass.

The young man watches the woman, who continues breathing. But soon, he touches a conglomerate mesh of organs inside her hand and attempts to pull away – he cannot. "My God," he says, squeamishly drawing backwards.

Yet, in her state, the woman continues to squeeze his hand. Unable to separate, the young man frivolously shakes and watches the woman's face turn transparent and ultimately become as her counterpart. It is only then that he notices her exposed heart beating within the gel-like substance of her transparent skin. Later, the beat comes to a ghastly end.

With tear stained eyes, the young man looks at the old man. "Did you see that? Did you see? She was conscience the whole time…the whole *fucking* time!"

"You can't know that!"

The young man breaks away, making haste in any direction possible. Mist fills the air, dissipating from the only remnants that remain of both individuals. Pandemonium breaks out as frantic observers seek what in their minds constitute a safe distance. Sadly, many learn that more tragic and similar deaths took place since the event, such that will change the face of London's West End forever.

In Texas, Walter paces the floor of Jade's apartment as though butterflies are wrecking his stomach. Jade can only render a concerning response. "I sent Gracella a message, telling her that we need to see her – that much, I understand. But this catch and kill thing you speak of Walter, I do not understand."

"Jade, you don't have time. It's what I've been trying to tell you all along. Whoever took out Tuan and Alexis can get to us. Make no mistake; those thugs in that van knew exactly who they were after. And you know something else? I bet 429 is somewhere in the middle of it. I can also bet you that Rowland has his fingers in it as well."

"Are you so sure?"

"Jade – do I look like a man that's lying?"

"Will police help?"

"And tell them what? That our former boss wants to kill us because we help create…an overgrown kangaroo-lizard; then secretly handed it over to the military – hah."

Jade sits quietly upon the sofa as Walter cautiously peeks through the Venetian blinds. Satisfied that all is clear, he resumes pacing, though speechless. Jade asks, "Walter, what do you ask of me?"

"Only that you trust me. It's not safe for us, not here…and especially, not for you."

"Then where do we go?"

"Anywhere, but here…"

"I cannot…just…leave."

"Don't make this hard Jade."

"If what you say is true, then where is proof of evidence…as you say?"

"Evidence…"

"Yes, that thing that proves your remarks – Walter."

Walter raises his wrists, exposing the underside scars. "So, what the hell is this, stigmata?"

Jade surprisingly stares, but suddenly, the doorbell rings, followed by a knock. Both stand quietly. The doorbell rings again. "*Shhhhh*...quiet," prompts Walter while holding a finger to his lips. Then, Walter carefully runs to the kitchen, grabs a knife and cautiously stares through a peephole. The doorbell rings again, and then it rings no more. Sweat forms upon Walter's forehead as he trembles. Jade remains perfectly still.

"Are you expecting anyone?"

"No," she whispers.

Walter slowly opens the door while exercising great discretion. He looks around, but sees no one. Then, he finds a small card wedged inside the molding of the door. He quickly retrieves the card and gets back inside.

Jade asks, "What is it?"

"It's a business card."

"What does it say?"

"Derek Wayne Harrison, U.S. Marshall, call immediately." Walter rubs the back of his neck and blankly stares at the ceiling. "Get your coat Jade, we're leaving."

They hastily exit the apartment, leaving behind much as possible.

Inside his home, Rowland sits quietly in a wooden chair. He activates a big-screen monitor but keeps the volume low. In a matter of moments, the local newscaster projects the decadence of society. "What have you today for me Claudia *Meeeells*?" Rowland's inert question strikes only the walls as he watches the monitor with acute interest.

Suddenly, the phone rings. "Krenshenkov speaking... *Ahh...eet eez* you... You have some...*ting*? Ah...wait...before you speak. The Mediterranean and Ukraine jobs went very, very good – Yes? (Silence) What, the leads I gave you did not work – grown cold you say? I see...anyway, *eet* has been long time since Langley and *hees* Ausie friend reported. We have to assume the worst! Some-*teen* is *rr*-wrong and I cannot wait any longer. Yes, I'm sure of *eet*! And I have just de' weapon of choice for the job."

Rowland grows silent, intently listening to the voice through the receiver; but his attention soon divides.The news broadcaster unravels her information as red and yellow letters scroll across the bottom portion of the screen:

'Breaking News' "Disturbing occurrences are reported from London within the city of Westminster. A large section of the West End district has been quarantined. Authorities say that a line of strange deaths occurred near the intersection of Regent Road within Piccadilly Circus. Witnesses say that people immediately underwent a very severe and most bizarre transformation into what some say, is a transparent jelly-like substance. Testimonies further depict that those who were affected…simply dissolved from plain sight. The gruesome reports also confirm that the only remains of the individuals are the clothing they were wearing. There is yet no official report on the total number of deaths, but local authorities are putting it somewhere in the hundreds. The London CDC is calling these incidents gruesome as well, yet bizarre and evasive. However, others are unofficially calling the incident, The Phantom's Death. Now on a more local note; the city of Dallas is bankrupt…"

Rowland quietly observes the monitor as faint verbal sounds emanate from the ear piece. No doubt, he hears the noise, but continues staring at the screen. Then, with a degree of assurance, "I'm sorry…I deed not mean to ignore you. Something interesting has happened. What *ez eet* you say? Perhaps you could turn your attention to Westminster London. Ver-*rryy* interesting *theeengs* has happened…Colonel."

Rowland slowly rocks back and forth in his chair. Afterwards, he smiles, clicks the phone off and places it on the table

~~~Nostalgia~~~

Again, the night sky looms heavily over Banks Laboratory as Arthur makes the final preparations on his latest project. The silent technician observes biomarkers on a transparent monitor, in effect, taking note of information uploading from several distinctly placed sources along the contour representation of his subject. The clear panel displays the outer form of a human female. Several markers continuously blink while suspended outside the subject's body. As text scrolls across a clear screen, Arthur intently observes the information. He misses nothing.

"Heart rate, body temperature, blood pressure, and tissue mass, and bone density, all look normal."

In such a modest setting, near the rear wall of the laboratory stands a tall fantastically crafted chrysalis. Cased within its transparent walls is a female whose body suspends effortlessly in blue fluid solution. Within the fluid, spectacular flames periodically erupt, vividly casting subtle displays of light, and then dissipating into a myriad of cascading bubbles. Arthur somberly gazes at his incarnation.

He quietly records, *"Even within the coaxing light of the lesser sun, her attributes of immortality enthrall the essential essence of evolutionary romanticisms. Skin; subtle in hues of orange yellow and green, deep in the pure color of cypress chestnut, smooth as refine glass; defined proportions conducive to a woman in her mid thirties. Shoulder length hair; black as coal with white ends, enchantingly framing the face of a celestial angel."*

Arthur glows with endearment. Soon, the doors to the laboratory slide apart. Angelica enters. Immediately, her eyes fixate upon the hybrid female.

"My, oh my…now that brings back memories – back in the day."

"Really…"

"Don't fool yourself kiddo, not only was I tight, but I had torque to go with it."

"I thought you were on cruise control."

"I am…but these days, I'm just under the speed limit."

"Aren't we all?"

"So…how is our girl?"

"Doing well... I'm just about to add a little seasoning."

Arthur presses several keys on the computer, after which the replicate's passive environment becomes a dazzling cascade of colorful turquoise and amber fluid turbulence. The spectacular barrage of igniting plasma engulfs the humanoid. Fire spontaneously erupt and dances within the watery volume, burning, purging, and purifying as it performs an astonishing transformation. After the chaos diminishes, the female hybrid floats within the life sustaining fluid. Arthur and Angelica both anxiously watch the event as the moonlight pierces the chrysalis, bathing the replicate in a subtle glow of light.

"There she is…your memory…Nostalgia."

Angelica places both hands over her heart as though to embellish the parental pride of a child's gleeful birth. Arthur watches.

"With this new procedure, accelerants and encoders get absorbed directly through the skin, making absorption into the organ tissue much faster and more efficient. The procedure also allows for the simultaneous genetic masking of the deer's heart and blood. I had to suppress her metabolic rate several times, as I warned you; or else she would have gone super nova. And since you couldn't wait, like I told you, you're going to have to take her real slow for the first week. I mean it."

"Well listen to you – Aren't we proud, yet?"

Angelica smiles, but takes notice of something. "Arthur, she's forcefully breathing. Is she in pain?"

"No, it's just harder to push fluid in and out of the lungs than it is for air, but once the cycle completes and she's exposed to air, she'll breathe normally. She is...quite peaceful."

"Remarkable..."

"Oh, by the way..."

"Yes?"

"Would you like to do the honors?"

"What honors?"

Arthur dims the lights in the laboratory; allowing only the moon's glow to stand paramount as it forms a glowing circumference around the chrysalis.

"As in natural child birth for any newborn, the same applies for replicates."

"Elaborate..."

"Her eyes just opened moments ago, and it's time to get momma's imprint. Stand near the chamber so she can see you."

"Arthur...this is amazing; look at her."

Angelica walks towards the chrysalis and places her hand on the side of the glass. Nostalgia immediately reacts to Angelica's presence and views her with a piercing stare. Then, a surprising act of unspoken benevolence occurs. Nostalgia touches the window of the chrysalis exactly where Angelica's hand presses from the other side. There, within the midst of the laboratory, in the cascading glory of the moon, Angelica makes eye-to-eye contact with her strange yet fascinating daughter. Their endearing connection continues for quite some time.

Arthur stands just beyond the shadows, but the moon light graces his face with a subtle luminance, making his appearance more ghostly than real. Strikingly, Nostalgia keenly perceives Arthur's position and beyond her crystal prism, she peers deeply into the eyes of her mystifying maker. She never breaks her stare; nor does Arthur, but Angelica discovers Nostalgia's curiosity.

"Well…I see I'm not the only one who's making a first impression."

Arthur remains silent, but steps further back into the shadows, leaving wordless matters to unknown interpretation.

On the following day, the employees of GenoSyss carry out their routine assignments. Among them, Gracella enters her work area and scans through documentation. With little effort, she searches through document after document. Suddenly, an alert on her computer draws her attention.

"Screen on." Soon a visual transmission appears. "Yes – this is Gracella, how may I help…you…Jade… Jade? "

"It is me…" Gracella cautiously glance above her partition, taking notice of any nearby co-workers. Afterwards, her voice lowers to a subtle whisper. "I can't believe this…it's you. Where have you been?"

"Can you meet me outside?"

"Of course; I'm on my way."

Gracella hurries outside the complex, gets in her car and drives to a nearby sandwich pavilion. She exits her vehicle and enters the building, searching. In a glance, she determines that two people are waiting inside, both wearing caps and dark shades. "Jade, Walter," she calls.

One person responds. "You recognized us?"

"Walter, you two are the only ones in here."

"Oh…"

Realizing a poor disguise, Gracella excitedly embraces Jade. "Jade, talk about timing, you caught me at the right time."

"Yes, I know, but listen Gracella; we do not have much time. Walter has something to tell you."

"Oh don't tell me… You both are getting married!"

Walter looks at Jade, who says nothing. "Oh, sorry," says Gracella while perceiving the language of their eyes.

271

"Well…okay. What do you have to tell me?"

"Gracella, I think I know what happened to Tuan and Alexis."

Gracella attentively listens, but before Walter could utter another word, her head lowers, as does her countenance. "They're *dead*, aren't they?" she asks.

Jade, sensing Gracella's dispondency, caringly takes her by the hand. Upon her response, Walter and Jade horrifically gaze at one another. Both become so still that the movement of a tiny spider crossing Walter's arm goes virtually unnoticed. Gracella leans back in her chair, slumping as tears stain her eyes.

"It all started with reports of a burned red car. No one thought about it at first; but then, his wife called looking for him. Then the administration office got word of Nathaniel missing. After that, the police came asking questions about Alexis', but they got nothing in the end. Suspicions grew. It made us all think about Frank's reassignment because we never heard from him. Many questions came but no answers. Then finally, the marshal came with his investigation, which grew more intense. He questioned us day after day as though we were the one's responsible for the disappearances. It wasn't hard to figure out that something was terribly wrong. I can't understand why any one would want to hurt them, or us." Gracella buries her head in her hands.

Jade comforts her, but the moment subsides as Walter addresses his former co-worker. "Gracella…Gracella, you have to hang in there – be strong."

"I know…it's just that no one knows why this is happening."

"None of us do. But how did you know that Alexis died? Did the marshal say?"

"The marshal mentioned some items, items that I know belongs to Alexis."

"Items…like what?"

"Gold bracelets... She always wore them at the meetings."

"Look, I don't mean to be insensitive, but you mentioned a marshal."

"Yes, he came by a few days ago questioning other co-workers as if some conspiracy is taking place."

"I knew it – I just knew it," says Walter. He reaches inside his pocket and gives Gracella a ruffled business card. "Is that the name of the marshal?"

"Derek Wayne Harrison – yes, yes that's him."

"We need to talk to this guy, now. But before we do, where's Arthur? I think he's also in danger."

"Arthur is out of town. He said only that he had a temporary part time project. He took leave of absence and asked Hollis and I to keep an eye on Gjhe'nan."

"You didn't mention him to the marshal – did you?"

"No…and there's not much more I can tell you."

"Where is Gjhe'nan?" asks Jade.

"You weren't supposed to hear that," blurts Walter.

"I am so sorry," says Gracella.

Jade confusingly looks at both of them. "Walter, what are you two talking about? Are you referring to Arthur's hybrid beast?"

"Just forget it Jade."

"Do not tell me to forget…my life in this too."

"Too much has been told already."

"I want to know who these people are – Who is Hollis and why is Gjhe'nan in Arthur's possession?"

"Shhhh! You're drawing attention, dear."

"We are the only three in here, but I will draw more attention than that if you do not tell me who these people are. I will go straight to police Walter, I need no more lies no more secrets – no more!"

"Okay, okay…fine; just calm down."

Gracella and Walter move closer to Jade and explain the scenario of misfortunes. As they do, Jade sits quietly in disbelief, pondering all that she hears. With each pressing moment, her countenance lessens. Then, as if drained of all hope, she turns to both, asking, "So, what do we do now?"

"Contact Arthur and the marshal. I think that in those two, we will find some answers," explains Walter.

Suddenly, a distinct sound captures everyone's attention. Gracella immediately reaches into her purse and retrieves a tiny device. Information scrolls down a small viewer.

"Something important?" Walter asks.

"Oh my God... It's Arthur. He's back in town."

"We better tell him – everything."

"I'll let him know where we are."

~~~Wayward Souls~~~

Across the North Atlantic, Aun'war sits behind an elaborate table that bridges 18th century Victorian craftsmanship with modern day high-tech sophistication. Built within the tabletop is a large monitor that displays the continents of the world in real time projection. Along both sides of the main viewer are three smaller monitors. Each of the smaller monitors displays various amounts of information such as time, date, events, and even satellite trajectories as well as city populations.

On one of the smaller monitors, a visual transmission projects to Aun'war as well as those who are with him. The speaker, a militant of some sort, conveys a direct message to Aun'war.

"Sir, all components for the extractor is in our possession. We have also neutralized all participants, suppliers, and financiers as you ordered. Nothing remains but the clothes they once wore."

"Excellent, we are now unaccountable to anyone. Now go! Finish your work and return immediately to base."

"Yes sir..."

After obtaining the information, Aun'war turns his attention to seven men who are sitting at the table. "My loyal friends…hear me. London's CDC cannot see us. Scotland Yard cannot touch us, and the Parliament of England will not deny us. Our plans are coming together. And once we land upon U.S. soil, we will take a band of men and disperse simultaneously to three large major cities, starting with New York, Houston, and eventually moving to Los Angeles."

One of the men, a tall scrappy militant with a heavy scar covering his right eye sequesters Aun'war's attention. "How many are we to kill this time?"

"Oh…I don't know. Depending where we strike; seven, eight, maybe fifteen thousand."

"Why such…larg…numbers, Sultan?"

"It is a numbers game my friend. The more, the merrier. Shoot until there are no more to shoot; however, shoot on a small scale, target high-class areas."

"I do not understand."

"Five to six dead among the rich and famous are more noticeable than sixty to a hundred in the slums."

"I see…"

"Good – "

"But now, we can take what we want. Perhaps you take more than you need?"

"Are you implying…that I am greedy?"

"No my lord… Please; no disrespect intended."

"Well spoken…"

Aun'war coldly stares at his questioner, yielding silence as his only response. He slowly rubs his forehead as though already fatigued with such an inquiry. Then, he takes a deep breath and walks only a few yards away from the table as if preoccupied with something else, twisting his neck as if to cast off a demonic annoyance. He turns towards his men again.

"Principalities cast their sanctimonious legislations upon gullible citizens, like human feces for a barren wasteland. These same governments create for themselves a life-style of luxury while their countrymen scavenge the land just to survive. Ah…but take good heart my friends, for in my world, the individual is as important as those who; supposedly, represent him or her from the office of the state. In my world the individual's voice should project louder than their magistrates. Politicians should be…more humble and appreciative of their positions – Don't you agree?"

"Of course my lord…"

"No ruling party should dictate anyone's way of life; especially mine. I should not have to pay taxes or obey laws forced upon me, nor should I have to fight battles that are not mine. And if barbiturates are the meal ticket of the day, then it is my choice - my right to choose such things. I am as unilateral as any person or institution in this world and I intend to make all the governments see that. Am I not above another man's law? Curse to them all - everyone has a voice."

"Some will think you a hero, Majestrate Aun'war."

"That is honorable my friend, but there is a small stipulation regarding my quest."

"A stipulation…how so?"

"Everything that transpires comes under my rules." Aun'war smiles; however, blank faced and beguiled members of his private party can only stare at him. "Look closely at North America – gentlemen. Here is our ticket for spreading the word. Fearful news travels fast in the land of the eagle and because of that, they will never sleep in peace. With that in mind, London was gracious to provide us with a name for our viral toxin."

"What is the name – my lord?"

"The Phantom's Death… And I have decided that such a name should not go to waste."

"After you release this…Phantom's Death, what will become of presidents, senators; governors…and to what extent will you carry out your demands?"

Hearing the question, Aun'war lights a cigar, much to the surprise of those around him. One of the men asks, "Emissary, have you taken a new interest in smoking?"

"No. I just like the taste…not only that, cherry plumbs smell good. I think the pipe also gives me a sophisticated look. Do you agree?" The man hears Aun'war's response, but dares not ask again, sensing that he may be pushing for an unwanted fate.

"Prepare to disembark," commands Aun'war. "Yes – sir..." All seven men immediately rise from the table, but before they could exit the room, Aun'war rises to his feet.

"It was once stated, regarding the two faces of liberty, *'A free man is he who is not hindered to do what he has the will to do.'* Governments control the people; I will control the governments. Imagine how grand it would be if I could get one third of the entire human race to follow me. That will leave only those who think as I, and that of course will make us one big family in the new world order."

"And…what of our mission in America?"

"Texas has a large commercial harbor. Be sure to use it wisely."
Aun'war puffs a somber cloud as fire singes the tobacco leaves. A

haunting stillness fills the room as baffling expressions cover the faces of the men. Yet, seeing no reason to add to their sultan's remarks, the men exit the room.

Late evening, Arthur, Gracella, Walter, and Jade assemble inside the city's West Precinct. Inside, a crude office becomes the meeting place. Among the participants, a middle-aged black man leads a series of questions as he holds a pencil and paper in hand.   With arms crossed, his mature sternness suspiciously captures each of the four listeners as the desktop serves as his casual chair. An officer's badge mounts boldly upon his belt, but his black sports coat suggests duties other than street patrol. His jacket partially covers a name tag that features the identity of Derek Wayne Harrison, U.S. Marshal.

Marshal Harrison's leg sways in a manner that is not so distracting, as though to direct the rhythmic heartbeat of those testifying. A thick, black mustache combines with attentive eyes to produce a face that is well seasoned for the task at hand; and yet, it is the same face that has most likely heard all the stories. If there is anything new to Harrison, it will have to come well beyond his line of work. He sits before his subjects and assures them that their input is not in vane.

"Again, I would like to thank each of you for coming down here; especially on short notice. For you new people, you can call me Harrison, my parents call me Harrison, my boss calls me Harrison, and you may keep the tradition going. Now without wasting time, I have heard some accounts on your behalf, but I would like to know if there is any thing that you have to add?" Silence looms as Harrison's eyes make contact with each person. "Nothing? Fine then..." Harrison takes a deep breath and slowly rubs his forehead as though to dispel aggravation.

Raising his head, he directs his inquisitive powers towards Arthur. "Mr. Robinson, Arthur?"

"That's me."

"Of all the accounts, yours is…intriguing. Tell me again. Did you have any contentions with Tuan?"

"There was a moment when he and I had a difference of opinion – all work related though."

"Really…"

"Yes."

"Professional differences like…"

"A petty disagreement…"

"I see… Do you have anything else to add?"

"No."

Harrison looks at Arthur but says nothing; however, his eyes search for more. Silence lingers yet again. Suddenly, Harrison slides off the desktop and scants to the door of his office. He opens the door, looks both ways down each corridor and then slams the door shut. Afterwards, he tosses a notebook and pen aside. All eyes widen as the marshal stares down each of them.

"Alright everyone…call me an unprofessional, a bigot, a charlatan, a child, or just simply a damn idiot; you can even call me the n – word…I don't care. My mother was a judge and my father was a street cop so that puts me somewhere between…less than a genius but smarter than a fool. For starters, when providing a declaration, you people should at least get your stories straight. One hour has passed, and I've heard each of your accounts, but it's quite clear to me that something *ain't* quite *jiving*. Off the record, stop…*bullshitin*…me."

Walter defiantly exerts, "Look man, what more do you want? We've just told you everything!"

"The hell you did science boy," recants Harrison.

Jade asks, "What more are you wanting from us?"

"Okay, let's start again with you this time, Ms. Jade Vjekoslava. You told me that you worked on a project with the missing four and…that two of them were reassigned to another department, while the other two found outside employment. Well, the personnel department for GenoSyss states that these individuals never left the agency – whatsoever."

Completely surprised, Jade stares at the floor.

"Now… Onto you Mrs. Gracella Andreas. Your account corroborates Jade's statement to some degree, yet it makes me think that you worked in the same building where the deceased presumably continued work. Your account says that you never saw either of them after a bogus reassignment, but your fellow employees confirmed sightings of the deceased – in the same building around the time of your affirmation. Did you also know that personnel documents provide no clue to the deceased traveling from the company at all? There are usually termination papers to go along with employees who quit jobs." Gracella does not reply. "I thought you would remain silent."

"Okay Walter Pierson. Your statement says that you survived a kidnapping. It also says that you don't know where you were taken and that you don't know why you were kidnapped in the first place. Yet, you somehow managed to escape – fair enough... However, did you know that blood samples, matching two of the deceased were found in a field near one of the streets you mentioned earlier – Coincidence?"

"I don't see the point!"

"The point isssss.... How convenient that you were kidnapped and taken to an undisclosed vicinity where two of the deceased lay?"

"Look Marshal...I told you everything I know.

"Everything?"

"Yes!"

"We shall see...And again, to you Mr. Robinson. I've been in this business for thirty-six years and believe me when I say – you could have won an Emmy, I mean they should put you on center stage – best acting job I've seen in a long time."

"I'll remember the compliment."

"Go for it, because you are very careful with your words, as if there is something more, as if you are hiding something."

"I guess now you'll tell me what the crystal ball says."

"Hah, now you're being a real ass. But for the record people, either GenoSyss fed you all a bogus story, or none of you really intend to solve this incident. Hell, call it ESP or an old fashion lawman's hunch, but you people have to work with me, otherwise the deaths of Tuan, Nathaniel, Alexis, and Frank is in vane. It's only a matter of time before I figure this out on my own. So what will it be?"

All remain silent, staring about the room, scratching their heads while displaying perplexing faces.

Harrison continues his relentless assault. He stares down Gracella and approaches her while noticeably holding a beige envelope. He reaches in and removes a clear plastic bag.

"Until now, there's been nothing but questions, so for the record. Recognize these?"

Gracella's eyes widen. "Oh God…those belong to Alexis."

"I thought these might jump start some memories. These match the same bracelets worn by a woman whose body was pulled from a fresh grave. She was assaulted. Do you want to see the photos?"

"That won't be necessary."

"I didn't think so. Now dry your eyes and get real."

"You're so rude."

"And you're wasting my time. So get use to it. Now if you all will be so kind as to indulge me. Let me paint a brief picture for you. Alexis Hawthorne; born in Palm Springs, California, worked part-time at Regis Blood Bank, then took an internship at GenoSyss, which is here in Texas. She worked on a project…came up missing, then dead – Need I say more? Frank Nunna'hi-tsune'ga Guilford, a Cherokee *brotha*, grew up on a reservation in Oklahoma, married and has two kids, came here to study for his degree, got employed at GenoSyss, worked on a project…came up missing, then dead. He was bludgeoned to death. Would you like to see the photos? Tuan Nguyen Vein, born in Hanoi, the land of distant misery, bright kid, bleak child hood though, comes here by way of immigrant parents, studies his butt off, gets smart real fast, acquires work at GenoSyss, works on a project…comes up missing, then dead – gun shot… Would you like to see the photos? Then, last but not least, Tennessee born Nathaniel Ulysses Keech, genetics veteran, genius by some accounts, married with kids, comes to GenoSyss…you know the rest – Would you like to see the photos?"

Harrison sits on the desk and slowly leans forward, visually dissecting every one present.

"Given the condition of the corpses we can only assume the worst. Were it not for a guy and his four-legged friend on a morning stroll, we probably never would have come across those four graves. Another grave was discovered and it looked as if it was prepared for someone. I can only imagine whom…it was intended for," says Harrison while sternly watching Walter.

"Convenient for us, all those graves were in one location. Our only link is that GenoSyss is the common denominator and all of you were part of some project there, at one time. We got your names from co-workers who described you all as having worked with the deceased…so here we are. As for the project in question, someone apparently believes it's worth killing for. Not to mention that it is the only element of this discussion that remains elusive. In summary, we have four dead people, conflicting accounts, and you people want my help."

"So much for serving the public," says Walter."

"Well…that's what I'm here for, but you all frustrate me. Know why? Because I have no motive and without a motive I can't build a case. If I can't build a case, I sure as hell can't help any of you. Sooner or later, I will find out what this secret project is, because I'm quite sure that who ever made a statement with your friends will soon make a statement with you. Now I'll give you people a couple of days to get your stories straight, but in the mean time. I'll try to find this Rowland Kreshenkov. He's the only consistency I've heard all evening."

The four glance at each other, and then rise to their feet. Within a matter of moments, they somberly tread the old wooden floor to the exit. Arthur is the last to approach the door. Instead of exiting, he briefly turns and sternly looks at Harrison. "Marshal, I do have one question."

Harrison, in a lethargic tone, asks, "What?"

"Why would a U.S. Marshal take on a case like this?"

Harrison pauses from his activity and takes a deep breath. He slowly looks upward towards Arthur. Then, in a brisk manner, he tells him, "Take this information on credit Robinson. Know that the FBI is interested in your former supervisor."

"Rowland…"

"There's more to him than even you know. And because of that…stipulation, I don't know if I'll be protecting or arresting him. Jurisdictions could become an issue."

"Our government wants Rowland?"

"Everything surrounding this investigation didn't just start yesterday. So don't plan any vacations. Got it?"

Arthur slowly closes the door.

Outside, Walter and Arthur hash out their suspicions. Walter's griping assertions pierce deeply within Arthur's ears; so much that his heinous verbal lashing comes as an unforgivable wave. "Lot of good that did!"

"What else were we suppose to do Walter? We can't leak out information on 429 or Gjhe'nan."

"Maybe not, but I say we tell the Marshal everything."

"We can't..."

"Why?"

"Breach of contract, besides, during the planning stages of 429, Rowland and Colonel Ducet clearly said that they would deny everything in order to protect GenoSyss from us or media slandering – nothing gets out, you know that."

"Ah…but don't forget, something did get out, and it's in a big white barn in the country."

"Gjhe'nan is far from this; so don't make it into something it's not. I'm warning you."

"People are dead because of that thing!"

"That thing…did not kill anyone!"

"Doesn't matter, he is property of the military and they're knocking us off just to get him back!"

"Oh…so now the military is doing the killing. Where in the hell did you get that nonsense Walter?"

"Arthur, how do we know that you are not helping them?"

"Are you serious?"

"Damn right I am! What's the real reason why you…of all people have Gjhe'nan in your possession?"

"Because… I'm not an idiot like you."

"You're a real piece of work pal."

"The hell with you Walter, I'm not taking your crap any more!"

"Get your ass back here!"

Walter lunges towards Arthur and wrestles him to the ground, commencing devastating blows to the technician's face. Arthur retaliates and the two become locked in mortal combat. Both sustain severe bruises until Walter pauses.

"You're the reason for all that's happened! Gjhe'nan comes up missing and we're dying for it!"

"You're full of *shiii*..." Again, Walter feverishly strikes Arthur and wrestles him to the ground, then standing, and kicking Arthur to no end as the technician attempts to block Walter's brutal attack.

Jade and Gracella watch in disbelief. Soon, both men wrestle to the ground again until Walter rises to his feet and stumbles backwards while placing his hand over his lower abdomen. "Son-of-a bitch! You stabbed me!"

Jade rushes to Walter's side and attempts to stop the bleeding. "You need stitches Walter."

Arthur slowly rolls to his side and rises to his feet as well, extending his arm with an erected blood stained blade. With body language poised for conflict and an attitude for vengeance, Arthur confronts Walter.

"Taking a life ain't hard; so if you're man enough to start something, then be man enough to finish it."

Gracella intervenes. "Stop it; stop it, both of you! Haven't enough people died already? The police couldn't find the killer's fingerprints on Alexis or Frank. How much more do you think they'll find anything on 429? For all we know, whoever killed them could be watching us right now. We need each other – we really do."

Walter covers his wound while staring at Arthur. Both men lay in deadlock silence as Jade and Gracella earnestly watch. Then, Arthur wipes the blade and slowly puts his knife away.

"If you want to take this further…it's your call."

"You're the real fool Arthur."

"Look man, I'm not trying to make this more than what it is."

"It's too late for that."

"How bad is the wound?"

"I'll live – no thanks to you."

"Walter, listen –"

"Didn't know you were carrying. Expecting trouble?"

"Let's just say I already have enough to think about."

"HARRISON is going to find out sooner or later and we can't stop him."

"Well you better pray that I'm in a listening mood."

"That's right…because wounds heal very, very, slow. And remember…*buddy*, you're not the only one who can carry a weapon – remember that."

Jade assists Walter as both depart.

Arthur stands, closing his eyes, breathing heavily as if troubled by a nightmare. Gracella walks near him, looking downward while placing her hands over her heart. "Just go. Don't try to make sense of this Arthur…just go home."

Afterwards, Arthur arrives home. Upon entry, he finds Aniah awake, sitting upon the couch while reading a book. "Hey honey, another late night… Whoa…what happened to you?"

"Nothing…" Aniah listens but perceives otherwise. "Are you guys working on another project?"

Arthur does not answer. Instead, he proceeds to the bedroom and sits quietly on the side of the bed. The bedroom door slowly opens. Aniah enters. She sits beside Arthur and gently lays her head upon his shoulder.

"Did your meeting at the job go well?"

"Yeah..."

"Do you want to talk about it?"

"No."

Aniah simply nods her head in non-verbal compliance, yet Arthur realizes it; but instead, he fixates upon a cabinet cased within the headboard of the bed. He stares, and stares until Aniah's nestling breaks his train of thought.

"Aniah, will you trust me regarding something?"

"Guess that all depends."

"You have to trust me."

"About...?"

"Listen, I may need you to go to your mom's for a little while."

"*Forrrr*?"

"I need you to do this."

"*Whhhyyyy*?"

"I'll tell you when you get there, but I need you to go, just for a week or two, maybe a month or so, hopefully no more – I don't know."

Aniah looks at Arthur with discontent. She asks, "Are you in trouble?"

"Things may get complicated."

"*Howwww*?"

"Will you just LISTEN?!"

"All right...all right...calm down."

"Don't tell me to calm down."

"Arthur…"

"I think someone is coming after me and I don't want you to be at risk. One week could make a big difference in whether or not my suspicions are true."

"See… I knew it! It's that project of yours – isn't it? Did you take that Gjhe'nan back to GenoSyss, like I told you too?"

"Anaih…"

"You didn't… Did you? Arthur how could you? I told you to take it back…now we're going to die for it!"

"Gjhe'nan is not the reason for what is happening."

"You told me your friends died and that scares me."

"I never should have told you."

Aniah strikes Arthur in the face, and angrily pounds his chest, senselessly beating him as if her act is a means to an end. Arthur manages to embrace her, despite being scared under such heretic wielding. Though her words lie immersed in subjection, she leaves Arthur with little reason to refute.

As her verbal lashing lessens, she tearfully tells him, "Arthur, I worry about you. Just give him back…give him *baaack…*"

"If only it were that simple…"

Aniah leaves the room, slams the door behind. Arthur focuses his attention on the cabinet once more. Opening a small door, he retrieves and holds within his hand, a gun. "Me, you, and the good Lord are going to see more of each other in the days to come," he whispers while loading bullets into the chamber.

Under the same cover of night, a tractor freight-class rig comes to rest along the side of an all but deserted street. The street lays adjacent to the GenoSyss building. Deep within the shadows of the surrounding structures, the wind sends flurries of leaves through nearby trees as well as under the rig, virtually masking any noises resonating outside. Lights quickly dim as heavy suspension coax radical movements inside the cargo area of the rig. Seconds later, large doors swing outward as two enans boldly, yet silently announce their presence. The beasts assert themselves position wise.

Then suddenly, massive hind-legs propel the assault nomads towards the GenoSyss building with staggering speed. Mounted cameras capture everything as the dreadful duo violently smash through the main entry doors of the building. Without breaking stride, the enans enter and quickly lay in pursuit of their targets. Though progressing with ease, an alarm dispatches a distress signal.

The enans separate. One makes its way down a corridor and eventually to the laboratory in the basement. Vaulted doors strongly secure the room, but the enan has an answer. The creature retrieves a device from its pouch and quickly secures a safe distance. The device explodes, sending glass, concrete and steel into several directions. Afterwards, the uncanny beast enters the room. Darkness is no hindrance as the enan acquires a small cylindrical canister. With canister in hand, the hybrid thief releases more devices upon the floor and immediately takes flight, hastily exiting as a trail of paper waves across the floor.

On the opposite end of the building, the other enan rummages through personnel documents. Locating an index of files, the hybrid tucks the documents inside its pouch and release several devices on the floor, thus taking flight as well.

Both attack nomads rendezvous within the main hall. Then, without warning, several thunderous sounds pound the hallways of the building, ripping walls apart while sending an inferno of chaos throughout the entire lower level. Shortly afterwards, explosions spur yellow and orange plumes of intense fire in all directions, rapidly sweeping the dark corridors of the building while rupturing more walls and collapsing every accessible space inside.

The enans rush for the exit. But then, a disoriented man staggers into the path of the escaping beasts. Unable to avoid the creature's fearsome approach, the man helplessly cowers to the ground. Fear grips him as contact is eminent. An enan collides with the man, sending his broken body crashing to the floor. Undaunted by contact, both hybrid beasts swiftly exit the building, leaving the fallen soul to his perpetual fate.

Several more explosions erupt until a sea of white fire engulfs glass and singes everything within its hellish grasp. Debris covers the parking lot and soon afterwards, the once magnificent high-rise building implodes, collapsing to the ground as mounds of wreckage succumb to the power of the white flames.

The enans successfully board the freighter. As the doors close, the creatures settle down inside and the freighter speedily moves down the road.

Inside the cab of the freighter, the female driver and her male accomplice observe the canister and envelope contents retrieved by the enans.

She asks, "Did the items get damaged?"

"No, the embryos are fine. They are frozen specimens of the enans."

"What about the paper work?"

"The papers are right here, but you would think such information would have been on a data capsule."

"Rowland says it contains all the specs on how to clone the enans."

"I think he intends to give it to an officer of the military."

"I don't care what he does with it; our job is finished."

"Yes, but other people were still inside the building."

"I only saw one."

"What difference does it make? One or a hundred and one, it seems we have gone from mercenaries to political murderers. Even our job in the Ukraine did not take the life of innocent people."

"Taking down Rham-kiev is worth the effort and worth one innocent life."

"I know, but it sounds like we have to divert our attention again."

"How so?"

"Apparently, Rowland's other hit men, Langley and his Ausie friend is dead. Now, our new orders are to take down four remaining possible threats."

"Our mission is changing again. Our employer has become…someone else."

As GenoSyss comes into full view, the burning remnants light the dark sky for miles around while leaving no question as to the demise of its current state. Deathly flames spiral upward, expanding far beyond the stone perimeter as it consumes nearby trees.

The woman skillfully maneuvers the iron rig pass approaching medical and law enforcement vehicles. In doing so, she draws no more attention than the rustling leaves that swirl in the brisk night air.

~~~Staging~~~

A small aircraft soars within a few feet above the taunting waves of the North Atlantic. The craft projects a heading towards New York liberty's main port. Ironically, the craft is a harbinger of individuals whose liberty is far from the subjugation of Western authority. On board, the pilot observes an aerial chart. He points to a location on the chart while drawing the co-pilot's attention.

"Flying below their radar is hard enough. It's even tougher without getting caught in the sea and the weather isn't helping."

"Some of those waves must be five to eight feet high."

"Scared?"

"No, but be mindful of the Coast Guard. You know how well they can smell a rat."

"I am aware of that…and you worry too much. All is under control. Our target is out there…now go and inform the others."

The co-pilot carries out his instructions. He flips a couple of overhead switches and the cabin lights immediately turn red. Both men monitor several instruments carefully. "Can you see?"

"No…no…not yet. Searching…Got'em!"

"Is it the Coast Guard?"

"No, just some sort of fishing troller."

"Compliment?"

"All depends… Do you wish to travel in third class or luxury?"

"I do not see any luxury ships in these waters; I choose not to take chances."

"We do not have many choices. We should take what is available."

"Agreed; the troller it is."

Upon approach, occupants inside the cabin of the plane quickly muster their weapons and ready themselves for the task. Four men, wearing specialized suits and water tight covering for their gear, approach the rear door of the craft. Each man motions his head with an enthusiastic expression, brining to full compliance their clandestine objectives. A man standing to their side addresses them. "Your destiny waits. We will rendezvous after all targets are seized…but if not…then we will meet beyond Jahannam. The waters may chill your bodies, but not your souls – *ma a salama* (go without fear)!"

Each man acknowledges with a bow and leaps beyond the aircraft, plunging into the waters below and ultimately disappearing from sight.

The aircraft flies dangerously close to the fishing vessel, thus causing panic while stirring excitement among the crew. On board the vessel, one of the men asks, "Captain, did you hear that?" "I sure did. What is a plane doing this far out without taxi lights, and flying that low at this time of night? There is no search and rescue going on that I know of."

"Do you think they are lost?"

"I certainly hope not. There were no emergency hails reported; anyway, they are going off now. Looks as if they are heading towards New York."

"Should we report it sir?"

"Nah…if they want to die out there, let them. Side's, there's nothing we can do about it anyway. Go check the trolling lines."

"Aye sir..."

Obeying the captain is the ship's mate. His loyal service carries with it the utmost respect and servitude that is becoming of all sea worthy hands. He stands at the edge of the deck and assures that the lines are fit and secure, but for him, such nobility is crushed as his body coldly drops to the wooden deck.

"Cossack, Cossack, are you okay man? Cossack!"

A crewman's shrieking call alerts others and soon the deck swarms with startled members who attempt to help their fellow seaman. Staring at the lifeless body, one of the men grabs Cossack's wrist.

 "My god, there's blood all over him. What happened?"

The crew's apparent fixation keeps them from noticing three bodies emerging from the dark water. Each figure boards the vessel, and covertly approaches while bearing high-powered weapons. Then suddenly, "Look, over there!" A crewmember's screeching yell alerts every one to an apparent danger. As members turn to reckon the matter, the approaching assailants open fire, brutishly slaying them all. Their bodies lie unconventionally in a crimson pool as the rain washes blood overboard.

In the control booth, the captain observes the incident and desperately activates his transmitter. "Mayday, mayday…code red, anyone hearing me? Harbor control…come in! My boat is under *attaaahh…*"

The captain never concludes his plea as he falls helplessly to the floor. Though alive, the sea commander squirms to a corner of the cabin and sits upright, leaving a smearing trail of blood. Pampering his gaping wound, the captain looks upward and beholds his assailant standing before him. The assailant slowly approaches the captain and kneels directly in front of him. In a casual manner, the assailant removes his hood and goggles, and then gingerly takes the bearded seafarer by the chin. Staring directly in the captain's eyes, the assailant moves closer.

"Tell me my ocean worthy friend. You have seven seconds to make peace with the deity of your choice. Should you choose wisely, you will have everlasting peace. Should you choose foolishly; you will partake in eternal misery. Which do you prefere?"

With blood pouring from his mouth, the captain scoffs. His breathing slows as he forces air in and out of his lungs. Yet, he beseeches the dark figure.

"Am I to know my murderer…who are you?"

The assailant positions the captain's head, making sure that he is conscience enough to comply with the solace request. "My sultan, for reasons of his own, admonishes us to say these things when we are in a position like this."

The captain stares at the man as strength pours from his body, causing him to slump even more to the floor. Then, in a weakened voice, he manages enough strength to tell the man, "Then…I forgive you as the Christ forgave me." The assailant nods his head in commendable acknowledgement, raises his weapon and sends the captain into silence.

Behind the assailant stands another of his accomplices. "Is that what Aun'war truly tells you to say?" "I saw him give a man a choice. I'd want a choice. Would you?" His accomplice says nothing as both men quietly watch the veteran seafarer slump onto the floor.

Suddenly, *"Harbor control to Sea Merchant vessel, come in. Harbor control to Sea Merchant vessel, come in..."* The message blares from a speaker, catching both men by surprise. "You better answer them," blurts the accomplice.

"This is Sea Merchant – go ahead..."

"We received a distress call...are you in need of assistance?" [silence] *"Remain where you are, we will be in route – over..."*

"Umm – Harbor Control...cancel that request – everything is fine."

"Sea Merchant – say again?"

"We are fine..."

"Is every thing okay?"

"One of the trolling lines broke and became tangled in our propeller. We thought it would hinder our ability to move. One of our crew was hurt and we panicked, but everything is fine."

"We are prepared to dispatch immediate assistance."

"Not necessary."

"Very well then, keep us informed. But do know that there is a storm approaching – so you may consider coming in."

"We are advised – out."

Both men sigh with relief as the assailant discontinues transmitting. "Too easy. It was not your voice they heard earlier. They will come."

"I know. Apparently the captain got enough information out."

"What are your orders now?"

"Weigh down the bodies and toss them overboard. Be sure to bleed their throats and let the sharks finish them off. Cut the trolling lines and we will resume our mission. He is correct about one thing."

"What is that?"

"There is truly...a storm coming."

Later that morning, in Texas, Marshal Derek Harrison and Detective Candice Hess drive to the home of Rowland Kreshenkov. The uncommon pair travel down a winding road that coasters the hilly terrain. Tall Aspens boarder the edge of the road as dormant vegetation covers the landscape. Sparse patches of foliage projects a scenic wonder as few pedestrians walk their canine companions. Some houses hide behind distant shrubbery while others stand panoramically upon high earthen platforms. Candice eyes their surroundings with splendid appreciation. "Wow, this guy's not hurting for money."

"So it seems."

"Maybe I should get into the custom cloning business. Create a pet that doesn't eat, poop, talk back; *oooor*...create a group of clones that can replace the IRS, or U.S government – all under my control. But then again, maybe I'll just settle for a male, a human male slave-pet."

"I take it he'll have no rights whatsoever."

"I did have one back home in Vancouver you know."

"Yeah right – and I'm the real Al Jolston."

"I can see the resemblance."

"Candice, I can't believe you left Canada for sage brush and tumble weeds, not to mention the heat."

"Well...if you can leave Detroit for a better offer, then I can leave my precinct as well; not to mention, leaving behind the jack asses who were trying to keep me down."

"I know, but a girl like you in this kind of work. You should be in a nice home with a good husband giving him beautiful babies."

"Oh, you mean knocked-up and a slave with some type of mental disorder – no thank you."

"There's nothing wrong with marriage and family. Madison and I are on a twenty-eight year haul and we ain't looking back."

"Good for you. My last boyfriend and I lasted twenty-eight days and I always look back."

"That's your problem. I'm going to be praying that the good Lord sends you a good man."

"Derek...if you don't get away from me with that pampas churchy bs, I swear..."

"All right Ms. Annie Oakley, calm down."

"He cheated on me..."

"I know...you told me already."

"But, the problem is..."

"Is...what?"

"I may have given him a reason."

"That can be a two way street. We don't have to talk about it."

"Your kind; besides, Texas has promise. At least down here, we can fry criminals. Not to mention, I can ride a mare and swing a hefty six shooter, thank you very much."

Marshal Harrison laughs openly until he drives into a long stretching driveway of one of the neighborhood estates. "We're here."

The officers gather their necessities and approach the front door. Harrison rings the doorbell while addressing Candice. "Controlling clones inside the IRS. Now that's a good one; I'm surprised it hadn't crossed my mind."

"I do have a brain."

"Just be mindful, should you manage to pull off such a thing, the Center for Cloning Ethics will eat you alive, especially if they find out about your male pet."

"CCE has been busy lately."

"You got that right. Besides, if you make such a thing as a male pet...what is he going to do for you?"

"What do you care, and who's going to tell the CCE?"

"If you behave…I may just forget."

"Just ring the doorbell Dereck. Again, the marshal rings the doorbell and then proceeds to knock.

"There's always the darker side of technology Candice."

"You are referring to what exactly?"

"Bringing clone hybrids; replicates into this world."

"Really…"

"Number one, they already have no rights – two, they're just property, and three, you can terminate them at anytime – whether moral or immoral. And let us not forget four – they are not aloud to have *babies* – whatsoever."

"I know."

"Good…now just remember one more thing, perhaps more important than any thing else in our line of work."

"And that would be?"

"All that glitters doesn't shine."

"Good point."

"I mean it. Now…if the Russian is here, let me do the talking."

"Yes sir…boss man."

"Did you say boss man?"

"You can be in charge, this time. But I'm supposed to do the investigating. That is why you brought me along – Right?"

"Sure…"

Harrison lifts his hand again, proceeding to knock, but before he could strike, the door opens. Standing in denim jeans with a bathrobe partially tied is Rowland. While flashing his badge, Harrison addresses the geneticist. "Mr. Kreshenkov I presume."

"Yes, that *eez* me. May I help you?"

"We just have a few questions. May we come in?"

"Sure…by all means."

Rowland invites both officers inside, but stops them shortly once they enter. "May I get you some-*teen*?"

"No…not at all. I'll be brief."

"Of course…"

"Mr. Kreshenkov, as you can see, I'm Marshal Derek Harrison and this is Detective Candice Hess. We're investigating the deaths of former GenoSyss employees who were part of a team in which you were the lead worker."

"Oh…*rr*-really?"

"Were you aware that some of your former team members are dead?"

"No."

"Were you aware that their deaths came shortly after a project that you were in charge of?"

"No."

"Can you tell me exactly what project you were working on during the time in which your teams were assembled?"

Rowland pauses for a brief moment, starring Harrison in the face. He proceeds to gingerly walk about the room as though to ponder the officer's question. Then, with skillful subtlety, "*Thaaht* question *eez*…matter of confidentiality."

"Really," squawks Harrison.

"Oh yes…"

"Confident enough to erase four people?"

Rowland, perceiving Harrison's implication does not answer, but Harrison refuses to direst. "Let me lay it on the line Mr. Kreshenkov. Four are dead, four are alive, you were the lead person, and we know that all of you participated in a secret project."

"How unfortunate…"

"I don't believe their deaths were coincidental."

"What suggests…you?"

"Do you have anything to add or would you like to come down to the precinct for further questioning?"

Rowland; puzzled to hear Harrison's statements strolls over to his bar and retrieves a wine glass. "Would you like *drr*-ink?"

"No."

"*Mees-ter…*"

"Marshal."

"Ah…Marshal Harrison. Tell me Marshal, who is the four survivors?"

"That's not important just yet. What I need to know at this point is whether or not your secret project is worth people dying for. But why do I feel that you are not going to tell me that?"

"We signed agreements of non-disclosure with our clients Marshal."

"You don't say – Then, does the words subpoena or warrant mean anything to you?"

"*Eef* you are to do that, might I suggest talking *weeth* Michael Gladestone, our lawyer, or Arthur Robinson, *eef* perhaps he is one of the survivors."

"Why?"

"Because Arthur *Rrr*-obinson played key role in project."

"Really…"

"Yes."

"Okay, thank you for your time."

"Of course…"

The officers approach the front door. Candice leads first, but Harrison stops shy of the threshold and looks at Rowland. "Oh, by the way."

"Yes?"

"I see that you have traveling luggage in the other room. Going anywhere?"

"*W…wh*…well that *eez* for my travels, but to no where here of late."

"Good, because we will be talking again soon. Good day Mr. Rowland Kreshenkov."

"Ah yes… Das Vidaniya Marshal and to you *Mees*. Hess." Rowland candidly waves the officers good-bye and closes the door, but suspiciously views the officers through the window.

Candice addresses Harrison. "Wow, I've seen you in action before, but wasn't your technique a little brass, even for you?"

"Brass is good, especially when you make them feel that you have the upper hand."

"Where are you going with this Derek?"

"Remember my meeting with Rowland's former team?"

"Yes –."

"Well…an officer found a partially burned van just outside the city limits. Thinking it was foul play for insurance, he called to have if towed in. But to his amazement, he found bloodstains in the cargo area. Well…that luckily led to a DNA match. The results of that match came in a few hours ago."

"Really?"

"Yes. And guess whose blood and fingerprints were in that van?"

"Who?"

"Walter Grant Pierson's."

"This is getting very interesting all the time."

"Tell me about it. And it is something he failed to mention during our little meeting."

"I see your point."

"Guess what else?"

"What?"

"Two unidentified bodies were found in the same field where the four GenoSyss bodies were uncovered. One of the two bodies was a blond-haired guy. A couple of slugs were cut out of him, but no murder weapon was ever found. This guy matches the same description that Walter gave me."

"Sounds like things are quickly adding up."

"You got it."

"But why did you not tell Rowland?"

"The boys in D.C. want to keep an eye on him. They have an interest in his expertise. He and Walter worked on a project together. I want to know what it is."

"But Rowland is not a fugitive Derek."

"Not yet."

"You withheld information from him."

"I wanted to see what he would tell me first – my prerogative. Not even Walter is aware of our findings."

"It's too soon for indictments or arrests."

"I think Rowland may try to skip town. He strikes me as an evading cockroach. As for now, we cannot connect Walter with a murder rap just yet."

"So where to from here?"

"To find Arthur Robinson. Here…take my phone and send a transmission."

Candice taps several keys and scans for Arthur's number. Upon finding it, she proceeds to transmit. "You know, Rowland seems like a nice guy."

"Of course he seems nice, they all seem nice. It's often said that in the court of law, you're innocent until proven guilty - Right?"

"You know how it works."

"Well, with me, your ass is guilty from jump-street…"

"But isn't that a bit pre-judgmental?"

"We're chasing something Candice and I think it is bigger than what they say it is. I also believe that project 429 is in the middle of it all."

"Tell me that you are not making this bigger than what it is."

"Candice, you're textbook all the way girl, but down here as you will soon discover."

"I know…I know… All that glitters doesn't shine."

"Now you're getting the picture."

As Candice attempts to contact Arthur, the technician is all but in anticipation of their call. The comforts of Arthur's home are far from solace, for his protective efforts have sent Aniah away; but, it leaves him deeply deprived of sleep. Tense, and ever growing with suspicion, he surveys his own premise while carrying nothing more than a gun in one hand and a glass of water in the other. Attentive to every sound, he finds no room for error in an attempt to identify periodic noises sounding throughout the house. Though the sun brightens the mid morning day, Arthur's world is growing darker by the minute. Faint prayers and a jittery disposition characterize the technician's temperamental actions.

Suddenly, the phone rings. "*Shhh…t!*" Arthur almost drops every item that he is carrying, but manages to hold on. He rushes to the monitor and stands to one side. Pressing the audio-only button, he says nothing, waiting for the voice to confirm itself from the other end of the transmission. The dial tone resonates as a green flickering light beckons his response. Arthur however, only stares at the black screen as silence lingers.

Then, in the most stillness of moments, *"Arthur, Arthur, are you there…is that you?"* A voice progresses loudly from the speaker. Arthur calls out, "Screen on!" As the screen illuminates, the voice continues to call for his attention until he blurts out, "Grace…is that you?"

"Yes – it's me! My God, I've been trying to reach you all morning. Arthur, did you hear?"

"Wh…wh…what, what happen to you…look at you; why are you crying?"

"GenoSyss was destroyed!"

"What?"

"Arthur it's true!"

"Hell…music to my ears! W…wh…wait a minute. I just called in earlier this week and took a leave-of-absence."

"I was concerned and called the police, then I tried calling you, then Walter and Jade, but no answer…but Arthur…listen. Robert went out this morning and he hasn't come back…it's not like him – and with all that was said yesterday…I'm scared!"

"Wait a minute; you're telling me that Robert isn't back. Did he say where he was going?"

"Just out to pick up a package he ordered; I've been waiting ever since."

"Have the cops arrived?"

"No. I called the office to tell them I would be late and that's when I found out about GenoSyss. Arthur, my husband…"

"Okay look…just stay where you are, lock the door, get your gun…I'm on my way."

Ignoring his own exhaustion, Arthur cautiously scans his yard through the front door, sets the house alarm and rushes into the garage. "Come on Ramsey. Don't fail me now," he says as he climbs into his transport. Upon firing the engine, he suddenly hears a loud, dull noise. The noise comes from within the house. Arthur grows deathly still.

Soon, the door of the garage rises, but then, the house alarm blares wildly. "What the…I just set that thing." The alarm breaks his stillness as the powerful engine comes to life. But Arthur denies Ramsey proper warm-up and hurriedly backs the long white transport out of the garage, and onto the driveway. As the truck approaches the end of the pavement, Arthur hears the flagrant shattering of glass and broken wood crashing to the floor.

While in the cab, Arthur turns his head and beholds the most disturbing visage that even he could ever fathom. His mouth hangs open as his eyes widen with a ghastly stare. "You got to be kidding me…"

Amidst the rubble, standing within the garage is an enan, poised and ready to attack. With talons drawn and a swirling tail, the creature views Arthur as debris trickle to the floor. Piercing ever intently are the creature's dreadful eyes, slightly casting a translucent reddish glow. Those eyes are all Arthur sees before the garage door completely closes.

"No!" Arthur's scream comes only moments before hastening his vehicle down the road. Yet, all is not secure as the creature violently smashes through the garage door, relentlessly tearing its way into the adjoining street.

With only a few leaps, the enan is side-by-side of Arthur's transport. Arthur takes note of the thunderous sounds pounding just outside the window. With terror in his eyes, the technician increases acceleration, slightly gaining distance, but the creature lunges even farther ahead and positions itself for the apt moment of Ramsey's approach. Arthur gazes in sheer horror. He turns the steering wheel, forcing his transport to take a less demising route, but to no avail.

The enan perches upon its massive hind legs, rears its tail and exposes the sharp predatory stave at the end. With one tenacious swing, the enan thrashes the side of Ramsey, ripping through metal while raising one entire side of the vehicle off the pavement and onto an embankment. Though gouged, the mighty diesel holds true to form and continues on course.

Surprisingly, the enan halts pursuit. Arthur takes advantage of the moment as a mysterious freighter stops near the creature. Rear doors swing open. "Get'em in before someone sees him," screams the driver. The creature enters the freighter and the big rig speedily lays in pursuit of Arthur.

Though swift, the freighter is yet to break free of the network of roads in the neighborhood; however, Arthur hastens Ramsey down the final stretch of roadway and quickly drives onto an access ramp that leads to the highway. Yet, in his determination, he passes Marshal Harrison and Detective Candice Hess as they drive in the opposite direction.

The officers quickly pass Arthur while Candice is the first to notice. "Hey…is that Arthur?"

"Yeah, that's him and he sure is in a big hurry. I'm turning around to pursue."

Marshal Harrison slams on the breaks and quickly turns his vehicle, but before he can engage, the large freighter surprisingly roars past the officers, shaking their car in its wake and leaving Harrison very upset.

"What the h…l! Plates, did you get the plates?"

"Only a glance…"

"They won't get far. There's not much on the road that can get away from this baby."

"Do you want flashing lights?"

"No, not now! I want to see where Robinson's going. Don't want to alarm him to our presence."

All three vehicles immediately take to the highway, driving fast while attempting to avoid speed patrols.

Arthur calls Gracella. "Grace…pick up!" The tiny monitor displays Gracella's visual transmission. *"Arthur?"* "Grace, listen. There's no more guessing! Someone is after us and I do mean that they intend to get us. Don't have time to explain, now listen. You have to get out of the house and meet me in the place where we all talked about you-know-who."

"Leave? Arthur I can't just leave!"

"Like hell you can!"

"What about the police?"

"Grace, someone is after us, now get the hell out of there, NOW!"

305

Gracella, dazed, quickly acknowledges Arthur and discontinues the transmission.

Arthur's awareness is commendable, but the occupants of the freighter are far from ignorant as their onboard electronics allow for the intimate monitoring of his conversation. "How clever... He seems to be aware that someone could be listening in on him."

"It appears that way."

"Were it not for her, we could pull along side of him and simply take him by force."

"With an enan, it shouldn't matter."

"Keep in mind love that time is almost gone and there are too many witnesses."

"Yes, but Arthur's poor judgment has lead us right to the correct target, this time."

"I know, and this time we better get it right."

"I thought we got her this morning."

"Apparently not..."

"That's because your hands were busy. I told you it is not good to mix business with pleasure."

"There is someone else's blood on the enan's claws; you also know how difficult it was to get a positive I.D."

"No matter; now we can make sure they both are silenced."

"Do you think Arthur saw us?"

"No. The truck was around the corner before we retrieved the enan; but I do believe that he now understands that only one other person is capable of handling these creatures – therefore Arthur and Gracella must die – today. Stay on him until the time is right? He can't run forever."

Pursuing in the distant rear, Marshal Harrison and Detective Hess steady their course. "Marshal, aerial trackers confirm that Arthur is still on this stretch of highway."

"Tech is good girl, but I prefer the old fashion way."

"Visual confirmation…"

"I'll speed up to get a better view."

"Hurry up before our window closes."

"Run the plates on that freighter."

"You're not going to stop them – are you? "

"I just smell a rat, but we got bigger fish to fry. Robinson's getting away." Harrison plunges the accelerator and darts into the right side lane. The powerful surge of the shiny vehicle presses both officers back in their seats. As the vehicle pulls along side the freighter, Harrison casually makes eye contact with the passenger. Both men suspiciously view one another, but then, Harrison speeds ahead, gaining a vantage point. The freighter reduces speed.

Far ahead, Arthur exits the highway and quickly arrives at the food pavilion where Gracella nervously awaits. "Grace, come on!"

"I can't believe this was where we first learned of Gjhe'nan."

"Yea, but that was a different time, we have to go."

"Go where Arthur?"

"Anywhere…but here."

As Gracella closes the door, Harrison stops his vehicle only a block away. "Derek, it looks like Arthur is about to leave. Maybe you should try to get near him."

"I want to see where he's going."

"What if he leads us nowhere?"

"Candice, All runners lead somewhere…be patient; we'll know the right time."

Suddenly, tires screech several yards in the distance as the freighter finally halts within inches of Harrison's car. "Steady," growls the passenger. But the driver's miscalculation draws Harrison's attention and the marshal exits his vehicle. Harrison's demeanor is all but cheerful as he leaves the door of the car open.

In an instant; both, passenger and driver observes Harrison. "He's got a badge." "Not good..." "Just play it low." As Harrison gets near the window, the freighter mysteriously sways side to side.

Harrison stands back in utter surprise. "What the...hell..."

Immediately, the passenger turns towards the driver. "The enans are restless. They are adjusting their weight to our sudden stop." *Shhh –* keep quiet." "Drive away or do something – we can't stay here." "Alright, hang on."

Arthur and Gracella notice the incident as well. "Hey, isn't that Marshal Harrison?" "It sure is and it seems that we're being followed, but who's he talking too and why is that big rig behind him?"

"I don't know; but Arthur did you see how that freighter moved." "Yes I did, and there's only one thing that can make a truck that size move in such a way. Let's go...GO GO GO – NOW!"

The driver of the freighter notices their departure. "They're on the move." "I know, but we got to deal with the law man." "We can't afford this...there's already been one major screw up today." "Then move – now!" Suddenly, the driver stomps the accelerator, drastically turning the freighter as it lunges forward, crushing the rear of Harrison's car. The driver then tries to get past the car, but in desperate haste, she smashes the driver-side door, completely severing it while pushing Harrison's car onto the sidewalk. Harrison throws his hands up in protest as the freighter goes into motion and scurries down the road.

Marshal Harrison stands in disbelief, but climbs into his battered vehicle and quickly presses the ignition. "Candice, Are you all right?" "I will be...after I sink six rounds in his..." "You very well may get that chance."

Farther down the road, Arthur attempts to put distance between he and his pursuers. "Back there, I notice the way that rig moved. I wouldn't doubt that an enan is inside the cargo hull."

"What...how is that possible?"

"An enan attacked my house. I'm sure it was trying to kill me."

"Are you sure?"

"How do you think this gash got in Ramsey's side?"

"Arthur, do you know what you're saying? There are only two people in this world that have that kind of control of the enans."

"Right – one wears epaulettes, but he ain't no singer, and the other speaks Russian, but he don't play tennis."

"Where are we going?"

"We have to get as far away as we can."

"You don't think they would send an enan to kill us in front of so many witnesses?"

"Grace, you know as well as I that those enas can kill us and then hide inside a truck that size, if not disappear from the scene all together. That's what they're bread for, that's what they do – Remember? And after they're done, no one will know what happened."

Gracella shakes her head in disbelief, burying her face behind sympathetic hands. "Oh God… They killed Robert."

"Grace, you don't know that; but if so – then you were the target."

Suddenly, Arthur and Gracella are thrown forward into the dashboard as the vehicle forcefully plows into a guardrail. Gracella braces herself as Arthur uncontrollably steers Ramsey into a concrete curb. Though dramatic, the front wheels strike the embankment; thrusting the vehicle high enough to clear the structure. Arthur's skills prove worthy as he maneuvers Ramsey back onto the road. "They're right behind us!" Gracella's scream causes Arthur to glance into the rear view mirror. Observing the freighter's deadly advancement, Arthur activates a visual transmission.

"Who are you calling?"

"Hollis."

"Why him?"

"He's the only man who can help us out at this point."

As the device attempts to connect, Arthur glances at the roadway ahead of him. "See that?" "Arthur, that's a huge incline!" "We're going off-road!" Arthur engages the vehicle's all-terrain capability as the freighter inches perilously closer. Closing the distance, the freighter makes its presence a deadly reality. Yet, despite an eminent threat, Arthur breezes past other vehicles and creates a cloud of dust as Ramsey clamps on to a hillside and jolts a staggering ascent.

Those within the freighter can only watch. "We cannot do that," screams the driver, striking the steering wheel.

"Relax…there are alternative measures."

The passenger leans outside the window and shoots a tiny device that grapples the tailgate of Ramsey. "There, that will track them until we can catch up. Look, there he goes - peeling off just south of here. We shouldn't be too far behind."

Meanwhile, Harrison and Candice watch the large freighter from a safer distance. Candice asks, "Are you going to call for back-up?"

"Sure, but tell them to stand-by. I want to see where this leads."

"This is not standard at all Derek."

"Yeah…but I guarantee it will lead us to the mother load."

The pursuit continues well into the evening as the sun begins to cast its reddish-presence. Ramsey finally comes to rest inside the large white barn where Gjhe'nan eagerly greets the bewildered duo. Soon, they prepare for the long night ahead. In doing so, Arthur finds time to speak with his bizarre, and yet peculiar consummation. The creature acknowledges Arthur with the usual head gestures and approaches. The uncanny beast presents more questions.

"No, not this time…" Arthur hastens Gjhe'nan to put the questions away but the hybrid stands as a child denied an anticipated reward. Gjhe'nan shrieks, but Arthur shows little concern for such bereaving as he gently caresses the hybrid's scaly head. Yet, in spite of such behavior, the powerful enan towers over Arthur, causing him to look upward. Eventually, Arthur entreats Gjhe'nan.

"Something is wrong. Danger will come – here…tonight. I need you to be quiet, but ready. Do you understand?"

Gjhe'nan's ears perk. Arthur presses his finger against his lips, giving the hybrid a gesture for keeping silent. Then, the technician slowly pulls from his jacket a firearm. Gracella does likewise and both sit quietly, waiting for whatever fate is to come. Though dark, Gjhe'nan sees clearly while taking special interest in the firearms. Heighten senses dictate to the hybrid that something unusual is about to take place.

As the night lingers, the freighter parks only a few yards outside of Hollis' property while the passenger and driver observe the large white barn with the utmost attention. "I told you we'd find them."

"Good. Now set both enans loose and this time make sure Gracella does not survive, as well as Arthur," exerts the driver.

In militant fashion, the enans exit the freighter, rocking the suspension as they embark upon their assignment. Armed with camera head mounts and natural weaponry, both hybrid beasts progress under the cover of darkness and approach the barn with incredible stealth.

Arthur and Gracella are asleep, but Gjhe'nan' is alert as ever. With ears perked, the hybrid sniffs the air and begins to move about the floor. In a simultaneous manner, the approaching enans halt, becoming idly still while presenting a moment of complete silence. Then, the enans begin to shake their heads and scratch the ground, tearing the earth while rising high upon their massive legs – both displaying hostile dominance.

Inside the cab of the freighter, the driver and passenger view the strange occurrence. The driver asks, "What is wrong with them?"

"Don't know…but something has their attention."

"They keep that up; we may have to finish the mission ourselves."

"I'll send the codes for them to proceed."

"Does that thing work?"

"I've always patched their messages thought the cameras. The wire is linked directly into their earpiece. It should work. Don't worry."

"Remember what happened the last time."

"You won't let me forget – Gracella is in there, I know. There will be no screw-up this time."

The enans proceed on course, but Gjhe'nan's stirring awakens Arthur and Gracella. "What is it boy?" The hybrid shrieks and stirs even more as the enans approach. "Something's wrong Arthur," whispers Gracella. Arthur cocks his weapon and takes shelter under the transport. "Grace…get under here, now." Gracella lunges forward, hastening Arthur's warning. Both lay motionless, laying so still that only the faint sound of their hearts beating resonates to the audible ear. All is quiet.

Then suddenly, a loud noise thunders within the wooden structure as wood fragments tatter the floor. Gracella's skirt tears along the ground as she quickly draws both legs under the vehicle. Her instinctive actions take place only seconds before locks upon the barn door tear away from the wooden mounts. Then, the main doors open, whisking dust everywhere while capturing the full attention of everyone.

"They're here, just keep quiet," whispers Arthur as rising goose bumps pattern his arm. "Oh my God…Oh my God," shrills Gracella, quivering in light of the moment. "*Shhhhhhh*," cautions Arthur.

Like apparitions within the fathoms of sea mist, the creature's red eyes pierce the haze of darkness, scanning left and then right for any trace of movement. They sniff the air, and then lower their heads to the ground. One enan departs into the aft section of the barn while the other enan continuously whiffs the air. Its thorough movements bring the creature closer to Arthur.

Then, without warning, the enan ferociously thrashes the grill guard of the transport. The violent surge triggers the alarm system. Flickering lights and a brass sounding horn can ward off any intruder, except an enan.

Arthur attempts to avoid injury, but his efforts mistakably reveal their presence. Gracella screeches, unwittingly causing the enan to hone in on her location. The enan swerves its powerful tail along the underside of the transport and lifts the vehicle high enough to expose their fragile hide-away. Yet again, Arthur peers deeply into the creature's eyes.

Stunned, Arthur stops all movement, acting as if a voice calls to him, persuading him to succumb to a demising plight, as have all who stood in the way of such perpetual darkness.

"So…this is what you've become," he says.

The creature shrieks, but Arthur is quick to the draw as he unleashes three rounds. But, the enan is faster, sustaining the first round at point blank range, dodging the second, and having the third bullet to ricochet off its scales. So intense is the incident that the enan releases the transport. The vehicle hits Arthur and sends him plummeting to the ground, dropping his weapon in the process. "RUN GRACE…RrrrrrrrrUUN!" Gracella makes her move.

Though preoccupied, the enan discounts her attempt as she fires off several rounds, effectively striking the creature in the side. "Take that…you…bitch!" Harsh words coincide with her desperate efforts, but the enan decides to move towards Arthur.

"Arthur!" Gracella's scream catches Arthur squirming on the floor like a wounded animal. Unable to run, he stares helplessly into the face of his would-be murderer; this creature, by his own hands stands poised and ready to deliver death without mercy. With dreadful intent, the enan lunges furiously at Arthur, who perceiving his own demise, quickly covers his eyes and turns away.

Black talons begin to pierce Arthur's skin; but as all seem hopeless, Gjhe'nan miraculously intercepts the enan and sends the creature plummeting into several support beams. High pitch shrills ring out as the enan rolls along the ground until finally ending upon its back, kicking and screaming while severely crippling the infrastructure of the building.

Gjhe'nan pounces and brings his massive weight down upon the fallen beast. With little resistance, Gjhe'nan ruthlessly tears away at the beast, clawing, pounding, biting, slashing, gouging deep into red flesh while frantically ripping scales apart until reaching the creature's bare skin. Then, in an act of sheer desperation, the enan strikes, but Gjhe'nan counters and slashes the enan in both eyes, showing anything but mercy despite its pleading cry.

Crippled and blind, the enan painfully attempts to rise, but Gjhe'nan sees otherwise. As if perdition curtails the blood lust of a soulless mind, Gjhe'nan raises his tail, positions the dreadful scythe, and mortally plunges it into the enan's throat. Drowning upon its own blood, the enan passes into silence.

While viewing the unfolding events, the driver turns to the passenger. "What is that?"

313

"That…my dear is the missing enan."

"Our price rises since there are three of them!"

"Not any more – one is dead."

"He did not say that there was another."

"You mean…our employer did not say that we were chasing another."

"That extra hybrid compromises everything," sulks the driver, slamming her hands into the dashboard.

"Settle down. That hybrid compromises nothing."

"Did you attach the explosives?"

"No – this was only a routine hit. They were not in a combat zone."

"You did not attach the explosives? What were you thinking – you idiot? At any given moment, the enans can become damaged!"

"Damaged? Taking an enan captive is not an easy task; that is…if you were paying attention."

"You men are so one-sighted."

"There was no time to set the explosives to the animals between GenoSyss and the hit on Gracella. Remember, our employer wants us to move quickly."

"Now we have to clean up this mess!"

The driver grabs a small device from beneath the dashboard. She clicks a few mechanisms, and then lays it aside. Afterwards, she sets the fourteen-wheeled mammoth in motion towards the barn. Though in route, their untimely approach is unable to prevent the unfolding confrontation of two of the most bizarre and yet powerful creatures ever seen by human eyes.

The second enan is unable to commandeer the situation, to either dispose of Arthur or engage Gjhe'nan.

But suddenly, Arthur emerges and draws the beast's attention. It attacks. The technician manages to fire several rounds until the heavy gun empties. Bullets strike the creature, but the red-eyed demon presses forward, hurling its massive weight as it lunges forward. Within moments, Arthur finds himself desperately grasping the creature's forearms in an attempt to avoid sharp claws. Swaying left, then right, and dodging. Arthur miraculously avoids getting impaled. To wits end, he relinquishes to the power of the beast as it slams his body into a mound of hay bales.

The enan swings its terrible claws towards Arthur, but in a split second, Gjhe'nan rushes in and grapples the torrent beast, pushing it away just before the extending claws could tear into Arthur's already bleeding flesh.

Gracella seizes the moment and crawls from under the transport. She takes Arthur by the hand and caringly aids him back underneath the vehicle.

Both creatures circle one another as though locked in an ancient arena, snarling, hissing, and scraping the floor with their sharp talons as if communicating a sentient affirmation of dominance. Having made their savage decree, both creatures hurl themselves at each other, tugging, and wrestling; locked in a gridiron death match. Dust rise as both hybrids contest for the other's demise. They damage equipment, crack boards, and smash more support beams.

Amidst the chaos, a dull, crackling sound spreads throughout the barn.

"Arthur, what is that?"

"Grace, we've got to get out of here."

"Can you crawl?"

"I can…*uuuuugggghh*…I *cn*…can make it – hell yes I can!"
Barely able to move, Arthur observes the torn structure. *"Uuugg"*

Gracella asks, "Is the pain is getting worse?"

"No…just that Hollis is going to kill me. I'd rather the enan did it instead."

"We're almost outside – hang on."

Within moments, the enans move their battle outside. They circle each other once more. Much to Arthur's surprise, both hybrids appear to render a stalemate. "Arthur, why is Gjhe'nan not attacking?"

"Gjhe'nan has not seen another enan since the lab. He killed the first enan because it was attacking me. Those two can easily drag this confrontation on."

"Even still Arthur, this enan has to be from the military. It's a trained killer."

"Are you saying that the enan is baiting Gjhe'nan?"

"What else could it be?"

"How much does that enan weigh?"

"Not sure. But Gjhe'nan is the larger of the two."

"How much does Ramsey weigh?"

"About 8000…oh, I get it. But Grace, you'll have to run back inside, and that barn can come down at any minute!"

Gracella quickly reenters the barn and climbs aboard Ramsey. With much haste, she clutches the steering wheel and sets the transport on a collision course for the enan. Yet, in her dire attempt, the enan grows alert and quickly braces for impact.

Gjhe'nan sees the unfolding event and slashes the unsuspecting enan in the chest, dropping the tyrant beast to the ground. Afterwards, Gjhe'nan presses his foot on the enan, preventing the beast from rising. As Gjhe'nan examines the enan, Gracella exits the vehicle near Arthur.

"This enan looks like the one that came after me this morning. And now I'm sure that it had something to do with Robert's disappearance."

"Oh God. Then this enan was meant to kill me."

"That's not going to happen. Gjhe'nan may have mortally wounded it."

"Good for him." Gracella's head hangs low as she gently kneels to the ground, burying her face into her hands.

Arthur's injuries are more prevalent as he approaches Gjhe'nan. "You always wanted to meet your brothers. Well…I'm sure you'll be meeting more…" As quickly as Arthur assures the hybrid of a family reunion, an ominous voice catches his attention.

"Not if I have something to say about that."

Arthur stands in utter silence. Then, he immediately comes face to face with the barrel of a gun. Wide-eyed and startled, Arthur's puzzlement distracts him from noticing that the woman's accomplice is pointing a gun at Gracella. Silence stirs, yet Arthur finds the courage to question the woman.

"Who are you?"

"That is not important, just know that; one, you have made a mess of things; two, that creature does not belong to you; and three, both you…and your friend will be crossed off my list. And when you die, we'll haul you away. But before you die, let me say that it has been one thrilling ride Mr. Robinson."

"Wait…please tell me why you want to kill us?"

"For what it's worth, Rham-kiev was our original target. We successfully took down one of their outpost in the Ukraine, but then, we were diverted to you."

"Did you kill my co-workers?"

"Not me personally, but the original intent was to hide you and your friends. Then things got complicated."

"You're telling me that someone wanted us temporarily out of the way? Why?"

"It was only until matters grew in our favor. You see…you are in the middle of a much larger scheme; a scheme in which your enans now play a key role."

"Did a man name Rowland Kreshenkov hire you?"

While brandishing a deceitful smile, the woman proceeds to pull the trigger. "You are bright…Good-bye Mr. Robinson."

Gunshots ring out into the night as two people fall to the ground. Silence grips the collection of remaining witnesses, but as Arthur and Gracella assess the situation, Hollis enters the area with a drawn 12-gage, ready to expire anyone else. "Hollis!" Gracella's gleeful expression turns into a sigh of relief.

"I got your message and came as soon as I could."

317

"Man, there is a God in Heaven," expounds Arthur as he embraces Hollis.

Gracella's celebration abruptly ends as she observes the fallen enan. She quickly departs, but soon returns with an axe. "You TOOK MY HUSBAND from me...I hate you, I hate YOU!" She hacks away at the fallen beast, barely able to tear through the scales. Gjhe'nan simply stands away while Hollis chooses to have anything to do with the incident. Arthur cautiously corrals her actions, though protecting his own well-being. Gracella's screams expound loudly until she pitifully falls upon her knees.

Her profound grief is unwanted, but Arthur knew her reasons as Hollis approaches. "Who are these people and why did they want to shoot you?"

"I'll explain later, right now we got to get these bodies out of sight, as well as those enans."

"Look big brother, I think you should get Gjhe'nan to drag the enans back into the barn until we figure out everything else. Not to mention that it's a bad thing to disturb a crime scene."

"I didn't know we had an option."

After Arthur makes his statement, a profound noise draws every one's attention. The barn collapses to the ground. Hollis stands with his mouth open as Arthur steps near. "You do have insurance?" Arthur's question is ignored as Hollis stares at the mound of crumpled lumber.

"Okay...plan b, we can burn the enans and bury them, then put Gjhe'nan in that freighter. Once that's done, we call the cops." Hollis does not answer, but continues to stare at the pile of lumber.

As Arthur prepares to carry out his plan, another sound carries a surprising discovery. "Hold it Robinson – no body moves and don't touch *nothin*!"

"You got to be kidding me," Arthur whispers."

Emerging from a covering of shrubbery is Marshal Derek Harrison and Detective Candice Hess. "Let me see your hands – and you...big boy, drop the weapon." Hollis complies.

With guns drawn, both officers approach. Harrison nears Arthur. "Well...well, Arthur Robinson...you do have an interesting testimony as well as a lot of explaining to do, but don't worry – I'll make sure you get the chance. Candice, where's my backup?" "All ready on the way Marshal."

Harrison inches closer, cautiously pausing as he views the dead bodies and the felled enan. "Looks like bad karma for those two; and whatever that thing is over there, I'm sure you can shed some light on it? I could have sworn that I saw another one of those things standing here, but..."

"Are you sure Marshal?"

"Shut up Robinson...and listen up. We got two dead bodies, a wrecked barn, and something laying on the ground. Soon, this place will crawl with med techs and field opts. So, what ever you have to say, at least get your stories straight – this time! Cuff 'em Candice."

Candice retrieves her handcuffs and approaches Arthur, but Arthur resists. As he does, Harrison pronounces his gun more visibly. "Get back...now," he warns, but Arthur is not so easily shunned. "Wait...please, not yet. Hear me out first."

"I don't know you like that Robinson. Put the cuffs on and then we talk!"

"Marshal, listen to me, or your killers will go free."

Harrison stares into Arthur's eyes and perceives that something may be of worth. "Alright, you got fifteen seconds, then procedure comes down, or – so help me I will shoot your ass."

Arthur slowly approaches the dead enan. He kneels beside the lane creature and observes its body within the luminance of headlights. His approach is methodical and strangely parental as he touches the corpse.

"Sometimes Marshal, things start out with good intentions, but then goes bad."

"No shit..."

"Good people get caught in the cross fire."

"Son, I need something that I don't know. You got eight seconds!"

"Fine... Project 429 was to benefit a nation. Nature became the medium and somehow; we, Gracella, myself, Tuan, Nathaniel and the others got caught in the middle of a war."

"Why?"

"Because of hidden motives by certain people in high places; people with power, people who can change the face of conflict from what you and I know; and we were not allowed to divulge information."

"Well...why don't you divulge such information now and let us handle it – like you're suppose too?"

"Because you don't have a clue as to what you're up against."

Harrison listens, but prepares to make his call. "Time's up. Candice...cuff 'em." "My pleasure... And Division 6 is five minutes away. They are aware that we got two henrys and a code-30."

"You two haven't heard a word I said," protests Arthur.

Harrison cocks his gun as Candice grabs Arthur's wrist. "Gjhe'nan!"

Arthur's scream reaches alert ears as the hybrid creature emerges from the darkness. As if appearing from hell itself, the beastly red-eyed demon pronounces an entry with a shriek and sinks its claws deep into the earth.

Candice immediately backs away. Harrison scarcely moves as he quivers in dismay, but his professional training compels Candice to proceed with their un-renounced protocol. "Division 6...badge number DH-7142a..."

Arthur quickly reacts to her response. "MAKE THAT CALL and nothing good will come of this situation!"

"Stand down, monster or not, I will shoot!"

"Even at point blank range, you can't kill him. So what will it be?"

Candice hears Arthur and slowly releases her transceiver. Harrison stands motionless but his expression publicly displays an apparent disagreement. Years of experience seat within the marshal's prowess, which strongly aids him in forming a decisive action, and yet, nothing within those years can counter his authoritative outcome. "Candice, have Division 6 standby."

"But they're already in route – it's too late."

Harrison sternly watches Gjhe'nan. The marshal is old school and will not stand down so easily. Prideful or not, he will go down fighting, taking away any chance of success from those he confronts. But Arthur yields no ground as well, telling him "We can all die here, but I promise you it will be for nothing."

Silence parades as Harrison reluctantly hastens Candice. "Candice, tell 6, situation clear, code-4…stand down." "Division 6, 10-108. Derek, they got the message but they're still coming." Both officers lower their weapons, though keeping their firearms drawn.

Arthur beckons Harrison's attention. "Now, I don't know what those codes mean but if you're lying to me, just know that whoever came after us knew of our involvement with 429, and now you can bet they'll be coming for you."

Harrison asks, "How would you know that?"

"Excuse me marshal, but everyone linked with 429 seems to be in poor shape these days and if these killers cannot get to you, then they will go after your families or any body else they can exploit."

"How can you be so sure?"

"How can you not be?"

"Don't play games with me son."

"Dead bodies are hardly a game, Marshal. Just know that if you inform others, we'll all disappear because there are bigger forces at work."

Harrison coldly eyes Arthur. Then, in a moment of unrehearsed action, Harrison raises his weapon. "Know what Robinson? You're full of shit…" The marshal fires upon Gjhe'nan. Shells plaster violently into dense scales as the hybrid lunges forward, smashing into the officer and forcefully drives him into the side of the white transport. Harrison drops his gun and falls to the ground.

Candice proceeds to shoot, but the hybrid's scales provide sufficient protection; so much that one swing of its tail sends her several yards into the open field.

As both officers lay motionless, Gracella glances at the fallen enan. "Arthur, look! The enan is burning into blue flames." The flames pierce through the animal's hide, singing and burning in white-hot circles until the corpse is engulfed in a fiery mound. The flames quickly incinerate every ounce of the creature until all that remains is an unrecognizable mound of ash. The strange incident occurs to the other enan as well.

"Guess he did it after all," whispers Arthur.

"Who...did what?"

"It was a failsafe designed by Rowland that if any of these enans escaped or were captured, they would be destroyed."

"What about Gjhe'nan?"

"No – I got him out before they could touch him. I did try to tell you."

"My God," says Gracella, standing with a baffling expression.

Harrison gains his senses. He slowly crawls on the ground while displaying a look of anguish upon his face. "All right Robinson, you've got my attention," he says, grunting every word with heavy breathing.

"Is your shoulder dislocated or your arm broke?" Harrison holds back and says nothing. "Fine, it doesn't matter. It's time for us to leave Marshal, and your friend over there can use medical attention."

"You can't leave the scene of a crime Robinson..."

"The hell I can't. I didn't kill anybody and you can't protect us from the real killers. I'm not waiting around for you to decide how I should live or when I should die."

"I can give you protective custody."

"Sure you can."

"Don't make me bring you in."

"You don't look like you're in shape to bring anyone in."
Harrison attempts to stand to his feet, but collapses to the ground. Hollis kneels beside Harrison, assessing the officer's condition. "He's not going anywhere; but both of you need too go."

"Hollis, you have no part in this. With Harrison out, give me your shot gun and we'll dispose of the two bodies."

"Not a good idea."

"This will only bring more attention to our situation."

"Arthur, you can not take the bodies with you."

"If we leave them here, we draw police attention – thought I said that already?"

"You're not thinking. Again Arthur, that is a bad idea."

"Who will miss two criminals?"

"If the cops can help – I think you should bring them in on this, at least maybe they can identify those bodies. It might give you a link."

"Don't know about that."

"And you intend to wage war all by yourself?"

"No."

"Let the cops handle the bodies while you get Gjhe'nan out of here."

"And leave in what?"

"Take that freighter."

"That thing's huge."

"Yeah, but I trained you for a class 5 hauler; you can handle it – now both of you – go, now!"

Arthur hesitates for a moment, rubbing his face as though wiping away confusion. "Who ever the marshal called will be here in 20 seconds. Will you be all right?"

"I'll be fine. I'll tell them self-defense. Besides, it's their word against mine and they got nothing on me anyway – now you, Gracella, and Gjhe'nan need to get out of here. Figure out what's really going on. I'll call you later. Oh…by the way, don't forget our other lake front property if you need it for a hide-out."

"You're a *God-sent* little brother."

"You take care of yourself." Hollis bids Arthur and Gracella farewell.

As Arthur drives the large freighter down the road, Gracella makes a startling discovery. "Arthur, did you see this?"

"See what?"

"This canister; it's frozen inside this compartment area. It looks like a small cryogenics chamber."

"Maybe they're chilling beer – hell…I don't know."

"Arthur, what were these people doing?"

"Who knows, is there anything else near it?"

"Just a binder with some kind of documentation located on the upper shelf."

"Open it up and see what it says."

"Get over here Arthur."

"Okay…let me engage the auto drive." Arthur hastily complies. As he approaches the rear compartment, he immediately observes Gracella's findings. "Wait a minute. That's liquid nitrogen running through those lines."

"I know that, but what is inside the canister?"

"Not sure, maybe this documentation will tell us."

As both scan through pages, a surprising countenance develops upon Arthur's face. "Well, how about that?"

"Embryos for the next generation of enans, and this documentation contains their entire genetic blue print."

"So…what do we know so far?"

"For starters, we were about to die, and that man and woman have enan embryos in their possession; apparently ready for delivery to someone."

"Aside from that, there's only one person that comes to my mind."

"Rowland..."

"Not too hard to figure out."

"Well, since Rowland took something valuable from me, I'll return the favor."

"Favor? Hey, where are you going?"

Gracella finds a metal rod and severs one of the lines that lead to the canister. A gaseous vapor discharges, and then she tosses the documentation directly in front of the expulsion. After several seconds, the paper crystallizes. "To hell with his delivery...and him." She strikes the documentation and watches it shatter.

Arthur sighs and sits upon the floor. "Feeling a bit revengeful?" Arthur's question lies heavily upon Gracella's mind. She senselessly stares at him.

"Let's just say that every little thing I do to take away from him will give me a degree of peace for the death of Robert."

"Be careful you don't cross over."

"And just what is that suppose to mean?"

"Grace, the past events can make us heartless, especially now. We are hurt, fragile; more vulnerable than before. Yes – we have good reason to want Rowland and the others dead. But anytime you, me, a person; any person looses focus, faith, or humanity in an act of vindication, we toss out everything that governs our actions."

"Who are YOU...to counsel me?!"

"I'm just saying that..."

"No...no, don't you dare; don't you dare do this to me..."

"Grace..."

"Robert is DEAD Arthur! I didn't ask for any of this!"

Arthur lowers his head; deeply sighing until his lungs dispels every ounce of air. Silence stirs. Then, he slowly looks upward, gazing at the ceiling. "Grace. We have to be careful, or else we will loose what God gave us in order to keep us from going over the edge. The law of survival says that we are no different than that man and woman who tried to kill us."

"I can't believe what I am hearing from you. Aren't you supposed to be the shoot now, questions later, no non-sense guy?"

"Grace..."

"Arthur, you sound as if we are...souls drifting through the universe and are governed by events that come our way; and...and that somehow...a coin toss decides how we respond."

"It's not like that."

"Then what is it like?"

"Grace, I'm just trying to say…"

"No, let me put it to you this way. I want Rowland DEAD! And you need to get your head out of your *ass*, because you know very damn well you would kill Rowland if he killed Aniah."

"If I do...then God means nothing."

"You are so full of sanctamoneous *bullshit* nonesense right now; sometimes I can't believe you… Just shut up – shut up Arthur! *SHUT* the fuck up!"

Gracella slowly looks downward. Her head hangs low as silence lingers.

~~~Specters in God's Shadow~~~

My eyes open, only to find that the howling wind forcefully whisks just beyond the window. The arid flow courses flagrantly, giving no relief for anything within its turbulent flow. Yet, as the season lingers, I begin to realize that dawn approaches and that my time with Nostalgia draws near to an end. Retrieving a glass from the kitchen, I soothe my throat with warm water and return to the den. Crouching Indian style, I draw the comforter over my bare torso and leisurely watch the coming of the new sun. As the night sky passively yields to the power of light, it soon occurs to me that the games we play are more needless than those of necessity; in essence, we attempt to become what we are not, conduct our lives in ways we should not, and try to possess things we cannot.

Perhaps, the simple contentment that the Apostle Paul speaks of is far beyond us mere mortals. But if obtainable, then surely it cannot come from modern religion or society – as we know. Maybe it comes from the epiphany of a tragedy, or the fear of an unknown situation, or perhaps something far simpler, like a consenting decision. Simple enough...

However regardless, those like me; contentment barely stands just beyond the fingertips of a curious heart. The curious heart manifests itself when we give deeply into our passions, so deep that we forcefully push the desire to perfect our own creations; whether song, art, literature – even imaginations, giving into such things until it consumes us or changes us into something else. It is as though we are objects playing into the greater scheme of good and evil; a scheme that borders somewhere between darkness and light; like the faint edge of a shadow in the sun. Simplicity is all but forgotten, yet still, we are given a choice in the end. Should we choose wisely, or foolishly, we will reap the consequences of our decisions.

Love, hate, kindness, indifference, truth, lies, cheating, honesty, stealing, giving, loathing, envy – joy, and sadness; all must co-exist, for we cannot value one without the other. And yet, at the seat of such deeds is the heart, a seat of emotion that is the root of every person's absurdity. Who can truly know such a thing as the heart?

Sadly, with willing pretense, I gave my heart away, only to find later that it would fester the very objects I failed to guard against. It was as though a spirit lurked deep inside, waiting, wanting until it swelled with such hunger that it became the driving force behind my most inner desires – I could not ignore it.

Even now, to destroy such a lurid spirit will mean an incomplete existence. But those spirits were so prevalent back then, and to all our shame, we willfully harbored such entities. Surely, God's glory would have destroyed us all – even me, but the slain Lamb stood between me and that of His glory, casting a shadow in which I found myself. It was strange, but a needful hiding place – and there I was. With that in mind, I close my eyes once more.

A mysterious aircraft lands at 6:45 pm on a vacant airstrip outside Houston, Texas. Two men exit the craft, commandeer a transport, and return to load supplies. Finishing their task, the aircraft takes flight and the transport travels far into the city limits. Aboard the vehicle, shadowy figures corroborate shady motives. "Everything is on schedule," says the driver.

Soon, both men locate a tall abandoned building and make their way to the sixth floor. One of the men unwraps a weapon, loads cartridges, and sits upon a crate. He peers out the window like a vulture perched for a kill.

Several unsuspecting targets lay below.

"There they are… Lambs for slaughter; red, white, brown, black, rich, poor…*hmmph*. What do I care? Soon, their meaningless lives will contribute to a worthy cause."

He takes aim at a man whose walking along the sidewalk and fires. The tiny projectile strikes the man, who barely notices the assault as he continues on his way. The shooter strikes a woman in which her jogging routine obliviously carries her down the road. Again, the shooter strikes a mother and child, and a mother with child. He fires cautiously at first, then freely, and then insatiably.

His partner joins in and doubles their effort. Busy streets become nothing more than a playing field. So effective is their marksmanship that they strike several unsuspecting victims while vanishing within the nearby surroundings.

Later, newscasters spread the word as the incident mercilessly exterminates hundreds within Sam Houston's establishment.

Deep within Red Sands Research Facility, Colonel Mortimer Ducet observes the progress of his enans from the observation deck. Standing firm, the colonel plans the next set of events. A sergeant approaches and gives the colonel a sealed envelope. "Sir, for your eyes only – this just came in." Ducet receives the document and locates a room far from prying eyes. He opens the package and holds a post card size monitor within his hand. Pressing his thumb to one side of the panel, the device activates. Once verified, a visual transmission of a ranking official appears. Instructions soon follow:

"Greetings Mortimer; hope all is well. I'll get to the point. Intelligence verifies that a Mediterranean outpost known for terrorist activities has been destroyed. The Algerian government denies involvement and there are no reports of conflicts from neighboring clans, even as far as Oran, Annaba, or the rest of the region for that matter. We do know that an extremist, by the name of Adir Sa'ood ran the outpost, and that he is tied to Aun'war Martinet. As you know, we've been after Aun'war for years. We believe Aun'war will retaliate because of this act – if he hasn't retaliated already…it's only a matter of time.

Oh, it may be of no consequence, but the authorities found strange footprints around the complex. These footprints do not match any animals within the region – more on that later.

The London CDC and Scotland Yard report numerous strange deaths around Piccadilly Circle. As of yet, they don't know if any of it is connected to terrorist activities. They call the phenomena the Phantom's Death. We know that Aun'war has used bio weaponry in the past but still, there's no link.

Finally, the U.N. and high councils continue to squabble over rules of engagement, especially those rules regarding foreign conflicts. As of now, the President doesn't seem too anxious to relinquish our position on independent confrontations. As a matter of fact, he wants to increase our troops and resources in the Gulf.

Hell, given our current state – that means more meat for the grinder on both sides.

Now for the bad news; and I'm sorry that you have to hear this from me. But in light of the situation Mortimer, I am canceling further research in your department at this time. Non-the less, I personally would like to commend you on what you've already provided this panel. Hopefully when all this is over, we will be able to get you back in action again. I'll be seeing you shortly – Caldwell Pendleton out."

Ducet quietly stands, rubbing the back of his neck, attempting to loosen his tense muscles. He presses a small red button on the tiny monitor. Smoke rises from the sides of the panel and he tosses the small instrument into the trash.

The colonel returns to the observation deck and views several enans standing upon the field. With one hand behind his back, he proudly paces the floor in high-class fashion, basking with assurance that his hybrid army can rise to any occasion. Perhaps an inner gloat, but his army is formidable.

While pondering his thoughts, a soldier approaches.
"Sir, will there be any thing else?"

"No."

"I see that you are quite taken with your hybrid army."

"Look at them Jamison. Aren't they murderously beautiful?"

"I never looked at them in that way."

"We use them mostly on land but you should see them in water – fantastic. They can swim for miles without end, hit targets and vanish without a trace. Despite their name, this group is mostly males, though a few females are added for flavoring.   Nothing like a woman's touch – Eh?"

"No sir, nothing like it at all."

"Did I ever tell you why we pursued this course of action?"

"Creating the enans? No-"

"You do realize Jamison that the only dumb questions are the one's we don't ask?"

"So I'm told sir..."

"Good. The question is – can a human soldier on the ground be replaced by an unconventional hybrid animal soldier?"

"That is conceivable."

"The counsel wanted an answer."

"And you gave them one – sir."

"Did I?"

"Of course…"

"What I gave them is an unconventional idea, an undisclosed concept."

"Is the counsel not pleased?"

"They want to continue sending men and women into combat zones where many will face a needless death."

"I take it that the council did not like your latest endeavor."

"Conventionalism is what the council wants…as long as it's not their butts getting shot at. Most people really don't care what goes on with soldiers on distant soil. I think its time we show them."

"But sir…you haven't told the congressional committee or General Pendleton about these hybrids?"

"No, and I don't intend too, at least while there is still time to get Aun'war."

"I see... Then it sounds to me as if you have two plans of action. First of all, I understand your take on the war, but secondly, where exactly does the other plan lead?"

"To Aun'war… And would you like to know how that plan will play out?"

"Yes sir…"

"Once we locate Aun'war; and we will, I will send in the hybrids, strapped with mini-nukes, and simply blow him to hell."

"Very direct…"

"The same applies for terrorist all over."

"But sir, what about the hybrids? Your actions will kill them as well as noncombatants."

"And?"

"You're talking about a suicide run."

"Casualties of war Jamison. Aun'war and those like him kill our civilians in such a way that would make the Devil himself cringe?"

"War is never a game sir, but..."

"Discretion Jamison, discretion will handle the noncombatants. As for the rest; we can not always pick and chose the outcome of circumstances – because our enemies sure as hell don't."

Colonel Ducet departs the observation tower and returns to his office. He activates a small device. In a matter of rings and dial tones, a distinct click resounds through an earpiece, thereby granting the colonel his moment.

"It's me. Don't worry...the signal is secure. Oh, can't talk now? Fine... Now you listen to me... I don't care about your little inconveniences; all I need are your ears, so listen up. Let me remind you that I kept my end of the deal. You are not rotting away in prison or better yet, standing in front of a firing squad. Got your attention already? Good. The time has come for you to deliver. My back is against the wall, so conjure up whatever *mojo* you need and rectify the relationship with your old boss. Also, too bad you lost your hit men, but GenoSyss and those lab techs are the least of my worries, and even if the surviving members of 429 go public – they can't prove any thing. So get busy!"

Ducet concludes his message.

The colonel's response reaches the ears of a woman. She resides comfortably in a motel room. Vermillion red fingernails course her distressed face as she lies underneath white linen. Silence grapples her intent to speak while yet, she disturbingly gazes towards the ceiling. Starring at nothing, all her frustration passes outward with a deep sigh – and then, she closes her eyes.

Another body stirs besides her, asking, "Was that your job calling?"

She hesitates to answer, but then, "Yes...I must go."

"Can you cancel for the day?"

"No, I must go out of town this time."

332

"I can make it worth your stay," whispers her counterpart as he proceeds to move his affections down to her thighs. She immediately sits upward. Agitation shrouds her face. Quickly rising to her feet, she drapes herself. "Walter, will you listen! Is this all you're good for?"

"Jade, okay, I just thought we had a moment. Things have been quiet for a while."

Walter grabs Jade by the hand and softly gleams into her eyes, but she reluctantly pulls away. He tries again until she succumbs to his charming mannerisms. "You don't know how much you mean to me."

"You mean much to me Walter, maybe more than I deserve."

"And, just what is that suppose to mean?"

"I have to work, I call you later."

"Jade, what's wrong?"

"Nothing..."

"Don't do this to me again – What's wrong?"

"Nothing...just –"

"Look, we got to trust each other – Alright?"

Walter senses more hesitation in Jade's voice. Jade leans upon the wall and begins clasping a towel while staring aloft. She turns her back to him, careful not to reveal her grief stricken soul. "Walter, the time I spent overseas..."

"You mean the pharmaceutical agency in the Ukraine?"

"Well...there is more."

"There usually is..."

"The less you know, better for us both."

"Oh...I see. Just shut me out again."

"No."

"Yes! It's like you're building another wall around a mystery and you expect me to climb over it while saying nothing."

"I can not explain right now."

"No one usually can Jade – go figure!"

"Please, no arguing with you."

"Then don't. Every time you get one of those calls, you turn different somehow - like Jeckle and Hyde."

Jade eyes Walter, emitting unspoken words through an emotionless face. Realizing his verbal chastisement, Walter extends his hand, but Jade abruptly enters an adjacent room. Locking the door, a deep breath precedes what only solemn feelings convey as she grabs a carrying case. Quickly dressing, she departs the motel under Walter's protest.

While in route, Jade activates a mobile device until a voice comes through. *"Pozdravi aut'saɪdər. Ostati evetanje in A'merɪkə?"*

"Aut'saɪdər ti govoriti? It had kod ti! Of course I speak Croatian you idiot, do you speak English?"

"Da –."

"Sarcastic you are. This is Jade and I must speak with Aun'war. Arrange meeting, and be sure to tell him an old acquaintance wants to see him."

Elsewhere, Rowland paces the floor of his home. The recent visit by Marshal Derek Harrison and Detective Candice Hess leave him very uneasy. A moment passes and the phone rings. Rowland simply stares until he finally answers.

"Yes. I know *eet eez yu*, but I thought you were police. Yes...yes I get your *massage* earlier. I was *beezy...prre*-occupation does not often allow for conveniences. Status you ask? *Vwell*..what can I say. As I told you, I'm *rr*-eady to meet, but *theengs* are getting worse. My team has not reported and two enans are missing after GenoSyss building destroyed. I see to it personally, but now, bigger problem comes. 429 team members, somehow dead. I only wanted to silence them for duration of time, until we finished our work. Authorities think I had some-*teen* to do *weeth* their deaths."

334

Rowland sinks into silence, digesting what he hears through the stylized earpiece. But soon, his anxieties give way to a calming demeanor as he leans against a table. Then, his coarse brown eyebrows rise to the sound of intriguing words. "What…you have proof that Jade is tied to Aun'war and that Aun'war is Rham-kiev's leader? I knew *eet*! Our suspicions *prr*-ooved correct! What else you speak of Colonel? How *eez thees* possible? Tell me more."

Silence looms as the geneticist takes in all that he hears.

Under a dense canopy of trees, fourteen wheels screech to a halt upon lake front property. As the moon sets high, warm air swirls around the silent freighter, but serene settings are far from comforting. Inside, Arthur and Gracella peer across dark placid waters. Words do not transpire between them for some time. Though weary, adrenalin forces them to relive the events of the day, every detail of every moment.

Both eventually make their way to the cargo section of the rig where Gjhe'nan silently waits.

Gracella's face flusters red while she gently rubs a ring on her finger. She slides along the wall until seating herself upon the deck. "I never said good-bye to him that morning." She pitifully cries while placing her head upon her knees. Arthur sadly stares at her and gently puts his hand on her shoulder. As she breaks into misery, a bracelet falls to the deck. Arthur reaches to pick it up but Gjhe'nan quickly takes the shiny wristband and immediately examines it.

The hybrid grunts, beckoning Arthur's attention. Afterwards, Gjhe'nan etches into the floor decking. Arthur examines the hybrid's handiwork.

"M A T H E W 1 9 6 - Oh, you mean Mathew 19:6. It's a common phrase between married people. You don't know Matthew; neither do I, and marriage is something you have no earthly idea about – forget it."

Gjhe'nan tilts his head, eyeing Arthur with inquisitive mannerisms. The hybrid etches into the deck again. Arthur sees the inscription, but does not answer. Gjhe'nan forcefully taps near the inscription.

Arthur perceives the hybrid's lack of deterrence, and stares at the inscription.

"God...Devine being...He is the Creator of all things – men, women, life as we understand. He is all-powerful, love, kind, mighty...etc...etc, what more can be said? He created me – as I see it."

The hybrid shrieks and begins to etch once more.

"Look, I know where this is going. God did not make you. You are neither man nor animal – as a whole."

Gjhe'nan stares deeply into Arthur's eyes.

Arthur terminates his discussion and moves near Gracella. He offers her a cloth; which she takes and begins drying her eyes. "You should get him a keyboard; keep him from scratching up everything."

"He'll break it."

"Arthur, he will eventually learn about himself."

"He's just having some kind of identity issues."

"And what's with this God thing; does he now have religion too?"

"He's just curious."

"You can't hide it from him forever."

"He's getting into issues that he was never meant to deal with."

"Really... Well I guess he's part of the club now."

"And your point?"

"What about the issues we were never meant to deal with?"

"Our issues?"

"Arthur, we're on the run, scared for our lives and those killers may still be out there, somewhere. They're probably waiting for us to come up for air so they can pick us off!"

"Maybe–"

"Arthur – you somehow act as if everything is going to...just be okay."

"*Shhh*..."

"Shush! Why, are you telling me to shush?"

"He'll hear you."

"Gjhe'nan? Arthur, people are dead, and my husband is gone and never coming back!"

"Grace, we don't know if Robert is dead. His body was never found."

"Arthur, I appreciate what you are doing but you must stop trying to cover me."

"Grace, I'm just trying to keep things in perspective - control our situation."

"Control – You?"

"Okay, maybe it was a bad word…"

"Control…that relative word that everybody thinks they have. Arthur, let me tell you something about control – since you can't figure it out. Control is a situation, a calamity, a hell bent whirlwind that you, our team, Rowland, Ducet, and even I…never had!"

"Grace…"

"No Arthur… You listen. Do you know why you cannot tell Gjhe'nan the whole truth about what he is?"

"He knows what he is."

"No. You're missing the point. You can't tell him…because he was never meant to exist!"

"Grace…you're just upset."

"I'm upset? I got a reason to be. And you know something? I think it's time to change this game of charades."

"What are you doing?"

"Since he wants to know what he is, let me be the first to tell him."

"Grace…no!"

Arthur can only watch in silence as tears course Gracella's face. She gets within inches of the hybrid; staring face-to-face. "YOU ARE AN ABOMINATION!!" Gjhe'nan flinches. Gracella slumps to the floor while holding back nothing.

Time lingers as both eventually succumb to the weariness of their travels. Gjhe'nan observes their slumbering, but the hybrid's mind is far from settling. For most, the shear magnitude of the creature's presence is overwhelming – perhaps even at times for Arthur; however, Gjhe'nan's appetite for knowledge is proving to be more of a domineering reality. Having heard Gracella's comments, the hybrid carves the word, 'abomination' into the floor and stares at the inscription while lying quietly in the dark.

Elsewhere, in the suburbs of Houston, Texas a mother and child cherish time together. "Mom lets watch TV." The child's mother embraces him and both sit comfortably in front of a large flat-screen.

Minutes into a movie, an urgent message broadcasts:

"We interrupt this televised program to bring you breaking news. Today, authorities are reporting a series of strange deaths that have occurred in Rochester, New York, Anaheim, California, and here in Houston. So strange are the incidents surrounding these deaths that local officials, along with the Center for Disease Control, have been called to analyze what they say are the remains of the victims. New York and California are continuing to piece together their findings. But for more information on the incident here in Houston, we take you live, to Tonya Walsh…Tonya.

Thank you Kalvin. Witnesses here, eerily testify that each of the victims seemingly turned into a glob-like gelatin and eventually dissolved into thin air, leaving nothing more than the clothing they were wearing. Currently, local officials will not allow me near the area for as you can see in the background, the press and all other non-essential personnel are banned for fear of contamination.

Hazmat units have been covering the area for the past several hours when they learned that, a man allegedly infected, simply dissolved in his wife's car while in route to Memorial Hospital. Based on the piles of clothing you see in the background, it is believed that the death toll is in the hundreds.

The CDC is trying frantically to rule out any possible air borne pathogens, yet still, no conclusion as of yet. They are currently advising people to stay in their homes. Similar reports are coming in from our sister stations in California as well as New York. Whatever happened here Kalvin is enormous. Strangely, there are no witnesses to whom or what may have caused the incident and authorities have no leads whatsoever.

Okay…the police are now telling us that we have to vacate the scene. I'll have more for you later…back to you Kalvin…"

As the transmission continues, the mother embraces her child even more while she, like many others, watch and listen in dismay.

Far away, inside a well protective bunker, Aun'war and his commandant watch the unfolding events. He rolls his head back while sipping a martini; laughing at the ill plight of his devised plan. "See…all you have to do is get their attention and they will spread the word."

"Well planned sir. Shall I recall the men and make preparations for departure to Kansas?"

"No – I've decided to set up operations on one of the eastern islands of the U.S. There is less traffic, excellent striking potential, and hardly any reason for inspection."

Suddenly, a man enters the room and humbly approaches Aun'war. "Sultan, you have a message. This transmission was relayed from one of the scouts."

"A personal call? Who would dare?"

"Someone of apparent acquaintance – sir."

Aun'war activates a nearby monitor and views the transmission. Jade's image appears on screen. *"Hello…or did you forget me? It does not matter. I have what you want and you got what I need so listen carefully: 32 degrees, 19 minutes, 43 seconds north, and 96 degrees, 45 minutes, and 38 seconds west. Two and half hours from now – I'll be waiting."* The transmission ends.

Aun'war's gleaming eyes widen as he grows more alert.

"Sultan, who is that woman?"

"A precious stone from an earlier collection."

Photo resistors begin the task of allowing street lamps to light the way for travelers. Aboard the freighter, Arthur and Gracella navigate their way through a maze of empty roads.

"Just got off the phone with Hollis. Marshal Harrison and his partner were taken to the hospital. The good marshal has a fractured arm and a bruised collar bone while his partner's ribs are busted. She'll need surgery, but will live."

"And you think Harrison will be thrilled to see you?"

"Hopefully…"

"Arthur, he's more likely to arrest you on the spot!"

"A chance I have to take. We need to see him. In the mean time, we'll get cleaned up at a motel."

"That sounds good."

"Grace, are you hungry?"

"I haven't had much of an appetite Arthur, as you can see…if you were paying attention."

"We have to eat. C'mon, I'll get us something. There's a place down the road."

After approaching the building, Arthur halts the freighter outside the parking lot. "Good lord Arthur, can you pick a more interesting place? This is a literal hole-in-the wall."

"Yeah, but it's near by; it'll do until we do better."

As Arthur enters the building, others take notice of his departure and that Gracella is alone. She sits quietly, pondering as if trapped in a maze of thoughtless wastfulness.

Then suddenly, the door opens and she soon finds herself face to face with the barrel of a gun. The perpetrator coldly addresses his intentions. "I don't care who you are…you scream, I'll cap you…Now get out!"

Realizing she cannot escape, Gracella reluctantly grabs the handle of the freighter and climbs down. As the door closes, the man grabs her by the arm, and covers her mouth.

With minimal resistance, Gracella demands information from her abductor as he casts her inside an unmarked vehicle. "What do you want with me?" One of the men raises his hand while presenting the handle of a gun. Gracella quickly cowers, as silence is her reply. "Shut up! Your boy friend must really be stupid. That rig of yours got a tracker on it and when you two came within our range, we picked up on it. Common sense says you should have gotten as far away as you could." "Who hired you?" "Money talks sweetness. You're the package and when your boy friend comes out, we'll deliver him too." Gracella lowers her head, staring silently at the floor.

Arthur steps from the building, only to see the rig is rocking and swaying in motion. Alertness covers him and he springs forth. Suddenly, shots ring out; piercing the side of the building as Arthur quickly enters the rig. He finds Gjhe'nan frantically trying to gain his attention. "Gjhe'nan, what's going on?"

The hybrid points in the direction of the windshield. Arthur observes an unmarked vehicle hastening down the road, but he also notices that Gracella is no longer in the cab of the freighter. "Grace! Grace, where are you?" Arthur's call falls on silent walls as the hybrid directs his attention towards the speeding van. Arthur starts the engine and immediately lays in pursuit.

Both vehicles enter the highway. Within moments, Arthur drives along side of the vehicle, taking note of Gjhe'nan's identifying gestures. He makes eye contact with the driver who cautiously looks at Arthur and then accelerates ahead. Distance increase between both vehicles, yet Arthur desperately tries to exceed the maximum speed of the rig. "Lord help me," he whispers as he presses the pedal. The chase leads to a dark residential roadway.

The van makes a sharp turn, but the freighter buries a passenger car and tears down several yards of fence while in pursuit. The van pushes further, but Arthur's relentless pursuit wreaks havoc on nearby homes and isolated structures; in effect, making his desire to press the machine much farther beyond its capabilities. Appearing to have an advantage; the van breezes through alleys and adjacent roadways until progress becomes difficult.

Perceiving such a turn of events, Arthur invokes his command assertiveness and summons the hybrid. "Gjhe'nan, get' em!"

Immediately, the cargo doors open and the wielding beast leaps from the trailer and onto the pavement. Agility spawns with tremendous effectiveness as the hybrid pounces from one location to aother.

In a matter of time, Gjhe'nan locates the van. Then, with a powerful surge of energy, Gjhe'nan propels higher than the surrounding two-story dwellings, and forcefully lands on the top of the van. Upon impact, all windows shatter, leaving only a fragmented windshield. The hybrid springs quickly to the ground as the decimated vehicle sputters forward. Yet, despite Gjhe'nan's efforts the occupants reach their destination. Though crumpled, one of the rear doors of the van surprisingly opens and immediately several shots ring out. A man forcefully pulls Gracella and they all enter a nearby building.

Dark paint covers the windows of the dilapidated structure as it lays in silence among other depraved dwellings. Arthur soon arrives and catches a few eyes peeking from beyond the windows of neighboring houses. He brings the metal giant to halt.

In an instance, two young men exit the side door, each brandishing firearms in a sideward manner. Their tattoos and red headscarf's alarms the technician. "Yo…what the f**k," yells one of the men as he quickly opens fire while re-entering the building.

Arthur dives to the floor of the cab. He sees Gjhe'nan, and then cries out in anger, "Kill'em…kill'em all!"

The hybrid shrieks and quickly plunges into the wall of the structure, smashing through mason and panels of sheet rock while breaking support studs. Once through, the creature boldly announces its presence as witnesses stand in disbelief. Gjhe'nan rapidly scans the area and distinguishes Gracella amongst the crowed. Then, without mercy, the red-eyed beast tears into flesh as it slashes person after person. Shots ring out but to no avail as the hybrid surgically dismantles all attempts of confrontation. Tough scales, engineered directly into the beast's skin thwarts bullets just enough for lethal talons to slash crevasses into raw flesh. Swinging its powerful tail, the torrent creature crushes the chests of three others while decapitating the head of yet another victim. Tearing through human-size entryways, Gjhe'nan ravages through room after room, leaving only pitiful cries for unsuspecting souls. No one escapes.

Realizing the time, Arthur cautiously enters the building and looses his footing. In the corner of a large room, he finds Gracella, shaking, yet quiet. Her delicate wrists are bound. Under the guide of a small flashlight, he carefully navigates thrashed bodies, broken fixtures, and smashed furniture in order to approach her. Then, he observes the bodies upon the floor. "They're all so young."

Money, condoms, broken wine bottles, and white powder lace the floor. All sorts of weapons lay openly upon tabletops with shell casings among the carnage. One mangled body lies partially imbedded within the wall as corpses dangle with syringes and plastic flex tubes intact in one arm.

Arthur, shocked and unsettled approaches Gracella and attempts to raise her from the floor. She flinches and immediately backs away. "Nnnnnno… GET AWAY FROM ME!!!" Under the high pitch squeal of her voice, her breathing becomes erratic. With pulse surging, her eyes cry out in vain. Arthur gently touches her wrist.

"Grace…Grace, it's me. Arthur." He carefully cuts her bounds, but she never looks at him. Arthur gently takes her hand and guides her out of the building.

As they approach the freighter, Arthur sees a youth crawling along the ground. His outstretched arms signify a failing attempt to flee. Arthur grabs him by the arm. "Don't think I would hesitate to kill you, but that's not my intent. The tattoo on your arm is like the ones on your boys back there. What is the meaning of the scorpion and hammer? Is this some kind of a new gang sign?"

The youth does not reply. Arthur brandishes him. "Who are you and why did you take her?" The youth shakes frivolously while crying and coughing blood. Yet surprisingly, his ghostly voice resonates, telling of just how much damage he has sustained. Then, the sound of crippling words comes forth. "Th…th…the lady…paid us to t…take her." Arthur stands back in astonishment. "What lady? What lady paid you?"

The technician's question goes unanswered as the youth's eyes roll back into his skull. He slumps to the ground. Gjhe'nan rejoins the two as they enter the freighter and depart the neighborhood.

Several minutes pass as Arthur engages the steering wheel. Gracella stares out the window, silently watching the yellow road markers intermittently dashing by. Her quiet state lingers until a small, frail, troublesome voice catches Arthur's attention. "They said she paid them. They wanted us both. I was a trap for you."

Arthur remains silent while observing the prominent bruises along her wrists. Her hands lay deadlock, clasped tightly together like a child clutching a parent for protection. She periodically shakes but never breaks her view from the window. Her countenance is completely destitute of emotion. Arthur engages the auto-drive, and places a blanket over Gracella as silence looms within the cab.

Eight-thirty A.M. An entourage of soldiers enters the observation deck of Red Sands Research Facility. High polished brass and pristine starched uniforms adorn all personnel present. The room snaps to attention as Major General Caldwell Pendleton enters. Greeting the General is Colonel Mortimer Ducet. General Pendleton dispenses with pleasantries and convenes with Ducet in seclusion. Both ranking officials sit opposite of each other as Pendleton activates a large monitor. The monitor divides into three separate sections, illuminating with three more visual transmissions. Soon, other high-ranking officials appear via the transmissions as Pendleton takes lead in their discussion.

"Colonel Ducet, joining us is Keanna Seung from The Department of Interior. Mr. Brice Sanders, Bio-Weapons Contractor to the Defense Technical Information Center, and Brigadier General Davenport, my boss - Thank you all for joining us." All constituents acknowledge Pendleton's acclimations as he turns to Colonel Ducet while smiling. "Colonel Ducet, I've asked them to join us and personally fill you in on occurring matters regarding the recent mainstream of events. I thought the well of information would be helpful." "That's fine sir – thank you."

General Davenport speaks:
"Caldwell Pendleton, good to see you again."

"You too sir, how's the wife and kids?"

"Fine…fine…and yours?"

"They are doing well…thank you. Sir, time is of the essence, I'll get to the point. Since the last time I spoke with you, it appears that we have another problem on our hands. It seems that the Phantom's Death, near London's Piccadilly Circus and the incidents of New York, Houston, and California are in fact, related. At present, there is no terrorist organization laying claim to the incidents but we are not ruling that possibility out."

"Of course not – And with that in mind General, you mentioned earlier about Colonel Ducet's implementation."

"Yes I did…"

"Colonel Ducet, your division was tasked with the burden of researching innovative counter measures for human combatants – is that correct?"

"Yes sir."

"Then you are aware that the board's unanimous decision to halt the alternative measures came immediately after the executive order to invade the Mesopotamia."

"I am aware of that also."

"Good…because as we speak, the President is pushing a large portion of all our resources into the Gulf."

"The world nanny," whispers Ducet with a smirk.

"Excuse me Colonel?"

"Nothing sir…just making an outward observation of the handling of our forces."

"Really… Well…, make it clear enough for all of us to hear otherwise, let me make this clear. We will follow the President's orders by deploying a conventional approach to the war – with humans. Do know that some people, human of course, will die – Colonel. Am I clear?"

"As mountain water – sir."

Ducet's shoulders sink into a slump. His hands close into a tight fist, smartly locked away behind his back as Davenport continues. *"At this point, Mr. Brice Sanders has more on the Phantom's Death. Mr. Sanders…"*

"Thank you General. A radical turn of events has aloud us to take a closer look at this strange reoccurrence. The CDC, in conjunction with HAZMAT units in Houston, was able to take a sample from clothing and rapidly analyze that sample before the larger portion completely dissolved. They found minute traces of osteon."

"English please," says Pendleton.

"Forgive me. Osteon, or osteons are predominating structures found in the bones of mammals, in this case - human. This cortical bone

structure is incredibly dense and makes up about eighty percent of the human skeleton's weight. It's extremely hard because it is formed of multiple layers and it is conclusive that it would be the last component to break down during the dissolving process. It was initially presumed that the bodies dissolve into thin air but we can officially rule that out. However, the agent that breaks down the tissue remains elusive."

"Thank you Mr. Sanders. If nothing else, Ms. Seung, let's hear what you have to say," adds Pendleton.

"Thank you General Pendleton. My concern is more of a relations matter that particularly involves the Native Americans; primarily, their curiosity regarding the Red Sands facility."

"Curiosity? Do explain," says Ducet.

"I am merely giving acknowledgement to a recent meeting involving the elders and tribal leaders. This...meeting... took place as the direct result of your your research center. The tribal leaders say that they saw something very unnatural on the outer grounds of your facility... Colonel."

"Is that so?"

"Yes. They say 'it'...walks on two legs and has a long tail and that there were several of them."

Chuckling fills the room.

"Well...I can assure you Ms. Seung that anything in this facility with two legs and a tail wears one inch heels, carries child-bearing equipment, and is properly clothed," replies the colonel, snickering along with Pendleton.

"Ahh...spoken with true infantile assertiveness. Perhaps you would like to explain your perspectives to Major General Davenport and the Chiefs of staff for the Congressional committee of Domestic affairs."

Their laughter dissipates as Davenport eyes both men.

"Just as I thought... As I was saying, the tribal leaders of this region saw something at night, upon the grounds of this facility that causes them great concern."

"Can they prove their claims?"

"As strange as their beliefs are, it is quite peculiar that each elder shares a common interpretation from eye witness accounts."

"Where...*exactly*...are we going with this Ms. Seung?"

"Colonel...these leaders, though modern, continue to hold ancient collective beliefs about humans and their relationship to the environment around them."

"And what does that mean to me exactly*?"*

"That means...the Department is working harder to keep good relations with these people. After all, our first meeting with these Native Americans wasn't exactly neighborly; not to mention that we now possess the land they once occupied – not very constitutional, even though it brutally worked out in our favor."

"I can't change history ma'am."

"Be that as it may, if what they say about the sightings around your facility is true, that could compromise our investment in the Red Sands Facility, and that is not acceptable. You know what happens when protesters and the media engulf government facilities. We don't need that type of attention colonel."

"I guess they have a name for...it."

"Your sarcastic response tells all, but as a matter of fact, they do."

"Would you be so kind as to indulge us all*?"*

"Certainly... The Navajo are calling this, apparition if you will... Ligaii Hastiin Nayee."

"English please..."

"They're saying 'white man's monster."

Silence falls as candid stares take place. Pendleton addresses the committee members. "General Davenport, do you have more to add?"

"No-."

"Any one else? Then if there's no further inquiry, I would like to thank each of you for your participation. God speed to you all." The transmission ends, leaving Pendleton standing before Ducet.

347

Pendleton watches Ducet while casually sitting upon a table. "I wanted them to brief you personally so that you wouldn't feel as though I'm under mining your efforts."

"No sir, not at all."

"Mortimer, I know that you hate their conventional approach but you have to understand that they set policy and that's...that."

"Sir, have you ever had to look several dying men in the eyes and tell them that every thing is going to be all right, even when you know very well that it isn't?"

"Yes - and you know what? Every soldier knows the risk of their chosen field."

"Even if they are blatantly sent to their deaths for some ambiguous mission with a hidden agenda?"

"Yes...we call it a-need-to-know mission..."

"And with all do respect sir, I think it's foolish rhetoric from old men who's out of touch with reality."

"Mind your place colonel."

"Sir, you know full well that there are lakes of black gold in that sand box, and we somehow have our leech-lines under the bargaining table."

"What do you suggest; send in a squad of animals to negotiate for the US?"

"Why not?"

"Repercussions..."

"You really think my approach is that vane?"

"Mortimer, sending in kamikaze dogs, cats, leopards – hell, whatever, we'd be scorned off the face of the earth. The United Nations and our allies wouldn't tolerate that kind of foolish barbarism of the animal kingdom."

"Since when did our personal tragedies become the UN's concern? War is war General."

"Humans negotiate war in order to keep it from becoming something much worse. We do not use animals to determine a man's fate on the battle field."

"You're telling me that human life is cheaper than a rat."

"Human life is cheaper to train and more controlled. It is also accepted in the field of battle rather than that of a rat...and has been since the first stones were thrown. And with regards to animals, what's this I hear about a two-legged white man's monster?"

"Just foolishness – sir. They keep their spies on the outer edges for some stupid reason. The redskins saw large props and thought they saw something else – that's all."

"Well...regardless to what they saw – conventionalism is the way to go."

"But that's old school General!"

"Dammit Mortimer! Do you think that I actually believe this is about hybrid animals on the battlefield? You know what this is about. Time and time again, I've gone over this with you; even covered for you on occasion."

"Don't go there."

Ducet leans against the table. Pendleton places his hand on the colonel's shoulder. "Like hell, I will go there. Joshua was a fine soldier, but you have to let him go. That cloud has passed."

Ducet tenses while Pendleton retrieves his hat. "I am personally touring this facility to ensure its readiness for ground forces deployment. But before I do, is there any thing I should know?"

"No – sir."

"Are there any projects that merit my attention?"

"None..."

"Good. Now, there's something you should know."

"Yes?"

"The local authorities came this morning and were asking about you. If there is something I need to know…you know where to reach me."

Ducet blankly stares at the general as he exits the room. Soon afterwards, the colonel sits in his chair and pulls from within his pocket a small photograph of a young man. "Josh," he whispers. The stoned hardened officer passionately clutches the still image while pulling it tightly to his chest.

Meanwhile, In Oklahoma, an aerial copter lands near a structure southwest of the Arbuckle Mountains. The structure lies deep in seclusion, protruding partially beyond the quiet hills of a steep and rocky incline. Camouflage covers the barren entrance with only a patch of ground as a landing pad. After the air ship settles, three people exit the craft and enter the structure.

Guards, alarms, and lasers line the entrance as the three individuals make their way down a sub-terrain corridor. "Aun'war is this way," says one of the men.

Sitting within the confines of his stronghold, Aun'war analyzes the events surrounding his recent excursion. Soon, a notification alerts him that visitors are within the bunker. "Enter!" The door to his chamber opens and the sound of foot steps echo through out the room. "Your guest is here – sir."

With his back facing his visitors, Aun'war continues to watch the monitor. Then, he raises his right hand and flicks his wrist. "Leave us." Both escorts depart. As the door closes, a devious laugh fills the air as Aun'war slowly rotates 180 degrees. He rises to his feet and stares ahead in wonderment, relishing every portion of what he sees. "Well, well, well…Ms. Jade Vjekoslava, or should I call you by your code name, Crystal."

"That name means nothing to me now."

"Ahhh… But your eyes are as green as the name you now hold. I wonder if you are hard, cold, ruthless, or simply a GenoSyss dissident? I thought surely that I would never see you again. But I must say you look rather charming, certainly none the worst for wear."

"It has been a while."

"If I recall, our communication on the information grid was cut short. INTEL only revealed that you had acquired work for a genetics firm. I can only imagine what transpired during the time of your silence."

"I had to be careful Aun'war."

"Even so... But you could have said good-bye."

"How cordial... There are many eyes and ears on the grid – you know that, and you also know that INTEL is not secure."

"Point taken..."

"I was in too deep to jeopardize my cover."

"I have no doubts – you always were my best."

"Was I?"

"Of course – what else could you have been?"

"I was nothing more than eye candy to you."

"Jade...Jade...you were my favorite assassin; come now. "

Aun'war attempts to kiss Jade on the neck. She immediately withdraws and slaps him. "Tell that to your other Hessian-bitches. I did not return to stroke your prodding ego."

"Still fiery...I see; but even more foolish than I thought. A brave enactment; however, should you EVER...touch me again like that!"

Cold auburn eyes pierce deeply into Jade's soul, dangerously warning her of her actions. She gratefully looks away. Aun'war wipes his face and returns to his chair, ill tempered and flustered. "Less you forget; death can visit you very quickly. But you have something I want. So tell me, what have you found out and who are the perpetrators?"

"A Russian by the name of Rowland Kreshenkov – the former head of GenoSyss Research Facility."

"Never heard of him."

"He was formerly known as Vladik Ivonovich Kreshenkov."

"Still...I do not know this name."

"No…but your protégé may have known. You were perhaps ten years younger than Rowland when his sister became victim in Uralmash incident."

"An ill sister…did she die?"

"Yes."

"And …this…Rowland retaliated?"

"He did."

"Even as youth; killing my predecessor and later going to U.S. for diplomatic immunity; all in exchange for bio-genetic information."

"That is correct."

"*Hmmm* – keep going."

"After Ukraine outpost was destroyed, my leads pointed to U.S. Once in, I gave myself to the military; as you instructed. I discover bioresearch programs were incredibly aggressive, competitive, and advance – mostly the result of the military. That is were I met Colonel Mortimer Ducet. He heads research for U.S. Marines genetic development."

"Ah, just as I anticipated. Tell me, does he believe that he is in control?"

"Of course he does. Arrogance often precedes ignorance."

"In most cases –"

"Colonel Ducet also believes he has me on a leash and…"

"You – on a leash," exerts Aun'war.

"You may laugh all you want, but as I was saying… he believes that he has me under his control."

"You bring much cheer."

"Do not be foolish Aun'war. They suspect your involvement with Rham-kiev, but your leadership of the organization continues to elude them. Even now, Colonel Ducet believes that I will give him your location."

"Amazing, he is as fool-hearted as he is misled. Now tell me again…why would you not betray an old friend, such as me."

Jade does not answer, but simply stares at Aun'war who relishes the moment while telling her, "Consequences…of course. You need not worry about the colonel's wantonness my dear, because in a few hours, I will notify the American government of my terms, and they will accept; then congratulations, your task is complete. You have done well my precious stone."

"There's more Aun'war."

"Of course there is, so why am not surprised?"

"Your attempts to create a hybrid carrier failed several times."

"Ah…you refer to the creature – yes."

"I saw the photographs of your hybrid Pan beast."

"I like to refer to it as a cryptic paradigm; yes, I remember. We successfully combined the animal and human. It was a good ploy in bio-hybrid weaponry…until the creature went mad. One of them eventually fell into the hands of the Americans."

"The photographs show that it was dead – nothing more."

"After the creature escaped, we had to destroy the others. We could not control them as we thought. But still…they cannot link that horrible looking thing to me. It continues to plague me that such an endeavor took place."

"You had your reasons."

"As did we all…"

"Aun'war, there is something else you should know."

"More information? This is getting better."

"Not that I have much of a choice since you were monitoring me; but Rowland's team succeeded where yours' failed."

"Intriguing..."

"They have non-human hybrid."

Aun'war stares intently at Jade. "Have you seen this hybrid?"

"Yes."

"What does it look like?"

"They call these creatures, enans and they appear as something you cannot possibly imagine."

"Remember your place woman."

"I speak truthfully Aun'war. These creatures have a magnificent covering of scales that protect them from most weapons. Here is footage of development stage."

Jade places a small device in front of Aun'war. The device automatically projects a visual image. Aun'war's fascination grows. He sits quietly, taking in all that unravels before him – until, "Wait a minute. This hybrid enan appears as a modified kangaroo, but more importantly, like the description given by the men surrounding Adir Sa'ood's outpost in the Mediterranean."

"I can assure you the creature exists."

"Remarkable."

"Truly..."

"How might I find this Rowland?"

"That may prove difficult. Rowland works with Colonel Ducet, but it is unclear that their superiors know of such a relationship between them. Since his departure from GenoSyss, no one has seen him."

"Then...how could you have let Rowland escape?"

"Things got complicated."

"Really..."

"By the time I was ready to deliver him; members of 429 were dead. Police questioned us all – watching every move we made."

"Yes…but allowing any person on the team to remain alive would be a mistake. They could replicate their success and sell it to others, in effect, making it easy for anyone to have the kind of control – I seek. Surely you understand why I could not allow that."

"You speak as if you knew of their progress all along."

"You have no idea my dear. After receiving your transmission from Red Sands, I realized that it was time to put my plans into effect. Bio-hybrid weaponry of this nature had to be concealed; and that is why the poor souls who knew about the 429 experiment had to die."

Jade's eyes widen as her mouth quivers upon a fragile word. *"Wh…wha…*what? *Yu…yu…*you knew of their deaths?"

"Foolish woman, are you so surprised?"

"But how?"

"Did you really think I would trust you as before?"

"I served you well, only you."

"Most men have a price Jade, and I could not allow the team to live, once I learned of their hybrid success. I knew all along of Rowland's scheme. His illicit desire to have his team hidden until his departure, but I had you to pay Rowland's henchmen, Langley and his Australian counterpart, to silence the team once and for all."

"I did as you instructed!"

"I believe your code name for the packages was, The Lady."

"You knew all along?"

"Did you truly think I let you run loose?"

"You sent spies."

"No my precious. That is too troublesome – ineffective. The small device in your arm not only gives you power to transmit information to me, but it also grants me the ability to listen in on you – even when you thought the transmission was terminated."

"You bastard…"

"My poor child…did you become friends with some of them?"

"I knew them Aun'war."

"Some information on you is, shall we say…cloudy, but enough came through. I know more than you think."

Jade lowers her head in sorrow. "Feels like old times," says Aun'war, smiling with devious contempt.

"Oh God…you ordered their deaths behind my back."

"Thanks to you, I already knew they created the hybrid – I just did not know what kind or how far they got. I also wanted to know if you were still loyal to me. Bravo for you – you passed the test…and now…you will live."

Jade closes her eyes. Her flustering visage all but discounts subtle movements, which yield its interpretations in a single, tear.

Aun'war approaches her. "Now, choose your next words carefully…for I know that some loose ends remain. Who is Arthur Robinson?"

"If I may…"

"Certainly…"

"He is responsible for the enans success."

"Ahhh, so…another potential threat does live. How many more survivors?"

"Please, sultan lord, none that are of harm to you."

"You have not called me Sultan or lord in an eternity. You are compromised."

"Please…Aun'war."

"Your original report tells of seven, and I know that three remain. Don't forget your little implant. Arthur is one of the survivors; now give me the names of the others."

"Please… I did what you ask of me."

"Are you sure?"

"Yes."

"The only time you failed a mission was when love-came-calling. So tell me…do you have affections for one of the remaining team members?"

"No."

"Who is he?"

"No one-"

"Is it Arthur?"

"No!"

"Or someone named Walter?"

"Absurd," she says, shaking as her eyes try to bury emotions deeper.

"Perhaps if you behave, I'll let him live. You see… I have arranged the services of someone else in order to assure that your mission succeeds."

Aun'war grabs Jade by the chin, forcing her to look directly into his eyes. "There is one immutable truth for all stones; even the ones that are flawed. As water carves a stone, the stone continues to remain hard. Apparently, you've been gone too long. You have forgotten what it is like to be here. You have forgotten what it is like to be with me. Perhaps if you can remember your true place, then I will be willing to forget your inperfections."

"Damn you Aun'war. Is your heart as cold as your soul?"

"You tell me…," he says; chuckling as deceit falls from his lips.

Jade stares at Aun'war, sensing that his eyes are crawling up and down every inch of her. She ubuttons her shirt as he views images which display the chronological progression of project 429.

~~~Allies~~~

In Texas, public hours conclude at Plaza Hospital, although family members often receive the common courtesy of visitation rights; compliments of the administration staff. Arthur successfully navigates pass the front office while raising little suspicion. He locates room 310 and enters. Hoping to find the ideal conditions of isolation with Marshal Harrison, he discovers a woman caringly tending to the marshal's discomforts. Arthur's presence startles her.

"Oh, hello, I didn't know Derek had more visitors."

"I'm sorry. I hope I'm not disturbing anything. I just came from out of town and heard of his condition."

"Well, he's in an out. I can wake him if you like."

"I don't want to intrude."

"Really, it's no problem, he's just lying there and I doubt he'll be moving anytime soon. Anyway, I don't recall ever meeting you before. My name is Madison; I'm Derek's wife." Though feeling awkward, Arthur recants with good mannerisms. Madison turns to her husband and whispers in his ear, gently touching his shoulder. "Hello *hunny*."

Harrison's eyes slowly open. "Whoa, I still feel like a truck hit me."

"There's someone here to see you; an old acquaintance."

"An old acquaintance…?"

Harrison sternly glances across the room until fixating upon Arthur. Silence stirs amidst as his eyes sternly focus. Madison observes her husband's expression and perceives that something may be out of order. "Is there anything I can get you?" Harrison's continued fixation prevents an attentive response until Madison touches him. "Derek…?"

"Oh…no…thank you. It's just that I didn't expect to see Mr. Robinson here – at least so soon."

"Arthur Robinson? Oh…I see." Madison acknowledges Arthur while rubbing her husband's bandaged ribs. Arthur notices it. "Well, it's sweet of you to at least drop in. I'll give the both some time alone."

Both men stare at each other until Arthur decides to speak. "She's a wonderful companion Marshal."

"Yeah, you got that right. She's the one spark of sunshine on a cloudy day…of filth, especially in my line of work. But then again Robinson, you're not the typical trash I have to walk through. Or are you?"

"I hope not."

"Your coming here suggests a bit of good intentions on your part – which means, I may actually like you. But then again, because I'm in this bed, that however constitutes a degree of after thought, which suggests - that maybe I should bust your ass right now. So tell me why I feel as though I won't have to do that?"

"Because I'm sorry..."

"I know you are – in the real sense."

"Wait, please let me finish. I'm sorry for what happened to you and your partner."

"So…what's your story?"

"I…we…can't keep running and we don't have the resources to fight. Nor can I protect my wife from these people."

"Well now… Common sense befalls another generation. You may actually be credit to the human race."

"I'll take that as a compliment."

"Robison, when I took my oath of public office, I became a servant to you. I don't know what you've been involved in or how you do what you do, but you need to trust me."

"That is why I came."

"Good. Now let's re-evaluate our time together. You people came to me and gave me partial information, which led me to follow a few leads. Those leads brought me to you, after which my partner winds up in ICU with busted ribs, a lung that can potentially collapse, internal bleeding, not to mention a slight concussion; which I might add, was brought on by an oversize thing that looks like a kangaroo on steroids. Fortunately for you…she will live – and recover."

"That's good to know."

"I'm not going to ask you what that thing was, but every time I take a deep breath, everything in me says it was all too real."

"How many more times can I say I'm sorry?"

"*Dammit*, until the pain goes away – won't hurt my feelings!"

"Okay…I'm sorry…I'm sorry…I'm so, so, sorry."

"Real smart …"

"That's good; get it all out marshal, now we're making progress."

"Shut up Robinson. Now talk to me."

"Marshal, I know you have cause to arrest me."

"Figure that out by yourself?"

"The information I have to offer may not help much, but Rowland Krenshenkov can probably give you a better lead."

"The Russian…yeah…he's a sneaky s.o.b; even I can see that. I did some checking on him. Since his arrival to the states, he's had a special deal with the government. He would get citizenship and other immunities in return for bio-cloning development. The man is good; I'll give him that much. The boys in Washington believe that he may have had ties with a radical group back home, but they ain't saying much. Personally, I would like to solve this case before they get too involved."

"Did you know that Rowland works closely with a colonel of the U.S. Marines."

"Who?"

"Colonel Mortimer Ducet."

Harrison's eyes widen. "Let's not waste time with this son."

"That's not my intention."

"I take it that you won't be filling out a report down at the station and that this conversation never took place – so therefore, I'm all ears; let's hear it – all of it."

"Ok. We all took a pledge of deniability. Even if you find Colonel Ducet, by the time you get through all the red tape, they would have buried project 429 so deep that it will make covering a landfill with a shovel look appealing."

"Well…let's hope that shovel has a wide scoop on the end, because, I'll be out of here in a day or so. Then I'm going to need more insight from you."

"Tell me what you need."

"You can start by telling me about project 429. What exactly is it and is it worth the death of your fellow workers, your family, and quite possibly - you?"

Marshal Harrison carefully listens as Arthur shares the information.

Deep underground at Red Sands Research Facility, Rowland enters the office of Colonel Ducet. He eagerly greets the commander and both men sit down for business. Rowland's gleeful smile parades a promising venture; however, the colonel is not as enthusiastic. "I was beginning to wonder if you got my message."

"I came as quickly as I could. You *rr-isk* much by my being here, but *eef* what you say *eez* true, *eet* holds great worth."

"Look at the monitor Rowland. I want to see what your thoughts are regarding this message."

The colonel activates a moderate size device. An image displays the silhouette image of a figure whose face is all but lost in a background of shadows. Audio of a morbid transmission soon follows:

"…deaths were no accident. If my demands are not met, more deaths are sure to follow. As it were in London, so it will be in the U.S. The Phantom Death is only the beginning. Rham-kiev lives…"

"Sounds like my ex-wife – Yes?"

"Rowland, a number of info-capsules were sent to news agencies as well as the governors of each victimized state; Texas, New York, California. Each data capsule contains specific instructions for each governor to carry out. Most of what we retrieved earlier suggests nothing more than thousands of dollars here and there at delivery points. They also want our government to grant them sovereign immunity. At best, we figure this guy uses the Phantom's Death to threaten any one who doesn't comply with his wishes."

"So *eet* appears."

"This can lead to something much worse. In a manner of speaking, he's the puppeteer and the governments are the puppets."

"Does *heez* request go abroad?"

"Yes – to any government that is willing or able to grant such privileges."

"*Een*-tresting that the *Prr*-esident has not been *een*-volved, only at state level – Yes?"

"Exactly, and aside from that, I want to show you something else."

"What *eez* this?"

"This is the satellite feed that covers the terrain of a rocky geographic region. But importantly, see the pulsating beacon?"

"Yes."

"That is where our precious little spy has led us."

Rowland's eyes fill with excitement as a dastardly smile spans his face. "Does Jade know you were tracking her the whole time?"

"I doubt it. Prior to 429, each participant was tagged for security purposes. When the laser print stamped Jade's wrists with the bar code, a tiny tracker was injected just beneath her skin. Too bad we didn't tag the others, but eventually, the tracker will dissolve."

"Misfortunate planning..."

"Not before we get what we want."

"I did not know of *thees* tracking."

"Only for those with a need-to-know."

"Yes – of course; you make strange bed fellow Colonel."

"Perhaps, but when I wake up in the morning, at least I want to know who's been lying next to me, especially if it's my enemy. Jade's pattern clearly indicates that she has made contact with someone of great importance. The information relayed back to me this morning strongly suggests you-know-who."

"Aun'war–"

"Checkmate."

"Does your superiors and FBI know?"

"Negative –"

"You wage personal war *weeth* this man – Yes?"

"I got my reasons. But if it's all the same to you, I wouldn't be surprise that Aun'war is Rham-kiev's leader."

"You know what you are saying Colonel?"

"Think about it. He is the same guy you wanted to take down in the Ukraine."

"That *eez* amazing Colonel; I chase *heem* for years, all over Ukraine. Now I have *heem*."

"Don't be too hasty – I said there is a strong possibility that he's in those hills. But whether or not, we're going in. Satellite telemetry pinpoints a very active base just inside the foothills of Oklahoma. This is where we will strike."

"I like what I hear colonel."

"I knew you would."

Ducet casually pours Rowland a drink. "You do realize that command has shut me down?"

"So I have heard."

"Soon, this facility will crawl with brass and become a training ground for troops. Before that can happen, I intend to kill Rham-kiev's leader and deploy the remainder of the enans on to the Mesopotamia, putting an end to this pathetic war. Are you with me?"

"Of course… You have the enans *rr*-eady Colonel?"

"Even as we speak, four are loaded in a convoy about a couple of hours away from the target."

"You do realize that there is thirty-*thrr*-ee that *rr*-ee-main. I'm not sure how the last two died but before their heart transmitters went silent, their neurological and systolic readings were off the charts. They confronted som-*teen* te-*rrible*."

"Really… Now what can be more terrible than a red-eyed enan?"

"*Dhey're* not indestructible comrade."

"True, but it is very hard to kill an enan."

"Absolutely!"

"Well…at least for now, I want you to meet with the team and assist Lieutenant Essington Jamison. His code name is Stalker. We'll fly you in. I, on the other hand will stay here and prep the other enans for departure overseas. We're looking at a two-hour window to take down Mr. Rham-kiev – if he is there."

"A very sound plan colonel and by the way… Good Scotch. Da svidaniya."

"Good-bye to you too Professor."

Outside Marshal Harrison's residence, Walter's visual image transmits upon a tiny screen as he and Arthur discuss their affairs. "No hard feelings about the wound*?*"

"*Naaahhh… But it's still sore.*"

"I hope you forgive me Walter, I am very sorry for what I did…but I know forgiveness takes time. I am truly sorry – I was wrong."

"*It was the moment. You lost your cool, but I provoke it.*"

"I won't let that happen again."

"*I hope not. By the way, where are you?*"

"I'm here with Gracella and Gjhe'nan. We're waiting for the marshal.*"

"So...you decided to work with Marshal Harrison after all."

"If I had listened to you in the first place, it would never have come to this. Now, we don't have much of a choice."

"I see..."

"That word has come to have great meaning. After the past few days, it's just good to 'see' anybody."

"Speaking of... Have you seen or heard from Jade?"

"No."

"I called her job but she isn't there, nor has she called me – it's not like her at all. I think something has happened."

"You have...obvious concerns."

"She's been gone a long time. It's messing with my head."

"Sounds like the love bug is stirring."

"We had an argument; I'm concerned about her. Besides, her people are overseas. If she goes home, I may never see her again."

"Just keep the door open for possibilities."

"Always..."

"Walter, we're not too far from you. We can pick you up."

"What? Oh...hey, no way man. We're getting picked off like flies; one by one."

"Which is all the more reason why you should join us? As a league, we have a lot more to fight back with."

"Arthur...look around you. What the hell kind of justice league are you talking about? You're dysfunctional, Gracella is distraught, and the marshal is all busted-up. How is my joining you going to help?"

"We have information and Harrison has resources; not to mention a weapon like Gjhe'nan, and most of all, we have prayer."

"Hah...sweet Jesus."

"Yeah, well...He's been working on our behalf so far. Just get your things ready; we're coming to get you. Stay put."

Soon, Marshal Harrison approaches the freighter. Gracella sees the marshal and alerts Arthur. In that moment, Arthur discontinues the transmission.

Upon approach, Harrison grabs the handle of the cab and opens the door. *"Whew!* Nice wheels – nice big wheels, all fourteen of them. Where did you learn how to drive this thing?"

"My little brother taught me."

"Your little brother...oh...you mean Hollis, big boy at the farm who nearly blew my head off."

"Yep –"

"Funny Robinson... You have a cargo trailer that's the length of The Mississippi. What's in it?"

"A...little surprise. We needed the space."

"Seems to me you techs live very interesting lives; surely I'm in the wrong line of work. What did you spring for this rig?"

"Oh...we...borrowed it...from friends."

Harrison's brow rises. "Right, don't ask; don't tell – fair enough." Harrison directs his attention to Gracella. "Hello again Ms Andreas. Glad to see you alive and doing well."

"Thank you Marshal. I'm glad to see that you are alive and intact, as well – no pun intended." Harrison stands in utter surprise of Gracella's comment.

"Alright Arthur Robinson; I've convinced my boss to play along with this unorthodox approach we have. Here's the deal; you stay out of jail – all charges dropped, if you help us nab the murderers of your friends – Got it?"

"Like ash on my skin."

"Speaking of skin, Candice; my partner, she's been downgraded from ICU and it looks like she'll make a full recovery, which is good for you."

"I want to tell her I'm sorry."

"Whoa…hold ya throttle... You got good motives, but bad timing. She's a pistol and needs time to heal, because she remembers how she got there."

"I could loose my head if I see her now?"

"Now you're catching on."

"Where do I stand now?"

"On one hand, if we're lucky, we bypass a lot of beaurocratic red tape, even with the department. On the other hand, this will be the fastest way to an epitaph."

Suddenly, a piercing shriek echoes from the aft compartment. Harrison turns towards the rear. "What the…?" "Follow me Marshal," says Arthur. Both men enter the cargo area of the trailer.

Anxiously waiting is a docile yet powerful contrivance of nature. Harrison's mouth slowly hangs open. He backs away while caught in sheer amazement. He attempts to blink, but his eyes fixate openly. Arthur taps his shoulder. "Marshal, let me formally introduce you to Gjhe'nan." Harrison observes the hybrid from toe to head. His perspective only gives a foreshortened view of the creature as its tail slowly wags from left to right. Harrison leans against the wall. His eyes never blink nor does he take a breath. With mystical fascination, the marshal peers into the deep, dark soul of the beast. Yet, the marshal's prolong observance renders him vulnerable. Seeing Harrison's dilemma, Arthur nudges the officer. "Marshal, Marshal..."

"Huh…what?"

"Don't stare into his eyes too long."

"I couldn't move."

"He has that affect on people."

"How?"

"Don't worry about it. Gjhe'nan, this is Marshal Derek Harrison…you two already met." The hybrid tilts its head, blinks, and turns away. Arthur and the marshal return to the forward cabin. Harrison breathes erratically, clinching his teeth while gently placing his hand over his chest. Arthur attempts to calm the marshal.

"Take one slow breath at a time. You don't want to arouse your injuries."

"That's the thing that attacked me."

"I know, but I did tell you not to shoot at him."

Harrison gives Arthur a look of disillusionment. Realizing the marshal's abrupt expression, Arthur sets the freighter into motion, then asking, "Where to first?"

"Let's visit your old director's house – Rowland Kreshenkov."

"Before we get there, we need to pick up someone."

"Who?"

"Walter."

"Oh…science boy. He finally decided to come out of his hole?"

"You could say that."

"Tell me something Robinson…you did say that there are more of those things back there…those g-nons?"

"Yes there are."

"And they are somehow connected with the military?"

"That's right…"

"If so, this whole thing may be way over our heads."

Arthur looks at Harrison but remains silent. The technician sets the large transport in motion as Harrison gently rubs his chest.

~~~Dawn's Early Light~~~

Heat rises off a grassy plateau, casting a wavering dance to assure all that the sun can be a good thing. The heat also envelopes convoys of Ducet's mercenaries as they set up occupancy outside Aun'war's camp. Inside an armor transport, one prominent monitor hangs as sophisticated electronics display information. Surrounding cliffs and sub-terrain caverns stretch in picturesque form; dispelling any potential hostile threat. More importantly, heat signatures vividly pinpoint hidden armies lurking beneath the hills.

A band of soldiers and four enans quickly scramble into position, surrounding the underground complex while closing off all possible escape routes. Rowland converses with Ducet and the unit's commander, Lieutenant Essington Jamison; code-name Stalker. Information connects through visual transmissions as each person listens carefully.

Colonel Ducet transmits his message.
"Stalker, can you hear me?"

"Go ahead Eagle."

"Are your teams in place?"

"They are sir…"

"Does the situation appear as the monitor displays?"

"It's a hornet's nest, but only a few hostiles guard the entry."

"Be advised that our SAT scan shows more numbers deep within. They're trying to conceal the location and douse outside curiosity. Now remember, confiscate what you can, but take no baggage – Understood?"

"Like elementary sir –"

"Professor?"

"Yes."

"Are the enans bio scans reading well?"

"They are *rr*-reading very well Colonel."

"That's what I need to hear- you may commence operations."

"Oh…Colonel, a small matter of inquiry."

"Speak…"

"What about Jade?"

"…And what about Jade?"

"*Vwell* she *deed* assist us in some way – Yes?"

"Against my better judgment. She infiltrated this country with intent to harm, lied her way into GenoSyss under your nose with intent to kill you, has affiliations with a known terrorist extremist, and God only knows what classified information she's leaked out over the information grid. She got picked up on our INTEL once we snuffed her out. Far as I'm concerned, she's one of them and will be treated as such. Professor, I thought you wanted the head of Rham-kiev?"

"Of course…"

"Then get your knives and forks ready…he'll be served up on a silver platter – commence operation Fox Burrow NOW!"

Commander Stalker raises his hand and gives the signal. A nearby sergeant informs the other teams as Aun'war's guards patrol the grounds. Though cool winds blow, sweat courses the faces of Ducet's men. Fingers gently touch triggers as deadly cross-hairs lock on to unsuspecting targets. Then, with sudden assertiveness, Stalker's hand lowers. Bullets fly as each projectile reaches its fleshly target. One by one, the guards fall victim to the kill shots.

"First wave, move in," commands Stalker.

Seven men immediately rush the entry to the bunker and attempt to gain access. "It's sealed," informs one of the men. "Blow it!" "Fire in the hole!" Suddenly, a blast of light signifies a job well done and first wave enters.

"Team leader to Stalker, I see nothing ahead…pressing forward."

"Team leader, you telling me there's no resistance?"

"Yes sir."

The team progress until they approach another section of a large hallway.

"Something's wrong… Still no resistance," expresses Stalker, who cautiously eyes the dark corridor before relaying another message. *"Stalker to Eagle, still no resistance."*

Ducet anxiously waits. *"Stalker, talk to me.What's happening?"*

"SAT shows multiple hostile readings but no movement – just ours. We're showing that first wave is right on top of the enemy, but they're saying otherwise – It can only be one thing."

"A trap – get'em out of there!"

"TEAM leader, ABORT, ABORT!!!"

"Mission abort – WE ARE LEAVING!" The men scramble for the exit. But then, without warning, a blistering stream of fire surges through the main hallway, scorching every thing in its path. The soldiers desperately hasten to escape the flames, but the surge of white fire engulfs them all. Piercing temperatures singe through their outer armor until raw flesh blackens upon hell fire's touch.

Unable to save his men, Ducet profoundly curses. As he does, a console technician attempts to gain the colonel's attention. "Colonel…" Ducet, fueling with anger looks at the technician. "Speak wisely son."

"Sir, we're picking up local authorities on short wave. They know we're here and are in route."

"What's their e.t.a?"

"Ten minutes…"

"How could they have known we were here? We didn't raise any outside attention."

"I don't know sir, but they are coming in large numbers as well."

Ducet signals Lieutenant Jamison. "Stalker…" *"Yes sir!"* "Send in the enans!"

Teams attach explosives to two enans and dispatch one of the creatures into the bunker. The enan enters without hesitation, but quickly encounters the same fury of flames as did first wave. Shielding membranes fall over the hybrid's eyes, therefore providing substantial protection. The creature shrieks and squalls, yet relentlessly proceeds forward. Though unable to see, the enan stumbles over chard bodies until clearing the fiery gauntlet; pressing its way far beyond the narrow corridor. Smoke rises off the dense scales as singed gear wrinkle from the intense heat. Standing powerfully with retribution, a high winding screech blares throughout the complex.

"Rowland, why has it stopped?"

"*Heez* eye covers need time to *rr-retract*."

A sergeant approaches Rowland as all eyes fixate upon the monitor. "Sir...hostiles on the move. They somehow lied to our sensors. They were expecting us." "They're preparing to defend their nest."

"*Rowland, I need those eye covers up, time's clicking,*" rants Ducet.

"Momentarily Colonel..."

"*No time – Stalker, send in backup!*"

"Done!"

Stalker deploys the second enan. As the creature enters the bunker, white flames quickly engulf the beast.

As the beast vanishes in a chaos of flames, Aun'war's men encounter the first enan, only to cease their approach. "This can't be," says one of the men. Another man asks, "What do you make of this thing?" Blank stares and puzzled faces are all that respond; until, high-powered projectiles impact the hybrid's side, ultimately punishing the beast with every devastating strike. Several bullets ricochet, but few penetrate the scales. Fewer bullets burrow deep into the hybrid's flesh. The creature screams. Then, powerful reflexes cause the hybrid to flinch. As a result, the enan runs blindly into a wall.

"WE HAVE IT! FINISH IT NOW!"

Dazed, the enan sends forth a terrifying scream as it stands in an act of defiance.

"Lieutenant Jamison, is the enan's earpiece damaged?"

"No sir Professor. It's lodged deep within the canal."

"Tell it *Vwhere* to go..."

Lieutenant Jamison verbally guides the enan, but the hybrid sustains an unmerciful attack. Aun'war's men empty several hi-powered rounds into the beast until the scales begin to tear open. Blood frightfully spatters the walls; yet, the hybrid remains standing, forcefully moving towards the intended target.

The second enan emerges from the fiery corridor, billowing as smoke rises from scorched scales, but the protective eyelids are not fully closed. Stepping wildly, the creature's presence quickly draws the attention of Aun'war's gunmen. Soon to follow is a torrential spray of hell fire, but the men's ill attempts fail to subdue the gangly beast as it scurries down another corridor.

The first hybrid, though badly wounded, continues to take on a brutal assault. Surprisingly, the creature strikes back as it succeed in decapitating two men with the deadly swing of its tail. Though twisting and turning, the hybrid begins to slow and become less effective.

Now confident, other gunmen move closer, loading and reloading their weapons. Some of the men discharge their weapons from a distance while others fire at point-blank range. Unable to sustain such a merciless onslaught, the enan tucks its head while coiling its tail around its blood-drenched body. As it does, human-like hands draw closely to its chest. Now in a fetal position, the enan sinks to the ground and endures a merciless punishment – until the very end.

Turquoise fluid pools beneath the hybrid's body as gaping wounds assure the gunmen of their success. Costly efforts to finally bring down the creature glisten upon disquieted faces. The men examine the fallen hybrid. "What is this thing?" "Don't know, but those scales are the reason it took so long to kill. Heaven forbid if it had weapons." "It took all this shooting to bring it down. Our ammunition is almost gone." "Doesn't matter...it is dead."

As the men speak, distinct sounds project loudly as others approach. "Where is that noise coming from?" "Look under the beast." The gunman takes a closer look and finds something of interest. Suddenly, the man rises to his feet and turns toward his fellow gunmen. "What is it, why do you look at us that way? Answer me," expels one of the men. No verbal response comes; only a wide eyed glance and a disturbed face. Soon, a loud sound erupts within the compound followed by a thunderous explosion.

In another part of the compound, the second enan encounters equal contest as Aun'war's gunmen attempt to defend their ground. Finding a position along the floor, the enan cowers into a fetal-like position. The hybrid's eyes turn from red to black, soullessly watching amidst, then slowly closing. The camera harness falls to the floor, but astoundingly relays information back to Rowland.
He watches in earnest.

Colonel Ducet sees as well, asking *"What is it doing Professor?"*

"I do not know…never seen such behavior; as though…expecting *itz* own end."

"You're telling me, that animal knows what's going to happen to it?"

"Why not Colonel? A very *een*-conceivable analogy you have."

"What are you talking about?"

"They do posses human intelligence – of course*."*

"We gave no clue to its demise whatsoever."

"They can sense *theengs* colonel and perhaps they know you *vweel keel* them *eef* they *rr-runawey*."

"They do not know the intentional outcome of a mission."

"They know when some-*teen* is *wrrrrong!*"

"If so…then it will not be known by those who watch."

Immediately, a soldier intervenes, telling Ducet, "Sir, local authorities are upon approach; e.t.a…two minutes." The colonel ponders for a moment.

"Stalker…"

"Yes sir."

"Explode the charges on the enan – do it!"

"Acknowledged…"

Disquieting sounds rumble throughout the remains of the complex as blistering heat precedes white surges of fire. Walls implode as ceilings collapse; allowing several tons of earth to fall within the entire bunker. Within seconds, the cataclysmic force silences forever the dreadful souls that dwell deep inside.

Aboard a military transport, a soldier gives Rowland a report. "Sir, SAT and thermal opts confirm that there are no signature readings from any one. If any body did survive, then it's nothing short of a miracle."

"No matter, the cave-in assures that no one *weel* come out."

Suddenly, a small green marker flashes on the monitor, attracting the technician's attention. Rowland asks, "What *eez* that?" "I...I don't know Mr. Kreshenkov. For a moment, I though I saw something. What ever it was, it's gone." Rowland listens but gives no verbal response.

Soon, Ducet's men, along with Stalker and Rowland depart from the area. Seconds later, local authorities arrive only to find an enormous sunken plateau.

Arthur and his companions depart the home of Rowland Kreshenkov. Their efforts of locating the former director turn fruitless and ultimately bitter. As the sun casts its reddish glow, the freighter barrels down the highway; carrying a compliment of battered passengers.

Marshal Harrison converses with headquarters through a visual transmission. "That's right chief; the bastard skipped town and I want a patrol car monitoring his house – just in case he decides to come back."

"I see... Very well then... Now hear me out Derek, this one took a bit of teeth pulling; but finally, I am sending you the last known assignment for Colonel Ducet. As you know, the military is tight-lipped and that means you boys will be taking the long haul tonight. Are you sure you're up for this?"

"I'm fine, just sore. Besides, these guys in this rig are more dangerous than any criminal on the street, believe me."

"Maybe you should deputize them."

"I hope you have a sense of humor."

"I hired you...didn't I?"

"There's so much love in this world…anyway, you got to trust me on this one boss."

"If you say so... Derek. I'll contact the New Mexico authorities and do be careful. After all, I don't need Madison coming after me because of something stupid happening to you."

"Aww…sensitive man." Harrison blows the chief a kiss and discontinues the transmission.

Arthur smiles at the marshal's playful bantering. "Didn't know you had it in you."

"Oh, I'm sweet alright; especially when it gets me what I want. In your case, it gets me a chance to sit back and collect a pay check."

"At the expense of Taxpayers?"

"Whatever… Look Robinson, there's a good chance that Ducet knows we are on to him. If I'm going to solve this case, we need to find him as well as the Russian."

"True…"

"You say that, but your eyes say something else."

"And what would that be?"

"You were going after him with or without my help. Weren't you?"

"After what he and his buddy did to me-"

"You're not the only one suffering son, and vindication by the hand of hatred is no way to go."

"No, but vindication sure can be one hell of a motivator."

Harrison looks at Gracella as she lays with a blanket drawn over her. "She's out cold. How long have you known her?"

"Ever since high school. I first met her brother, nice guy…then she comes along."

"She got family?"

"Relatives – but no kids."

"I see..."

"Marshal, you are aware that her husband is missing – or dead."

"No."

"We think an enan got to him, but the attack was meant for her."

"Nothing was reported, not even on the local channel."

"That's what I've been trying to tell you all along. They can strike us at any time and no one will ever know that we were missing. I hope you understand why we can't sit still and wait for something to happen. At least on the move, we have a chance."

"Point taken; anyway, you look tired."

"I am."

"Who's your replacement driver?"

In a timely manner, Arthur steers the freighter into a nearby parking lot. "Him," he says. The large vehicle halts, and Walter Pierson climbs on board. Harrison sternly eyes Walter, "Look who we have here."

"Greetings gentlemen."

"Well I'll be d…"

"Careful Marshal. After what we've been through, you don't need any more damnation upon yourself as well as us." Arthur releases the steering wheel into Walter's hands and the large vehicle is once again, in route.

Lying quietly sprawled on the floor is Gjhe'nan. His hands lie across each other while his tail leisurely sways to a soundless rhythm. The hybrid's posture also gives Arthur much solace as the technician chooses to seat near the beast. As though a domestic canine; the hybrid nudges his maker while bestowing affectionate mannerisms upon him; such that are conducive to that of human adoration. Gjhe'nan gleefully pushes Arthur who responds with head nudging. Then, the placid hybrid lays its head upon Arthur's lap. The technician squirms to reinforce support under the weight as Gjhe'nan closes his eyes. Arthur observes several wounds and damaged scales. "You're healing well," he says while coursing the hybrid's finer scales, realizing that such biological plates house enormous strength. Arthur gleams as he stares over his creation.

As time passes, Arthur lays his weary head against the wall and closes his eyes. As he does, he catches a glimpse of two books on the floor. Curious attempts to identify the literature vanish under the subjection of sleep, but only Gjhe'nan would have such items; yet, with regards to the hybrid's wantonness, the books; a dictionary and a bible lay visibly accessible. All is quiet as they journey to New Mexico in the still of the night.

~~~Intentions Beguiled~~~

Within Red Sands, Colonel Mortimer Ducet convenes with a small assembly of soldiers inside the control room. Everyone listens with great interest as the colonel boldly parades before them while invoking his patriotic constitutions.

"Long before now, you men and women have worked with me in a co-op effort to silence criminal and ill-humane acts of a terrorist nature; such acts that were imposed upon the American people many years ago. Well guess what – those threats are alive and well...even today. In an attempt to combat such barbaric notions, we were given the assignment to introduce a non-human element into war so that our troops would not foolishly fall into harms way.

Well, the committee has decided that conventional warfare is the answer to the over-all madness of this world, and that our military should deal with it accordingly. Frankly, I find the committee's point of view quite disturbing, especially when our men and women are being picked off like flies...every day. And those numbers keep growing. It gets worse, because in three days, this facility will house another staff and many of you will come under their administration; thereby serving the mission of a new commander.

With that in mind, I have received orders for deportation over seas– Now guess what? I'll take those orders, but before I do, there's only one final mission to carry out. I want you to understand that I cannot order you to do what very well may be your last mission – if we're successful. Nor can I order you to participate in mortal conflict that could result in a court martial – if you return.

I'll only need a few of you. Once implementing factions are in place, I intend to use the enans to bring this war to an end! I have personally picked those of you in this room because of your loyal dedication to the project; the vision that we started a long time ago. If you feel that you should come with me, then you have one hour to decide. God speed to you all."

Ducet exits the room. Flanking the colonel is Rowland, who proceeds to clap his hands in a mockingly gesture. "Impressive...a true testament to the power of insight. Now *weeth* Rham-kiev crippled, it *eez* time for your final act."

"I've got some bad news..."

"Oh?"

"Aun'war may not have been in that bunker, but I know his men were and you can bet that if he's alive, he will retaliate."

"As *eef* we *deed* not know."

"Non-the-less; but good job on your victory in Oklahoma."

"*Spasibo, spah-see-boh*; very much comrade, but it *iz* our victory. But tell me Colonel, so sure are you to allow your soldiers knowledge of your plans already - *hmm*?"

"The group that I have chosen is loyal to me; besides, there's no turning back. And you know full well that I can't carry out this mission alone."

"Of course..."

"It's time to make my move."

"Your approach *vwill rr*-aise serious questions colonel."

"My approach will put a bogus conflict to rest."

"What about your Articles of Conflict?"

"Which one?"

"The rules for engagement..."

"Here's a bit of advice regarding the rules of engagement Krenshencov. April 17, group of soldiers stand near a wall talking, playing the peacemaker without hostile intentions. A little child comes along, plays with them; they smile, give her candy – whatever. Others join in – one big happy family until seconds later – Boom! Like to know which parts were scraped off the pavement?"

"Terrorism has no mercy Colonel."

"Then why the hell should I?"

Ducet reaches within his pocket and retrieves a handheld device. He presses a small viewing screen; which illuminates with data. "Remember this?"

"Our *mee*-shon in Oklahoma."

"This is the terrain of the bunker we hit. Now, listen to the audio. Hear that? That confirms Aun'war's voice in the same location as Jade. This data was uploaded a few hours ago. Now…notice that all the little flashing markers are gone. That means you have a confirmed 100% kill ratio of Aun'war, his men, and Jade – everyone."

"Moments ago, you were unsure that Aun'war was in the bunker."

"That's because no bodies were recovered."

"Skepticism *has itz* place – yes?"

"We will know soon enough. But if we got the head of Rham-kiev, your mission is over – so smile a little more."

Rowland's face inflames red as he stares down Ducet's finger pointing directly in his face. "Your tone suggests recklessness Colonel. I never *keel* others to get Aun'war. One man hurt my famil-*lee*, one man destroyed the life of my *sees*-ster, my friends; and one man is *rre*-sponsible for deaths of many more. I track *heem* down and *kill heem* – *heem* only."

Ducet glares coldly into Rowland's eyes. "Bravo hunter," he says. "You now have the good sense to recognize vengeance, so that makes you and me the same. Your target is a man; mine is the face of politics, so don't piss off the chance. I scratched your back, you scratch mine. In a few hours, we move."

Rowland stands quiet. His stern eyes tightly squint as his ruffled ego bears the onslaught of Ducet's recollections.

Subtle shades of amber paint the low-lying New Mexican valley as the sun's brilliance begins to cover the earth. Desolate fields lay in every direction, while the pristine cycle of darkness to light unfolds, as it has done for ages – leaving an intrinsic trademark by the Maker himself. Light gently bathes the sandy landscape, forcing iron oxides to reveal the tantalizing color for which the Red Sands facility is known. However, those guarding the entry are all too familiar with the sun rise as the pressures of daily life unfold. Their senses immediately heighten as the headlights of a freighter class rig approaches. With weapons raised, one of the guards orders the metal giant to halt. He approaches.

"Sir, may I help you?" Harrison flashes his badge and the guard looks at it with baffling astonishment. "A U.S. Marshal…"

"I'm here to see Colonel Mortimer Ducet. I know it is early, but it is important that I speak with him." Each guard eyes one another with suspicious caution. "Sir, I have to contact central command."

"Do your thing. Just get me through to the good colonel, or tell me where I can find him."

"I have to ask you to wait here sir."

"No problem."

The guard retreats inside a small building. Several minutes pass while the other guards eye the monstrous transport with curious intent. Finally, the guard returns. "You can enter, but you'll have to wait at the research bunker. But before you enter, we'll have to inspect your vehicle. Please turn off your motor, and step outside."

A thorough investigation takes place, but the moment of truth lies in the opening of the cargo area. Slowly, the ramp door extends outward and touches the ground. With weapons drawn, the guards enter only to find nothing. They retreat and allow the transport to pass through the gates. Further down the road, the freighter slows, leaving the ramp door within a few inches above the ground. Suddenly, a tremendous fireball lights the sky in the far distance. The incident draws the attentinon of the guards and turret gunners.

As they stare, Gjhe'nan quickly immerges from behind a nearby hill, leaps over the perimeter fence, and quickly enters the cargo area of the transport. The door closes, concealing the hybrid inside. While the guards continue to focus their curiosity upon the odd phenomena, the freighter travels farther inside the complex until it halts near the research building. In addition, bustling workers increase in numbers as the transport draws their unwanted curiosities.

Within the cab, calmer tensions resume. "Not bad; especially for a boy from Dayton, Ohio…huh? A few gallons of gas, matches, hairspray, wires, and a kitchen timer, then wallah! You got the whole world at center stage," says Walter, raising his hands while taking a theatrical bow.

"Wow, aren't we proud of yourself," notes Gracella.

"Impressive," replies Arthur.

"Only proves that ninety eight percent of the population is ingeniously psychotic," mumbles Harrison.

Walter taps Arthur on the shoulder. "Ducet should be in the office by now."

"I hope so, the temperature is rising and Gjhe'nan is going to feel the weight of it. Due to current fuel consumption, a/c is out of the question."

"Point taken, but don't you think all of this is a bit convenient?"

"What is?"

"I mean – you were in the military once – right? Shouldn't there be a police escort, guards watching us, nearby reconnaissance or something like that?"

"The gate check wasn't good enough for you Walter?"

"No, but I'm just saying…"

"This is a research facility, not a SAC or MAC base with military strike capability."

"Are you telling me that Red Sands is considered low priority on the totem pole?"

"If their mission is research, it is for now."

Harrison seizes the moment. "Haven't you heard? Congress is in the process of drafting their decision for an all out invasion over seas. It's expected that they will arrive in full support by noon. Should that happen, it's unlikely we will find Ducet." Arthur takes a deep sigh. "I hope you're wrong," he says.

Again, Arthur looks at his watch and then notices a woman entering a building. "Marshal, I think its time to move." "You just let me do the talking Robinson." Both men exit the transport and hasten towards the approaching woman.

Harrison asks, "Excuse me ma'am. Can you help us? We are looking for Colonel Ducet. It's important that we speak with him. Do you know where we can find him?" The woman sternly eyes both Arthur and Harrison with reasonable suspicion as Harrison displays his badge.

She asks, "And…who's looking for him?"

"U.S. Marshal Harrison, like the badge says."

"I don't know where the Colonel is, at this moment."

"But you do know him?"

"Of course, we all know of him. But I don't know where he is. You may have to consult central command."

"C'mon. Your telling me that we have to see the League of Nations just to talk to one man who's stationed at this facility?"

"I can't answer that sir."

"Then can you show us where his office is?"

"No sir. But you may have better luck inside that building."

As the woman departs, Arthur and Harrison enter the building. As they do, a commanding sound precedes a guard as he storms on approach with one hand extending forward and the other hand on his firearm. "Halt! No one is to enter this building without proper clearance!"

"We had clearance from the front gate," responds Harrison.

"Who are you and why are you here?"

"We're here to see Colonel Ducet."

"Under whose authorization?"

"The front gate, just like I said."

"I need you to step outside – now."

"Does this badge mean anything? I said, U.S. Marshal and I'm just here to see the colonel on official business – no need to get hostile."

"A U.S. Marshal? I didn't know the Colonel was classified as a fugitive."

"I Never said he was - So what can you tell me about that?"

"Again, I need both of you to step outside the building and wait for proper clearance."

"You refuse the entrance of a U.S. Marshal?"

"Military law presides here…don't make me tell you again."

The guard pushes Arthur. "Don't touch me!" Arthur shoves the guard's hand away and stands defiant. Harrison intervenes. "Hold ya throttle son." In the midst of the situation, the commotion draws the attention of yet another guard. "Stand down! Both of you are in direct violation of standard entry procedures."

"And just what the hell is standard?" rants Harrison.

"Higher clearance or direct authorization from the Colonel; both of which you do not have."

"I'm not going anywhere until I get some answers."

"Then we're going to have to take you down."

 With baton sticks drawn, the guards quickly rush Harrison and Arthur, and wrestle them to the floor. Other guards join in and take both men to a room. Inside, Harrison's heels resonate loudly as plain white walls echo sounds of talk outside the door. Harrison furiously pounds the door, venting his frustrations.

"This is a federal offense! You cannot detain me without probable cause – YOU HEAR ME?!"

"Marshal? They're deaf by choice," declares Arthur while rubbing the bruises on his arm.

"No *kiddin*. The front gate lets us in, tells us to come here. Our presence gets the storm troopers underwear in a tightwad, and we wind up in containment. And for what?!!"

"Marshal, did not the guard say that he did not know Ducet was a fugitive?"

"Yeah..."

"Why would he imply such a notion?"

"Most people think marshals only go after fugitives."

"Yes, but if nothing suggests otherwise; why then…assume?"

After hearing Arthur's question, Harrison paces the floor while scratching his head. The stalwart lawman looks at the ceiling, as though to gather some form of spiritual insight. "I don't know," he answers.

"Sure you do. Think about it. The colonel did not know we were coming; therefore, he can't be running from anyone."

"You're saying that; if he is gone, then his departure is by choice."

"That's right. Rowland; however, working with the colonel, did know that you would probably have questions – so he decides to run. And those guards are over protecting a non-mission critical portion of this base, rather than offering assistance."

"And…the point to all this?"

"Either Rowland ratted us out to Ducet, or the colonel simply is not here – by choice."

"There are still variables Robinson."

"Always… But I bet you within one hour, someone will have questions for us – if not answers as well."

Suddenly, the sound of unlocking mechanisms dominates the moment. The door opens and three men enter the room. Their silhouette faces are all but identifiable within the aft lighting. Soon, the luminance of the room reaches full percent as the men display their firearms and conclude their approach.

Harrison explodes, "Who the hell are you? I want some answers NOW!"

One of the men steps between the other two. He does not hold a weapon; yet, his presence is more predominant than the others. His cold ironclad stare is anything but casual. His voice is completely authoritative as he stands with commanding assertiveness. "My name is Caldwell Pendleton, General, United States Marines, and for your answers – please follow me." Each person makes their way down a long corridor of the building and eventually into another room.

Inside the room, several monitors line three walls. Elaborate décor of military scenery; from ancient sailing ships to modern armament displays brilliantly from a walled showcase. Subdued lighting creates a tranquil mood as intricate instrumentation line an oak-top desk. Tiny flickering lights continually signify the functionality of built in components.

Harrison scans the room. "So, this is where our tax dollars are going."

Pendleton laughs. "Hardly... You, me, anyone with adequate means, and some what normal intelligence can do this."

"If...you say so..."

"I do... Now take a seat gentlemen. Guards, you may leave us. I don't think the marshal or Mr. Robinson intend to cause me any harm."

Harrison scoffs aloud. "After what happened to us; what makes you so sure?"

"Because they will kill you, put your body in a bag, and no one will ever find you for the next twenty-eight years." Harrison remains silent.

Folding his arms, Pendleton sits upon the desk top and casually views his guest. "I'm terribly sorry for the earlier incident; sincerely I am. I hope no injuries were sustained by either of you; especially you Marshal."

"My chest was sore, but under the circumstances – You may just get a slap on the wrist."

"Forgive my men, please. I offer you the full services of our infirmary."

"We'll see..."

"Then...if nothing else...let me get to the point. I am well aware why you are here. Needless to say, I am not surprised. This whole place is uneasy because of something that transpired two days ago."

"What might that be?"

"It appears that Colonel Ducet has taken a group of soldiers with him and departed for the Mesopotamia; somewhere in the Middle East."

Harrison looks at Arthur whose raised eyebrows signify a facial concurrence. "General, I want to question the colonel."

"I know why you want him Marshal. I just don't know what you want him for."

"Just want to know his relationship to a man named Rowland Krenshencov."

"What kind of relationship?"

"Whether they're communist; or just simply good old Amish boys gone bad – maybe I'd like to know if they're banging each other…"

"You don't say…"

"Yes – I do say..."

"Well Marshal…if that's all you want, then…a simple phone call would have sufficed. Yet, you made a long trip instead."

"Some questions are pertinent only for the questioner – in person with the one being questioned."

"Indeed."

"Indeed…"

"Just so you know Marshal, I am Mortimer Ducet's commanding officer - and I have a right to know what involvement or trouble he may be in – if any."

"Just, how much do you need to know?"

"If this situation, you're referring too, is going to affect his performance in the field; then I need to know."

"It seems to me that he is quite capable of performing his duties – in the field."

Harrison takes a deep breath and slowly paces the floor as though to conjure the right response. He leans against the wall, but then, stares the general in the eye. "Look – I realize you want to protect him. After all, that's what the military does. I did time in the Navy, so I'm familiar with *we-protect-our-own* concept."

"We try –"

"I'm sure you do… But I will tell you that your golden boy may be involved in a conspiracy; in which deaths occurred."

"Really… And how did you come to this conclusion?"

"His relationship with a man name Rowland."

"Oh, I see…"

Pendleton scratches his head and let goes a miniscule chuckle; however, years of military sternness grips his face once more. He rises from the desk and stands directly in front of Harrison. "Is Colonel Ducet or Rowland Krenshencov charged with murder?"

"That all depends."

"Then you have no conclusive evidence."

"None that you know of…"

"Then I'm afraid…that this…Rowland is your concern, and Mortimer Ducet is a military matter. But if we find anything on the 'good colonel,' then he's yours – after we deal with him first. Hate you wasted your time on the road." General Pendleton approaches the door.

Arthur quickly addresses Pendleton. "Wait a minute. Is that it?" "We're done here Robinson…, "informsHarrison. "No way! After all we've been through; driving all the way down here?"

Arthur shakes his head and approaches Pendleton. "General, I too am aware of the need for military discretion, but there's something I'd like you to know."

"And that would be…?"

"Four people are dead! I have a friend out there who's crying her head off because her husband is either missing or dead! Our research facility is gone; not to mention that there's a hole in my house! If we don't talk to the colonel, do you know what that means?"

"The marshal just said that you have no…"

"Wait…let me finish. Colonel Ducet worked with Rowland on a secret project that was supposed to give soldiers an edge in warfare – or better yet, ultimately take their place. It took four hundred and twenty-nine attempts before that goal became a reality. Since then, I've been on the run, threatened with death, and have no sense of closure! We need to speak with the colonel…now."

Pendleton's eyes widen as his mouth partially opens. His head tilts upward as his body composure looses all military bearing. With shoulders slumping, the general slowly takes a long deep breath. Then, in a hardened exhale, he asks, "What are you telling me?"

"I'm telling you that Colonel Ducet has within his possession creatures that are intended to take the place of soldiers. Even as we speak, these hybrids are primed and ready for combat. Make no mistake, they are effective killers and can very well carry out any agenda that the colonel has."

Pendleton rubs his face and paces the room.
"Can you prove any of this?"

"Damn right he can," says Harrison.

General Pendleton, Marshal Harrison, and Arthur enter the large freighter and approach the compartment door that leads to the cargo bay. The general sternly looks ahead, perhaps more anxious than anyone to see what Arthur has in store.

Halting their progress outside the entry door, Arthur places his hand on the handle. "What I am about to show you must be kept as quiet as possible. No one knows about him." "Him?" "Yes sir, it's a...him." As Arthur opens the door, the general gives consent for passage, telling Arthur, "You first."

Arthur precedes Pendleton. But as the general enters, he immediately takes a step backwards. He stands with his mouth open, pupils fixate, and a momentary pause in breathing; vividly displaying the type of reaction that would easily have been his death, if the creature were to attack. Yet; for him, the hybrid beast is docile and trusting of his creator's acceptance of those around him.

"General, let me formally introduce you to project 429 – better known as Gjhe'nan." Pendleton is flabbergasted. He takes small incremental steps towards Arthur; in effect, making sure the technician stands between him and the creature. Gjhe'nan simply observes the general.

"Arthur, tell me this is an isolated travesty?"

"I can tell you that Gjhe'nan is real and there are more like him. I can also tell you that your colonel has a plan that involves them. I can also tell you that he's not too impressed with you."

"You're telling me that this…thing… is Ducet's handiwork. This is what he's worked on under our noses?"

"No…not this one. The colonel collaborated efforts with Rowland to supply a hybrid prototype. I gave them our friend here – as a blueprint."

"My God… Is that blood on those claws?"

"Yes."

"How did it get there?"

Arthur frowns in an absurd manner, denoting a ridiculous expression upon his face. "Sir; we need to speak to Colonel Ducet. Can you help us - please?"

"Not so fast young man."

General Pendleton walks towards the cab of the transport. He leans against a window while staring outward onto the compound. Then, he closes his eyes; tilting his head downward as though his face has taken on the weight of the world. Humbly, he addresses Arthur and all who are listening.

"Four years ago, a young man by the name of Joshua served in what was to be a routine exercise. There were three patrols in the Bad Lands that day and the insurgents feared that our troops would take the region. They set fire to nearby oilfields, which blackened the sky for miles. As the group of patrols got near the capital, an ambush took out two of the patrols. The remaining third patrol barely made it back to base – but Joshua was not on board. They said…'the place crawls;' and LAN-Sat confirmed it. Survivors claimed that Joshua was alive, but it was too late. Their distress call had already summoned the mighty 43rd. By the time we got people in there, those machines had already crop-dusted the place. Only smoke and ash remained. Joshua's body was never found. It's never easy to forget, because civilians were mixed with militants. Colonel Ducet held then, and still holds now, that indiscriminate bombing should have preceded the patrols; kill the innocents and the guilty; then let God sort them out –he said. But central command thought otherwise. Forgiveness was not in the colonel's heart, and later, trouble followed. I thought enough time had gone by."

"That explains a lot."

"You have no idea."

"Let me guess. Joshua was the colonel's son."

"Yes. And the rules of engagement are a son-of-a-bitch."

"That's why you gave the colonel an opportunity for redemption."

"He spearheaded several projects to spare soldiers an unmerited death – none of which were successful. Now with the war raging overseas, the timeline, funding, and personnel are greatly suffering under tremendous political constraints. Who would ever guess that such resistance could spur out of a desolate place on earth?"

"Now what?"

"We take him down – if we're not too late."

"What do you mean?"

"He may already be in the Middle East by now."

"General, if Ducet is in the Middle East, then it is conceivable that he will carry out his plan. That will look really bad for this country."

"You needn't remind me of the repercussions son. I've been serving in this man's army before you were born."

"No disrespect intended."

"I'll have to summon the joint-chiefs on this one. You and the marshal may have to accompany me."

"But general, what about the enans? No one is supposed to know."

"At this point, it doesn't matter. The colonel has falsified documents, withheld crucial information from his superiors; guilty of insubordination, and derelict in his primary duty. If that thing you call a g-non is his answer to replace infantry; at least in Ducet's mind, there can only be one outcome."

"Vengeance..."

"Wake up son...I'm talking genocide."

"You never knew about the colonel's project, did you? "

"Not this one."

"Is Colonel Ducet capable of genocide?"

Pendleton quickly opens a door and steps down from the freighter. He summons a guard and gives him instructions. Once the guard departs, the others draw near to the exit as Pendleton casually clasps both hands behind his back. Standing with poise, he stares beyond the threshold of greenery. The officer breathes deeply, and then slightly glances at Arthur. Then, in a soft, sincere voice, he tells Arthur, "A man scorned is capable of anything."

Arthur sternly watches as the general walks away.

Santa Monica, California. Thousands pack a three-mile coastline to enjoy the majestic Pacific. Deep cool water coaxes, pacifies, soothes, and even hypnotizes many visitors; putting them into a world of flourishing lullabies and placid imaginations. One by one, each shore-side occupant rest within his or her seductive state. But their indulgences make them nescient of two dreadful mysterious observers.

Two men post within a building far away. The structure sets high upon an elevation that provides excellent visibility of the city's greatest natural asset. Inside the building, carrying bags, boxes, and other acquirements line the floor of a room. Two long–barrel guns set upon tri-pods. One of the men reaches for a box and hands it to his partner.

"Here are the new projectiles. With these, we get the same effect from eight thousand yards – a little more than our distance from the beach."

"Good."

"Not only that, the viral toxin can take out several people with one shot."

"Ah…they did add several needles to one casing after all. I told you they would."

"How many can it effect?"

"Aun'war never said…only that the decay process would take a little longer because the dose is much smaller. So time your shots carefully."

"Here, take this."

"The bag?"

"Yes. It is full of new canisters and it will keep you busy for a while. After we're done, we are to wait for Aun'war's instructions."

"Did he set a count?"

"Never."

Both men affirm their allegiance to their dissident sultan. Afterwards, they each load the weapons and take aim in the direction of the beach. Using topside scopes, the men find their unsuspecting groups. "I have a man in my cross-hairs." "And I...a female, and another, and another... Today will be a good day." Asserting their declarations, one of the men pulls the trigger.

The weapon repeatedly fires, barely dispersing sounds as sleek projectiles pierce the air. One by one, the tiny capsules burn away, thus allowing a small whisk of smoke to discharge only a few feet from several congregating groups.

Sun tanned bodies flinch as unsuspecting victims swat at something amidst, and yet hitting nothing. Each person gently rubs the area of impact upon their flesh, but so tiny are the needles, that suspicion fathoms the culprit to that of a tiny insect. The instance occurs again, and several more times. All are completely oblivious. As the other gunman disperses his rounds, no one on the beach seems to notice the simultaneous reactions from other sunbathers as the result of their untold demise. Both assailants continue to shoot until projectile cartridges litter the floor.

Then, a short while later, beautifully fine sand that once covered the feet of young and old alike now mixes with the blood remains of internal organs. Medical teams quickly arrive on scene and quarantine the area, but the frightened crowds impede the teams much needed efforts.

Mass panic erupts as men, women, and children alike break quarantine barriers. Others pitifully kneel beside an associate or loved-one and watch in disbelief as bodies dissolve into a gelatinous pool of organic matter. A rising putrid scent of decomposing flesh fills the air as Santa Monica's finest are powerless to arrest the degrading onslaught known as the Phantom's Death.

The census bureau estimates far more than one million people live in the coastal state; however, at the end of day, the official report decreases that number by several thousand.

Beneath the desert, at Red Sands research facility, crucial footsteps echo within a wide corridor; such that are the steps of despair, hope, and desperation – The steps of Major General Caldwell Pendleton and his unlikely associates.

Armored centurions, whose dark shielded faces reflect their surroundings, step aside to allow General Pendleton and the others to enter the central briefing room. Plants, brass vases, and other items beautifully adorn the prestigious chamber as well as keeping all participating parties mindful of the serious discussions that take place within these walls.

Arthur, along with Harrison, Gracella, and Walter seat themselves behind Pendleton. Seven large monitors, suspending from the ceiling, hang only a few feet above a highly polished oak table. Six of the screens provide an independent view of each panel member, whom already awaits the general. The seventh screen provides a group display of the Joint Chiefs of Staff.

Chairman of the joint session, Berkshire, addresses Pendleton. *"General, we assembled as quickly as possible once we got your message. If what you say is true – my God man…we're here to help."*

"Thank you Chairman Berkshire…and believe me, this came as a surprise to me as well."

"I took the liberty of speaking with the Secretary of Defense and he gives his approval for any course of action. Now…in the case of Colonel Ducet, it would be prejudicially bias to punish a man for a crime he has not yet committed."

"Of course Chairman…"

"Do you know where the colonel is?"

"We're almost certain that he is somewhere in the Mesopotamia by now. A military manifest confirms his signature, but the transport destination is questionable.

"I see... What are your contingencies?"

"Depending on his depth of presence, I'll get the field commanders to detain him until our arrival. At that point, we'll question him and bring him back; *if…* convincing evidence supports our speculations. Once complete, we'll bring him before the board to face a military hearing."

"Very well…"

A female member of the committee addresses Pendleton. *"General, what of these enans or g-nans as you call them; how do you intend to subdue such a bizarre infantry?"*

"We have contingencies in place ma'am. If we encounter these creatures, we should be able to contain them with current tactics and weaponry."

"Your report sounds very fascinating. We may actually want them on our side."

Laughter resonates amongst the panel, but Arthur's eyes immediately widen as he sits on the edge of his chair. His face grapples with pure astonishment.

Pendleton sees Arthur. "Sorry Arthur, I had no choice. If we want their help, then they have a need to know."

Arthur clinches his teeth as unsound words scarcely pronounce. Harrison places his hand on Arthur's arm. "Calm down Robinson. What did you expect – you brought that animal right to them and you did say that you needed help."

"Yeah," replies Arthur.

"You must excuse Mr. Arthur Robinson. He expressed his desire that these enans remain anonymous to outside knowledge."

"Really... Then how does Mr. Robinson intend to thwart the colonel's intentions?" Silence looms as Arthur relaxes, yet continuing to brandish a hateful stare.

"General, if you think Arthur or whomever, can be of worth to you, just make sure the U.S. stance in this matter is not compromised – Understand?"

"Yes ma'am."

Berkshire intervenes. *"Very good Caldwell, we are scheduled to meet with the Secretary of Defense and the President, and with other cabinet members of Congress to discuss the Phantom's Death."*

"Excuse me?"

"You do know that the Phantom's Death struck again, this time in Santa Monica."

"No, I was not aware sir."

"Rham-kiev claims responsibly. And General?"

"Yes."

"Anything short of continents falling in the ocean or meteors sticking the Earth, you need not bother me. We back you 100 percent; therefore, you represent us – This situation is in your hands. If matters escalate, only then will we bring it before the President. Until then…Godspeed."

"To you too sir…"

The transmissions end as everyone exits the room.

Within the corridor, Arthur walks side-by-side with Pendleton. "General, what will happen to the enans?"

"Your enans are part of a larger picture. You must understand that even without these creatures, the colonel can still compromise our country's position, especially in that region of the world. He could also virtually destroy any positive relationship with all our allies. Your enans will only make his job that much easier. You must also understand that I'll do what it takes to bring this situation to a close, but I thought you said that two of those beasts tried to kill you and your friends."

"They were just following orders."

"Aren't we all?"

"So what happens to Gjhe'nan?"

"He'll be taken care of."

"Just like the rest of them. Why don't you just shoot him in the forehead when you're done."

"Excuse me?"

"That is what you intend to do to him?"

"Mind your place Mr., besides…you don't seem to be the type who practices such methods."

"What is that suppose to mean?"

"Don't confuse the issue here son. As I've explained, there's a hell of a lot more going on than you realize."

"I understand that."

"Do you?"

"It seems pretty clear to me."

"See that room we just came from?"

"Yes –"

"See those guards?"

"So…"

Pendleton draws within a few inches of Arthur's face, snarling while never breaking a stare. Then, he tells him, "No information leaves that room and I have been authorized to apprehend Ducet by any means necessary. Got it? So…if you're up to it, I'll make you an offer."

"A what…offer?"

"Names can be overlooked, dates falsified, and data can disappear - plausible deniability."

"Then you will keep Gjhe'nan, as a secret – safe?"

"I'm bringing you in on this mission because I don't know how these…hybrid enans, as you call them, will affect our troops. I'm not sure how they will respond to modern warfare tactics. Help us bring in Ducet in exchange for Gjhe'nan's esoteric existence."

"Sounds good…"

"Then pack your bags, because we're leaving for the biggest sand box in the world."

Pendleton resumes his walk as Arthur watches in bewilderment.

Far away in the dessert northwest of Baghdad, Colonel Ducet and Rowland travel into the realms of isolation. A band of soldiers in alliance with him carries supplies and powerful weaponry that can easily repel most hostile assaults. Radar, computers, and other instruments of fantastic sophistication ride securely within the walls of two highly mechanized vehicles, such that are known as Land-Amphibious All-Terrain-Transports (LAATT). Many soldiers have given the LAATT the unofficial name Iguana.

The heavy armored LAATT, or Iguana, is known for its high impact resistance and maneuverability. The LAATT is also known for an ingenious adaptation, in that it can burrow into the ground and become a formidable bunker. It is Ducet's vehicle of choice and it secretly carries his band of dissident combatants to their destination. On board, the colonel observes a place of opportune significance. "There…behind those rocks will be fine. Let's bury in."

As both vehicles halt, the lead Iguana begins the ingenious transformation. Immediately, four lifter-jacks extend outward from the side of the transport and lowers to the ground, lifting the vehicle completely off all six wheels. High tensile strength blades extend from beneath the chassis and expand outward, thus compensating for the full length and width of the transport. Powerful turbines engage, causing a massive forward shaft to rotate clockwise while the rear shaft rotates counter clockwise.

Now balanced; the blades lower and begin to efficiently plow away the earth from beneath the transport. Plums of sand and rock expel outward as the lifters retract inward and the transport sinks into the earth, lowering until the top of the vehicle is surface level; leaving the exhaust and airshafts barely protruding above ground. A radar antenna extends upward as the topside turret hatch opens. Out climbs Ducet and Rowland while soldiers finish manually covering the vehicle and setting up their base of operations. The second Iguana burrows in as Rowland observes in fascination.

"We have nothing like *thees* back home colonel."

"Iguanas are fascinating. No one can see us from the air or the ground. Even heat seekers and infrareds can't detect us, nor can they dig us out. We can also lie to sonar if we have too. We can take down an entire city from this vantage point; a buried mobile command center – we are. No one can touch us."

Looking skyward, both men observe stars twinkling above the foreign landscape. Birds quietly pass overhead as mountains cascade in the distance, silently paying homage in a state of timeless solidarity. Ironically, sounds of gunfire cast a ghostly terror in the distant horizon, reminding everyone that a greater evil is present. Ducet observes the vast expanse as Rowland accompanies him. "*Eez* everything well colonel?" He does not answer, but walks several feet ahead.

Colonel Ducet reaches within his jacket and retrieves a photograph. He stares at the paper image until his face flusters red. "Yesterday, our forces took a nasty hit. A carrier bomb explodes and nineteen marines were killed. It goes on and on, and on – I honestly do not think it will ever end. For the most part, the locals are decent people. They're just trying to make ends meet. You will not see many of them out here, but if you're lucky enough to get to know some of them personally, it can be a rewarding experience. They hate this war as much as we do. But there are the fanatics; those who see an opportunity for some damned cause that can be the death of us all. In the end, every one becomes a pawn in a global game of chess, fighting another man's war at the expense of killing innocent bystanders. But that is what we do –right?"

"More or less, but you made it *thees* far – so view bright side Colonel. *Eef* command knew you were here, they would have apprehended us both in Baghdad."

"That's true, but surely they know by now."

"Perhaps…but this mission must succeed. Afterwards, Canada may be good choice for me – Yes?"

"Maybe…"

"I hope you find peace Colonel."

Ducet lowers his head, staring intently at the ground. His demeanor is all but reminiscent of one whose face is stone. Dry weeds roll across the cool sand as tiny night crawlers begin their activities. Silence dictates, but then, in a low, solemn voice, "Face up on a stretcher; without an ounce of breath…is the only way out for me," he says. Rowland silently stares.

Then, a soldier approaches. "Sir, the beacon tracks are lighting. They are approaching the mouth of the river."

"We better get going."

Inside the transport, soldiers monitor the control panel while entering information. Other systems denote geographical coordinates as the colonel enters. One of the men, Essington Jamison, provides Ducet with a report. "Sir, British patrols are moderately low, but they're training *Shia* soldiers to guard their own ports."

"The Britts are practical – I'll give them that."

"It seems that much of their immediate focus is on maritime vessels; the ones large enough to transport troops."

"Good… So – what about our hybrids?"

"I've pggybacked instructions on a low-frequency carrier beacon to guide them right to us." "Good." "Also Colonel, sonar clicks from satellite telemetry indicates excellent water passage as far as Tikrit. Levels within all five reservoirs – the Saddam, Dokan, Al Azim, Darbandikhan, and Diyala, have each dumped their payloads into the Tigris. There is minimal flooding in the south as well as a slight matter of current; but the enans can efficiently navigate their course with excellent timing."

"Timing is everything."

"And finally sir, when the hybrids are north of Baghdad, they will have only a few minutes to find us. The water will cool their heat signatures, but when they're on dry land at night, our window of execution dramatically decreases."

"Excellent work Jamison. Now go and introduce our enans to the Eastern world."

"Will do – sir."

"Oh…by the way… Congratulations on your promotion to captain."

"Thank you sir…"

"Carry on captain," replies Ducet as he inhales deeply while relaxing his shoulders, brandishing a rare smile across his face. His men look on as enthusiasm rises amidst the cabin.

~~~Enter the Enans~~~

Gjhe`nan is their namesake. They are genetically enhanced joey-hybrids that are *evolutionized* as nocturnal assault nomads. But they are officially known as enans. Each enan is highly adaptable to numerous geographical regions, and with no permanent residence, they move from place to place at the beckoning of one militant's vision. Though deadly on land, they are formidable at sea. Partially webbed hands act as ores in conjunction with strong tails to propel the enans through miles of fluid expanse. Dorsal ridges act as rudders; giving the enans excellent maneuverability under water. Specially enhanced eyes provide incredible vision in darkness; a superior advantage during night reconnaissance. Skin, comprising of transient colorful scales grant the enan with remarkable protection as well as resisting watery drag. Massive hind legs allow the hybrid to travel great distances within a short time span. Razor sharp talons extend from their fingertips; giving the enan a deadly offensive capability. In conjunction; a scythe-like blade at the end of the enan's tail serves as nothing less than perhaps the hyrbrid's most dangerous weapon. Enans think as humans and posses the astounding ability to comprehend literature; though high pitch squeals and shrieking sounds suffice for wordless communication.

One by one, the enans secretly pass from the Persian sea into the mouth of the Shatt al-Arab, a two hundred kilometer length river system formed by the convergence of the Euphrates and Tigris rivers. The union of the rivers joins near the town of Al-Qurnah, a place in the Basra Government of southern Iraq. Though convenient for the enans, the river system is the treacherous boarder separating Iraq and Iran. It is also the entry point for few watercrafts.

Overhead lights converge upon merchant vessels entering the mouth of the river. Each vessel is subjugated to coalition inspection. As boarder patrols conduct on-board assessments, several enans swim underneath the hull of the vessel, stealthily maneuvering, thus remarkably gaining entrance into the harbor. More arrive and soon, all hybrids eventually pass far beyond military checkpoints long before boarding patrols conclude their inspections.

Rowland and Colonel Ducet watch in earnest. Ducet resounds with much enthusiasm. "Remarkable... They knew the heavy freighters could not make it too far into the harbor, so they use the smaller trolleys as cover. We never mentioned a word about doing that."

"They learn on their own."

"Yes and all six groups are accounted for. They have just past Al Kut."

"Excellent *prrro-gress*; but day light *iz* upon us. We should not push our luck Colonel."

"Of course not... We should bunker them in. Any place near the water's edge will do."

As Ducet prepares to render his order, one of his men hastily approaches. "Sir, VID-com shows population on the water."

"What...now?"

"Yes sir...and our enans are heading right for them."

"I guess curtailment didn't make it this far."

"Don't know who they are sir, but in this area, the river is about thirteen hundred feet wide and only seven to eight feet deep. These markers show two boatmen, likely local fishermen. But the other two markers are definitely skimmers, and they're heading right for our enans."

"Who are these people?"

"Not sure sir. It's not uncommon for locals to go fishing this early – if they're lucky. Also, if skimmers are coming, they probably have sonar."

"But the second group of enans is passing right under the raft."

"Sir, I think it's safe to say, that the other enans won't make it past the rafters before the skimmers discover them."

"Is it possible to veer them outside the location of the raft?"

"Not all of the enans will elude them sir. Discovery is eminent."

"The skimmers are likely on a routine patrol. They will scan the fishermen, and when they do, our cover will be blown. Rowland, do you think we can make it to land in time?"

"An enan *rr*-equires at least six feet of clearing; at best...when crawling on *itz* belly. You must get them out – now."

"All right. Listen up people! Advance the first two enans to intercept the skimmers, redirect the third enan to the rafters, and put the others in the ground."

"Aye sir," respond the men.

The command goes forth. Like volcanic eruptions, the hybrids burst through the surface of the water and make their way towards shore. With only a few leaps, the enans land several yards inland, but their stalwart actions attract unwanted attention.

Curiously watching, two locals witness the event through night-vision optics. In sheer horror, the men clutch the sides of their strewn raft as the make shift floater bobbles in the wake of the enans exodus. Frantically screaming, the men jab poles into the water, desperately pushing in an attempt to further themselves from the lurid creatures.

Ducet watches both men fleeing as well. He leans closely to one of his sergeants, softly speaking in his ear. "The monitor does not lie son. If those men get away…they will compromise our mission. You know what to do." The sergeant's flickering eyes sternly creates folds over his brow. His hands grasp tightly the side railing of the chair upon which he balances himself. He places one hand over his face; slowly exhaling, as though the next move will be his last, as if his decision teeters on the threshold of ethical conviction – or moral indictment. However, his ponderous intentions are squeamishly made known. "No sir. I can't do that."

Ducet coldly stares at the young man as everyone fixate on the moment. Then, in a slow attentive manner, Colonel Ducet leans near the man. "Then…step aside sergeant," he says.

Trembling with uncertainty, the subordinate breathes deeply, but surprisingly stands defiant. "This is not right – sir."

"Excuse me…what part of this assignment did you fail to understand? Step aside sergeant; you knew this might happen when you agreed to come."

"How can those two men possibly hurt the mission - sir?"

Suddenly, Ducet pulls from within his holster a gun and points it at the young man. He stands tall; yet, expressing a look as if already annoyed. "Soldier…I'm warning you."

"Colonel, *pleez*," exerts Rollin.

"Sergeant, for the last time... Don't stand in the way of me and my mission."

"Sir, you wouldn't shoot me – That's just not like you... I know it."

Silence stirs; granting nothing more than an interlude for pounding hearts. Some members back away while others sit idle. Then, in the fraction of a second, Ducet fires upon the sergeant, striking him in the thigh. Blood speckles across the console as the sergeant falls to the floor. His galling scream fills the internal compartment, yet becomes abstract in the light of Ducet pressing buttons. "Someone, get this idiot out of here! Listen people, *priority eagle command, take'em* out...both of them!" Rowland turns away from the monitor as instructions reach the third enan.

Lurking silently, the third enan barely raises its head above the surface of the water. Assessing the moment, the creature submerges, but continues to observe both men from beneath. The hybrid's eyes subtly reflect a red luminance as it crouches. Then suddenly, a dynamic thrust from the creature's legs propel the beast upward as swashing water draws the men's attention.

One of the men excitedly turns to observe the noise. He sees only the trickling radiance of waves. His interest peeks, but soon dispels as the enan crashes down upon him. The shear impact shatters the small craft into several pieces. Soon afterwards, the hybrid submerges with its victim beneath the dark water.

As wrecked pieces of wood bobble upon the surface, the other man drops his pole and looses his cargo. Fear grips him in cold silence as a desperate scream projects nothing more than a whimpering plea. While trembling, he frantically paddles; attempting to gain forward momentum. Stroke by stroke, he meagerly attempts safe passage as he continues to project soundless cries amidst the darkness. Sadly, disorientation sets in and the man ceases his escape. Now idle, he leans upon the floating wreckage, convulsing feverishly while gazing afar. Freighters cast distant lights; projecting a helpless glow well beyond his reach. His head hangs low, until he slowly looks upward.

Then, for a brief moment, the man discovers that a pair of red eyes is staring directly at him. Closing his own eyes, he slowly sinks into the water and inevitably, another violation occurs until all that remains are wood fragments and rags that bear the corresponding marks of a Bedouin tribe.

"Sir, skimmers are closing, e.t.a, fifteen seconds."

"Engage them."

"But colonel, NAV-com signatures indicate *friendlies*…how should we proceed?"

"There can be no witnesses – you know that."

"Understood…"

As both skimmers approach, one of the watercrafts reduces speed and slowly circles the area. Searchlights find nothing more than wooden debris. Strangely, the fragments attract the attention of the soldiers. A discussion convenes on deck. Suspicion ravels the men, but each quickly realizes that a presence other than their own is near. Suddenly, the sound of thrashing water erupts. Both skimmers shake in the rippling waves. A dull noise follows as two enans climb aboard one of the skimmers, hissing loudly with talons fully extending. The craft begins to sink; yet, despite gunshots, the enans brutally tear their way into the cabin. Terrible screams echo loudly as hardened claws rip through complex instruments and unmercifully into the flesh of everyone on board.

The craft violently rocks in a jerking manner as the hybrid assailants conclude their vicious onslaught.

With the demise of one craft, an enan leaps onboard the other skimmer, recklessly thrashing away while wielding its horrid barbarism. For both accounts, all that remain are two derelict hulls. The beasts drag both laden vessels to the center of the river and forcefully sink each one. Astoundingly, the hybrids recover the bodies of the soldiers and make their way to the burial rendezvous.

Exiting the water, both enans find their location and conspicuously camouflage the area. Lowering their forearms to the ground, the hybrids brace themselves as acrobatic gymnasts and use their hind legs to burrow into the earth.

Aboard the LAATT, Rowland stands beside a console technician who observes the event. The young man draws Rowland's attention. "Mr. Krenshencov, what exactly are they doing?"

"They are hiding from eyes *een* sky."

"Sir?"

"Satellites. The sand *weel* hide their body temperature from thermo scans as they lay in ground."

"Oh...clever..."

"As you can see the enan's tails and forearms prove quite efficient for raking sand and rock over themselves. One enan remains outward and makes sure the others are completely covered...only a small air hole remains."

"Very clever indeed sir..."

"Yes, *eef* I say so myself."

Ducet sits quietly, staring at the monitor as if it holds mysterious secrets. He observes the resting areas of the enans, as well as the place where two sunken skimmers lay. But soon, the images move continuously and then...he sees nothing more. Rowland approaches. "Not what you planned – no?"

The colonel provides no immediate answer. Then, in a slow monotone voice, he tells Rowland, "Where is the wisdom of God when human insight becomes the redemption of fools?"

"Depends on the fool's ability to interpret the insight given to *heem*. Does it not colonel?" Ducet remains silent as both men sit quietly and prepare for the long day ahead.

In another part of the desert, time passes as sand blankets the distant horizon. Two military vehicles and one large transport carrier glide along makeshift roads. The small convoy arrives at a place known as Canvas City, one of several American military outposts eight miles beyond the boarders of Baghdad.

On approach, members of the ranking hierarchy prepare to greet the inbound party as each vehicle comes to a halt. General Pendleton along with Arthur, Walter, Gracella, and Marshal Harrison exit the transport. Each is given clearance badges and later enters one of the tents. Inside, Pendleton and the others gather to discuss matters with ranking officials.

Commanding Officer Dwight Ellis of the 438th Infantry Division spearheads the discussion. "General Pendleton, it's good to see you; however, your arrival is...much unexpected. Matter of fact, just to know of your coming has got us jumping around like fleas."

"My apologies Dwight, and speaking of fleas, I understand you guys have been referred to as – *Sand Fleas*?"

"Hah, you could say that. We're not like the other guys, but in point of fact, we're scattered everywhere, jumping from one place to the next…sucking the blood out of this eastern dog with every confrontation…that is, until a few months ago. As you know, we've been taking serious loses. And not only that… Neighboring countries are becoming a problem. RECON shows large numbers of insurgents creeping in from outside boarders. One might think they actually don't want us here."

"I get that feeling as well."

"In any case, what can I do for you General? COM gave no details, and only said that you will provide information upon arrival."

"That is correct, but primarily, I am here because of Mortimer."

"Mortimer – the name rings a bell."

"It's Ducet."

"What…you mean Colonel Mortimer Ducet?"

"That's right."

"Wasn't he indicted for dereliction of duty?"

"Yes he was, and this time, I fear that he's gone rouge."

"I remember reading something about him. Oh yes – wasn't he the one who wanted drastic changes to the engagement of warfare on distant grounds, or something like that?"

"Right again. He also wanted justification for the death of his son, Joshua."

"Joshua…"

"Yes."

"Poor guy."

"I think our good colonel is well beyond self-pity. I also have good reason to believe that he intends to make us all aware of his intentions – in a profound way."

"And he came all the way to this blanket of sand in order to do just that?"

"He's quite able…and, he still holds a grudge against us for Joshua's death."

"Us…as in you and I, or the whole military?"

"I was his commanding officer for the operation that day. The air strikes were a tactical precaution once RECON showed hostile engagement. Josh's patrol was believed to be dead after we received the reports from another surviving patrol. There was no way we could have known just how wrong we were. By then, it was too late. Somehow, I knew this day would come."

"Sounds like a personal grudge."

"At this point, it doesn't matter. We believe he's somewhere within the boarders of Iraq, maybe somewhere on the outskirts, but nonetheless…he's on a mission without command authorization. He's planning something Dwight; something that could put us in tremendous opposition with the entire Middle Eastern world, our Allies, and quite possibly the entire galaxy – hell, who knows."

Dwight eyes Pendleton with intense attentiveness. He tells the general, "I have men standing by to assist."

"Of course…and you do have my gratitude."

"So tell me… Who are your friends?"

"I want you to meet my four colleagues, primarily Marshal Derek Harrison."

"Greetings Marshal Harrison. I've been informed about your interest; though keep in mind that Colonel Ducet is a military matter."

"I'm well aware of that general, but you keep in mind that if your little golden boy has any ties with deaths surrounding my investigation – he's officially my matter…as well."

"Point taken…"

Pendleton intervenes, "I think it's fair enough to say that we all have the same interest. Each of my colleagues has their own quintessential perspectives on this matter, but Mr. Arthur Robinson is whom you will need to coordinate your efforts with – if we encounter the abnormal."

"Say again?"

"There is something of current concern that we need to investigate, along with Ducet...of course; pending if *it* becomes a concern at all."

"What exactly is...*it*...you are looking for – if I may ask?"

"Classified Dwight..."

"Really...."

"Yes – even in this case. Though we're the same in rank, I do respect your position. But you must believe me. The issue of which I speak requires the utmost secrecy."

"Guess I'll have to take your word for it old friend. And what of my men?"

"I can assure you they will not be harmed – at least by us."

"I see... Now this excursion of yours will not conflict with my current duties, will it?"

"Let me assure you again, this event will not conflict with your current duties unless we encounter something far more threatening."

"What could be more threatening than live ordinance with your name on it?" Pendleton stares Commander Dwight Ellis directly in the eye while allowing his back to partially face the gathering of onlookers. He glances momentarily at Arthur, and then scratches his head as if sequestered by a Grand Jury. Then, in a stern voice, he tells the commander, "Something that can potentially withstand live ordinance, and has your name as a target." The entire ranking assembly listens, providing nothing less than puzzling stares.

Clouds of dust spiral in a mystic swirl as warm air skim across barren plains. The sun, having brightened the sandy realm now sinks beyond the western hills; again relinquishing its cycle to the celestial powers of the night. For now, time is what Colonel Ducet needs as he prepares for the next stage of operation. His stern, brackish voice commands the buried centurions to summon their powers and emerge as valiant warriors for the cause of his righteous indignation. Sand disperses outward as adjutant bodies unearth themselves and hop to the river's edge, plunging into the shallows to resume their northern trek once more.

The enans travel swiftly, making good their distance by several miles as they silently elude gunmen in the marsh. Ripples softly dissipate upon the water's surface, barely noticeable as blasts of yellow and white fiery bursts light up the distant sky, displaying the climactic encore of the savage fury from both warring forces. Skirmishes continue to erupt as advancing armies of coalition troops encounter the merciless retaliation of insurgents.

Colonel Ducet and Rowland closely observe the monitor as satellites relay the unfolding events; however, Ducet's concerns are mounting. "The enans are only one mile from Baghdad and the fighting is getting worse."

"We've been very lucky colonel. Hopefully luck *weel* continue un-*teel* the enans pass through."

"I know, but as the fighting draws closer to Baghdad, the greater the odds our enans will run a watery gauntlet. We got insurgents on the far east side and our guys encroaching from the west side of the river. The fighting could hinder us."

"Yes – but the river Tigris can be a formidable ally when you know how to use *eet*. Any human crossing *weel* be immediately identified and shot. But an enan can still pass."

"Let's hope so."

"Certainly colonel, because eyes in sky look for humans, not enans."

Rowland's statement is worthy of merit as the hybrids pass under the watchful eye of insurgents and allied forces alike. While submerged, the enans swaying motions leave mild topside wakes that draw no more attention than fish swimming along the surface.

Despite hopeful outlooks, Arthur and his associates, along with two members of the 438th travel eastward aboard a large transport while Gjhe'nan sits quietly in the cargo bay. In the cabin of the transport, Arthur sits in the front passenger seat beside the driver. He relays information along a visual transmission to General Pendleton.

"General, even if the colonel is here, the enans will have to travel across vast distances just to get somewhere."

"True, and there's also the possibility that several big transports could ferry them across land. Yet, such a convoy would not only attract attention, but could easily come under enemy fire. Not to mention running the risk of encountering large cannons. It will take some serious balls to pull that off – even here."

"In order to get the enans into the country, the colonel will have to exploit some natural geography, something that could hide an animal with the enan's proportions as well as provide an easy route inland."

"What features hold such characteristics in a place like this?"

"There is nothing but mountains in the north and the shallow marsh to the east and west. I'll see if we can get a display of Southern IRAQ.

Within seconds, Gracella activates a transparent three-dimensional display which appears on the overhead monitor. "There it is," she says.

"See where the Euphrates and the Tigris merge into the Persian Gulf? We should concentrate our efforts on the rivers – even if they are shallow. After all...the enans are modified for water. This time of year, the two rivers could easily hide the enans, not to mention that RECON would not know what to scan for."

Pendleton asks, *"Arthur, how far can these enans swim in a day?"*

"If you're asking me can they swim from the open sea to the Persian Gulf, and then into Iraq in two days – I believe they can."

"Then it appears that Ducet may have a bigger lead on us."

"Since the rivers are shallow, he may use the night as cover when moving them."

"What about the day?"

"I'm not sure, maybe he hides them somewhere...somehow."

"Yes, of course. It would be helpful if there were clues as to which river system he might be traveling. Good luck people, keep me informed – Caldwell out."

The transmission ends.

Watching with tremendous interest is a veteran figure that stands confidently beside Arthur. Lieutenant Lillian Sullivan, leader of the mission, makes her entrance among the others. Wearing sand camouflaged fatigues, she displays a knife strapped to her right thigh and a side arm nestled within a waist holster. A slim physique suggests qualities of an athletic lifestyle though housed inside the baggy confinements of military linen. Short, dark hair, with a stringing twirl just above her right brow nicely conforms to a narrow face and a small chin.

Arthur responds. "Hello Lieutenant Sullivan, I didn't see you."

"No problem," she says as she struts past Arthur and views the onboard consoles.

While Lieutenant Sullivan views the instrumentation readings, simultaneous conversations catch the ears of a tall dark-haired sergeant who seems to relish a conversation with Arthur. His name is Thibodaux Guidry and he drives the heavy armored-class transport. His bronze skin and short wavy hair gives him the markings of a Middle Easterner, though more characteristics about him strongly suggest otherwise. His heavy eyebrows encompass an attentive visage, yet a light-hearted drawl often precedes his warm personality.

Lillian commands his attention. "Tell me sergeant about the incident from HQ."

"*Ma'am*, we received a *repoat* earlier *bout 'two* British patrol *skimmas* that didn't *repoat* in this *moan-nin*."

"That's unusual."

"How unlikely is that Lieutenant?"

"We don't know. What else do you know about the report?"

"Well *ma'am*, they *sey desturbances* woke the *areah*, but *nothing on radahr*."

Arthur obtains the lieutenant's attention. "May I recommend we head for the Tigris? Search that river system from every bridge if we have too, starting with this one." Arthur points to a map, but Lillian daunts a surprising stare. "Mr. Robinson, that's the Sarafiya."

"So…"

"That bridge has long been destroyed. Many, many years ago, a bomb sent at least thirty people to their deaths and many more injured. Click on the info box underneath the image."

"Oh…I see. Well, according to the map, there is a bridge that links Al Kazimiyah and An-Nassah."

"That bridge is called the Al'- Aaimmah."

"Then…why don't we start there?"

"Sounds reasonable…"

"Do you have security there?"

"Of course – there is a war going on. Besides, Commander Ellis informs me that we have a few secured areas along the river and the Aaimmah is one of them – So, what's your plan?"

"If the enans are in the river system near downtown Baghdad, then we wait for them. If they're gone, then we sniff them out one section of river at a time."

"Very assertive Mr. Robinson. I must admit, you struck me as a slow-minded individual, but you seem to be coming along as time unfolds."

"Ummm-yeah…I get that a lot these days."

"Although I cannot tell you which section of the river…you need to wait on, the least I can do is take you there. Sergeant Guidry, set coordinates for sector five grid two-two seven." Lillian's command bores deep within the ears of the sergeant and the large transport immediately powers through the sandy road leaving only dust behind.

Elswhere, several enans course the Tigress through downtown Baghdad. Yet, in regards to Baghdad, the name itself invokes feelings of exotic travels, mystic people, capricious delights, and biblical archeology. But for the men and women who survive those fallen in combat, the name invokes the horror of humanity's downfall, the plight of a civilization, and the perils of a merciless leadership. Yet, ever so often, an endearing smile, a gentle waving hand, or an ecstatic cheer brings a degree of dignified humanity. Sometimes, a kind hand of

417

gratitude stretches forth to members of the coalition in a place considered by many to be the cradle of life as well as a refuge from turmoil. Though admirable, such gracious mannerisms are of little concern for the hybrid beasts. Swimming past bridge after bridge, they leave behind a treasure trove of historical artifacts that extend from ancient history to the present.

Ducet and Rowland continuously observe the enans progression. All is well, until Rowland curiously leans closer to a console monitor. "Colonel, what *iz* that?"

"*That*…my friend…is a floating bridge. The coalition must have put it up. It's not uncommon. Why do you ask?"

"Can the enans pass under *eet*?"

"Don't know, I never…oh…I see your point. And it's well lit, with guards – not good."

"Our hybrids *weel* be upon that bridge in one minute."

"They will have to tunnel under. Sergeant – send info. Instruct the first three enans to dig under the bridge, but keep the others at bay."

"Yes sir!"

Within moments of their approach, the first enan raises its head, barely breaking the surface of the water. The hybrid takes in air and submerges once more. Gliding beneath the surface, the beast encounters the side of the bridge. Finding the edge nearest the bottom, the hybrid begins to dig. Progress is good, until exertion sets in. Raising its head, the hybrid bumps the under support beam of the floating platform, thus drawing the attention of nearby soldiers. The men quickly investigate. Bright lights bathe the watery surface as they search.

Ducet's monitor reveals all. "Shit – someone's on to them. Keep the enan under, keep them all under."

"Might I remind you Colonel that many of them are already submerged and have exhausted their air; they are not *feesh*."

"I can see that Rowland. Sergeant, punch up all monitoring cameras."

"Yes sir."

Immediately, the second row of monitors reveals the entire convoy of hybrids, however, one monitor drastically catches Ducet's attention. "Look, Rowland, what is he doing?"

"*He's* convulsing – near asphyxiation. He will surface to survive."

"If that guard sees him breathing, this whole mission is over – Do you hear me?"

"Yes."

"So be mindful that I am not going to let that happen."

"What do you intendto do Colonel?"

"I calculated only ten to fifteen enans to pull off this mission and that makes the others collateral damage."

Rowland gets within inches of the Colonel's face. "There are thirty-three enans. Must needless deaths line your path?"

"No Rowland. There are now only thirty-two enans – left...thirty-two. Get it?"

"Colonel, what have you done?"

Ducet pushes Rowland aside while leaning near another one of his men. The brazen officer lowers his head; his face tenses, glaring red while full of anguish, but the young man never takes his eyes off the console. In a barren voice, Ducet affirms his declaration. "Execute Judas-Mercy." "Aye sir, executing order six-seven-six, Judas Mercy. Locating beacon signature of hybrid number 28; now executing." Without hesitation, the operator raises a protective lid and flips a lever, in effect, sending the command to reach the intended enan.

As it does, a small explosive discharge ignites at the base of the hybrid's skull and the creature falls into a mortified state.

Ducet grits his teeth. "Why is it still moving?"

"Post-mortem reflexes Colonel...like shark gutted open, the body *steel* moves."

"It will draw attention."

"Colonel, this procedure was unnecessary."

"Shut up," shouts Ducet.

Again, the colonel turns to his Sergeant. "Signal the others – put it down for good."

"Aye sir!"

Immediately, three enans move in and forcefully brace the defunct hybrid. The creatures weigh the beast down, twisting its neck until all motion subsides. Dorsal ridges braze the water's surface as the enans perform their task, but the hybrid's body floats. As it does, the other enans push it away from their location. Now floating motionless, blue sparks erupt upon the dead enan's body.

Immediately, a sergeant alerts Ducet. "Sir, allied soldiers are watching. And who knows – we may even have a few insurgents as well." "Damn! Wait a minute. This may not be bad after all. Sergeant, move all of them!" "Yes sir!"

As the flames draw the soldier's attention, all remaining enans quickly take breaths of air. The first few enans finish tunneling through to the other side of the bridge. Afterwards, one by one, each make their way up the river as patrols move in to investigate the burning phenomena. Alert soldiers stand aboard skimmers with drawn weapons, staring at the burning mound of flesh. Suddenly, before their eyes, blue flames ignite and eventually consume the hybrid's entire body, even bone. The event also takes place beneath the water until ash is carried downstream – until nothing remains.

Distrusting eyes glare at nothing as one of the patrolmen receives a call. *"Blue Patrol, this is watchtower 2, what's going on – do you copy?"* Bewildering stares coincide with open mouths as each soldier aboard the skimmer utters a voiceless response. The apparent hesitation spreads to the others as the inquisitive voice repeatedly calls for information. One of the men presses his communications badge. Then, in an apprehensive manner, he slowly raises his hand and wipes his face. "This is Blue Patrol, go ahead."

"Blue Patrol, is there a situation – over?"

"Ahh…Blue Patrol copy…ahh…. whatever was here…is gone. There's nothing."

They all scratch their heads. However, with every one's attention captive by the spectacle, there is little regard for the dense clouds of silt pooling upward as the enans press their way underneath the bridge. With success in hand, the hybrids proceed on course – once more.

Though their journey is successful, Rowland brandishes Ducet. "How convenient *eet eez* to *fleep* switch and poof – all gone!"

"Oh give me a break! You knew that could happen. Besides, our situation is a lot better now than before."

"I caution you Colonel; do not *keel* enans so soon. You are foolish as you are *een*-sensitive!"

"Planting an explosive at the base of the skull proves to be a lot more humane than a bullet to the head! Not to mention that the blue phosphorus singed any remains of that animal, in effect, covering our butts."

"So say you!"

"Rowland, are we on the same page – you and me? You know what can happen if an enan falls into the wrong hands – get real! As far as what happened out there; it's called insurance - and you better get use to it."

"Insurance! Cannon fodder perhaps!"

"Don't get self-righteous with me Krenshenkov; you know what's at stake."

"Perhaps Arthur Robinson was *rr*-ight."

Ducet angrily approaches Rowland with his finger extending only a few inches from the geneticist's face. "Let me tell you something. Mr. Arthur Robinson doesn't know JACK, about warfare, death in war, or loosing someone to the politics of war. He, like many other self-righteous idiots, sits on his tail at a sweet nine-to-five and never has to worry about waking up with his nuts shot off, nor does he have the luxury of informing parents about the deaths of their sons and daughters! Arthur, like anyone else, can kiss my ass – and so on!"

"The nerve of you Colonel."

"Those enans are just fifteen miles from us, fifteen miles from doing the duty for which they were put on this earth, fifteen miles from shoving those extremist hell raisers back into the sand from which they came, fifteen miles from liberating our troops from this foolish cursed-crusade holocaust, fifteen MILES!"

"There are better ways to get around *thees* problem."

"Open your eyes Rowland! For Pete's sake man, the greatest technological militia in all of history has been humbled by a simple belief…an idea, a religious dictation, a theological paradigm; to die as you kill your enemy, to become a suicide mercenary or martyr is a weapon that's almost imposible to fight against. That act alone is killing far too many of our men and women out there. And you think I'm merciless. With the war progressing like it is…tell me Rowland, what would you do – tell me…what would you do?" Rowland remains silent.

Showing no signs of despondency, the colonel sets the next phase of his operation in motion. "Sergeant, set optical spectrum to 800 nanometers and cast the beam." "Are we too soon sir?" "Just do it. The enans will be in range in a matter of minutes." "Done sir," replies the sergeant.

"Alright Rowland, lets hope they can see what you say they can see."

"Of course they can colonel. Most human eyes respond to color wavelengths between 390 and 750 nanometers in the color spectrum. Beyond *thees*, there are ultra-sensitivities in *colours* of violets that are visible to the enan, but beyond *thees* color range, we cannot be sure as to what the enan sees."

"Didn't ask for a lecture Krenshenkov."

"Arthur adapted their eyes for *thees* ability."

"Well bravo for him."

Within moments, a long-range beacon projects a single beam of light into the sky. The beam stretches as far as Baghdad, silently glimmering, catching only the eyes of the enans as many are already far north and waiting to exit the river. Responding to their silent call, the hybrids slowly wade the shallows; systematically emerging upon dry land like prehistoric leviathans, then crawling behind rocks and near by foliage under the cover of night. With vast dessert before them, the enans see the beam and quickly leap into the night. Pouncing from one place to the next, the enans efficiently reach commendable speeds. However, the last enan approaches the Al'-Aaimmah Bridge.

Aboard the transport, an array of complex electronics captures Arthur's attention. He scans the dazzling sophistication until he sees an imprint in the console panel. "Praetorian," he whispers. His preoccupancy draws the driver's inquisitions. "Roman guard..."

"What?"

"The name, Praetorian. In ancient times, Roman emperors would pick an elite group of guards from the ranks as personal body guards."

"The best of the best."

"Yep, and as far as protection – that's exactly what my baby does."

"Your baby... I see. And the pride of your baby is written all over your face."

"This *heer* transport... Oh, *scuse'* me. The name's Thibodaux Guidry. You can *call* me Theo *fa* short, or *Sarg* Guidry – that's what everybody else calls me."

"Well...please to meet you Sergeant Guidry. So tell me... How did a transport this size receive a name like Praetorian?"

"As chief mechanic, I get to give it a name."

"You're the mechanic and driver of this transport?"

"Yep! The Army feels that if you fix it, then you *woun't* be trying to break it."

"So...they let you personalize it with an official name."

"Do other transports have names?"

"Why *shoa. Wah – Hammah*, Head *Huntta*, and Clad Iron *Killa*."

Arthur smiles while attempting to hide his laughter. "It's *awl*-right Mr. Robinson. I *wuz* bourn and raised in Mantachie, Mississippi and later grew up on a farm in south Louisiana. Got a girlfriend and a little boy...but I *ain't* married just yet. How *bout* you?"

"Fort Worth, Texas – born and raised."

"You don't sound like a Texan, but you *shoar* do talk slow."

"*Hah*…I guess so – however, I do have a wife but no kids. My Grandparents raised me in the city. But I do have an outback hat, a rusty pair of boots, one shotgun, and two trucks – Ramsey and Gertrude."

Thibodaux laughing aloud, "That's right, when you *luv'em*, you *gottagive'em* a name."

"You got that right."

"So tell me *Artha*, *bout'* the *cah-go*. I *mean*…I know you *caint'* tell me *wut* it is, but will it help us in this *wahr*?"

"I sure hope so."

"Well…just *wount* you *t'know* that *ol'* Praetorian here will *git* you were you need to go."

"That's good to know Sergeant…that's good to know."

The ensemble of travelers intently scans monitors for any clues of enan activity. Lieutenant Lillian Sullivan visits each person until finally ending her inquiries with Arthur. She attempts to understand the various amounts of information. "Can you see them from the satellite coverage Mr. Robinson?"

"No. Their movements are far too subtle to produce highly noticeable wakes or ripples on the water's surface. The murkiness of the water hides their outline form from above and the ambient temperature of the water masks any heat signatures their bodies produce."

"It sounds to me as if you have really given thought to the colonel's approach."

"The more I think of the situation, the more it can only make sense to bring the enans in by water. The Tigris by far is the perfect route."

Suddenly, Walter draws their attention. "Lieutenant, Arthur, every one… I've been monitoring communications from some of the troops on the river. I'll increase the volume so you all can hear. Several voices are coming through, but there's only one conversation I want you to hear. There…got it…now listen…"

"...yeah well if you asks me, they've been on the river too long. Something about seeing blue fire, and then nothing... Sounds like garbage to me but that's their official report..."

Harrison asks, "Is that all? What are we suppose to be listening for science boy?"

"At first, something was reported, but nothing came of it. This conversation came from the mouths of two guards involved in meager conversation. They're stationed inside downtown Baghdad. Earlier, the dispatcher mentioned something about a floating bridge, but the interesting thing here are the words – blue fire. Now where have we seen that before?"

Lillian asks, "What exactly is a blue fire Arthur?"

"Insurance."

"Insurance?"

"Blue fire is a type of phosphorus which consumes the body of a dead animal – even the bones."

"I take it that this *animal* is part of the secret that I am not supposed to know about?"

"Possibly..."

"Then could it be a military adaptation by Colonel Ducet?"

"With Rowland's help...no doubt."

"According to that transmission, this big secret may be closer than we expect."

"How many Army bridges are on the water?"

"According to the map, there's only two. One is near the harbor, and the other in downtown Baghdad."

"Lieutenant, what two bridges are north of the Army's floating bridge?"

"Difficult to pronounce the name of one, but the other is the Al'-*Ammah* – and believe it or not, we're about fifteen miles from the check point."

"Sunni territory...even to this day."

"That's right, so watch yourself," whispers the lieutenant as she pulls out her I.D. and activates a console.

A visual transmission appears. "My pardon Commander Ellis, but we may need your assistance sir."

"Very well Lieutenant, do explain."

The transport eventually halts in front of six guards. Each guard approaches with weapons drawn. One of the guards commands that the lieutenant lowers her window. "This is a restricted zone ma'am. What is your business here?" "We're on official business from Canvas HQ for reconnaissance."

"Lieutenant, let me see your clearance please, and prepare for boarding."

"I am First Lieutenant Lillian Sullivan, mission leader of this excursion, and you are hereby authorized to grant us passage without search. Cargo in the rear of this transport is a top-secret priority."

"Really? So let me guess; First Lieutenant, top-secret cargo, but no on board security... Ma'am...in all do respect, there's me...and then there's Congress – I set the law. Comply or we will deny you passage."

"I'm not interested in a bipartisanship!"

"Then you can kiss your efforts...good – bye."

Lillian smirks at the sergeant; then, she positions a monitor for him to see, whereby Dwight Ellis is staring directly at him.

"Oh shit...," expounds the guard, while standing more attentively.

"And that's exactly what you'll be shoveling if you deny them passage. Their cargo is mission-priority- top-secret. Grant them PASSAGE on my direct order – NOW!" The visual transmission ends and the transport Praetorian passes through the checkpoint.

Continuing their journey, Gracella makes a visual inventory. "Lieutenant, are those rusted I-beams? It looks like ancient metal, suspension cable, and rebar?"

"That is the old bridge."

"Old…"

"It's been there for a while."

"I'm sure it has a story."

"They all do. For this one, as the story goes, close to a million sojourners were marching toward the Al Kadhimiya Mosque. The mosque sits on the Sunni side of the river. As the travelers were in route, rumors about a suicide bombing got out and caused wide spread panic. Hundreds ran towards the bridge while hundreds more were already on it. There was too much weight, and the bridge collapsed. Some say that bones still lie at the bottom of the river."

Silence looms within the cabin until the transport comes to a halt. "Fortunately, this bridge can hold much more than its predecessor, so don't worry about falling in." "That's good to know," replies Gracella.

Lillian approaches Arthur. "Okay…we have arrived at the middle of the bridge. Just look straight down. There, you will find the water at its deepest point.   Here is your moment to shine Arthur Robinson – so shine well."

"Show time..."

"We are about thirty meters above the surface. Time is of the essence."

Arthur peers out the side window of the forward compartment and looks down into the water. "Nothing… Not a single thing. There's not even a trace on any of the monitors." Arthur slams his hand against the side of the transport as Lillian watches. She flagrantly asks, "You actually expect to see something?"

"And…"

"We barely arrived. You're not too bright – are you? Hand me those binoculars," she says, as Arthur remains silent, eying her with contempt.

Looking into the water, Lillian begins a methodical scan, panning back and forth in a zigzagging manner, working her way from downstream to upstream. As her methodology nears the edge of the bridge, she stops. "Well it appears that you are either too early or too late. How long do you think we should stay?"

"I don't know."

"You don't know."

"It's hard to say Lieutenant."

"I see… Well…bit of advice Mr. Robinson. Do your home work a lot better so you don't appear as foolish as this assignment."

"Is there a problem Lieutenant?"

"I'm merely saying that given the number of bridges, your little *water lily* could be anywhere. The odds of locating such a *thing* are far beyond reality."

"Sounds to me like you would rather be somewhere else."

"Oh… Do you think?"

"Say it then…"

"Alright… I have been on countless assignments but none as miniscule as this one. I have friends out there dying, and would much rather be spending time fighting the enemy – doing something much more productive than helping to look for a lost pet!"

"Lost pet?"

"Well you haven't found it, have you?"

"There's the door – why not use it."

"Commander Ellis thinks this is a worthy cause; therefore, I'm inclined to accept, but…"

"Hold it right there Lieutenant! As far as this being a war and your friends dying; I can see the writing on the wall."

"How could you?"

"The same way I realize that you don't piss on rattlesnakes; so let me tell you something about this lost pet."

"Please do…"

"It's a hell of a lot more than you can handle and very capable of changing the entire outcome of this war."

"Then bring it on. I would much rather know that this is not some little piss-ant assignment."

"You wouldn't last five seconds with this *pet* – so shut up."

"The hell with you Robinson…go ahead and put me on report!"

Arthur walks away as Lillian stares at him.

Radiating wakes ripple on the topside of the water's surface as the last enan tilts its nose upward. Taking in air, the hybrid submerges and swims several yards upstream, passing directly beneath the bridge as well as the transport. Arthur, with binoculars in hand, increases the magnification of the optics, and turns to the opposite side of the transport. He scans the surface of the water over and over but finds nothing.

Sergeant Guidry enters the cabin of the transport and taps Arthur on the shoulder. "You know…back home, when I use to go *mudfishin,* I sometimes use a tuning fork. *De* sound make *dem go crazeh'*, make *em'* dance in *da wotah*."

"You used sound to drive them out. Are you suggesting sonar and if so, do you have sonar capability?"

"Why *shoah.* This is a military vehicle *Artha.* I'll drop a line and start to…"

"Listen…"

"Not only that, but also look."

Guidry lowers an acoustic dispenser into the water. He and Arthur observe the screen of the sonar finder. An undulating barrage of colors resembling the contour of the riverbed and distinct low-lying objects separate as the images scroll across the screen, until… "I'll be… Look at that."

"I see something *Artha*"

"This little group distinction of lines looks really wired."

"Its far north if you want to catch a view."

"That gives me an idea…thanks sergeant. I know what to look for on a spectral analysis."

Arthur immediately grabs a pair of binoculars, rushes out of the compartment, and on to the bridge. "I'm setting this thing to infra-red at forty-two hundred yards; set my thermo imaging to the lowest for black body radiation – let's see what we can see." Arthur scans the surface of the water due north of their location. In an instant, a grizzly smile sprawls upon his face while rising to his feet. "Gotcha," he says.

Profound curiosity grips the others as Marshal Harrison approaches. "You see something Robinson?"

"Two nostrils heading upstream."

"What? Listen son, you ain't Jesus, so stop speaking parables."

"It has to come up for air marshal."

"Sounds like we're on the move, it's about time – strap in…we're moving out," says Lillian, who signals Guidry to set the transport upon a northerly course.

They track the elusive creature until their progress becomes more difficult. Guidry maneuvers Praetorian around large objects and upon wet earth. Seemingly unstoppable, the metal giant clashes with larger objects, forcefully smashing through small brush and eventually onto smoother pavement. The crew manages to hold on as they shake vigorously within the compartment. Then, in the midst of darkness, the forward lamps illuminate five men just beyond the weathered road.

The transport startles the men and they quickly brandish their weapons. Arthur asks, "Guidry, who are they?" "Don't know." Sergeant Guidry leans forward to get a better view. As he does, one of the men raises his hand. Proximity lamps reveal the militant regalia of a heavily dressed and well-armed field soldier.

"They're one of ours," says Guidry as the soldier approaches the driver-side window. Beating on the side of the transport, the man demands Guidry's attention. "What purpose have you in this sector Sergeant?"

"That's classified."

"Well classify this; you are in a hot zone. Small cells of insurgents broke through our defense perimeter. Though we've taken this sector, it looks like we're going to have to fight to keep it."

"This must be recent information."

"Hell man...how can you miss the fireworks in the sky?"

"Sweet Jesus..."

"Turn around, because there's *unfriendlies* in this area."

"It was my understanding that this sector of river is a non-combat zone."

"Not any more."

Arthur grabs Guidry by the sleeve. "We turn around now, we loose what we've come for...and there *goes* our only lead!"

"I know *Ahtha*, but if this place crawls, then we may not have a choice. We *cain't* jeopardize civilians in a military skirmish – we have to find another way." Hearing Guidry's words, Arthur tosses the binoculars on the console.

"Contain that behavior of yours Mr. Robinson," blurts Lillian.

"You do not understand what I've been through lady. Loose that creature – *we*...loose our lives – Got it?"

"Creature – *eh*? It would thrill me to death to know what you're going after. I can't even enter the aft cargo section without your authorization code. What is it Arthur; an animal, a weapon...exactly what are we chasing?"

As the lieutenant drills Arthur, a thunderous explosion rips through the area, hurling debris in several directions, even striking the soldier outside the transport. "In *ya'* seats people; switching to combat mode!" Upon Guidry's command, cabin lights turn red as outer metallic shields unfold, covering forward, side, and aft windows. Though remarkably concealed, every one inside can see outwardly through the shields. Forward head beams that project white light now project an illuminating green; piercing the night, yet barely seen from a distance.

"Incoming!" Guidry's scream fills the cabin as Praetorian sustains a hammering blow. The sheer force of impact raises the transport several inches on one side before it contacts the ground again. "Get us out of here," commands Lillian.

Guidry floors the pedal, increasing the distance from the occurrence; however, the transport proves difficult to steer, plunging into a wooden structure as it barrels over corpses and imbedded craters.

"Base camp, this is Lieutenant Lillian Sullivan calling…please respond!" Lillian continues to relay the situation to base camp as columns of fire rise from impacting mortars.

Arthur scrambles to retrieve a few items, asking, "Sergeant, where are we?"

"Hell fire!"

"No! What's our geographic location?"

"*Nowth-east* quadrant…sector A-49. Punch it into *tha* squawkingbox.*"

"What?"

"*Tha* computer *Ahtha*."

"Oh."

"*What'cha needin* it *foar*?"

"Georeferencing our proximity to our fugitive. Can you push us farther north?"

"Can't; have to pick another route or return to base command."

Arthur shakes his head, but locates their position on the electronic grid. "You can run but you can't hide – I'll find you."

Bullets tatter the hull of the transport, enforcing the realism of their situation. Then, within moments, a larger explosion in the distance draws Guidry's attention, yet he sees something directly ahead. "Hang on everybody, it's *gonnagit* ugly real fast!" Quickly turning the wheels, Guidry's actions hurl every loose item against the compartment walls while everyone tries to secure themselves.

Lillian shouts, "What are you doing Sergeant!"

"*Ma'am*, enemy directly in our path and *movin* heavy guns!"

"Can they see us?"

"Not *shoah*, *we'ah* in the *dahk*. But our green beams got him lit up like a China Berry. Pretty *shoah* I can *take'em* down but it's your call *Ma'am!*"

Harrison quickly intervenes. "Lieutenant, we can handle our own; to hell with the combatant waivers!" Harrison's expulsion casts a stern glare upon his face as he grimly watches the unfolding events. "Very well marshal," she says.

An eerie silence looms through out the cabin as Lillian looks forward. "Do it quickly sergeant – let's help who we can."

A wounded soldier rolls on the ground and attempts to crawl away from his tormentors, yet some are already dead, and while two more are only moments from impending doom.

Like an arriving cavalry, Praetorian rushes in, dispels the enemy and halts just over the body of one of the solders. "Open the floor hatch!" "I'm on it," responds Walter, who waists little time as he pulls the soldier from the ground and into the armored transport. "Go – I got him!"

The transport resumes for the second soldier, but his attacker is upon him. Seeing the approaching transport, the attacker drives a long blade into the chest of the wounded soldier. Agonizing cries spill into the night as the soldier's limp body sprawls across the desert floor. But in his haste for blood, the attacker misjudges Praetorian's approach and attempts to flee. Guidry sees him and accelerates. Forward lamps converge upon the attacker as his fleeting efforts fail. Raising his hands, the attacker despairingly waves as Praetorian's impending tread sends him to the ground, after which tons of high tensile steel imbeds his body deep into the earth – never to be seen again.

Later, Guidry and his passengers arrive at the Al'Amma Bridge as units of coalition forces make their way into the encroaching bands of insurgents. Wounded soldiers are taken aboard helicopters and other emergency aircraft.

Lillian approaches Guidry. "Sergeant, once we get pass the bridge, I want you to take us to the med-evac ramps. We'll have this soldier transported to a nearby infirmary and then I want you to put us on a northern course to resume operations." Without question, Guidry complies.

Arthur hears the lieutenant's command and acknowledges her with a smile. She, in turn, grants the technician a casual head gesture of friendly compliance.

Resuming their search, the team travel as far as where Arthur last saw the enan, but their journey places them on the opposite side of the river. Lillian approaches Arthur. "All right Mr. Robinson, you may resume your search, but I must warn you, a degree of urgency is needful."

"I thought we were returning to base."

"Let's just say that I intend to carry out my mission – all of my missions."

"I want to apologize about my earlier behavior."

"You mean to say that you are sorry for allowing testosterone to rule your actions."

"You don't have to be so mean."

"I thought that was the normal downfall for all males, and that you were simply acting out on what evolution has caused you to become."

"Another comedian…"

"You appear less agitated, but surely, you do not think we have come this far just to turn around. Do you?"

"I thought it was over."

"General Pendleton did not go into detail about your intentions, but he made it quite clear that I would be exposed to things of a classified nature and that this little excursion of yours is to succeed – now that bit of information was free. And though formidable, Praetorian's hull cannot protect us indefinitely."

"Point taken…"

"I am also quite sure that this thing you are looking for is no longer waiting around at the previous location. So tell me again, how do you intend to find…it?"

Arthur looks directly at Lillian. Her peering light brown eyes and authoritative voice mandates nothing less than dignity and respect. She is a veteran, a military success story, and an intriguing conversation piece. Arthur gives her full attention, but displays an impish grin as he walks towards the cargo bay. While in stride, he tells her, "I intend to find it, by following a nose."

Lillian simply stares at him.

As Arthur enters the aft cargo bay, Lillian cautiously follows, and realizes that he did not lock the door behind him.

As usual, the solemn technician greets his hybrid-child with a rub and a gentle head nudge. "Hey *fella*…got some things for you." Arthur places a torn piece of clothing near Gjhe'nan's nose. "Here…smell this. This piece of clothing got torn off while trying to survive in the barn fight. It's got your kinsmen's smell all over it. And speaking of kinsmen, I need you to find one of them and show us where he went; so hopefully we can find Colonel Ducet. I'm putting this earpiece deep inside your ear so you can hear me."

The tiny device lodges securely within and well out of sight.

"There…you can hear me now. Do you understand?" Gjhe'nan shrieks softly. "The instructions I gave you earlier are still in effect. Also, there is gunfire out there – so be careful."

Arthur moves to the rear of the cargo bay and activates the aft door. The heavy door slowly opens, but then, Lillian enters. She sees Arthur and Gjhe'nan standing near the exit. Like many before her, she too succumbs to the grappling effects of astonishment. *"Whh…whh…*what is that?"

Both ignore her and suddenly, the colorful beast lunges outward; into the darkness of the arid wastelands. As the door closes, Arthur walks pass Lillian and returns to the forward cabin. However, Lillian's distraught demeanor leaves her with a hasty recourse. "Can you explain *that*…thing to me? What is *that* and where did it go, and how was it possible to be on my mission without my knowledge? I'm asking you a question Mr.!"

Hearing her questions, Arthur slowly turns to face Lillian, and stares her in the eye for several seconds. Then, with no expression, he tells her "That thing is hope." Lillian looks about the cabin, silently requesting a response from the others, but no one volunteers a word.

Outside, the sound of distant gunfire fills the air as Gjhe'nan leaps towards the last known location of the enan. Under the cover of darkness, the hybrid finds the water's edge and begins to investigate. Gjhe'nan sniffs the ground, scouring the barren earth while sampling what little foliage becomes available. Finding nothing more, the hybrid beast wades into the water, tasting and smelling the fluid surface for several minutes at a time.

Celestial bodies cast a subtle shine upon the water as a bobbing image of Gjhe'nan faintly reflects passively along the surface. The hybrid lowers its head just shy of the surface and observes the reflection staring back. In curious human fashion, Gjhe'nan touches his face, slowly coursing both hands down the ridge of his snout until finally reaching the tip of his nose, then standing as though time is frozen. Nothing moves nor stirs about, only a cold dark silence and the subtle blue illumination that currently marks the hybrid's deep dark eyes. Then strangely, Gjhe'nan lowers a claw into the water and disburses the reflection. Looking afar, he stares in the distant, watching, and pondering - until the hunt begins.

His searching patterns encompass several yards north and then west until the watery surface finally yields a clue. Taking a deep breath only a few inches above the surface, Gjhe'nan Immediately moves across the shallows and onto dry land, but soon becomes curiously drawn to the sound of engines.

A small band of coalition troops are on the move. Gjhe'nan crouches low to the ground and remains motionless as the convoy draws near, yet their progression leaves the hybrid undetected. As the troops increase distance, Gjhe'nan reestablishes the scent trail.

Though safe from discovery, something in the sky catches his attention. Looking upward, Gjhe'nan observes a narrow beam of strange light that stretches across the sky. Intrigued, he determines that the beam of light extends from Baghdad to a point of origin extending somewhere in the darkness of the distant valleys. His fascination grows. Seconds pass, then the light mysteriously disappears. Gjhe'nan resumes following the scent trail, which yields a path directly to the origin of the beam.

Aboard the LAATT, several monitors relay information to Rowland and Ducet. The atmosphere within the cabin grows with tremendous excitement as the last enan rendezvous with the others. "That a boy soldier…reel him in, reel him in – yes," says Ducet, patting everyone on the back while singing praises to his sworn commitment.

"All present and accounted for sir…thirty-two strong and resting. Also, when the satellites are close enough, I'll be able to bounce a signal directly off their dish and link it to the enan's cameras. We'll be able to see them in combat."

"Great news… I love it when a plan works," says the colonel.

Rowland intervenes. "Congratulations Colonel. You *deed eet*. I would have never believed *eet* possible."

"It's always after the fact. All right people, listen up. According to this map, we are here, and they are there. When the time comes, I want you to raise seven enans. INTEL and SAT shows that the heaviest fighting is about seven klicks from us. Four more cluster skirmishes are taking place in these areas, near Kuwait and Fallujah. The night is early and I want to hit them with their pants down!" Ducet continues to unfold his elaborate plan as the last enan buries itself beneath the sand.

AS time progresses, the scent trail proves quite sufficient. However, Gjhe'nan finds something more interesting and waits. Eventually, the transport Praetorian stops along side the hybrid, to which a series of shrieks and high pitch squeals signals Arthur that something of great value have been found. The technician exits the transport and utilizes a tiny flashlight to unveil the hybrid's curiosity.

"Look at that. It's a footprint…and there is several more…way out here. It appears that our fugitive is not alone after all." Arthur smiles and pats Gjhe'nan on the head. "Find him, follow these prints but be mindful that satellites can see you. Put this oil on, it will help mask your heat signature, but don't get too far in front of us."

Suddenly, Lillian exits the transport; and yet, with one powerful leap, Gjhe'nan's massive body becomes air borne and disappears into the distance.

"Wait, wait! Arthur, I saw that. What was that? Why won't you talk to me? Tell me what that…that thing is? That is the secret, isn't it?" Lillian attempts to make eye contact with Arthur, but the solemn technician stands quietly, staring in the direction of the hybrid's departure.

Lillian repeatedly sequesters Arthur's attention until finally, a subtle response comes forth. "As I said before lieutenant; that thing is hope."

~~~Assault~~~

Walter holds a picture in his hand. He gently rubs the small photo with his thumb while intermittently closing his eyes. Then, he pulls a silver ring from his pocket and dangles the dazzling piece of jewelry on his index finger. "Fret not *thyself* because of evil doers," he whispers, over and over. Gracella hears him and approaches. Walter becomes alert.

"It was a fun time," she says.

"Oh…what part…the madness or the mayhem – or both?"

"I mean you and that person in the photograph."

"Yeah…she means a lot to me."

"Of course she does, the shiny ring says it all."

"Stranger things have happened. She and I, not much in common, yet the more time I spent with her, the more I thought about her."

"Only likenesses attract; so maybe you two have more in common than you thought."

"I can't stop thinking about her– it was a good time. Imagine…a guy like me from Dayton Ohio winds up with someone like her – all the way from Croatia."

"I think she wants a nice guy and that just happened to be you."

"You're being kind."

"No, you're laughing, but really. Jade and I would have our girl talk and you were very much in it."

"Sometimes, I would try to talk about her work overseas, but strangely – she almost never gave any detail."

"There are times when the past is not worth the hurt."

"Everybody has a past."

"Some – more complicated."

"Whatever is back there, she tries hard to get away from it."

"Something doesn't add up."

"Maybe with all that has happened, I may have misunderstood her."

"That's not important right now. Anyway, you two found each other at a very difficult time. Surely that has to count for something."

"I'm sure it does Gracella, but she and I moved faster than we intended. At first, we're tearing into each other; then the next thing you know…we're discussing a family."

"Wow…you really did move fast."

"It wasn't *my*…our initial intention."

"There are always consequences Walter, but I'm not here to preach to you."

"I just want to make it right before God. With all that has happened…I started thinking about how fragile our lives are. Tuan, Frank, Nathaniel, Alexis. At any given moment, we all could be wiped out. After a while, this stuff gets to you."

"Sure it does."

"After those thugs tried to kill me, reality started to set in. Jesus sounds like a good start; at least that's what you and Arthur imply; although, Arthur admits to being a poor example of a believer."

"If he can stop cursing and throwing things…"

"I guess we all have issues; but I do give him credit for his honesty. Someone has to make the first step; guess it starts with me – Right?"

"As with us all…"

"Gracella, do you think God hears a man's desperate cry?"

"He has too."

"Then, there's nothing left, but to accept Him."

"I am so happy for you. That's the best news I've heard in a long time."

Gracella embraces Walter.

Aboard the LATT, Captain Jamison approaches Colonel Ducet. "Sir, it's time." Several miles away, a silent army awakes. Like stalwart draught horses, the hybrid sentries shake their heads while moving their massive bodies in a swaying motion; dredging the sand with sharply staved talons; prating unspoken words as though to inflict their deadly anxieties upon an unseen enemy.

"All right people. The enemy is dug in like a Norwegian tick, and you can bet civilians are mixed in with them. That's their disguise. And since the enemy refuses to have peace talks; we'll just have to show them a little bit of negotiating diplomacy. Jamison!" "Sir..." "Send in team 1 to the north and team 2, to northwest. SEND THEM IN!" "Aye sir!"

Immediately, three enans travel north while four take to the northwest; moving as if a boisterous wind aids their progress. The enans display remarkable agility for their size; but unlike their much smaller cousins, their leaping ability is slower, yet covers a far greater distance; in effect, putting them near an isolated skirmish in a very short time.

Aboard the LAATT, Ducet's men earnestly watch. "Sir, satellite coverage in five minutes. They'll be hot."

"We only need two minutes. Just keep them outside the grid as much as possible."

"Acknowledged..."

Team 1 reaches an overlying cliff as coalition forces lay a few hundred yards to the west. Insurgents occupy territory to the east. Mortar rounds fly in the night as fighting already takes place. The enans disburse and lay in a course for the insurgents. The first enan finds a small band of fighters and pounces on them, instantly breaking their necks while slashing four more unsuspecting members. Other fighters open fire upon the beast, but the hybrid makes a hasty retreat. As the creature seemingly disappears, several more gunmen focus their attention in the wrong direction. As they do, another enan captures them off guard and ruthlessly rips out chunks of their flesh while severing their spines.

Some fighters become aware that a compromising situation is growing and group together to challenge what they cannot see. Threatening red eyes barrel down upon the approaching hopefuls; missing nothing while determining the heighten moment of an onslaught. Suddenly, the men raise their weapons, but the enan spins its body; wildly swinging its tail with calculative precision as it destroys several gunmen in one thrashing motion. Gunfire desperately rings out, but their efforts prove far too foolish as more gunmen lay in decapitation. Headless bodies litter the streets as blood courses dark rivers into the earth. Internal organs spew outwardly as deep cuts burst open; leaving no hope for those misfortunate to sustain such markings. Many insurgents continue to fire into the direction of the coalition troops, but screams quickly erupt along a shallow trench as the third enan pummels the unsuspecting gunmen. Without mercy, the creature relentlessly clears the trench, thrusting its victims while severing more bodies in half and casting the serrated corpses aside. For many, there are no screams, no suffering, and no time for pity – no time for fear. The enans leave as quickly as they came; having dreadfully testified their skills for a political cause in the sheath of the night.

Ducet's team cheers as the commander preludes a defiant rally. "Now that – is how it is done gentlemen. Guide the other enans to this location," he tells the technician as he points to a monitor.

Team 2 locates another cluster of insurgent fighters. This time, the gunmen sense nearby movement and fire in the direction of the curious unknown. Surprisingly, their blind miscalculating efforts remarkably strike an approaching enan. The enan shrieks loudly, but the darkness makes difficult for the gunmen to pinpoint their aim as the creature continues to advance.

Despite the hybrids approach, night vision technology assures the gunmen that the nightmarish pack is all too real. Several gunmen immediately fire in desperation. Their aim is for something that they were not expecting. Deadly rounds strike the hybrids' chest, but the effects are too little to keep the thunderous juggernauts from pounding and viciously mauling several men to death. Afterwards, havoc spreads quickly.

One insurgent gunman remarkably survives and runs directly into the arms of the advancing, yet surprised coalition forces. He approaches the troops with frantic screaming and hand waving. *"Ahtaaju Almusa'ada',"* he cries. The soldiers intently watch. The man cries out again; yet this time, the soldiers are not as trusting. Failing to heed several warnings, the man's gestures are sadly mistaken for something else and the soldiers fire upon him, striking him down in his tracks. The man suffers a decisive but merciful fate than his brothers in arms.

Ducet's team cheers.

One of the enans of team 2 comes upon another group of insurgent fighters. The fighters are already engaging coalition forces. The skirmish takes place outside a large establishment. Exploding rounds brightly light the sky as each side exchange their perpetual savagery. The enan stops shy of the insurgent's boundary and looms behind rocks; silently observing.

Ducet and one of his men observe the situation as it unfolds upon the monitor. "Where did they get that kind of firepower to strike back with sir?"

"From neighboring boarders and shady friends."

"I'm showing a large concentration of people in that village. There must be at least three-hundred surrounding the buildings – not to mention those inside. No air strikes from base command colonel?"

"No. Tactics of this nature dictate a systematic gorilla-style expulsion of the enemy…door-to-door evacuation. But such a method can take too damn long…"

"I see…"

"As I said before, situations like this raise the possibility of killing innocent civilians."

"But sir, reports suggest the enemy at eighty percent."

"Command wouldn't want to get their hands dirty, now would they?"

"The enemy was easily identified in the old days; Black Hawks and snipers could decisively take them out."

"That was a different kind of war – son. Insurgents quickly learned how to use the allied forces sense of compassion against them."

"But sir, are you sure that civilians are inside those buildings."

"Infrared tells all."

"We have to assume that commanders know."

"Sure they do. Why do you think those buildings are still standing?"

"I understand."

"Good, now send them in!"

"Will do; message sent…commencing operation."

The enan receives the instructions; but then, surprisingly lowers its head, giving off a low whining shriek, and does nothing.

Ducet watches. "What the hell is it doing? Why is it just sitting there?" No one answers. The colonel turns to another one of his men. "Jamison! You are aware that day break is in a couple of hours and our forces will have satellite coverage of this whole area in forty seconds." "Yes sir." "Good, then I need that enan to carry out its mission – put it in a language it can understand!" "Yes sir!"

The captain presses a button on the console and slowly turns a large shinny dial. As he does, the hybrid covers its ears, shaking its head as though to ward off an excruciating occurrence. Jamison continues to turn the dial. Then, agitation sets in and the hybrid plummets to the ground, smashing into rocks and nearby foliage while kicking dust into the hollow midst of the dark.

"For God's sake colonel," rants Rowland, scorning Ducet. The colonel glances at him, but gives no reply.

Blood stream from the enan's ear as the creature staggers upright and yet staring wildly until painfully advancing towards the settlement. An untimely rhythm marks the hybrid's gating trot as it falls to the ground, suffering the deadly predicament of visual exposure.

Some insurgents hold allied forces at bay while others divert their attention to the hybrid. Sensing a threat, high-powered projectiles strike the beast until tearing through the creature's scales. Despite the brutish onslaught, the enan progresses forward. Gunnery cannons takes aim at the enan, but the hybrid falls to the ground again.

Several insurgents move in for a closer examination. All become quiet as they curiously observe the laden beast. One of the men asks, "What manner of demon is this?" No one answers. Then suddenly, a piercing sound erupts and soon to follow is a bright fiery sphere of yellow and orange expanse. The event horizon expands outward, consuming everything within its incinerating grasp while shaking the scorched ground beneath. Peering eyes afar witness the pyrotechnic fury as nothing of the buildings or the insurgent stronghold remains.

Personnel aboard the LAATT observe the event with astonishing reprieve as one female soldier summons the colonel. "Sir, INTEL discloses that the coalition forces are now progressing without resistance whatsoever! All remaining insurgents outside the blast area are on the run and best of all…there are no casualties of allied troops!"

"That's what I want to hear," says Ducet, gritting his teeth from ear to ear while boasting of imminent success. But the soldier has more. "Also sir, only six of the seven enans returned. They are now buried for the day."

"One enan for three hundred or so possible gunmen, and maybe a hundred civvies *accidentally* caught in the blast zone…not bad, just collateral damage ensign; every thing comes with a price. We'll simply grow another enan and do it all over again. By the way, good job on coordinating the teams, now get some rest."

Ducet closes his eyes in sheer gratification and parades in silent celebration. So deep are his indulgences that the soldier rises from her seat and addresses the commander once more. "Sir…"

"Yes, what is it?"

"Thank you for the earlier compliment; however, there is something else you should know."

"Such as…"

"COM indicates something rapidly approaching our vector."

Ducet stares at the woman as his smile completely disappears.

Impacting the ground is Gjhe'nan. The hybrid hones in on the final set of footprints. Amidst the dust, heighten senses enlighten the hybrid's predatory instincts as he moves systematically in the direction of Ducet's buried camp.

Ducet and his combatants carefully watch the monitor as the image sensor unravels their most dreadful fear. "Sir, is that what I think it is?"

"I'll be d…"

"I thought all the enans were buried."

"That can't be one of ours."

"Then whose can it be?"

445

"Arthur's," says Rowland.

Ducet harshly asks, "How the hell did Robinson get way out here?"

"One can only suspect – assistance no doubt."

"Can it find us?"

"Why can it not?"

"Then be quiet – all of you, lay still, and quickly shut down the generator and all non-essential equipment – NOW!"

Sensitive whiskers cover the ground, sniffing, scouring, and seeking out potential clues, earnestly scavenging for the lost remnants of an obvious trail, but the ground gives nothing in return. Soon, Gjhe'nan fixates upon an intriguing layout of dense sand and rock in the immediate area. Curious by nature, the hybrid distinct sense of sight reveals an unnatural terrain only a few yards ahead. Placing his whiskers to the ground, Gjhe'nan sniffs while listening.

"*Shhhhhh*…every one be quiet," whispers Ducet, placing his finger upon his lips.

Gjhe'nan passes directly over the LAATT, but then, onto something far more compelling. Moving faster, the hybrid locks on to a scent trail. So powerful is his driving force that he discovers a mound of disturbed sand. One sniff and Gjhe'nan is thrown into an overwhelming frenzy. He sinks his powerful talons deep into the mound and plows away.

Ducet watches in disbelief. "Good Lord man – that's an enan…it's big."

"We call *theem*…bulls."

"A bull… Well, male or not, it's digging up one hell of a surprise. We better stop it!"

"*Thees* one does not *rr*-espond to our controls Colonel."

"You seem nervous Rowland."

"Not nervous, only concerned."

"For what…"

446

"*Eef* Arthur controls *dis* creature, then surely we have more problems."

"Maybe, but how did that enan find us?"

"I don't know, but more importantly, should *eet* unearth apparent suspicions – then we are surely compromised."

Rowland clinches a fist while rubbing his flustered thick-skinned face.

Then suddenly, Captain Jamison draws Ducet's attention. "Sir, look."

"Look at what…"

"The other monitor sir…"

All watch in earnest as amber fields of radiance slowly span from the east, climbing over distant mountains while stretching beyond the capacious valleys of the arid sand. As the yellow sun heightens, a spectacular beam of light cascade down upon the hybrid as it borrows deeper into the earth.

Rowland taps Ducet on the shoulder. "Daylight *eez* upon us comrade, and that enan has found one of our buried enans." "Then kill it – NOW," commands Ducet as strict orders come with the brandishing contact of fist upon metal.

Gjhe'nan uncovers the face of a buried enan. Surprise engulfs the hybrid; however, the enan revels nothing less than bloodthirsty eyes and an abhorrent attitude. With hissing sharpness and a snarling vehemence, the creature rips its way topside. Gjhe'nan steps back. Suddenly, two more enans tear from their earthen coffins as well. Gjhe'nan surprisingly watches.

Aboard the transport Praetorian, everyone witness the horror as three enans surround Gjhe'nan. Arthur recognizes the situation as Walter approaches. "He can take'*em*, he's done it already at Hollis' barn – Right Arthur?"

"One of those enans was a syren and the other was a smaller bull. Here, it appears to be one syren and two bulls. And in case you haven't been paying attention, one of those bulls equal Gjhe'nan in size and I'm sure in strength as well. Not to mention that all three are closing in on him. Gjhe'nan's in danger."

"Then you better get him out of there."

"The thought had occurred – in case you hadn't notice."

Arthur relays information to Gjhe'nan and immediately, the agile beast takes to the air, pouncing from one place to another, showing no sign of slowing down as his uncanny pursuers engage pursuit. With each leap, Gjhe'nan's pusuers effectively close distance behind him.

Also, daylight intensifies as allied forces draw near; yet Arthur guides Gjhe'nan into a valley just behind a large out cropping of sandy bluffs. Astoundingly, one of the pursuing enans reaches Gjhe'nan first and immediately attempts to thrash him. Gjhe'nan avoids the deadly appendage and counters with a powerful kick.

The enan decisively counters Gjhe'nan's nimble reflexes; but lances a murderous frontal assault. Gjhe'nan dodges the enan's death strike. Yet, unable to seize the moment, both creatures lock talons in a deadly battle of noxious mayhem. As each attempt to subdue the other, dust rise, shrieks clamor as both bodies tumble upon the ground.

Then, in sheer madness, the attacking enan gains a foothold and strikes Gjhe'nan with its deadly scythe; leaving a ghastly scar as a fervent warning. Both hybrids encircle each other, until, the enan lunges forward for the murderous kill, and yet again, Gjhe'nan evades the attempt. Missing its target, the enan wildly slams head first into a palm tree. The stalwart plant cracks directly in the center.

Seeing an opportunity, Gjhe'nan quickly pounces to the front of the disoriented beast and delivers a rear kick to the creature's forehead. The fatal blow sends the enan's limp body several yards backwards while leaving a shallow trench in the wake of the forceful surge. Amidst the settling dust, the unstable enan stares Gjhe'nan in the eyes as its legs collapse.

Falling to ground, the creature's massive weight dispels clouds of dust. The beast slowly turns and lays sideward. In that brief moment, the enan's eyes turn from a fiery red to the deepest of black as blood pours from its nose. Gjhe'nan approaches the enan, sniffing and touching the hybrid's scaly face while tilting his head; as if to quietly bestow a sense of farewell to a fallen compatriot.

But the placid moment ends when the second enan approaches. Pouncing high, the enan lands on Gjhe'nan's back and viciously tears into the hybrid's dorsal ridges. Unable to shake the smaller attacker, Gjhe'nan rolls along the ground and radically squirms. The noble effort proves worthy, which creates space between the two. Snarling fangs cast forth a message of ill attempt as the enan lashes out towards

Gjhe'nan, striking feverishly into the air as to undo the hybrid by any means necessary. But Gjhe'nan's awareness of the third enan causes him to quickly eradicate the situation. Keying in on the moment, Gjhe'nan slashes towards the enan, causing the beast to flinch; then rams the creature in the side, sending the hellish beast over a rocky ledge. Clouds of dust cast high as the head-mounted camera breaks and the enan tumbles out of sight.

With no time for assessment, the third enan grapples Gjhe'nan from the side and violently wrestles the hybrid to the ground. The beast holds Gjhe'nan in its tenacious grip; yet, somehow, Gjhe'nan breaks free. Like conceptualized gladiators, both hybrids engage in perpetual bloodshed, shaking the ground beneath, slashing, hitting, snarling; creating small earthen craters with every thunderous slam upon the parched surface.

The battle stalemates, but Gjhe'nan is only as indestructible as he is mortal, and fails to take down his opponent. Instead, he hops away, but his pursuer hastens after him with a bloodlust rage.

With nowhere to hide, Gjhe'nan leads the enan far into the arid wasteland, gaining ground with every leap. As distance increase, the enan discontinues pursuit. Sensing no imminent danger, Gjhe'nan stops and looks for the enan, but instead, sees an encroaching army of coalition forces in the distant hills. The potential for discovery is far too costly and Gjhe'nan recourses a path along the outer realm, a path that takes him directly back to where the skirmish began.

Attempting to remain elusive, Gjhe'nan finds an enan laying on its side, yet conscience. Upon approach, the laying creature rises, displaying claws and snarling while exposing an open wound. Gjhe'nan sees the wound but does not attack. Somehow, Gjhe'nan recognizes the enan. It is the same enan he fought earlier and pushed over the ledge.

Obscure senses render the warring beast to subdue predatory intentions as he slowly approaches the injured creature. With ears laid back and a relaxed tail, Gjhe'nan gets close enough to write something in the sand. The words 'NO HARM U' vividly displays before the enan. Moments pass as the wind sweeps white sand between both hybrids – though neither beast dare relinquish their gained footholds.

Soon, a once snarling demeanor becomes silent and a readiness for attack lessens into a relaxing acceptance. Heavy breaths and a waning posture tell of the enan's misery as blood trickles to the ground. The smaller enan scribes in the sand as well, a benevolent gesture for either hybrid attempting to kill each other. Gjhe'nan breathes easier.

Strangely, the enan makes a gesture, referring to the base of its skull. Then, for a moment, both observe each other.

Suddenly, Gjhe'nan sustains a terrible blow and surprisingly finds himself on the ground battling for his life. The third enan has found him and has no mercy to give. The murderous attacker draws its sharp talons and claws away at Gjhe'nan, tearing scales, biting, scratching, and eventually pushing the hybrid deeper into the ground.

Sensing a triumphant encore, the enan relentlessly pounds Gjhe'nan, whose mouth begins to hang open. Gjhe'nan's crimson stained teeth are more than a white flag as the enan secures an un-benign victory. Then, the creature raises its tail, strikes a lancing pose, and readies the tip-end scythe of its tail.

Gjhe'nan lies pitifully upon the ground, staring at the sharp scythe of bone as it quivers for a strike. In a human like manner, Gjhe'nan gently closes his eyes.

Suddenly, the enan lances on a downward thrust, but before impending doom can strike; the smaller enan interrupts the deadly act and slashes the monstrous warmonger's throat, sending the torrent creature into a raging fit as blood spews everywhere. Profusely bleeding, the enan's massive body slams to the ground; transforming the gold sand into a red-soaked quagmire.

Standing silently, the smaller enan watches, casting a stare as cold as black ice. It is as though poetic justice prevails – but the underlying mystery for such actions remains elusive.

Then, a high pitch wine draws the enan's attention. Gjhe'nan calls and the enan approaches. For several minutes, the smaller enan gently touches Gjhe'nan's wounds while staring into the hybrid's eyes; staring as if a concernment beyond words is taking place. A tender conveyance occurs as the hybrid attempts to move Gjhe'nan out of the sun, but the creature becomes jittery at the sound of an approaching vehicle.

Guidry's transport, Praetorian, makes its way near Gjhe'nan and stops. Arthur immediately rushes to the hybrid's side. "He's hurt pretty bad. Get me the first aid kit. Walter, you and Harrison prepare the wench."

Once straps are in place, Walter reels the hybrid inside the transport; but then, Gjhe'nan grabs Arthur's hand and points to where the smaller enan's inscription lies in the sand. Surprised, Arthur investigates.

"HELP U. What's this?" Arthur rushes back to the transport and consoles the lain beast. "Help is here, I will help you."

Gjhe'nan musters what strength he can and slowly shakes his head, pointing a finger past the technician.

Discerning the hybrid's intention, Arthur turns and sees the smaller enan staring at him. "Whoa…where did you come from?" The enan does not run away, but curiously watches Arthur while maintaining distance. Arthur entices the cautious creature to come closer.

As Harrison stands near, Gjhe'nan grows restless. "Arthur, get over here, this damn thing's going crazy…doing stuff."

"What is he doing?"

"You tell me… Looks like he's putting his hand to the back of his head; trying to get our attention for something."

"He's pointing to the base of his skull, then towards that enan. It's something about the back of his head and that enan out there. We need to get that enan in here."

"How can you be sure that…that, thing won't attack us?"

"I saw two sets of writings in the sand marshal. One says *'no harm u',* and the other says *'help u.'* I just don't know who wrote what."

"You're scaring me Robinson."

Arthur beckons the enan to approach and enter the aft compartment.

Everything transpires under the watchful eye of Lieutenant Lillian Sullivan, who quietly approaches Arthur. She asks, "Is that a *g-non*?"

"No Lieutenant. Gjhe'nan is over there; this enan is what we call a syren. Syrens are the females of the enan species. Originally, we intended them all to be females but there was a change of plans."

Lillian gazes at the creature as though staring at a precious gem. Her mouth partially opens with no sign of breathing while her hands cover her forehead. She stands motionless. Arthur chuckles aloud. "Well Lieutenant, you act as everyone does when witnessing an enan for the first time. There is always that moment of aw."

"She's beautiful; so many colors," whispers Lillian while spellbound.

"I did not know such words could be used in the description of an enan. Fortunate for you, this syren is not in a killing mood."
Lillian scoffs at Arthur.

"In any case Lieutenant, Gjhe'nan's antics regard a more pressing matter. His actions are making me suspect something. Something I hope is not true. Is there a metal tracker of some sort on board?"

"I believe I know what you're trying to do. Hold on."

Lillian scrambles through two compartments until she locates a device. She gives the device to Arthur who activates the small instrument. The syren trustingly allows Arthur to approach and begin procedures.

Lillian asks, "What exactly are you looking for?"

"I'm searching for a disposal policy."

"What kind?"

"There was talk between Rowland and Ducet, that in the event an enan is captured, killed, or fall into the wrong hands, no traces of the enan would remain."

"The cover your ass policy... Does it come with a premium plan?"

"I didn't know you had a sense of humor Lieutenant."

"Not today. Just tell me if this premium plan includes the destruction of others – like us for instance; who just happen to be standing around this…syren."

"I don't know the specifics, but I would rather not be in close proximity when such a policy activates."

Arthur moves the device in a systematic manner until he nears the back of the enan's head. Soon, a series of lights and sounds begin to flash on the instrument. "You've found something."

"Look, there it is on the monitor."

"It's metallic in nature and there appears to be a wire leading from it. The wire does not appear to be attached to any thing."

"Whatever it is, I'll have to remove it manually."

"And you assume...that is what you should be doing – how?"

"Well...the syren feels that it shouldn't be there – so, I'm removing it."

Arthur reaches behind the enan's head and separates the scales. He makes a small incision upon the enan's skin. With methodic tenderness, the technician removes the blunt object from the base of the enan's skull. Trailing the object is a long thin wire. All eyes fasten upon the device as Arthur immediately brings it to Lillian's attention.

"Definitely something electronic."

"Where does this wire lead?"

"Not sure but don't pull to hard."

"It's as if it leads to something."

"What ever this thing is attached to surely runs deeper inside."

"Hey, wait a minute."

"What?"

"Do these enans have some kind of mutual existence with instruments?"

"Not that I'm aware of."

"I mean...do they have some kind of pace maker in order to live or function."

"If you're suggesting that these enans are remote controlled, the answer is no – I think."

"Does your Gjhe'nan know?"

"Only one way to find out."

Arthur draws Gjhe'nan's attention. Pointing to the device, he compels the hybrid to identify it, but only a hard stare complies with the technician's request. Suddenly, in a strange yet purposeful act, the syren comes near and inscribes something on the floor.

'DANGR 2 AL.' Immediately, Arthur's eyes widen.

"Oh my god! Now I know," screams Lillian as she pushes Arthur aside.

"Give me that!"

Lillian's demand grants her possession of the device. She activates the lower cargo door. "Hurry, hurry, hurry!" Without looking back, the lieutenant decides to crawl beneath the steel border as the door continues to rise. Upon exit, she hurls the device far into the air. Suddenly, an explosion occurs, dispersing shrapnel in all directions. The discharging force imbeds shards into the lieutenant's face – even before she could make contact upon the ground. Walter and Harrison desperately rush to the side of the ailing officer and carry her back inside the transport. Her blood drenched hands attempt to soothe a bitter anguish. Arthur sees Lillian and quickly locates Guidry. "Sergeant Guidry!"

"*Whut* was that noise?"

"Can you take us back to where we encountered the enans?"

"Why *shoah,* but I need the Lieutenant's authorization."

"Trust me; it's because of her that we need to go – now!" The sergeant looks at Arthur for a brief moment, and then earnestly complies.

Aboard the LAATT, Ducet intently observes information regarding the recent incident. Sensors relay something of importance as he presses Captain Jamison for an acceptable explanation. "Did it explode?"

"Sir, the implant did explode. Once the readings indicated that tampering was conclusive, we followed standard procedures – as…*you*…instructed. Again, our protocol dictates that when there's no detectable heartbeat, detonation or incineration is put into effect."

"I don't need you to remind me of protocols Jamison."

"I assure you Colonel; the syren is gone – just like the other two."

"I hope you're right Jamison."

"The only thing we don't know is if our enans succeeded in killing that other enan, when they were in pursuit. The last camera clearly shows a favorable outcome for us – even if the other two were destroyed in the scuffle. As of yet, we still have no idea where the other enan came from."

"Where ever it came from, I'm quite sure it is dead. Nothing can survive the onslaught of three enans."

"In any case, we got bigger fish to fry. INTEL reports that the largest concentration of insurgents is outside Mandali."

"How many sir?"

"That number could be well into the thousands."

"Strictly enemy?"

"About sixty percent."

"That region is near the Iranian boarder. A small band of our guys stumbled across the insurgent's presence, but were soon discovered. They called in for help, but aid is yet to arrive. Needless to say…they are now taking on heavy fire."

"What is their current condition?"

"They are trapped in the surrounding valley. If we handle this carefully, this can be the turning point in this war."

"But sir, there is also a major concentration of refugees fleeing the area. They could potentially get caught in the crossfire, if they are not part of that number already."

"Collateral damage Captain Jamison... Remember, the bad guys are counting on our humanitarian compassion. That's why they surround themselves with innocents. I have good reason to believe that this encounter will break their strong hold – should we win."

"Are you making a point sir?"

"LANSAT shows heavy artillery in the enemy's possession. You know as well as I that if our guys take the diplomatic approach, the enemy will hide any ounce of evidence. By that time, it will be too late."

"As always..."

"My gut feeling is that…they probably know the coalition forces are more than thirty clicks away."

"Too much time will pass before they can reach the allies in the valley."

"We can engage the enemy in far less time."

"What are your orders, sir?"

"Prep all the enans; prepare for a decisive frontal asault."

"But sir..."

"I intend to take down the entire northern sector."

"Aye sir..."

Rowland enters the compartment. "Colonel, *eeennn*-teresting development..."

"What is it now?"

"Radar shows object coming *thees* way on an intersecting path directly *weeth* us. See the trackers?"

All eyes fasten upon the beacon as it moves across the screen. Rolland asks, "Who could possibly be knocking at our door colonel?"

"Don't know, but we don't have to answer. Retract all topside feeds," commands Ducet. Soon, the air exhaust and radar dish sinks beneath the ground.

Evasive maneuvers are put into action as Arthur and Walter step outside their transport. Both men scan the area, searching the ground, combing the sand while trying to unravel clues. Success wanes, but soon, they stand directly near Ducet's underground encampment.

"THERE, in the ground", shouts Walter while pointing, moving in closer to investigate. Both begin to dig until Walter rises in astonishment. "I'll be... Those airshafts and that radar dish don't grow in these parts. Guidry's information on the LAATT was right. Arthur, I think we're about to have company." "I think your right." Both men quickly depart.

Ducet watches from on board in disbelief as his fortress is no longer hidden. "Damn," he whispers.

Rowland nears the screen. "I *rr*-recognize *dose* men. *Arthur Rrr-obinson* and Walter Pierson."

"It appears that their enan has found us, but are you surprised to see them?" Rowland does not answer. Ducet stands cold and brazenly stares at the monitor. With fists tightly clenching, he yells, "We are compromised – but we will not go down without a fight!"

As Arthur and Walter enter the transport, mounds of sand and rock burst into the air. Several enans emerge from beneath the ground, tossing while pushing outward in all directions. They pronounce their formidable presence to the world. Abandoning their earthen tombs, the enans depart the scene one by one.

Soon afterwards, both LAATTs begin to unearth from beneath the ground as well. Powerful hydraulics push the armored vehicles upward, dispersing sand and creating a cloud of highly visible dust.

Once clear of the ground, lateral support arms fold outward, extending well beyond the pit to become the support for the entire vehicle. All wheels begin to roll as hydraulic arms close forward and place the vehicle beyond the empty hole. Both vehicles speedily set off in the same direction as the enans, but they are not alone.

Aboard the Praetorian, Arthur turns to Guidry and strikes the console with the palm of his hand. "We have him – now we have to let him go!"

"I know *Ah'tha*, but Lillian needs medical attention. I got to follow protocol."

"I know sergeant, I know." Arthur's head hangs low.

But as Arthur watches the departing LAATTs, a hand gently touches his shoulder from behind. The stunned technician turns and faces the countenance of endearing turmoil. His eyes widen as speechlessness overwhelms him; and yet, he receives subtle words, which revive a vanishing hope. "No…press forward…"

"Lieutenant?"

Lieutenant Lillian now stands before Arthur. She has one eye patch and several bandages covering a portion of her face and left shoulder. Harrison stands along side her. "After we patched her, she was persistent in coming," he says, while assisting her to sit. Lillian painfully turns her head to see Arthur, grunting while trembling in anguish with every movement of her body. Her speech is slow, yet her wits are fully intact.

"General Pendleton cleared us for pursuit and dispatched a unit…to aid in capturing Ducet."

Guidry looks upon his commanding officer with compassion, standing momentarily silent. She bestows him the servitude of courage in a head gesture while her hands tremble even more.

"You may carry on sergeant – that's an order."

"Aye ma'am…we'll find him – or else."

Lillian reaches for Arthur'. "The army uses…those types…of bombs to break…small structures. Ducet is marine; we know each other's…weapons."

"We all owe you Lieutenant."

"No – Ducet has been under suspicion for a long time… He can hurt us. Pendleton knew this…"

"You knew about the enans?"

"Only about the colonel's program – for a better soldier."

"I see…"

"If he controls your creatures – must stop him…"

"We will Lieutenant, we will."

"Your *g-non* is not like the others?"

"No."

Surprisingly, Lillian chuckles while leaning back into her chair. She gently rubs the bandages as her hands faintly tremble. "I'm not…some, skinny, weak, cover girl."

"Not at all…"

"Arthur; get that son-of-a-bitch – make him pay. We should…"

"Shhhhhhh," says Arthur, gently touching Lillian's hand as her eyes close.

Harrison intervenes, securing Lillian in the seat while propping her head. "Guess the pain killers are taking effect. You don't mind me saying…we are probably alive because our golden boy couldn't tell if that syren was dead or alive. And Sergeant *Cajin* – over there, told me that this hull we're in can block a lot of transponder frequencies."

"Thank God for small miracles."

"Amen to that... Not to mention, her actions may have saved us all."

Suddenly, "Iguana at two o' clock!" Guidry's scream draws Harrison's attention. The marshal leans near the sergeant, asking, "Iguana…what are you talking about now; a lizard?"

"The name given to the Land – Amphibious All Terrain Transport; better known as the LAATT. Highly prized for its ability to dig underground and travel in pretty deep *wau-ta*. It's a fast *lil'* bugger, but we're on its tail."

"What about weapons?"

"*Nothin* we *cain't* match; but the outer hulls of both transports can take a pounding, but Praetorian is stronger. *Woun't* profit much to shoot at us; problem is…we *ain't* much faster."

Seizing a moment, Arthur asks, "Sergeant, are these the controls to one of Praetorian's guns?"

"Yep…easy to operate; press button, aim, *set n'* click – but turn *ya* safety off."

"Like this?"

"That's right *Ah'tha*, you *ain't* as slow as you talk."

Arthur activates the topside cannon and unleashes one projectile. The destined explosive impacts the starboard side of the LAATT and catches Ducet's undivided attention.
"Return fire," commands the colonel.

A direct hit off the hull of Praetorian sends the entire transport swaying off course. All inside suffer degrees of infliction. The incursion immediately draws Guidry's agitation. "WHAT THE HELL DID YOU DO *AH'THA*? Now don't you go *stahtin-nuthin!* I *sed* we can take a *poundin*, but we *ain't* indestructible!"

"Just assuring the good colonel that we're on his tail."

"I *thank* he knows that!"

Guidry sets the transport back on course and closes distance on the LATT. As he does, he attempts to contact the colonel. "Colonel Ducet, respond. This is Sergeant Thibodaux Guidry of the 438th Infantry Field Division, come in. I stand on behalf of Lieutenant Lillian Sullivan and General Caldwell Pendleton. We request that you halt your course…at once."

After several attempts, a visual image appears on screen. Staring at the crew is Rowland, standing chin high with one arm behind his back. Astonishment covers the faces of everyone as Rowland's peering eyes scan the cabin. His mannerisms display vividly as though he already knows what questions are to come. By his side is Colonel Ducet, adorning full desert camouflage and sitting with one leg crossing the other in gentleman-like fashion.

Ducet asks, *"Where's your commanding officer sergeant?"*

Before Guidry could utter a single word, Lieutenant Sullivan surprisingly, yet painfully summons enough strength to stand while Harrison assists. Ducet curiously stares at the lieutenant, who stands in a torn uniform and dressed in white bandages. Though silent and barely able to view the Colonel, Lillian's distressing state profoundly communicates the uniform code of justice. With one eye, Lillian sends the higher-ranking officer a sense of unforgivable temperament as he leans forward. Ducet addresses her.

"At ease Lieutenant, and good afternoon."

"Colonel," she replies.

"I trust your injuries were not self inflicted."

"I doubt that sir – as well as you.*"

"Surely you realize that stopping this vehicle is improbable."

"Perhaps, but certainly not impossible.*"

"Well said," replies Ducet, dauntingly smirking. He asks, *"What exactly do you think is going to happen here Lieutenant?"*

"That depends on you – sir."

"Are…you a religious person?"

"Irrelevant Colonel..."

"Oh, I think it's very relevant. The good book says all things are possible. Do you believe that Lieutenant?"

"With proper support and determination, anything is possible – sir."

"Then, do you believe that you could be in error by interfering with a covert operation, which is hidden far beyond your knowledge?"

"No."

"Lieutenant, do you..."

"Colonel, in any regards..."

"I'm not done lieutenant!"

"Sir, with all do respect, you are finished, and transports are on their way to assist in your apprehension. In case you haven't noticed, these bandages tell of something more than just a mere coincidence with a freakish animal – which by the way...is still alive. As for what I believe, you should simply turn yourself over to General Pendleton, then...the both of you can settle your dilemma. My job was to find you; and that...I have done - sir."

"Well...isn't that the problem. You see...I believe that what I'm doing is possible, probable, and needful, and soon you will too. Right now, you're too young and inexperience to break free of conventional ideas but I'll give you credit for a job well done. You haven't seen what I've seen nor have you lost as I have lost. But soon enough, crossroads will force you to the point of no return and sometimes when that happens – deaths occur. You'll understand that when you take on a true command."

"This is all very interesting Colonel, but this is not a father daughter session. You may explain yourself to General Pendleton."

"Then, tell the good General thank-you for all he's done; but there's something out there that needs curtailment and I intend to carry out that mandate. Also Lieutenant, you can very well come after me, but do know that you will...suffer the consequences." Ducet immediately walks away.

Harrison glares hard at the monitor as his stern face frowns with deep expressions. "Men like him make the uniform look real bad!"

Standing before them now is Rowland whom noticeably eyes Arthur. *"Meester Rr-obinson, we finally meet again."*

"Well...you don't appear the worse for wear, but I can't say I'm thrilled to see you."

"Always a candid remark with you...but as you say, the show goes on."

"You're living proof."

"Your work weeth the enans has proven quite prrr-omising; however, I'm sure you have many questions. But know that your presence suggests that you and yours are safe."

"Is that a confession?"

"To what?"

"You tell me."

"I am merely stating truth."

"Somehow, Tuan, Frank, Nathaniel, and Alexis may think differently."

"Perhaps they would...eef they were here."

"Did you kill them?"

"How dare you...of course not!"

"Then who?"

Silence lingers within the cab as all anxiously await Rowland's answer. Slowly, the geneticist leans closer to the monitor. *"Meester Walter Grant Pierson should know eef not by now."* The transmission ends as all eyes turn toward Walter, who stands utterly speechless.

Mystic wails fill the air as warm winds gust across auburn landscapes. Sandy shoals give way to the brazen sun while dunes cast their peaking crests throughout the grainy sea. Far in the distant from beneath high bluffs, wayfaring gunmen stare into the bright blue sky, attempting to discern the origin of the strange noise. Puzzling expressions cover their faces as disquiet eyes scowl the land through vagabond rags, piercing the empty terrain that lies all around.

Several cock their weapons while others slowly move away from the hillsides in a defensive maneuver. Communications stir amidst the large encampment as more gunmen depart into the surrounding hills. They further their investigation of the strange sounds. Few reach the summit and scan the horizon for any thing out of the ordinary – yet see nothing; but their distressing masquerade speaks for their silent voices, with only the sound of the wind prevailing.

Suddenly, shots ring out as several gunmen unload rounds into a nearby embankment of trees. Darting into the sandy plateau is a heard of camels. The gunmen, lightly humored by the incident turn to join the others below. Speaking their native tongues, the men converse as they descend the hill sides.

Cheerful gaiety rises among them; until, without warning, massive scaled bodies sail high above their heads and thunderously descend into the valley below, rapidly scurrying after impacting the ground. Chaos sprawls the land as dust pillars into a towering haze.

The enans arrive and they bring a dreadful force unlike anything seen by human eyes. Immense legs rapidly propel the beasts to several targets as their chilling red eyes pierce the brightness of the day. Gunshots blare loudly as insurgents fire upon the beasts. Though responsive, acts of desperation turn horridly sour as gunfire take down non-combatants, leaving the rampaging enans to crush several people to death – mercilessly destroying all they cannot forgive.

More enans enter the scene and pounce upon victim after victim; stomping their terrifying image into the faces of those who fall victim to their demise. The enas are indiscriminate and utterly thorough; thrusting bodies, severing limbs, decapitating heads, gouging chunks of flesh while ripping through bone; actions continuously repeating over and over until all life within the area dwindles.

Artillery cannons rain devastation in the direction of the creatures, blasting piles of rock and sand several feet into the air. So effective are the canons that each systematically destroys any thing in the line of fire; even their own; but agile movements make targeting the enans far more difficult, bringing many gunmen to a merciless surrender. Some enans pair off and attack persons fleeing while other enans perform a sweeping, thrashing motion with their tails, taking down several people at once.

Fear rises amidst the encampment. Explosions rip through several structures and tear hidden bodies apart. Remaining gunmen take refuge wherever found, but the enans quickly seek them out and constitute their horrid judgment. Sorrowful screams give way to anguishing cries of affliction, but silence under the ravaging onslaught of predatory indiscretion. Headless corpses speckle the crimson roadways as innocent and guilty lay besieged in decapitation – a hellish testament to the enan's holocaust.

Remarkably, one man and a woman escape the wave of destruction as they climb over debris and beyond the outer sandy bluffs. Looking back, both secure their salvation as they witness how vicious maulings scarred their shanty borough with human remains.

The man stands to his feet and presses his hands toward the sky. "These dogs belong to Satan!"

Tears course rivers upon his ragged face as he pitifully observes vultures circling the morbid carrion.

~~~Darkness of Heart~~~

Colonel Ducet and his men finally arrive. Both LAATTs halt within a few feet of overlooking the valley. The colonel exits the vehicle and walks to the edge of the bluff. Gazing down, he scans the carnage. Numerous clusters of fire send smoke and ash spiraling into the air, thus providing a devilish beacon for all to see. Then, the colonel observes the entire region, slowly panning from left to right as his chin begins to hang low. He barely draws a single breath.

As if summoned by a mysterious force, his hollow eyes peer towards the heavens – but nothing happens. Afterwards, he gazes upon the expanse of lifeless bodies scattered among the ruins. Some lay with their eyes open, as if telling the story of where they were when the attack came. Though intact; or not, misfortunate souls lay in inhumane piles as scarlet spatter covers the surrounding structures. Such barbarism leaves no doubt that many were fleeing for their lives, even children. "Dear Lord, what have I done," he whispers, closing his eyes while leaving only the sound of the wind to howl pass his tortured soul.

In an abrupt moment, Captain Jamison approaches. "Sir, this was definitely a major strong hold! Probably the biggest yet Colonel. You did it! There has to be well over three thousand of the enemy dead. If this doesn't merit higher headquarters approval for the enans – surely command will grant you an extension. What now Colonel?"

Ducet remains silent.

"Sir – the mission is accomplished – this is a major take down in the enemy's stronghold. There are stockpiles of weapons everywhere! This is what we've been looking for – What now?" Jamison's dire question falls on deaf ears as Ducet glares across the lifeless field.

Vultures accumulate, ravaging the cadaverous souls, gorging themselves at the expense of one man's audience.

Jamison becomes jittery. "Sir, time is of the essence, are we to terminate the enans as planned?"

The colonel remains silent. Instead, he steps towards the edge of the bluff and gets a closer view of the enans far below.

Each creature stands with hostile form; awaiting the next order. Intense red eyes pierce the noon day as blood-stained talons leave no doubt to their intentions. Their powerful tails sway in the holocaustic aftermath. While standing over dismembered corpses, all the enans mysteriously look up and see Ducet, who gazes directly back at them. There, stands his rogue demon army.

Tears course the colonel's face. His eyes relay wordless trepidations as Jamison presses for a response. "Colonel, I just got word that coalition troops are moving this way as well as a large transport. What are your orders?"

Still, the colonel does not respond.

Finally, Arthur and his group arrive at the seen as the transport Praetorian stops only a few yards behind both men. Captain Jamison orders the second LAATT to lock guns on the transport and pulls his weapon as he hastens back on board.

Sensing no retaliation from Ducet's crew, Guidry brings the transport closer to the colonel, but continues to point the topside cannons towards the LAATT.

Marshal Harrison and Arthur prepare to disembark as Lillian stands at the open door with the aid of Walter. She quietly assesses the situation. "Careful you two… This is still a hostile zone and a military operation."

"Hah, you should tour some parts of Chicago," replies Harrison.

With weapons drawn, Arthur and Harrison exit Preatorian and cautiously approach Colonel Ducet from behind. Harrison places one hand on his pistol while extending his other hand forward. Systematically, both men approach the colonel. As Arthur covers for potential unknowns, Harrison takes lead. "Colonel Ducet, this is Derrick Harrison, U.S. Marshal. Let's talk about it."

Ducet hears Harrison, and acts as though he senses Arthur's presence, yet his contrite motions yield a performance oblivious to their arrival as he slowly reaches inside his pocket and removes a small photograph. With slumping shoulders, his brown hair ruffles in the breeze, contrastingly opposite of his stony face. His eyes bear the mark of a soulless drifter who wonders between purgatory and hell, yet subtle enough to touchingly burn his image deep into Harrison's mind.

While clutching the photograph, the colonel lowers his hand. Then, in a slow, humble voice, he asks, "What is justice Marshal?"

Harrison stands silent for a moment. "Let's go back and talk about it."

The colonel's speech is slow and almost non-responsive. He takes a deep breath and glances into the distance. "Some say it's the law punishing the unjust– Right detective?"

"Possibly..."

"Even if the unjust makes the rules..."

"The law does get shady at times Colonel – fair or unfair."

"What...do...you...know...Marshal?"

"I know it was unfair for Joshua."

"If that is true, which rules do we play by?"

"The courts...but you know that... Then again, it's not my call to make."

"And yet...you are here, Marshal..."

The colonel smiles as he slowly turns around, now facing Harrison, and yet wildly exposing his watery eyes for all to see. Harrison says nothing. Ducet's chin sinks deeper into his chest.

Time passes as silence stirs. He takes a long deep breath, and tells Harrison. "The heart Marshal...the heart. It is a very, very deceitful thing. Even the good book calls it wicked. Did you know that?"

"I've heard it a time or two."

"I see... Then be careful how you follow it lawman...be very careful...how...you...follow..."

Ducet's eyes null with emptiness as sweat forms upon his forehead. He slowly blinks and looks towards the heavens, smiling, quietly speaking soundless words. Then, his eyes close.

Harrison inches towards the distraught officer. As he does, Ducet immediately pulls from within his holster a gun and points it directly at Harrison, but Arthur grows alert to the situation. "Marshal – no!" Arthur's scream alarms Harrison as Ducet quickly raises his weapon. Then, in the shadow of a moment, acute reflexes decisively give credence to three bullets piercing the heart of
Colonel Andrea Mortimer Ducet.

Lillian and Walter turn their heads and quietly retreat inside the transport.

Wind gently blows sand over the colonel's body as Harrison and Arthur rush to examine the fallen officer. Harrison removes the gun from Ducet's hand and ejects the cartridge; but then, stares in amazement while raising both hands in discontent. "Shit," he says. "What is it?" Harrison circles Ducet's body.

"He could have killed you Marshal," implores Arthur.

"Yeah…right, a trained shooter missing a target like me at close range."

"He baited you."

"Tell me about it."

"What was it for?"

"It's often said that a man's life reflects in front of him before he dies."

"What… You think the colonel wanted to die?"

"I think he saw something that made him take the eternal leap."

"I don't understand."

"The heart – Robinson. He was trying to say that deceit is the true darkness of the heart. He put his heart into his mission but it was all misguided."

"That can be said for us all, but Ducet blamed the military for Joshua's death; then he took his retribution out on the insurgents of the war, but winded up killing a lot of innocent people in the process."

"Would you or I be any different?"

"I didn't walk in his shoes, but I think he wanted you to send him to the only *One* who could judge him."

"Such a waste…"

"He could have been a spark of hope in this war."

"Could have…but look at the cartridge."

"What am I looking for?"

"It's empty."

"He didn't have to go down like this."

"Maybe, but remember one thing Robinson."

"And what's that?"

"All that glitters doesn't shine."

Harrison examines Ducet's gun and tosses it aside. A warm subtle breeze blows across the arid plains as sand covers the small photograph of Joshua Ducet.

Suddenly, an audio transmission alerts both men. *"Artha…Artha!"*

"Talk to me Guidry."

"Get in here…you need to hear this!"

Harrison hears Guidry's beckoning. "You better go son. I have a lot of explaining to do. Our troops are just over those hills and heading this way."

"Will you be alright Marshal?"

"After all I been through with you…hell, I may be looking at early retirement."

"Oh, one more thing…"

"Don't worry Robinson – your secret is safe with me. I still don't believe it."

"Thank you."

Arthur rushes inside the transport as Guidry sets the monitor audio for all to hear. [*"Judas mercy…repeat, Judas mercy commences in five seconds."*]

"Mercy is very kind, but the only Judas I know had no mercy. So what does that mean to us Sergeant?"

"While *yall wuz* talking to the colonel, I monitored the Iguana earlier. Some guy calls himself Jamison; he says the *enuns* are waiting for instructions, but it sounds like he *waunts* to do something to those e-nuns. *And it ain't pretty.*"

Perching upon their hind legs, the stout hybrids continue to await instructions as all crews within their transports observe each one from a distance. Suddenly, a faint explosion erupts within the back of one enan's neck. Blood spews in all directions as the creature's neck severs. The enan immediately collapses to the ground. Then, a gaseous cloud engulfs the beast until a blue flame appears and consumes every ounce of raw flesh. Another enan falls, and then another.

Everyone aboard Praetorian watches in sheer horror. Walter slams his hand against the console. "They're killing them off!"

Gracella asks, "What can we do?"

Arthur turns to Guidry. "Are the topside cannons still in place?" *"Yea!"* "Then hit them. Hit their transmitters." Guidry looks at Lillian who gives him the go-ahead. Then, with pinpoint accuracy, two projectiles directly impact the topside transmitters of both LAATTs.

Afterwards, Guidry sets Praetorian on an intercept course towards one of the vehicles while Arthur sits beside him at the forward console. Arthur asks, "What are you doing?"

"Closing the distance beside them so they *cain't* hit us with full impact."

"Smart guy… Now you do just that and I'll take care of the rest of them." Arthur pats Guidry on the shoulder and runs toward the cargo bay of the transport.

As Arthur enters the bay, the transport heavily shakes, sending the technician to the floor. Guidry's voice emits throughout the transport. "Brace yourselves, second Iguana at two o' clock!" Projectiles impact Praetorian's hull, pounding the wheeled fortress with an unyielding assault.

Walter scrambles towards the sergeant. "There's two of them things?" "Yep! Problem is, we kill pursuit – loose your leads, or…even the numbers." "How do we even the numbers?" "Aft section, on your left; click, press, aim *n* shoot!"

Walter quickly grabs the controls to Praetorian's topside canons. "They're still shooting at us!" "And they would be Mr. Pierson!" "Setting for fully auto...I got one of them in sight!" "Whatever you *gonna* do, you better do it – sensors show they're about to...hang on!" Guidry immediately swerves the massive transport, thus avoiding the second LAATT's frontal assault.

"Can you make that any closer?"

"Shoot the gun Mr. Pierson!"

"Fire in the hole!"

Immediately, three projectiles pound the front assembly of the LAATT. An explosion occurs; effectively tearing away metal while projecting parts of the chassis into the sand. The impacting devastation forces the vehicle to halt in its tracks as black smoke testifies of a successful strike.

"*Yeeeeeeeaaaaah!* Now that's how it's done baby!" "*Alriiiigt!* One down, one to go!" All share Walter's ecstatic celebration.

Surprisingly, with topside transmitters gone, the crew of the first LAATT manages to fire more projectiles, striking another enan to death. Quickly, blue flames engulf the fallen beast and consume every ounce of its existence.

Shrills horridly fill the air as disorientation clamors throughout the remaining herd. Like children cowering to the brandishing blow of punishment, several enans lower their heads to the ground and wrap their tails around their bodies.

Guidry watches in earnest. "What's they *doin*?"

Gracella approaches and sees the hybrids behavior. "Oh God...they're afraid...confused."

"Like soldiers cut off from their command."

"They carried out their orders, but don'tunderstand why they have to die for it."

"They are acting as if the colonel can still hurt them. *Artha* says they were receiving commands to kill those people. Like a *dawg obeyin* his *masta* but then gets punished for it."

"So it seems."

"They won't kill no more if I can help it."

"What are you going to do?"

"Take a seat ma'am – now."

"My God, you're going to ram them."

"This mission must succeed; the general's very words."

Immediately, Guidry sets Praetorian on course. However, the crew of the LAATT fires at will, but their intentions misjudge Guidry's actions and they quickly find themselves the victim's of a brutish onslaught; thus, missing Praetorian as an intended target. However, the skilled crew of the LAATT is quick to recover and spur the vehicle into the arid wasteland. Their desperate actions strike two more enans, wounding one while sending the other to its death. Observing the travesty, the remaining herd disbands and flees the area.

Dust spirals upward as both transports head into the distant hills. Soon, the vehicles are side-by-side, pounding and scraping metal as Guidry savagely rams the smaller LAATT.

In the aft cargo section, Arthur approaches Gjhe'nan. "It's time my friend and we're not going to get a smoother ride. Are you ready?" The hybrid shrieks. "Good. You're still a little bruised, but you will heal. Now listen…you will see things you may not understand, but stay focused. Find the other enans, hide them and wait for my instructions. Now go, I will find you."

Immediately, the cargo door rises, and both, Gjhe'nan and the syren leap outward. Eventually, the two hybrids locate the herd of enans and lead the beasts into the far-reaching landscape, virtually vanishing from sight. Their hastening departure takes place only moments before coalition forces arrive.

Above the surrounding hills, the LAATT and the transport Praetorian continue to exchange rounds as if each were mechanized boxers. Both transports tactfully impact the other, slamming sides while savagely scraping metal. The LAATT rams several trees while smashing through rocks, plowing the edge of a hillside, and yet discharging several projectiles into the side of the advancing Praetorian.

"We got to end this now!" Frazzled, but undaunted, Guidry's rallying cry revels his skills as he lines directly along side the LAATT. Metal shavings frizzle into the sand with each grinding contact. Eventually, Praetorian pushes the smaller LAATT into an embankment, which violently halts the vehicle in its tracks.Praetorian's topside guns purposefully express an attitude for cooperation.

Later, furious whirlwinds radiate outwardly as two aerial gun ships hover above the stricken vehicle. Ground forces deploy and apprehend the crew of the LAATT, as well as an embittered Rowland and an angry Captain Jamison.

~~~The Day of Reckoning~~~

Beige tarps sway heavily under the force of the Sunni winds, projecting a familiar scent as the smell of canvas fills the air. Inside one of the larger tents, fans oscillate the coolness of the eve while an array of sweet odors permeates the atmosphere within. Such fumes are exhilarating; yet repugnant, as the scent of body odor lingers upon sand-ruffed clothing and formaldehyde laced skin. White bandages testify of an irrefutable skirmish, displaying as badges of courage over stitched wounds.

Overhead lighting provides sufficient lumination of faces, which emerge like ghostly apparitions from the dark corners of oblivion. Full armored centurions brandish their weapons, poised to vanquish uninviting mischief. Seated around a table, Commander Dwight Ellis and General Caldwell Pendleton address Captain Jamison, whose gauze-covered hands conceal partially burnt flesh. Jamison stands at parade rest. Behind him sits Rowland, Arthur, Gracella, Walter, Marshal Harrison, and other observers.

Acting as tribunal adjutant, Pendleton's abrasive method maliciously scours Jamison. Persisting conversations silence as the general takes lead, making fully known his intentions towards the silent officer.

"You appear nervous – Well…you should be. Because now; you're on my turf. So tell me Jamsion, just what the hell were you thinking when you signed on with Colonel Ducet? Oh…by the way, our official records deem you as a lieutenant, so your field promotion to captain don't mean squat in the eyes of the Marines, since it came under a rogue commander's commission. You will be addressed as Lieutenant Jamison in this hearing. Got it?"

Jamison looks forward, never blinking, never revealing a stint of emotion. His mouth quivers as though to produce words but quickly abate under the brandishing onslaught of Pendleton's inquiry.

"Are you deaf? I can't hear you… Good, because just as you are now, is the way you should have been when Ducet propositioned you!" "But sir…" "BUT WHAT?! You finally got something to say – stupid? Well you just hold that thought you little piece-of-filth! You told us earlier that you were familiar with The Marine Corpse Close Combat Manual. If so, then you ought to be aware of the assessment level that clearly designates lethal force."

Jamison slightly nods.

"I'll be…the good little zombie has a brain and by God it's attempting to use it! Then if you can understand that, then why in the hell could you not understand the part in the clause that says; 'the subject (hostile encountee) usually has a weapon and will either kill or injure someone? At what point did that clause give you the right to assist in the murder of un-armed, non-combatant, elderly civilians and children, which may have been held against their will? According to RECON, a large portion of those people had no weapons whatsoever; especially to harm YOU!!!"

Jamison holds his peace as Pendleton makes facial gestures, perhaps in an attempt to provoke the junior officer to speak. A dreary silence lingers until Pendleton speaks again.

"LANDSAT records confirm that something went down in that settlement! Our ground forces found that place covered with decapitated bodies, blood everywhere, destroyed buildings, endless shell casings, several chard mounds of ash, and…oh get this, claw marks as well as footprints – which I might add are not in any of our data records. If I didn't know any better, I would say that they were under attack by animals! Now with regards to that, your crewmembers testify to some of the craziest unorthadox…*shit*, that I have ever heard…something about Ducet trying to end the whole war with a pack of wild kangaroo-like reptiles, as well as going after Aun'war – What the hell is that supposed to mean…and you expect me to believe which part?"

Jamison still remains silent.

"Son…even if there is a small chance of validity to those statements; you have to understand that, with the colonel gone; that left you in charge of the mission. So let me break it down for you. You resisted Lieutenant Lillian Sullivan's orders to stop and you fired upon a transport carrying civilians. We have repeatedly asked you questions regarding the colonel's secret army and you go brain dead on us, or give us some kind of statement – pulled from the back of his *ass*…that winds up in a hole. I can't work with that. Now tell me who the real enemy is."

Again, silence lingers.

"Lieutenant Jamison, you were well aware of that settlement… and by heaven's gates, you either can not or is unwilling to tell me just how those bodies were ripped to shreds in the way we found them. So – whomever you are trying to protect, surely cannot help you now. Do you have something to say?"

Jamison remains silent. Pendleton furiously slams
his hand upon the table.

"Oh…it's great for all the bad guys who died! Some call it poetic
justice, but what about the innocent men, women, and children in that
town…for Christ sake - are you hearing me son?! And let us not even
get into the number of deaths. Shielded Cross stopped counting after
three hundred – BECAUSE THEY COULDN'T MATCH THE DAMN
BODY PARTS… In a place that RECON says over three thousand
DWELLED! So how about we just focus on one person. According to
one report, there is no way those insurgents could rip the entire body
of one child into pieces in the way that they found her."

Pendleton reaches into a binder and throws several photos
in front of Jamison.

"See that…that one. See that little girl? Look at her face. Best guess,
she's six…seven. She is just one of several whom our labs examined.
The coroner says she suffered severe distress trauma around the time
of her mutilation. My guess is that she saw something; something that
scared the living hell out of her before being ripped to shreds. But you
were not aware of that – were you?"

Jamison offers a subtle blink.

"Let me tell you something else. In this part of the world, we try hard to
get our act together, because we are trying to figure out just whom we
are dealing with. You know why we do that Jamison? We do that,
because it helps us to determine whose head to take to the chopping
block. It is called discreteness, or discretion, for lack of a better word.
In this case, what gets me is that, you somehow saw fit, to go buck-
wild Sodom and Gomorrah! WHO THE HELL made you JUDGE, jury,
and EXECUTIONER?!!! "

Jamison resentfully looks at the photos. Tears creep from the corner
of his eyes as his military baring grows fragile. Pendleton continues.

"Let me tell you something lieutenant. Rules of engagement, ROE, are
what make us different from those extremists who say that Allah
sanctions their efforts. And whatever Colonel Ducet was thinking puts
us in direct violation of those rules, in effect, making his efforts alone,
produce more problems in one day than our entire military has caused
since the time of our arrival! And the whole wide world is now pointing
a finger at us for the insanity that those terrorist heathens started in the
first place. Whatever the colonel's plans were has severely
undermined our stance in this part of world. I'm quite sure that you are

asking, why we are being blamed for the incident in that village – well…go figure."

Pendleton rises from his chair, throws paper to the floor and walks directly towards the lieutenant. Within seconds, the brandishing two-star slowly leans within an inch of Jamison's nose making certain that eye contact registers, as well as lowering his voice, almost to a whisper.

"Your dog tags denote some form of religion. Well, I don't claim to be religious, but the hell that went down in that settlement is about as far from God as a horse *fuckin* someone in the ass – and I hope that when they ship you to the CONUS, you will remember the genocide of Rwanda, a pathetic situation that took place way back in the year 1994. You…disgraced the uniform – damn you."

Pendleton arises while continuing to stare Jamison in the face, though never yielding to the lieutenant's distraught face.

"Now let the record stand. YOU…are hereby charged with misconduct, dereliction of duty, insubordination, attempted murder, unlawful use of military property, and the unlawful aid in the destruction of a settlement without command authorization, which resulted in the deaths of civilians. And though your excursion uncovered a stockpile of weapons it doesn't erase the means by which you obtained that discovery. Therefore, YOU will receive a court marshal – and may God **not** intervene on your behalf, in that you **will not** escape the end of the rope! Guards, get him out of my sight!"

All watch as a broken young man is forcefully taken away. Pendleton turns to Rowland.

"Mr. Krenshencov. It appears that your *ass*-kissing lawyer, Michael Gladestone has instructed you well, thus leaving us without conclusive evidence of your involvement in this matter. Everybody is lipped-lock and that makes me suspicious about you. Therefore under military law vested in me, I hereby release you into the hands of United States Marshal Derek Harrison for immediate transportation back to the states."

Pendleton moves closer to Rowland. With hands sprawling the armrests of the chair, Pendleton causes Rowland to lean backwards and turn his head in an attempt to shun the officer's overbearing presence. As with Jamison, Pendleton gets within an inch of Rowland's face.

"Somehow, you were Ducet's accomplice...I know it. At present, detaining you will not help our cause out here. Though there's no direct evidence to connect you, I can still make your life a living hell; but we got bigger fish to fry. It's hard enough to save face value in a world full of judgmental hypocrites and ignorant idiots, especially when the world loves to hate us as much as they hate to love us, and the annihilation of that village does not help any of us...at...all. You may have gotten by, but I'll be damn if you're innocent – We will see each other again, I promise. You are the filth of a cockroach you son-of-a..."

Pendleton straightens, standing tall and domineering while eyeing Rowland. The geneticist stares back at the officer, offering no constitution for the matter at hand. Harrison places handcuffs on Rowland and escorts him away.

Gracella whispers in Arthur's ear. "Pendleton knows about the enans, but he didn't divulge his awareness."

"He wants Jamison's testimony. That way, it will legitimize his investigation into the enans, but also keep him out of it as well."

"The deal he made with you?"

"Yes...to help bring in Ducet for Gjhe'nan's esoteric existence."

"Plausible deniability..."

"That's our government."

Later, Arthur awaits departure for the states. He sits in isolation, away from his comrades. Within his hand, he holds a small visual transmitter, which broadcasts the image of Lieutenant Lillian Sullivan. Arthur, sporting a boyish smile, listens with cheerfulness of heart. The Lieutenant has his full-undivided attention.

"I know you were concerned about the report I delivered to my superiors. Just know that I can only report what I saw. Speaking of which, the doctor says I must have surgery on my right eye – as you can see. Do realize that there is no guarantee that I will receive a hundred percent of my vision back, once the surgery is over. So...I'm at their mercy."

"I'm *sooo*...sorry to hear that. I know you were only doing your duty."

"Yes, but again, I can only tell them what I saw – which after the explosion, I didn't see much of anything."

"Doe's that mean Gjhe'nan is safe from the military?"

"That means the military will intervene in what they think is necessary. Without hard evidence, you might say that they have better things to do."

"I cannot thank you enough, Lieutenant. You are...quite a lady. I wish I could know you more as a friend."

"Awww...sensitive man, well...aren't we benevolent. I hope your mission was successful Arthur and I hope you and your friends have a safe journey home."

"I will pray for you. But Lieutenant..."

"Shhhhh," she gently whispers, placing a finger to her lips and then softly touching the screen.

"Just call me Lillian and yes, you are a friend. Good-bye Arthur Robinson."

Lillian softly casts a gentle kiss to Arthur as Sergeant Guidry rolls her away in a wheelchair.

Arthur rejoins the others and sits directly opposite of Rowland. Visually tarnished, the geneticist looks upward, finding only Arthur in his field of view.

"Vwell meester Rr-robinson... Find what you were looking for – hmm?"

"You tell me. What *'were'* I looking for?"

"A monster perhaps..."

"That being the case, I found one."

Rowland grimly laughs, and then leans forward. "Then perhaps you find good reason to hate me – yes?"

Arthur stares at Rowland for a moment. Then, he glances at the floor as though attempting to gather his thoughts, as if trying to connect with a hidden agenda. At that moment, in a mild narrow tone, the technician tells him, "No. I don't."

"Sure you do. *Eet izzz* only…fitting – of course."

"Maybe; but not today, or any other day after... But there were moments."

"I see... And why should you be modest *weeth* such clemency Arthur - *hmmm*? "

"I know it sounds old and out dated, but…Jesus forgave me – and still does."

"Oh…I see…"

"It doesn't make me better than you, I'm just saying that some things should not linger. I'm also quite sure that Marshal Harrison has grilled you, the military panel has prodded you, and your conscience convicts you – otherwise you would not be talking to me."

"Stranger *theengs* happen – yes?"

"You would know, but here is something for you. What is stranger than an enan trying to kill the person responsible for its existence? Not to mention the deaths of four people who worked on a project that promised to deliver results."

"The universe is big Arthur *Rrr-obinson*."

"Sure, it is…but even if you escape all this, your involvement with Ducet will eventually implicate you. Our testimonies have been delivered."

"Yes, I am quite sure they were."

Rowland observes Arthur, silently watching as if discerning the ponderous notions of unspoken questions. The technician preludes a deep exhale before his mouth partially opens. Then, in a sincere voice, Arthur draws Roland's attention moreso. "Rowland, there is something I want you to tell you."

"Oh?"

"In light of all that has happened; I wish I were someone you could have trusted."

"I am not sure I understand."

"On a personal note, if you saw more of Christ in me, I feel as though..."

"*Ahh*...the son of God. You come here to *geev* sermon for me - Yes?"

"No."

"I was orthodox...but no longer..."

"No, I'm not here to preach to you and this is not about religion, but relationship."

"Human character *Rrr-obinson*?"

"If you saw more of Him...in me, maybe you would have trusted me enough to help you handle your situation with the enans, or even your personal dilemma in regards to Dunyasha."

"*Ahhhh*...I see. Well...it is noble entreatment, but allowing God to become ones very own scapegoat? Bah...foolishness *eet iz*! Such beliefs become *rr-ecourse* for those *weeth* troubled minds Arthur *Rrr-obinson*. Deity-ship was not my intention during days of 429, nor days before, or days after."

"But despite our differences, I could have helped you with a better approach to this whole matter."

"You speak as *eef* you would have joined the colonel and I – Yes?"

"I'm trying to tell you that I was hateful towards you and offered no alternative resolution – and I was wrong...and...I'm sorry."

"Your words make sense, but in truth...sometimes, when a man sets upon journey, *heez* purpose is al-*rr*eady set in *hiz* heart. You know this – I *theenk*. Choices are made whether man lives accordingly or not. YOU...have no control over one's decision."

"I know that."

"Very well then... So tell me...would God have spared Dunyasha and others?"

"Not all people live."

"Then perhaps seeing *Heem* in you would not have changed my actions Arthur *Rrr*-obinson."

Arthur quietly listens, peering at Rowland as though a strange manifestation instantly appears before him. Though such a thing could be far from his mind, he looks downward to the floor as if searching for something. Rowland's poorly bending physique bestows the image of a man who has nothing more to offer, watching amidst quietly as light flickers across the cuffs that bind him.

Walter approaches and sits beside Arthur. The solemn countenance of all three fosters a moment void of conversation. Then, Rowland slowly looks upward and leans directly towards Arthur. He opens his mouth to speak, but the words are slow to come. "*It* is never simple, these things. Initially, one man was too pay for murder of my *seester*, but many pay high *prr-ice*. Dunyasha was innocent, as was most in my neighborhood that day. When she took ill, *eet* was I who helped her – not doctors. They look to their books and peers but I knew some-*teen* else was *wr-ronng*. My *seester* was dying. Eventually, I find Aun'war Martinet *rr-respon*sible and set upon journey to des-*trrroy heem*."

"You mean…Aun'war, the terrorist?"

"*Da…*"

"Rowland, should you be telling us this?"

"*Eet* is okay…my fate in balance now."

"Mercy…"

"You mentioned trust Arthur. Then I trust you *weeth* this. Long time ago, Aun'war conducted experiments on humans and animals. *Heez* work *prr*-oduce chimeras – like creature you saw in photos – Yes? But *heez* post-product methodologies caused deadly radiation, *eet* poisoned many."

"Like Dunyasha."

"*Da…* When found, I go after Aun'war, but could not touch *heem*. Soviet government covers up everything. They wanted *heez* hybrid-weapon but could not use *eet*. So, I come to America to pursue means to get *heem* – make *heem* pay for *hees* crime. But I wanted hybrid weapon also."

"You were as ambitious, as the colonel."

"Soon, I meet Colonel Ducet, only to find that he too was tracking Aun'war."

"Apparently, Aun'war pissed off a lot of people, foreign and domestic."

"You could say that. The colonel makes proposal…good arrangement – he and I. GenoSyss was born…And became a staging platform for me…"

"To get revenge on Aun'war."

"Da… But there is much more."

"The colonel used the pursuit of Aun'war as a means for political reparation."

"*Eet* was justice in *hees* eyes for death of Joshua."

"Yes…I know."

"When successful creation of your *g-nan* became obvious, the colonel needed to test the cloned enans in field. Later, he raided the house of Adir Sa'ood."

"He was calling Aun'war out."

"He was also trying to make good on *hees* hybrid soldier for Department of Defense."

"But Ducet crossed the line."

"Apparently…"

"But, what was your primary role in all of this?"

"I simply wanted, as you say…poetic justice for Dunyasha."

"Is that all?"

"Long time to hold hatred – Yes?"

"My God Rowland…all this…just to get revenge on one man."

"Not just any man…no…not just any one man."

Walter conveniently nudges Arthur aside and positions himself directly in front of Rowland; pointing his finger in the geneticist's face while leaning forward and snarling with ill favor. "Poetic justice...well let me tell you something...you sick, twisted *bastard*! No matter what you call it, your personal vendetta put four innocent people six-feet under, not to mention what it's done to me. YOU deserve the same fate as those you killed!"

Redness swells upon Rowland's face. He too leans forward, gritting his teeth with eyes wide-open. "So righteous are you Walter Pierson! Sitting there judging...spewing ignorant words for testimony you know no-*theen* about – damn you as well!"

"Tell that to those you murdered!"

"I *keel* no one – no one!"

"Keep telling yourself that."

"It *eez* truth! My job was to deliver enan hybrids to the colonel and put 429-team workers *een* isolation until time of my departure...but they wind up dead!"

"You cold heinous...*motherfu----!!!!*"

"Take it down a notch Walter," cautions Arthur.

"They're dead because you killed them," screams Walter.

"SOMPLETON! There WAS NO reason for me to *keel* anyone!"

"Then why the need for isolation?"

"Not everyone *weeth* higher plans kill in order to cover their *trr-acks*. Who do you *theenk* cleans up after mess *eez* made?"

"The Community for State Security."

"KGB? Nice try, even for you Walter. As far as getting what one deserves, you should know better than most – I *theenk*. That is...*eef* your lover has not told you already."

"What did you say?"

"Come now...who else do you think I mean, or has she told you already?"

Walter glares at Rowland with a wild raging stare. His tight lips quiver with a speech bound readiness while moving under the bridge of flaring nostrils. As he clinches his fist, he comes under the watchful eye of Arthur. "Easy guys," cautions the technician, but Rowland fearlessly resumes.

"No. I *theenk* it is time science boy knows. Did you not *theenk* I know? The colonel and I find her out...discover who she was. A former life *weeth* Aun'war she had, or did she tell you, or were you so caught up *weeth* her? Even then, at GenoSyss, no secret you and Jade were like hounds in back alley."

"Watch it old man."

"*Eet* was I who destroyed her old boss' plans in the Ukraine; so, she comes to GenoSyss to kill me. Why you *theenk* the colonel co-operate *weeth* me? We took care of her."

"You killed her you...you...*son-of-a-bitch!*"

In a split moment, Walter lunges towards Rowland, wrapping his hands around the geneticist's neck. Rowland gasps for air. Arthur attempts to separate both men just as Marshal Harrison enters the room. Walter violently lashes out with verbal onslaughts towards Rowland as Harrison forcefully pulls him away, leaving Arthur and Rowland alone once more.

Arthur asks, "Are you alright?"

"Yes."

"Every thing you said, is it true?"

"Of course *eet* is."

"Why silence the team Rowland?"

"I wanted team out of way so I could destroy all documentation of 429, leaving nothing to find; putting them away long enough – until my departure."

"You wanted to remove 429's complete existence, keep it for yourself as well as Ducet, and then cover your tracks in the process."

"Bright mind you have..."

"But how does Jade fit in all this? She was our friend."

"Perhaps, yet she was more. *Eef* you knew her as the colonel and I."

"I can't believe this."

"You mentioned trust earlier – did you not?"

"Yes."

"Then I trust you w*eeth* new information, so listen carefully. We attacked Aun'war's camp in Oklahoma, but soon discovered that *hees* body was not amongst the dead. He *eez* alive – somehow, and you are not safe at all."

"Why?"

"He knows the power of your enans and make no mistake, he *weel* desire them, and come looking for you. He *weel* find you Arthur *Rrr*-obinson."

"I'm honored."

"Not joke… The colonel's death *eez* dreadful misfortune – severely hurting our operation – *heez* and mine."

"This will never end, will it?"

"Only *eef* you *brr-eeng* Aun'war to justice – or, *keel hem* in the process; your God forbid…of course."

Arthur scoffs at Rowland, laughing while turning his head. But the geneticist remains ever stern. "Why do you *theenk* I tell you? Fate of enans now in your hands *Meester Rrr-obinson*. …And your *g-nan* trusts only you – no other. These creatures can assist you in ways unimaginable. Do you understand?"

Arthur quietly stares at Rowland as footsteps echo towards the two.

Rowland leans closer to Arthur, whispering, "Before the colonel died, we trace information to states that confirms *heez* association with Phantom's Death. Follow the Phantom's Death and you *veel* find

487

Aun'war. No more of this will I speak…and may your God be *weeth* you Arthur *Rrr-obinson. Das vidaniya*."

Arthur leans backward, slumping on the bench as Marshal Harrison enters the room and escorts Rowland away.

~~~Brackish Horizon~~~

Deep within a dense jungle, an elaborate subterranean fortress hosts the next phase of a hellish scheme. A man carrying documents hurriedly makes his way through a labyrinth of concrete corridors and stairways. He passes several guards and ends his trek at a room deep in seclusion. He opens the door, only to find that the room is placid and spectacularly laden with electronics. The rear wall of the room is an enormous walled aquarium, in which several species of large fish dwell. Their watery realm projects a subtle mood as ceiling lights cast warm columns of illuminating brilliance in soft ambient forms, complimenting the entire mood of the atmosphere therein.

The carrier leaves his shoes at the edge of the entry and approaches the silent figure of another man, who stands in front of four large crystal monitors. Each monitor portrays different landmasses; representing America, Britain, Canada, and China. The man halts progress and stands behind the figure. Before he can utter a single word, the figure barely raises an arm, commanding silence as if he foreknew the man's intent to speak. The deliveryman complies and steps backwards, bowing with a sense of humility.

As he does, a faint sound draws his attention from another part of the room. Indulging his curiosity, his eyes follow the lavish paintings along the wall and the gold trim along the base moldings; continuing throughout the spacious dwelling, passing marble statues which stand upon a picturesque rug. The rug lies over plush white carpet and in front of a tantalizing fire where two granite lions stand guard. Strikingly, upon the far side of the room amongst other fabulous statues of gazelles and leopards, the man catches a glimpse of a body.

Moving to get a better view, he discovers that the body displays as a prized token amongst the other magnificent exhibits. His curiosity grows. He cautiously steps sideward, barely making a sound; and there before his eyes, a woman.

The woman leisurely reclines upon an exquisitely crafted lounging chair. She and the chair are contained within a compartmentalize prism. Gold bands hold fast around her neck and thighs allowing only enough movement within a controlled radiance. She is completely nude, yet adorned in the finest of jewels and diamond rings on her ears, fingers, and toes. Colorful jasper bracelets parade her wrists while onyx lockets lace her ankles. Her hair is as black as coal and styled as an Egyptian queen. Though bound; her tanned-skin glows in the subtle beam of a track light.

She sees the man, but displays little concern for his intrusion.

The man stares in anguish, wrestling as to whether or not he is observing what he actually sees.

Then suddenly, disquiet words chill the subtle ambiance.

"If she passes the frame of the prism, the bombs in her bracelets will explode; but do know that she bestowed her acquiesce when given an impending choice," says the figure, breaking the deliveryman's puzzlement.

Astonished by the heavy electronic sound, the deliveryman focuses back on the figure, yet continuing to look downward, careful not to stare at the figure's face.

"Forgive me Sultan Aun'war; I did not realize you had such a...exhibit."

"Forgiven," says the figure, who is Aun'war while mildly laughing as though nothing occurred.

Aun'war approaches the man. "Rise," he says.

"These are the transmittals, Masseur Aun'war."

Aun'war Martinet reveals his face. The once elegant and handsome prince now stands with such a hideous appearance. Small deep holes now reside where his nose and ears once were, prominent features that gave a complimentary addition to his royal visage. However, Aun'war's eyes continue to pierce the souls of onlookers, though sunk within twisting pink flesh – flesh that is now contained behind a clear plastic mask. A prosthetic hand lowers to receive the documents. With no lips to cover his teeth, Aun'war's' words project as muffled jargon, though still quite understandable.

"Excellent. The states of the U.S. concur with my request. It is well. We can now move in and out of any territory in the world and virtually take what we want, when we want – destroy whom we want. I would have been so kind to bargain, but my unfortunate incident in Oklahoma changed my heart."

The deliveryman slowly looks up, but doesn't make eye contact with Aun'war. "Masseur, there are skilled surgeons at your disposal."

Aun'war laughs. "Your own actions personify what lurks within the hearts of EVERYONE who deals with a monster. My poor man, surgeons will only provide a shell; a shell that cannot feel, sense, or touch. I already have such, for this plastic casing covers my entire body. I feel nothing, touch nothing…sense nothing. Look at this hand. It is merely a cover for missing fingers."

Aun'war shoves a nearby vase to the floor, watching senselessly as the fine pottery shatters.

"At first, I thought my demise was surely at an end; but now, I am resurrected in a new light. I am the reaper, the judge, the punisher, the carnage of humanity. I will remind the world of Evil's demising folly, especially those who perpetuate themselves above others; they all shall fall under my reign. And with this face, they shall never forget, with this face, they shall live in fear, with this face; they will always know darkness. And now, I will add this face to the Phantom's Death. Even as we speak, high-altitude dispensing units are near completion and will soon rain down the viral toxin upon millions!"

"But Masseur, you bring a new message of hope and the governments are now willing to cooperate."

"I allow the super powers to think that they have negotiating involvement, but they do not."

"So be it Sultan."

Impending curiosity draws the man's eyes as he briefly looks at the woman, thus alerting Aun'war's attention. Aun'war slowly walks toward his prized display and leans closely near her. She turns her head away as her bare breast rise and fall to the discontent rhythm of breathing. Aun`war takes his prosthetic finger and slowly courses her.

"There are art works…and then there are works of art. This one…is a continuing working masterpiece. Do you agree?"

"It is…as you say, your eminence," says the man.

"After bombs reeked devastation upon us in Oklahoma, the authorities found her locked away in one of the inclusion shelters. Coincident? I think not."

"But how do you know, Sultan?"

"Her intriguing talents lie not in her ability to survive, but in that she came away virtually unharmed, with no questions asked. My fate however was not as forgiving. I stepped outside my chamber just as the explosion ripped through my door. My trustees grabbed my torched body and rescued me. The fire ravaged my entire being. When I awoke, I realize that only three key people knew of our location that day. One perished in the flames, one returned from Texas, and I certainly would not have put myself in this ghastly existence. So there is only one explanation for how we were discovered."

Aun'war leans closer to the woman. She keeps her head turned away, but unable to contest his appalling mannerisms. "Ernesto, please let me go," she says.

"Ahhh…you remember my name…Jade. But that name; especially the way you say it, meant something – a long time ago."

"You will always be Ernesto Armani to me."

"Then at least this way, we will always be together."

Aun'war walks around the prism, eying his token prize. "She is a true artisan in her ability to seduce whom she will – I taught her well. And though I cannot enjoy her as I once did, I am very proud to have her as the latest crowning centerpiece to my collections."

"Don't do this Aun'war…please let me go."

"As you wish…my dear… Simply cross the barriers and your soul shall be free."

Aun'war abruptly turns towards the delivery man while laughing. "Let us go now and oversee the progression of the first dispensing unit."

Aun'war leaves Jade behind as he and the man exit the room.

On a moonless night, stars radiate far in the distant heavens. So far is their celestial dance that it dwindles long before reflecting upon the dark Mediterranean waters. Yet, such acts do not go completely unnoticed as several ships travel upon the black horizon. Some ships carry a compliment of people and cargo while other ships carry soldiers to their impending doom. Among the aquatic vessels is the U.S.S. Derringer. Its sheer size makes it nothing less than a mountain of steel as it carves a watery chasm across the surface of the sea. It even carries an audience that beholds the starry performance.

On deck, Arthur gazes into the sky as well as the black abyss, yet unaware of a presence behind him. Gracella approaches as he quietly leans against the railings. "Oh…sorry to bother you."

"It's okay Grace; I was just…standing…here."

"That wasn't hard to figure out."

"With darkness everywhere, you can imagine any world you want."

"I see… But your face is asking – Is she okay?"

"Who?"

"The only person brave enough to take on your name."

"Aniah – oh sure... She's devastated about the house and feeling somewhat vulnerable, but hanging in there."

"You will see her soon."

"I look forward to it. What about you?"

"Things happen, what else can I say."

"You do not have to pretend to be strong."

"Who's pretending Arthur? Robert is dead – nothing can change that."

"Only God and time..."

"I will be spending time with my sister; and when it all settles, keep a line open."

"For you; always... Besides, Aniah misses you. She really loves your hot sauce. You're never a stranger Grace."

"Thanks, but…Arthur, you do know that Walter and I are scheduled to depart on the next transport to the states."

"I found out this morning."

"It seems that Marshal Harrison needs our testimonies in order to put Rowland away. He is convinced that there is enough evidence to indict Rowland on the charge of obstruction of justice as well as his

493

involvement that lead to the deaths of Tuan, Nathaniel, Frank, and Alexis. But it's your testimony that Marshal Harrison really wants."

"I know, but there is something I have to do...and he knows."

"So – you are going to do it after all – aren't you?"

"It seems that way."

"Can some one else take care of that for you?"

"Name one person; then I walk away."

"Arthur, Aun'war is not just your local thug."

"Which is exactly why I have to do this."

"Do you even know what you're getting in to?"

"If what Rowland says is true, then the least I can do is locate Aun'war, especially with the help of the enans."

"I can't believe what I'm hearing...and to think that you trust Rowland after everything that has happened."

"It was not a black and white decision."

"For God sakes Arthur, let the military deal with Aun'war!"

"But Grace, haven't you heard? As cruel as it was, the destruction of that village may have finally given our forces a turning point in this war. If the military secures more areas, they can finally come home to be with their families – alive and in one piece."

"Which is all the more reason why you should let the officials handle Aun'war."

"That may not be an option Grace."

"Why?"

"It is only a matter of time before Aun'war comes after us – personally."

"How do you know that?"

"Because he knows we're alive and that we have the enans."

"I'm tired of running Arthur. If Aun'war wants to kill me, then so be it."

"It's not like you to give up a fight."

"I'm tired of fighting Arthur – I do have the right to stop."

"Quitting is not an option Grace."

Gracella shakes her head, disapproving of Arthur's assertions and walks toward the cabin door. Forcefully grabbing the doorknob, she halts her progress and gingerly looks over her shoulder. "I just lost Robert and Jade. Do I need to loose you too? For Aniah's sake, I really hope you know what you're doing."

Gracella opens the door and quickly vanishes from sight. Arthur quietly stares over the dark waters.

Later, inside the ship, a soldier approaches Arthur. "Mr. Robinson, General Pendleton is ready to see you." The soldier opens the door and escorts Arthur inside an office where the general awaits. Arthur settles into a chair, quiet, yet poised, nervous, but observant. Pendleton pours two drinks and offers one to Arthur. Soft spoken with less agitation, the general dismisses the soldier and sits casually within his chair. "Well now… You don't seem all the worst for wear Arthur."

"Thank you sir..."

"I personally want to thank you for helping us find Ducet, though his last moments were quite unfortunate."

"I'm sorry as well sir."

"You wanted to see me about something – so…what can I do for you?"

"Sir, thank you for taking time to see me.
I know you are a very busy man."

"Aren't we all?"

"General, what exactly do you know about Aun'war Martinet?"

"Hah, now you're tapping on a-need-to-know situation."

"Is it that classified sir?"

"Enough to say yes, but I will tell you this. He's a royal pain in the ass. In the end, we know only about as much as you. The chiefs of staff are working diligently on finding the guy, but information is as readily as it is available."

"Is there something I can do?"

"I don't know… Is there something you can do?"

"Surely any assistance is better than none."

"I thought you were going back to the states."

"After the recent incidents, I think I may be able to help."

"How?"

"Remember your encounter with Gjhe'nan?"

Pendleton sternly gazes at Arthur as though a ghoulish apparition appears. He leans back into his chair, wiping his face while barely breathing. "Yes…I remember that…*thing*."

"Well sir…that *thing* can help us."

"How?"

"It's complicated to explain, but in the end, I need your help to get him transported."

"Well, tell me what you got in mind."

Arthur expresses his candid deliberations before the general. As time passes, both men find themselves engrossed in the unveiling plans of action.

Far away, Aun'war leads a small band of faithful men across a catwalk. He oversees the production of an aircraft deep within the bowels of his home base. Basking in the glory of his accomplishment, praise of adulation rises as a shiny black mask conceals his fleshly appearance. He motions his arm, pointing to the operation in progress as finger-fixed appendages give the impression of human hands. The men pan the construction site while cranes move large metallic sections into place. New technologies connect high carbon alloys to the frame while welders seal the craft's outer skin.

Aun'war marvels as if granting the entire world to those who follow him.

"As you can see, we are nearing completion and after a few trial runs, I should seriously think that we can move the dispenser into position within a few days. It will have the ability to move in and out of radar like a fish in water. Once we have secured our place in the arms race and made every nation yield to our voice, then I will sell this weapon to the highest bidder."

One of the men asks, "Will that compromise our control over this instrument?"

"Not if I am the only one holding the means to destroy it." Laughter fills the air as Aun'war brings attention to a large carousel. "See the dispensing unit? This device will attach to the belly of the air ship. Using the craft's power, it will disperse over 1 billion tiny units of the Phantom virus in less than fifteen seconds. This is our finest moment gentleman."

One of the men beckons Aun'war's attention. His benign actions sanctions Aun'war's approval while inching closer. The others can only watch in astonishment. He asks, "What are we to do once this is all over?"

Aun'war scoffs at the man. "Over...over you say? Several heads of state have granted political immunity to me already. Key people in certain positions assure my stake in a much greater scheme. With one word, governments will flinch. Hundreds of thousands, of infidels...as my associate kinsmen call them; will vanish upon a single command. Our reign is never over. Democracy is for the weak. Do you not understand that only through fear can we obtain true respect?"

"Yes my lord."

"It is said...give the devil an inch and he will take a mile, and another – and another. No – my friend, our task will never end."

"Then, the original plan has changed."

"No. The original plan has always been. It is never wise to tell everything before its time. Through the course of our progress, trust worthiness became an issue."

"Even now...at this point in your quest?"

"Certainly... Even God smiles upon the strong who can rid the world of infectious-vile vermin. I can take such a role in the world while bringing every nation to its knees."

"But...to what end?"

"Until I offer them hope."

"What you suggest is that we create global chaos and then offer a solution?"

"How wisdom graces the mind of such – simplicity. I am telling you that I am the *only* one who can offer a cure for the Phantom's Death."

"Do you know what you are saying Sultan?"

"Of course small one – And what does that make me?"

"I dare not speak; for fear of a foolish tongue."

"Wisely said..."

"Then tell us...Eminence."

"It makes me, the one true Messiah..." Aun'war releases a hellish laugh as the man steps backwards, staring in disillusionment with eyes wide open. In the moment of a disquieting chill, silence covers the entire group.

Sparkling waters herald the crisp newness of blue skies as the U.S.S Derringer plows through white caps. Inside one of the Derringer's cabins, Arthur sits quietly as General Pendleton briefs four men on an upcoming mission.

"Okay...listen up people. The celestial higher-ups in DC sent our boys in Santa Monica a direct line – sanctioned by the President himself. That line contains information that caused our boys and the FBI to jump like Alabama ticks on a dog's *ass* in July. Word has it that civilians saw a man walking away from the scene of a Phantom's Death incident. In his haste, he dropped an item that contains fingerprints, but he himself manages to escape into a building where local authorities are having trouble trying to get him out. What that means to us, is that if this old boy pans out to be who we think he is, then the biggest break in the Phantom's Death and the link to Aun'war has just been delivered on a silver platter. Somebody's been praying. Also, I've been assigned to coordinate efforts with the FBI; that's where you fine gentlemen come in. I'll brief you later. For now, you are hereby dismissed."

Hours later, five massive anchors plunge into the watery depths as the Derringer berths far outside the Santa Monica Pier. Large crowds gather to watch the enormous sea fortress as it settles amidst the turquoise surges. An air shuttle taxis Pendleton, Arthur, and the four men to the entry steps of the seaside entrance. As the men walk the pier, camera flashes immediately light up the boardwalk. "Gentlemen, eat it up, because today…you are movie stars," Pendleton expounds in a savory manner, waiving his hands to the curious hoards of onlookers. Awaiting the men are two cab drivers.

Later, fluorescent lights fill a simple room where bare walls and a concrete floor are the only matching commodities. A detainee sits upon a black steel side chair. One hand is cuffed to the armrest while his ankles are chain-linked. A well-armed centurion stands at the entry door along with a casually dressed FBI agent. The agent sits upon a table, facing the detainee. Behind a one-view sided mirror, Pendleton, Arthur, and two other staff members watch as the interrogation process is underway.

The agent wastes no time with the detainee. "Again, what is your name?"

The man stares at the ceiling and says nothing.

"I'm not going to ask any more. You are here because you were caught running from the scene of a crime. One account testifies that you dropped an item before being taken by force. That's right; keep your mouth shut, because we will soon learn of your true identity. But you can make it easy on yourself just by telling us what you were doing at the scene of the Phantom's Death, because we already know that the operation is much bigger than you."

The man says nothing, only staring into an imaginable void. His face gives no assurance that he is even registering what the agent is saying.

General Pendleton addresses Wiley Garrison, the center's director. "Wiley, are they all ways this tongue-tide?"

"Apprehension alone is usually enough to get results. But occasionally, they can be a tad bit stubborn. However, there are other matters regarding this one. But I'm quite confident he will eventually – educate us."

"How soon do you think?"

"I consider myself a man of legal persuasion."

"What you're telling me is that this interrogation can take much longer."

"That is quite possible…"

"Well…pray that he doesn't contact some idiot lawyer."

"Yes, I know…the evidence is cold by then and we simply hold him on suspicion."

"…And then, you eventually set him free."

"That is usually how it works."

"But your men are sure he was at the scene of a Phantom's Death incident."

"The report says he was running from a small enclosure and witnesses verify that he was carrying a riffle of some sort. The weapon was never recovered but his behavior towards the whole matter is questionable. In any event, we may not be able to hold him for long."

"I see... Perhaps this is not what I thought. As you know, anything regarding the Phantom's Death is very concerning to the military. Thought I'd drop by to see what was going on."

"Oh really? Come now… You simply stopped bye – did you?"

"I miss you Wiley – didn't you know?"

"I have known you far too long Caldwell Pendleton and surely, this matter does not merit the full response of a nine million- ton ocean battle fortress parked outside the bay area."

"Hah…the crew needs a little r-and-r and we…just happen to be in the neighborhood."

"I bet you were."

"Thank-you for your time Wiley."

"The pleasure is all mine. By the way, we cannot thank the military enough for the jobs they do. I will see to it that you find your way out."

Pendleton and Arthur exit the building.

7:45 pm. The detainee is held in lock-down. Armed guards parade before the chamber; each tapping the cell wall while harrasing the man. The detainee sits quietly on a bench as an overhead monitor pipes in mundane sitcoms.

Surprisingly, Arthur enters the building and approaches the front desk. The night guard confronts him. "May I help you?"

"Yes – I think my car keys in one of your rooms. Can you help me?"

"I don't recall any lost and found reports. Besides, visiting hours is over, so you need to come back tomorrow, and then you can make a full report of the matter."

"I understand… At least for now, could you please check for me? I have a long way to walk home."

"Is there no one you can call?"

"That's just it, my phone, wallet, everything is in the car."

The guard continues to ask Arthur several more questions and soon attempts to usher him out the door, but Arthur recants a savory manner. He is quite good, but his efforts are failing as the guard begins to grow tiresome.

"Sir, I'm going to have to ask you to leave – now!"

"But you don't understand…I need my keys."

As Arthur contests for the items, two men, each wearing masks enter the facility and sneak past the commotion. Both men make their way to the cellblock where the detainee is held, but soon encounter a guard. "Hey," the guard shouts.

He attempts to retrieve his side arm. One of the intruders stuns the guard and takes his keys. His partner efficiently apprehends the detainee at gunpoint. Afterwards, the men set off charges that emit dense clouds of smoke. The smoke rapidly fills the corridors as unsuspecting guards succumb to thick fumes. With little resistance, the detainee accompanies the intruders into the lobby and exits the building.

They shove the detainee into a nearby car and depart.

As the vehicle enters a neighborhood, the detainee grows suspicious regarding his situation and decides to question his apprehenders. "Who are you and why do you not remove your hoods?"

Neither man answer, but instead, they drive a few miles more until the ravening sound of yet another vehicle halts directly in front of the car. "Get out," says the driver. The detainee complies.

Out of the second vehicle, two more men exit and take the detainee. Both vehicles quickly exit the scene.

While in route, one of the men addresses the detainee. "Aun'war sent us for you, but you are not to see him yet."

"Who were those men that took me from the holding cell?"

"They were working for us. We could not risk being identified and it is important that you get to your location. We were followed, so you have to be quick."

"I'm not sure I understand what you are saying."

"If we take you to Aun'war, we risk exposure; so, we're going to have to release you. From there, you're on your own."

"Clever…you sound like us and you look like us, but how do I know that the sultan has sent you?"

"Go to hell for all I care… Nor do I give a rat's ass – about your suspicions! If you cannot raise your contacts, this money will at least get you far from the city – so…shut up and take it and be grateful his majesty did not allow you to rot in jail; or maybe you prefer the just punishment for a failure such as yours."

The men stop the car and allow the detainee to exit.

502

Standing in the road, the detainee watches in utter amazement as the car rolls away. Confused, he scans the surrounding area and walks away in an inconspicuous manner.

Meanwhile, the four men and Arthur return to the U.S.S. Derringer.

Later, General Pendleton debriefs the four men as well as Arthur. They all observe the former detainee's behavior on screen. One of the men addresses Pendleton. "Sir, the trackers are in place. We also have a man in the field transmitting the audio link to us. It would appear that our John Doe detainee is just wondering around. He has been that way for a couple of hours."

"I wonder what is going through that head of his."

"He may be suspicious of being followed or watched, or he may be determining how to make contact with his connections."

"I surmise that you are not pleased with the outcome of the operation – sir?" Pendleton scoffs aloud as he hears the report. "I have seen animals behave more predictable."

"You don't trust the INTEL on this guy – do you?"

"He may prove useful, but the local police move too slow on these maters and there is not enough on John Doe to hold the FBI's interest."

"I am sure we did not help the situation by breaking him out of jail."

"I thought you wanted to see where he would lead us – Did you not?"

"I did…and it's always better safe than sorry. I fear that Aun'war is planning something big and we don't have a lot of time."

"Maybe John Doe is aware of that."

"Take a good look at him. He is groom too nice to be homeless and I doubt that his spouse, if he has one, is worth his wondering blindly about the neighborhood for such a long time."

"More than likely, he is suspicious."

"Wouldn't you be?"

Arthur moves near the console, asking one of the men, "Where is he going?"

"He's making tracks to that convenience store.
Let's see what he does."

"Why would he enter that store?"

"We will soon find out. The transmitter we tagged him with is untraceable and should give us a visual even from inside the building."

"He's making a call."

Soon, a van enters the parking lot and the former detainee hurriedly gets in.

"Well I'll be…the rat has taken the bait," says one of the men.

"Get satellite to track him," says Pendleton.

"Already on it sir…"

Within moments, the van rolls into a driveway near a refinery and halts just shy of an old warehouse. An overhead lamp casts a silhouette of three men exiting the vehicle and entering the building.

Pendleton and the others watch the events through the monitor with great interests. Then, one of the men grabs his earphones. "Sir…incoming audio…" All listen carefully to the information until the words; *"Aun'war is attempting to move in two weeks…"* brazes the airways. Pendleton slams his hand on the table. "Enough said! They know the heathen and that's all I need."

Pendleton immediately activates a transceiver.
"Wiley Garrison, how are yah?"

"Greetings again Caldwell… It would appear that your hunch is correct."

"You have enough to bring *'em in?"*

 "We certainly do – at least for further questioning, I should think."

"Can your boys handle this little situation or should I use mine?"

"You keep your cowboys to yourself and let the real professionals show you how to apprehend in a more civilized manner."

"Just shoot the s.o.b."

"After all these years, you have not changed at all."

"Yeah…well why should I? I like me just the way I am."

"And God surely has mercy on your putrid soul.
Until further notice – out."

"Yeah…well I love you too, you lanky-ass Britt."

A detachment of Garrison's Special Forces encroaches upon the warehouse. Their methodology produces little excitement; however, with great stealth, the forces advance closer and systematically dispense canisters within a nearby window. Plumbs of smoke pour from within the building as exterior lights goes out. Darkness paints eeriness throughout the area. Infrared instruments hone the eyes of elite squads as their deadly riffles lay in wait of anything unsuspecting. Suddenly, a loud noise erupts and the main front door of the building forcefully swings open. Heavy smoke precedes the hastening exit of several men; yet, some of the men frantically spew vomit while falling to the ground. Tactical units quickly deploy and apprehend all occupants inside the building. Wiley Garrison's former detainee is among them.

On the following morning, all in apprehension present nothing more than that of the earlier day. The detainee and those with him sit idle, providing no words, no confessions, and no cooperation. Silence is the only bounty that the tactical units seem to have harvested.

Pendleton furiously takes his point to Wiley Garrison. "Hot *fuckin* meals and a shower! After all this time, you'd think we learn by now that this is what the American taxpayer provides for terrorist. Wiley, there's a nut case out there liquidizing people and for crying out loud, we finally have the best link to that sadomasochist *son-of-a-bitch*, that we ever had, and now you're telling me that the detainees have a right to obtain fair representation! In case you don't get it my friend, time is of the essence!" Pendleton slams his hand upon the desk, shaking nearby glasses while shattering a once tranquil atmosphere.

Then, Wiley Garrison transmits. *"Calm down – will you, and for Pete's sake watch your language. Our raid was not entirely fruitless. At least we know how they deliver the viral toxin to its victims, and soon, we will know more about the chemistry makeup of the Phantom's Death. Now regarding the acquisition of information from our detainees, there has to be more of a humane approach. Yes, I want them to pay for their crimes as you; yes, I want Aun'war as much as you, but we cannot extract that information as barbarically as other uncivilized countries. Remember, the face of democracy has to be smarter in the face of stupidity – you know that already, so spare me your childish whimpering."*

"Cry me a got–*damn* river! Those men who we detained, are all descended from Al-Qaeda and will stop at nothing to kill you, me, our families, and…hell…they'll do it…just because..."

"Caldwell..."

"Hold on Wiley… I hope you can appreciate why I joined the military and not the police department!"

"Thank you for your insight – That went over very well. Now, when you acquire a chance to think, do understand this one very important thing."

"Go ahead, I'm listening."

"Did you happen to know that there are a few Americans among those apprehended?"

"Well…shoot their ass too!"

"This bickering is pointless. You know the laws just as I. If only there was another way to interrogate these men without physical indictment."

"My experience says otherwise – sometimes, torture is necessary!"

"What do you propose, drill their skulls, water droplets, tar and feathering, or perhaps tickling them to death?"

"A lobotomy sounds good!"

"The Joint Chiefs trust you to represent them in this matter, so give me something to go on."

Pendleton scratches his head, and then wildly rubs his face. He clicks off the monitor and paces the room in sheer agitation. After several minutes, the brazen officer looks at Arthur and the other team members in the room. Taking a long deep breath, Pendleton slowly wipes his forehead, saying, "Gentlemen…it appears that they have us by the balls."

~~~Terms~~~

Arthur acquires shore leave from the Derringer. Operating a small watercraft, he maneuvers the vessel around the sandy shoreline until finding an area deep in seclusion. Arthur lowers two fingers into the water and performs a circular motion while periodically tapping the surface. As his performance is well underway, cascading waves gently sway the sleek craft to the evening tide of an oceanic rhythm while stars begin to cast an ominous spectacle high above the heavens. Arthur's prevailing ritual continues until prominent ridgelines break the surface of the water and a distinctly smaller wave moves out of sync.

The wave moves directly towards the craft. Arthur continues tapping the surface until the wave dissolves only a few feet away. As though to conjure a mystical event, he holds his hand above the water until pulsating ripples begin to appear. Soon, whiskers rise from beneath the surface, followed by a nose, and then a face, which inevitably pushes Arthur's hand upward. He smiles. "Gjhe'nan, there you are." The creature's eyes radiate a subtle luminescent blue in the darkness as masculine hands gently rub hardened scales. As always, the hybrid nudges Arthur as to encourage a warm gesture from his maker's response. "Are you well?" The hybrid acknowledges while maintaining buoyancy beside the craft. Arthur wondrously gazes into Gjhe'nan's eyes. "We are getting closer," he says.

At the detention center, the men who were taken into custody earlier from the warehouse lay in quiet slumber as guards observe their holding cell. The detainee, apprehended on both accounts, also lay sleeping. A guard makes his routine rounds throughout the facility as silence fills the atmosphere – until, he places his attention on the exit door.

Faint sounds eminate from the other side of the door, catching the guard's attention. He watches with extreme caution. Suddenly, the steel hinges that secure the door thrust outward, spewing concrete rubble in his face. The officer frantically clears his eyes. As he does, he witnesses a large indentation protruding through the metal surface.

"What the hell? Code 799, we have a..."

Immediately, a loud noise ruptures within the hallway as the door propels forward, violently sending the guard to the ground. His alarming call for help is cut short as he now lays motionless beneath the battered piece of scrap metal.

507

Entering with uncontested dreadfulness is Gjhe'nan. The hybrid steps directly on top of the door and makes a path towards the detainees' holding cell.

Alarms scream, insanely warning all within the building that danger is near. Guards quickly muster in earnest to apprehend the situation. The detainees are behind a large wall-size translucent panel.

Upon approach, Gjhe'nan pommels the wall until the entire barrier moves, allowing just enough separation from the walls.

Soon, several guards swarm the room, but succumb to the bizarre appearance of the beast. Sensing a hostile threat, the creature smashes all lights, destroys security cameras, and then presses through the makeshift opening. Screams fill the darkness as bodies are randomly hurled against concrete. The sheer force of impact rips flesh apart, tainting the floor with blood until a slippery cover spreads. Those on their feet spontaneously mount a feeble escape, but their efforts turn horridly futile. More guards enter the room only to find that darkness impairs their vision. Several pleas for help ring out, but assistance cannot be found. With nothing more to loose, the guards unleash hell fire. An enormous pile of lead penetrates the translucent barrier, until it shatters into a crystallize pile. "Something big is in there," yells one of the officers.

Flairs dispense into the darkness; and to their favor, the momentary blast allows a brief glimpse of the hybrid. Immediately, the guards fire upon the beast. "SHOOOT THAT DAMN THING!!!"

The brandishing onslaught is relentless, but Gjhe'nan locates the detainee and secures him. Then, in an amazing feat of strength, Gjhe'nan protectively covers the man and smashes through the rear wall. Several rounds of gunfire follow as the hybrid forcefully tears through the ceiling and into the main hallway. With only a few leaps, Gjhe'nan exits the building as guards pursue; but their attempts are cut short as they helplessly watch the beast disappear into the night.

Gjhe'nan finds Arthur waiting at their previous rendezvous. The hybrid holds the detainee above the watery surface, but does not allow him to see Arthur. Arthur leans over the edge of the watercraft and gets close to the man's ear. "I know you understand English and I am quite sure that you are committed to your ways. But before you die…ask yourself – will your death eliminate all the infidels you hate?" The man says nothing. "Good, then we are off to a wonderful start. I'll make this simple. Give me Aun'war's location, so your death will not be in vain. But if you do not know where he is, then give me the general area. I know that you intended to meet him, somewhere." Still the man says nothing. Then strangely, the man begins to vigorously shiver and shake uncontrollably.

"Right about now, you should feel claws pressing into your liver. I will see just how much pain you can take." Arthur shoves a rod into the man's mouth, forcing him to bite down on the metal shaft. Then, he wraps a scarf around the man's face as to prevent him from screaming. Gjhe'nan pulls the man beneath the water, momentarily submerging from sight. When both reemerge, the man's eyes are extremely wide and void, and his body feverishly shivering as he trembles uncontrollably. "Still have nothing to say? Take him down." Again, the hybrid pulls the man under. Moments later, both reemerge, but this time, the man glares coldly at Arthur. Soon, mumbling words raggedly project outward as Arthur removes the scarf. "Ready this time? Good for you." Satisfied, Arthur retrieves a pen and a torn piece of paper from his pocket. Holding both items, he prepares to write.

Later that night, several observers gather near the outside pavilion of a local restaurant. Paramedics rush to the scene as policemen stave off curious onlookers. After pressing through the crowd, the medical staff discovers a man's body slightly imbedded in the wall of the restaurant. Perplexing faces tell all as medical personnel remove pieces of mason from around the distraught figure. As though suspended in time, all eyes sternly fixate on one location. Remarkably, Wiley Garrison's former detainee is alive.

On the following day, the U.S.S. Derringer casts off for open waters. Its ironclad hull plows the salty waves as sea birds bid the arborous journey blessings of benevolence. The crew performs their daily tasks.

Inside, General Caldwell Pendleton sits before a crystal monitor with keen interest. Wearing an under-shirt and boxers, the general pronounces his appearance before his cyber spectator; Wiley Garrison, without conviction. "Wiley…what are you telling me? I'm looking forward to a good day," he growls.

"If you remove the cigar, I can understand you better."

"Done."

"Thank you. Now listen, I'm telling you for the fourth time already, our former detainee was wearing no pants. Again, I say, medics found him partially imbedded in a wall with slabs of skin ripped from his thighs. The torn pieces of flesh stem all the way up to his groin."

"My…my…oh my; poor bastard."

"I am serious! The man's testicles were found hanging beneath his kneecaps. And aside from the fact that he will never bare children, a torn piece of paper with numerical values were recovered from his trousers earlier this morning."

"I thought you said he had no pants – so… How would you know that?"

"I just happen to know that, because I discovered his trousers on my desk, ripped to shreds with his blood on them. God only knows how they got there."

"Sounds like you had a busy night. So, tell me –
What does the note say?"

"Our analysts conclude that the numbers are coordinates of some sort, latitude and longitude values of a geographic location."

"Really... Were exactly is this location?"

"That information is being analyzed as we speak."

"Why wasn't this mentioned last night after the raid?"

"Because there was nothing in the man's pockets after the raid…unless…you know something."

"Who…me?"

"Who else?"

"Well…I was here…jacking off – What do you think?"

"I think you were hatched, and certainly in need of counseling."

"Don't we all."

"I do not have time for you. Listen to me Caldwell, if this means anything to you, then you best look into it. As for the other detainees, there are a lot of cuts and bruises on them, but they will live.   For the most part, our holding facility is in direct need of repair. Several surveillance cameras were destroyed, and the reports I am hearing are anything but average."

"Sounds like you will be busy."

"I will. Until next time old friend..."

"Thanks for everything Wiley. Thank you for all your hard work."

"Godspeed to you as well – old friend."

The transmission ends.

Pendleton sits in his chair and slowly wipes his face. He faintly stares at the ceiling and slowly takes a long deep breathe, exhaling while whispering aloud, "What have you done Arthur Robinson..."

~~~The Phantom's Shadow~~~

Deep beneath a jungle canopy, large doors slide apart within a hillside. The outer metal surface mimics the surrounding area so well that the appearance of the earth opening is all that becomes visible. From within the blackened pit, an unusual machine rolls beyond the doors and jettisons on a vertical assent high above the canopy. The craft speedily soars into the distant sky.

Later that evening, the mysterious craft returns, descends and reenters the earth through the sliding doors. As the doors close, the machine powers down only yards from the entrance. Workers rapidly provide attention to the aircraft.

Aun'war and an entourage of men approach the machine as the pilot climbs out.

"*Assalamu alaikum (peace be with you)* Sultan," says the pilot.

"*Walaikum assalam Shemi* or as we say in my homeland; bonjour *shemi, a emploi bien done,"* replies Aun'war with outstretched arms.

"Today is a good day. We have infected hundreds of thousands with the Phantom's virus. Soon, you can infect millions with one disperse, but for now, you can have anything you desire and no one will appose you. They will have to turn to you in order to live."

Aun'war smiles and turns to his band of followers. From beneath the black shiny mask, muffled words project loudly as Aun'war captures their attention. "See what a little persuasive jester can do? Today the world witnessed the beginning of the cleansing. Today, they have seen the paradox of heathen nations come to an end as well as the start of a new global order. When one third of this world is with me, the others will either follow - or die. *Le époque de age a venir (the time of age has come)*," he says as a celebration erupts from everyone.

Aboard the U.S.S. Derringer, General Pendleton addresses his staff. "Well...it's official. The Phantom's Death struck again, in yet; another unlucky coastal city, taking nearly nine hundred and eighty thousand lives in matter of minutes. I know that sounds terrible, but it's fortunate for us. Shortly afterwards, LANDsat caught a mysterious unidentified craft of some sort, flying just below the equator. Well...it disappeared. We're not entirely sure if the craft is associated with the Phantom's Death, but serious questions did arise. In conjunction to this strange

UFO, Wiley Garrison's forensic analysts removed geographic coordinates from the pants of our…former detainee."
Laughter fills the room.

"At ease…at ease people – get your heads out of the gutter. People are dying – don't forget."

A woman in the audience asks," Sir, how did the coordinates get into the man's pants?"

"Still a mystery, in itself, but Wiley's team concludes that the coordinates point somewhere to an area in the Morona Santiago jungles of Ecuador."

"Do the Joint Chiefs or the Secretary of Defense deem this information credible?"

"The Joint chiefs believe it's worth looking into. The Secretary – haven't heard from him as of yet."

"So – what are our options?"

"We are sending in a small unit to check out the information. If there is nothing else, you are dismissed."

As the room clears, Pendleton approaches Arthur.

"Mr. Robinson, you got a minute?"

"Sure."

"I don't have much time, so I'll get to the point. A lot of questionable things happened at the detention center, especially with regards to where and how the detainee was found. Would you happen to know anything about that?"

"No sir…"

"Is there anything you want to tell me, or that I even care to know, with regards to that matter?"

"No."

"Then you have the qualities of a good lawyer and the mannerisms of a politician, but make no mistake; this is my turf. Screw up – your ass is mine."

Pendleton daunts an impish grin, staring Arthur directly in the eyes. Arthur remains silent as the general turns and walks away.

In the jungles of Equador, the sheer force of a torrent down draft frazzles palm leaves as two aerial gun ships land in one of several plush green outcroppings. Dozens of armed men, dressed in camouflage regalia, deploy from the airships and forcefully penetrate deep into the dense jungle. Each team methodically plows their way through twisting vines and wild folding trees, slashing and parting the leaves in order to make progress. Their journey finally brings them to an opening. One of the men relays information to the U.S.S. Derringer where General Pendleton observes with intent interest.

"Sir, we are nearing the coordinate zone."

"Proceed with caution Captain," replies Pendleton.

Minutes turn to hours as the men meticulously search the area, watching, waiting, and scanning the unusual terrain. Time painfully passes. "Sir, if something is here, we would have found it by now."

"Of course captain. Increase your search radius by fifty, then by four-hundred yards."

"Yes sir."

The men comply. Soon, dusk falls and the captain relays more information. Pendleton listens but disappointment quickly sets in. He takes a deep breath and strikes the table with the palm of his hand. *"Oh well... I thought this was a worth-while lead. Captain, wrap up and come home."*

"Very well sir..."

The Captain recalls the men and they depart, unaware that darkened eyes watch from well-hidden instruments.

Deep underground, Aun'war and his trustees stare at several surveillance monitors. One of the men beckons his master's attention. "Sultan, they are leaving. What are your orders?"

"Do nothing."

"But they are getting away."

"Their deaths will only attract others."

"They did come."

"Yes, they found where we are. Now how do you suppose that happened?"

"I do not know."

"If a purpose is no greater than the life it sustains, then what reason does the purpose have to exist? And if a cancerous cell can infect the whole body, will not that body eventually rot? It appears that there is an infection amongst us and I must purge it before it destroys us all." Several of Aun'war's men back away as their sultan tightens his left-handed grip atop an elaborate cane. Aun'war walks towards a nearby wall where more monitors display satellite imagery. He presses a few buttons and three monitors simultaneously illuminate, each displaying the faces of three other men. The men see Aun'war and addresses him *"Sultan,"* paying tribute with the bowing of their heads and the pressing of a clinched fist over their heart.

With outstretched arms, Aun'war beseeches them. "My brothers, salute not me, but rather the cause of a higher purpose. Our recent deployment of the aerial dispenser proved most effective. Your task in the field is now complete and you are to return here. Each of you has proven your worthiness with much valor. Now…before you return, see to it that you cover yourselves. Bid those who have served you well their due benevolence…into eternity's embrace."

Each man preludes a gesture of allegiant subordination. Then, the terrible sound of cocked firing pins systematically echo through the speakers. Afterwards, pitiful screams of many fade to silence as each transmission discontinues, one by one.

Aboard the U.S.S. Derringer, Arthur sits quietly in a waiting area. With two fingers, he rubs the temple of his forehead as though lost in a distant world. His relax posture suggests a nonchalant awareness that someone else is with him. Rapid keystrokes in periodic spurts constitute nothing less than Corinne Sears performing administrative duties. As Arthur tilts his head, he focuses on her hands. High glossy cuticles taper into finger tips, complimenting the sleek form of every digit. Green veins barely rise underneath the surface of pastel skin as ambient light reveals a fleshly smoothness, a genetic trait that is typical of divine perfection.

516

Arthur's fixation soon collapses as a buzzer sounds off. Corinne presses the tiny fixture. "Yes sir…he's here. Okay. Mr. Robinson, you may go in now. Right this way," she says.

Arthur enters Pendleton's office and sits directly across from him. "Thank you for seeing me again General."

"Sure… Can I offer you a drink or something?"

"No, no…no thank you."

"Okay – let's get to it then. I received your message the other day about leaving. Before you go, I just want to know what are your intentions for the…the…"

"Gjhe'nan…"

"Ah…yes…the…*g-non*…enan things as you call them."
Arthur leans back into the chair and clasp both hands behind his head. Taking a long deep breath, the technician slowly crosses his legs. Then, in a brisk, sharp voice, he tells him, "To find Aun'war."

Pendleton lets out a hearty laugh. "Arthur, I figured you to be a church *fella*. Everybody knows good Christians don't lie."

"Who says I was lying?"

"Well…number one, you are no kind of law enforcement - whatsoever; number two, you have no resources, and number three; you don't have a *damn* clue as to where he is."

Arthur lowers his hands and firmly places both feet on the ground. "General, give me transport to Ecuador. I'll take Gjhe'nan with me and together we will find something, if it is there."

"Robinson, you sure know how to change a subject. Can I have what you're on? Hell son…you are telling me that; you can find something that sixteen highly trained Special Forces soldiers couldn't?"

"I'm telling you that if something is truly there, Gjhe'nan will find it."

"That *g-non* must have a gold plated nose."

"He has abilities that your marines don't."

"Is that a fact?"

"There are things he can do that even I am just now beginning to understand."

"Does he walk on water?"

"General...please..."

"I see... Does the *g-non* have any abilities that may have had something to do with what happened at Wiley Garrison's detainment center? Or is there more to those coordinates than what we were led to believe?"

"Possibly..."

"You place a lot of faith in this g-non creature of yours."

"My faith is in God General, and I trust Gjhe'nan's proven skills."

"Spoken like a man with experience..."

"As far as his fate, GenoSyss was not very kind to him – so...what ever happens I personally feel that it should be his decision."

"His decision?"

"Why not?"

"You speak as if it is a...a..."

"...Human?"

"Arthur, we are extremely grateful for your role in the apprehension of Rowland and Ducet, but I still do not know much about this creature. Why exactly was it created and where are the others?"

"All I can tell you sir is that he can help you and it will not cost you anything."

Pendleton sternly eyes Arthur. The general leans backwards, openly pondering the technician's words. Then, in a stern voice, he tells Arthur, "I see in you a determination that makes for restlessness. Yet, such energy can be beneficial when used properly. I cannot give you a personal transport, but we do have cargo ships going into that area. Maybe I can arrange something for you. All I ask is that you don't go doing something stupid. But should something happen to you, I need to make sure that you do realize what you are getting into."

"Yes I do sir."

"Then as of today, my official word is that you departed the Derringer under you own volition – against better judgment. You are therefore no longer under military protection. Is that all?"

"Yes sir."

"I hate to see you go son...but; a man's gotta do what ever mission besets him. Godspeed to you Arthur Robinson."

A handshake confirms all that Arthur requires as both men depart from each other, perhaps for the last time.

Sea birds perform aerial spectacles, hovering only inches above white caps as turquoise waters stretch far into the horizon. The sun provides no less than a brilliant performance, complimenting the fluid surface with glistening highlights. Leaning against topside railing, Arthur closes his eyes and breathes in the salty mist as deeply as his lungs can pull in. He relishes the moment until the journey finally ends in the Ecuadorian Port of Guayaquil.

The cargo ship, *Semeyontal-jenah* docks into harbor where the loading and unloading of prized merchandise takes place in a timely manner. Arthur departs the ship and finds seclusion within a nearby motel. His simple accommodations suites him well as he unpacks and finds comfort in a single bed.

Eating and resting fills the day, until nightfall, the time when he decides to venture out. As he makes his way along the coastal shore, he finds an area hidden well in seclusion. Arthur removes from his backpack a hand-held instrument and submerges the device just beneath the water. He presses a button and the device begins to pulsate.

Time passes and Gjhe'nan finally appears. Arthur pulls from his backpack several pounds of meat and a large sack of oatmeal. "Here, yum yum...eat up." Gjhe'nan eats heartedly.

Gristle and fat; all disappear. "Whoa! Slow down...I cannot burp you. Hiding you in the cargo bay of the Derringer's hull and having you swim all the way here has taken a lot out of you." The hybrid shrieks, but then inscribes something in the sand. Arthur flashes a tiny light and reads the inscription. "Eat, rest, go… Yeah, the sooner the better." Both rest for the evening.

As the following night approaches, Arthur prepares to disembark. Gjhe'nan hoists Arthur upon his back. Tightly holding makeshift reins, Arthur lowers his head and the beast lunges into the night air, disappearing while traveling into the outer edges of the city, and finally into the dense jungle. The hybrid moves as easily through the foliage at night as humans move by day whiletaking sustenance from the surrounding terrain in the process.

Later, both arrive at their destination. "I have the lat and long values. The GPS says we have to stop here. Okay boy, instead of looking for something tangible, we will move a little stealthier. Use your eyes to look for metallic signatures or any thing out of the ordinary." The hybrid scans the area several times, moving in small increments. Gjhe'nan's approach is methodical, much like Arthur's, but more thorough. Arthur flanks the hybrid, scanning for metallic objects through night vision sensors. Time passes, but then, something catches Gjhe'nan's eye. "What did you find?" Gjhe'nan parts the brush and unearths a tiny object. Arthur further examines the finding.

"A pipe of some sort. There's air coming out of it. I see why Pendleton's men missed it. Only your eyes can differentiate this type of material from the surrounding brush. There are no nearby facilities, at least way out here. The air is warm and the flow is strong."

Suddenly, white light floods the area, temporarily blinding both Arthur and the hybrid. "Gjhe'nan…you know what to do – GO!" Arthur's scream sets the hybrid in motion. Shouts ring forth amidst the ominous glow as dark figures rapidly emerge with weapons cocked and ready. "Get on the ground – now," demands one of the figures, shoving the butt end of his weapon into Arthur's back. The mysterious men forcefully take Arthur away while sending deadly rounds in the direction of Gjhe'nan's departure.

Later, Arthur finds himself lying motionless on the floor, though slightly trembling in the presence of his captors. Small prayers rise in a disdaining manner as he stares downward, making no attempt to draw unwarranted attention. But his subtle pleads to beckon divine intervention heightens well into the ears of the lord of his captors.

Aun'war enters the room and circles Arthur as a predator circling prey. "You may summon His Majesty all you want but He will not come. I have found that it pleases Him to watch those committed to His sorrowful religion to suffer prior to their pitiful end. You are no exception – my dark-skinned brother. I can say that because never in a million years would I have expected seeing you here – of all places. That means that you and I are alike in many ways. It also means that I can make this very easy for you. Simply tell me what I want to know and I may find a place for you in my regime. If not, then your death will come quickly."

Arthur says nothing, leaving Aun'war less enthusiastic. The masked sultan forcefully drives the tip end of his cane into Arthur's shoulder. Cringing even lower, Arthur embraces his shoulder, but Aun'war leaves nothing to imagine.

"In time, I would have come after you; but your presence here makes me aware that you have substantial knowledge about me – else why would you come? I also realize that a beast accompanied you hear and took flight upon your command. A fantastic creature of some sort, but I doubt that you will grant me the honor to know what and where that creature is." Arthur remains silent.

"So, perhaps a new proposition for you... Deliver that creature to me, and I will keep you alive so that you may serve me, personally – a benevolent offer for you, I should think."

Again, Arthur does not speak. Only mildly trembling in the presence of his captor, but Aun'war refuses to desist. "Perhaps…my initial introduction to you may have been a bit overwhelming; therefore I shall try this one last time. I am Aun'war Martinet, as you may have already guest by now. I can give you much in return for your cooperation. I know about the beast that came with you. I want it. So tell me – what is it you want?" Arthur does not respond – yet agian.

"I can give you so…much, but you are not as easily moved as I thought you would be. Contemplate your situation well Mr. Robinson. In the meantime, I want you to meet someone whom I am quite sure that you will find fascinating."

Aun'war raises his hand, signaling the guards to take Arthur away. Arthur watches a large door silently closing. As the distinct sound of latching mechanisms reaches his ears, it becomes obvious that he is going nowhere. He scans the silent walls, but finds nothing of interest. As he faces the interior of the room, he pauses. Then, in shear amazement, his speechless state expresses a heighten sense of awe.

The walls in the room are high and laden with pink marble as a spectacular glass ceiling provides a shimmering crystal canopy. White tiles artistically line the floor, concluding the perimeter with crystal squares. Huge fantasy-size figures stand powerfully on both sides of an enormous fireplace. Each figure remarkably resembles the nude physiques of men, with the heads of lions, holding a hammer in one hand while displaying the imbedded image of a scorpion in the other. Untamed flames radically dance between the stone gods, teasing a seemingly unseen audience with mystical gestures.

"Who is this guy?" Arthur's whispers echo amidst the spacious room as if a voice softly taps his mortal conscience. In the midst of the room lies a long white table. Eight exquisitely crafted chairs line the edges of the table. Gold forms the outer support of the chairs as purple royal cushions line the high back rests and seating portions. Arthur's amazement grows as he soon focuses upon something more intriguing.

Further entering, he sees a woman sitting in a chair with her back towards him. He slowly approaches her, but the glistening brilliance of several jewels vividly radiate upon her smooth barren skin while casting a glare upon his face. Flawless gems seated in gold bands adorn her wrists and ankles as gold rings tantalizingly sparkle upon her fingers and toes. Stylish sandals grace her delicate feet, the only garments to touch her bare body. Arthur sits across the table and catches a full view of her.

The technician blinks several times as if the shimmering jewels blind him. Subtle attempts to hide his startling surprise cause him to slowly turn away, but not before the woman's eyes catch his. Showing no signs of disconcertedness, the woman holds her head up and looks directly at Arthur.

"All that glitters doesn't shine," she says.

In pure astonishment, Arthur leans back in his chair. "Jade," he whispers.

"Who else…?"

"I…I…thought you were dead."

"Apparently not…"

"How did you get here, what is this all about, who did this? And why are you…"

"I know you have thousand questions Arthur; I only tell you what truly happened. You must be quiet, Aun'war is coming."

The door opens and Aun'war, flanked by two guards, approaches.

"Ah...Arthur Robinson, I see you two have made acquaintance while under the watchful eyes of Gautier and Damien; my annular gods of justice." Aun'war, points towards the figures near the fireplace.

"God's of justice – right. If that's so, then why do you need those guns?"

"Precaution – of course, Mr. Robinson; and though my overseers are divine in nature they are...made of stone. They host the body of a man, which denotes humanity. Their head is that of a lion, which denotes courage; and the hammers are the martinets of justice; sanctions to validate war if need be."

"...And the scorpion?"

"Ah yes...the mark of excellence, to strike with fear. I find them rather appealing – Don't you?"

Aun'war walks towards Jade and places his cold un-human hand upon her shoulders. "She is a magnificent work of art and I just love to show her off before my entire guest. I bet you are curious as to how our paths crossed."

"It has to be the second greatest story ever told."

"Almost...but not quite. Years ago, you could say that she came to us after the death of her husband, Constantine. She was a reckless youthful renegade; seeking vengeance for his death – no doubt. Destitute and impoverished, she had no direction and what little family she claimed, offer little...if any assistance to her state of mind. So, I provided her guidance. In a turn of interesting events, she became my trustee, then, one of my top assassins, and later...my lover...long before my deformity of course; and now...my glistening work of art. She is, as her name implies, a beautiful hard stone."

"Interesting..."

"Did you know that our earliest ancestors found that by sharpening such a stone just right, it will cut you? I have found that by sharpening this...*Jade,* in like manner, she will cut you as well; but you already knew that. Judging from your expression, I gather that she never told you about us – pity. When a stone cuts - Arthur, it is imperative to expose the sharp edges; else it will cut you again – especially if you rub it the wrong way."

"Sounds double-edged to me..."

"Precisely..."

"And...you're telling me all this because...?"

"Every man deserves a sense of closure; but since you are here, this scenario could mean everything to your dead co-workers."

Arthur stares directly at Jade. "Now I understand why you didn't talk about your past. But for the sake of our team, did you kill them?"

Jade, teary-eyed and distraught, looks at Arthur. "I had no choice."

"Is that what you told Walter or did you tell him anything at all?"

"No."

"I can only guess that you 'cut' Aun'war as well. Was it worth it?"

"Aun'war...would k...kill...me."

Jade lowers her head in sorrow and begins to sob as tears stream upon her glistening jewels, much to Aun'wa'rs delight. "Ahhh...Walter it is. Remember, I told you that love would make you fall short of your mission. As it did then, with Constantine, so it does now. You cannot have a normal life Jade – you simply cannot. Not in the cards for you."

Arthur asks, "Do you have to treat her this way?"

"Concered are you? If I recall, Arthur Robinson, the last time water flowed from a rock; it upset your God, did it not?"

"I know Jade. Can't say I'm proud of what I'm hearing..."

Aun'war immediately strikes the top of the table. "Then hear this! Rowland Krenshenkov was her target. He destroyed one of my earliest biological facilities in the Ukraine. We were conducting test in creating chimeras. You saw the photographs...hideous creatures those animals. Radiation leaked out and poisoned the inhabitants of a small town. It was afterwards that I learn of Rowland's sister, Dunyasha. She was dying as the result of that infernal test, but it was not intentional – truly. My protégé' died from the radiation poisoning as well. We tried to save him, but techniques back then were atrocious. Afterwards, Rowland took vengeance upon us. Need I say that his actions hurt us tremendously? From then on, his very existence became a nagging threat to my mission."

"Mission, what mission?"

"We wanted to see if we could produce a non-human hybrid army. We took some of Russia's brightest minds and sequestered their talents."

"Let me guess…you killed them once their task was complete."

"Close, but not all of Mother Russia's brightest volunteered, so we had to ensure our position. I hope this is all somehow beginning to make sense to you."

"After your failure to produce the perfect hybrid non-human soldier, you found out about project 429 and you wanted it for yourself."

"Very good... It was only fitting to oblige Rowland for his actions. We find him in your country, but your CIA discovered our intentions and Rowland's association with Colonel Ducet. Both elements became infractions, or shall we say – problematic."

"I thought Rowland only wanted to silence the team until he could leave GenoSyss."

"Yes, another miscalculation, which put more eyes upon him. I could no longer just walk in and kill him."

"And that's when you sent an assassin."

"My best... Jade's mission was to destroy Rowland and erase all his work – but then…you…you *black bastard!* You created infernal beasts that became a hellish thorn in my side; yet ironically, much to my liking."

"You seem to have things under control."

"How would you know? As I lay recovering from the fire in Oklahoma, it occurred to me that such hybrids would make a wonderful addition to my cause. I saw how your military used them. Now that you are here, you will create the same hybrid army for me."

"Then you will kill me. So why should I help you?"

"Because, the face behind this mask is the direct result of your enans."

"I don't even know you."

"Do say Robinson…compliments to you regardless, since no one else from the outside could even come this close to me."

"I had nothing to do with the fire in Oklahoma."

"Then you should know that I am willing to bestow the same grace upon you that gave me this face. Now tell me Mr. Robinson. Did God grant you reassurance?"

"I made my peace with Him."

Arthur stands straight and tall, pronouncing a silent defiance before all. With fists clinched and tightly aligned, the technician sternly observes Aun'war. Intrigued with Arthur's behavior, Aun'war curiously draws closer. "I am quiet sure that you have made your peace, and you are going to need it; yet, you continue to – tremble."

"I don't want to die like this."

"You don't have too."

"I will not help you Aun`war, so get on with it."

"With what?"

"You brought me here to meet Jade, so…I guess you intend to kill me now."

"Meet…Jade?" Aun'war bolsters a gut-wrenching laugh, leaning his head back while holding his belly. As he gains his composure, he tells Arthur, "Oh no…no my poor man. It is not she."

Arthur's eyes widen with a curious sternness. "Then who?"

"Why do you think your existence continues Arthur Robinson? Why do you think I entertain you in such a way?"

"Divine intervention…"

"I am thoroughly amused. Look at you. You are as poorly suited for retribution, as you are pitifully predictable with ignorance." Aun'war laughs as Arthur sternly eyes him.

The guard's open the heavy door as Arthur anxiously anticipates who will enter. Suddenly, in steps a woman. She gracefully makes her way to the table and seats herself with the others. Her attire is nothing less than astonishing; from an antelope skin hat that covers her head, to the matching extrusions of Zambian Saber embroidery covering her breasts; even down to the elaborate shoes that adorn her feet. Bare shoulders reflect smooth brown skin as lengthy black gloves fit snugly over her arms. Tilting her head upward, overhead lighting bears witness to her identity. Aun'war candidly preludes her introduction.

"Allow me to introduce – again for you Mr. Robinson, Ms Angelica Banks."

Arthur leans back his chair, awe struck. He cannot find the words to address the moment. Widen eyes coincide with a partial mouth opening, perplexing such wordless expressions.

Angelica places both hands upon the table, one over the other, leaning forward as though to give Arthur a full view of her presence. Then, in a sultry overtone, she tells him, "You are looking at me now as you did when we first met. How have you been Arthur?"

"I've seen better days."

"I'm sure you have. Now aren't you just dying to know why I am here?"

"The thought had occurred."

Angelica laughs.

"You're so trustingly cute."

"You can't be in this for the money."

"Oh…not at all."

"Then what could possibly bring someone like you, to someone like him, in a place somewhere like this?"

"In a word – legacy."

"Legacy…for the love of God… What kind of legacy?!"

"One in which an entire populous can be controlled without the moral *humanistic* involvements."

"It's called vitro fertilization – can you help me understand?"

"My, my…we're not so timid anymore."

"Yeah well, my current situation is having an effect. So – what about this legacy?"

"The outlook is more complex than that."

"I bet it is."

"We can regulate over-population, kill off all criminals with death records, end starvation, and eliminate greed. We will control everything."

"Control, there's that…*delusional* word again."

"Oh…listen to you."

"Angelica, the world you describe means the eradication of humans and the infiltration of mindless clones. This is the wildest thing I have ever heard!"

"Only a certain percentage of humans will remain."

"How many?"

"A third..."

"A third of the earth's population? Even if you have the power to pull off such nonsense, do you really think you can do it with out a fight?"

"You saw what the Phantom's Death can do; now couple that with an army of enans and any thing is possible."

"An army of enans…"

"Why not?"

"You are just as delusional as he is."

"Arthur, look at your parents and grandparents. What purpose do they serve when unable to perform tasks beneficial to society or they loose the ability to live a full meaningful life?"

"It's called aging! It sucks, but it's a hell of lot more humane."

"Sure it is, if you're not *hooked* to some kind of machine."

"That's what makes our daily human experience well worth the moment. Cherish the here and now!"

"But what we offer is mercy."

"Mercy my ass..."

"Calm down."

"Calm DOWN? LOOK DAMMIT, aside from being shot at, threatened, chased half way around the world; I just found out a few minutes ago that this naked lady here tried to kill my former boss, who tried to kill a terrorist, who's trying to take over the world. And to top that off, I befriend my former employer who is here in another country – discussing plans to kill off two thirds of the world's population along with Mr. Hitler reincarnated! Excuse me while I have a *got-damn* conniption fit!"

"Oh, shut up Arthur. You sound like a trifling juvenile. Aun'war is a brilliant man. Though his methods are questionable, his means is precisely what is in need for carrying out such a grand endeavor."

"The hell you say."

"Yes – the hell I say. As ruthless as it was, Hitler's rule did bring Germany from the brink of social and economical collapse. Hiroshima's destruction put Japan on the roadmap as an economic contender, and the brutalities of the American government towards true Native Americans paved the way for modern America as we know it – remember the unification of Japan and England?"

"Don't go there. What you're trying to justify is propaganda genocidal garbage!"

"The events stand true."

"All that says Angelica is that my gun is bigger than yours and I want what you have – to hell with moral ethics!"

"Arthur, would you like to still be living in a hut, drinking putrid water, or wiping your ass with fig leaves?"

"With out tyranny – yes."

"I don't think so."

"But who are you to decide?"

"Great strives in progress demand greater sacrifices!"

"No, no, no!"

"If you were not so simple…"

"You cannot do this…"

"Yes we can!"

"ENOUGH," commands Aun'war, cracking the table with the head of his cane.

Angelica leans very close to Arthur, touching the side of his ear with her nose, whispering, "And how many creatures died before your hybrid became successful? How many humans died giving you the knowledge you now possess, allowing you to uncover such wisdom that laid the foundation for your proven methods?"

Arthur quickly moves his head and resentfully eyes Angelica. Angelica reciprocates the action and gets within inches of his face.

Arthur sternly tells her, "Progress comes with a price. Who are you to set the amount?"

"Out of chaos comes the next stage of evolution."

"This is not evolution."

"When the next stage happens, I want to be at the forefront. Such a society will extend well into the next millennia."

"Try dying in Christ."

"Don't be so coy, after the language I heard coming from you."

"Never said I was perfect."

"Nor did I."

"Beckoning God's damnation upon an evil scheme like yours is very Christian."

Angelica smiles while leaning back in her chair. Arthur sits as well, brandishing a cold stare towards her. Then, the technician slowly leans forward. "This explains why you had me increase Nostalgia's accelerants. Now I know why you were in such a…big hurry."

"As you know Arthur, GenoSyss was of one my contenders in the pharmaceutical arena. Once I caught wind of the military's interest in that company, I knew that something big was underway – and I just had to know more. Needless to say, I'm not the least bit disappointed in what I found. I learned later that your association with Rowland, and your disheartened feelings towards the administration put you at odds with the company, and it was that situation that made you the best candidate for what I had in mind; not to mention your ties to Jade as a co-worker."

"You've been spying on me all along."

"For the most part… Then, I became aware of Colonel Ducet, as well as Rowland – exactly how I found out is not important."

"I'm sure a woman of your talents is quite resourceful."

"Do tell. Once I learned of Aun'war, I became very intrigued with his vision."

"Let me guess, you got to Jade and she spilled the beans."

"Wrong again, but at least you're trying. At the time, Aun'war needed assurances that he could trust."

"What kind of assurances?"

"The kind that assures dead men don't talk."

"So, you became the clean up woman."

"No, just making sure that Jade's mission went through."

"You must have been the *other woman* Walter heard about."

"Plural to singular, both Jade and I; were the other woman, but at the time, Jade did not know. Aun'war began to loose faith in Jade when he figured out that the four of you were alive."

"He suspected that she grew soft – or was in love."

"Now you're catching on, and that is where I entered the picture."

"You do realize that you are an accessory to murder."

"Our plan was almost full proof, that is – until you became a catalyst Arthur. You simply would not go away."

Aun'war steps forward. "I did not know just how far I could trust my precious Jade, so I needed to make sure that the plan would not die. It was Angelica who made Jade's mission quite successful. Rowland wanted to scare your team into silence until he got away. I sent Angelica to reassure that your friends were taken away, thus eliminating each of you, one by one. What do you think of that?" Arthur remains silent. "It doesn't matter. Angelica made us aware of Colonel Ducet's intention. Needless to say, his actions were most detrimental to us in Oklahoma - the one part that Jade left out. But as fate would have it, your enans played a pivotal role in the good colonel's misfortunate death."

"I'm quite sure you feel sorrow for him," says Arthur.

Aun'war activates a large monitor, after which a video begins to play. "Speaking of your enans...see this? Jade took this footage from the GenoSyss lab. It documents your enans progress and training. This beast of yours will make the perfect biological assault weapon."

"Your army of men are not good enough?"

"On the contrary... Even though I have an aerial dispensing unit, it becomes a visual risk when deployed or it could be shot out of the sky; however, combine your enans with the Phantom's Death and the two will make a most formidable union. Your creature's can enter and exit areas with such precision and stealth that no one will ever know they were there. With an army of enans, I can clone them, grow them and dispose of them at will. Because of that, I do not need as many men."

"Seems to me like you have a pretty loyal following."

"People are hard to control, even trust. Once they grow disenchanted, they will turn on you. Unlike your enans, they will simply do what they are told – with the right conditioning of course. Beasts of burden need no rewards – merely purpose."

"And you, of all people, think you can control them."

"Control – a relative term Mr. Robinson; but I also understand that they comprehend language – which makes them far more valuable to me. And just in case you are wondering…this is why you are still alive." Aun'war gives Arthur a bold look of confidence, but the solemn technician turns away and remains silent.

However, Aun'war grows impatient and approaches Arthur, getting within inches of his face. "Look at me my benign brother. Men like you stare death in the face as if it is a trivial token, perhaps because of a defunct belief in someone or some thing higher than you. Do know that it is I who designed this mission, it was I who controlled Jade, and now it is I who will cause you to either live or die. My point is simple Arthur Robinson. Build an army of enans for me – to protect my operation, a clone from your enan perhaps – and I will let you live. My word is law – for I have spoken it."

Arthur stares at Aun'war, coldly offering no reprieve.

"Very well Mr. Robinson, your actions suggests otherwise – therefore. Since you will not summon your creature, then perhaps I can persuade your indecisiveness."

Aun'war removes from within his coat a saber and hatefully thrusts it into Jade's chests. A loud cry rings out as Jade grapples the blade. Her initial reaction is to remove the sharp instrument, but she is unable to follow through as Angelica surprisingly turns away. With petite hands covering her wound, silence befalls the despairing princess as she now lays face down in a crimson pool.

"You're a barbarian Aun'war."

"No...Arthur Robinson. I am an eccentric idealist; something far from you. I believe that seven is the number of completeness, so I will give you seven minutes to make your decision. Work with me and live or do not and die."

Aun'war exits the room, flanked by Angelica. Arthur desperately attempts to flee but the guards restrain his hands and press him back into the chair. The frightening sound of silence fills the palisade room, lending no comfort to Arthur's seeming demise. He sits quietly; realizing that another attempt to flee will produce the same results. But the guards will not kill him, for that honor belongs solely to Aun'war.

Arthur stares at Jade, and then stares at the ceiling as if a celestial host beckons him. He slowly approaches Jade. While raising her head, he observes her misfortune and attempts to remove the saber. Jade's forbearing cries ignite into a sorrowful moan. "Jade, we have to get this out. Only a hard pull will work – just one quick pull."
"Do it," she says. Pressing one hand upon her chest, Arthur gently grabs the handle of the saber. With one swift pull, he removes it. An agonizing yell fills the room as she falls forward. Arthur places the saber on the table, courtesy of the guard watching.

Later, the large door opens and in walks Aun'war with his hands behind his back. "Well Mr. Robinson, have you come to a conclusion?" Arthur looks at him and motions his head in a disaffirming manner.

"So be it... Guard, kill him."

"Suddenly, Arthur rushes the sultan, knocking him to the floor. He desperately fights for his survival. The guards rush in but Arthur runs to the rear of the room. Aun'war rises to his feet, straightening the mask upon his face. He and the two guards corner Arthur, much to Aun'war's anger.

"A foolish act on your part – IDIOT! Now you will die like the *damned* fool you are." The guards bear their arms and aim directly at Arthur, who closes his eyes, and turns away.

Suddenly, an alarm echoes within the room followed by a voice, "INTRUDER ALERT...INTRUDER ALERT!"

Sirens echo throughout the room as Aun'war gives the order to halt. He presses a small device on his sleeve, "Yes!" Silence carries, but then Aun'war focuses back upon Arthur.

"It would appear that several perimeter breaches have occurred; friends of yours no doubt. Perhaps this is a good thing. Once I have dealt with them, I will return to savor your slow torturous death – and yet, beneath that foolish hide of yours exist a man capable of a valued recourse. You can coral your enans, but you will live a dreadful life while serving me, a fitting example for those who dare defy me."

Aun'war and one of the guards exit the room.

As the door closes, Arthur and the remaining guard face off, each glaring eyes of contempt as if daring the other to make a wrong move, as though tied to a fate of destiny. Then strangely, the guard makes several erratically jerking motions as blood oozes from his mouth. He convulses, dropping to his knees with his head slumping upon his shoulder.

Arthur steps backwards and focuses on something strange.

Emerging from the guard's neck is a shiny pointed object. The object protrudes with such force that the guard's eyes roll back into his skull. While gasping for air, he endures the sound of crackling bones and falls forward to the floor, barely able to set off one shot. Hearing the noise, Arthur's eyes widen, and there before him, slowly rising from behind the fallen guard, is Jade.

Arthur rushes to her side as she helplessly collapses. Carrying her in his arms, he positions her within a chair. Arthur tears a portion of the guard's shirt and begins to gently wipe away the blood from Jade's body. Forming a tourniquet, he precedes to wrap her chest. As he does, Jade gently places her hand on his shoulder. Her eyes fill with tears as she humbly sequesters his attention.

"Please...hear me..."

"*Shhh*...you need your strength. If I can't stop this bleeding, you will die."

"Death may be good thing for me."

"Nonsense... You're alive – that means hope."

"Aun'war murdered my family – and threatened to kill me if I did not join him. When I realized who he was, it was...it was so...late."

"Tell me later. Right now, Aun'war wants me to do something for him and that gives us time."

"*Auuuuggggg!*"

"Sorry... I know this is tight but we have to stop the bleeding."

"Go to fireplace and put edge of blade in fire."

"Aun'war's saber?"

"Do it Arthur...part of survival training – just do it."

Arthur plunges the blade into white-hot coals and later removes it. He approaches Jade in earnest. She skillfully guides him to the decisive moment, after which a disquieting scream fills the room. Arthur removes the guard's uniform and clothes Jade, securing the pants with torn strips of fabric and allowing the jacket to hang loosely, though partially tied. Then, he carefully moves Jade to the side of the door, seating her on the floor. Retrieving the guard's weapon, both patiently wait. Arthur sternly watches the door.

"I don't think Aun'war considers me a threat – at all."

"He is brilliant man, but not thorough. His loose ends…everywhere, if you know where to look. Notice how he leaves one incompetent man to guard a bio-technician and a trained assassin, in a room with no cameras."

"Maybe, but we are going to have to fight them as much as possible."

"There is only one way in."

"Then, whoever comes through that door, will get it from behind."

"I feel weak."

"You just hold on, because Walter really wants to see you."

Jade smiles.

~~~Retaliation~~~

Aun'war looks deeply into a nearby monitor. "Are you sure something is out there? All I see are trees and the darkness."

"Sir, whatever they are, they keep attacking the main doors. Sensors indicate movement and we are having difficulty tracking the signatures; one moment they appear and then disappear."

"Express your point man!"

"Look at the doors. Whatever is out there is powerful enough to put indentions in the hanger doors. The attack comes in waves and their approach seems to concentrate on one point in the center of the doors."

"...And?"

"Sir Martinet, the doors are beginning to separate."

"Hmm...it appears that Arthur's creature has returned, but not alone. GATHER YOUR MEN – NOW!"

"You want us to go out there, but sir, what about...?"

Aun'war strikes the man in the face.

Blustering alarms engulf the underground complex while setting myriads of armed allegiants into motion. The men swarm the exterior of the compound, setting forth piercing beams of light that reveals nothing more than broken branches, torn foliage, and a dusty cloud of haze. Silence befalls the elusive event as attentive eyes scour the surrounding area. With each turning head, deadly weapons follow suit. Disciplined field units slowly advance; assuring that their tactical approach discounts nothing.

White light devoid the darkness, but nothing of hardened intent is revealing – until, an alarming cry rings out. *"Par-dessus ici!"* The striking cry of *(over here)* causes the army to separate into several teams as they pour into the identified area, pointing their weapons with an attitude for attack.

Then, a large cluster of brush ruffles wildly. Soon afterwards, a staggering spray of bullets unmercifully shreds the nearby foliage, mowing down several plants until a large opening appears. The harsh reaction sends birds frantically flying above the high canopy as bottom dwellers disperse in mass panic.

Amidst the smoke and rubble, some of the men quickly inspect for biological residue, but find nothing. Sweat clings to harden faces as rhythmic heartbeats tighten under the adrenaline rush. All that remains is the backdrop of darkness.

"Sir, what ever was there, is gone," accounts one allegiant as many stare in disbelief. Aun'war's units remain vast in number, poising for anything unsuspecting. All are quiet, until…

Whisking sounds spur the air and immediately, one allegiant violently slams into the ground. Another gunman observes the strange happening while trembling with agitation. Stricken with fear, the gunman focuses on an enormous foot, pressing upon the lain man's back. He scans upward, surely interpreting that what he sees is not human. Though bearing a weapon, his trembling grows worse. Soon, his eyes fixate upon another pair of eyes; red and furious – yet sadly, those eyes become the last thing he sees. A distressing scream gives alert to other bands of allegiants who respond with nothing less than a spectacular barrage of fiery rage.

"What the hell are they?" Several men repeat the same question in shear horror as two enans engage one of the groups, pouncing on one gunman, then another. With incredible agility, the enans crush the gunmen necks and shatter bones; viciously mauling their victims while slashing with sharp talons, leaving many allegiants disemboweled or worse. Other misfortunate souls are cast high into the air; impaling tree limbs while more are trampled to death and snatched into the darkness of the jungle. Serrated edge blades on the tips of the enan's tails wildly thrash bodies in half, effectively cutting human limbs and beheading weary victims in one sweeping motion.

An enan takes down an allegiant fighter. The man desperately fires several rounds into the creature's side. Seeing no damaging results, the shooter cries out, "*Le Diable's chien.*" Others stare at the incident, only to realize that those were the man's final words. Another gunman falls victim as well, screaming "*Chaitan's chal-leb*" repeatedly. With one deadly slash; more enans rip bodies apart while thrusting more victims mercilessly. Surprisingly, some gunmen desperately escape, running in shear terror, barely realizing the human parts that litter the ground. Afterwards, the creatures lunge forward and vanish into the night, leaving behind the silent chill of a gruesome massacre.

Observing the demise of his soldiers, the captain sends word to Aun'war through a miniature viewer. "Sultan, the situation...these... beasts are attacking. We hit them with our guns, but..."

"...Quiet! I hear only silence Captain. Are you the only survivor?"

"The seers you put into service have killed many who tried to run away. We also strike our own men in an attempt to slay the creatures. I...I...did what I could lord masseur – hear me."

"You have almost half of my army Captain – and yet you survive."

"Please, please Sultan Martinet."

"I heard my French and Arabic brothers in the background; what did they say?"

"They said these creatures are the Devil's dogs!"

Aun'war remains silent. "Advise me Sultan Aun'war," beckons the captain.

Aun'war's mask lies fixated as his hollow eyes provide the only clue to a contemplation of thought. He folds his arms and turns away from the monitor, looking as though to find a solution, giving no consideration for the captain's distressing plead. Then, in solemn voice he says *"Captain, I have bestowed upon you a prestigious position; one which denotes your abilities and loyalty. You presided over a very large unit...but the unit is no more; however, the unit must be kept as one."*

"Sultan, please...I have more service to give you. I did all that I could!"

"Not all. The saber you carry will assist you in a most honorable act of gratitude."

The captain responds with an abrupt nod. While trembling, he positions the tip of the blade to his throat. But suddenly, an enan approaches and thrusts him from behind. The creature savagely rips the officer until a crimson cloak covers the monitor – which is all Aun'war sees.

Carnage continues as blood spills into the night. Each hybrid beast decapitates gunmen after gunmen, spurring a blood lust that rivals a medieval massacre. Several enans play off the success of another as each gunmen falls victim to the hybrids' scythe. In some cases, an enan renders a victim helpless while another enan finishes the assault, either tearing or slashing a gunman before an impending doom sets in. Many of Aun'war's men attempt to flee but are gunned down by seers, who also become victims of their own destruction.

Two gunmen escape an attacking enan, only to find refuge under a large tree. One of the men watches as his comrades fall several at a time. He turns to his fellow combatant. "If we return, our fate is worse. Our lord will expect no less. Either there or here – mercy will not be given." He pulls a device from within his pack and straps it to his side.

Creeping from beneath the tree, the gunman finds an approaching enan. The beast lunges for him; and yet, his timing is perfect. Both engage each other at the moment of impact. An explosive discharge ignites and incinerates the gunman while engulfing the enan. The creature falls to the ground, startled, shaken, but alive. Distressing squawks testify of a gaping wound as the hybrid lies on the ground.

Curiosity grips the other gunman as he scans the area for activity. Satisfied, he quietly crawls near the enan. Upon approach, he cautiously observes the beast, assuring himself that his fellow combatant has rendered the hybrid dead. But the lurid creature's eyes open and fixate upon the approaching gunman. Alert as ever, the enan stares down the gunman who slowly backs away. Exhaling in anguish, the gunman falls to his knees, draws his saber and plunges the blade deep into his own heart. A shameful death grants him the grace to escape, but not until he hears the pitiful screams of fellow gunmen under the dark canopy, as wave after wave of hybrid onslaught ultimately destroys Aun'war's army.

Aun'war repeatedly slams his prosthetic hand upon the monitor, shattering fingers while tearing the appendage to pieces. His muffled speech resonates loudly, touching the ears of everyone. Then, the disdained commander summons a guard. "You there!" The guard snaps to attention. As he does, a loud pounding commences upon the bay hanger doors. Both men watch in horror as the doors slightly separate. Aun'war grows angrier.

"Dispense with every thing we got, and see to it that Arthur is brought before me now! Do you hear me?"

"Yes sir…"

"Should you fail, such incompetence will cost you your life!"

"Understood sir…" The guard immediately departs.

As Arthur and Jade wait patiently beside the door, Jade continues to apply pressure to her wound. "It's not as bad as it looks," she says.

"I hope he didn't puncture a lung or cut an artery."

"I would know by now – if he did. Aun'war hurts me so you will join him. Believe me, he would kill us if he really wanted too."

"But what purpose will killing you serve?"

"None... He taunts me. I am his eye candy."

"I'll say..."

"How is Walter?"

"He misses you."

"He is kind."

"Maybe, but at least I know why he's alive."

"Please do not...Arthur."

"What is there to say, if you love the man,
surely you would protect him."

"You have reason to hate me now. I am a monster."

"I don't hate you."

"Aun'war made me wear transmitter under my skin – he tracked me all the time."

"That explains how he found out about me."

"Remember Red Sands, and the death of Gearhardt?"

"Yes."

"The failure of the computers was no accident. They were sabotaged."

"Do I want to know anything else?"

"After 429 successes, Rowland hired a man named Langley and a blonde-haired accomplice. Their job was to silence our team."

"I know."

"But Aun'war wanted to destroy Rowland."

"So, you stepped in and deaths occurred."

"No. When I learned who Rowland hired, I offered more money for their services to silence or hide the team from Roland."

"Silence...? But Jade, Nathaniel, Frank, Alexis, and Tuan were killed."

"Aun'war ordered their deaths, and threatened me if I did not provide the information to Langley. Big problem occurred when Walter killed Langley and the blond haired man."

"Is that when Aun'war grew suspicious of you?"

"Yes. He knew I would never fail a mission."

"Then... Who where the man and woman, that tried to kill me at Hollis' farm?"

"They must have been Rowland's hit men. They use enans to destroy Aun'war's outpost in Ukraine."

"My God Jade, how many teams did Rowland have?"

"Only two... By time GenoSyss building explodes, Aun'war no longer trusted me. Then I learned that Angelica was involved, and carried out Aun'war's original instructions."

"Then you became a marked target."

"Once Colonel Ducet forced me to go back to Aun'war, I knew I could never leave – so here I am."

"Ducet used you, to get to Aun'war – clever. So tell me, have you given up now?"

"I am tired of this, Arthur."

"You just hang on; stay awake... and definitely stay alive."

"There is something else you should know. I do not think Angelica is fully aware of Aun'war's intentions. He will use her until he gets what he wants – I speak truth."

"At least your testimony will have her acquitted, if we live. But there's one more thing Jade."

"Which is?"

"Was I on your kill list?"

"Please do not do this."

"Where you going to kill me and Gracella?"

Tears quickly fill Jade's eyes as she slowly turns away. She refrains from looking at Arthur, as unnerving water course her quivering lips, yet she holds the grace to maintain. While exchanging blood soaked rags, Jade removes every precious gem and uncaringly tosses each item on the floor. Her back firmly presses against the wall as her coal black hair drapes upon slumping shoulders.

"*Shhhh*...someone's coming..." Clacking sounds eerily coincide with a turning doorknob as the heavy closure sways open. In steps a guard, who untrustingly pans left to right. Arthur immediately seizes the moment. He rushes the guard from behind and violently plunges the saber into the man's chest. Another guard enters and sees the skirmishing situation. In haste, he reaches for his alarm, but Jade's actions end his hopes for assistance.

"Nice shot, but I think it's going to attract attention."

"I am an assassin…"

"Speaking of…we need to get out of here as quickly as possible."

"What is your plan?"

"I suggest we get to the nearest exit and use it, or else face the chaos that is about to come."

"Someone comes to rescue you – yes?"

"Jade, listen…we have to get you medical help, but first, we need to find a safe place outside these walls."

"Then you must follow me."

Arthur places Jade's arm around his neck and the two cautiously enter a series of complex passageways.

In the launch hanger, mounting concerns put several allegiants on high alert. The men quickly form a barrier between the bay doors and the command center. Continuous poundings separate the bay doors, moving the barriers a few more inches apart. Surprisingly, an enan reaches through the separation, clawing at anything accessible. As it does, several allegiant shots compound the creature's efforts thereby forcing a rapid withdrawal. Silence fills the hanger once more.

But then, the main airshaft supports begin to cringe and buckle under the pressure of an unseen force. The noise captures the men's attention. Soon, the vent covering falls to the floor. Alert gunmen point their weapons in the direction of the vent opening and proceed to fire. While engaged, more attacks commence upon the bay doors.

"Their drawing our fire," yells one of the gunmen. The men divide their attention to both disturbances. In a matter of moments, an enan viciously tears its way through the ventilation corridor, ripping fragile tin and concrete supports as it enters the bay. Falling from the ceiling, the creature belts a stoic roar, yet sadly takes the full magnitude of allegiant firepower. Though armored, the enan's scales fail to repel the onslaught. Horrible screams erupt as the enan coils its tail and quietly passes into silence.

Angelica stands beside Aun'war as he consults with one of his trusted allegiants. The man approaches the sultan, bowing with a degree of humility in his voice. "What would you have me do Aun'war?"

"I want you to finish loading the dispenser with the Phantom virus. Once the aircraft takes to the sky, prepare to destroy this facility."

"All of it?"

"Every ounce..."

"Yes sir," responds the man as he departs.

Angelica, purposefully positions herself in front of Aun'war. She takes his hand and caresses it as though touching live flesh. Embellishing her senses, Aun'war's piercing eyes gaze upon her through the windows of his mask. She asks, "Are you really going to destroy all this?"

"A necessary loss."

"…For the greater good – of course."

"Always…"

"There is Canada."

"Too pervasive, for we have come so far."

"Then salvage what we have and start over."

Aun'war presses Angelica closer to him. "What are you trying to tell me…my Nubian Temptress?" Angelica moves her finger along the contours of his mask and moves even closer, putting her lips to his ear, whispering, "Live today, attack tomorrow." Aun'war faces her and then looks afar.

He walks towards a console and activates a transceiver. "Main hanger – status."

"Sultan, we've just killed one of those things."

"Well done."

"Better yet sir, we captured another one. The men are bringing it into the hanger at this moment. Also, the attacks have stopped, but we're sure that several more are still out there."

"Excellent work! I want to see the creature up close."

Aun'war quickly enters the main bay area flanked by several trustees and Angelica. Spectators increase as the men wheel another enan into the hanger bay. Heavy nets and twines appear to subdue the creature. As the men position the hybrid beside the body of the dead enan, Aun'war approaches and closely examines the netted beast.

"So…this is success where others have failed. It is also the testament to a true thorn in my side."

"Clever creature; especially to have found your base out here," says Angelica.

"Yes, but an incredible looking creature and most formidable."

"Arthur can create more of them."

"Arthur. Ah yes – Mr. Robinson," says Aun'war, chuckling while turning towards his allegiant force. The men begin to smile and chuckle along with their dissident leader, until, "WHERE IS HE?" Immediately, the men make haste in multiple directions.

Angelica leans closely to Aun'war. "All is not lost. We may not need Arthur. You can simply take a tissue sample and some blood work; clone from that."

"Then we will have our own army of enans. You are truly my intuition – Angelica." She smiles.

Suddenly, blue flames ignite and incinerate the entire body of the dead enan. As the smoke clears, a mound of chard ash remains. Confounding stares gaze upon the blackened pile as Aun'war screams aloud, "What happened?" Several men shake their heads in disaffirming acknowledgement while backing away from the scene, but Aun'war stands with shrewdness. "What is this?" Again, he asks, but his men do not respond.

Suddenly, the sound of footsteps emanate from within the shadows of the room, drawing the suspicious attention of everyone. A tall thin figure of a man enters the light, and immediately, shooters take aim. "It is an insurance policy," the figure says. Such words mysteriously echo to Aun'war's question. Raising his head, the figure allows light to reveal his identity.

"Amazing… Arthur Robison," whispers Angelica.

Aun'war sees Arthur and angrily confronts him. "At least tell me how they got past my sensors."

"The scales; those wonderful, remarkable multi-colored scales. In most cases, each of those scaly tiles can divert a projected signal – like a plane deflecting radar."

Aun'war claps in an unsavory manor. "Brilliant to the end… But did you know that there are species of cockroaches that live and are much harder to kill, even after the exterminator has passed time and time again?"

"I wouldn't know."

"YOU, Arthur Robinson are definitely the two-legged species."

"Maybe, but I do recall you as the one surviving fire."

"Amusing, now tell me – what kind of policy?"

"White phosphorus; copper capsules, napalm gel caps – with other additives of course. All set at the right mixture to make sure that these enans will not fall into your hands or any others – like you."

"Bravo Arthur…bravo, you are as cunning as you are clever. Broadway should have been your choice of occupation – I will give you that much; and yet, I never would have thought that a descendant of slaves would be so – intellectually troublesome."

"I guess that makes me a smart *Niggah* – doesn't it?"

"Interestingly put, but you are a fool and you are equally stupid, just like your co-workers. Now comprehend this; you were destined to die – and die you shall." Aun'war, trembling with rage, turns to his men; "Kill him – NOW!" Upon hearing the command, Arthur quickly ducts behind a console. His actions transpire only moments before shooters unleash hell fire, shredding everything in their path. Smoke fills the room as fixtures hang loosely and debris blanket the floor.

"Even a cockroach eventually dies," spouts Aun'war as he abruptly walks towards the second enan. He quietly observes the beast, yet daunting a suspicious countenance, even behind his mask. "This creature is strangely, silent. How was this beast captured?"

A man raises both hands, denoting his uncertainty. Aun'war turns to another. "You there – how was this creature taken?"

"I'm not sure, we found it netted."

"Found it where, and netted by whom?"

"I…assumed our men did it."

"Did you see if our men netted this beast?"

"I…I did not."

Aun'war quickly strikes the man, sending him to the ground. "FOOL! All our men died out there! Get me protection!"

Aun'war' steps backward while taking one more glance into the hybrid's eyes. In his dire need for curious appeasement, Aun'war sees the illumination of red staring back at him. His eyes widen as he makes a sharp wistful inhale, drawing his distrusting attention as he stepps away. Aun'war retreats, but as he does, the hybrid immediately jumps off the cart. Three gunmen fire upon the beast, but the hybrid swiftly thrashes two of the gunmen in the chest and hurls the other gunman several feet into the air.

The hybrid quickly enters the main hanger and systematically disposes of all cannons and other large deadly weaponry. More allegiants enter the area, but the hybrid reaches the main console and activates the door controls. Sustaining much gunfire, the hybrid watches the doors open just enough for several enans to enter. With barely enough separation, the hybrids make their barbaric entry, shrieking as though to commence the impending doom of Aun'war's allegiants.

Moving swiftly, the enans demolish several instruments as they lay in deadly pursuit of their targets. Light fixtures fragment under the impact of bodies as the enans cast their victims upward. Headless corpses litter the floor as razor sharp talons decapitate unsuspecting marksmen. Allegiant canon fire pulverizes walls, equipment, and even some of their allied combatants in an attempt to strike down the creatures, but mayhem spreads. Pouncing upon person after person, the enans ruthlessly mutilate their victims; even overtaking those in frantic retreat.

Faint sounds of gunfire echo in the halls as horrid screams fall deathly silent.

All actions transpire under the watchful eye of the enan that was once netted; the creature that remains at the console, the hybrid beast Arthur calls Gjhe'nan.

~~~Denounce~~~

Thunderous explosions rip through the underground complex as several enans continue their merciless assault. Few enans sustain brutal retaliation from Aun'war's dwindling army, but not enough to render the creatures immobile. Hallways, once clean and nicely laden with organization now lay in destruction, hidden beneath rubble and red covering. Several allegiants attempt escape, but fall victim to enans or their own shooters mishaps.

Among those in retreat is Aun'war. Sensing his demise, the sultan desperately runs toward an aircraft. Approaching the airship, he activates a hydraulic door and stands just beyond an extending ramp. Upon entering, the door retracts.

Angelica pursues, but finds her hand pressing against the cold exterior of the craft. "Let me in…Aun'war, it's me…let me in!" Her pleads go unanswered as she frantically pounds the sterling surface.

Soon, a rumbling noise begins to roar, shaking the ground while overhead fixtures lightly sway. An orange glow lightens the hanger as the noise of engines intensifies. Angelica pounds continuously upon the craft. "Aun'war, open up! Why are you doing this?" Aun'war does not answer.

Angelica pleads repeatedly; however, her beckoning cry draws the attention of an enan as it emerges from the shadows. With claws extracting a readiness for death, the creature slowly approaches her. Angelica's eyes fixate upon the terror. She steps backwards, shaking, trembling, and then finally dropping to her knees. "Oh God," she pleads while covering her face. Blood mingles with saliva as the enan's fangs display. The beast prepares to strike, but then, Arthur quickly steps between the two. "Stop," he says, compelling the creature to ward off its dire intentions. Arthur sways the enan to back away. Reluctantly, the beast lowers its talons and steps backwards.

Afterwards, Arthur aids Angelica to her feet. Her eyes quickly widen as astonishment paints her face. "You control them?"

"No – Gjhe'nan conveyed my message to the others –
if I were still alive."

"Arthur, I thought you were dead – I thought they killed you."

"A small foxhole proved to be a good investment. Now let's get out of here before that enan changes its mind." Arthur pulls Angelica away from the enan and moves beyond the wings of the craft.

The craft shifts slightly to an exit trajectory. Yet, standing afar is the enan whose eyes begin to turn blue. As Arthur looks into the hybrid's eyes, fire from the wake of the engines instantly singes the creature, but the enan manages to escape a burning death.

Aun'war peeks through the window of the craft and sees Arthur standing with Angelica. His mask gleams through the portal as though smiling, as if casting the adulations of farewell.

"Aun'war! You...bastard!" Angelica screams as she and Arthur stand helplessly and watch the craft steer towards the main hanger doors.

Angelica looks at Arthur and slowly closes her eyes, shaking her head in disbelief. "Arthur...?"

"Now's not the time Angelica. The enans have littered the runway with bodies, but Aun`war is still moving ahead. We have to get out of here. This place is about to explode and I don't want those enans mistaking us for Aun'war's men."

As both seek cover, an enan surprisingly approaches. Arthur, fearing a worse fate holds Angelica as a deep concern grips his face. "Gjhe'nan!" Arthur exhales a sigh of relief. The hybrid responds to the call of its maker and displays a conveying feeling as fiery eyes softly turn to a subtle blue. Gjhe'nan beckons Arthur to climb upon his back. "Angelica, go through the bay doors – hurry before an enan sees you. We will try to stop Aun'war."

"Okay," she says.

"Go boy – let's go!" Arthur and the beast immedieatly pursue.

Pouncing with tremendous agility, Gjhe'nan speedily gains distance in front of the aircraft as it slowly taxis the runway of the hanger. Aun'war sees his pursuers and accelerates. The chase intensifies. As it does, the technician observes something in the debris. "Gjhe'nan, get that piece of furniture!" Arthur directs the hybrid to strategically take position directly in front of the approaching craft. "Throw it into the intake – NOW!!" Gjhe'nan immediately thrusts the side of a desk with his tail and lifts the damaged piece of furniture high above the ground. With only moments to spare, the hybrid hurls the item at the craft and jumps to safety. So great is the impact, that metal shatters in all directions. Powerful surges from the craft's intake sucks down portions of twisted metal until razor-like turbines imbed crumpled fragments. The engine violently bursts into flames. Fire begins to ravage the internal cabin and the craft comes to a staggering halt. Aun'war jettisons the escape hatch and flees into the jungle.

Under the overcast of a cloudy sky, Arthur and Gjhe'nan pursue Aun'war. They find him crawling on the ground. His mask is broken and partially imbedded in his face. Smoke lightly rises off his singed garments. One leg is severely severed while blood oozes from his mouth. Arthur dismounts from Gjhe'nan and stands over Aun'war.

With veins coursing his neck and a tight grip on the handle of a gun, Arthur raises the weapon and points it at Aun'war. The technician slowly presses the trigger, but then, quickly releases pressure in a tentative manner. Arthur finds the recourse to press the trigger again, yet yielding no detrimental action. Then, he surprisingly lowers the weapon, as if consenting to an inner voice. Instead, he grabs Aun'war by the neck and presses the gun at the base of his skull. "You squirm like the snake you are," he tells him.

"Surely there could be more to this," replies Aun'war, laughing as he rolls on his back and stares upward at Arthur.

The sultan's broken mask hangs partially from his face. Arthur grabs the mask, yanks it by the edge and tosses it aside. Blood spatters upon the ground as a stationary hand covers the wound, thereby reaching the limits of its prosthetic design. Arthur shunts little disdaining behavior for the gruesome unveiling of Aun'war's face, while yet, the sultan's battered body frantically shakes, desperately compensating for loss of strength as he struggles to support himself. With blood-red eyes and a gargle cough, Aun'war summons what little strength he has in order to prop his back against a large stone.

Drizzling rain pours as Aun'war tilts his head to one side, viewing his would-be prosecutor with difficulty; but nonetheless, Arthur stares him down. Both men eventually square off.

"You will not escape this time Aun'war."

"*'Not escape…?* That be a statement, a paradox, or a dichotomy Mr. Robinson? What exacty is your act now?"

"Speak English –."

"Whether dead or alive, I have already escaped, but for you; my point is…your infantile mindset will never let you grasp that which is bigger than you."

"I've seen your world and I have no desire to live in it."

"Such, possible future frightens you?"

Arthur presses the gun into Aun'war's forehead, forcing him to lean.

"Taunting me with your weapon is senseless; either you will shoot or not."

"A taste of your own medicine; hard to swallow – isn't it?"

"Those who can see the demise of a society and possess the power to change it – can and should. Is this not what you did when you made your infernal creatures?"

"They were not trying to change the world."

"Then what was their purpose?"

"To help a sick society…"

"Sick…? According to whom?"

"You know what I mean."

"Do I?"

"We have an obligation to fight for the life we choose to live; an inherent right to fight back against our foes."

"Fight back? Is this not what I have begun to do? Is this not what God did when He flooded the Earth – to fight back? What exactly are we fighting back, Arthur Robinson?"

Arthur stares silently at Aun'war as though a deep connection is occurring. He slowly releases pressure from the trigger. An indentation remains upon Aun'war's forehead as he painfully reestablishes his position upon the stone. While breathing heavily, Aun'war closely observes Arthur, yet leaving nothing to chance. He takes a deep breath and draws Arthur's attention even more.

"Remember your history Mr. Robinson. Ancient cultures, whether primitive or deemed unacceptable, have always suffered under the hand of the stronger power."

"True, but motives determines actions Aun'war."

"Yes, but who determines motives?"

"God sets that threshold."

"Did He set the threshold for those who invoked slavery, the rise of Germany in the First World War, the wrath of Japan in Pearl Harbor, or the abominations of moon base colony Cellist 3?"

"Those were out right attacks on innocent people and you know it!"

"Such events were actions committed by those who had the courage to create change. Their endeavor is only a hindrance when it affects your apathetic life style; things you hold with such high value, the life by which you choose to live."

"My right...and I have the right to defend the life that suits me."

"You, like many – my poor boy, uphold laws that were sanctioned by your government, a government that took lands from its original Native American inhabitants. Now tell me, did those inhabitants have rights?"

"Everyone has rights."

"Yet, you now enjoy the barbaric fruits of what your government did to those people, and you say that God endorses your current actions as well as your pathetic beliefs."

"God sets the threshold that determines right and wrong, and I cannot be held responsible for the actions of others; especially those before me."

"But you – as a man relish in the fruits of their labor."

"Rules govern us Aun`war."

"Then man determines behavioral rights – yes?"

"Man determines the course of action by which God's rules apply."

"Really… Then pick a subject, a category of all the ills in the world and tell me if MY COURSE of action is wrong to wipe them out!"

"Your course of action violates the innocent in the process."

"As did your government – even England!"

"NOT MY PROBLEM!"

"The men your enans killed; did they have a right to fight for a better life – a life they chose to live?"

"They have no right to kill others for the life they choose!"

"FOOL! Strangers create a law and force you to follow it, where by disobedience punishes those the law will not forgive."

"God creates the law by which men live."

"Then tell that to the black slaves and Native Americans whose blood cries out from Democracy's soil; the Jews of the early World War. Tell that to those who choose to live in a land where there is no god. Tell that to those who died in countless wars over money and lands under the name of righteous crusades; those who died wrongfully, which gives you the power to stand before me now!"

"Contentment eludes man's thirst for gain; difference between those who killed for their selfish cause and me, is simple greed. When it's all said and done, everybody answers to someone…now go cry your pathetic river while explaining it to the judge."

"You poor child…" Aun'war brands a fiendish grin while expending more energy to remain stable. Rain pours heavily as the sultan spews blood from his mouth, but he manages to keep Arthur at bay.

"Your enans Robinson... What are they? Did you make them knowing their purpose?"

"Shut up."

"You know what they are."

"I said shut up!"

"They are – freaks of unwise human intervention."

"You just won't quit – will you?"

"Your enans are unnatural abominations."

"Shut up...shut up!" Arthur's outburst is soon followed by a harsh kick to Aun'war's side. But the lain sultan continues his Luciferian observance. "How many people did they kill because of your intervention?"

"You got a lot of nerve."

"Nerves are what makes us strong – dear boy, because we can feel, and that makes us all fight for the life we choose. I kill to create a better society, you kill to subdue what you refuse to embrace and understand."

"Reasons justify the cause and if I am a killer – then I have good reason!"

"So...you are a killer."

"My reasons are not like yours."

"Reasons separate us? Well...if that is so; Arthur Robinson, then you and I...are...exactly alike."

"Like hell we are."

"You are indeed shallow; for we are all guilty of an evil more trifling than death itself, an evil that lurks within us all, causing us to make decisions that no one else will. It is a grimacing shadow that inbreeds in us from generation to generation. One that follows our daily façade as we tell the world that our way of life constitutes the best existence for everyone. It is the essence of what makes us who we are!"

"You were born in sin."

"And you were *shapened* by the hands of iniquity...Arthur Robinson. And because of that; guess what...my naive simpleton? You, me; every one like us, rich, poor, saint, sinner, peasant, monarch, master, slave; it makes us all...specters in the shadow of God!"

Lightning cracks the sky as Aun'war belts a devilish laugh; and then, impending silence falls upon him as he leans forward, sucking as much air as his frail lungs will allow. Arthur stares into the depths of the jungle. His tall sleek figure slumps against a nearby tree as his head lowers and the gun falls to the wet ground.

Gjhe'nan quietly observes his maker's reaction. Silence looms. Then, Aun'war reaches within his shredded clothing and removes a gun. Trembling, yet accurate, he points the weapon towards Arthur, who never sees him. Gjhe'nan shrieks loudly. Then suddenly, three shots ring out as the sound echoes in all directions. Arthur falls to the ground as thunder pounds in the distance.

Moments pass; but quietly staring through the dense canopy, Arthur examines his clothing – finding a mild flesh wound. He slowly rises to his feet and observes Aun'war slumping to one side. In complete puzzlement, he approaches Aun'war. Upon the sultan's chest are two deadly wounds, accurate and sure, widely gaping from which blood drains into the earth. Aun'war lies motionless with his eyes glazing towards the heavens. Arthur stands in amazement, slacked jawed and rattled, but he soon looks over his shoulder and discovers another staggering element. "Angelica," he whispers.

Angelica stands with frantic disillusionment, holding a weapon as smoke rises from the barrel. Arthur cautiously approaches her. "Easy…easy," he says while slowly removing the weapon from her trembling hands. Her magnificent glow now shadows under the canopy of stress, making Angelica barely noticeable to the eyes of her familiar acquaintance.

"Not like this…it wasn't suppose to happen…not like this," she says, shaking her head to denote a noncompliant situation.

"Shhh…it's okay." Arthur embraces Angelica as she buries her head into his chest, but his ill attempt to console her only brings more tears. Jade silently watches while gently placing her hand over her chest in an attempt to ease her own pain.

Explosions burst throughout the remainder of the complex, collapsing walls, tearing floors; virtually destroying everything beneath the ground therein. White fire savagely scours everything in its path, decimating nearby trees as well as creating an earthen tomb. As such chaos lingers in the face of a downpour; the remaining heard of enans departs into the surrounding jungle – vanishing from sight as though they were never there.

~~~Kindness~~~

Sea faring gulls stretch their wings against the vivid backdrop of a bright blue horizon. Turquoise waters glisten as pristine white caps peak and crash against moss layden rocks, casting a salty mist high into the air. Rays of warmth cascade upon barren skin as hundreds frolic along sandy shores. Not far from the congeries, Arthur converses with General Caldwell Pendleton through a public visual transmission port. The officer's information clearly weighs heavily upon the technician's mind, but the light-hearted Arthur casts a smile and offers Pendleton an encouraging word.

"I'm fine, thank you sir. I did go; and came back, nothing more to tell."

"You are aware that this is a secure line."

"I know sir."

"Well, needless to say, the official Ecuadorian report will not make the evening news – especially the part about human remains scattered throughout the jungle. Good news is…the vials containing the viral toxin have all been destroyed. Some samples are in CDC's possession and soon we will know how to counteract the effect of the Phantom's Death."

"What is the official word General?"

"The official conclusion is that Aun'war lost his mind and had all his men killed; and then turned on himself. The government is hoping to curtail would-be martyrdom by changing some things regarding Aun'war's death, but you and I know better. Don't we?"

"I have no comment sir."

"Hah…spoken like a true politician, but at least with servitude. Arthur, I know what you told me, but I must ask; is it possible that any thing of salvageable value remains?"

"I'm not sure I follow –"

"Could I prove that what really happened down there – transpired in the way that you said it happened?"

"No sir... Nothing of that tragedy remains..."

"Except you..."

"Miracles…do…happen, General."

"I see... Anyway…in the near future, someone from the Department may wish to speak with you."

"How near?"

"Near enough...."

"I'm no longer involved in genetics – sir."

"Change of heart?"

"Let's just say that I'm not in the mood to focus on another test tube."

"You could have a bright future with the department."

"Only time will tell..."

"Of course; but what about your g-nan? Hello…hello…Arthur, did you hear me?"

Arthur whisks a smile and then becomes void of all expression. He glances towards the outer stretch of ocean and candidly smiles. Then, he looks downward as though to elude Pendleton's question. Silence stirs, but then, the words slowly come forth. "I don't know where Gjhe'nan is."

Pendleton observes Arthur and slowly leans back into his chair with hands clasping behind his head. He sits there momentarily, staring.

Then, he tells Arthur, *"Son, I've been in this man's military too long and I believe you should reconsider. In all fairness, I did promise to keep information on that creature safe in return for your assistance – you did well. Robison, I'm not gonna pretend that I didn't see anything; but you know more than what you are telling me, and I sure as hell hope that you rethink your decision. If those enans…can be controlled, then we may truly have something of worth."*

"That's exactly the problem. The enans cannot be controlled."

"Everything can be controlled. The question becomes – to what end."

Both men stare at each other, until Arthur begins to smile. "Thanks for everything General Pendleton."

In like manner, a smile faintly graces Pendleton's face. *"You take care of yourself Arthur Robinson. It's been one hell of a ride. You know how to reach me should you change your mind. Godspeed..."*

"Godspeed to you too..." The transmission ends.
Arthur makes his way beyond the cover and finds Angelica sitting at a table. He conveniently sits opposite of her and awaits their order. Sitting amidst the crowd, both quietly watch cascading waves dissipate upon the sandy shore. With eloquent mannerisms and lady-like posture, Angelica crosses her legs and silently observes Arthur.

She glares at him as though to pierce his soul, but then turns her head as if to contend with thoughts well hidden from the world. However, Arthur's senses are finely tuned to Angelica's seemingly subtle innuendoes. Their drinks arrive and both sip down the beverages as though nothing matters. But the chafing reality of prior experiences quickly sets in. Angelica tenderly looks away from Arthur, takes a long deep breathe, and mournfully sighs. She asks, "What do you want me to say Arthur?"

"What is there to say?"

"Think me not harsh or some foolish woman."

"I've heard that before."

"Please..."

"What were you thinking?"

"Please, let me finish..."

"Do I need to know?"

"I want you to know."

"Some things are best left buried Angelica, and only God can save your immoral soul."

"I wanted control of my own destiny."

"Who doesn't?"

"Yes but...I wanted something far more continuous than just children, or heirs."

"It's only greed Angelica."

"Arthur, in the early days, you cannot know what it was like to have endured what I have. My father was gone…and no one else was there."

"Yes, you did a tough thing to keep the company going…but this, this thing that you have done is something far more complicated. It's far deeper than just wanting a continuing legacy Angelica."

"Those were hard times that I never knew. Then Aun'war comes along and – and there was my ticket to this dream of mine - freedom."

"Freedom… Angelica, you found out about Aun'war because of your snooping around GenoSyss. What you saw in him was only part of a much bigger sadistic picture. Those private messages you delivered to Rowland's hit men is what got my co-workers buried six feet under."

Angelica's persona frails before Arthur as her watery eyes convey something deeper. Arthur stares at here, hardended by what he hears. She consoles her anguish within the confines of a hankerchief.

"Arthur, please…please hear me on this. I did not know that Aun'war had those people killed – I swear it. And don't you let it cross your mind that a single day goes by without me seeing their faces over, and over…and over again! How many times must I be crucified? I believed Aun'war to be a ticket to something grand – to something larger than a menial existence."

"Aun'war was your ticket to becoming an accomplice to murder while endorsing his idealistic brand of terrorism – Hitler style. And remember, a lot of people died out there because of that man."

"I did not know Arthur…I just…did not know."

"Should he have spelled it out on a sheet of paper for you? First Rowland, then Jade, now you –"

"Do you want me on my knees – begging for forgiveness? I have no more tears to shed Arthur."

"*Dammit* Angelica. You paid those hit men money to carry out Aun'war's encrypted messages; messages that ordered the deaths of my co-workers, my friends – even me. And you never bothered to find out what kind of messages you were delivering."

"Sometimes, we do foolish things Arthur. I am sorry – so sorry."

"Jade told me everything, but my guess is that all this is simply an unfathomable quest for control on your part. And sadly, it is a control of which you never had. I guess a moderate lifestyle is out of the question for someone like you – or is it. I hope you finally realize Angelica, *'all that glitters doesn't shine...'*"

Angelica's mouth quivers under the brandishing of Arthur's outspokenness; in effect, causing her to show something far deeper than even he realizes. She clutches her hands in prayer-like fashion and slowly bows her head, gently rocking to an emotional rhythm. Though her eyes are closed, it is as though she can see Arthur as deeply as any one.

"*'All that glitters doesn't shine.'* Very well then... If that is so, there is only one thing you can do for me that will shine for the both of us?"

"And what is that?"

"Forgive me...please."

Arthur places both hands over his face while leaning back into the chair. He rubs his eyes under the earnest request of Angelica's frail sequestering.

"Did you hear me?"

Arthur says nothing as Angelica gently pulls his hands and stares directly into his eyes.

"Arthur, I need to know that all is well between you and me – no...matter...what."

Arthur does not answer, but Angelica asks again. "Is it well between you and me – tell me?"

"And what if it is or isn't?"

"Then it is...what it is, but I need to know."

"Do you want closure from me?"

"Please..."

"Angelica, I have no heaven or hell to put you in."

"Nor should you..."

"I trust you."

"I make no excuses Arthur. I made a choice that caused others harm."

Arthur's lips move to the sound of wordless conjecture. Angelica glares at him, locking his hands in her tight grasp. In the distance, a policeman approaches the pier. Arthur abruptly fastens his eyes on the officer as he is several yards away. Angelica sees the officer as well and gently releases Arthur's hands.

"You owe me nothing Arthur, nor do I ask for anything. Now do what you must."

In a sorrowful manner, Arthur gently kisses Angelica on the forehead. He rises from the table and leaves her behind, heading in the direction of the officer. As he nears the lawman, Angelica gingerly sips her beverage and gazes towards the open sea. Minutes pass as birds fly overhead and the sun moves farther on a westward course. Eventually, Angelica turns her head only to find that the officer is much farther down the pier, continuing on his beat, and that Arthur is nowhere in sight.

Later that evening, a large transport travels along a distant highway. Arthur sits quietly as Hollis steers the rig. In a tranquil moment, Arthur attempts to bury his tense forehead into the palm of his hand, massaging his head as he rotates his neck from side to side. Securing relief, he peers out the window as if hoping for an intangible occurrence. With nothing to hold his interest, he turns to Hollis.

"Thanks for coming."

"I was glad to hear that your little Ecuadorian excursion went well, and you didn't get killed."

"God looks after idiots too."

"I'll say. By the way, Aniah is fine and anxious to see you. Your extended family misses you too."

"I appreciate that, thank you."

"If you don't mind me saying, you look like a calf staring at an open gate."

"I'm tired Hollis."

"Sure you are, but you have to hold out just a little while longer. Now before you fall asleep on me…"

"I'm not sleepy."

"Yeah…you always say that, but I know better."

"I'm fine."

"Considering every thing else, that means you have something on your mind and it can only be one of two things."

"You're acting like you actually know me."

"Since childhood, but to the point, it's either Gjhe'nan or you know who; and since we're in route to see your scaly contrivance that leaves only one thing – the two-million dollar question."

"And survey says…"

"Did you turn Angelica in?"

"No…"

"And why not?"

Arthur says nothing as he leans against the door while rubbing his eyes. Hollis observes Arthur's sluggish reactions. "Owe, I see…I won't go there."

"It's okay little brother. At this point, I don't care."

"Does it have something to do with what we talked about in the past?"

"Everything…"

Hollis takes a long deep breath and exhales in a moment of discontent. "Oh well. I'm done preaching to you about it; just as long as you can see that some things should never happen."

"But Hollis, things do happen – and I am the one who made that choice – not the devil."

"Get some rest big brother."

Hollis drives the dark road as Arthur leans against the passenger-side window. He places his hand upon his forehead once more and closes his eyes; softly breathing until all around him becomes faint, and he falls to sleep.

Hollis sees a small device lying just beneath Arthur's hand. He stares at the device for a moment, until curiosity sets in.

Activating the auto controls, Hollis retrieves the device, though trying not to awake Arthur. After pressing a few buttons, several images of Arthur's artwork pan the tiny screen. Hollis lightly scans the works of art, but becomes intrigued with a drawing of a woman, whose sheer form basks in a subtle light.

While viewing the subject, an audio begins to play:

Whether by guilt or the confession of a poor soul, denial is not an option. Yet, either testimony comes as a meager attempt to dislodge an unbearable weight. In the darkness, the moonlight cast upon her like soft rays beaming through the canopy of a dark forest. It was then that my curiosity begun to stir. As the soft light graced her face – that was when I truly saw her for the first time. She had matured and was fully capable of the tasks awaiting her. Until then, I had never seen her before. There she was…quiet, serene, but quite vibrant.

Her eyebrows delicately arch with the gracefulness of Devine's penmanship, pronouncing an accenting start to a finely tapering end. Chestnut color eyes lay in placid form just beneath fleshly covers, covers that noticeably bears the darkest lashes of natural apparel. Accentuating cheeks bask in the subtlety of maroon tint while dimples mildly compliment bone and muscle. Fuchsia masterfully paints her tantalizing lips as a picturesque smile sways before hidden pearls of white. All enchanting facial features culminate to a small rounding chin, encompassing nothing less than the face of interludes most fairness. Her head sits prominently upon a sleek neck as black vibrant strands of her crown's glory prances just shy of slender shoulders, draping a two-tone vibrancy of black with white highlights. Her breasts are shapely firm and proportionately round; renditioning the power and style that defines femininity, from the satisfaction of a suckling's need to the alluring foreplay of a lover's delight. There is no naval, but her abdomen is smooth as glass, soft as white downing, faintly revealing the underlying muscles that maintain its oval form.

As she promenades across the floor, her sultry hips move like heavy branches swaying in the wind; like the nimble surge of an ocean's wave, or the fall of a leaf upon a light layer of air; all converging upon the reception point where seeds of future generations penetrate therein. Prominent muscles flex, commanding a waltzing stride as her statuesque legs move in harmonious balance. Her hands are small and skin slightly wrinkling over each joint of slim fingers, casually adapting to every move set forth by arms of ornamental distinctions. The palms of her hands are smooth, very much like the soles of her feet, in which high arches accentuate extending toes upon the delicate pivotal placement of every step. To see her once is to remember her for a lifetime. To see her twice is to forge her image for all eternity. She is Nostalgia, and she moves as graceful as the memories she bestows.'

"Didn't know you were a poet big brother," whispers Hollis while smiling. But his slight gesture disappears as more words unfold.

'But Nostalgia's impending existence spawns from the imagination of a purpose so misplaced that only the Creator can make sense of it. Angelica's hope for this fleshly machine is to perpetuate a fool-hearted notion concerning the memory of a legacy's beginning. Nostalgia is Angelica's heiress and it was I who gave her life. Eight hours of imprinting has culminated into a person whose age ranges somewhere between mid to late thirties. Her brain can only handle so much information. She had entered the maturation point for the mid-level stage in her development. If she were too young, she could not represent the face of Banks Industries; though ironically, she will age far slower than her human counterparts, almost remaining as she appears until the span of her conclusion.

As usual, I made my routine check-ups and monitored her progress. That night, the moon glared brighter than normal. She was standing there as if waiting for me. It was never wise to have made her aware of my presence. She saw me and approached; unsuppressed, unashamed, and undeterred – unstoppable. There was no weakness, no temptation, not even a wrestling conviction, not even an affair – I chose to remain.

A part of me wanted to see if it were possible. God was always speaking, and his warnings did not fall upon deaf ears. Before me stood a being of profound mystery, yet such a creature is far more than just flesh and bone. She took my hand and held it to her chest. As I felt her heart beat, I saw a pureness un-tattered by the pollution of this world, an extension of a soul tie that beckoned the desire of intimacy, the lure of the ultimate expression of one's own self, the thing that all men see in a woman's capacity; the power to become the raw embodiment of his own being; of his true essence; an expression on multiple levels. No words can entirely explain the plight of human foolishness, the wantonness of another, the yearning to envelope the curiosity and folly of a thousand generations; even the game to seek and conquer – but Nostalgia was never a game to me.

As my hand pressed against her arm, hues of pink, orange, and brown began to blend in an illusive palette of provocative sweet skin. She gently wrapped her arms around me and pulled me to the floor. Telltale sounds of copulative indulgence rose in the ambience of moonlight - all that I gave; she willingly received, pulling – beckoning for more. I desired her, I wanted her and this was our moment.

It wasn't until days later that I received a call from Angelica. Only then did I discover that accelerants were still active during the final stage of Nostalgia's maturation, something that I did not know. No one fully understood the total effects of accelerants, not to mention the yielding need for a replicate to satisfy an innate drive, which was never accounted for. To all our surprise, Nostalgia never had time to adjust to foreign bacteria, and her body was shutting down.

I found where they kept her. She was lying quietly in a chamber. I forced my hand inside a sterile glove, watching, hoping for some sign of reprieve; but on that that mournful day, she looked at me and smiled, then died while holding my hand – she was with child.

Banks Industries could not allow the outbreak of such news, but Angelica refused to have the child aborted. The child was removed and secretly taken to another facility. No evidence of Nostalgia remains – Angelica made sure of that… and covered me as well. Every full moon, I see Nostalgia's face. May God have mercy on my soul, because I certainly do not.'

"Whoa," whispers Hollis. He attempts to replace the device, but Arthur awakes. Both stare at each other. Arthur sees the device in Hollis' hands. "Now you know…"

"I didn't mean to pry; I just thought…that this was your artwork."

"It is – in one way or another, I painted it."

"That was your voice on the recording and those were your notes."

"Yes..."

"Did all this happen when you were working for Angelica?"

"After Angelica told me to increase the accelerants; that's when I went back to monitor Nostalgia's progress."

"And… that is also when you…"

"People call it weakness; I call it curiosity…whatever…"

"The end game is the same; but you never mentioned the child. Is the child real?"

"He's real."

"Does Aniah know?"

"She does."

"What was her response?"

"What do you think?"

"And where is the child now?"

"Angelica is caring for him.

"What happens now?"

"The boy becomes heir to Angelica's empire – so to speak. For apparent reasons, he will mature just a bit normal."

"Now I understand why you did not turn her in."

"Checkmate."

"I don't know what to say."

"What is there to say? I fathered a hybrid's child."

"What happened to Nostalgia is why there are laws regarding that."

"No kidding… Well guess what? I also created a killing machine with scales, bent laws to bring a being into existence, violated a sacred trust, stole military property, and… I caused the death of my son's …" Arthur covers his tear stained eyes. Hollis sorrowfully observes him and convenes an apathetic consolation by shaking his head. After hearing Arthur's broken voice, Hollis now bears the haunting impression as well. He regains manual control of the rig and continues down the highway.

Dark shoals lay vastly across a silent horizon as the moon lit sky stretches the heavens and a cool wind breezes above surging waves. Hollis navigates the rig to a remote area just around a rocky outcropping where the sea coaxes the sandy shore. He brings the machine to halt and climbs out. Arthur joins him. Under the cover of darkness, both men venture close to a ridge where the roots of a large tree grow. Arthur plants a device in the water and they wait.

Soon there after, Gjhe'nan forcefully emerges from the surging waves and meets them near the rocks. Arthur gently rubs Gjhe'nan's forehead, softly speaking aloud as the hybrid beast stands quietly.

"You're no longer the awkward, playful juvenile I once knew. Look at you. You're all grown up...and...you're healing very well," he says, while observing deep scares and broken scales lining the hybrid's outer skin. Gjhe'nan mildly shrieks in response and abruptly turns away.

"What is it...where are you going?" Gjhe'nan scribes in the sand. Arthur pulls from within his pocket a small pin light and illuminates the ground. 'PURPOS,' he says, and then asks, "Yours or mine?" Gjhe'nan shrieks, lightly tapping his chest. "Yours? I see..."

Arthur breathes deeply and rubs the side of the hybrid's head while looking directly into the creature's eyes. As always, Gjhe'nan responds in kind. "My god, you are farther than I realized. There is no need to request purpose from me any longer. But listen, my time is short, so try to understand. Your purpose was to locate and destroy enemies to our way of life – my way of life; but sometimes, the real enemies are much closer than we know."

Gjhe'nan stares at Arthur so attentively as if nothing else matters. Again, the hybrid scribes in the sand. This time, the inscriptions bestow Arthur's unprecedented attention. Of all the markings, Gjhe'nan taps directly on one word. Arthur turns away, but the hybrid's awareness makes Arthur's gesture far too obvious, causing the technician to confront the issue.

"I can see that you want to know whether or not you fit such a description, but I can assure you, that you are not...that...word. You are NOT an ABOMINATION! Where did you get this from?"

Arthur's boisterous question comes in earnest as he angrily kicks sand into the air and throws his hands in futile disgust. His face tenses in anguish as he tries to keep from drawing needless attention.

"Gjhe'nan, you are different, and you must believe that. You're trying to make sense of things you were never meant to know." The hybrid gently places its head against Arthur's; nudging him, sequestering a gleeful response, but such never manifests. Arthur slowly lifts his head and touches the face of the beast; but Gjhe'nan senses an abnormality. In doing so, the hybrid's eyes fall into the misty shadows of a deep bluish hue, subtly illuminating under the darkness of the shoals. Arthur looks upon Gjhe'nan with a degree of paternal concern, yet barely able to project broken words – though perhaps to his own satisfaction.

"Human irony is something not easily explained – and no less understandable. The first time you asked me, I thought you would consent to die, though foolish of me. Your humanness has grown far beyond what even I imagined – surely, you must understand that you were never meant to know these things. Again, you ask if you are an abomination. Well… without Christ – aren't we all."

Gjhe'nan shrieks softly as Arthur wipes his face and rises to his feet. Arthur reaches inside his pocket and retrieves a tiny device. Afterwards, he climbs on Gjhe'nan's back.

"The military is your rightful owner. I took you from them, which makes me a liar and a thief, something far worse than you. At some point, they will come after you." Gjhe'nan responds with a menacing growl. "I know they hurt you and the others but they will come…and when they do, I cannot protect you. This tracker will let me know that you are alive – somewhere."

Unable to curtail his fragile emotion, Arthur forcefully wedges the tiny device between the hybrid's scales. He embraces Gjhe'nan, whose response is nothing less than solemn.

"You are free now. Find the others and go somewhere far from humans. Stay hidden as much as possible and most of all…do not trust anyone – especially humans…now GO!"

Arthur pushes against Gjhe'nan, but the hybrid yields no ground, only staring in sheer bewilderment. Arthur finds a stick and strikes Gjhe'nan, attempting to drive the hybrid away, but Gjhe'nan does not move. "Go AWAY…get out of HERE!"

Arthur's harsh screams fall upon attentive ears as he turns and walks away, leaving the hybrid to shrill a boisterous screech. As if by instinct, Gjhe'nan steps forward to follow, but quickly halts. Shrills project yet again, but Arthur never returns a glance.

Finally, upon reaching the rig, Arthur stares at the moon. "You were there when I embraced a life, and now you are here when I release a life." The technician lowers his head while closing his eyes. His actions are nonetheless sorrowful, occurring under the disquieting sounds of Gjhe'nan's lamentations. As Hollis engages the engine, Arthur turns his head as though to see if his prodigy continues watching, but he never concludes the act. Instead, he looks into the eyes of Hollis and asks, "Is he there?"

Hollis looks at Arthur for a moment, observing the face of a tired beaten man. While gently placing his hand on Arthur, Hollis looks towards the sea where Gjhe'nan stands. His eyes then flow into the dark heavens, glancing at stars twinkling as though dancing to a mystical orchestration while waves dwindle upon sandy shores. Again, Hollis glances at the sea and then observes Arthur, whose face is tucked so low that it remains virtually hidden from the world. Audibly, yet faintly, Hollis tells him, "No."

~~~I'll Tell You a Story~~~

That was the last time… I saw Gjhe'nan.

I'd like to think that he's found a place somewhere unknown to humans; free of near-sighted judgment, free of cruel prejudices and the careless intentions of others – free of the military's clandestine purposes, and even… free of me. My love for him was too costly; I had to let him go. I like to think that he's running happily on a secluded island somewhere with the other enans. Maybe he's with a syren, maybe he has offspring, maybe he understands his place in this world, and maybe…just maybe, he has found purpose…

…And now…I hear a voice…

"Arthur, get up sweets; it's time to get up." My eyes open to the sound of Aniah's voice. "Get up…it's time," she says while shoving me in the chest.

Rising from the couch, the immediate brightness instantly signifies that morning has come and it is time to commit to the task ahead. But Aniah continuously presses the issue. "Get up. Gracella called earlier and wants us to let her know how everything goes today. She and Lionel want to go to a movie tonight after we finish – so hurry up – old man." "Alright…alright; I'm coming. Give me a minute."

Jumping to my feet, I return the photo albums to the rightful places upon the shelf. While powering down the computers, I take note of one photograph. Displaying proudly are the immortalized images of Walter and Jade, holding hands as their wedding rings glisten in the sun. Dharma, their little girl, sits happily upon Jade's lap. They all have smiles; therefore, it is only fitting that I grace this moment accordingly.

After showering, I dress and meet Aniah at the door. "Today will be a good day. I prayed for you. Are you ready?" Aniah's question is no less to the point as hesitation sets in. No verbal response comes; however, her offer is as an obliging comfort as we walk out the door. I kiss her and for a brief moment; gaze upon her. Sometimes, the best things are taken for granted.

The sun's warmth moderates the brisk air, making it possible to enjoy the scathing breeze rushing past my face. The coolness fills my senses while reminding me of the time I spent at sea, but the wind also blows red and yellow leaves across the streets, engulfing every pedestrian caught in its swirling embrace. However, there is a time factor, but a quick stop by the deli to secure a dozen macadamia chocolate chips is a much needful act. Once acquired, the drive resumes with much haste. By noon, we reach our destination.

Upon approach, a high arched gate becomes the only remaining obstacle in our path. I press several buttons upon a keypad and soon a voice ecstatically projects from a speaker. *"Yes...yes...I've been expecting you. You're running late."* As the gates slide apart, we enter.

Towering Evergreens stand in the distant. Their deep color provides a pictorial glimpse of the ongoing season. The last time I entered these gates; those trees were only waist high. The driveway is very long and nicely lined with maples; each sporting red foliage that spectacularly canopies the bright white gravel beneath. While in route, several magnificent appaloosas speedily approach and run along side of us as though we bring them gifts. But their interest wanes and soon they are off to something more appealing.

We finally arrive at the house, which is far beyond moderate. Several architectural compliments display upon the brick structure, ranging from arched windows, contemporary Roman pillars, and six waterfalls flowing from huge vases. Each vase sits upon the shoulders of large male statues. Crescent shaped stairs formed of marble, lead from two side-by-side entry doors spanning downward to the base of the driveway.

After parking, I climb out of the car and open the door for Aniah.

Before she could plant one foot upon the ground, one of the tall doors open and out comes something that changed my life in such a way that I never thought possible. Running down the stairs with a smile as large as the lone star state, is Adrian. Seeing him renders me motionless. I barely breathe. It is difficult to accept that I am actually looking at a living breathing being.

As he approaches, sheer excitement grapples every ounce of my being, and yet, several thoughts pierce my soul. Each memory recalls countless scenarios of guilt and shame – even sorrow. An epiphany takes hold of me, and then it all goes away.

"Uncle," he shouts. I fall to my knees as a thousand feelings engulf my emotions. Adrian bypasses the last five steps and hurls his small body into my outstretched arms. What cannot translate into words quickly convenes through a teary eyed embrace. We hug and laugh, but only I shed tears.

Our laws forbid human hybrids as parents, and children born to them constitute death for the offspring, without plea. Lobbying partisans dictate that such beings are nothing more than sub-human creations by unnatural intervention and are therefore by-products of society. They say hybrids have no soul and are considered walking abominations. But Adrian shows no signs of such mindless notions…but, perhaps it is too soon to tell.

Adrian touched something within me that I thought would never come across my path. Fatherhood, in this unorthodox sense has come to me, filling a void that I never knew existed – or so I tell myself. I cannot walk away from him, nor can I wipe away the past. Perhaps it is just another way to secure a new experience, or the beckoning of an unknown horizon, perhaps one that caters to the adulations of growing old.

Adrian was never meant to exist, thus making him as rare as the rarest of stones. His preternatural conception puts me in a world that is so different from my very own childhood. Nostalgia did give birth and my son lives. But if Adrian is discovered, he will more than likely die as a test subject, which is something I cannot bear. My fate; however, would be nothing less than questionable or worse. I will have to answer for my sins. Someday, the truth will cross his path; but for now, he will know me as a caring uncle while his innocent world and those of us around him is all he has.

He combs through my pockets, searching, testing, earnestly mission oriented until he stands back. "Uncle, did you bring them?" His commanding request demands my admirable attention.

"Yes I did." I give him the bag of cookies and he relishes them as only a youngster can. I smile.

Soon, Angelica emerges from within the house. She stands at the door with one hand covering the other as though to bestow prayers for those entering a monastery. A weathered smile graces her face, yet it is none the less bright – like the days of old. Her hair, more salt than pepper now, is more complimentary of a person who is well seasoned, wiser, and of all things - settled. While smiling, she excitedly requests Aniah to enter.

At that moment, I take Adrian by the hand. "Uncle, where are we going?" His small voice rides upon his question so innocently that I can only reminisce of the pureness of my own childhood. And yet, while looking into his chestnut colored-eyes, Nostalgia hauntingly appears. Adrian offers a puzzling look, as all children do; but then, after a sudden blink, I voluntarily concentrate on the current matter at hand. In doing so, Nostalgia disappears. Last night marks a long time since our first meeting. Soon, I know that we will meet – no more.

I smile, and so does Adrian. "You want to go see the horses?"

"I always see the horses Uncle."

"Then would you like to go to the lake and see the horses again?"

"I guess..."

"But this time, would you like to row the boat – with me...while we see the horses - again?"

"Yeah," he gleefully responds.

Angelica eagerly embraces Aniah and both greet each other as if they were lost sisters from another time period– acting as if nothing of the past ever happened. But wishful thinking is only as prevalent as the mind's ability to either conjure or forget; while the distilling truth often renders nothing less than a striking reality. Yet somehow, through it all, a consoling reprieve comes when Angelica conveys a gentle nod to me, and they both enter the house.

Engrossed with his treats, Adrian periodically looks upward. While tugging my arm, he asks, "Will I see Nostalgia - your friend?" I gaze upon him and gently rub his head. Taking him by the hand, we begin to stroll towards the pond. My words fail to come so readily; even the heavens offer no answer. Only silence of thought lingers.

But then, words slowly come. "Th...there...there are things you will not understand right now, but in time – you will."

His little eyes look downward, but quickly enlarge with excitement. "Uncle, do you got a story?"

"Always... And would you like to hear a really good story?"

"YEAH!"

"Well, let me tell you about another friend of mine."

"Do I know him?"

"Not yet."

"What's he like?"

"Well...he's got a really big tail and big, big legs and he can jump; jump as high as the moon."

"Nu-uuun!" Adrian laughingly shouts with wide-eyed wonder. "Is he a dog?" he asks.

"Oh no... Not a dog, but something more."

"Is he like... God?"

"Not even close..."

"What's your friend's name?"

As Adrian's question fills my ears, I gleam far across the horizon where the earth meets the sky. The wind blows softly upon my face while several thoughts come and go. Some thoughts conjure the joyful triumphs of the past while others epitomize the hurt caused not only to me, but what I've caused others.

Despite the recollection of failures, crowning this new day is to understand that, I no longer have to walk in God's shadow, but finally realize the assurance of living in the light of His forgiveness. Understanding this makes me realize that in the shadow of His hand, he somehow conceals me; even in times past. And now, for the first time in several years, a tremendous weight is gone.

Adrian looks at me with ponderous attentiveness. I look back at him as a tear trickles down my face, and I tell him,

"His name… His name is Gjhe'nan."

~~~**The End**~~~

www.ingramcontent.com/pod-product-compliance
Lightning Source LLC
Chambersburg PA
CBHW080942020726
47505CB00009B/2116